Praise for L.E. Modesitt Jr.'s world of fantasy:

"This is a very special fantasy, original . . . in its slow and thoughtful use of familiar fantastic elements and its skillful development of character."

Asimov's SF Magazine, on *The Magic of Recluce*

"This lively tale of two strong-willed magicians' coming of age chronicles the founding of the island nation of *Recluce*."

Publishers Weekly, on *Towers of the Sunset*

"Extremely interesting."

Andre Norton, on *The Magic of Recluce*

"The universe he's built is fascinating. I hope he visits Recluce, Candar and their neighbors again in the future."

Amazing

"An exceptionally vivid secondary world."

L. Sprague de Camp

TOR BOOKS BY L. E. MODESITT, JR.

THE SAGA OF RECLUCE
The Magic of Recluce
The Towers of the Sunset
The Magic Engineer
The Order War
The Death of Chaos
Fall of Angels
The Chaos Balance

THE ECOLITAN MATTER
The Ecologic Envoy
The Ecolitan Operation
The Ecologic Secession

THE FOREVER HERO
Dawn for a Distant Earth
The Silent Warrior
In Endless Twilight

The Timegod
Timediver's Dawn

Of Tangible Ghosts
*The Ghost of the Revelator**

The Soprano Sorceress

Adiamante
The Green Progression
The Parafaith War

*forthcoming

THE TOWERS OF THE SUNSET

L.E. Modesitt, Jr.

TOR
fantasy

A TOM DOHERTY ASSOCIATES BOOK
NEW YORK

THE TOWERS OF THE SUNSET

Copyright © 1992 by L. E. Modesitt, Jr.

Edited by David G. Hartwell
Cover art by Darrell K. Sweet

A Tor Book
Published by Tom Doherty Associates, Inc.
175 Fifth Avenue
New York, N.Y. 10010

TOR® is a registered trademark of Tom Doherty Associates, Inc.

ISBN; 0-812-51967-1
Library of Congress Catalog Card Number: 92-4527

First edition: August 1992
First mass market printing: August 1993

Printed in the United States of America

0 9 8 7 6 5

For Eva,

    and Susan,

        For yet unforgotten memories,
            and the lessons I should have learned,
            and still have not.

THE TOWERS OF THE SUNSET

I.

BLADE-MASTER

I

CAN YOU SEE how the pieces fit together? Not just the visible ones, like the towers of the sunset, but those unseen, like the heart of a man or the soul of a wizard.

Not that you will believe. Patterns work that way, for each individual is captured by her patterns, even as she must reconcile them.

The lady named Megaera, if indeed merely that, sees all the patterns, yet for all she sees and says, for all the truth in the Legend, logic and the towers fail. Logic indeed is a frail structure to hold a reality that must encompass both order and chaos, especially when Black supports order and White is the sign of chaos.

Even logic must fall to understanding, to those who can laugh at their chains and shatter chaos and upend order, even more so than the so-called gods and those who call upon them. Or the Furies that followed the fallen angels of Heaven.

Has there been a god in Candar? Did the angels in truth fall upon the Roof of the World? How true is the Legend? The patterns supply no answers, but any story must start somewhere, even if its beginning seems like the ending of another tale, or the middle of a third epic. And patterns never tell the entire story, the order-masters and the chaos-masters notwithstanding.

As for the towers of the sunset . . .

Though the musician has seen them—the towers of the sunset—rearing above the needle peaks of the west, who has dwelt there?

Another look and they are no more, just towering

cumuli-nimbi, strafing the foothills with the lashes of the gods. In the gold light of morning, the rivulets of ice would verify the anger of . . . ?

What does a house tell of its builder? A sword of its owner? Or of those who stop to admire the lines of each?

The musician smiles briefly. That is all he can do. That, and bring to music what his eyes have seen, for he will sing to the Marshall of Westwind, ruler of the Roof of the World, about the towers of the sunset.

Who else looks at the towers of the sunset? Who built them? The angels of Heaven? The musician knows no answers except those of his music, and of his heart, which lies colder than the strings of the guitar he bears with him.

Suffice it to say that the castle is called Westwind . . . founded by a long-dead captain: Ryba, from the swift ships of Heaven.

Her many-time daughter's son—but that is the story to come.

II

"REMOVE WESTWIND'S CONTROL of the Westhorns, and Sarronnyn and Suthya will fall like overripe apples."

"If I recall correctly, that kind of thinking cost the prefect of Gallos most of his army."

"Light! We're not talking about arms." The skeletal man in white jabs a finger skyward, the mouth in his young face smiling. "We are talking about love."

"What does love have to do with removing Westwind?"

"I have sent Werlynn to Westwind. Do you not like the sound of that? Werlynn to Westwind?"

"But . . . how? Werlynn never comes here; his music ruins the work of the White brethren. What—"

"That's the beauty of it. One little charm . . . to ensure

that he will bring the Marshall a son . . . first. And the charm was even order-based."

"You've never liked Werlynn, have you? Ever since—"

"That's not the question. The question is the Marshall. Just think—*think*—she is a woman. She won't kill her firstborn, male or not, Legend or not."

"You seem certain of that. But she has no children, nor even a consort."

"Werlynn will see to that."

"Even if he does, that's a long time from now."

"We have time. The road is still not through the Easthorns."

The other man shakes his head, but does not speak further.

III

THE GUITARIST STRUMS an ordered cadence, almost a march, so precise are the notes, so clear are the tones. He does not sing.

A single look, underlined with a brief flare of light from the middle stone seat, the one upholstered with the black cushion, stops the guitarist. He nods toward the woman. "Your pardon, grace." His voice is as musical as the strings he plays, evoking a sense of dusky summer that has yet to come to Westwind, even in the centuries since its construction.

"Perhaps you should consider a trip to Hydolar, or even to Fairhaven."

"Perhaps I should, if that is your wish." His eyes darken as he looks toward the boy.

In turn, the silver-haired toddler hanging on to the stone arm of the chair bearing the green cushion glances from the silver-haired guitarist to the black-haired woman, and back again.

"Play another song of summer," she orders.

"As you wish."

As the notes cascade from the strings of the guitar, an unseen fire lifts the chill from the stone walls of the room, and even the guitarist's breath no longer smokes in the dim afternoon of the Westhorns' endless winter.

The toddler sees the notes as they climb from the strings into the air, lets go of the stone support and clutches at a single fragment as it passes beyond his grasp.

Neither the woman nor the guitarist remark upon his sudden drop to the gray granite beside the chair he has released. Nor do they notice the glimmer of gold he clutches within his pink fingers and how he turns to seek the light it bears.

Nor do they see the wetness in his eyes when the gold dissipates from within his grasp even as he watches.

His jaw set, the chubby-legged child struggles upright until he stands next to the chair that is his, his hands reaching out once more toward the order behind the sounds he sees and hears.

But the song of summer has come to an end, with tears unshed in the eyes of the guitarist.

Beyond the gray granite walls, the wind howls and . . . again . . . the snow falls.

IV

"I HAVE TO wear this?" Against the warm light that floods from the open double-casement window through the thin, close-woven silksheen of the flimsy dark trousers, the young man can see the outline of the man who stands holding the garment at the foot of the bed. "Galen, you can't be serious."

The older, round-faced man shrugs helplessly. "The Marshall ordered . . ."

The youngster takes the trousers and tosses them onto the bed next to an equally thin white silksheen shirt. His image— that of a slight, silver-haired youth in a light-gray flannel shirt and green leather vest and trousers—is framed in the full-length, gilt-edged mirror that hangs against the blond wood paneling. His eyes are a steady gray-green. The silver hair and fine features overshadow the wiry muscles beneath the flannel and the weapons calluses upon the strong, squarish hands.

"Why did she even bother to bring me? I'm no consort to be paraded around."

Galen straightens out the clothes so they lie neatly upon the green-and-white-brocaded bedcover. "The Marshall thought that you should learn about Sarronnyn firsthand. And like it or not, you are a consort."

"Ha. She has more in mind than that. Llyse will be the one who must deal with Sarronnyn."

Galen shrugs again, almost helplessly, and his shoulder-length white curls bob. "Your grace, I can but follow the Marshall's orders."

The oak door connecting the spacious single room with the suite provided to the Marshall by the Tyrant swings open. A tall woman, slender and deadly as a rapier despite the flowing green silks that cover her figure, steps into the room. A single guard, her short-cut brown hair shot with gray, followers the Marshall, a pace behind.

The youth looks from the silksheen clothes to the Marshall and back to the clothes upon the brocaded spread.

The woman smiles faintly, but her eyes do not mirror her lips. "Creslin, if I am wearing silksheen, then you certainly can. The garments are a gift from the Tyrant, and spurning them will only make the negotiations that much more difficult. Unlike you, I prefer to save my resistance for those times when the issue matters."

Her blue eyes are as hard as the dark stones of Westwind. The contrast between their adamancy and the green silks that flow around the lithe muscles—muscles she has developed and maintained over nearly four decades of training and warfare—reminds Creslin of the snow leopards that skulk the edges of the Roof of the World.

He inclines his head as he removes his green-leather sleeveless vest and lays it on the bed. "I will be ready in a moment."

"Thank you." She steps back through the entry to her suite but does not close the heavy oak door behind her.

Creslin tosses his flannel shirt next to the vest, then strips off the leather trousers.

"Where did you get that?" asks Galen, pointing to a thin line of red down the consort's left arm.

"Blade exercises. Where else?"

"Your grace, does the Marshall—"

"She knows, but she can't object to my wanting to be able to take care of myself." Creslin frowns as he holds up the dark green silk trousers, then begins to ease his well-muscled legs into them. "I keep telling her that if I'm too emotional I must need the training even more. She just shakes her head, but so far she hasn't actually forbidden it. Once in a while I have to smile, but most of the time I can appeal to reason. I mean, how would it look if the son of the most feared warrior in the Westhorns doesn't even know which edge of the blade is which?"

Galen shivers, although the room is not cold.

Creslin pulls on the shirt and arranges it as he looks in the mirror.

"Your grace . . ." ventures Galen.

"Yes, Galen? Which fold did I do wrong?"

Galen's hands deftly readjust the collar, then add the silver-framed emerald collar pin provided by the Marshall.

"Do I have to wear that, too? I feel like property."

Galen says nothing.

"All right, I am property, courtesy of the damned Legend."

"Your grace . . ." mumbles Galen, his hands not quite going to his mouth.

"Are you ready, Creslin?" The voice comes from beyond the door.

"Yes, your grace. As soon as I retrieve my blade."

"Creslin—"

"Galen, would not any eastern male wear a blade?"

There is no response, and a faint smile crosses Creslin's lips as he buckles the soft leather of the formal sword-belt into place. The blade, the short sword of the guards of Westwind, remains securely sheathed therein.

Creslin steps through the connecting door. The guard follows him with her eyes, but he ignores her as he joins his mother the Marshall.

They walk out through the carved doorway of the guest-wing entrance. Creslin moves to the Marshall's left, a half-pace back, knowing that is as far as he can push.

"Creslin," begins the Marshall in the hard-edged soft voice that is not meant to carry, "do you understand your role here?"

"Yes, your grace. I am to be charming and receptive and not to volunteer anything but trivia. I may sing, if the occasion arises, but only a single song, and an . . . inoffensive one. I am not to touch steel unless I am in mortal danger, which is rather unlikely. And I am not to comment upon the negotiations."

"You did listen." Her voice is wry.

"I always listen, your grace."

"I know. You just don't always obey."

"I am a dutiful son and consort."

"See that it stays that way."

During their exchange of words, their steps have carried them down the hall and into a wider hallway leading to the dining room of the Tyrant's palace. A herald, scarcely more than a boy, has appeared to escort them into the Tyrant's presence.

As they turn into an even broader corridor, wide-glassed windows on the left show a garden with a hedge of short, green-leaved bushes cut into a maze centering on a pond with a central fountain. From around the fountain's statue—an unclothed man well-endowed in all parts—shoot jets of water that arch upward before cascading into the pond.

The wall to the right of the two from Westwind is of pale pink granite, smoothed and polished. Gold-fringed tapestries depicting life in ancient Sarronnyn hang against the stone, a space perhaps equal to three paces between each scene.

Creslin, having studied the hangings earlier in the afternoon, ignores them, instead fixing his eyes on the doorway ahead, where a pair of armed women guard the entrance to the dining room.

The Marshall waits as the herald steps into the hall. Creslin waits with her, still a half-pace back.

"The Marshall of Westwind!" announces the young herald. "Accompanied by the consort-assign."

The Marshall nods and they step inside, following the herald toward the long table upon the dais.

". . . handsome lad."

". . . a blade yet . . . but can he use it?"

". . . like to see his work with the other blade."

". . . too feminine. Looks like he trained as a guard."

Creslin purses his lips, trying not to hear the whispered comments of the court as he trails the herald and the Marshall. Some of the comments are all too familiar. Two places are vacant at the high table: one next to the Tyrant and one at the end, between two women.

"Your grace . . ." A serving boy pulls out a chair for Creslin.

Creslin nods to the graying woman at his right, then to the girl at his left. The girl's unruly and shoulder-length mahogany curls flow from a silver hair band, and she is the only woman at the table with long hair.

"Your grace," begins the older woman.

With regret, because he understands the seating, Creslin turns to her. "Yes?" His voice is nearly musical, much as he rues it at times such as these.

"What might we call you?"

"Creslin, but no names are really necessary among friends." His stomach turns at the lie, and he wonders if he will ever be able to twist the truth, as he has been taught, without paying his own personal price. His eyes flicker to the center of the table, where the man to the left of the Tyrant has raised his knife.

The others turn to the sectioned pearapples on the yellow china plates before them, and Creslin lifts his knife to pare the sections into even smaller slices.

"Do all men in Westwind wear blades?" asks the older woman.

"Your grace," he defers, "Westwind is upon the Roof of the World, and all those who leave her walls must beware of the elements and the beasts that brave them. The Marshall would leave no soul unprotected, but was generous enough to grant my request to be able to protect myself."

"You appear rather . . . athletic."

Creslin smiles, and his stomach turns yet again. "Appearances may be deceiving, your grace."

"You may call me Frewya." Her smile is only slightly less overpowering than her breath. "Would you tell us about Westwind?"

Creslin nods but first finishes a small section of pearapple and wipes his lips with the linen napkin before speaking. "I doubt that I am the most-qualified individual to describe Westwind, but I will do my best." He turns to the red-haired girl. "I would not exclude you, your grace—"

"If you would tell us about Westwind . . ." Her voice contains a hint of laughter as she pauses in raising her goblet. She wears a heavy, dull, iron bracelet, almost as wide as a wrist gauntlet and set with a single black stone.

Creslin senses that the bracelet is not exactly what it seems to be before he quickly returns his glance to her face. Her hidden laughter has pleased him, and he bestows a smile upon her before turning back to Frewya.

"Westwind sits upon the Roof of the World, anchored in gray granite to the mountains themselves, walled against the weather, and armored against all assailants . . ." Creslin did not compose the words he employs, but calls them from his memory of words written by another silver-haired man, kept in a small volume addressed to him.

". . . and during the storms, the great hall, with its furnaces and chimneys, holds all warm against the winter and worse. Outside the walls of Westwind and beyond the walled road that leads to the trade routes, near-unbroken whiteness sweeps from below the south tower and up toward the still-shimmering needle of Freyja.

"Freyja" Creslin explains more conversationally, "is the sole peak to catch the light of the sun at dawn and at dusk.

"Beyond the Roof of the World are the depths, the cliffs that drop more than a thousand cubits into ice and rock. Beyond and below them lies the darkness of the high forest—massive spruces and firs that march both north and south toward the barrier peaks of the Westhorns." Creslin stops and smiles, then shrugs. "You see, I can offer you only images."

"You offer them well," responds Frewya.

The red-haired girl, or woman—for Creslin has perceived that she is somewhat older than he is—nods.

In the interim, his plate has been removed and replaced with a second and larger one, also of yellow porcelain, on which rests a slice of browned meat covered with a white sauce. To the side are cooked green leaves.

Creslin slices a presentably small section of meat. He ignores the spicy and bitter taste, although he calls the slightest of breezes to carry away the perspiration that threatens to bead on his forehead.

"How do you like the burkha?" The question comes from the redhead.

"It's a bit spicier than what is served at Westwind," he admits.

The woman laughs. "You're the first outsider I've seen who didn't totally burst into sweat with the first bite."

Creslin smiles vaguely, wondering whether to feel insulted or complimented. "I take it that's a compliment."

"Yes." But before she can say more, she turns to the man on her left in response to a question from him.

Creslin realizes that she wears a second bracelet upon her left arm. Both bracelets are concealed by the flowing blue silksheen of her gown, except when she raises a hand to pick up a goblet or to gesture. The man on her left, who wears a laced and frilled shirt open nearly to his waist, displays a broad and tanned chest, although one which seems soft to Creslin. Still, the man is taller than Creslin, as are most of the Sarronnese men, and his laugh is easy and practiced. The tone grates on Creslin's ears, as do all falsehoods—his own and others'.

"What do you think of the progress of the negotiations?" asks Frewya.

Creslin finishes another bite of the burkha. "I trust that they are going as planned, but since the higher matters of statecraft are best practiced by those with their responsibility, I can but hope." He takes another bite, this time of the mint leaves that help to cool the fire of the hot brown sauce.

"Are the guards of Westwind as fearsome as they are reputed to be?" pursues his tablemate, sending another gust of highly charged breath into his face.

"Fearsome? Certainly they are called fearsome. Their training is rigorous . . . that I have seen. But since I have not seen them in battle, only in practice, I might not be the best one to answer that question." He cuts another slice of the highly spiced meat.

"You seem rather unable to comment about much, Consort-Assign," breaks in a new voice, a deep masculine voice, belonging to the man on the other side of the red-haired woman.

Creslin lifts his head, takes in the artificially waved blond locks, the even tan, and the stylish shirt. "I'm afraid I have little practice in saying nothing, and perhaps my lack of training in the art of diplomacy shows through."

A bemused smile appears on the redhead's lips, but she says nothing.

"Your words belie your assertions, for again you have said little."

"You are absolutely correct, but then, I need to say nothing. Nor do I have the need to prove anything by my words." Creslin turns his head fractionally from the blond man to the redhead. "Your pardon, your grace, for such bluntness, but the Roof of the World is not a soft place, even for a consort, and I am not skilled at evasions."

With a smile that is half-bemusement, half-laughter, she responds with a tilt of her head. "I accept your bluntness, Creslin. It is a shame that you will not be here much longer. Some . . . could learn from your words." She turns from him to her companion and adds, "Dreric, I am certain that our guest would have more than enough to say in a less formal setting."

Dreric nods, then turns to the woman to his left and asks, "Your grace, have you heard the Sligan guitarists before?"

For all the politeness, Creslin suppresses a wince at the iron behind the words of the red-haired woman and at Dreric's reaction.

"What do you think of Sarronnyn? That should be a question harmless enough," laughs the redhead, whose name Creslin has not yet learned.

"I don't know what to think," he begins, "except that it appears prosperous. Certainly the roads are well maintained, and the people we passed on the way scarcely looked up from their work. Some even waved, and that would indicate general contentment."

"You *are* cautious, aren't you?"

"One learns a certain caution upon the Roof of the World."

"And as the only male of standing in a garrison of the Westhorns' most fearsome fighters?"

"Standing?" Creslin laughs, and the laugh is not forced. "Your grace, I have no standing, save by the Marshall's wish."

"You are the consort-assign?"

"While the Marshall holds Westwind."

"I fail to see the distinction."

Creslin shrugs. "Given the Marshall, and given my sister Llyse, there probably isn't one. But the succession isn't automatically hereditary. The guard captains can theoretically chose another Marshall."

"Is that likely?"

"Now? Hardly. I suppose the tradition is a protection in case there should be a weak Marshall. Those who live by the Legend hold to their strength."

Thrumm. A single note hums from the platform to the side of the high table, where sit three musicians in bright-blue tunics and trousers. Two are men, one a woman. Each cradles a guitar, but the three instruments vary in size and shape.

Creslin can see the faint golden-silver of that single note as it ascends toward the high, dark-timbered ceiling.

"The guitarists from Sligo are supposed to be rather good," he ventures.

"Yes. Although that is like saying that Werlynn was good."

"Werlynn?"

"The music-master of Southwind. Did you ever hear him? He spent some time at Westwind, they say."

"More than one musician has spent time at Westwind.

The Marshall is fond of music. I do not recall a man named Werlynn."

"You might not. He disappeared somewhere in the snows of the Westhorns years ago. But the older folk still mention him. He had silver hair like yours, and not many people do."

"That is true," Creslin responds, "and I may have heard him if he had silver hair. His notes were true."

"True? That's an odd comment. Some time, perhaps you could explain."

While her words invite a comment, their tone is perfunctory and vaguely threatening, as if discussing the trueness of notes were a subject better not mentioned at table. Creslin takes the hint gratefully, for to explain would reveal too much, and to lie would hurt even more. Instead he shifts his eyes to the guitarists as they begin to play.

V

AFTER WHAT SEEMS the hundredth look out the open casement windows at the formal gardens below since his breakfast, Creslin snorts. "Enough is enough."

"Enough what?" asks Galen.

"I'm going out."

"Creslin! But the Marshall—"

"She didn't say I had to stay in one room. She said I had to stay out of trouble. Walking in that garden down there isn't going to get me in trouble. It's entirely inside the palace."

"Let me at least get you a guide."

"I don't need a guide."

"Not for that reason. A guide will signify that you're a visitor."

"I'm leaving."

"It will take only a moment."

"A moment's about what you've got."

Galen scurries through the connecting door to the Marshall's suite, returning even before Creslin finishes adjusting the formal sword-belt over the silksheen trousers that slither against his skin.

"Creslin, is the sword—"

Beside Galen is the young herald who had escorted Creslin and the Marshall the evening before.

"I feel undressed without it. Wearing this . . . bordello outfit is bad enough. Besides, it's not in a battle harness." Creslin turns toward the boy. "Is there any reason why I can't walk through the formal garden there?"

"Many of the . . . men of your situation do, your grace."

"A diplomatic answer, young man. Well, there's no one there anyway. Lead on." Creslin ignores the fretful look on Galen's face and opens the door to the hallway. *Clunk*. He has not meant to shut the heavy oak door so firmly, but the hinges are well oiled.

For the first dozen steps, neither Creslin nor the herald speak. At last the youth asks, "Is it true that you wear battle leathers, your grace?"

Creslin laughs softly. "I wear leathers, but so does everyone in Westwind. You'd freeze in silks like these. Our summers are colder than your winters."

"But how do you grow crops?"

"We don't. We have some mountain-sheep herds for milk, cheese, and meat. We trade for the rest. We pay for it by maintaining the western trade roads clear of bandits, and—"

"—and hiring out to the western powers?" asks the boy. "Are the guards as good as the Tyrant says?"

"Probably," admits Creslin, as he follows the herald down the wide stone steps. "But I don't know what the Tyrant said about them."

"She said that even the wizards of Fairhaven could not stand against them."

"I don't know about that. Wizards don't like cold steel, but the eastern wizards are supposed to be able to split mountains."

"Each year they move a little closer, they say."

Creslin shrugs. The affairs of a kingdom ruled by wizards on the eastern side of the Easthorns—two mountain ranges east of the Roof of the World—scarcely seem urgent. "Is this the entrance to the gardens?"

"This is the east door. There's another door from the men's quarters."

"The men's quarters?" Creslin steps onto the white gravel path. The shadow that has darkened the garden lifts as a small white cloud drifts away, revealing the white-gold sun, and as the blue-green of the sky brightens like a fire emerald.

"You know, where the unattached consorts and the other . . . male guests . . ."

Creslin raises his eyebrows. "Hostages for good behavior? Sons of suspect houses?"

The herald looks down at the fine and polished white pebbles.

"Never mind. Tell me about the garden."

"It's nearly as old as the palace. The tales say the second Tyrant built it in memory of her consort. That was Aldron, the last consort to ride in battle. He was killed at Berlitos when the Tyrant crushed the Jerans."

"Jera is southern Sarronnyn now, isn't it?"

"Yes, your grace. Very loyal. This maze is sculpted from just one creeping tarnitz."

"Just one?"

"That's right. If you look down, you can see how the roots intertwine."

Creslin kneels to study the base of the tarnitz.

"Very clever gardening. We couldn't do this sort of thing at Westwind."

"Oh?"

Creslin laughs briefly. "Only the evergreens grow there, and not well. Show me some more of the garden."

The herald leads Creslin around a series of turns through the maze until they emerge near the statue in the midst of the marble-walled pond.

"Aldron?" asks Creslin, gesturing toward the well-endowed male figure.

"So it's said, your grace, but no one knows for certain."

Creslin turns at the sound of footsteps and a voice saying, "Ah, I do believe it is the honorable consort-design of Westwind. You know, Nertyrl, the one who had nothing to say at the banquet."

The speaker is Dreric, the broad, blond companion of the unnamed redheaded woman. He wears matching royal-blue silks that under the white-gold sun set off his tan and his flowing golden hair. Beside him is an older man, wearing gray silks, a pointed and drooping mustache, and a long blade.

Although he smiles faintly, Creslin has nothing to say to either man, particularly since he has no doubt that any wit he might display would be far less practiced than that of two men who have spent a lifetime mastering the innuendo.

"Good day, I say." Dreric's voice oozes from his lips, honey-coated.

"A pleasant day, indeed," agrees Creslin, knowing that he cannot refuse to respond to a direct greeting.

"He wears a blade, you see," comments Dreric, with a pronounced look at the older man. "Perhaps because his other blade is less than adequate, you think, Nertryl?"

"That would be for the . . . women . . . to decide, your grace."

"Ah, yes . . . assuming that women are even—No matter . . ."

Creslin swallows as Dreric halts perhaps four paces away. Dreric turns his back on Creslin and begins to study a miniature pink rose set in a waist-high box of white marble.

"Your grace," whispers the herald, tugging at Creslin's sleeve.

Creslin remains immobile.

"Do you think he really merits the title, Nertryl? Grace? Ah, well . . . what we must put up with to obtain a little more security. We could do him a favor, I suppose. Maggio likes boys, the thin ones like this mountain . . . lordlet. Do you suppose we could manage an introduction?"

Creslin can feel his face flush, not from the direct sunlight.

"I do believe he shows some interest, your grace." Nertryl's voice is simultaneously flat and languid.

"One must be so dreadfully direct with . . . mountain . . . nobility."

Creslin turns to the herald. "It is truly amazing to hear such vulgarity posturing under polite language. I would like to see an area of the garden not spoiled by . . ." He cannot finish the sentence.

There is a moment of silence.

Creslin turns as a hand touches his sleeve.

"I do believe you have slighted my lord. Grievously," admonishes Nertyrl. The smile on his face is not mirrored in his eyes.

"One cannot slander a toad," snaps Creslin. "They live in the mud."

"Your grace . . ." whispers the herald.

The long blade clears the scabbard.

Creslin swallows.

"Well . . . do you wish to beg his grace's pardon . . . humbly, and upon your knees?" Nertryl's voice remains hard and languid.

"I think not." As he speaks, Creslin steps back, and his own shorter and fractionally wider blade is in his hand.

"Well, well . . . he has some nerve, if not much in the

way of intelligence . . ." The grating voice is that of Dreric.

Nertryl says nothing, his eyes fixed upon Creslin's.

Creslin smiles, remembering the sessions with Aemris and Heldra, and his blade moves without his eyes moving.

Nertryl steps back, involuntarily, at the nick on his forearm, then moves forward.

Creslin's blade flashes, almost faster than his thoughts, and the long blade lies upon the white gravel.

Nertryl holds his right arm as heavy red wells through his fingers and over the gray silks.

Dreric's mouth is still open as Creslin steps forward, blade flickering.

". . . you wouldn't . . . barbarian . . ."

The sword caresses the blond man's cheek, and two thin lines of red appear.

"That should be enough, Lordlet Dreric, to remind you that insulting one's betters is dangerous." Creslin bows to Nertryl. "My apologies, of a sort, to you. You might also remember that the Guards of Westwind are far better at this than I am. I am merely a poor Consort-Assign."

Creslin turns to the open-mouthed lad. "Let's go. I detest the stench of blood." He swallows as he thinks about the Marshall's reaction. She will not be pleased.

"Your grace . . ."

"Which way?" Creslin starts toward the path by which they had entered the garden.

The herald shrugs and leads him back along the white-pebbled stones. Behind him, Creslin can hear the rapid crunch of footsteps grow fainter. He forces himself to walk slowly after the herald, wondering where Dreric is heading in such haste.

His own steps are deliberate. He will not be stampeded by any male harlot, especially one without enough nerve to handle his own dirty work.

"Are you all right, your grace?"

"I'm fine. Just thinking."

In silence they approach the golden-varnished door leading from the garden into the palace proper. The herald opens the portal, which swings wide on the same well-oiled hinges as had the door in Creslin's room. Still wondering about Dreric, Creslin steps into the relative gloom of the stone-walled corridor.

"Lord Creslin!"

Darkness swirls around him, as though night had descended from nowhere. His hand darts for his blade. Before his fingers reach the hilt, they are jarred loose as he finds himself slammed against the granite wall, with more than one pair of arms trying to pin him.

His thoughts reach for the winds, and the bitter gusts of winter suddenly swirl silks and scarves, lashing them toward faces and eyes. A line of cold stabs at his arm even as he falls away from the blade. The darkness lifts, and the winds depart, and he stands alone—except for the herald, his eyes downcast.

"What . . . was . . . that?" Creslin gasps.

"What, your grace?" asks the boy, his eyes clear. "Someone called, and you stopped to talk with her. I didn't see who. Since you stopped, I thought you knew her." The boy looks at Creslin's disarray. "Are you all right?"

"You didn't see who it was?"

"No, your grace. I mean, not clearly. She was in the shadows."

Creslin looks back at the door. Although not as bright as the garden, the corridor is well lit by the windows several paces away. There are no shadows. "Oh, well. I wish I knew who she was," he temporizes.

"She must think a lot of you, to be so open," marvels the herald.

Creslin smiles falsely, and his stomach turns again. Dreric's doing? But why would anyone start an attack and then leave as soon as they she pinked his arm? Creslin does not look at his arm, although his senses tell him that it bears a needlesized hole, and the slit in his silks is so narrow that it cannot be seen.

Compared to the mess in the garden, the incident in the corridor is mild, best forgotten, and quickly.

Still, he wonders.

VI

"YOU TOOK A considerable risk, Creslin. What if he had been a master-blade?"

"He wasn't. He wore the silks too well."

The Marshall shakes her head. "You realize that this will make your life much harder?"

"My life? I was more worried about your negotiations." He glances toward the window, where the silken curtains billow in the wind preceding the rain clouds yet on the horizon.

"You couldn't have helped me more." The Marshall steps toward the window, then stops and fixes hard blue eyes on her son.

Is she jesting? He waits for her to continue. For a time, the sitting room of the suite is silent.

"A consort, scarcely more than a boy, disarms one of the most notorious blades in Sarronnyn. Nertryl has killed more than a score of blades, male and female." The Marshall laughs harshly. "And you apologized because you weren't up to the standard of the guard. Your friend, the herald, had that all over the palace within moments of the time you were back in your room."

"I fail to see the problem," Creslin admits.

"What ruling family would willingly accept a consort more deadly than any man west of the wizards and more dangerous than most of the fighting women in Candar? It doesn't exactly set well with those who respect the Legend." The Marshall smiles. "That artistry on the other fellow's cheek was also a bit much. Oh, I know it was justified, but it also shows that you don't play games. Then, we all learned that a long time ago." She looks to the window. "In a way, it's too bad we didn't get along better with the Suthyan emissary last spring. We'll do what we can . . ."

Creslin suppresses a frown. At least he hadn't killed anyone. In view of the Marshall's mood, he decides not to mention the strange episode in the corridor. The wound in his arm is no more than a pinprick, and his senses and his health tell him that no poisons were involved.

The guard in the doorway shakes her head ever so slightly, mirroring the gesture of the Marshall of Westwind, until Creslin looks in her direction.

VII

Ask not what a man is,
that he scramble after flattery as he can,
or that he bend his soul to a woman's wish . . .
After all, he is but a man.

Ask not what a man might be,
that he carry a blade like a fan,
and sees only what his ladies wish him to see . . .
After all, he is but a man . . .

The chuckles from the guards at the tables below grate on Creslin's nerves, but the minstrel continues with his elaborate parody of the frailties of man. With each line, Creslin's teeth grate ever tighter.

The Marshall's face is impassive. Llyse, on the other

hand, smiles faintly, as if not quite certain whether the verses are truly humorous.

The minstrel, dressed in shimmering, skintight tan trousers and a royal-blue silksheen shirt, flounces across the cleared end of the dais, thrusting—at times suggestively—a long fan shaped as a sword.

". . . and, after all, he is but a man!"

The applause is generous, and the minstrel bows in all directions before setting aside the comic fan, retrieving his guitar, and pulling up a stool on which to perch and face the crowd as the clapping and whistling die down.

Creslin listens, watches as the silver notes shimmer from the guitar strings and observes the guards' reaction to the more traditional ballad of Fenardre the Great. The silver-haired young man recalls hearing the words from another silver-haired man.

The minstrel is good, but not outstanding. Creslin is nearly as good as the performer, and he has no pretensions about being a minstrel. The applause is only polite at the end of the ballad. The minstrel inclines his head toward the dais with a wry smile, then turns back to the guards below and begins to strum a driving, demanding beat.

Several of the guards begin to tap the tabletops to match the rhythm as he leads them through the marching songs of Westwind.

Even as he enjoys the familiar music, Creslin feels that he does not belong on the dais, or even in the hall. The refrain from the comic song still echoes in his thoughts: "After all, he is but a man . . ." His lips tighten as he becomes aware of the Marshall's study of him. He meets her dark eyes. For a time, neither blinks. Finally Creslin drops his glance, not that he has to, but what good will it do?

The thought comes to him, not for the first time, that he must leave Westwind, that he must find his own place in the world. But how? And where? His eyes focus, unseeing, on the minstrel.

At the end of the dais, the singer is standing now,

bowing, and nodding toward the table where the Marshall, Llyse the Marshalle, the consort, and Aemris, the guard captain, are seated.

As the whistling again dies down, the Marshall leans to her left and murmurs a few words to Aemris. In turn, Aemris's eyes flick to Creslin and then to the approaching minstrel. She shakes her head minutely.

Creslin strains to bring the words to him on the wind currents generated by the roaring fire in the great hearth, but can catch only the last few murmured by the Marshall: ". . . after Sarronnyn, he'll always run the risk of being challenged. He has to be as good as he can be."

"As you wish," affirms Aemris, but her tone is not pleasant.

Creslin wishes he had paid more attention to the first words between the two.

The Marshall stands as the minstrel approaches. "Join us, if you would, Rokelle of Hydlen."

"I am honored." Rokelle bows. He is older than his slender figure and youthful voice, with gray at his temples and fine lines radiating from his flat brown eyes.

Creslin suppresses a frown at the wrongness of the eyes and smiles instead.

In turn, Rokelle takes the empty chair between Llyse and Aemris, reaching for the goblet that Llyse has filled for him. "Ah . . . singing's a thirsty business, even when you're appreciated."

"And when you're not?" asks Aemris.

"Then you've no time to be thirsty." Rokelle takes a deep pull of the warm, spiced wine.

"Any news of interest?" asks the Marshall.

"There is always news, your grace. But where to begin? Perhaps with the White Wizards. The great road is well past the midpoint of the Easthorns, and now they are building a port city on the Great North Bay, where the town of Lydiar used to be."

"What happened to the Duke of Lydiar?"

"What happens to anyone who defies the White Wizards? Chaos . . . destruction." The minstrel takes a smaller sip of the wine and reaches for a slice of the white cheese on the plate before him.

"And those who supposedly revere order? The Black ones?"

Rokelle shrugs. "Who can say? Destruction is so much easier than order."

A number of the older guards have left the tables below, but the younger women at the front tables continue to pour from the wine pitchers. Creslin glances across the tables, hoping for a glimpse of Fiera's short blond hair, but he does not see the junior guard. His ears miss the next few sentences, until he realizes that Fiera is no longer in the hall, if indeed she has been there at all.

"Ah, yes . . . well, the wizards and the Duke of Montgren seem to have come to some sort of agreement, now that the Duke has completed his fortification of Vergren and Land's end—"

"Land's End? Out on Recluce?" asks the Marshall.

"Montgren has claimed Recluce for generations, your grace."

"An empty claim," snorts Aemris. "A huge, dry, and forlorn island. Just right for a few coastal fishing villages."

"It's easily ten times the size of Montgren," observes the Marshall. "But neither the Nordlans nor the Hamorians were able to make their colonies pay. Montgren's claim was never disputed because no one ever wanted the place. The fact that the Duke has committed anything there is . . ." She breaks off the sentence.

"I thought the Duke of Montgren was connected to the Tyrant of Sarronnyn," Creslin volunteers.

Aemris and the Marshall turn toward him, both sets of eyes cold at his statement.

"He is, lad," responds the minstrel, "but Sarronnyn looks down on him because he's a man with a tabletop kingdom, and he's angry because the Sarronese won't give him more than token support against Fairhaven. He claims that he's the only one left who hasn't caved in and joined the White Wizards."

"Is that true?" asks Creslin.

"Ah . . ." smiles the minstrel, with an odd and wrong smile, "he is but a man, and who is to say what exactly is true? It is certain that he pays Sarronnyn no tribute, and it is also certain that he has increased his army and the tax levies, to the point that his peasants, those who can, are leaving their fields for Spidlar and Gallos."

"It's that bad?" asks Aemris, turning her eyes from Creslin to Rokelle.

The minstrel does not answer immediately but instead takes another long sip of the lukewarm wine.

Llyse refills the empty cup.

"Is it that bad?" repeats the guard captain.

Rokelle shrugs. "You know what I know."

The Marshall nods slowly and looks toward Aemris.

"What about Jellico?" asks Llyse. "Last year a traveler said that the city was being rebuilt."

"It is not as grand as Fairhaven, but far more welcoming to those who sing," observes Rokelle, between mouthfuls of cheese. "You should see the stonework . . ."

Creslin lets the man's words drift by as he considers what he has heard this night: the guards laughing at the frailties of men; the Duke of Montgren standing alone against the White Wizards and being mocked by his female relatives; the Black Wizards silent; the Marshall and Aemris displeased with his questions. Under the cover of the table, his fingers tighten on the carved arms of the chair even as he leans forward with a pleasant smile on his face.

In time, the conversation dies and Creslin leans back, although the Marshall has already left, her face as impassive as Creslin has ever seen it.

Aemris turns toward him. "You start working with Heldra tomorrow. With blades." Her voice is short, and she stands as she speaks. "You'll need it all." She bows to the minstrel and to the Marshalle.

Llyse turns with a puzzled look toward her brother.

Creslin shrugs. "You think they'd tell me? After all, I'm but a man."

The minstrel sips the last of the wine as the consort and the Marshalle of Westwind rise. Llyse gestures to the guard at the end of the dais.

Creslin takes the inside stairs to his quarters, leaving the sleeping arrangements for the minstrel to his sister.

VIII

THE RED-HAIRED woman wearing the iron bracelets glances into the mirror, her lips tight. The surface wavers, but no image appears. In time she loses her concentration and plunges her wrists into the bucket beside her chair.

The hiss of the steam mingles with her sigh.

Later, after pulling the combs from her long red hair, she looks over at the miniature portrait of herself where it rests atop the ornate wooden desk. Ryessa had insisted that the artist paint her hair short, even though she has never bowed to the military fashion sweeping Sarronnyn. Her sister the Tyrant has never let reality interfere with the images necessary for a successful reign.

The redhead's fingers stray toward her left arm. She wills the itch to depart, as she has willed for too long. Imagination? Her blood swirls with the roar of the winds.

"Still getting stronger, isn't it?" The voice coming from the woman who has just entered is cold, as cold as though her ice-blond hair were indeed fashioned partly from the winter ice.

"I don't feel much of anything," the redhead lies.

"You're lying."

"So I'm lying. Hang me. You'd like to. You're just offering me another form of bondage . . . maybe one that's even worse than these." She holds up her arms, letting the silks draw back. The iron slides away from the welts and scars. She lowers her arms, and the silks again conceal the marks.

"You still don't give up?"

"How can I?" The redhead looks down. There is silence before she looks up. "I was thinking . . . remembering, really, back before . . . Anyway, you and I used to play in the old courtyard, and you used to get so mad because I could always find you, no matter where you hid. But then you'd laugh, at least some of the time—"

"That was when we were children, Megaera."

"Aren't we still sisters? Or did your ascension make me illegitimate?"

"The White has never been legitimate under the Legend."

"Am I any different now, because my talent is classified as White?"

"That was never the question." The blonde shakes her head. "In any case, the negotiations with Westwind may offer you a way out."

"A way out? By enslaving me to a mere man? How could a real sister do that?"

"You think my choice is unfair?"

"When have you ever been fair, Ryessa?"

"I do what is best for Sarronnyn." The blonde shrugs. "In any case, this is fairer. I don't trust Korweil, and I especially don't trust Dylyss."

"You don't trust the Marshall, deadliest fighter in Candar? How skeptical of you."

"Not skeptical. Just practical. Dylyss fights hard, and I'll bet she loves as hard as she fights. He is her son."

"You think she will turn you down?" Megaera laughs harshly.

"After the way you set up Dreric? And Creslin's reaction?"

"Creslin is good, almost as good as a guard."

"From what I saw, he's better than some." The Tyrant smiles.

"He doesn't think so."

"You think Dylyss would let him know? It doesn't make any difference. From what I hear from Suthya, Cerlyn, and Bleyans, they're not likely to welcome such a wolf in lamb's clothing. They'll use the Legend as an excuse."

"You believe it's only an excuse? You're a bigger hypocrite than Dylyss, or Korweil."

"None of us were alive in the time of Ryba."

"How convenient for you."

The Tyrant smiles. "It's convenient for you as well. If I really believed in the Legend and the demons of light—"

"Please don't remind me again."

"Can you sense what he feels?"

"I sense nothing. I told you that. Just go back to your scheming."

"It's for your benefit too, sister. Who else could stand to your fury, to the power within you, bracelets or not?"

"And how long will either of us last once I'm with child?"

"You with child? Without your consent? Spare me."

"Against a blade better than your best, sister dear? You act as if I really had a choice."

There is no answer, for the blond woman has left.

The redhead looks at the decorative but solid iron chair molding that encircles her quarters. Then her eyes flicker to the iron-bound door.

Should she call for Dreric? That, at least, is within her purview. At the thought, her blood seems to storm, and she shakes her head. Two tears fall like rain from the storm within.

IX

IN THE SPACE before the largest window, Creslin strums the small guitar, cradling the crafted rosewood and spruce firmly in fingers that feel too square for a master musician, though he knows that the shape of his fingers has little enough to do with skill.

The room contains a narrow desk with two drawers, a wardrobe that stretches nearly four cubits high—a good three cubits short of the heavy, timbered ceiling—two wooden chairs with arms, a full-length mirror on a stand, and a double-width bed, without canopy or hangings, covered with a quilt of green, on which appears silver notes. The heavy door is barred on the inside. The door and the furniture are of red oak, smooth with craftsmanship and age but without a single carving or adornment. The only reminders of softness are two worn green cushions upon the chairs.

Thrum.

A single note, wavering silver to his inner sight, vibrates in the chill air of the room, then crumples against the granite of the outer wall.

Never can he touch the strings so that the music appears golden, the way the silver-haired guitarist did, the one whom he is forbidden to mention. Even the autumn before the fabled Sligan guitarists had not played solid gold, but only touched upon it.

For the time, he places the instrument on the flat top of the desk and walks to the frosted window, touching his finger to the glass until the rime clears, melting away as though spring had touched the frozen surface of a lowland lake.

Outside, the snow dashes against the gray walls of

Westwind and strikes at the window, the window that is opened seldom, even if more often than most windows within Westwind. As the glass refrosts, he picks up the guitar.

Thrap!

With a sigh, he places the instrument in its case and slides it under the bed. While his mother and Llyse must certainly know about the guitar, neither of them ever mentions it. Nor does either mention music, for that topic is forbidden at Westwind, for all that it is a talent best cultivated by men.

"By men!" he snorts softly. "Coming." His response is soft, like the green leathers that he wears within the castle, but it carries.

Thrap!

He frowns at his sister's impatience, lifts the bar, and opens the door. Llyse stands there.

"Are you ready for dinner?" Her hair, silver like his, dazzles, though it barely reaches the back of her neck, a brief torrent of light flashing even in the dimness of the granite-walled corridor. Only by comparison to his short-cropped head does her hair seem long and flowing.

"No." His smile is brief, lasting only the moment before his guts warn him of the dangers of even flippant untruths.

"You never are. How you can stand to be alone so much?"

He closes the heavy door as he steps out onto the bare stone floor.

"Mother was not pleased—"

"What is it this time?" Creslin does not mean to bark at his sister, and he softens his voice. "About the time alone, or—"

"No. If you want to be alone, that doesn't bother her. She makes allowances for men being moody."

"Then it must be the riding."

Llyse shakes her head, grinning.

"All right. What is it?"

"She doesn't think your hair is becoming when you cut it that short."

Creslin groans. "She doesn't like what I wear, what I do, and now . . ."

They pause at the top of the sweeping circular staircase, comprised of solid granite blocks that would carry the weight of all of the Marshall's shock troops. Then they begin the descent to the great hall.

"Really," begins Llyse, and her voice hardens into an imitation of the Marshall's voice, "you must learn the proper manners of a consort, Creslin. You may simper over that guitar if you must, but riding with the guards is not suitable. Not at all. I am not pleased."

Creslin shivers, not at the words but at the unconscious tone of command that already pervades his sister's voice, beyond and beneath the imitation of their mother.

"She's never pleased. She wasn't pleased when I sneaked out and went on the first winter field trials with the junior guards. But I did better than most of them. At least she let me go on the later trials."

"That's not what Aemris told her."

"Aemris wouldn't cross her if the Roof of the World fell."

They both laugh, but furtively, as their feet carry them into the main entryway of the castle.

"How is the blade-work going with Heldra?" Llyse asks as they reach the bottom of the stairs.

"I get pretty sore. She doesn't care how much she hurts either my pride or my body."

Llyse whistles softly. "You must be getting good. That's what all the senior guards say."

Creslin shakes his head. "I've improved, but probably not a lot."

A pair of guards flanks the archway to the main hallway. The one on the left Creslin recognizes and nods to briefly, but she does not move a muscle.

"Creslin . . ." reproaches Llyse. "That's not fair. Fiera's on duty."

Creslin knows his informal greeting was not fair. He shifts his glance to the far end of the great hall. The table upon the dais is vacant, except for Aemris, unlike the tables flanking the granite paving stones upon which the Marshalle and consort walk. At the lower-level tables have gathered most of the castle personnel, the guards, and their consorts. The children are seated to the rear with their guardians, near the doorway through which Creslin and Llyse have approached.

Creslin concentrates on walking toward the dais, knowing he will hear too much as he nears the forward tables of the guards, the tables frequented by those yet unattached.

"My, we are grim today," prods Llyse.

"You aren't the one they examine like a prized stud," he murmurs between barely moving lips.

"You might as well enjoy it," comes back her calm reply. "You don't have much choice. Besides, it's honest admiration."

In the beginning, it might have been, when he insisted on joining the sub-guard exercise groups and on learning blades, and when he stole rides on the battle ponies. He knew, because he could not spend as much time at it, with all the demands for writing and logic placed on him by the Marshall, while he had the strength and basic skills, most of the guards he once held his own against could probably outride him in the field. Only with the blade could he continue to hold his own. Even Llyse, now, was receiving that concentrated field training he envied.

He almost shrugged. Then again, that was the point of it. The guards of Westwind could outride, outendure and outfight virtually anyone. They were why his mother the Marshall ruled the Roof of the World and controlled the trade routes connecting the east and west of Candar.

". . . still a handsome boy."

". . . sharp like a blade. Cut your heart and leave it bleeding."

". . . not soft enough for me, thanks."

Creslin can tell that Llyse is having trouble in refraining from smiling at his discomfort, and he tightens his lips.

"I'd still try him . . ."

"The Marshall would have your guts for breakfast."

As they step up to the dais, Aemris rises from her seat at the far right end of the table. Four places are set.

"Your graces . . ." The guard commander's voice is low and hard.

"Be seated, please," indicates Llyse.

Creslin only nods, since any words from him are merely decorative.

Llyse raises her eyebrows. Neither she nor Aemris will seat themselves until he does. Then everyone will rise when the Marshall arrives. Creslin could keep all three of them standing. He has done it before, but tonight it is not worth the effort.

He sits at the end opposite Aemris, and Llyse lets out her breath slowly, in turn sitting next to her brother but in one of the two chairs facing the hall and the tables below.

Aemris turns to Llyse. "The winter field trials start the day after tomorrow."

Llyse nods.

Creslin had hoped to participate in the trials, using the skis and holding to the winds that howled off the Westhorns—those winds that might give him an edge—but Aemris is saying that Llyse will be there and he will not. Still, he looks toward Aemris.

The Guard Commander ignores his glance, instead turning to the curtains behind Llyse and rising. Creslin and Llyse follow suit as their mother steps forward, raising her hands to prevent the assemblage from rising.

The dark-haired woman in the black leathers with the square face and well-muscled shoulders that belie the intelligence behind the dark flint-blue eyes glances at her guard commander, her son, and her daughter. Then she sits without ceremony.

A serving boy springs forward with two trays, and Creslin begins to pour the lukewarm tea from the heavy pitcher into the tumblers.

"Thank you.." His mother's voice is formal.

"Thank you," echo Llyse and Aemris.

He nods in return, pouring his own tea last and setting down the pitcher.

A low, roaring whisper rises from the guards and those below as they are served the same food as that of those on the dais.

Creslin's eyes flicker down to the front tables, glad that the meal has stopped the ogling for the time. Llyse holds one of the platters. He spears three thick slices of meat from one end of it and a heavy roll from the other.

Another platter contains various honeyed and dried fruits and pickled vegetables. Though scarcely fond of the vegetables, Creslin takes his share, even if he will have to wash it down with tea.

"Creslin?"

"Your grace?"

"Aemris has doubtless indicated in her best manner that it will not be possible for you to participate in the field trials. That was my order."

"I'm sure you had the best of reasons."

"I did, and I do. Which I will announce shortly. Do you know the Tyrant of Sarronnyn?" The Marshall waits.

His stomach tightens as his mother speaks, but he keeps his gaze level upon her face. "We guested there last fall." He remembers most of it all too well, including the incident in the formal gardens, the one which the Marshall will not let him forget.

The Marshall smiles. "Your expertise with a blade was noted."

"I remember."

"At the time, not much was said," she adds. "Apparently

Ryessa was quite impressed. The negotiations were rather involved, since a proposal from the Marshall of Southwind had also been considered."

Creslin does not understand. Throughout the fall and early winter, he has heard of how his rash action has destroyed any chance of his becoming a respected consort outside of Westwind. And he cannot stay much longer in the citadel of the winter. For his own sanity, at the very least, he must depart.

Beside him, Llyse draws in her breath, like the whisper of the winds just before the mistral.

"I'm somewhat in the dark. Are you indicating that—"

"Not exactly. You will be the consort to the sub-Tyrant, Ryessa's younger sister. Offhand, I cannot remember her name." A signal passes somewhere, and the serving boy brings forward a tray to Creslin. On the black enamel tray lies a sheet of blue velvet, and upon the velvet is a golden frame. Within the frame is the portrait of a red-haired woman, handsome despite the extraordinarily short-cut hair, the piercing green eyes, the strong, straight nose. The corners of her lips are upturned slightly with the same cynical smile as he had seen displayed by the Tyrant throughout the eight-day stay in Sarronnyn. She looks vaguely familiar, but Creslin knows he has seen no woman with red hair cut that short.

"I see."

"You will indeed. You could not have done better, and you're lucky that she prefers feminine men over the more traditional western man. She was intrigued after hearing of how you insisted on undertaking the field trials, and pleasantly amazed at your standing. She even applauded the . . . incident in the formal garden, the Temple only knows why."

Creslin swallows the sick feeling in his stomach as the Marshall stands. A silence radiates from her out into the great hall, a darkness sweeping from her proud, pale face and black working leathers.

"We have an announcement."

She waits.

"Our consort-to-be has been honored, highly honored. He will be leaving Westwind within the eight-day as the consort-intend of the sub-Tyrant of Sarronnyn." A half-turn and a gesture toward Creslin follow.

A pale smile pasted upon his face, he rises.

"Creslin . . . CRESLIN . . . *CRESLIN!*" The chant builds as he stands there acknowledging it with a hand that turns the winds back, though gently, and waits for the words to fade away.

As the sounds trail off, he sits down, wanting to wipe his damp forehead but refusing to show any weakness, other than the stiffness of his jaw caused by his clenched teeth.

"Very nice, brother, considering you're ready to dispatch the sub-Tyrant with your blade."

The breath hisses from him at Llyse's whispered remark.

The Marshall indicates that all should resume eating, and most do, save the handful of single guards in the front tables, who regard Creslin directly.

He takes a sip of tea, then refills his tumbler. He has not finished the last slice of meat upon his plate, and now he has no desire to. How can he escape becoming little more than a prize stud?

His mother has reseated herself.

"It might have been nice to have had a bit more warning," he tells her.

"The sooner, the better . . . for your own protection."

"My protection?"

"Your peers—those who would consider you a consort— are scarcely appreciative of one who is both skilled in arms and tumbled by the most attractive guards of Westwind." Her laugh is throaty, the real laugh he has heard so seldom.

The laughter leaves him speechless for a moment.

"And, as you well know, you cannot stay here, not unless . . ."

He shivers, knowing what she has suggested.

"I really didn't think that would meet your approval. And Ryessa's sister is handsome, perhaps too gentle . . . too masculine."

The Tyrant's sister? Had he met her? He takes another gulp of tea.

"Is she as . . . does she look like this?" asks Llyse, studying the portrait.

"A bit softer than that," comments Aemris. "She'd do well to have a strong consort like Creslin. Sarronnyn's strictly by lineage, and Ryessa already has two daughters. A strong consort like Creslin," Aemris nods toward him as though he could not hear the conversation, "protects her from those who would use the men's quarters against her."

The Marshall looks at Creslin. "Tomorrow you need to consult with Galen to determine what you will take with you to Sarronnyn." She smiles. "It's for the best." Then she stands and is gone before Creslin can respond.

As soon as she is past the hanging tapestries, Creslin stands, nods, and departs. His steps carry him through the back entrance and to the narrow old stairwell, the first one built within Westwind, the one with the hollowed stone risers and the rough edges of the outside wall stones. Upward he climbs, one quick step upon another, until he stands on the open wall and stares southward.

As cold as the gale makes the parapets of Westwind, they are warmer than the atmosphere within the great hall. A thin line of white rises from the tall chimney set squarely at the north end of the hall, the smoke bending eastward into a flat line as it clears the shelter of the castle walls.

Creslin looks out at the near-unbroken whiteness that sweeps across the snow bowl below the south tower and up toward the still-shimmering needle of Freyja, the sole peak yet lit by the sun that has already dropped behind the Westhorns. Even in the twilight, the snow glistens, unbroken, untouched except for the cleared gray stones of the high road leading to the forests below, and to the east.

He wants to sing, or to scream. He will do neither, the

former because now is not the time for song, and the latter because he refuses to give either Aemris or the Marshall any satisfaction, any hint that he might be a weakling like the other men.

Instead, he reaches for the winds, weaves them and hurls them against the walls until his face smarts and sweat flows from his face to freeze upon his leathers. Until the walls are coated with a layer of ice as hard as rock. Until his eyes burn and he can see only with his thoughts. Until the winds slip from his thoughts and go where they will.

Then, and only then, does he slowly trudge back toward the warmth of his room, ignoring the pair of guards who have watched, wide-eyed, as the consort of the sub-Tyrant flails against the destiny that others have arranged for him.

X

CRESLIN'S STEPS CARRY him along the east wall to the covered passageway leading to the tower, called Black for all that it was built of the same gray granite as the rest of Westwind. Within the Black Tower are the fallback winter stores and spare equipment, the not-quite-discarded packs and oil cloths and old winter quilts. They will have to do, for the newer equipment is within the guard armory below, where is posted a live guard.

His short silver hair blows away from his unlined face, and his strides are quick in the darkness of morning just before dawn. The gray-green eyes are set above dark circles, for he has not slept well, not after learning his future. Despite the snow film on the stones, his steps are firm, his boots clearing the risers mechanically.

Creslin glances at the narrow white expanse that drops off into the sheer cliff defining one edge of the Roof of the World. Beyond the thousand-cubit drop, beyond the jumble of ice and rock below, the darkness of the high forest thrusts through the deep snow, massive spruces and firs that march both north and south toward the barrier peaks of the Westhorns, those peaks that separate the eastern lands from the civilized west. Between and upon the high forest giants, the snow glistens, untouched. Beyond the high forest lie the unseen trade roads.

Creslin looks away from the dim vista, turning the corner into the darker shadows, more preoccupied with the past than the present.

"Ooffff . . ."

He staggers from the impact and finds himself half-falling, half-drawn against a blond guard, nearly as tall as he, nearly as strong.

"Fiera—"

"Sshhhh!"

Her lips burn his. Then they are standing separately, thrust apart by the practiced motions of her training as a Westwind guard. Creslin is sorry to lose the warmth he has so briefly held.

"Greetings, honored consort."

"I'd rather be a guard."

"Everyone knows that, including the Marshall. It doesn't change things."

"Fiera . . ."

Her eyes are level with his. "I could be sent to North-watch for years for what I just did."

Northwatch? For a kiss?

"Yes," she answers, her narrow face severe in the shadows. "For daring to kiss the Marshall's son, for leading him on."

"What difference does it make? Llyse follows the Marshall, not me."

Fiera frowns, but the expression is gentle. "Men. It matters. And the sub-Tyrant would not be pleased either, though a one-time love would be difficult to prove."

Her words are meaningless, and Creslin has no response.

"Good day, sweet prince."

He reaches out but she is gone, battle jacket and sword, cold cap and helmet—down the inner staircase to the barracks below.

Again he shakes his head.

The covered section of the parapet is empty, and he fingers the key in his belt pouch. Fiera will not speak of their meeting, and he must obtain what he needs from the storeroom and return to his quarters before the day's formalities begin.

He steps toward the lock. Better old supplies than none.

XI

"SEE? LIKE THAT." The arms-master adjusts Creslin's formal sword-belt. "It did some good to let you learn the basics. The Marshall should have stopped there. All you needed was enough to put up some defense." Her voice is impartial, stating facts.

"Defense? Just defense?"

"I'm not fond of armed men. The Legend dies hard, your grace. But I can't grudge you the right to take care of yourself. And the Marshall can't either, once you leave, you know." The arms-master's mouth puckers as if she has swallowed a bitter plum.

Creslin has heard rumors about the western rulers and their stables of men and boys; he has even seen the men's quarters in Sarronnyn. But he has never considered that he might become part of such a stable. "Perhaps I should have learned more about knives."

She says nothing.

"How might I do against the easterners?"

"You'd be a good blade there, maybe better than that. With their wizardry, they don't hold much stock in blades.

If you ever go there, keep the cold steel blade. It's twice as strong as theirs."

Since Creslin has had drummed into him the reason that no one wears steel in the eastern reaches—cold iron binds chaos—he only nods. Fairhaven may be his goal, but kays indeed, as well as the winter itself, lie between him and the White City, not to mention his mother's guards, and the Tyrant of Sarronnyn, whose sister's consort he will be, like it or not. The redhead in the miniature portrait within his pack, as striking as she appears, bears at least a half-decade more experience than he.

"In the east, it's said that men—"

"Barbaric." The arms-master steps back. "A patriarchal empire is what they're building, based on wizardry." The revulsion in her voice turns her formerly impartial tones acid. "They'll recreate the Legend, but worse. The whole western continent will look like Recluce."

He has heard the same bitterness from his mother, and indirectly from most of the other western rulers.

"You'll do," declares the arms-master, studying him. "A little too feminine probably, with your sword. At least it's not in a battle harness."

Creslin keeps his expression polite. The battle harness is in the pack he has switched for the one that Galen packed.

"You still ride like a trooper, not like a consort, but that's probably what intrigued the Tyrant. She doesn't care much for soft men, that one, and she's the one who asked for you. Someone was needed—"

"For what?" Creslin has not heard this before.

The arms-master's face closes like the castle gate before a storm. "I'll see you below, young Creslin. Her grace will see you after you pack up the sword and finery."

Creslin is less than certain that he wishes to face his mother—or Llyse—right now. But he has little in the way of choice, not since his mother is the Regent of the Western Reaches and the ruler of Westwind and of all the peaks that can be seen from the high castle, not to mention the dozens more that cannot be seen.

At the same time, he is more than eager to escape from the soft silks and leathers that have been fitted for him. Everything has been packed, including his guitar, except the sword and the last ceremonial outfit he wears. He has saved the Guard blade he has practiced with for the trip. His mother would not deny him the right to a solid blade for self-defense. He hopes.

Even before the arms-master has left his room, he begins to strip off the green cotton shirt and matching thin leather trousers, ignoring the lingering look from Heldra as he flings them upon the green-and-silver coverlet and begins to pull on the guard leathers. Glancing up, he catches her stare.

She turns brusquely.

Creslin shakes his head. "Even Heldra . . . was Fiera right?" He does not wish to consider the rightness of his mother the Marshall's words, but he stuffs himself into the heavy leathers more violently than necessary.

Then he starts to fold the ceremonial outfit before dropping it on the bed. Galen will scuttle in and pack it while he talks with his mother.

His head still shaking, he opens the door and leaves it open, walking toward the opposite wing of the quarters, past Llyse's closed door. His sister will not be there but in the field, deep within the winter of the Roof of the World, trying to prove her right and skills to succeed the Marshall—a test she must undertake and overcome each and every year.

Creslin must worry only about palace intrigue, and about pleasing the sub-Tyrant. He snorts. Not if he can help it. Yet he knows so little about real life beyond the guards, beyond the Roof of the World.

Before the sound of his knock dies away, the door is opened by a guard, gray-haired and muscled. She lets him enter, glancing at his guard blade.

He makes his way into the study.

"Creslin!" The Marshall stands. "Even with those leathers, you look good. Except for the hair. Sooner or later you'll have to let it grow."

"Perhaps. Then again, things may change."

She laughs, her manner less formal in the study with only a pair of guards, and those a room away. "Still fighting destiny?"

Creslin grins ruefully. "Since I have no idea exactly what my destiny will be, I couldn't say what I'm fighting."

She touches his shoulder, then withdraws her hand. "You'll do well in Sarronnyn, son, if you remember that you can run to destiny, but not from it."

"That sounds like a rationalization of fate."

She shakes her head. "You need to be off. Shall we go?"

They proceed back out into the hall and down the stairs. Outside the castle's front entry, an honor guard awaits.

The consort swallows. An honor guard? Not including the armed-escort squad? He steps away from the Marshall and toward the single riderless battle pony. The parka he has not worn lies across the saddle, with the cold cap and gloves. Galen has forgotten nothing, except that being a man means more than expertise with domestic details.

"Have a good journey."

Creslin inclines his head as he pulls on the parka. The cap and gloves follow, and he swings into the saddle. The Marshall, in her normal black leathers, stands at the top of the stairs, the wind ruffling her short, gray-streaked black hair.

Creslin raises his arm in a farewell salute, then flicks the reins.

The sound of hooves is the loudest noise as the cavalcade heads out through the open gates onto the high stone road across the corner of the Roof of the World and toward the nations below.

XII

"NOW WHAT ARE you going to do? The last thing we need is an alliance between Westwind and Sarronnyn. It's bad enough that the Black weaklings are muttering again about our abuse of the Balance. With Ryessa's power and hold on the southern trade routes, and that mad bitch Dylyss and her guards—"

"You still don't understand, do you?"

"What is there to understand? Ryessa needs some way to keep that . . . that abomination, her sister, under control, and both Creslin and Megaera need the appearance of being forced into the alliance. We need to keep them apart, and you need a lever over Montgren. That's the clear part. But how on earth this mad scheme will promote anyone's ends but Westwind's and Sarronnyn's, or your feelings about . . ." The heavy, white-clad man continues for many elaborate sentences.

"Enough. Your words are interesting. You feel that Ryessa's sister is an abomination because she was born to the power and chose the White route. Yet the White is right for you? Or is that because she is a western woman who was born to the Legend?"

"The Legend, that involuted rationalization!"

"Who had the idea for the betrothal insinuated?" The older and thinner man cuts off the intricate phraseology.

"You did."

"And what will happen if the boy never makes it to Sarronnyn?"

"Accompanied by Westwind guards? Who'd be fool enough to tackle them?"

"You're assuming that the boy will go along with the

bethrothal. That is a rather large assumption. What happens if he flees to escape his well-planned destiny?"

"The Westwind guards will chase him and capture him."

"And if he won't be taken, or if he dies? Or if the Black ones attempt to help him?"

"Can you be sure of that?"

The thin man shrugs. "The seeds have been planted. Carefully, and he's good soil. After all, Werlynn's music was never chained. That was too bad; no one could sing like he could. He was a Black, I'm certain, but too smart to admit it."

"This is far too theoretical . . ."

"No, it is very practical, because our success rests on the failure of the improbable alliance. When it fails, the Tyrant will have to destroy the . . . as you call it, the abomination. Either that or recognize the White way, and she and Dylyss will be at each other's throats." He laughs softly. "The Duke already has pulled some of his garrison from Recluce. None of them can win . . . no matter what happens now."

"I would still prefer something more direct."

"Like chaos against cold iron? Be sensible."

XIII

CRESLIN HAS NOT memorized the road as well as he would have liked, but there are two likely points where his plan might work, provided he can reach the skis and the pack undetected.

He rides, as any valued consort would, in the middle of his entourage, behind six fore guards who trail the outriders by nearly a kay, and before the rear guard. There are no sleighs or wagons, for neither are used by the guards of Westwind, only the battle ponies or the skis.

For Creslin, the ponies offer no answer. He is but an average rider for the guards. On skis, with the slight chance of winds at his call, and if the conditions are right . . .

He clamps his lips as Heldra rides up beside him.

"You ride silently, Lord Creslin."

It is the first time she has ever addressed him as "Lord," and he ponders the meaning before answering. "I suppose it is a time of reflection. I had hoped to ski the winter field trails."

"Not everything happens as planned. Not even the winds control their own course, for all their powers."

Creslin does not start at the veiled reference to the way the winds behave around him. Despite his care, some rumors have always surrounded him, and his thoughtless behavior on the night of his betrothal announcement scarcely helped quell them.

Still, he has two other small advantages: sheer nerve, and his long hours of practice with the skis on open slopes. His night sight may help later, but not in the afternoon, which is the earliest they will reach a point where he can flee.

He does not respond further to Heldra's presence, and after a time she rides ahead to check with the fore guards. As he rides, he visualizes that point where the road runs exposed along the ridge line between the Roof of the World and the shield range. There the wind always blows. Over long winters and too-short summers, it has driven the snow on the north side into ice covered with hardpack, covered in turn with shifting, drifting, and treacherous powder that flows downward for kays into the top of the forest below. The grade is not particularly steep, not for the Westhorns, but there has never been a reason to ski a slope that leads only northward into the winds. The guards do nothing without reason.

"You do not seem pleased to be the consort of the sister of the most powerful ruler in the west." Heldra's voice rises to surmount the whistle of the wind as she drops back again to accompany him.

Thin, dry flakes stream across the raised stone that leads from the Roof of the World back to the shield peaks. To the west of the shield peaks lie the warmer lands of Sarronnyn, Suthya, and Delapra.

"Should I be?"

"Does the Marshall have any choice? A dozen guards have tried to find a way to you." Her smile is brittle. "Sooner or later one of them would have succeeded. What would the Marshall do with an heir, particularly if anything happen to Llyse? How would the easterners have viewed it?"

Creslin has lost the logic. Instead, he considers how many nights he has spent alone, wondering if Fiera had been one of those guards. How likely was it that a virgin such as he would provide a guard with a child? "That has to be an excuse," he says curtly. "No one can threaten the Marshall."

"Does it really matter?" responds Heldra dryly.

She has a point, he realizes. But he says nothing more, and in time Heldra rides ahead once more to check the fore guards.

The sky remains filled with the shifting, dull-gray clouds of winter, and the wind has begun to pick up as they reach the long drop from the plateau that is the Roof of the World toward the ridge that will connect it to the shield peaks. There is no connection between that plateau and the barrier mountains that comprise the eastern half of the Westhorns, only the canyons and the howling winds.

Creslin slows the battle pony slightly so that, in the descent, the pack ponies, those with the emergency skis, will close the gap. He also reaches out for the winds, catching a fragment, twisting it through his hair momentarily to ensure that he can before releasing the energy.

Now he must ride and wait, ride and wait, and hope.

The sky darkens, then lightens, as the guards and the consort they guard near the ridge that bridges the gap between the Regent of Westwind and the softer rulers of the lower world.

The consort begins to lift those energies he can control to pull loose snow from the north side of the ridge until even Heldra can scarce see her hand before her face. Then he reaches out for his pack, pulls it clear and onto his back.

His pony is barely ahead of the left-hand pack animal as he leans back. The skis are too tightly bound to wrench free. He drops lightly from his mount and slaps it on the flank, then slashes with his knife to free the skis, still walking quickly to keep up with the pack beast.

His own mount stops, and he dodges to get around the beast, grasping the reins with one hand and threading them over the arm that holds the knife. The arrangement works, even as the blowing snow screens him. At least both ponies are moving, and no one has noticed his actions. Not yet.

The first ski hangs loose. He leaves it hanging and works on the second until it too is loose. He pulls both skis free, almost sliding on the slippery stone underfoot, tottering for a second while trying to match steps with the pack pony and keep the wind whipping the snow.

"Where's the consort?" bellows Heldra.

Creslin looses his pony's reins, knowing the beast will stop and the rear guards will run into the empty-saddled animal. Then he clambers up on the low stone wall on the right side of the road and begins to tighten the thongs around his boots, first on the left ski, then on the right. As he tightens, he wills the wind to gust around him.

"He's fallen off his mount!"

"Find him!"

"Can't see shit in this wind . . ."

". . . the hell are you?"

With the second ski as tight as he can make it, he yanks the heavy gloves from his belt and over his nearly numb fingers, then eases his weight off the stone and onto the skis, pushing away sharply so that he does not sink immediately into the deep powder.

"Captain! He's off the road! The skis are missing!"

Creslin wobbles, the powder piling to his knees before his desperate weight shift and downward momentum bring the ski tips upward. He is moving, the wind tearing at his face, his eyes, his body—reaching even through the heavy parka.

He totters at a scraping on the right ski but leans left and back, slowly forcing his track at an angle to the slope. Heading straight downhill would be a death sentence, even for him.

Scccttttccchhh . . .

Once more he corrects, leaning into the hill, hoping he can maintain his balance at least until he is out of easy range of the guards. With only a few pair of skis left to them, he has a chance—more of a chance now, in the kind of terrain he knows—than in the intrigues of court life of the west.

Rrrrrr . . . *sctttt* . . .

A mass of rocks appears out of the lighter curtain of snow ahead, and he begins a sweeping turn, the only kind he dares.

The wood vibrates under his boots; the thongs bite through the heavy boot leather; but he stays on the skis through the turn and into the narrow, snow-filled bowl downhill.

Behind him stretch the twin tracks of his skis, arching down the snow that cover the rock and ice beneath, not that he can afford to look back. Instead, he concentrates on the powdered surface ahead: untouched, virgin like him, but with hidden depths he would rather not find at the moment.

Also like him, he reflects with a grim smile, nearly frozen in place by the wind, for he still flies downhill too fast to control the air that slashes at his waterproofed and underquilted leathers and unprotected face.

Frumppp . . .

As he lurches, flying, he tucks the short skis as close to his body as possible and rolls into a ball, flailing . . .

When he comes to rest, his buttocks are smarting and one

ankle is twisted sharply. Snow is wedged in improbable parts of his body, and his torso is lower than his legs.

Slowly he twists around, levering the skis over himself and to the downhill, even though he cannot see. Cold snow is packed against his bare back where the quilted leathers and wool undershirt have ridden up.

His footing semi-secure, Creslin wipes the snow from his face, studies the area around him. He has rolled nearly a kay downhill, stopped at last by a raised snow hummock through which poke a few thin branches of elder bushes.

He pauses, wiping both the instant ice-sweat and snow from his forehead. Above the silver eyebrows, a single lock of silver hair falls across the unlined forehead from under the hood of his leather and quilted parka.

His body, still too soft for what he is putting it through, let alone what must follow, rests on the threshed snow he has carried downhill with him.

Less than a hundred cubits downhill, the evergreen forests begin. He takes a deep breath and checks his pack, relieved that it has clung to him. So has the short sword in its shoulder harness. Creslin struggles upright, ridding himself of the clinging snow, distinctly less powdery and dry than on the slopes where he began his wild descent.

His ankle is sore, but not tender to the touch. He eases himself onto the skis and makes his way down toward the forest, careful stride after careful stride, knowing that he must keep moving to outdistance the determined guards who follow him as though their lives depend upon it.

His skis swirl the powder like the wind. As he passes, the air congeals behind him, and the winterseed beneath the frost line draws deeper into the thin, stone-hard soil. He pushes onward until he is nearly a kay into the forest, panting with every sliding stride.

After a time, he stops to concentrate, and the wind rises behind him. On the slopes above, the snow re-forms into an unbroken expanse, almost as pristine as before a fleeing consort crashed through it. His breath continues to rasp through his lungs like an ice saw, for brushing the winds across his tracks is more effort than physically moving himself.

He rests, leaning against a dark-trunked fir whose branches do not spread until far above his head, trying to breathe deeply and evenly through his nose rather than gasping for breath, remembering the damage that air will do to his lungs with too much deep mouth-breathing.

He cannot rest long, and he begins his strides once more even as the shadows of the twilight increase, even as he looks for a place of shelter and some way to conceal his tracks. While he can see in the depths of the looming snow-lit night, his legs ache, and his jaw is sore from the effort of keeping it closed so as to protect his lungs.

In time, Creslin locates another clump of elder bushes, and, after removing the near-frozen thongs that hold boots to skis, he uses one ski to dig down into the natural hollow beneath a frozen overhang. Between the oil cloth, the winter quilt, and the protected space, he will be warm enough. Not comfortable, but warm enough to survive.

As he pads the hollow where he will sleep with mostly dry needles over the fir sprigs he has carefully placed, a shadow flickers in the corners of his eye. Barely, just barely, he does not jump. Instead, he moves his head slowly around to view the pair of spruces where the figure might lurk. The trees stand perhaps ten cubits from his hollowed-out den.

Between the branches of the low, bluish-needled trees there is a distance of less than two cubits, an expanse untouched even by hare prints. Behind the spruces, the wind gusts shuffle and reshuffle the white powder that has already covered most of the lines left by Creslin's skis.

Unmoving, he watches, his left hand ready to pull the sword from the scabbard set on the pack by his feet. The wind reshuffles the fine ice dust again, moaning without tone in the darkness that has dropped on the high forest.

Creslin sinks into a lower profile within his hollow,

drawing pack and sword within, still watching the silence.

Woooooooooo . . .

He ignores the bird of prey, wriggling only his toes to warm them within his still-dry boots.

Click . . .

A frozen limb, or a pine cone, drops against a tree trunk.

Wooooooo . . .

The shadow is back, although it appears from nowhere.

Creslin sucks in his breath silently, for the shadowy figure wears no parka, stands on the powdered snow crust without making a track, and stares across the space between them. She wears but thin trousers and a high-necked and long-sleeved blouse. She is clearly female. Her eyes burn.

Creslin stares back, but says nothing.

Then the shadow is gone as if it had never been. Creslin shivers, for he has never seen the woman before, nor one like her. Yet she hunts him. Of that he is certain.

Although he is not cold, he draws his parka around him. The morning will be early, and he has hundreds of kays upon hundreds of kays to go before he can escape the regent of Westwind and the Marshall of the Roof of the World. And that is just the beginning.

But first, he must escape. If he can ever escape. He purses his lips, studies the two spruces for a last time before leaning back into his den, fully out of the wind.

Wooooooo . . .

Click . . .

XIV

EVEN BEFORE DAWN, Creslin wakes stiff, but pleased that no shadows await him, female or otherwise.

Moving slowly in air so cold and still that the crystals of his breath fall like snow upon his parka sleeves, the would-have-been consort wriggles his toes to ensure they are still functional before he extracts the small packet of battle rations from his pack, chewing the dried-apple slices first. Each small bite is a chore for his dry mouth.

He moistens his lips with a thin trickle of water from the melt bottle carried in his trousers. When he is finished, he scoops more snow into the bottle and replaces it, then nibbles on a piece of hard cheese from his pack. The remaining dried fruit and cheese he repacks.

Silent is the high forest, except for the faintest whisper of branches and breeze stirring the dry powder snow that lies on the heavier whiteness.

Creslin must also meet other needs, and before too long, despite the chill such necessities will entail.

The night winds have swept clear his tracks, or enough that it would take far more guards than accompanied him to find him. With that thought he proceeds, beginning with physical necessities, then with packing, and covering his shelter. Standing on the skis, he brushes away as much as he can of his traces, trusting to the snows and winds to do the rest.

His pace is measured; he takes even, long-sliding stride upon long-sliding stride. Before the cloud-shrouded sun has lifted dawn into gray day, he has covered another three kays or more through the high forest that falls and rises, falls and rises, as he heads toward the northeast and the eastern barrier peaks of the Westhorns.

The dry whisper of wind through fir branches, loose snow sifting down from the trees, and the faint scraping of his skis: the sole sounds he hears as his legs drive him onward.

No roads, no trails, mark the northeast route he takes, and it is for this reason he takes it, knowing that where lies a surface uncovered by snow, or by a road, there the guards would find him.

Food? He has enough for an eight-day, in battle rations. Water? He has melted snow with body heat and drunk it before, in the winter training of the years before his mother declared such training unseemly.

Slide, lift, slide . . . cubit after cubit, until it is time to rest. Then slide, lift, slide . . . slide, lift, slide.

The gusts from the north rise with the day and rattle loose another frozen cone. Underneath the forest giants—spruces so enormous that his arm span would not circle even a third of the smaller trunks—the snow is uneven, the light muted.

Creslin concentrates on following ridge lines, on holding toward the north, using the pyramidal peak in the distance as a guide when there are breaks in the trees sufficient to see the barrier peaks.

Slide, lift . . .

Frummmp . . .

The cold powder sifts inside his parka, chilling his neck while relieving the heat of his exertion. He struggles to right himself in the waist-deep depression into which he has plowed. At first he slides in even more deeply, until he is engulfed nearly chest-deep by the heavy powder. A fir limb offers hope, and he pulls on it gently, trying to lever himself upward. The limb breaks, and more snow sifts against his chest, no longer even half-welcome in its chill.

With a sigh, Creslin begins the slow process of easing himself out of the deeps, realizing that no quick pullouts are possible. Inching the skis—now bearing stones' worth of snow above their tips—sideways, he pauses, takes a deep breath. Again he inches the unseen skis toward his right, until finally he can feel the frozen ground against his leg and hip.

Once more, he rests. Then he grasps the narrow trunk of the spruce sapling. It bends but does not break as he draws his boots and skis out of the deeper snow.

In time, his wool-lined leather trousers damp from snow and pressure, he lies draped on more solid snow, his breath rasping as the wind rises and icy flakes drift through the high branches and down upon his woolen cap and dampened soul.

He sips from the narrow bottle that he soon refills with snow and places in the special trouser pocket, gnaws upon hard, half-frozen cheese, and takes a deep breath.

"Onward, Creslin, you noble idiot . . ."

Noon, or its approximation, and dusk fall too close together. In the growing dimness, despite ever more frequent rests, Creslin's legs ache continually. He falls frequently, even on the gentle downhills.

The barrier mountains look to be no closer, and the wind continues to rise, driving harder and thicker whiteness into Creslin's face.

Slide, lift, slide . . .

Is that a shadow behind the tall fir? Or behind the slender spruce?

Slide, lift, slide . . .

Frummmmppp . . .

"Enough . . . is . . . enough."

Creslin sits upon the snow, untwining the leather thongs, knowing that he cannot get back on the skis.

Twenty cubits downhill, through nearly waist-deep snow and the falling white curtain, he finds a fallen trunk. It will have to do.

In time, with frozen needles, the crushed branches beneath the trunk, and the striker in his belt pouch, he manages a small fire to warm himself as he prepares another hollow, one which, when lined with small branches and ample needles, may prove warmer than the last. He forces himself to eat and drink, and then not to sleep immediately, but to carve small branches with the knife and feed the small fire that helps warm him against wind and snow.

The snow hides the shadows; the flakes fall so furiously that no traces of a trail can survive.

Creslin wonders, not for the first time, whether he will either.

XV

"THERE IS STILL no word from either the road posts or our sources at Westwind. The Marshall refuses to declare mourning, but half the guards are wearing black on their sleeves when they're not around her."

"It is as though he vanished. How could she have let that happen? She doesn't even realize what he is." Frewya looks perplexed.

"Do you know that for a fact?" asks Ryessa.

"What do you mean?"

"Westwind must always be held by the daughter. That does not mean she does not love her son. Or that she is blind to what he is." The Tyrant frowns. "There was a rumor that Dylyss also had the talent."

"That would be horrifying, if true."

"Why? She's bound not to use it. Besides, that's not the issue, although it would explain—"

"Why did she let him ski into the winter storms?"

"Frewya, the boy was allowed to train with the guards, at least until I inquired. He could out-ski most of them. Our sources indicate that when he was refused permission to work out with them, he copied their workouts on his own. He was taught blade-work, or so we were told, in order to protect his honor and to deflect any criticism by the easterners. You saw what he did with a blade here. Yet after that, the Marshall had him taught more by the guard arms-master. I'm sure that the rationale was that after the episode here, he needed even greater skill. How convenient. He was also taught the traditional skills of numbers and rhetoric, and the old Temple tongue." She smiles a smile that is colder than most women's frowns. "And he does have some mastery of the winds, or so Megaera has assured me."

"But the guard source insisted he was not up to guard standards with blades. That is what you told me."

The older woman shrugs. "That may be true. How many men, even easterners, are up to guard standards?" Her face turns colder. "But I suspect he is better than most Westwind guards, given his parenting. Dylyss tends to omit the important details."

"You're saying that she had him taught enough to survive on his own?"

"Only if he wishes—she could not teach desire. He is bound to be naive about the ways of the world. Experience cannot be taught. She saw more than she was supposed to here, but even then, she refused to make it easy for him. She makes it easy for no one." Ryessa pauses. "Still, our turn will come."

"Insist that she find him!"

"How?" asked the Tyrant dryly. "How would we force the Marshall? With our might of arms?"

"What if he died on the mountain? Or what if he makes it across the Westhorns? Or even the Easthorns?"

"I don't think he died. After all, Megaera is still alive. I'm tempted to take her to Bleyans and strike the bracelets. She has to find him, you know, like the Furies. As for the easterners—if he makes it that far, and if Megaera finds him, in time they will regret it."

"You aren't planning to take on the magicians?"

"Why should I? Let us see what he can do, especially once Megaera is after him."

"Would the guards . . ."

The woman in the high chair shrugs. "Ask them, or find him, if you can. If not—"

"That is a dangerous game."

"Do we have any choice? Each year the wizards drive their road that much nearer us." The woman with the cold green fire in her eyes that complements the white-blond flame of her hair watches as her advisor departs.

In another room, a red-haired woman stares into the mirror that brings forth no reflection, only swirling gray.

Just one image, one clear moment—that is all she has glimpsed, the image of a man buried in snow—before the pain had become too great to hold the link.

Each time she reaches out, the bracelets burn, but she only bites her lips when they glow red-hot and when she can no longer bear the heat. Now her eyes flicker toward the iron-bound door, and they burn with a heat deeper than the iron on her wrists.

XVI

As HE SEES the clearing on the hillside, Creslin pushes slightly harder, despite the drudgery of forcing the skis through snow that has become steadily heavier and wetter as he has moved eastward and gradually lower. He has followed the ridge lines as much as possible.

The warm weather of the past two days has made sleeping damp and uncomfortable and the traveling slow. Outside of the several deer, a handful of snow hares, a few scattered birds, he has seen no living creatures. No other travelers, not even a trail. Through the trees, the eastern barrier peaks appear less than another range of hills away.

Now, nearly an eight-day after escaping the Roof of the World, he is almost through his meager supplies, and his jacket and trousers hang noticeably looser on his frame.

"Even Heldra would feel that I'm not carrying extra weight . . ." Talking to himself helps, at least some of the time.

The massive spruces and firs of the high forest have given

way to thinner-trunked pines and firs, interspersed with oaks and other bare-limbed trees he does not recognize.

His skis almost catch on a branch scantly covered by the heavy snow, and he lurches, but regains his balance. He listens. He hears nothing except the whispers of the wind, and those whispers bear no news. He studies the opening in the trees ahead but discerns no tracks, no structures.

Then he wipes his forehead. Even with his parka strapped to his pack, even in the shadows of the hill forests, travel during the day is hot.

Finally he slides the skis between the gaps in the trees and through a scattering of sparse branches poking up through the snow until he stands in unshadowed winter sunlight. The line of blackened trunks marching downhill bears witness to the reason for the clearing.

Creslin smiles. While the fire may have burned unchecked, the path of the devastation is to the northeast, and the snow, while heavy, is mainly open. He squints through the brightness of the mid-morning sun, a glare to which his eyes are unaccustomed. A narrow line of brown winds around the base of a hill and toward the barrier peaks and the east.

He shakes his head in wonder. Somehow, in some way, he has managed to find the trade road to Gallos. At least that is what he thinks it is. After withdrawing his hand from his heavy glove, he finds the melt bottle and takes a drink, careful to kneel on his skis and to replace what he has drunk with some of the cleaner snow.

After straightening up, Creslin brushes his finger across his uneven growth of beard; silver like his hair, he suspects, but he has brought no mirror. With a sigh, he puts the glove back on.

One way or another, he will reach the trade road by evening. Then his problems will really begin. While the road is beyond the control of the Marshall, he will have to avoid any guards she may send looking for a silver-haired youth. For he knows only too well that he is not a man . . . not yet.

With a glance behind him at the distant clouds overhanging the Roof of the World, he glides forward and begins the descent toward the valley and the road beyond.

Leaning, shifting his weight, he peers ahead, trying to anticipate the rough patches, seldom even having to turn because the heavy snow is so slow under the wooden skis. With each instant, he is farther from Westwind and from the sub-Tyrant of Sarronnyn. In time, through turns, lurches, and one fall—which leaves a damp stain on his leathers from his left leg to his shoulder—he glides, strides, and puffs his way through the snow and thicker underbrush until he can once again see the lower line of trees that marks the road.

By now the skis are heavy, the snow heavier, and the scraping of the branches, needles, and other debris beneath the snow more frequent. He slows to a halt and wipes his forehead with the back of his glove. His wool undershirt is damp, more from sweat than from snow. The lack of wind in and among the trees makes the day seem unusually warm.

The ground before him slopes gradually uphill toward where he believes the road to be. With a sigh, he starts out again, plodding uphill. Here the trees are farther apart, creating patches of ice and frozen, exposed branches and bushes.

Creslin eases himself along and begins to unthong his skis, wiggling his toes and stretching first one foot, then the other, as the tension from the leather straps is lifted. Deciding to carry the skis until he can see whether the road in fact lies over the hill crest, he marches across snow that barely covers the toes of his boots and plunges through white-crusted surfaces into powder nearly to his knees.

After all his uneven progress, he arrives, breathing hard, on a level stretch. Less than two dozen cubits away is the road he had observed from the hills behind him. Creslin sets down the skis and ponders.

He first strips off the leather thongs, winds them into a ball, and places them in his pack. Then he hides the skis in a deadfall, for they would be a giveaway. The sword he leaves in the scabbard strapped across the pack.

Less than ten cubits from the road, he stands in snow halfway to his knees, snow that would have melted were it not shaded by the pines.

Terwhit . . . terwhit.

The call of a bird he does not know, for there are few birds indeed upon the Roof of the World, whispers through the bare branches of the oaks and the green needles of the pines.

Terwhit . . .

With the gentle echo of the unseen bird still in his ears, he steps toward the road, if he dares to call it a road—more like two clay tracks surrounding a center space of dirty white. The clay lanes represent the sun's light upon the two wagon wheel tracks, melting them outward until each is nearly a cubit wide. The center snow is marked with irregular holes remaining from earlier footprints.

Creslin studies the road and the prints—just a single wagon and one rider, perhaps a pair of travelers walking, all of them heading to the west several days ago.

At least the day is pleasant, and walking on the cold and packed clay of the road will be a welcome change from slogging through the damp snow of the lesser mountains. He does miss the crisp cold of the Roof of the World and the easier strides across dry power.

"Do you?" he asks himself, recalling the powder-filled pits he had tumbled into. "Maybe not everything . . ."

He glances back along the winding road to the west. Nothing. His footsteps carry him from the snow that is little more than ankle-deep by the roadside onto the dark surface. Underfoot, the clay gives way, as if the mud is neither fully frozen nor completely loose.

He turns to the east, the sun at his back, and stretches out his legs. After so much time on skis, it will be good to walk for a while. The novelty will pale quickly, he knows, especially as the sun stands low in the western sky.

Are there any way stations on this road that should lead to Gallos? He does not know, nor does he know whether it would be wiser to use them or to avoid them. He does know that the coins in his belt pouch will not go far and that the heavy gold chain concealed within the belt itself is too valuable to display. Even a single link would betray his origin and make him a target. More of a target, he corrects himself.

At least the guards have not reached this far east. Not yet.

XVII

CLUNUNNNG . . . CLUNNGGG . . .

The impact of hammer and heavy steel chisel on cold iron echoes through the near-deserted smithy.

A red-haired woman kneels on the stone pavement, one wrist extended onto the anvil.

"That's one, your grace." The smith holds the heavy hammer and glances from the woman in traveling woolens kneeling before the anvil to the blond woman wearing the white of the Tyrant.

"Go ahead. Strike the other," orders Ryessa.

The kneeling woman extends her other wrist to the iron, her lips tightly pressed together.

"As you wish, your grace." But the smith shakes her head. The hammer falls.

"Thank you." As she rises, the redhead's words are addressed to the smith. She turns to the Tyrant. "And you also, sister."

"An escort awaits you, Megaera."

"An escort?"

"To Montgren. I thought it would make your task somewhat easier. I prevailed upon the Duke—"

"What did it cost you?" Megaera's fingers touch the heavy scars on her wrists, almost as if she cannot believe that the iron bonds are gone.

"Enough." The Tyrant's tone is sardonic. "I hope you and your lover are worth it."

"He's not my lover, and he never will be."

The Tyrant shakes her head. "Who else could there be?"

"You think that I intend to let you and Dylyss dictate my life? I may have to keep Creslin alive to save myself, but that doesn't mean I have to turn my body over to a mere man as if I were . . . a bond slave."

"That's not what I meant. Besides, you'll repay me, in oh-so-many ways."

Megaera raises her hands, and the Tyrant steps back involuntarily.

"Yes, my sister dear," the redhead responds, "you are right to fear me, but I pay my debts, and I'll pay this one."

"Don't try to repay me until you have left the western lands. There are three watches upon you."

"I scarcely expected less." Megaera has dropped her hands. "And in a strange way, I do owe you." She pauses. "Unlike you, I have never forgotten that we are sisters." She walks toward the stone stairs that lead to the stables. Unseen bands of fire still encircle her wrists, and her breath rasps in her throat. She swallows, but her head is held high.

XVIII

TERWITT . . .

The echo of the unknown bird vibrates through the near dark as Creslin peers into the gloom before him, seeing only empty road and bare-limbed trees between the thin ever-greens.

The sun has dropped behind the still-looming shadows of the mid-ranges of the Westhorns far earlier, not long after Creslin had set foot upon the scarce-traveled trade road to Gallos. In the lingering light, he has walked perhaps another four kays along the gently turning road.

Real evening descends, and no inn appears out of the gloom. Despite his sturdy boots, his feet feel the hardness of the frozen road clay with each step. For all his tiredness, Creslin keeps his tracks well within the hard clay patches upon the road rather than in the snow, determined not to leave a betraying trace for the guards should they have pushed this far eastward.

Has it been that far? How many kays has he covered in the more than eight days since he threw himself off the Roof of the World?

His thoughts drift back to his lessons, back to the Legend. Why did the angels come to the Roof of the World? Were men really so blind? How could anyone believe that either men or women had the right to rule by their sex?

He continues to put one foot before the other, looking all the while for a sheltered place in which to spend the night. Somehow, beyond his flickering vision, he can sense a structure. Not an inn, for there is no warmth to surround it, but . . . something.

Through three long turns of the road he trudges, feeling the strength of the mental image increase, until his eyes confirm his senses. The way station, half-buried in snow, has a solid roof and a squared arrangement of timbers and planks that can be tugged to cover the entrance.

Creslin approaches and steps over the drift in the stone-framed opening and peers inside. A small stack of dust-covered logs rests by the narrow hearth under the blackened chimney stones.

"Good enough . . ."

Setting his pack on the cold stones, he begins to peel

slivers of wood from the thinnest log until he has a pile at the back of the hearth. He steps back outside, breaks off several green fir branches and carries them within. His efforts with the striker are successful, and soon a small fire warms the hut. Later, he enjoys hot tea and nearly the last of his field rations. In time, he sleeps, his body relaxing in the comparative warmth.

Before dawn, he awakes with a shudder. Has something been searching for him: a white bird flying in a blue sky? Or a mirror filled with swirling white? For those are what he remembers, and the memories are stronger than a mere dream.

"A white bird . . . " Still within the winter quilt, he shakes his head. First a shadowy woman, and now a white bird? Guilt? Is that what he feels? For leaving his sister? For thwarting his mother the Marshall? Or is he suffering from exposure and hunger so that his mind is creating such illusions? And the mirror? What does the mirror mean?

Creslin takes a deep breath. The image of the woman he saw, long before exposure or hunger could have affected him. But the bird, the white bird, and the mirror—they could only have been a dream.

Is his whole life based upon dreams? Is everyone's? Dreams of a Legend? Dreams of a better time, and of a better place named Heaven? What really is he . . . besides a youth not yet a man who seems to fit nowhere?

His stomach growls. He draws himself from the quilt and into his boots and parka.

Outside the rough door barrier, in the gray darkness just before dawn, the wind moans. Creslin reaches into that grayness and touches the wind, samples the chill, and nods slowly. A dark day will dawn, leaden and windy but without snow, at least not until later.

After refolding and packing his cloak, he eats the remaining honey grain bar and a small lump of rock-hard yellow cheese, washing down the cheese with water from his melt bottle.

After sealing his pack, he brushes the ashes of the fire into a pile at the back of the hearth with an evergreen branch. He uses the same branch to obscure his steps through the snow from the road. With a few gusts of wind and a day or so, no one will know when the hut was last employed.

A hint of pink tinges one corner of the heavens, then fades into the dull gray of a cloudy day. Creslin's legs stretch out toward the eastern barrier peaks of the Westhorns, whose less-angled slopes rise not more than a handful of kays from where he walks.

A twinge in his shoulders reminds him of how far he has already carried his pack, although it is lighter now. With a deep breath that billows white fog before his face, he continues, even step upon even step, toward the east, his boots following the wagon tracks that have melted and refrozen, melted and refrozen.

XIX

"There were in Heaven in those days rulers of the angels, and the rulers had rulers above them, and, in turn, those rulers had rulers over them.

"More than half of the angels of Heaven were women, yet only some of the lowest of the rulers were women; fewer yet of those rulers of rulers were women; and none of the highest rulers were in fact women, nor even the Cherubim nor the Seraphim.

"The angels of Heaven were each like unto gods, and each could throw thunderbolts from a hammer held in her hand; each could travel vast leagues in chariot drawn by fire, either over the ground or through the skies.

"So when it came to pass that the angels of Heaven girded themselves for the battle with the demons of the light, those who were women asked this thing: For what reason do we fight the demons?

"The rulers of the rulers of the angels replied: We fight the demons of the light because they opposeth us.

"And the angels who were women asked again: For what reason do we fight the demons?

"They revere the light of chaos and they opposeth us, responded the Cherubim; and the rulers were sore affronted at the question.

"Still a lower ruler, an angel, yet a woman, bearing the name of Ryba, called for an answer from the Seraphim: The demons seeketh not our lands nor our lives, yet you would sacrifice our children, and our children's children, because the demons are not as we are.

"There can be no peace between angels and demons, not in the firmament of Heaven, not in the white depths of Hell, answered the Seraphim, girding up their loins and clasping unto themselves the swords of the stars that are suns and the dark lances of winter that shatter lands with their chill.

"You declare there can be no peace, when there has been peace, and you cannot yet answer why that peace mayest not continue. Thus persisted Ryba of the angels.

"And the Seraphim and the Cherubim were most wroth, and they gathered unto them all the angels that were men, and the white mists that tell of the truths that are within men and within women, be they angels or mortals. And they encircled all of the angels within the white clouds.

"Yet Ryba and lesser of the angels who were women broke from the circle and gathered themselves, their possessions, and their children unto themselves and unto their chariots, and they departed Heaven in their own way.

"The Cherubim and the Seraphim drew unto themselves all the angels that remained and armed all with the swords of the stars and the lances of winter, and carried destruction and night unto the demons of light.

"Across the suns that are stars, and even through the depths of winter between stars, the remaining angels pursued both the demons of light and the angels who had fled.

"But the demons of light drew unto their own ways and resources and builded for themselves the mirror towers of blinding light that dispersed back unto the angels the energies of the swords of the stars and the lances of winter.

"The stars dimmed, and the firmament that contained Heaven and all the stars and even the darkness between stars shook under the powers of the Cherubim and the Seraphim, and the change winds roared across the faces of the waters and blotted out the lights.

"Yet the demons were not dismayed, and mounted into their towers and hurled them against the angels, and again the firmament trembled and tottered, and this time, the stars fell into winter, and Heaven was rent in many places, and smoke that poisoned even the angels rose from that burning, and the Cherubim and the Seraphim, and the host of the angels perished, as did all but the strongest of the demons of light.

"Ryba, the least of the rulers of angels, thus became the last of the rulers, and the angels, having fallen from the stars after the time of the great burning, came unto the Roof of the World, where they gathered the winds for shelter and abided until the winter should lift.

"Yet upon the Roof of the World, as a memory of the fall of the angels, winter yet remains.

"So in that time, Ryba sent forth her people unto the southlands and the western ways, and told them: Remember whence you came, and suffer not any man to lead you, for that is how the angels fell . . ."

—*BOOK of RYBA*
Canto 1, Section II
(Original text)

XX

THE INN BARELY distinguishes itself from the trampled ice and heaped snow. It squats in the center of what might be meadows in the summer, its low stone walls not more than eight or nine cubits high, topped with a steep-pitched roof of gray slate tiles.

Creslin, his silver hair concealed by the oiled-leather parka hood he has tied tight as protection against the winds that have swirled around him for the past several kays, stands where the road widens out onto the flat valley holding the inn.

From the structure's two chimneys—one at the right end and one in the middle—white and gray smoke forms a thin line, flattened by the wind and barely visible against the overhead clouds and the snow-covered slopes behind the inn.

The sound of a horse's neigh echoes across the ice and the packed snow. Why would a horse be in the stables so soon after midday? Unless the beast was part of the party that had preceded him to the inn. With a shrug, Creslin takes a deep breath and starts toward the long building. Smoke continues to rise, but no figures brave the gusting winds.

A wooden door, braced with timbers, swings wide at the left side of the inn, and a bulky shape lumbers out and stops under the overhang of the eaves, facing Creslin and waiting.

Creslin continues along the stone road until he is less than two rods from the hitching rail that is nearly buried with snow shoveled from the two clear paths at the front of the building. One path, wide and filled with frozen hoofprints, leads leftward to the heavy door behind the solitary man. The other, narrow and covered with boards, leads straight to the inn itself.

Creslin glances to the left of the covered walkway, from where the odors of animals waft, and then to the right, where peeling paint on a battered board above a closed double door bears the imprint of a cup and a bowl.

"Who's the traveler?" asks a voice from behind the doors.

"Sort of thin to be out in the Westhorns alone. Bet he's a plant for Frosee's band." The heavy man grunts from before the stable door, his voice rumbling, his accent on the first syllables of the Temple tongue, a sure sign of a free trader, according to Creslin's former tutor. The trader's hand rests loosely on the hilt of a belt knife.

The inn door opens, then closes as a thin man wearing a sheepskin vest steps out.

"Nah. Clothes are his, but they're loose, like he's lost weight." The thin man wears a hand-and-a-half sword across his shoulders, much the way Creslin wears his shorter blade.

Creslin looks from the heavy man to the thin man and back again.

"Doesn't look all that strong," rumbles the big man as he steps forward.

Not knowing exactly what to do, Creslin nods politely. "You're right. The clothes are mine. But who is Frowsee?"

"Frosee," corrects the big trader. "He's a bandit."

Creslin steps onto the boardwalk. The thin man does not move.

"I beg your pardon," Creslin states quietly.

"Boy has manners, at least," observes the big man.

The thin man studies Creslin without speaking.

Creslin returns the study, noting the mustached narrow face, the hard gray eyes, the heaviness in chest and gut that may signify a mail or plated leather vest, and the short knife that complements the long sword.

"Younger son?"

Creslin considers the question, then nods. "It was a little more complicated than that, but I had to leave." Even the incomplete truth gnaws at his guts, but he fights back the feeling and continues to watch the thin man, for he is the more dangerous of the two.

"The blade?"

"Mine."

The thin man looks at Creslin again before turning.

"You just going to let him in, Hylin?" grumbles the trader.

"You stop him if you want. He's no danger to you, unless you meddle." The thin man opens the inn door.

"So, boy . . . why are you here?" The trader waddles toward Creslin.

"Because it's on the way east. Now, if you will excuse me . . ." He steps around the trader toward the inn door.

"I was talking to you!" A heavy hand grasps his shoulder.

Creslin finds that he has reacted, that the guard drills have fulfilled their purpose in a way not intended by Aemris or Heldra. He finds himself looking over the prone figure of the trader.

"I'll have your head . . ."

"I think not," interrupts a new voice. A woman, gray-haired and heavyset, stands in the open doorway. "The young fellow was trying to be polite, and you grabbed him. Besides, Derrild, you haven't got sense enough to come out of the west-blows. Your man told you not to mess with the young fellow. He could see a fighting man, even if you couldn't. Young doesn't mean unskilled." She turned to Creslin. "And you, young fellow, looks and skill are fine, but coins are what buy hospitality."

"I did not mean trouble, lady." Creslin inclines his head and upper body. "The tariff?" he asks in the Temple tongue, knowing that his accent differs from the innkeeper's.

"The tariff?" The woman looks bewildered.

"The amount for food and lodging."

"Oh, the charges. Four silvers for a room, another silver for each meal."

While Creslin can afford such charges, at least for a time, he knows the numbers are high and tries to let his face show some astonishment. "Five silvers?"

" 'Tis high, but we must pay dearly for the food and spirits."

"Three would be larceny, kind lady, but five is high extortion. And that would be for a room fit for a queen."

A smile crosses her face, perhaps at his language. "For a fine face such as yours, I would settle for mere larceny, and even throw in a hot tub. With so little trade, you can even sleep alone, though . . ." Her eyes rake over him.

"Humph," rumbles the trader, who has lurched to his feet. "Baths. A nuisance designed by women."

"And a meal?" pursues Creslin, ignoring the innuendo.

"And a meal. Without high spirits, though." Her voice turns harder as she lifts the broom. "You pay in advance."

Creslin looks at the clouds overhead, then nods.

"Come on in, before we lose all the heat from the fires."

Once inside, with both doors firmly shut, the woman waits as Creslin fumbles out three silvers. He is thankful that the larger coins are concealed within the heavy travel belt.

The room she leads him to contains one double-width bed, a table scarcely more than two hands wide, and a candle lamp. The stone floor is uncovered and the window barely more than a slit.

"Even a pillow and a proper coverlet!" exclaims the gray-haired innkeeper.

"You mentioned a bath?"

"Ah, yes. The bath comes with the room."

"And a good towel, I'd wager," Creslin adds cheerfully.

"You will break us yet, young sir."

"Perhaps we should just head for the bath," Creslin suggests, catching a whiff of himself.

"As you wish."

Creslin continues to carry both pack and sword, oblivious to the unspoken suggestion that he leave them in the room.

When he sees the bath, Creslin understands the snort from the heavy trader. The small room contains two stone tubs into which hot mineral waters slowly flow from a two-spouted fountain. Despite the faint odor of sulfur, the hot water is more than welcome, and Creslin uses his straight razor to remove his sparse beard, nicking himself only once or twice.

After the innkeeper leaves him by himself, he washes out his underclothes, wringing them as dry as possible before pulling on the spare undergarments from his pack and re-donning his leathers. Then he returns to his room.

The towel and damp clothes he smoothes out across the footboard. After barring the door, he drops on the bed. Within moments, he is asleep.

Cling . . . cling . . .

At the sound of the bell, Creslin jerks upright. How long has he slept? All night? The darkness outside the window could mean either early evening or predawn. He sits up, fumbles the striker from his belt, and coaxes the candle into light. The clothes on the footboard remind him of his garb, and he rises and touches the garments. Too damp for morning, he decides.

Finally he pulls on his boots, slings the pack across one shoulder, and unbars the door, stepping into the dimly lit hall.

Four of the dozen tables in the Common Room are occupied. After taking a small table for two, Creslin eases the pack under the table and ignores the looks from the heavy trader and from a red-bearded man who sits at a circular table with a woman and three male blades.

Another gray-haired woman, even thinner than the innkeeper, wipes her hands on a once-white apron as she eases up to Creslin's table. "We have a bear stew or a crusty fowl pie, and either ale or red wine. The wine is extra."

"What would *you* eat?"

"They're about the same. For another silver, there's a pair of lamb cutlets."

The silver-haired youth smiles faintly, wondering if he could have bought the entire lamb for a silver. "Stew and ale."

"Will that be all?"

Creslin nods. As she scuttles past the hearth toward the kitchen, he glances toward the red-bearded man, who has returned to the meat before him, presumably the lamb. One of the blades, a grizzled man with a short salt-and-pepper beard and a single ear, glares back at Creslin, who returns the hostile look with a polite smile.

The blade who had studied Creslin earlier at the inn's

entrance begins to talk to the trader. Derrild shakes his head. Once, twice. Finally he nods, and the blade stands up.

He steps over to Creslin's table. "Mind if I sit for a moment? Name is Hylin. Road guard for Derrild. He's a trader."

Still waiting for the stew, Creslin gestures to the battered chair across from him.

"You handled Derrild pretty easy there."

"Rather stupidly," admits Creslin, still not comfortable with the Temple tongue. "I did not think."

"You're from the far west, I take it?"

Creslin raises his eyebrows, not wishing to admit anything.

Hylin shrugs. "You talk Temple like some fellows I knew from Suthya, but you're fair, and I never saw anyone with real silver hair before."

"Nor I, either," laughs Creslin, though he has to quell his turning stomach as it reminds him of Llyse and a silver-haired man.

"We're headed to Fenard, and then to Jellico. Derrild wouldn't be adverse to having another blade. He's tight. Probably wouldn't pay more than a copper a day, but he's got a spare mount. Berlis stayed in Cerlyn." The thin man looked at the floor. "Could be better than walking. Faster anyway."

"You are worried?" Creslin senses the uneasiness in the other man, like a dark fog hovering behind his eyes.

"Me? Devils be damned, I'm worried. A cart, two pack mules, and a fat trader, with just one blade?"

Creslin nods. "Two would be the right number?"

"Right. Three says Derrild's carrying jewelry and perfumes, and one and an empty saddle says that we're hurting."

While he does not follow the logic, Creslin understands the feelings. "I am interested."

"Show up at the second bell in the morning."

Creslin raises his eyebrows again.

"You are from a long ways away. Second bell is right after the early breakfast for the hard travelers. Same in all the road inns, leastwise from the Westhorns east. Cerlyn's as far west as I've been."

"Second bell, then," Creslin affirms.

The thin man starts to rise, then pauses. "You can ride?"

"Better than I walk," Creslin responds with a chuckle.

Hylin nods and walks back to Derrild's table, where he resumes his seat and begins talking in a low voice to the trader.

Creslin shifts his attention to the tall man seated alone at another table for two in the far corner, dark-haired and with a mustache, but wearing no beard. After a glance, the silver-haired youth looks away from the white mist that looms unseen around the single figure.

He almost laughs as he wonders what he would see were he to look at himself. Would the naivete be as obvious to others as it is to himself?

"The white bird and the shadow woman . . . trouble for someone tonight . . ."

Creslin's ears burn at the low words, but he cannot distinguish from whose lips they issued, save that a man spoke them.

With a thud, a chipped gray mug filled with a soapy-looking liquid lands on the table. The thin serving woman is already two tables past him, unloading the rest of the meal from her wooden tray onto the table of the largest group: the man and woman with the three male blades, clearly an eastern party, beyond the impact of the Legend.

As he surveys the public room through the smoky haze from the fire and the kitchen, Creslin realizes that he is the only totally clean-shaven male in the inn. Most are bearded. Only Hylin and the dark man in the corner have no beards—only mustaches, and both seem clearly hired blades.

Is that coincidence? And what does being clean-shaven mean?

He takes a sip of the warm ale, carefully. His caution is rewarded as he is able to swallow that bitter sip rather than choke it down. As he waits for the stew, he listens, picking up fragments that those who spoke would not have believed could be overheard.

". . . swear those are leathers of the Westwind guard . . . woman playing at being a man?"

". . . heard him speak . . . doesn't sound like a woman."

". . . weather witch says a cold blow coming out of the north . . ."

The smoke from the fire and haze from the kitchen thicken until Creslin's eyes begin to burn. A pair of men in scuffed herdsmen's jackets shuffle their worn boots across the stone floor and drop themselves at the table next to Creslin. Sheepherders or goatherders, by the smell, Creslin decides.

He gestures absently, his ears on the conversations surrounding him, and the smoke gently sifts away from his eyes.

". . . look," hisses a low voice. "The smoke . . ."

Creslin abruptly releases his hold on the air and the smoke, letting them swirl where they will.

"What about the smoke?"

"I could have sworn . . ."

The silver-haired youth takes a slow, deep breath, not quite cursing himself for stupidity, and continues to listen.

". . . took the big trader without even touching his blade."

". . . assassins' guild . . ."

". . . you don't have to talk to him, Derrild. Just pay him . . . couldn't get his like for two golds anywhere else."

Creslin smiles faintly at the overestimation of his abilities.

". . . what do the wizards want now, besides everything between the Easthorns and Westhorns?"

". . . thank the light . . . never have to go back to Land's End. Why anyone thinks the place is worth having . . ."

". . . you can buy anything you want, dearest, once we get to Fenard."

The chipped crockery bowl of stew arrives in the same unceremonious way as the soapy ale had. A battered tin spoon protrudes from one side of the bowl, and the thin brown liquid drips onto the table, almost onto the wide and crusty slab of bread strewn beside the bowl.

Creslin lifts the spoon. Although the stew is nearly as heavily seasoned as Sarronnese burkha, the combination of peppers and assorted spices drown out the taste of whatever had been passed off for bear. Still, the spiced potatoes, wilted carrots, and shredded meat are an improvement over the field rations he has eaten since he skied off the Roof of the World. The bread is harder than anything carried in his pack, but both stew and bread are improved by eating them together.

"Doesn't look like a wizard. Too young . . ."

"A wizard can look any age he wants."

Creslin ignores the speculations, although his foot nudges his pack and sword to reassure himself of their availability. He spoons in the mixture, interspersed with bites from the heavy brown bread, until the bowl is empty. The ale, warm as it is, and even with its faintly soapy tang, cuts the bitter aftertaste of the so-called bear stew. But he is careful to drink as little from the mug as possible.

Creslin has not finished the ale when he stands and shoulders his pack.

"You be done, ser?" The serving woman, who has scarcely seemed to notice him, suddenly appears.

Creslin represses a smile and slips her a copper, guessing that her presence signifies her belief in an undeserved reward of sorts.

"Thanks be to you, ser." Her voice is polite but not edged.

Creslin swallows his relief at his judgment, and with his pack half on his shoulder, slips around the two sheep-reeking individuals, brushing the shoulder of the nearer with the edge of the pack.

"Hey . . ." The man, with a scraggly black beard, looks at Creslin as if to stand.

"I beg your pardon," Creslin offers flatly.

The man takes in Creslin's face and the short sword on the pack and sits down. "Sorry, ser."

Creslin nods and continues toward the doorway.

"Polite . . . like one of the prefect's killers."

"Still say he's a witch."

Once outside the Common Room, Creslin turns left and down the stone-walled corridor that leads to his room. A single oil lamp flickers halfway down the hall. Before he enters his room, he pauses, listening, trying to sense whether someone might be within, although he cannot fathom why anyone would take the trouble. The room is empty, and he eases open the door. From what he can tell, no one has been there since he left, and his parka remains on the hook, his gloves protruding from the pockets.

He closes the door.

The bar in place, he sets his pack on the far side of the bed, where he can reach the sword instantly if need be. Then he sits down on the bed, which sags but does not creak, and eases off his boots, followed by the leathers. He folds the leathers on the table.

With the warm coverlet, underclothes are enough, and Creslin still does not like sleeping in his clothes. As an afterthought, he walks to the foot of the bed and checks the underclothes spread out there. They are only damp now. Likely they will be dry in the morning, at least dry enough to put in his too-empty pack. The stone is not as chill under his bare feet as he would have thought, perhaps because of the thermal springs underneath the inn.

His eyes are heavy by the time he slips under the coverlet and blows out the candle.

The room is still dark, pitch dark, when he wakes. He does not move, for someone is in the room. He knows this even though there has not been a sound. Through slitted eyes, and with his other methods of sensing objects, he studies the room as well as he can. The bar on the door remains undisturbed.

Finally he rolls over, as if turning in his sleep, not sure that he is really awake.

"That is unnecessary." The voice is low and husky, feminine. "You know that I am here, and I know that you know."

Creslin sees a woman in a pale garment seated on the end of the bed. In the darkness, he cannot tell the color of her hair, except that it is not blond or pale. That darkish hair glitters with the tiniest of red sparks.

He struggles to a sitting position, not sure but whether he isn't dreaming. "Who are you?"

"You can call me Megaera."

"That's an odd name."

"Only if you do not know the legend behind the Legend." She moves closer to him. "Unfortunately, I am yours, and you do not even know me."

The huskiness of the voice causes him to shiver even as he reaches for her, not knowing whether she is real.

"But . . ."

His hands part the pale garment. Her body is warm against his, and her lips burn . . .

But Creslin awakens alone in the middle of a rumpled bed, the predawn light as bright as any sun to his night sight. He squints and turns.

The shadowy lady is gone. Creslin frowns, looking from the rumpled coverlet beside him to the barred door and the narrow window. The dark-haired beauty has vanished, yet no human frame could fit through the hand-span clearance of the window, even were it full open. And how could she have barred the door from the outside?

Yet the bar remains in place across the door, and the dust on the floor by the window and on the window ledge remains unmoved. Though the fragrance of ryall had seared his nostrils as he had crushed her to him, no fragrance remains on the coverlet where he thought she had lain. Had it been a dream?

He flushes as he recalls the details.

Megaera—is that her name? What is it that she had said? The words that had seemed so portentous in the evening are near lost in the sunlit morning. Near lost, but not totally lost. Creslin begins to recall the darkness . . .

". . . the Legend. Unfortunately, I am yours, and you do not even know me. Now, harsh wizard, though you try, never will you escape me, neither through purpose nor deed, for I am sealed to your soul . . . and for that, you will pay."

Who is she? How did she find him? And why will he pay? She had resisted—but not for long—and she had shared his bed.

He swallows, not quite believing that he could have forced himself on her . . . but had he?

He swings his feet onto the stone, recognizing that one reason he is not chill is that he wears his underclothes. He had worn underclothes to bed, taking to heart the innkeeper's admonition that the nights in the Westhorns were cold, even with the inn's fires stoked high. Yet he recalls warm skin on warm skin. Even in the empty room, alone, he flushes.

So why is he shivering as though the ice of the Westhorns has knifed through his heart?

Megaera?

He shakes his head and stands, shuffling to the basin of cold water, where he splashes another kind of chill upon his face. Thinking about the natural hot baths at the other end of the inn, he stops, then purses his lips.

After a moment, when he looks out through the narrow window at the patterns of frost upon the grass in the field across the road from the inn, he continues his ablutions with the clean, cold water he had not used the night before.

After he dries his face and hands, he folds the towel over the wooden peg on the edge of the table and then unfolds the heavy leathers. By the second bell, he must meet Hylin and Derrild.

But his eyes flicker back to the pillow as he pulls on his boots, and his thoughts linger on a mirror, although he cannot say why.

XXI

IN CONTRAST TO the ice-rain and the gloom of the day before, the morning dawns bright and clear, the sun thrusting its light through the sole gap in the eastern peaks of the Westhorns and thus through the narrow windows of the Cup and Bowl long before half the travelers have struggled awake.

In the stable, his breath steaming like the caldrons in the kitchen, Creslin studies the horse, taller and more fragile than the battle ponies of Westwind's guards. Finally he touches the chestnut gelding's shoulder, avoiding an old scar, and concentrates on reassuring the beast. In time, he checks the bridle and the rest of the fittings before beginning to saddle up.

"I never got your name . . . or what you'd be called if the name's a problem." Hylin watches but for a moment before saddling his own horse, a heavier and younger gray. "Derrild'll be here 'fore long."

"I'll be ready." Creslin wears his sword in the shoulder harness, as he has been battle-trained, outlandish as it may appear to the easterners. Only on ceremonial occasions do the guards wear sword-belts. "Call me Creslin."

"Creslin . . ." The thin man rolls the sound across his tongue. "Weren't for that beard you had the other day, and that silver hair, you'd pass for one of those devil guards."

"Devil guards?"

"You know. Haven't you heard of them? Those women fighters off the Roof of the World. The ones that destroyed Jerliall two years ago." The small man tightens the straps on a pack mule, then stacks the fitted bags onto the harness.

"Jerliall?" The name is unfamiliar, but then, Creslin realizes, there is so much he does not know.

"You really don't know, do you?"

Creslin shakes his head.

"Stop the jabbering, and let's get on the road." Derrild's voice is even thicker than on the day before. The trader jabs a heavy arm at Hylin and then toward the half-open stable door.

In turn, Hylin turns toward the youth. "Give me a hand, would you, Creslin?"

Creslin skirts the gelding and begins to hand the cargo bags to Hylin one at a time as the trader wrestles another mule out into the yard and into cart traces.

Silently, Hylin and Creslin load a second pack mule while Derrild mumbles and stacks bags and boxes in the cart. "Frigging cold. Hell of a time to trade . . . got to be crazy to be a trader."

Creslin looks toward the hulking and bearded man, then toward Hylin.

"Don't mind him." Hylin checks the harness. "He talks to himself a lot, but he's careful. He doesn't get drunk, and he pays. Can't say that about too many traders. It's a hard life, being a trader."

"Must be harder being a guard."

"Some ways, but we get paid whether he makes money or not."

Creslin frowns, not having considered that a trader might well lose money. "Does he do . . . well?"

"Can't say as I know. But he's still in business, and has been for a long time, and he has a solid house in Jellico, with a stable. His son takes the shorter runs, north to Sligo, or south to Hydlen."

Creslin nods as he hands the last bag to Hylin. "What about the east?"

"Ha . . . no money trading there. Not much risk. Not even someone like Frosee messes with the wizards' road guards." The thin man tightens the last of the straps and begins to lead the pair of mules out of the stable. "Same thing's true out west. Between those devils of the mountains and the Tyrant, not much thieving goes on. So anyone can be a trader."

"They just think they're traders," rumbles Derrild as he finishes loading the cart. "They carry a wagon load of cabbage twenty kays and they're a trader. Bah!"

Creslin holds the reins of both the gray and the chestnut; his breath steams in the chill air. He has strapped his pack behind his saddle, between the near-empty saddle bags that contain grain cakes, presumably for the horse.

"Let's go. The sooner we get moving, the sooner I can warm myself before the fire at home." Derrild levers himself onto the cart seat, his right hand touching the leather-wrapped handle of some sort of weapon.

After readjusting the stirrups, Creslin swings into the saddle.

Hylin merely grunts.

"Where to?" the younger man asks.

"You haven't been this way?"

"This is as far east as I've ever been."

The mercenary raises his eyebrows under the hood of his stained leather cloak but says nothing as he nudges the gray forward.

Creslin rides half a length back, his eyes already on the narrow cleft at the edge of the snow-covered meadow—a cleft that points eastward. The weight of the blade on the shoulder straps reminds him that he is, for now, a guard of sorts, with a horse that will carry him eastward faster than his legs will. He eases up closer to the mercenary. "Tell me about Gallos . . . whatever you can."

Hylin snorts, then half-smiles. "We're headed for Fenard, named after, I'm told, the great King Fenardre. The storytellers claim he was the one who beat back the Legions of the West. And his was the first kingdom that didn't swallow the tyranny of the Legend. Fenard sits on a high plain and has two walls. The lower wall is more than ten times the height of a man . . ."

XXII

THE COACH RUMBLES northward along the main post road from Bleyans, through Suthya, northward to the port of Rulyarth.

Megaera looks down at the white leather case that contains the mirror, then shakes her head. Why is it that using the mirror now leaves her stomach twisting? Can it have something to do with the lifelink? She tries to call up the familiar sense of the whiteness. Her wrists tingle, even though the iron bracelets are gone.

So far, she has managed to send her soul out after the silver-haired target three times—once to even touch his mind, the evening before, from her inn to his inn. Her lips tighten. "Men—even the most innocent—are violent beasts, even in their thoughts."

Her eyes fix on her sleeves, long enough to cover the scarred wrists, but her eyes fail to focus, and she feels lightheaded. Is it her imagination? Is there a reason why, at times, her head spins like the winds she can sense but cannot touch?

"No! Why him and not me?"

"Are you all right, my lady?" The guard leans down and peers through the open coach window.

"The Legend be damned if I know . . ." Megaera glares at the guard. Her eyes spark with a white flame even as her head begins to ache.

The guard's visage jerks back, vanishing from Megaera's sight, just before a line of fire flares through the window.

Megaera purses her lips and listens to the driver and the guard, straining to hear their low voices above the rumble and the rattle of the coach.

". . . careful there . . . Tyrant warned you . . ."

". . . be damned glad when we get to Rulyarth . . . damned glad."

"Look at it this way, mate. Anyone tries to stop us, and look what they'd get! Ha!"

". . . sooner she's headed east where she belongs, the happier—"

"Relax. Just be glad you're not after her boyfriend. He's worse, they say."

"He's not my boyfriend!" The words hiss through Megaera's teeth and rattle in her mind. "Damn you, sister . . ." But the tears roll from the corners of her eyes as she recalls two girls stalking each other in a courtyard. Then it had been in play.

XXIII

THE ECHO OF the hooves resounds from the stone walls at Creslin, even as he can see ahead to where the canyon widens and the shadows of the hills rise beyond the last stone ramparts of the Westhorns.

Ahead of him, Hylin touches the hilt of the sword at his

belt, leaning forward as if straining to hear someone, or something.

Creslin wonders why the mercenary appears so concerned now when they are about to reach the rolling plains of Gallos after nearly three days on winding mountain trails. Still, the man has far more experience than he does. Creslin gathers his senses and spreads himself to the winds, especially to those eddying around the trail where it opens into the brushy valley ahead.

The effort brings beads of sweat to his normally cool forehead, and he sways slightly in the saddle. After a time, however long it takes for the horses to tread another half kay, he straightens.

"Hylin . . ." His voice is raspy, for his throat has dried out. "There are two or three people down there, behind that ridge that faces where we'll leave the protection of the rocks."

Hylin's sword is out and pointed toward Creslin. "You said you'd never traveled this far."

"I haven't. I just know they're there."

Hylin studies the youth's face for a long moment. "I don't know, but it doesn't make sense you'd be with them."

Creslin waits.

"But how do you know, damn it?"

Creslin shrugs. "Sometimes . . . I can feel where people are, if there are winds around them. That's part of what got me in trouble." His stomach tightens at the partial deception, and he wonders if every untruth or incomplete truth will continue to torment him so. He blinks, and when he clears his eyes, he sees that Hylin has lowered the sword and dropped back to the cart, where he is talking with the trader.

". . . damned witch as well . . ."

". . . damned . . . or not."

". . . have him do it . . ."

"Creslin? Can you handle a bow?"

"Not as well as a sword," confesses the silver-haired

youth, without the slightest tremor in his guts. "But I can usually hit the target."

Hylin is holding what might be called a short longbow. "If you know where these bandits, or whatever, are, could you slip down to just short of the gate rocks up ahead and arch an arrow over the ridge? There's not much cover there."

Creslin frowns. "What good would that do? I don't know how much power an arrow would have from that far away."

"It just has to get there. Most of these types want to surprise you. I think an arrow or two might send them on their way. If it doesn't," Hylin shrugs, "it sure doesn't cost us much."

Creslin understands both elements of the man's logic— that, and the fact that Hylin will be guarding Derrild and whatever the trader's goods are.

Creslin takes the bow and ties the quiver to the free brass ring beside his right knee, realizing his own naiveté again. He has not the faintest idea of what goods the trader carries, nor has he ever asked. Keeping to the side of the road so as not to be visible from beyond the exit of the pass that will lead to the rolling plains, Creslin nudges his mount forward.

In time, he reins up, holding the bow. Before he nocks the arrow, once again he sends forth his senses upon the light breezes.

The three figures remain behind the ridge.

He draws the bow to the full, then releases the arrow, feeling it as it soars, then drops toward the three.

Creslin can sense the impact of the iron arrowhead as it strikes the boulder before one of the waiting riders.

"Demons!"

"Where are they shooting from?"

He releases a second shaft, correcting slightly and touching the winds, as if they may help guide the feathered missile.

The shaft penetrates a heavy shoulder.

"Move!"

"Can't fight what you can't see . . ."

"Devils!"

The muffled clops of the hooves echo back up the canyon as Creslin nudges the chestnut back toward Hylin and Derrild.

Hylin smiles faintly. "They're leaving, all right."

Creslin nods. "Two arrows."

"Hit anyone?"

"One, I think, by the sounds." Creslin's stomach twists at the misrepresentation. When will he learn not to volunteer unnecessary and misleading information, he wonders.

"Thought you said you were better with the sword."

"I am." The words slip out before Creslin can catch them.

"Oh . . ." The trader's involuntary comment drifts upward from the cart.

Hylin's lips tighten for a moment, then he swallows. "Let's take it easy, just to make sure."

Only faint traces inform the three of the would-be bandits: smudged hoofprints, a shattered arrow, and a few dark splotches on a low boulder.

XXIV

FOR THE LESS than half a day it takes the three to cross the rolling plains from the edge of the Westhorns to the plateau on which the city of Fenard squats, Creslin is largely silent, wondering about his success with the winds and the arrows, wondering exactly how far beyond the winds his talents lie, if indeed he has talents.

Twice he sees a white bird, one he has never seen before except in his dreams, circling overhead before disappearing. Neither time does he see it appear or vanish, and the second time, on the stone-paved bridge crossing the river to the northwest gate of Fenard, he shakes his head.

"You're right, young fellow. Those are witch birds. That's what the Suthyan women told me, anyhow. Witches watch people through their eyes."

Is the woman who called herself Megaera a witch? Is her name even Megaera? And what does it mean? And why will he pay? With a second shiver, he drops the questions. She has to be a witch. But why does she follow him?

"Careful. The guards here are sort of touchy," Hylin volunteers.

"Oh?"

"They worry about everyone being an agent of the White Wizards," rumbles Derrild from the cart. "As if worrying'd do them much good."

"I don't know much about the White Wizards—" begins Creslin.

"Later," hisses the mercenary.

Three guards in black leathers greet the travelers at the post on the far side of the bridge. A low stone wall runs along the eastern bank of the small river, broken only by the bridge and the stone gates.

The main city walls are a good kay ahead. Fenard appears to have been designed to withstand a prolonged assault, yet Creslin cannot recall any tales about battles in or around the city.

"Your business?" asks the middle guard.

"Trade," wheezes Derrild. He flourishes a heavy leather folder, letting it fall open to a page on which is embossed a gilt seal over purpled wax. "My seal . . . from the prefect."

The guard nods politely. "And what are you trading this season? Any hempweed or dreamdust?"

"Demons' brew," Derrild snorts. "None of that. A few trinkets; some spices, like ryall seeds; some vials of cerann oil; purple glaze paste from Suthya for the potters of Jellico."

"Let's see." The guard steps toward the bags on the cart.

Derrild sighs as he slides off the cart's bench seat. "What's a poor trader to do?" He loosens the largest sack. "If you would like to see for yourself . . ."

The guard peers into the sack.

Derrild thumps the sack, and a faint, dusty haze surrounds the guard's head. "Just dried glaze powder . . ."

"ChhheeWWW . . . AHHHCHWEEE . . . ACHWEEE . . ." Tears stream down the guard's cheeks as he continues to double over with violent sneezing.

"Now, in this pack . . . here is the cerann oil. Each vial is stoppered with wax. That's because the oil can burn your skin . . ." Derrild's voice rumbles on as if nothing has happened.

"CHHWEEE . . . ACHWEEE . . ."

The trader gestures toward the third sack. "And here—"

"Just . . . CHWEEEE . . . move on . . . ACHHWEEE."

Hylin's lips are pressed tightly together as they lead the mules past the two lesser guards. One of the guards, a youth not any older than Creslin, also has his lips pressed tightly together.

Not until they are almost to the main walls, with an open and unguarded gate, does Derrild comment. "Damned officious fool. Waste of good glaze powder. They never learn."

Hylin shakes his head. "Even his own guards were trying not to split their sides laughing."

"Why didn't he use his weapons after that?" asks Creslin.

"Because he can't. He turns on one of the trade guild, and we'll threaten to send everything to Kyphrien."

"But Kyphrien is still part of Gallos," Creslin points out.

"True enough, but the guards are paid out of the *city*'s trade levies. Would you want to explain to the prefect how you caused all the traders to leave Fenard?"

"Besides," adds Hylin with a laugh like a barking dog, "the traders have been looking for a reason to make the trade center of Gallos in Kyphrien. It's warmer, and the prefect is here."

"Wouldn't he just move?"

"It's not that simple," Hylin responds. "The foretellers have said for generations that Fenard shall not fall if the prefect holds the Great Keep."

Creslin raises his eyebrows.

"Ah, yes, it's superstition," interrupts the trader from the creaking cart. "But rulers have to follow superstition. What happens if Vaslek moves to Kyphrien? Then the peasants and the soldiers immediately believe that the city will fall, and they start looking for the worst. Their belief encourages some fortune-seeker to split off northern Gallos and live in the Great Keep, and before long, you've got a war and then some."

"Just because of beliefs?" Creslin shakes his head.

"Don't laugh, young fellow," rumbles the trader. "What about those women guards? They're the deadliest fighters on either side of the Westhorns, and it's at least in part because they believe in that damned Legend about the Fall from Heaven being caused by men."

Creslin says nothing. Is the Legend enough reason for the Westwind guards' success? Or is that just what other people say, while they ignore the precision and the training that create a guard?

The lowlands between the river and the walls bear the green haze of a recently planted crop, but there are no farmhouses, no fences. Creslin turns in the saddle to look back to the river, then smiles as he understands the city's defenses. Doubtless there are hidden gates in the levees that would flood the lowlands, turning those fields nearly a kay wide into marsh and mud.

The hooves of the horses and mules clatter on the causeway leading to the outer city wall. Although the gates are massive and sit on steel hinges and pillars guarded by even more massive granite walls, only a pair of guards, and those high on the wall, oversee the actual entrance to the city.

"Let's get to the Gilded Ram," wheezes the trader. "Long day tomorrow. And you'll get an education, western boy. Will you get an education!"

"Education?" Each question Creslin asks makes him feel less sophisticated, but there is so much he does not know.

"That's Derrild's way of saying that while the prefect may be rather distant, the women here can be very friendly."

"They can be so friendly that they end up with everything you own and then some," grouses the trader without looking at either of his hired guards. "Take the second wide street we come to. The Ram is on the left side, by a woodcrafting shop, before we get to the Great Square."

Not understanding how he is supposed to take directions from places he will not even reach, Creslin throws his senses to the light spring breezes that swirl around him, trying to locate a great square.

A Great Square there is, thronged with people and small merchants. But beyond and behind, or perhaps above and behind, Creslin also finds a mist, a reddish-white smokiness invisible to his eyes, that hangs over the city like an unseen pall, or fog. Even the lightest touch of that smokiness twists his stomach, and he is forced to withdraw into himself almost as soon as he has located the Great Square.

He sways in the saddle for an instant before his reflexes and training take over.

"You all right?"

"Yes." Creslin wipes his forehead with the back of his sleeve. "It will pass." Yet he wonders what it is about the city that bothers him, even after they are unsaddling in the stable behind the Gilded Ram.

Derrild appears from the inn with a grim look on his face. "Get those mules unloaded. That locker there!"

Hylin and Creslin exchange glances, but not words.

"You have to clean out the stalls before we leave in the

morning," announces Derrild while the two guards begin unloading the bags and transferring them into a solid red-oak locker encircled in black iron.

"We're not stable hands," snaps Hylin, halting with a bag in his arms.

"I know. It's worth an extra day's pay."

"Just this time," concedes the thin mercenary, handing the bag to Creslin, who stacks it in the rear corner of the locker.

"Agreed," sighs the trader, and he begins to remove certain small packages from the cart and place them within his own pack. He looks at the locker and shakes his head. "They say it's safe." He shakes his head again. "Keep the glaze powder until the last."

Hylin nods. "You want it tipped so that it falls if anyone else opens the locker?"

Derrild nods glumly. "Waste of good glaze powder, but what can you do? Robbers even here in Fenard. They're all thieves."

"They wouldn't let you bring the stuff into the inn?"

"No. Some order of the prefect's. I tried the Brass Goat across the way, but they said the same thing. Two inns caught fire last year. The idiots were carrying cammabark."

Creslin looks up blankly, then staggers under a bag of heavy and lumpy objects Hylin thrusts at him. "Cammabark?"

"It's a wet root that grows in the southern marshes. When it dries, it burns almost like demon-fire. Anyone with any sense carries it in wet canvas." Derrild lugs bags from the cart to the locker.

In the background, a small boy is dragging a bale of hay through the stable doorway.

Derrild turns. "Boy! Which stalls are five, six, and seven?"

"Ser?" The boy straightens.

"Stalls five, six, and seven?"

"Those empty ones right before you, ser. See the numbers . . . on the beams up there?"

"Ah. I see. And what about some feed for our poor animals?"

"Soon as I get this in, I'll be with you, ser." He resumes dragging the bale, nearly as large as he is, toward the first stall, wherein resides a tall black stallion.

Creslin and Hylin finish with the pack mules and begin to help the trader in emptying the cart.

"They're crowded, so we'll be sharing the same room. I got two cots for you." The trader grunts as he waddles toward the locker with a heavy bundle.

Creslin stacks two more leather bags near the front, then stops, for there is nothing else to place within the locker except for the two bags of glaze powder that Hylin moves, ever so gently, toward the narrow oak doorway.

"Right. Edge them here so we can catch them." As Derrild speaks, he eases the locker door shut and places a heavy iron lock through the hasp loops.

"Now, you get the animals in the stalls and let me find that stable boy." The heavy-set trader shoulders his pack, filled with the smaller bags he placed within it earlier, and trundles toward the front of the stable.

Creslin unties the gelding from the railing and leads him into the second stall, then returns for Hylin's gray, since the stalls are doubles. The mercenary, in turn, has managed to get both pack mules into the third stall, leaving the first stall for the bigger cart mule.

"They promised feed, and we'll have feed . . ."

Creslin ignores the trader as he racks the saddles and blankets.

". . . here and now . . . ."

"Ser . . ."

Hylin looks across the stall barrier and grins, shaking his head as the trader's voice begins to echo off the stained plank walls.

By the time Creslin leaves the stall, closing it behind

him, the stable boy, now muttering to himself, is filling the mangers while the trader watches.

"Let's go eat," Derrild says, looking from the stable boy to his guards.

"Sounds like a good idea," answers Hylin, shouldering his pack.

Creslin nods, leaving his pack slung half across his shoulder.

The Gilded Ram has one public room, smoky with burned grease and close with the odors of spilled ale and wine. Of the three empty tables, Hylin chooses one nearest the wall and sits facing the doorway.

"Expecting trouble?" asks Creslin.

"No. Not here. It's a good idea to keep up the habits, no matter where you are. Besides, avoiding a fight is usually worth more than winning one."

"That's an odd comment from a hired guard." Creslin adjusts his chair on the uneven, wide-plank floor.

"Smart comment," grumbles Derrild. He turns to Creslin. "Your speaking's gotten a whole lot better. Sometimes I hardly hear the accent."

"You see," adds Hylin, "anytime that you fight, you can get hurt. Or you could hurt or kill someone. In lots of towns, you hurt a local, and they want to lock you up, or worse. So you don't get paid, or you end up on a road crew, or hanging from a tree. When you're in a town, you only fight when the alternatives are worse." He gestures to the serving woman, thin and of an indeterminate age. "Some drinks here!"

"We have red wine, ale, mead, and redberry. What will it be?" The woman's voice is simultaneously bored and tired.

"What's redberry?" asks Creslin.

"Berry juice, red. Ladies' drink, no alcohol."

"Wine," announces Derrild.

"Same here," adds Hylin.

"Redberry," says Creslin slowly. Whether he will like it

or not, he scarcely knows, but his guts tell him that alcohol is not a good idea.

The serving woman looks again at the silver-haired young man, then catches sight of the sword and harness attached to the pack by his feet and nods. "Two wines and a redberry. How about dinner? Fowl pie or stew for two coppers, four coppers for a cutlet. Black bread with any of them."

"Stew."

"Stew."

"Fowl pie."

The serving woman again refrains from looking at Creslin. "Eleven coppers. Four each for you two with the wine, three for you." She inclines her head toward Creslin.

Derrild drops a silver and a copper on the table, then covers them with a heavy fist.

"Just make sure they're there when your stuff comes, trader."

"Don't worry, lass. Don't worry."

"I guess I can trust *you*, trader."

Hylin manages not to grin until she has turned toward another table. "Such charm you have, Derrild."

"At least someone trusts me," snorts the trader.

Creslin glances around the room. His eyes sting from the greasy smoke, and he wishes he dared to summon the slightest of breezes, but with the sullen white vapor that infuses the city, he refrains. He blinks his eyes against the stinging. The tears help.

"Now, isn't that some lady?" observes Hylin.

Creslin follows the other's eyes toward a corner table where a slender man dressed in white sits beside a dark-haired woman. Even through the smoke, Creslin can sense the allure of the woman. He can also sense the white wrongness that surrounds both of them and spills over onto the two armed men seated at each side. The armed men do not eat, but watch the other diners.

"Let's have those coins, pretty boy," rasps the waitress as three metal tankards come down on the battered wood.

Derrild surrenders the coins reluctantly. "Let's have those meals, pretty woman," he roars back.

"If I were younger, I might believe you." She smiles briefly, revealing blackened teeth.

Creslin lifts the tankard of redberry juice. His eyes catch Hylin's. "When we rode in, you said something about beliefs, and why the prefect has to stay in Fenard . . ."

Hylin finishes a slow mouthful of the wine. "Ah, better than that mountain ale. Much better."

Creslin waits, and Derrild says nothing.

"Oh . . . about the prefect. I don't know—"

"You're right. You just know blades," interrupts Derrild, his voice surprisingly soft and low. "There's another reason why the prefect won't leave Fenard, another prophecy in the Book."

He pauses for a gulp of wine, then wipes his mouth with a large cloth he has pulled from his belt; it might once have been fine white linen. "The Book says something like the Plains of Gallos will stay united under one ruler until long after they are split by the mountains of the magicians, when then they shall be ruled by a woman with a sword of darkness who will hold the highlands of Analeria and the enchanted hills." He shrugs. "So one prophet says the prefect has to stay and the other says he can't lose the southern plains anyway. I mean, mountains in the middle of the plains . . . how could that ever be? And who'd ever want the highlands, anyway? Goats ruled by princes from round tents, that's all Analeria is. Damned foolishness."

A chill touches Creslin, and he looks past the trader toward the man in white at the corner table, who smiles a knowing smile, not at Creslin, but at Derrild's back.

Three heavy, chipped crockery platters drop on the table, a bent and battered tin spoon resting in each.

"See, pretty boy? I always deliver. It's you men who can't deliver when you get up there in years!"

Creslin smiles in spite of himself.

Hylin grabs the spoon and begins to slurp up the stew.

Derrild shakes his head at the broad backside of the serving woman. ". . . still can deliver, thank you."

Creslin eats slowly, methodically, wondering about the pervasive whiteness of the city, the White Wizard in the corner, and the white birds that have trailed him, on and off.

He watches, absently sipping the redberry, as Hylin smiles at a woman on the far side of the room. She sits with other women, and even Creslin does not need to see their painted cheeks to appreciate the women's looks and expertise. But only to appreciate them from afar. The last thing he needs is to be involved with another woman.

Megaera . . . who is she, and why is she still on his mind? The images tell him— But what do they tell him?

He shakes his head as Hylin looks from him to the women and back. "Not tonight. Not now."

"Wise man," rumbles Derrild as Hylin winks and leaves the table.

"Him or me?"

"You. Can't buy love. Can't even buy real sex." Derrild raises his heavy arm. "Another wine, pretty woman!"

Creslin sips his redberry, pursing his lips. How much he has yet to learn.

"Another wine, pretty woman!"

XXV

ONE OF THE mules swerves and plods through the mud at the edge of the road.

"Gee . . . ah!" Hylin methodically herds the pack animal back onto the road. "Damned mud. Slows everything."

"How much farther?" Creslin again glances at the rolling

hills that will in a day or so, according to Hylin, lead them to the western edge of the Easthorns. The horizon is dark. Looking over his shoulder at the hills behind, he sees the orangish-pink glow that reminds him of the towers of the sunset, those incredible sunset clouds seen from the Roof of the World.

But there are no towers on the eastern plains of Gallos, just fields and hills and occasional orchards, interspersed with rain and mud. The afternoon has been clear and still, almost springlike steamy as the sun has heated the puddles and quagmires resulting from the morning downpour. Creslin has sweated most of the afternoon, and his tunic is as loose as he can get it, though he must brush away the gnats and flies even more often.

Hylin and Derrild still wear their jackets.

Whhhhnnnn . . .

Smaackk.

Creslin removes from his forearm the pulped remains of the mosquito that has plagued him for more than a kay in the still and humid air.

Whhnnnn . . .

Should he call up the slightest of breezes now that they are well away from the white presence around Fenard?

Smmackk!

Whhhnnnn . . .

"Shit," he mutters. No one had talked about the mosquitos when they mentioned the fertile plains of Gallos or the eastern lands. Nor the flies. Nor the stink of the back alleys of both the cities and the towns.

Whhnnnn . . .

A flicker of white catches his eye, and he turns toward the southern sky, but the bird, if it is a bird, has vanished.

Whhhnnnn . . .

Smacckk!

Wwhhnnn . . .

"Don't like the little buggers? They sure seem to like you," Hylin observes.

Smmackk!

His exposed neck is sore, but the mosquito population of the Gallosian plains is one fewer. "How much farther?"

"Another couple of kays. Just far enough that it will be dark when we get there." Hylin's voice is dry.

"Be good to stand up," rumbles the trader from the cart. "You two don't have to sit on hard wood."

Hylin looks at Creslin. Both have remarked upon the thick cushion that insulates the trader from the seat about which he is continually complaining.

Whhnnnnnn . . .

"How far is this place?"

"That might be the kaystone ahead . . . if we're lucky."

The orange-pink glow has faded, and the oblong stone is a light gray against the darker gray of a fast-falling twilight by the time Creslin reins up the gelding to make out the characters.

"Perndor. It says three kays. Is that where we're headed?"

"Yeah, I think so."

"You think so?"

Whnnnnnn . . .

"He's giving you the knife, youngster."

Hylin grins, despite Derrild's explanation.

Smaacckkk . . . Creslin sways in the saddle, off balance after his attempt at the latest attacker. Then he flicks the reins.

Squuusshhh . . . squuushhh. Mud flies from the gelding's hooves as he carries Creslin back onto the highway's stones, mud-coated but far firmer than the clay shoulders of the road.

"Shouldn't be that much farther."

Whhnnnn . . .

The silver-haired youth—sweat dripping down the inside of his shirt and insect welts rising on his neck—sighs. Before too much longer, they come to another gray stone, which says simply, "Perndor." A tumbledown hovel looms off the road behind an equally decrepit railed fence.

The stones of the highway vanish, to be replaced with local clay . . . and worse. While the rain has long since stopped, the road remains filled with mud and water.

Creslin continues to sweat, even in the gloom of the cool twilight that is fast becoming night. He dare not shift the winds to cool himself or to keep the insects away, not with the skeptical trader and the sharp-eyed Hylin riding almost next to him.

"Hate being this late." Hylin's hand reaches up and touches his sword hilt.

Creslin merely shifts his weight and throws his senses out upon the light breeze that seems to have sprung up from the west, from behind the trader's mules, and toward the dark shapes of unlit buildings before them.

"Anyone live here?" he asks as they pass another deserted hovel.

"Supposed to have an honest inn."

Creslin sees a single bright light perhaps half a kay ahead.

Clink . . . whufff . . .

Creslin stiffens at the sounds and the feelings of mounted men gathering behind an abandoned barn beyond and to his right, then reaches and flips the sword from his back sheath.

At the same time, he can feel the bow being drawn, and in desperation, twists the winds and the moisture in the air and flings them into the face of the bowman.

"Bandits!" rumbles Derrild unnecessarily, snatching at least twice for a heavy nail-studded club.

Dropping flat against his bony mount, Creslin spurs the gelding toward the half-dozen riders, blade ready.

"HYYYYYY!"

"Bastard!"

His blade flashes once, then again, as he ducks and lets his body follow the patterns drilled into him.

"Devil! Where is he?"

Creslin gathers the now-wailing winds and flings them once more, even as his mount starts to crumple. He leaps, using his momentum to drive the sword through the throat of the heavy bandit, who has tried to back away.

"Go! There're more! They got Frosee!"

"Hell . . ." he mutters as he tries to unseat the dead man.

Hylin reins up beside him.

"Who's coming?" Creslin asks.

"No one. Just me." Hylin's face is pale, even in the dim light.

"Where's Derrild?" Creslin succeeds in toppling the dead man.

"On his way to the inn, as fast as he can drag the mules."

"What?"

"We're paid for this. Remember?"

"Oh . . . yeah." Creslin looks around. Besides the heavy man lying facedown in the mud, two other bodies sprawl on the ground . . . and the gelding that had carried him for so many kays.

"You got one more, but he's dead in the saddle." Hylin's voice is flat.

Creslin shakes his head, as much to stop the quaking of his hands and body as to deny what Hylin has said. "Couldn't be. I rode through just twice." He sees one bowman lying on his back, his face covered with ice. How can there be ice? How can there possibly be ice? The evening is cool, but not that cold. Creslin swallows, not wishing to think about how he has called the winds from the Roof of the World.

The other man, smaller, and in dark tunic and trousers, lies with his face in a puddle.

"I don't know what you are, Creslin, and I don't want to find out."

Creslin shakes his head again. "I'm nothing . . . nothing at all." He wipes his sword on a fragment of cloth dangling from the saddle, then automatically replaces it in the sheath.

"So is death, friend." Hylin drops off his mount, bends over the bandit chief, and slashes. He comes up with a heavy leather purse and tosses it at Creslin. "Put that away."

Creslin slides it into his pack, numbly, as the other man remounts.

"Shift your bags, and let's get on with it. We need the locals to clean up the mess. They can at least do that."

Creslin hands the reins of the well-muscled black horse to Hylin, wondering how it happened so quickly. One moment the archer was about to spit him with an arrow, and the next, four men, if he can believe Hylin, are dead. "I couldn't have done that . . ." He shakes his head again, then wades through the ankle-deep mud to the gelding. Dark blotches streak the dead horse's muzzle. Whether they are mud or blood, Creslin knows not, nor does he care as he retrieves the mud-smeared bags. He ties the saddlebags and his pack in place quickly, behind a far better saddle than Derrild had provided.

He touches the black, trying to reassure it, and the horse steadies as he swings up into the saddle in close to a fluid motion, as close to fluid as his tired legs permit.

From somewhere, thunder rolls, and unseen clouds begin to mass.

"Hard to believe you're not one of those devil guards . . . so at home on a horse, and you fight just like them."

"They trained me." He might as well tell some of the truth.

Hylin keeps his face turned from Creslin. ". . . believe that now . . . still don't understand that bowman."

Neither does Creslin, exactly, but he knows well enough that it was his doing. He takes a deep breath as they make their way toward the inn. He does not want to talk about the bowman, not tonight. With each new action, he discovers that he knows himself less. He shivers in the saddle, though he is not cold.

Whnnnn . . .

He shakes his head tiredly. Some things don't seem to change.

The rain begins to fall again, cold drops—unlike the morning rain.

XXVI

CRESLIN GLANCES TO the right of the trail—rock and more rock, interspersed with patches of old ice, in the deeper crevices. Although the Easthorns are not nearly so high as the Westhorns, they are more barren, with fewer trees and bushes, and drier, as if the snows that fall on the Roof of the World never quite reach across the plains of Gallos.

Yeee-ahhhh. A black vulcrow's shriek echoes along the narrow trail, followed by the flapping of wings as the scavenger retreats farther eastward down the winding road that leads to Jellico. Creslin feels the white wrongness about the black bird without even extending his sense. At least in the mountains, there are no mosquitos, no flies, and the chill is welcome.

Although Creslin's parka is full open, Derrild huddles under a heavy fur coat as he sways on the seat of his cart. Hylin's fur-lined jacket is closed.

The black, more spirited than the bony gelding, sidles edgewise for a moment. Creslin pats the mount's neck. "Easy."

The cart wheels almost scrape an outcropping of stone as they round a sharp turn. A wagon would have far more trouble then Derrild's two-wheeled cart.

"Isn't there a wider road across the Easthorns?" Creslin calls to Hylin.

"The southern road is nearly twice as wide."

"Why don't we take it?"

"It takes almost five days longer," rumbles Derrild. "Five more days I have to pay you, pay inns, and five days that I cannot sell goods."

"Oh . . ." Creslin's voice trails off. His pay is cheap, but Hylin probably draws a silver a day. At five days each way, plus the inn and food costs . . .

"Don't forget, silver-head," shouts the trader, "that I can make more trips, or run the shop in Jellico, if each trip takes less time."

Creslin takes a deep breath, wishing he had never raised the issue.

"And," rumbles the trader's voice from the cart behind him, "this road is safer because all the fat caravans take the southern road. Sometimes we don't see a single bandit. That's not often, but . . ."

Hylin turns in the saddle and grins, then looks forward and nudges the chestnut to widen the gap between cart and guard.

". . . and I'm not in this for the thrill, not at my age," Derrild rumbles on. "A man has to do something when he has a wife and three daughters and but one son. Besides, should I sit in a shop and nod and grow fat? But the travel—at times, I never want to sit upon a horse or a cart ever again."

"What about the roads?" Creslin asks desperately.

"The roads!" snorts the trader. "What roads?"

The cart scrapes around another switchback, and the road dips toward the plains of Certis.

"These aren't roads," the trader continues from atop his cushioned seat. "The only real roads are the ones from Lydiar to Fairhaven, and from Fairhaven to the Easthorns. The wizards build good roads."

"So why don't we take them?"

"Because, young idiot, there's no money in taking roads that everyone travels. You do what everyone does, and you're poor. Look, you're a blade. If you're just as good as the average blade, you're dead. Right?"

"I suppose so," ventures Creslin.

Yeee-ahh . . . The vulcrow flaps on down the gradually widening stone-lined valley to perch somewhere out of sight.

"You have to be better, do things others don't do. That's true with anything. More skill and more risk—that's where the rewards are. And," adds the trader, "more speed. You understand that, I know, by the way you use that sword. That's why we're not stopping and trading along the way. It's all worth more, much more, the quicker we can get it east."

Creslin nods, looking ahead toward Hylin's back.

"And another thing, that's being honest . . ."

In spite of himself, Creslin listens. He has always heard that traders are among the most corrupt of the merchants.

"Honesty pays, boy. Not in any darkness-loving, mealy-mouthed way. No . . . it pays in cold, hard cash. People trade with you. They hold goods for you, because you keep your word. Good guards work for you, because you pay what you promised. And the other thing is, if you're honest with yourself, then you don't lie to yourself, and you don't try and tell yourself you can do something that's stupid. Lying to yourself'll kill you, if it doesn't ruin you first."

Creslin frowns, looking ahead. Now that he thinks about it, Derrild has been foolish once or twice. He has been loud. He has bargained hard, but he has never tried to cheat anyone.

"But it's still hard, with all the travel . . ."

XXVII

CRESLIN LEANS FORWARD in the saddle. Ahead and to his right, the sun glints off the river below. To his left, the road widens into a broad, stone throughway that leads toward the open gates. The wheels of the trader's cart echo on the hard and even pavement.

Unlike the smaller towns of Gallos and Certis, Jellico has walls, walls rising more than fifty cubits. The southern gates stand open on massive iron fittings. The grooves for anchoring those gates and the stones in which they have been chiseled are swept clean.

A full squad of men—twelve or more—in gray-brown leather patrols the gate, inspecting each traveler entering, each person departing.

"Master Derrild, it's been a while. Some were a-saying you'd gone too far." The serjeant's voice is respectful, but friendly. His paunch does not quite bulge out of the leathers.

On the wall overhead, barely visible behind the parapet crenelations, a pair of crossbowmen sit lazily in the sun, their weapons resting on wooden frames within a cubit of each man.

"These your men?" asks the Certan serjeant, inclining his head toward Hylin and Creslin, who have dropped back abreast of the cart.

"You've met Hylin before," rumbles Derrild. "Creslin, here, joined me out of Bleyans after Berlis took a fancy to a lady whose family decided he'd taken too much of a fancy. Hope he likes being a cooper!" Derrild's laughter echoes against the stones.

The serjeant smiles politely. "It is good to have you back, Master Derrild. Have a good day." His eyes do not smile with his mouth, and his glance has rested more than once on Creslin's silver hair.

The three move on into the town. The houses are mostly of fired brick; narrow, two storied structures with pitched roofs, and heavy, iron-bound oak doors, closed despite the sun and the spring warmth.

"I'll get you, Thomaz! I'll get you!" The high-pitched voice comes from a small, ragged figure chasing another toward the trader's party.

"Watch the horses!" screeches a woman in a leather skirt as the two boys run along the rough stones of the byroad. "Watch the horses!"

"Watch the side!" snaps Hylin.

Creslin tears his glance from the children and the woman and glances toward the alleyway on the left, perhaps thirty cubits ahead. Even without the breezes, he can sense someone waiting there. "Someone in the alleyway ahead." He reaches for the bow, grabbing for an arrow.

Hylin reins up short. "Make them come to us."

As Derrild pulls the mule to a halt, the two boys stop their race and turn, scuttling toward the right side of the narrow street. The woman halts and reaches for something.

"Stop!" shouts Creslin, arrow nocked and ready to release.

The woman, not a woman at all, but a thin youth, drops the bow, then looks nervously toward the alleyway.

Creslin smiles faintly as he hears the scuffling of footsteps fading away, leaving the youth and the two boys standing there alone.

"They're gone," sniffs Hylin. "Couldn't get us by surprise. So they'll not stay and fight."

"Please . . ." pleads the youth, eying the arrow drawn upon him.

"Pot him," rumbles Derrild. "Don't need another thief growing up here."

"Take off your clothes," Creslin commands. "Now!" He waits. "Step toward the door. And stay there."

Although the day is not chill, the youth shivers. Absently, Creslin notes that the two small boys have vanished into some hidey-hole or another.

"Now what?" asks Hylin.

"You pick up the bow, and we keep going. I doubt he'll attack us, and I have no desire to explain a body."

"Softhearted bastard," Derrild grumbles from the cart. He flicks the reins and recovers the bow hastily, but only to slash the string and throw the bow stave into the alleyway as the three pass.

As they draw abreast of the wide-eyed youth, standing only in baggy shorts, Creslin's eyes fix the dark-haired youngster. "Keep this up and you'll die before your next birthdate." His voice chimes silver, like spring thunder, and the youth shudders.

The two guards continue their ride toward an intersection with a larger avenue ahead.

"You know, Creslin," Hylin observes in a low voice, "you're one scary bastard. I believe every word of your warning to that kid. So did he."

"It's true. How I know, I couldn't tell you, but it's true. Sometimes I can know things." Creslin shrugs. "Other times, I know nothing." He half-turns and looks back over his shoulder, but the youth has disappeared.

"What are you? Some kind of wizard warrior?"

"I wish . . ." Creslin laughs ruefully. "Then again, maybe I don't."

"Enough jabber, you two," interrupts Derrild, catching up. "There's the warehouse."

"I recognize it," mumbles Hylin.

The warehouse is a stone-walled building the width of several houses; it is three stories high, with a high-pitched roof. While taller than the adjoining structures—a wood-crafting shop toward the square and a linens and dry-goods shop toward the city gate—the warehouse is more than matched by the white stone facades of even taller structures around the square, another hundred cubits down the narrow street.

Derrild's establishment offers three doors: The first is an open sliding door, level with the rough stones of the street and wide enough to admit Derrild's cart; the second door is iron-bound and barred; the third door, nearest to the square, is of carved oak under a blue-painted cornice.

Looking upward, Creslin sees that the third story contains household windows. He returns his attention to the sliding doorway, before which Hylin has dismounted. The thin mercenary pushes the slider all the way to the left. Creslin then draws the black gelding out of the way as Derrild guides the cart into the dim light within.

"Need any help?" Creslin asks Hylin.

"No. I'll close this. Just follow Derrild."

Inside, to his right, Creslin finds a row of open wooden bins, most of which are empty. In one there are wide-necked pottery jars. One jar is cracked and unstoppered. Other stoppered jars rest firmly on the red clay. The bins rise two stories. Stairs and wooden walkways allow access to the second level, where most of the storage is taken up by wooden lockers with locked doors.

Creslin reins in before the six stalls on the rear wall. In one stall, the one closest to the doorway to what Creslin presumes are the trader's business offices, there is a black mare. The other five stalls are vacant.

Despite the dim light afforded by two high windows on the rear wall and an oil lamp on the wall beside the first stall, Creslin has no trouble in determining that the warehouse is litter-free. His nose confirms that the cleanliness extends beyond the superficial and that the trader maintains order within his premises. Beneath the grumbling, rumbling facade, Derrild is well-organized, as is Hylin.

Creslin pauses. Is that why he had had so little trouble on his trip across the mountains of Candar?

"Let's get going!"

Creslin dismounts. After leading the black gelding into

the third stall, which seems appropriate somehow, he begins
to unsaddle the mount, racking the saddle and shaking out
and folding the blanket.

The black snorts.

"I know . . . I know. It's been a long trip. But you get
to rest now."

"Don't take forever," Hylin calls.

"I know," repeats Creslin. "We're the ones who have to
unload the mules, right?"

"Right."

It is not the unloading that is difficult, but the climbing up
the stairs and the determination of which items go to which
bins or lockers.

"Not there! The purple glazes go in the next locker, that
one," calls the trader. "The cerann oils, just carry them one
at a time. I couldn't afford it if you broke two at once.
Neither could you. They go on the second level, fifth door
down, with the green leaf."

"The one that says 'cerann'?" asks Creslin.

"Yes. How did you know that's what it says?"

"I can read," the former consort snaps. "How else?"

"Oh, I didn't—"

"Never mind. I never said."

Some of the unloading goes more easily from that point,
since Creslin is handed the goods that bear clearly labeled
destinations. He suspects that everything labeled is either
heavy, delicate, expensive, or all three, and tries to watch
his footing.

"It figures . . ." he mumbles under his breath as he lugs
up the last jar of something called porthernth, the sweat
streaming down his forehead.

"You about done?" calls Hylin.

"Yes. Finally."

As Creslin clumps down the unrailed steps, Derrild
motions both men toward him. The trader stands by the
doorway that leads to the quarters. "You get a dinner, a bed,

and a meal in the morning, plus your pay," he explains expansively. "We'll settle the accounts after dinner."

"How about a horse?" Creslin suggests.

"The horse is worth more than you, young fellow, good as you are." Derrild turns toward Hylin.

"Wait," observes Creslin. "You had the gelding. The black's a far better horse."

Derrild pauses, his face twisting for a moment, then smoothing. "There is that. I do owe you for the upgrade. Probably two silvers' difference, and I'll split it with you."

Creslin sighs. "More like a gold's difference."

"I can't sell the black," notes Derrild. "It's really too good for a trader, but I'll give you two silvers instead of one. If I go through the horse brokers, I won't get more than three or four silvers."

Creslin reaches out faintly, senses that the trader is both scared and telling what he believes to be the truth. "All right. Two silvers it is."

Derrild lets out a heavy breath. "You can wash up. Hylin can show you where. By then, dinner should be on the table." He turns with another heavy breath.

"Good," snorts the mercenary.

Creslin pulls at his sweaty and stubbled chin. Derrild, the trader—scared? Creslin reaches for his pack. He not only wants to wash up; he wants to shave and more.

"Anywhere I can wash out what I'm wearing? Not the leathers, the rest of it."

"Since the washroom's where we get to lather up, I doubt that anyone would mind," Hylin answers, hoisting his own pack.

Creslin follows him, not that they go more than a dozen steps. Two large tubs filled with lukewarm water await them. Almost wishing that he could submerge himself, Creslin contents himself with a thorough wash and shave.

Following Hylin's example, he leaves his sword and pack hanging on a post in the washroom. Unlike Hylin, he dons a fresh shirt, without a tunic over it, and he has cleaned his boots as well as he can. His other shirt hangs on the drying rack, as do his underclothes.

"You'd think this were a castle, the way you clean up," Hylin says.

"Compared to some places I've been, it is." Creslin follows Hylin to the dining room.

The long red-oak table is polished, oiled, and only slightly battered along its near eight-cubit length, and there are wooden armchairs, not benches, for the nine who gather.

Derrild, his beard now trimmed and wearing faded and comfortable red tunic and trousers, nods toward his household. "My wife Charla, my son Waltar and his wife Vierdra, and young Willum, and my daughters Derla and Lorcas."

Creslin inclines his head to Charla, then bows slightly. "Honored, lady, and I thank you for your hospitality."

The blond daughter named Lorcas leans toward her sister and murmurs something that Creslin cannot catch.

"Let's sit down," rumbles Derrild. "You're there, Hylin, and Creslin, between Charla and Lorcas."

Knowing that men are the empowered ones in the east, Creslin holds the chair for Lorcas and eases her into place, assuming that Derrild will do the honors for his wife.

"Ah, Derrild, it's good to see that some chivalry remains in the world."

"Chivalry never paid for dinner," grumbles the trader.

Lorcas and Derla exchange glances across the table.

A white-haired woman appears from the next room with a large steaming bowl, which she places before Charla. Next come two wooden platters, each containing a fresh-baked loaf of bread. Two pitchers already sit upon the table, and before each diner is a wide crockery plate, rimmed, and a heavy brown mug.

"Ale's in the gray pitcher, redberry in the brown one," Derrild says.

"Where are you from, young man?" says Charla, her

not-quite-round face pleasant under her short thatch of gray hair.

"From the other side of the Westhorns," he answers.

"That is a long way. Where are you headed?" She breaks the end off a loaf of bread and hands the platter to him.

"Fairhaven, I suspect. I have not decided for sure." He takes the bread, tears off a chunk, and puts it on his plate. Then he picks up the redberry pitcher, offers it to Lorcas, who nods; he pours for both of them.

"Are you a good fighter?" asks Willum, the boy whose tousled blond head barely clears the edge of the table.

"Willum!" scolds the blonde named Vierdra.

Creslin laughs softly. "That depends on who you ask. Those you defeat will say you are a good fighter. Those who beat you say otherwise."

"You're a good fighter!" affirms the boy cheerfully.

"He sees right through you, Creslin," Hylin mumbles through a mouthful of bread.

"Best I've seen," adds Derrild.

Creslin takes his turn and ladles the thick stew—composed of heavy noodles, a white sauce, and some sort of meat—onto one side of his plate. He manages to do so without dripping or otherwise disgracing himself.

Hylin attacks the huge bowl with the serving spoon, and there is sauce on the polished wood and noodles oozing from his plate onto the table.

Creslin suppresses a wince at the mess, but no one else seems to notice.

"Are you a professional fighter, then?" asks Lorcas.

He finishes a mouthful of the peppery stew, which is not as hot as the burkha of Sarronnyn but still highly spiced, before answering. "No. I have seen the real fighters, and I'm not that good."

"I haven't seen them," adds Hylin. "If they're that much better than Creslin, I never hope to meet them."

"Why are you thinking about Fairhaven?" asks Charla.

"It seems to be the place where the unknowable can be discovered."

"Sometimes it's better left undiscovered," mumbles Derrild. "Especially if it involves wizards." He pauses. "They're a jealous lot, Creslin."

"Jealous?"

Splooshh . . .

"Willum!"

The brown pitcher has succumbed to the strong arm of young Willum and disgorged redberry across the lower end of the table.

"Jarra!"

The white-haired serving woman appears with some rags and mops off the table, presenting a clean rag to Vierdra, who shakes her head and says, "Eating with youngsters is always dangerous."

Creslin grins, though he is glad that the juice sprayed away from him, and turns his head so that the boy does not see his expression.

Young Willum submits to being patted relatively free of juice, chewing on a large piece of bread the while.

"You going to make any more trips?" asks the dark-bearded but already-balding Waltar.

Creslin shakes his head. "I was glad to be of service, but—"

"Good men are hard to find."

"Even harder to keep," adds Derrild. "Somehow, I don't think the young fellow would be all that happy on the trading runs, even if I could afford to pay what he's worth."

". . . he's really good . . ."

Creslin ignores the words whispered between Derla and Lorcas, breaks off another piece of bread, then ladles out more of the stew.

"There are a few sweets later," notes Charla.

For some reason, Derla coughs, Lorcas blushes; and Hylin grins at Creslin.

Creslin can feel the red creep up his face and reaches for his mug.

"What's so funny?" demands Willum.

"Nothing . . . nothing." But even Vierdra is having a hard time keeping a bland expression on her face.

Waltar sees nothing humorous in the situation, as shown by the sour turn of his lips. "Women . . ." he mutters, so quietly that only Creslin hears him.

Even Derrild smiles, shaking his head. "To be young again . . ." Then he looks at Charla, bends close to her, and his lips brush her cheek.

Creslin swallows, realizing he has never seen, never experienced, such banter. He sips the redberry slowly.

The sweets do arrive: a heavy, dark pudding accompanied by thin, honeyed biscuits. Creslin has only a small portion of the pudding, sensing it is far too rich for him. Neither the Marshall nor the guards indulged in such solid sweets, insisting instead on fruit or plain biscuits. He glances toward the end of the table, where most of young Willum's face is covered with dark goo. He manages not to smile.

"Good!" smacks the boy as he crunches another honey biscuit.

"That's enough!" snaps Waltar at his son.

Vierdra lays a hand on the man's sleeve.

"He's acting like a hog," mutters Waltar.

"He's acting like a boy."

Creslin swallows again, feeling his eyes burn, but not quite understanding why, and takes refuge in another sip of redberry. His glance strays to the small guitar hanging on the wall.

Lorcas's eyes follow his.

"Do you play, too?"

Creslin shakes his head. "Not well enough to play in public. I used to amuse myself with the music. It seems like a long time ago."

"Got that guitar in Suthya, years ago," rumbles Derrild.

"Tyrell could play it, but I think he was the last guard who could. Sometimes I could get Vierdra to strum a melody . . . you up to that, lass?"

The young mother smiles. "With my friend here? Not tonight, I think."

Derrild glances around the table, then clears his throat. "Let's go over to the account room," he suggests in the silence that has followed his daughter's polite refusal. "Get that taken care of." He rises.

Creslin stands, then turns to Charla. "My thanks again, lady, for a tasty and hearty meal." He steps back. "And to all of you, for making me feel welcome." He grins at Willum, then turns to follow the trader.

". . . no hired blade. Bet he's a duke's bastard or something."

". . . that silver hair . . . you ever see anything like it?"

Both unattached daughters keep their eyes on Creslin even as they rise from their chairs.

Again Creslin ignores the whispers and follows the trader.

Derrild is lighting the oil lamp on the wall of the small room. A set of racked strongboxes fills one short wall, enclosed in a cage of cold iron bands thicker than a man's wrist. A table and four chairs take up most of the floor space. One chair, the one behind the table, has a thick pillow on the seat.

"Sit down while I get the ledger and tote up the numbers."

Hylin slouches in a chair; Creslin eases into another. Derrild removes a heavy bound book from above the iron cage.

Hhhmmm . . . Creslin started on the eighth, off of the Cerlyn road. Let's say we give him the benefit of the whole leg. That's be two silvers for straight pay, and another— say, four—for the two attacks, and the two for the black stallion. That's be eight. We got back with what we started, and no breakage. So there's a bonus there of half a gold. Say a gold and a half."

Derrild does not look up as he jots down numbers with the quill, dipping into the ink pot.

"You, Hylin . . . you get the straight pay, plus four for the attacks and a half gold for the bonus."

Hylin nods. "Seems fair enough."

Creslin senses that both men feel the pay is fair, and nods.

"Now, you also get breakfast and a bed, and that's worth something in this thieving town." Derrild looks up from the ledger at Creslin with a sad expression on his face. "Those girls of mine, Creslin . . . well . . . they think a pretty face and a quick blade's everything."

Creslin understands. The trader is bound by his own bargain, and he knows he cannot threaten Creslin. "I understand. You don't mind a little sweet-talk, but one grandchild's enough for now."

Derrild looks at the ledger; the silver-haired youth senses his relief.

Hylin nods, as if to say that he approves.

"One moment, gents. If you'd wait outside . . ."

They stand, and Creslin follows Hylin out while the trader closes the door, trying not to be too obvious about the bar he sips into place.

"Habit . . ." Creslin murmurs.

"You're a strange one, Creslin," Hylin says slowly. "You don't know the east, but you act like a prince and fight like a demon, and sometimes I think you can hear what people think . . . and then you want to risk it all by walking into Fairhaven."

"I don't know that I have any choice. Nobody else can teach me."

"They might not teach you either . . . just might want you dead. You better be real careful. Don't let them think you're anything but a blade for hire."

What the thin man says makes sense, unfortunately. Too much sense.

"Here you go, gents . . ."

Derrild hands each man a small leather bag.

Creslin slips the coins from the bag into the inside pocket of his belt, folds the bag, and tucks it into the belt also.

"Hylin . . . can you show Creslin where to sleep?"

"No problem."

"See you in the morning. I have more to do with the ledgers yet tonight."

After recovering his pack, Creslin follows Hylin up a narrow stairway from the second level to the third. "We're at the end of the family quarters."

The room has two large, if single, beds and an oil lamp in a heavy brass sconce on the wall. A high table with open shelves underneath provides space for packs and other small gear.

"I may see you later." The thin mercenary sets his pack on one end of the high table.

"You're not sleeping here?"

"That depends . . . I need to see an old friend." Hylin grins. "Besides, I'm sure that Derrild's daughters wouldn't appreciate me hanging around to interrupt their sweet-talk. Which one do you prefer?"

Creslin shakes his head. "Prefer? I'm—"

Hylin grins again as he walks out, whistling softly. Creslin sits down on the edge of the other bed, listening to the mercenary whistle his way down two flights of stairs before closing a door.

Shortly thereafter, Creslin hears light steps. He listens carefully. He can't even straighten out his feelings about the nighttime visit—or was it just a dream—by the lady called Megaera, and now he is about to have visitors.

A blond head peers in the doorway.

Creslin laughs. "Hello, Willum. Come to say good night?"

The child's face is clean and he wears a long nightshirt.

"How many men have you killed? Grandpa said you were the greatest blade he ever saw."

Creslin sighs. "I have killed a few—"

"How many? I'll bet it's a whole lot."

Creslin shakes his head. "It's better to avoid killing, Willum. Grow up and be a good trader like your grandpa."

Two other blond heads stand behind the boy.

"Rather profound for someone so young . . ." Vierdra smiles as she speaks. "Say good night, Willum."

"Good night."

"Good night, Willum."

Vierdra scoops up her son and leaves the other blonde, Lorcas, standing in the doorway. She has the small guitar in her hand.

"Why did you say that to Willum? You can't have killed that many men."

"Killing one person is too many." He motions to the bed across from him, then stops. "Would it be better if we went downstairs somewhere?"

Lorcas closes the door softly and sits down on the bed opposite him. Her eyes are brown, Creslin realizes. He also realizes that she has not answered his question.

"Would you consider playing a song or something . . . ?"

With words phrased that gently, how can he refuse? He slowly takes the guitar, runs his fingers over the strings, realizing that the instrument must have been the property of a master musician.

He tightens the strings until all of the single notes are the hidden silver that he alone seems able to see.

"Something from your home . . ."

Creslin smiles faintly. He doubts that Lorcas really wants to hear the marching songs of Westwind. What shall he play? For some reason, he recalls a song from the court of Sarronnyn. Slowly, slowly, he begins . . .

> Ask not the song to be sung,
> or the bell to be rung,

or if my tale is done.
The answer is all—and none.
The answer is all—and none.

Oh, white was the color of my love,
as bright and white as a dove,
and white was he, as fair as she,
who sundered my love from me.

Ask not the tale to be done,
the rhyme to be rung,
or if the sun has sung.
The answer is all—and none.
The answer is all—and none.

Oh, black was the color of my sight,
as dark and black as the night,
and dark was I, as dark as sky,
whose lightning bared the lie.

Ask not the bell to be rung,
or the song to be sung,
or if my tale is done.
The answer is all—and none.
The answer is all—and none.

He lets the words of the short song die away, and stands. He places the guitar on the high table, then resumes his seat on the edge of the bed.

Lorcas leans forward. "Where are you from, really?"

Creslin decides to discourage her by telling the truth. "The Roof of the World. Westwind."

"I thought the women were the fighters there." Her forehead wrinkles in perplexity. Then she brushes a stray wisp of hair back over her ears and smiles.

"They are."

"But you're a blade. Hylin said that you're the only blade he'd run from. He never runs. Father watches you like a vulcrow."

"It's a long story."

She edges from where she sits and slips over next to him. "We have time. Hylin won't be back, and Vierdra won't say anything."

"Your father?"

"Mother has him in hand."

Creslin smiles wryly. Some things don't seem to be much different in the east.

"My name is Creslin, and I was born in the Black Tower . . . the trials? Now . . . I suppose they knew—" He answers her questions. "Aemris never liked teaching me the blade. Heldra, I know, had her own reasons—One whom I liked? There was Fiera, but she was a guard first . . . mostly," he amends, thinking of that single kiss outside the Black Tower.

Lorcas continues to sit next to him, warm and soft, as he details his rather short life. She still wears the blue tunic she had worn to dinner, although now her hair is completely unbound.

He finds that his arm has gone around her waist as they have leaned back to rest against the pillows and the wall. Some things he had not mentioned, like Sarronnyn, or the midnight visit of Megaera.

"You really are a prince?"

He laughs gently, glad for the moment to lie next to someone who will listen. "No. It doesn't work quite like that. Only Llyse can be the next Marshall, if she has the ability. She needn't have the best blade, but she has to be as good as any senior guard, and she has to know trade, tactics . . . everything."

"You like your sister?"

"Sometimes, and sometimes she's just like the Marshall."

"Why don't you ever call her mother?"

"She never let me."

"But . . . it sounds like she risked a lot to get you trained."

"If you look at it that way." Creslin pauses, leans his head against Lorcas's cheek, closes his eyes for a moment, then forces them open. "I don't think I can talk much longer."

"Don't." She turns to him, her arms going around him as he slides back, enjoying her softness against him, her lips on his, his arms around her.

That time comes when he must release her, and he does. She draws away gently. "If you hadn't promised . . ."

His mouth drops open.

"You think we don't know what Father's up to?" Her words are gentle, but not mocking. Then she kisses him again before speaking. "Besides, there's a princess out there for you, and you deserve her."

"But—"

"Think about me. Often . . ."

Lorcas is gone almost as quietly as she has come, and Creslin understands the phrase "women . . . ," delivered with a headshake, just a little better.

He manages to get his boots and trousers off before he collapses. The lamp snuffs out with a tongue of the breezes he calls, and he sleeps, dreamlessly.

XXVIII

CRESLIN PICKS UP his pack, slings it over one shoulder.

"Well, young fellow, I wish I could afford your like," Derrild rumbles softly. "But trading's a thin business."

Creslin nods. "I appreciate the thought." Derrild cannot afford him for more than one reason, one being the blond girl in the next room. He shifts the pack and puts it over both shoulders, the sword harness where he can still reach the hilt. "You think Gerhard is the best bet?"

"Gerhard's the only one who travels regularly to Fairhaven, the only one who makes money at it. Demons know how, so watch your step. But it's a sight faster than walking, if he'll take you on. Or cheaper than paying wagon rates." Derrild shrugs. "Take care, young fellow." He eases toward the doorway.

Creslin takes the hint and follows.

"Father?" Lorcas steps down the stairs from the kitchen. "Is Creslin leaving now?"

"Yes," Creslin answers, to spare Derrild the admission. "It's time to go." His eyes rest on her as he remembers how soft and warm she had felt.

"Then I need to say good-bye." She steps around her father and up to Creslin, hugs him and kisses him, full on the lips and hard enough that Creslin starts to kiss her back before he remembers that her father is standing there.

Creslin is still blinking when she lets go of him.

"Good-bye . . ." Her voice is soft, telling him she knows that any platitudes about seeing each other again would be false.

"Good-bye." His throat is dry, and his throat catches. He does not move until she steps back toward the staircase. "Good-bye," he repeats.

She darts up the stairs.

"Well, best you be going."

Creslin nods mutely and almost stumbles out the doorway onto the street.

"Try Gerhard."

"I will."

Click . . .

The door shuts before he is two paces away. He looks toward the house but can see no faces in the windows.

"Go see Gerhard," Derrild has suggested, and having no better ideas himself, Creslin starts down the street; as good as the trader has been, he knows that his welcome will become thin indeed should he attempt to remain.

Hylin has not returned, and there is no point in leaving a note, since Hylin could not read it in any case.

Although his breakfast was as hearty as his dinner, although the sky is a clear blue, and although Lorcas has bestowed upon him a good-bye kiss that was not the most chaste of farewells—his steps lag, and when he whistles, the notes are coppered silver notes that do not quite materialize, notes that tremble upon the morning. At the end of the first block, he turns left, heading downhill, recalling what Derrild had not said about Gerhard.

Down in the yards next to the winding stream that flows into the river, he finds Gerhard. Unlike Derrild, who is big, Gerhard is fat, bulging out over his wide, brown-leather belt.

"Much as I would like the added protection, I cannot pay for another guard." Gerhard shrugs.

Creslin knows that the man is both lying and telling the truth, but he cannot tell which half is true. "Fine. I need to get to Fairhaven. You need another guard. You pay a token wage—say, a copper a day—and I'll go with you."

"That's still too much. You have no horse, and you probably eat like one. You thin men are all alike, all appetite."

Creslin shrugs, begins to turn away.

"All right. Take the dun mare at the end. You'll have to put the bags on the main wagon. But you don't get paid if you break anything."

Creslin nods. He fully expects Gerhard to find some way not to pay him, but his main consideration is to get to Fairhaven, to see the eastern wizards, and to observe quietly. There may be a place for him there. Cost is not nearly the consideration it once was, not with the nearly dozen golds he found in the dead bandit's purse. Before he had left Derrild's, he had slipped two of the coins into Hylin's pack, hoping they would help the thin man.

His thoughts turn back to Fairhaven. Can he discover what he is there? Or what his destiny might be? Or is he still just blindly running from Westwind? He shakes his head. If not Fairhaven, then where can he turn? Certainly not back to Sarronnyn, but the Duke of Montgren might welcome any help.

As he unstraps the extra packs from the dun mare, another man approaches. He is heavy like Gerhard, and sloppy to boot, with stains covering a leather vest worn over a woolen shirt so faded that the original colors have melted into grays.

"You the extra guard?"

Creslin turns. "Creslin."

"I'm Zern. You answer to me. Why are you unstrapping the packs?"

"Because Gerhard told me to. Told me to put them on the wagon, and to use this horse."

"All right. You start up front with me as soon as you finish. We're late already."

Creslin's expression is sober as he looks around the assemblage, taking in the two overloaded wagons, two pack mules, and the two other guards.

XXIX

THE PALE-GRAY granite surface of the road does not glitter, although, from certain angles in full sun, the stones look nearly white. Each massive stone block is fitted to the next more smoothly than the fine marble floors of many palaces. Broad enough for more than two wagons abreast, this road stretches so precisely east and west that at high noon no shadows fall upon its surface, even where it drives between the ridges of the Easthorns and the not-quite mountains to the east and west of Fairhaven itself.

Gerhard's wagons roll onto those granite blocks from the packed clay of the Certan road, past the toll station manned by white-clad road guards.

Derrild had not mentioned tolls, but the economics of the wizards' efforts and the military implications are clear enough. The road is a weapon in itself, enabling cavalry and supplies to travel through the mountains and across the rolling plains and fields far faster than otherwise, even faster than on the flat and winding roads that cross Certis and Gallos. But the road has not spanned the Easthorns yet, although rumors indicate that the wizards continue to press forward, boasting of the not-too-distant day when it will and of the time when they will at last challenge even the mighty Westhorns.

But why has Certis let the wizards construct such a road? Creslin asks Zern.

"Who knows? Gerhard told me once, but I forgot. Something about the viscount getting a tithe. He gets some sort of cut and the free use of the road for his troops . . . something like that." Zern's face screws up, almost as an afterthought. "What's it to you, pretty boy, anyway?"

"Not much. First time I've seen anyone charged to use a road."

"Bet they don't have roads like this where you come from."

"You're right," Creslin agrees. "I've never seen a road like this." He hasn't, and while the engineering and the stonework are magnificent, he has that familiar sense of white wrongness shrouding the area. Not the road itself, but the rock walls flanking the sections where the road passes through the hills.

"Bet they don't have much of anything where you come from."

"Not much," Creslin answers absently.

"Can you use that toy on your back?"

"I have, once or twice." Creslin studies the almost

unnoticeable grade of the stones and observes that the road is much lower than the surrounding hills, almost as if it were designed to rest on the underlying solid rock.

"For who? Some spice merchant with a private army?"

"A merchant named Derrild."

"Who'd you work with?"

"Hylin."

"Oh . . ." Zern's heavy face screws up as though he is trying to remember something. "Wait! Is he a thin man, long nose, who just finished a run from Suthya?"

"Yes. I joined them on the way back."

"Shit. Forget I said anything, all right?"

"Fine," Creslin agrees, still preoccupied with the road and the white wrongness behind and around it.

Zern drops back . . . slowly, until he is even with the lead wagon, where Gerhard sits next to the driver on the high bench.

Creslin, puzzled by the sudden change in Zern's attitude, extends his senses on the light breezes, fighting his way through the unseen white mist.

". . . know who he is. The killer . . . the one I told you about. Took all of Frosee's band single-handed."

". . . thought he might be—"

". . . dangerous."

". . . Hardly. Dangerous to anyone who attacks us. Good cheap protection." Gerhard laughs.

". . . attack us? When has—"

"Forget it."

Creslin, absently, widens the gap between himself and the wagon. Already the fields of southeast Certis have given way to forested hills that rise on each side of the road, which is climbing, though less steeply than the hills, so that the roadbed almost seems to dig deeper into the rock from which it has been carved.

Feeling eyes upon him, he glances overhead but sees no white birds flying, nor any other bird.

The guards ride mechanically, and the wagons creak

eastward on the hard granite, rolling solidly toward the white city, bearing sacks and boxes of who knows what from who knows where. In time, the guard named Pitlick rides up and suggests they trade places. Creslin then rides behind the wagons, still feeling the eyes of an unseen watcher, or watchers, upon him.

XXX

MUCH AS THE wagons rolled onto the wizards' road and past the toll station, they roll off. Except that this time there is a paved road, also of smoothed granite blocks, leading at right angles to the main highway.

Gerhard is talking to the toll collector, another of the guards dressed in white and wearing white armor. Whatever the trader has said, the collector appears interested, nodding his head before waving the merchant on.

Creslin looks at the gentle slope upward. Beside the road grows only a thin, crawling grass, not even bushes or low trees—just grass, reaching halfway up the slopes of the hills.

The road-building is something that Creslin still fails to understand. Why does the road tend to be slightly lower, straight and fine as it is, rather than higher than the ground around it? But the builders have taken the runoff problem into account, as shown by the continuous stone-lined drainage ditch on the right-hand side.

He frowns. The military uses of the road are obvious. But why build a road where an enemy could hide above it in some cases? He almost gathers the winds to cool him as he ponders, for they tend to blow above the road rather than upon it.

Then he nods. The wizards do not fear archers. They fear other wizards, those who can lash fire—presumably—at an exposed target. Even Creslin has trouble in directing the breezes onto the road.

Still, he suspects that either Heldra or Aemris would have little difficulty in turning the road against its builders.

"Straight ahead," Gerhard bellows. "The trade stop is straight ahead."

Creslin nudges the dun mare in the direction indicated by the fat trader's voice, letting the sun warm his back as he rides northward. In less than a kay, he reaches the top of a hill from where he can see before him tents of all colors and sorts, many of them patched with odd-shaped and off-colored cloth.

"Pitlick! Get on up there and scout out a site. You know what we need. Damned wizards. Rules . . ." Gerhard's voice drops off.

Creslin tries to discern the meaning behind the mutterings, but there is neither meaning nor coherency.

"Zern!"

"Yes, ser!" The guard leader drops farther behind Creslin and matches pace with the trader's wagon. He leans toward the trader as he rides.

". . . once we get passes . . . Pitlick . . . location . . . pay off silverhead . . ."

". . . before we set up?"

". . . not until you get Turque . . ."

Creslin strains to pick up the words passing between the two men, but with the low pitch of their voices, and the squeaking and rumbling of the wagons, he is unsuccessful.

". . . pay him . . . agreed, plus a silver as a bonus."

". . . a silver! I . . . we . . ."

". . . you want to be in his boots, Zern?"

". . . Turque . . . I wouldn't bet—"

". . . you want Turque . . . after you?"

". . . all right . . ."

Creslin is not surprised, but wonders who or what Turque is. In the meantime, he rides the dun mare toward the tents, toward the dust and the noise of trade.

Zern eases his horse up beside Creslin and his mount.

"Why don't we go straight to Fairhaven?" asks Creslin.

"We can't. Only food gets traded in Fairhaven, unless you live there. They don't like traders in the city."

"You can't even go into the city?"

"Didn't say that, young fellow!" Zern's booming laugh sounds hollow. "They'll take your money. You'll see. They don't talk to outsiders, not much anyway. So all the young fellows like you—I've seen 'em walking through the streets, and the streets are . . . you wouldn't believe them—but none of the old-timers go into Fairhaven. It's no fun there, no one to drink with, no games, and the local girls . . . forget that, too."

"Everything is here?"

"Everything you'll need."

Not everything he will need, but Zern will not understand that. Creslin is silent as they stop by yet another gate for Gerhard to pay still another fee, this one to permit them to enter the trading grounds.

"Pull the gate!" calls the gatekeeper, and the single beam swings wide.

Creslin follows Zern, trying not to sneeze at the fine dust that sifts upward with each step of the horses. After traveling for several hundred cubits down a snaking path between tents, Zern points to a red-and-gold flag waving on a slight incline at the north side of the grounds. Waving the flag is Pitlick, and the wagons roll up to him.

Within instants, Gerhard is on the ground, bellowing. "Get the tent, the big one, unrolled . . ."

Zern joins him, leaving his reins and mount to Creslin. In turn, Creslin ties his mount and Zern's to the post where Pitlick's mount is already tethered, then unstraps his pack.

He checks his gear, debates unsaddling the mare, then decides against it, since he does not know where the saddle and blanket should go.

The site Pitlick has chosen is to the north and perhaps three cubits higher than most of the rest of the trading grounds. A stream winds lazily across a field on the other side of a rail fence that marks the boundary of the traders' activities.

Creslin surveys the vast spread of tents and listens to the sea of voices; he hears nothing except the sounds of greed and trade.

". . . the best sea emeralds this side of the Westhorns."

". . . spices! Spices! Every spice you can imagine."

". . . firewine, get your firewine here."

The former consort wipes his damp forehead and looks toward Gerhard's wagons. The trader still gives orders, but Zern is headed toward Creslin with a bag in his hand. "This is . . . where we . . . Creslin." Zern's voice stumbles, as though he has tried to rehearse what he says but has forgotten the script.

"The job's over?"

Zern nods. "There's a half-silver bonus there."

"Very generous. I should go thank Gerhard, or was that your doing?" Creslin tries to keep his face blank, although his stomach twists at his words implying that he does not know.

"His doing." Zern clears his throat. "Anyway . . . good luck."

"Thank you." Creslin affixes the sword harness to the pack, then shoulders both pack and sword. Zern watches as he adjusts the pack.

Before he steps away from Gerhard's wagons, where Pitlick is beginning to unroll a shapeless heap of canvas that will soon become a tent, Creslin slips his pay into the inner pouch of his belt, glad enough for a few more small coins. At least he will not have to show the golds from Frosee or convert the gold links of the cabin into coin. Not yet.

". . . famous pots from Spidlar. The best purple glazes of Suthya."

"See the copper as hard as steel."

Creslin snorts at the boast of the armorer. No bronze could match good Westwind steel. He raises his eyes and surveys the tents and the men and women coming and going. Not ten cubits from him, a black-haired woman, shapely and garbed in almost transparent silksheen, trails a thin man with a huge curled mustache. She wears sadness and a set of chains, light iron shackles, almost decorative in nature. Her eyes catch his, fall on his silver hair. She shakes her head minutely and mouths words he cannot catch before a jerk on the chain sends her reeling toward the mustached man, who has not even looked back.

Creslin sees the whiteness trapped behind the cold iron, and swallows. Seeing beyond the merely visible gives him more than chills at times.

". . . raw woods. Cedars from Hydlen. Hard pine from Sligo."

". . . ointments for any ill! Any ill at all!"

He has taken no more than several dozen steps, crossing behind a wagon filled with lengths of lumber, when a white-blond woman, enormously endowed, revealing those endowments through silksheen that hides nothing, steps forward. The white-blond goddess of love is followed by a man who, at first glance, stands more than a cubit taller than Creslin. Creslin's second glance also catches sight of wrists as thick as roof beams.

"A western man . . ." Her voice is a throaty whisper meant only for him, and her smile is an invitation. She steps closer, and the scent of ryall and woman enfold him. She takes another step.

Creslin waits, his eyes taking in the erect nipples on the high, full breasts, the delicate collar bones, the not-quite-full and pouting red lips . . .

Idiot!

From whence comes the thought, Creslin does not know, but he blinks and forces himself to look beyond his eyes.

He swallows, nearly retching. While the woman is not ugly, the whiteness that swirls around her, suffused with angry red, reeks of evil, and the white-blond hair is merely white, the eyes promising another kind of oblivion.

"So . . . he can more than see." The words are still throaty, whispered but rasping, like those of a speaking snake.

No one seems to notice them; a heavyset guard walks by less than a cubit away, oblivious to their presence.

"But they cannot—"

He starts to step back, but his muscles do not seem to move.

The giant behind the white-shrouded woman steps forward, and each step vibrates the hard ground. The only saving grace Creslin can see is that the man carries a broadsword big enough to use as a lever for boulders. A sword . . . perhaps. Except that Creslin cannot each reach for his own sword. He reaches for what he can—his thoughts—and they grasp for the high winds overhead, for the thin line that ties them to the storms and thunders that rule the Roof of the World.

"Struggle, little silver-head. I love to watch men struggle."

The giant pauses, his hand on the hilt of the massive sword.

Creslin strains, bending the high winds down . . . down . . . grasping for the water, for the ice within the air.

. . . *wwwhhhsssssSSSTTTTT!*

Around him, Creslin can hear the canvas of the tents begin to flap in the wind and sense the haze forming in the air above.

The woman's mouth turns into an "O," but her movements seem gelid as Creslin seizes the winds and flings them across the whiteness that infuses her.

Lightning flares somewhere, and hailstones begin to patter down on canvas and traders alike.

Aeeeiii . . . The cry is snuffed out, and the whiteness vanishes.

Creslin jerks out of his paralysis. So does the giant, who takes in the ice-covered figure on the ground and brings forth the broadsword. Creslin darts back, grabbing his own sword, shrugging out of his pack, and moving fast.

The big man is quick, very quick, and Creslin cannot try to reestablish his hold on the winds, not if he wants to survive beyond the instant. So he dodges, parrying. Blades caress, for Creslin knows that he can do no more than slide the other's blade.

Cling . . . clunk. His whole arm rings, but he steps inside, twisting . . .

The giant tries to swing the sword for a last time, but Creslin's arm blocks the swing at the locked wrists. The man looks stupidly at him and collapses into a heap.

"What's that?"

"Turque and her man!"

Creslin replaces his sword without wiping it clean. Then he sweeps up his dropped pack with one hand and hurries away, twisting behind tents, hastening toward the road, betting that more than a few traders will not be displeased to see the giant dead. Turque is another question, but he did not seem to have a choice.

A silent question strikes him, and he looks overhead just in time to see the wide-winged white bird vanish into empty air, air that swells into more than the brief hailstorm Creslin has called.

The wind continues to whip through and around the tents, and the warm air has already begun to cool as Creslin reaches the road. He swallows, thinking of the white bird. Megaera? Had she voiced the warning? Why? Who is she, and what does she want? He shivers, feeling colder than the ice he has flung around the White Witch called after him by Gerhard.

Is it wise to go to Fairhaven?

But where else can he discover who and what he is?

XXXI

QUICK STRIDES HAVE taken Creslin more than three kays from the trader's grounds and to another flat, if rutted, road. Glancing back over his shoulder, he looks for the faint haze that has hovered over the traders' grounds, a natural haze of not exactly natural moisture and smoke from the many cook fires in too small an area. Instead, a thundercloud continues to mushroom into the sky, growing darker underneath, with white cotton plumes on the top reaching toward the sun.

A thunderstorm out of a clear sky? From a single call to the high winds?

The road he walks is clearly a farm road, with wheel ruts, heavy hoofprints, and horse droppings. He may find a farm wagon headed into Fairhaven. If not, his legs will eventually bring him there.

After another kay, Creslin looks back toward the clouds that have spread well beyond the traders' grounds and cast a shadow across the road he walks. On top of the rolling hills behind him, he sees a farm wagon, with two figures on the wagon seat. He keeps walking.

He can feel the wagon's ponderous approach, pulled by a draft horse a third again as big as the black stallion he had taken from the dead bandit. A spare man, his black hair shot with white, holds the reins. A thin-faced woman, her hair still pure black, sits beside him.

"Looking for a ride, young fellow?"

"I would not turn one down, ser."

"Then don't. Climb aboard, if you can avoid the baskets."

Creslin looks over the sideboards until he sees a narrow area free from baskets of what appear to be potatoes and assorted greens. Then he vaults in, teetering on the jolting boards before catching his balance and easing down on the dust that has sifted from the produce bushels.

"You some sort of acrobat?" asks the farmer.

"No. I just couldn't think of any other way to do it."

"You are headed for Fairhaven?" asks the woman.

Creslin nods.

"Not much for soldiers, the wizards aren't," adds the man.

"That's what I've heard. I can use a blade, but I'm not really a soldier." Creslin's stomach agrees with the statement, and that agreement sends a chill down his spine. If he is not a soldier, what is he?

"Hope you're not a wizard, either," adds the man. "They don't care much for wizards, excepting their own, of course."

"They don't sound terribly friendly," observes Creslin. "The traders say that they don't like traders. You tell me they don't like soldiers and wizards. Who do they like?"

"It's not that bad," laughs the farmer. "They like merchants and children and farmers, and people who live their lives without messing into other people's ways."

Creslin nods, listening.

"Fairhaven's a good city. You can walk the streets day or night and feel safe. You can find some place to eat day or night, and the money and the people are honest. How many places can you say that about?"

"Not many," Creslin admits. "Not many."

In time, they reach another road, wider, smoother, and of stone, heading south along a wide ridge. Overhead, the thunderclouds have continued to mass, cutting off all but scattered sunlight.

"This leads straight into the city?"

"Sure enough does, young fellow. Sure enough does. What are you planning to do there?"

Creslin shrugs. "Look around, watch, have a meal, find a place to sleep."

"Hope you have a few coins."

"Some."

"The wizards are death on theft. First time, you're on the road crew. Second time, you're dead."

"The road crew?"

"The great east-west highway. Someday, they say, that highway will cross all of Candar." The farmer flicks the reins.

"Be after our time," adds the woman. Her voice is almost as deep and husky as the man's.

"I don't know, Marran. I can recall when it wasn't barely into Certis. Now they tell me that they're near as to halfway through the Easthorns.

Creslin listens, asking a question or two, as the wagon creeks along the stone highway.

A messenger, dressed in white and with a red slash across his tunic, gallops past, and horses and carts continue to pass in the other direction.

"Is this rather late to be going to Fairhaven?" he asks.

"Works better this way," explains the farmer. "Things get picked over in the morning, and the vegetables sort of wilt. Don't know why, but some stuff doesn't long stay fresh there. Does in our cellar, but not there. Too much magic, I'd guess. Anyway, our customers know we come in late, and their servants are there waiting for us. Don't have to fight the crowds, don't waste the whole day."

Creslin nods. So there is something in Fairhaven that wilts the vegetables sooner than elsewhere. Curious, but why vegetables? Or just some vegetables?

He rises to his knees on the swaying floorboards and glances ahead toward a pair of buildings.

"Those are the old gates," says the driver, following Creslin's gaze. "From back when the wizards ruled just the valley."

Creslin looks at the gates, at the green trees and bushes beyond them, and at the whitened granite of the gate house and the pavement and curbs. His stomach twists. "Think I'll get off here."

"Square's a good two or three kays farther."

Creslin straightens up and shoulders his pack. "I need to . . ." He finally just shrugs, unable to explain why he needs to walk into the town from the old gates.

"We could take you all the way to the square, young fellow," the farmer offers. "Long walk from here." He holds the long leather reins to the swaybacked horse loosely, waiting for his passenger to reconsider.

"Thank you, but I need some time . . ." the silver-haired young man says, knowing that he must stop and reflect, try to think out what he hopes to attain in Fairhaven, the White City, before he descends into the center of all that is Candar and will be Candar for generations, if not for millennia, to come.

"If that's what you have to do, we'll not be telling you otherwise."

"Thank you." Creslin repeats, then grasps the sideboard and leaps from the wagon, landing lightly. The stone is hard, and he staggers.

"You sure?" asks the bronzed farmer, flicking the reins.

"I'm certain," confirms Creslin. "But thank you, anyway. I need some time to think."

"Geee . . . ah." The farmer flicks the reins again. "Don't think too much. It isn't what you think that counts. It's what you do."

Creaakk. The wagon pulls away, heading east down the wide, divided boulevard that the east-west highway has become as it enters the White City.

White is the city, as white as the noonday sun on the sands of the Vindrus Desert, as white as the light from a wizard's wand. White and clean, with off-gray granite paving stones that glisten white in the sun, and merely shine in the shade.

From just outside the west-gate towers, Creslin looks across the valley, amazed at the confluence of white and green. Tall trees with masses of thick green leaves thrust themselves above the intertwining lines of white stone walls and boulevards. Yet for all the grace and curved lines, the great avenues—the east-west highway and the north-south road—quarter the city like two white stone swords.

Slowly he moves past the empty old buildings, across an invisible line inside which almost all the buildings appear white. Even under the roiling gray clouds that promise rain, the streets of white stone seem to glitter with an inner light.

Creslin takes a step along the boulevard, where a central strip of grass and bushes, curbed in limestone, separate two roads. Despite the mist of spring, he sees no flowers, no colors except for the green of shrubs and grass and the white of the curbstones and pavement. He studies the roads for a time before realizing that all of the horses and carts headed into the city are using the right-hand road, while those leaving the city use the left-hand road. Those who walk use the outer edges of the roads.

Toward the center of the shallow valley, the whiteness becomes more pronounced, the greenery less. None of the buildings exceed three stories.

Creslin takes a deep breath, then casts his senses to the wind . . . and reels in his tracks, withdrawing into himself at the swirling patterns of whitish-red that seem to fill the entire valley, that seem to twist and tear at his whole being. For a moment, he thinks that he has sensed a patch or two of cool blackness amidst the unseen turmoil, but the strain is too great for him to seek further, not until he has learned more.

He wipes his suddenly dripping forehead with his sleeve. Wizardry indeed, and it seems to underlie everything around him, for all that the stonework appears laid by the most skillful of masons and the trees and grasses fully natural.

With another deep breath and another attempt at wiping the moisture from his brow, he pushes forward, one cautious step at a time.

XXXII

"Report." The dark-haired woman's face is as impassive as always, despite the circles under her eyes and the long, strong fingers of the left hand resting on the knife hilt.

"He made it off the Roof, down the Demon's Slide on skis—"

"How do you know?"

"We found enough traces in the high forest, and the patterns were all guard patterns. No tracks remaining, of course. In that respect, he was careful." The senior guard stands before the Marshall.

"You couldn't catch up to him—a mere man?"

The senior guard lowers her eyes. "He had somewhat of a head start, and we didn't know where he was going. Once we could estimate his direction, it got easier."

"Then why isn't he here?" The Marshall's voice remains cool, distant, as if she were discussing troop deployments.

"Because you ordered us not to enter Fenard or to cross the Easthorns." The guard swallows. "By now, he's probably in Fairhaven. At least, that's where all the signs point."

"He traveled quickly," observes the Marshall.

The guard lowers her eyes even farther. "Will you require my departure?"

The Marshall laughs, a harsh sound that echoes brittlely against the stone walls. "For what? You did what I asked. You could have caught him only if he had failed or been injured. Have you asked the arms-master about his abilities?"

"No, ser."

"Don't bother. You'd find that he meets all of the guard standards, and most of the senior-guard levels. He doesn't know that, and it was difficult indeed to ensure that few guards knew it."

"Oh. Why are you telling—"

"I sent you out under a deception. I don't want your performance hampered by false feelings of failure. Ask Aemris. No son of mine would be helpless, yet I may have played him false by allowing him such training."

"Ser . . . why?" The guard refuses to look to the black leathers, but her back is straight.

The Marshall stands, turns, and looks at the heavy flakes beating against the leaded windowpanes of her study. "In his place, would you have wanted to stay here, or to have been a pampered pet in Sarronnyn?"

There is no answer.

"Of course you cannot answer that. It was an unfair question." She continues to watch the whiteness outside the citadel. "I only hope he finds something to run to . . . in time."

She stares at the falling snow long after the guard has left, watching as the thick flakes cover the tops of the parapets, watching as the night drops to enfold that impenetrable whiteness.

XXXIII

IN THE GOLDEN light of the pre-twilight sun, a handful of people gathers around three carts in the paved open space. From the closest cart, the one painted green, a woman plucks something off the grill at the rear, wraps it deftly within a flat pastry and hands it to a bearded man. She repeats the process with the next customer, then slaps two more slabs of meat on the grill.

The smell of roasted fowl drifts toward Creslin. His mouth waters. He has had nothing to eat since an early breakfast many, many kays westward, and now it is late afternoon.

He steps toward the green cart and takes his place behind a stout man dressed in green trousers and a sleeveless green tunic with no shirt beneath.

"Grilled fowl pie." The voice drifts back.

"That's two." Two coppers change hands.

Two younger women and the husky man stand between Creslin and the woman serving the food.

". . . Father thinks that he's so upright."

"Ha! Should see him on Winden Lane, or ask why Reeva went to live with her aunt and uncle in Hrisbarg . . ."

". . . believe ill of a cadet in the White Guard? . . . must be joking."

"Do you have any lamb pies?"

"They cost three."

"Lamb and fowl, then."

"And you, ser?" the woman asks the man directly before Creslin.

"Two fowls." The man steps partly aside.

"What about you, silver-hair?" The woman is perhaps as old as Aemris, but she has a friendly smile, and her figure cannot be concealed entirely by the baggy brown tunic.

"A fowl pie." Creslin extends the coppers.

"Oh, Certan coins."

"Is that a problem?"

"Hardly. We just don't see them that often." She smiles again, then turns and plucks two more slabs of meat from the grill, deftly rolling them in the flat pastries she pulls off a stack on a platter beside the small grill. She presents them to the girls. "Here you are, one fowl, one lamb."

The two girls wander toward one of the stone benches, not looking back.

". . . Father will be furious. Late . . ."

"Let him . . ."

Beyond the bench where the girls have settled, three bearded men, wearing identical green-and-red surcoats and

holding flasks, have stopped at the edge of the open space
that is too small for either a park or a square, and they stand
on the grass behind the benches.

> . . . *thirteenth day, they said that he was dead,*
> *but up he rose and bashed the captain's head* . . .
> *Ohhhh . . . wild was the sailor, wild was the sea,*
> *and wilder still the girl they called Maree* . . .

This is the first music that Creslin has heard in the entire day
he has been in Fairhaven. He looks behind him, but he is the
last one in line, at least for the moment. No one stands
around the two other carts, and he cannot see what they
might be serving.

"Here are your two fowls."

The other man takes the two meat rolls and waddles
toward the bench to the right of the one taken by the girls.
At one end sits an older man, nearly bald, dressed in drab
olive, walking stick in hand. His eyes are fixed on a pair of
brown pigeons that scurry under the benches for crumbs.

"Silver-hair . . ."

Creslin jerks his eyes back to the vendor "I'm sorry . . ."
He takes the chicken in the roll, warm to his hands.

"Are you an outlander?"

"It shows that much?" He doesn't have to force the laugh.

"What do you think of Fairhaven?"

"It seems to merit the name. A very clean city, and the
people seem happy."

Behind them, the song grows louder, and more off-key.

> . . . *he blew so hard the sails came down,*
> *But he rose with the prefect's crown* . . .
> *Ohhhh . . . wild was the sailor, wild was the sea,*
> *and wilder still the girl they called Maree* . . .

> *Threeppp* . . .

Creslin winces at the piercing nature of the whistle.
"What's that?"

"Wizards' guards. You'd better stay right here for a little bit. All right?" She hands him a small flask. "Have a drink."

THHHREEEPPP . . .

"Might I ask why?" Creslin looks around, then notices that no one else is paying attention, that the girls look only at each other and that the old man stares at the ground. He looks back at the vendor.

Her smiled is strained. "Singing . . ." Her voice is so low that he can barely hear it.

> . . . *wild was the sailor, wild was the sea,*
> *and wilder still the girl they called Maree* . . .

Despite the whistle, the revelers continue to sing, waving their arms in a rough semblance of rhythm.

THHHHREEEEPPPP . . .

"That's enough now." The harsh voice jolts Creslin, but he follows the example of the vendor and the girls and does not look over at the guards whom he knows have surrounded the three men. "You three know better. Sure, it's the road camp for you."

"Frig you, White boy!"

Thud . . .

"Come along, you two. Lerrol, call the waste crew."

Creslin swallows, catching the vendor's dark brown eyes with his, questioning.

"The lamb pies are three," she says cheerfully, but there is a trembling edge to her tone.

"Come along . . ."

The vendor exhales slowly as the footsteps of the guards and the former revelers fade away.

No one looks at the body lying on the ground behind the benches.

"Drunkenness?" Creslin asks hoarsely.

She shakes her head. "Public singing. Upsets the White magic. They say people have been killed."

Creslin finally takes a swallow from the flask he has been holding. "Thank you. What do I owe you?" He returns the flask.

"Nothing. I'm glad you were here. I'm not from Fairhaven either." She takes the flask and starts to turn back to the grill, then stops. "Be careful. You're an outlander carrying cold steel." Then she sprinkles water across the grill. The coals hiss as she begins to pack up the pastries.

Creslin takes the bench farthest from the body, one where he cannot be seen directly by the clean-up crew—whatever or whoever that might be. He takes a bite of the fowl pie, still warm, although the flaky pastry has become somewhat sodden with juice from the sauce on the meat.

Despite the tangy taste of the pie, Creslin has to force himself to take another bite. As he does, the two girls pass by, not looking in his direction.

". . . can you imagine . . . as if being a White Guard meant anything . . ."

". . . late. Father will be . . ."

". . . let him . . . always mad about something."

By now Creslin sits in shadows, for the sun has dropped behind the low western hills, yet the small square is not gloomy. The vending woman has finished stowing her supplies in a wooden locker in the cart. Then a cover goes over the grill, and the tailboard comes up.

As he watches, she wheels the cart out of the square and northward along the gentle incline. The other two carts have already left.

Three more slow bites, and he finally finishes the roll. As he stands, so does the old man, who peers at him for a moment as if to ascertain in which direction Creslin intends to walk.

Creslin turns south and back onto the boulevard.

The old man turns north, the direction the vendor has taken.

One by one, the oil-fired street lamps flicker on, and as

each one lights, Creslin can sense a brief touch of redness, of flame.

Fairhaven murmurs, like all towns murmur, and his ears, cast to the breezes, catch but the loudest of the murmurs. He has to strain against the encircling mist of White magic.

". . . not here. My father . . ."

He grins at that.

". . . the same old story . . . never enough . . ."

". . . and I told her that it was nothing to me. If he wants to think something . . ."

". . . thirty, thirty-one, thirty-two. Not a bad day . . . a good number of outlanders, and they pay more."

". . . a lot of white coats out tonight."

Down the boulevard, another pair of white tunics on the other side of the divided road stroll slowly uphill.

"What are we looking for?"

". . . didn't say. Just said we'd know it if we saw it."

"Funny orders, if you ask me . . ."

". . . didn't ask."

The silver-haired man drifts to the outside of the boulevard and bends down, as if to adjust his boot. Then, as the two pass abreast, not even looking beyond the low bushes and the rolled grass, he slowly straightens and continues on his way.

Should he turn and leave? But why would they be looking for him? No one knows about the incident at the trader's camp, at least not one who would have recognized him. And there is no way that either the Marshall or the Tyrant would ever ask anything of the wizards.

Still, he shakes his head. He needs to know more. He continues until the gradual slope of the boulevard levels. With measured steps, he comes to another square, where he finds a shadowed bench. Even as night descends, the slightest glimmer from the oil-fired streetlights is magnified ten times over and white light sparkles from the stones, the red tinge apparently invisible to anyone but himself.

Creslin sits on the bench next to the fountain in the warm evening, listening, trying to sort out the city. On one side of this central square is a long arcade, lined with shops of every variety—cabinetry, cloth, baskets, coopers, silversmiths, goldsmiths—every variety except one. There is no establishment that handles cold iron. Many, but not all, of the shops are closed. A woman's laughter, chiming like off-key bells, rings from the open café on the far side of the boulevard.

The more he learns, the more confused he becomes. He is called a Storm Wizard, yet cold iron does not bother him, while an entire city of wizards far more powerful than Creslin shuns the metal.

The other strange thing is the ban on public singing, and the fact that everyone ignores the killing by the White Guards; it is as if the people do not want to have to acknowledge the guards' power.

Finally he stands and heads for a doorway through which he has seen a number of outlanders pass and from which issue the muted sounds of a guitar and singing. Perhaps he may find out more there, and perhaps the White Guards do not patrol the taverns quite so thoroughly. Then again, he reflects, they may patrol the taverns even more thoroughly.

No one accosts him as he enters the smoky room and peers around at the tables. At one end of the stone-walled structure there is a low stage, and upon the stage is a single figure; a man who strums and plays a song of some sort.

> . . . la, la, la, la-la, and the cat would play
> with the dog on the spring's first day . . .

The notes are copper, if that. Creslin could do better, scarcely trying. A small table along one wall is vacant, although two empty mugs rest there. He edges forward.

"Careful there!" snaps a voice.

He turns to see a pair of young men, with a woman between them.

The man who spoke, his hair curled in ringlets, thumbs a knife. "Don't like outlanders much. Maybe you ought to go back to the outlands, huh?"

Creslin's eyes flick down at the man. "I'd rather not." His voice is flat, like the wind before a storm.

The man looks away, and Creslin continues to the table, where he eases down his pack and slips it under the table next to his feet, the hilt of the Westwind blade within easy reach.

"What'll you have?" The serving girl has already collected the two mugs as she speaks, and she smears a damp cloth across the wood.

"What is there?"

"You a singer?" She has a round face under black curls that tumble not quite to her half-covered shoulders, and a cheerfully hard voice.

"Not here," Creslin laughs. "What do you have?"

"Too bad. They say the next one is better, though. What do we have? Cider, mead, red wine, mead . . ."

Creslin shrugs. "Cider, then."

"That's three."

His face expresses amazement.

"You're paying for the singing, bad as it can be. This is one of the few places that's got a license."

Creslin digs out the coins, puts them on the table but leaves them there.

"Fair enough. But no magic. They'd better be there when I get back." The lilt in her voice indicates that she does not seriously believe he will cause the coins to vanish. Her hips brush him ever so slightly as she turns toward the trio he had dodged on his way in. "Ready for another?"

"Here . . ."

". . . not yet," adds a feminine voice.

"Fine."

Only a few hands clap as the guitarist stands and departs the stage.

While he waits for his cider, Creslin slowly observes the

others. Besides the three who sit two tables away, there is a table of four outlanders, garbed in varied livery, the wide belts and equally large swords proclaiming a familiarity with violence. Next to the outlanders sit two couples of indeterminate age. As his eyes continue their circuit of the room, Creslin picks out what appear to be two traders, three men in garb that he guesses may mark them as seafarers, although why a set of seafarers would be in Fairhaven is beyond him.

Five women, each with short hair and a belt dagger, sit at a corner table, and the entire corner seems shrouded in white. As quickly as he can, but without hurrying, he lets his study move onward. Another table contains five outlanders—one woman amid four men—but only two wear swords, and one of them is the woman.

"Here you go!" The professionally cheerful serving woman delivers a heavy brown mug.

Creslin smiles. "Here you go. No magic."

"Thanks, fellow. They tell me the new guy is better, much better." Her head turns toward the stage, where a stocky man is seating himself on a chair, cradling a guitar, and facing the audience directly.

". . . better be better, for what these cost," someone says.

Creslin agrees with the sentiment.

". . . hush. Just listen."

The silver-haired man leans forward and takes a sip of the cider, heavily spiced and warm. The taste is of apples and spices, with the faintest of bitter undertastes, though not enough to mar the overall effect. He glances toward the stage, then continues to watch.

He can see the order behind the notes played by the guitarist—almost as if the notes are pasted on the heavy, smoke-filled air. He sips from the weighty brown mug, no longer really tasting the mulled cider. The faint memory of another time drifts behind his eyes, the memory of a guitarist with silver hair, of grasping at a note floating in the air.

With a smile, Creslin shrugs, concentrates, and reaches forth with both hand and mind.

Thrummm.

The guitarist's fingers falter as the single tone lingers on past the instant he played it, and his eyes widen as he looks toward the corners where it resonates, where the dimmest of silver glows issues from the fingertips of the silver-haired man sitting alone in the shadows of the table for two.

Creslin releases his capture, ignoring both the faltering of the guitarist and the raggedness of the rest of the ballad.

"What—" whispers the heavy serving girl, watching the glow vanish from his fingertips.

"Just a memory," he says, as if the words explained anything at all.

The girl swallows, turns, and makes the sign of the one-god believers as she picks up another set of empty mugs from a table of dicers. "Another round, girl. Same as the last."

Smoke from the burning oak swirls from the hearth, mixing with cold air rushing in from the open doorway.

Creslin sips again from the dark-brown mug, tasting for the first time the edge of autumn buried in the cider, drawing forth that sense of ripening fruit and that hint of something else that he noted with his first sip.

Plop . . .

Wobbling on the table is a red apple, streaked with green. On one side are both a large dark spot and the dark antennae of a fruit beetle. Creslin's mug is now less than half full, though he has taken but three sips.

"I think I would have preferred not to know." He takes another sip of the cider, discovers the taste is unchanged and nods at the understanding that the infested apples become cider.

"Where'd you get an apple this time of year?" asks the clean-shaven young man who has seated himself at the adjoining table. Hard-faced, he wears the white leathers of the wizards' guards.

So does the woman pulling out the other chair; there is a black circle on the lapel of her white-leather vest. Her eyes glance at Creslin, catch the silver hair, then rest upon his face. Finally she looks away and gestures.

A small point of fire appears before the face of the serving girl, who turns quickly, sees the white leathers and scurries toward the two guards. "Yes, your honors?"

Creslin takes a deep breath. To leave at this point would call even more attention to himself. He takes a small sip, as much to bring the mug before his face as to drink.

"Cider and cheese, with the good brown bread," states the woman.

"Same here," says the man, returning his attention to Creslin. "About the apple."

Creslin shrugs, bemused, and picks up the apple, extending it to the guard. "It's a little spoiled."

The man takes it, then employs his narrow-bladed and white-hilted bronze belt knife to cut away the brown spot, expertly carving the remainder of the fruit into identical crescents. He offers a crescent to the other guard.

Her eyes still scanning the half-dozen occupied tables, she begins chewing, then stops. "Harlaan, where did you get this?"

"From him. What's wrong?"

"It's fresh. That's what's wrong." She turns toward the corner where Creslin sits.

"Fresh? That's a problem?" mutters the young guard.

"You! What school are you from?" Her flinty gray eyes bore in on Creslin.

"School? I beg your indulgence, lady blade, but I am a stranger here, not a student, though I would learn what I could if I knew how to."

Her lips tighten. "A pretty statement, especially for a western wizard." She stands, and her thin sword shimmers white-gold in the dim light. "Let us go, you and I. And Harlaan."

Creslin stands slowly, his hands empty, his eyebrows drawn. "I would appreciate knowing what offense or crime I may have committed."

"Definitely an outlander, wouldn't you say, Harlaan?" Her words are addressed to the guard although her eyes remain on Creslin. "Possibly the one we might be looking for?"

"He speaks the Temple tongue too formally, too well," agrees the guard, leaving two apple crescents on the table as his white-bronze blade extends toward Creslin.

Creslin remains standing, though he glances down at his pack.

"Step away from the table. Harlaan, get his pack. I thought I felt something odd about you, stranger."

"Holy wizards . . ." breathes Harlaan as he straightens up with the pack. "Look at that blade."

The serving girl has retreated through the smoke to the kitchen, and the rest of those in the room pointedly ignore the two White Guards and their captive, just as the bystanders had done earlier on the boulevard.

"What about it?"

"Cold steel, and it's a Westwind guard blade. You can tell by the length."

"Be careful with it—the Westwind guards are women. He's a man; he probably stole his way across the mountains."

Creslin smiles sadly.

Harlaan shakes his head. "You don't steal their blades. It's either his or he was good enough to take it from a guard."

Creslin's eyebrows knit and unknit, but he says nothing, suspecting that any answer will get him in deeper trouble.

"Interesting," snaps the woman. "Let's go."

"Would you mind if I left a copper for the serving gir'?'"

"Be our guest."

Creslin takes a single coin from his purse and sets it on the battered wood. "Where to?"

"Out the door and turn uphill. I wouldn't try to run, not unless you want to have your guts burned out."

Creslin has heard of the White Guards, who mix weapons and magic, but he regrets that his first encounter with them has turned out the way it has. And all because he was wondering about the taste of the cider. He purses his lips and steps through the heavy wooden door, emerging into the misty twilight, where a fine and cold spring rain begins to filter down his neck. The earlier warmth of the day has vanished. While the air seems near summerlike to him—which is the reason his parka is in his pack—the dampness of the rain is annoying. Yet, with a wizard bearing a blade at his back, he dare not channel the wind and moisture away from himself.

"Uphill, stranger."

Absently, as he follows the command, Creslin notes that the smoke from the tavern has emerged with them. He also notes that the man is close to a head taller than he is.

"Do you really think he can use that blade?"

"Yeah, but I couldn't tell you why," answers Harlaan. "I don't think I'd want to be around if he got his hands on it, either."

Creslin chuckles.

"Think that's funny?"

"No. It's just that you have assumed I am dangerous, deadly with a weapon, and some sort of criminal, and all I have done is to sip cider in a tavern."

Neither guard replies, but Creslin can sense an increased tension in the pair and wonders if he should have said nothing. Still, silence would have presumed guilt.

As the light from the western sky decreases, the pale, white stones of the street seem to reflect a dim light from somewhere, enough that the oil lamps hung by each doorway seem almost unnecessary.

The hill is not long, nor is the square building seated at the crest large.

"In here."

A quick look to the right and Creslin can see a line of white that seems to be the main highway through which he had entered Fairhaven so recently.

"Syrienna? A tavern roisterer so early?" A thin man in black leathers sits behind a flat table. His lips curl away from even white teeth as he speaks, making him seem old, though Creslin doubts that he is much older than the woman.

"Call Gyretis."

"My!"

"Call Gyretis, or—"

"Are you threatening me, dear lady?"

"No. But I might give this fellow his sword and do nothing at all."

"That would pose a problem."

"You Black types can't defend yourselves against anything but another wizard," sneers Harlaan.

"Not quite true, Harlaan. Would you like to grow another beard, right from your eyes?"

The young guard swallows.

"Would you just call Gyretis?"

"Could I tell him why?" asks the Black Wizard.

"Unlicensed Black wizardry, able to carry and use col steel, and the sword is a Westwind blade."

As the Black Wizard studies Creslin, Creslin feels unseen fingers across his thoughts.

"You're damned lucky that he's essentially untrained, Syrienna. There's enough power there for three Blacks Unlucky for him."

Creslin frowns in spite of himself. Power? Black power In him? What are they talking about? Surely his meage ability to channel the winds—or to recreate an apple from cider—is not to be envied or a cause for alarm.

"Where's Gyretis?"

"He's been notified." The man in black smiles wryly.

Creslin's eyes feel heavy and he wants to yawn, but his knees shake and he can barely get his hands out to keep himself from toppling to the floor in sheer exhaustion. At the same time, he throws up a mental arm against sleep, but . . . the floor is deep and black.

XXXIV

"ARE YOU SURE he's the one?" asks the High Wizard.

"How many are there who can bend winds and wield blades?"

"Why can't you just kill him?"

The questions circle the table of white-clad men like vultures circling a carcass.

"We know that the Tyrant of Sarronnyn has a lifelink to him, assuming this is the same youth. What happens if he dies?"

"So does the lifelink, of course."

"And?" pursues the skeletal man in pure white.

"That means the Tyrant knows he's dead. So what?"

"The Tyrant and the Marshall suspect that he is in Fairhaven," responds the High Wizard.

"You worry about two women across the Westhorns?"

"I worry about the only two rulers remaining in Candar with armies worthy of the name. I also remember what happened to the expeditionary force you encouraged so effectively, Hartor. Besides which, the Tyrant is the cousin, if by consortship, of the Duke of Montgren."

"Oh . . ."

"Exactly. If this youth were to become weaker over time and die, of course . . ." He shrugs. "It wouldn't be that bad, in any case, but why give either the Marshall or Ryessa another affront when we don't have to?"

"I'll ready the cell," Hartor offers.

A sigh replies. "Don't you ever think? If his life-signs stay in one place, that's a sure indication. The other thing is that we really don't want it known who he is quite yet. Then we can spread a few rumors about the barbarian nature of the western wenches, driving a poor boy to his death. That certainly can't hurt."

"But we're the ones—"

"So, who will know? We're not exactly constrained by Black-order considerations." The man in the blinding white smiles his non-smile.

"The Blacks won't like it, Jenred."

"They don't have to know. Even if they did, how could they prove anything?"

"I see. What about the main road camp?"

"That will do splendidly, with one minor addition. He doesn't have to know who he is."

"Won't the White prison wear off?"

"Not for a year or so. And by then . . ."

The white-clad men around the table nod sagely, except for one, but his blank face is lost in the nods.

XXXV

THE RED-HAIRED woman staggers to her feet, blotting her forehead with a cloth. "The bastard. Why doesn't he take care of himself? Why? Damned fever, damned headaches. What did they do to him?"

As her eyes fail to focus, she sinks back into the wooden chair bolted to the deck, her fingers grasping the arms carved into the representation of leaping dolphins. The white scars on her wrists tingle, and a touch of redness suffuses them, almost as if the cold iron still encircled her flesh.

"Sister . . ." She chokes back what she might have said, glancing instead at the rack above the narrow bunk, her eyes picking out the white-leather case with the mirror inside. Her left hand lifts itself from the carved chair arm as if independent of the rest of her body, then falls back on the arm of the chair as the deck lurches under her.

The coaster bearing her to the north shores of Sligo, to Tyrhavven, continues to pitch in the heavy seas, but her stomach remains calm, unlike her thoughts or the fevers that wrack her body.

Both hands grasp the arms of the chair, her fingers tightening as if to lever her slender body erect on the smooth red-oak deck. Then the fingers spasm, and she shudders.

"Sister, you deserve . . . all the hells of the eastern wizards." She closes her eyes, as if the words alone have exhausted her, but she remains in the chair, behind those closed lids recalling the mirror and the swirling white that blocks any contact with her lifelink.

"Darkness damn . . . him and damn . . . her." Her breath rasps through chapped lips and a parched throat. "Damn . . . damn . . ."

XXXVI

THE SOUND OF hammer upon chisel clangs, off-key, disordered, in the morning shadows that cloak the canyon.

The silver-haired man trudges back from the leading edge of the construction, past the first of the deep, straight clefts that separate one foundation block from another, each block a rock cube more than thirty cubits on a side. As he steps up to the unloading stand, he leans forward to balance the weight of the rocks in the basket upon his back, ignoring the ache in his shoulders and the crease-edged pain of the basket's canvas straps.

Before him stretches the newest canyon of the mountains, a knife-sharp raw gash open to the east. At the base of that gash are the joined stones of a roadbed that strays not a thumb's width to the left or to the right, a roadbed that runs from Fairhaven to where he stands, or so he has been told. Behind him, scarcely four hundred cubits distant from the square timbers of the unloading apparatus he approaches, the canyon's clean-cut walls terminate in a barrier of solid stone. The trees and soil, more than two hundred cubits above, have been removed, and the dust and white ash from that removal drift into the notch below, causing the workers to cough occasionally, and to squint and blink away the ash and grit.

Halfway between the unloading platform and the mountain wall that blocks the road's progress stand two figures in white: white boots, tunics, and trousers.

With the ease of habit, the silver-haired young man turns and presents his burden, slipping from the straps and standing aside to wait for the return of the empty basket. His eyes skip over the glittering arc that flows from the northern wall of the canyon a kay eastward from his work: a stream that tumbles into the watercourse beside the road, clawing futilely at the massive granite blocks and smooth-fitted stonework that support the road. Some of the mist from the falling water drifts back toward the silver-haired man as the light morning breezes shift.

The fill-master swivels the unloading spout to direct the smaller granite chunks into the space between the two base blocks and above the stone drain. The watercourse beside the new construction remains empty except for scattered puddles from the rain of the afternoon before.

"Next!"

Stepping to the other side of the unloading platform, the man who has no name, none that he can presently remember, reclaims his empty basket and trudges back toward the wizards in white.

Tweet! Tweet! A shrill whistle splits the morning shadows, for the sun has not yet climbed high enough to strike the bottom of the canyon.

"Stand back! Stand back, you idiots!" The order—conveyed in a disordered, grumbling growl—tumbles from the fleshy lips of a man in white leathers who wears a sword and a white bronze-plate skullcap. "You! Silver-top! Stand by the stone. Behind the barrier!"

After edging behind the low stone wall that rests on wooden skids, the nameless worker takes his place among a dozen huddled figures.

"Close your eyes! Close your eyes!"

Remembering the pain, the silver-haired one complies. Has there been a time without pain? He feels that once such a time existed.

CRACK! CRACCCKKKK!

A flash brighter than the noonday sun, sharper than the closest of lightnings, flares across the stone face that rims the canyon.

Once-solid rock fifty cubits deep splinters, fractures, separates, and slides into a rough pyramid at the base of the remaining rock wall. Rock dust mushrooms above the shadows and into the morning light, blurring the sharp edges of the canyon walls.

"Head out. Load up," calls the road soldier.

The two wizards walk slowly, tiredly, back toward the golden coach that waits where the smooth-finished paving stones end.

The silver-haired and nameless man squints as the younger wizard passes by, less than an arm's length away. He cannot grasp the memory, recognizing only that he should know something, and that he does not.

"Load up, you idiots! That means you, silver-top!"

The memory and the moment boil away with the mist and shadows as the sun clears the southeast edge of the canyon rim and glares upon the road-builders. The nameless man blinks and steps toward the pile of granite that must be removed for fill or for reshaping by the stonecutters. Then the wizards in black will come and bond the stones and mortar together. While he has seen the men in black, again he can only remember what he has been told their actions signify. In any case, the stones will be used, and the road will proceed westward toward the sunset.

"Load up!" comes the command once more.

His steps carry him forward toward the loading rack that other prisoners are sliding into place beside the tumbled stones, even before the dust has settled.

"Just the gray stones . . ."

The words wash over him as he waits in the line of men wearing baskets identical to his.

Clink . . . clink . . . Behind him, the stonemasons resume their work, crafting the flush-fitted gray walls and storm drains that link the base-blocks of the road.

The loading crew begins placing the square stones into the loading bin, and the first porter eases his basket into the rack.

"Next!"

The nameless man racks his basket, waits until it is full, then strains away from the rack and staggers onto the heavy plank walk that leads back to the unloading rack, leaning forward and squinting against the rising sun.

"Next!"

Heavy leather boots protect his feet against the splinters of the planks and the sharp edges of the rocks, but not against the casual fit and the blisters. The inside of his right boot is damp with blood. Each step sends a twinge up his leg.

"Silver-top!"

He looks up blankly to the road soldier, not halting his progress past the overseer.

"Unload and go to the healer's tent. Then get back here." The soldier's voice bears exasperation. He is not as tall as the nameless man, but he wears a sword and gestures with a heavy white-oak truncheon.

The nameless man can see a white glow tinged with red

around the scabbarded sword. That same glow surrounds all of the swords of the road soldiers, swords that cut like the fire they contain.

He stumbles up to the unloading platform, performs the routine, and staggers back along the boards. Instead of turning right, toward the shattered pile of rock heaped like a rough pyramid at the end of the slowly growing canyon, he turns left, toward the canvas tent which bears a white banner emblazoned with a single-lobed green leaf. There he sets the basket down.

The woman in the crisp green blouse and matching green-leather trousers and boots looks at him. "Right foot?"

He nods.

"Sit there." She points to a short wooden bench. "Take off the boot. Let's see." Her voice is matter-of-fact.

He is pleased with the music in her words, submerged as it is beneath the duty, and smiles faintly as he seats himself and removes his right boot. Thin lines of red have splashed away from his heel, from the bloody and yellowed sore there.

The woman shakes her head, talking to herself as if he were not present. "Idiots. Don't put oversized work boots on bare feet." Her fingers touch the skin around the wound. He winces in anticipation of pain, but there is none, so gentle are her fingers.

"Hmmm . . . not too bad." She takes a white cloth, dips it in an acrid liquid. "This might sting." The wet cloth touches his foot as she begins to clean away the pus and blood.

"Sssss . . ." The breath hisses through his lips as liquid fire bathes his heel, but he does not move.

"While you are here, let me check something else." Her fingers touch his temples, and a faint warmth stirs within his head, then vanishes. She steps back, even before the burning sensation leaves his foot.

From a full two cubits away, the healer looks at him

through dark-lashed eyes, shakes her head imperceptibly. "Sit over there. Let it dry."

He moves to the stool she has indicated.

"Healer?" Another voice intrudes.

They both look up. A road guard stands by the tent, followed by two other prisoners carrying a stretcher.

The silver-haired man knows one of the stretcher-bearers—Redrick—because they share the same bunk wagon.

"Smashed leg," announces the guard, his voice flat.

"Set him on the table. Gently."

The nameless man watches as Redrick and the other prisoner ease the injured man onto the long, battered table. The guard watches, along with the two stretcher-bearers, while the healer examines the leg.

"I can splint this, but the master-healer at Borlen will have to handle the bones."

"Darkness . . ." mutters the road guard.

"It's your choice. Two bones are shattered. I can keep him from losing the leg, but it will be nearly half a year before he can get around without help, and he'll never really be able to use the limb."

"Fix him up as well as you can. I'll ask the squad leader. You two—" the guard jabs with the hand not holding the truncheon"—come on and get back to work." He glares at the nameless man. "How long before this one's ready?"

"Not long. This time you sent someone before the whole foot was diseased."

The guard purses his lips, then turns without speaking. Redrick and the other prisoner follow him.

"My leg?" asks the bearded prisoner, an older man with streaks of gray in his straggly beard and remaining hair.

"They'll send you to Klerris. They don't like to, but they will." She rummages through a long trunk as she speaks, finally extracting an apparatus of canvas and wooden braces. "You, silver-head. Give me a hand here."

"What?" mumbles the older man.

"We're just splinting the leg temporarily. That's so the ends of the bones don't rip up your leg any more than it is when they throw you in the wagon."

The nameless man stands up and takes the four steps that bring him beside the table. The pain in his bare foot has subsided to a dull throbbing.

"When I tell you . . ." The healer explains how she wants him to hold the injured man's leg. "Do you understand?"

He nods.

She takes the apparatus in hand. The prisoner screams but does not move as the healer and the nameless man do what they must. The healer's hands never falter.

The silver-haired man clamps his lips as he does his job, but his hands remain steady. He knows that he should do something besides what he has been told, but what that should be, he does not remember, if indeed it is an action that he should remember from the past he does not recall.

At the end, the man on the table lies half-comatose, sweating. As the healer sponges away his sweat, her eyes fall upon the nameless man. "You don't belong here."

"I don't know where I belong. Do you?"

She looks away, then shakes her head. "Let's check your foot."

Her hands are deft. She places a thin cloth, sticky at the edges, over the sore, which is no longer yellow but merely white beginning to crust. Then she rummages in the trunk under the table.

"Oohhh . . ." comes a murmur from the table.

The healer straightens and touches the unfortunate's forehead. "You'll be all right." In her other hand, she lifts what appear to be two strips of cloth. She turns to the silver-haired man.

"Wear one of these each day on the injured foot—today, over the pad. Tomorrow, wash the foot and take off the pad. Wear the clean sock. Wash the socks out as well as you can and wear a clean one each day until the foot heals. If it gets worse, come see me as soon as you can. Just tell the guards I told you to." She holds up her hand. "You won't work at all if it gets really diseased."

He takes the socks and sits down on the stool, easing one sock over his injured foot, careful not to move the pad over the sundered blister. Then he reaches for the heavy work boot, looking at the healer. Does she resemble a shadow he should remember? He looks down, uncertain.

She smiles faintly, then turns back to the man on the table.

The nameless man pulls on the boot slowly. The healer does not look at him until after he picks up the empty shoulder basket and heads westward to the pyramid of shattered granite.

XXXVII

"RIGHT NOW THEY only pay lip service to the Balance, and they ignore the Legend totally."

"Can we really believe the Legend?" asks the healer.

"Look at Fairhaven, and the way things are heading. Then look at Sarronnyn, and tell me."

"What about Westwind?" The healer purses her lips.

"The Marshall's almost as bad as the High Wizard. How Werlynn ever stood it . . . He loved her." The man in black shakes his head. "And he went there only to do his duty. His son is a miracle, and we owe him that much." He appraises the healer. "Are you willing to try to lift the memory block? It could be fatal if they discover your efforts."

"They won't. He has an injured foot. He's been to see me once, and I have already started the process. He may be able to do the rest on his own. If not, I can stage it in a way that he looks out of his mind."

"You wouldn't use a Compulsion?" The sound of repugnance chokes his voice.

"I'm not that far gone, Klerris. He's bright, very bright, and still struggling hard under that White prison. He can speak and understand, and that's a wonder in itself. Next time they won't catch him."

"If he gets away . . ."

She looks down. "There's no risk to us there. He either escapes or they kill him."

For a time, both are silent. Finally she stands. "Do your best with the leg."

"That's easy enough, compared—"

She waves him off. "The Whites serve only chaos. If we don't serve the Balance, who will?"

"If we don't serve the Balance, who will?" Her words ring in his mind long after he has mounted the steps and begun to repair a prisoner's shattered leg under the watchful eyes of the road guard.

XXXVIII

THE REDHEAD FIXES her eyes upon the mirror once again, ignoring the damp patches on her forehead and cheeks, and the hair matted with sweat.

On the dark oak-paneled wall two oil lamps burn steadily, flickering only when she casts her thoughts into the silvered depths before her.

"Damn you . . . damn . . ."

She senses the thinnest of threads . . . a touch of whiteness, smooth, and the swirl of winds beneath that barrier—her teeth bare in a fierce smile as she throws her energies along that thin line of sweat and blood.

Crack!

On the heavy oaken table, the mirror lies shattered. The lamps on the wall behind her are snuffed out.

Blood oozes from a cut on the redhead's forearm, above the scar that circles her left wrist. Her head slumps onto her arms, tears and blood and glass mixing as shudders take her body.

"Damn . . . Creslin . . . and damn you, sister . . ." The words are low, nearly a hiss.

Behind her, the heavy door silently swings open. A short, slender man, dressed in green and gold, stands in the light from hall lamps bright enough to show his white-streaked red hair and the creases in his forehead.

He stares at the slumped figure, the shards of glass and the black lamps, and his mouth opens, then shuts. He makes a gesture of protection, steps backward into the hallway and closes the door as silently as when he entered.

Within, the shudders continue.

XXXIX

THE MAN WITHOUT a name limps into the wagon, his right foot bare and carrying a boot in one hand and a damp sock in the other. He ignores the road guard who has followed him back from the water trough.

"No more roaming around, not after dark," growls the rail-thin night guard. Unlike the day guards, the night guards wear knives and swords. The white-red glow of both is clear to the limping silver-haired man.

"The healer said—"

"Before dark, silver-top. That's it. You know the rules."

The prisoner moves into the darkness of the bunk wagon, not that the darkness slows him, for he has found that he can perceive objects equally well in darkness or in light. And at night his eyes do not have to squint to block out the distracting brightness of the summer sun. Again, it seems to him as though he should know these things. He wants to know them, but his thoughts find nothing save a great void where there should be memories.

". . . guards . . . hassling, hassling, hassling." He hears the voices of the other prisoners in the wagon.

"It's one of their cherished pleasures, Deiter. Wine, women, and song, you remember? No wine here. The only women are other guards, and they're tougher than the men. And you know how the wizards feel about song."

The nameless man sets his boot on the bottom of the top bunk and prepares to climb up. No women? What about the healer? And song? But he does not ask. There is too much he does not know. Finally he puts his foot on the edge of the bottom bunk.

"Careful there, silver-top."

"Sorry."

He climbs toward his bunk and the planked roof of the wagon, where he wiggles into the narrow space and removes his other boot. Then he attempts to stretch out and sleep. His muscles ache, though not nearly so greatly as when he remembers first carrying the stones.

Although the soreness in his heel has disappeared, the low whispers of the other prisoners persist, and sleep does not find him.

"A song . . ." hisses a voice.

The silver-haired man eases to the edge of the cramped bunk, looking down.

Redrick sits on the narrow space next to the bottom bunk of the opposite row, glances from one side of the wagon to the other, clears his throat softly, swallows, then looks toward the open doorway and the blackness beyond. Like three others in the wagon, he half sits, half leans, between the lower bunk and the narrow floor space that separates the twin row of pallets upon hard wooden frames.

"Go on . . . a song," insists the older man with the hairless and tanned skull, the one with arms like small trees.

"A song?"

"A song."

"Shhh . . ." hissing from a top bunk. That noise'll have the wizards' men back here as fast as storm bolts."

The single lamp flickers in the wind that gusts through the doorless opening in the wagon.

"Shit . . ." The mutter comes from the bottom bunk, the lowest in the stack of three beneath the nameless man.

Redrick glances nervously toward the emptiness outside and clears his throat once more. Then, without strings, without flute, his thin voice, as clear as a mountain stream at dawn, creeps through the wagon, one note, one word, at a time.

> *Ask not the song to be sung,*
> *or the bell to be rung,*
> *or if my tale is done.*
> *The answer is all—and none.*
> *The answer is all—and none.*
>
> *Oh, white was the color of my love,*
> *as bright and white as a dove,*
> *and white was he, as fair as she,*
> *who sundered my love from me . . .*

Even in the flickering light of the lamp, the singer appears drawn, as though each word is a struggle against an unseen opponent, each note an arrow thrown against a white-red flame that seeks to consume it.

To the silver-haired man, those fragile notes climb like silver ghost-lights from the singer toward the flat plank roof of the wagon, lights more intense in their insubstantial glow than the yellow flame of the lamp itself. He extends a hand, cupping it around a single ordered vibration.

Tweet! Tweet!

Redrick's voice falters, halts . . .

The note shatters into less than dust, and the nameless

man stares blankly at the emptiness between his palm and his fingers, feeling tears welling in his eyes. Tears? For a fragment of nothing?

"So . . ." rumbles the gravelly voice of the road soldier. "Singing, is it? Such a happy little group here. And who was singing?" The white wand he carries twists toward the thin man with the reddish-blond hair. "You again? Still the troublemaker?"

Redrick does not look at the soldier.

The wand jabs at the singer. "Move. The wizards want to see you. You know what they think about singing here."

Slowly, Redrick slouches to his feet.

"Now, my fine singer!"

Before the silver-haired man can focus on what has happened, both singer and soldier are gone and the lamp flickers in the wind of their disappearance.

"Singing disrupts the road work . . ." The sotto-voce imitation is nearly inaudible, cruel and bitter in its mocking overtones.

No other voices rise in protest. None.

The silver-haired man wipes away his tears and turns his face to the wall, but the unsung words resound in his mind, their tones echoing in his ears.

> . . . *the answer is all—and none.*
> *The answer is all—and none* . . .

In the darkness of the wagon, long after the others have drifted into exhausted sleep, he lies awake, staring at the planks less than a cubit from his face. Through the blackness whisper the small sounds; the snores of exhausted men, the creaking of bunk frames as those men turn in their sleep, even the few murmurs of Hamorian as a foreign prisoner mutters into the depths of his dreams.

The nameless man's muscles no longer ache as they did in the first days he worked on the road, and his pale skin has bronzed and toughened. But he has no name, no past save

the whispers of voices within his skull, voices so faint that
he cannot make out their words, barely comprehending that
they are there. Only one thing does he recall clearly: the
shadow with a woman's face.

In time, he sleeps, dreaming about golden notes that
glitter against gray stone walls and endless white snow.

Tweet! Tweet!

"Let's go! Up and out!" The gravelly voice of the
morning guard grates more harshly than normal.

Outside the bunk wagon, a faint drizzle fills the canyon,
but even the mist bears the grit of crushed and shattered
rock. So does the porridge ladled out to each road-work
prisoner. Only the water is pure and cold, and the cold
reminds him of falling white flakes, and of song.

The wooden bowl bounces off the rock underfoot, the
porridge splattering across the stone. His eyes open, seeing
not the fog and mist above, nor the prisoners around him,
nor the guards behind him.

"NOOOooo!" The scream goes on and on, never ending,
and the silver-haired man wonders why the guards do not do
anything, even as he realizes that the tortured voice is his
and that the guards are moving toward him in slow motion.

The cold and whiteness of his thoughts, the rushing
images of . . .

—*an endless expanse of snow beneath peaks that touch the*
  sky
—*silvered notes shattering against gray granite walls*
—*eating in green leathers at the high table*
—*riding a narrow, stone-worked road . . .*

He totters on wobbly legs, not lifting his hands to fend off
the blows. The images are dispelled with the second blow
and the rush of darkness it brings upon him.

When he wakes, he cannot move, for he is bound upon a
table, and overhead, damp canvas sways in the wind.

Plip . . . plip . . . Droplets of water collect in the

depressions of the tent above his head, some seeping through the worn fabric and falling onto the stone, others falling upon his half-bare body.

The dark-haired healer glances over at him, although her hands are dressing the gash in the arm of another prisoner, a thin, bald man who once was fat.

"That should do it. Try to keep it clean." Her voice was flat, as if she knows that the dust and rock powder will infiltrate anything.

The silver-haired man closes his eyes, tries to keep his breathing regular.

"Is he ready?"

"This one? Yes."

"What about silver-top?"

"His breathing is more regular, but until he wakes up, I can't say. A second head injury isn't good for anyone."

"No loss. He didn't even know who he was."

"He may never know if you keep beating his skull."

"He went nuts!"

"Did he strike anyone?"

"He started screaming 'No!' at the top of his lungs. Wouldn't stop. The wizards were real upset. Gero had to crack him. They would have done worse."

"I'll let you know."

The slooshing footstep sounds of the guard and the bald prisoner retreat.

"They're gone."

Her voice is almost on top of him, and he jumps. "Easy. I'm going to untie these."

He relaxes, as much as he can, while moving his stiff arms out of the spread-eagled position where he has been restrained. His skull aches, more than his shoulders ever did.

"Don't try to sit up yet."

He opens his eyes slowly to see the healer studying his face, looking from one eye to another.

"What happened?" she asks.

"I . . . don't know," he mumbles, feeling the once-familiar tightening in his stomach. "Exactly . . ." he adds to relieve the tension.

She nods slowly. "You could probably go back to work tomorrow, but you will have to be very careful. You won't see things exactly as you have, and the adjustment will be difficult." Her eyes turn toward the opening in the front of the tent and follow the stone pavement stretching eastward. "There's a beautiful valley five kays back toward Jellico. The wizards left it for a future inn or a resting spot. The stream leads up to where one could cross into the northern valleys of Certis on the way to Sligo."

Heavy steps sound in the rain outside.

"Let's see those eyes again."

"So silver-top is recovering?" The growling road guard stands just inside the tent.

"He's still dizzy, but you didn't hit him hard enough to kill him. He might even recover, provided you let him rest today. He could have dizzy spells for several days. So if he sits down suddenly, it's probably real."

"How long will he be like that?"

"It might last for just a day. It might last for three or four. If he gets through three or four days, he'll recover. There's nothing broken, and I can't do much more."

"Fine! He can lie on his bunk as well as here. Let's go, silver-top."

The healer looks at the guard. "Not yet. He may not even be able to stand without getting dizzy."

"I'll be back."

The drizzle of the morning has turned into a flood of water from unbroken gray skies. For the first time in days, if not longer, the odor of dust and rock has vanished.

"Try to sit up."

He swings his feet over the side of the table. For an instant he feels as though he is two separate people, sitting side by side, yet together. Even the rain seems to fall in two separate patterns.

"Stand up."

The urgency in her voice spurs him to his feet. She studies his eyes as he sways upright. His hand grasps the table to steady himself.

"You can sit down." Her voice is flat again.

The guard steps into the tent, ducking under the sagging and damp canvas.

"He's still unsteady, but there's not much else I can do."

The silver-haired man, for he now knows that it is dangerous even to admit he has a name, follows the guard through the rain to the bunk wagon, which is filled with the other prisoners.

"Silver-top's back."

"Must have a skull like armor. You see how hard Gero cracked him?"

He makes his way to the top bunk, gingerly, trying to ignore the single empty bunk once occupied by a singer. Soon the bunk will be filled with another hapless prisoner, but the song will remain unsung.

Escape . . . there is little time before the White Wizards will recognize him. While he knows what once he could do, he does not know his present abilities.

Light sears the canyon through the rain, followed by a roll of thunder. The rain continues to drum on the roof, with an occasional gust of wet air blowing into the doorless wagon.

In time, the throbbing of the lump on his skull subsides into a dull ache. He eases himself to the side of the bunk and begins to clamber down, his booted feet clumsy on the wood.

". . . stay in your place."

". . . just silver-top."

He says nothing, trying to keep a vacant expression on his face as he stumbles toward the doorway, where he halts, apparently staring out into the rain.

The old patterns reassert themselves, though each look

sends a wave of agony through his eyes. The heaviest rain will continue, but not for long.

The bored guards stand under canvas, talking.

After a moment he lurches into the rain and begins to amble eastward, angling toward the incomplete wall that separates the raised roadway from the sunken drainage channel on the left.

". . . silver-top. Crazier than ever."

". . . don't do it!"

He is not crazy, but saner than in many eight-days, for only in the storm can he possibly escape the wizards.

"Gero! Get the idiot!"

The prisoner shuffles faster, heading toward the wall, and the torrent a good five cubits below.

The tall guard hesitates, then pulls his sword and moves after the silver-haired man, not at a full run, not on the rain-slicked stones.

"Run! Run, silver-top!"

"Quiet!" snaps the other guard, the one who does not pursue.

Like a silent play, the action unfolds through the blurring of the falling torrents. The prisoner totters toward the edge of the uncompleted wall, momentarily staring at something below. The guard scurries forward, sword at the ready.

The wind whips a violent blast of air and water into the guard's face, and he slows, shaking his head.

The prisoner swings over the wall until his hand alone can be seen, clutching at the wall stones.

The guard lifts the sword, bends . . . and steps back. "He's gone. He's in the river." His voice is muffled by rain and wind.

"In the river? What river?" The second guard joins the first at the edge of the unfinished stone wall.

Then they hasten toward the elaborate wheeled wagon that houses the White Wizards, each looking back over his shoulder at the wall where the prisoner has escaped.

Clang! Clang!

Tweet! Tweet! Tweet!

Another pair of guards races eastward along the completed road, one glancing at the raging waters below, his glance moving farther and farther ahead of his body as he runs.

". . . damned water!"

Amidst the torrent, the silver-haired man tries to relax, tries to let the water carry him where it will, at least for a time. Before he has taken two breaths, he is swept past the temporary gate on the road itself that blocks the prison work area from the completed road, past the small universe that is all he has been aware of for . . . how long? He does not know, for his life is in two parts: the part he is beginning to regain, and the part he has spent as a prisoner of the White Wizards. The last part, and its mindlessness, could have been for days, or for seasons, or possibly even for years.

The water flow smoothes out as it carries him toward the east, away from the storm and into the mist, which is the deluge's forerunner.

He studies the terrain beyond the road and paddles southward, toward the roadbed, the side punctuated by drains. In another two kays, the current slackens to that of a swift stream. His booted feet begin to bounce off the rocks beneath. His eyes watch the upper peaks.

Then he sees the bridge, a fast-approaching blot across the small river. Splashing wildly and thrusting with his feet against the rocks, he half-swims, half-bounces toward the north side of the channel and is just in time to grasp the rocky abutment.

He clings there, his lungs rasping.

"Accuuugh . . . accugghh."

The fingers of one hand edge toward the thin line between the carved stones, dig into the narrow groove and lever his water-tossed body nearer to the rocky escarpment. The other hand crosses, grasping another tenuous stone edge. By repeating the tedious process, the fugitive drags himself clear of the water and onto the stone riprap that slopes toward the valley mentioned by the healer.

After more heaving, he is at the top of the stones, putting one water-filled boot onto the grass. The meadow is empty except for scrub oaks and small junipers around the perimeter. He leaves behind him the stone-paved bridge crossing the subsiding torrent.

Before long, the riders will come trotting down the wizards' road, and he must be out of sight. The mist is turning to rain as the clouds from the west move eastward over the Easthorns.

He forces his walk into a labored jog through the knee-high grass and toward the edge of the meadow, where, if necessary, he can drop behind the low junipers and scattered pines. Intermittent rain beats across the rags on his shoulders, but the water is scarcely cool to him.

"Accuffff . . . cuffff." He coughs out the last drops of water from his laboring lungs and pushes onward toward the narrow end of the valley, where the pines rise toward the higher peaks and cover a jumble of rocks jutting through patches of thin soil.

As the sound of horses' hooves echo down the wizards' road and the artificial canyon that contains that road, the silver-haired man reaches the cover of the trees. His steps slow, but continue upward. The sound of pursuit grows, then fades as the fugitive works his way through the firs, glad for the skimpy underbrush.

The rain falls again in waves, each wave pushed by gusting winds and restricting vision to mere cubits. He struggles upward, knowing that he must cover as much ground as he can before the cover of the falling water vanishes and either the White Wizards or the trackers' dogs can follow his trail.

At times he stops, but only long enough to regain his breath, to rebuild his strength. And thus he proceeds throughout the rainy morning and into the afternoon, following the trees over the crest and into the decline that will become a river valley leading into the Certan plains north of the valley where sits the walled city of Jellico.

He rests again in the late afternoon, under a sky filled with white clouds scudding across the clear blue-green and next to a berry patch. Even with the goodly distance between himself and the wizards' road, he is careful to tuck himself into a hollow created by a boulder and a fallen tree, shielded from the view of high-flying dark birds. There he slowly ingests the dark-purple berries.

Curled into his shelter, thankful that he was raised in real cold on the Roof of the World, he tries to put the pieces together, the rain of memories that the nameless healer has allowed him to recapture. Was she Megaera? Or another tool of the Fates and Furies of the Legend?

As he rests, dreams, half-sleeps, his thoughts drift back.

XL

"It is hard, I admit, to function when part of one's mind is blank, but I have overcome greater obstacles." Megaera smiles wryly.

"You have been here from late spring, and now the end of fall approaches. How long yet do you plan to be here?" the Duke of Montgren inquires.

"I do what I can, cousin. But under my handicap . . ." She smiles again, a twisted smile. "For as long as it takes."

"You can't mean—"

"For as long as it takes. He recovers, escapes, or dies. Dying, of course, would be the easiest on you and sister dear. I am doing my humble best to help him break the spells." She pauses. "I'm not well trained, though. Sister dear ensured that. So it could be a long time that I may have to enjoy your hospitality."

"Which I must supply," notes the Duke coolly.

"Ah, yes. We all have burdens to bear." She turns toward the antique desk on which she has placed her crystal goblet. She blinks, then reaches out toward the desk.

He shakes his head slowly, not noticing her hesitation.

"Aeeeii . . ."

The redhead sinks to the floor under the weight of the kaleidoscope of memories and twisted images that scream through her skull like nightmares riding on warhorses with spiked hooves.

The small and precisely dressed man who has held her arm but a moment before whirls, nearly dropping the goblet of red wine. Instead, only scattered, dark-red splotches mark the ancient Hamorian carpet dating back to the prosperous days of his grandfather.

Before he can replace the half-empty crystal goblet on the desk, the redhead is flat on her face, unconscious, though still breathing.

"Now what?" he mutters. "Helisse! *Helisse!*" He looks down at the woman, then finally kneels beside her. "Now what?"

II.

STORM-MASTER

XLI

The dashing young man on the wind-bearing skis,
He flew down the cliff with the greatest of ease,
A sword on his pack and his soul in the breeze,
That dashing young man on the wind-bearing skis.

With fury to heel and his gray silver hair,
He stepped from the heights out over the trees,
And he dropped from the Roof to the magic so fair,
That dashing young man on the wind-bearing skis.

His eyes on the dark and his soul upon ice,
He flew from the Tyrant, a life filled with ease.
He left behind wealth for love without price,
That dashing young man on the wind-bearing skis.

The soldiers, they searched for many a year.
They ripped down the mountains and tore up the trees,
But never they found what they never could hear,
That dashing young man on the wind-bearing skis.

"Dashing Young Man"
Sarronnese—Anonymous

XLII

FROM BENEATH THE overhang, Creslin studies the unnaturally clear sky to the south. There, a pair of vulcrows circle, spiraling outward from where the wizards' road drills its way through the Easthorns.

From where did he receive the strength and the courage to swim the torrent that carried him from the White road guards? Did the healer's hands help break the block on his memories? Or was it someone or something else? Whatever the cause, he has escaped the White Wizards for now. He will not escape again, not alive, and that means he cannot be caught again.

Toward the east circles yet another pair of the sharp-eyed predators. And he has felt the disruptions of the winds and the skies, the storms being shunted to the east and west. With an indrawn breath, he rests under the rocks, his eyes taking in the thin line of rushing water: another stream that may lead him eastward.

Inside his skull, memories twist like the winds, for he is two people at the same time—silver-top and Creslin—and each remembers a different yesterday. One remembers the road crew; the other remembers the glittering white stones of Fairhaven and a guitarist who could barely reach the silver notes, and only in a well-shielded tavern.

Music . . . why don't they like it? The questions are all too many, the answers too few. *So who are you?*

He is a man. A man who can sense the music, and the order behind the music. A man who can wield bow and blade better than all but a few. A man who can grasp the winds and bend them to his wishes. A man who knows little of life apart from the Roof of the World, and even less of women, for all that he has been raised around them. A man who has no idea of his destiny.

Unbidden, another set of words drops into his thoughts: "You can run to your destiny, but not from it."

But what is his destiny? Neither musician, nor soldier, nor student—what is his role? Why do white birds and vulcrows circle above, searching for him? Such questions will not help him to escape from the wizards. Or to find food.

In the cloudless sky, the vulcrows have begun to circle farther to the north, closer to his cover. His heel twinges, but outside of keeping the sore clean, he does not know what else he can do. Yet, besides tending to the infection, the healer had touched the soreness and somehow hastened the healing. Creslin recalls her hands on his foot, and then on his forehead.

But . . . who? Why? Someone else opposes the White Wizards, enough to help him without saying why and to give him a set of directions, even though such actions could have been exceedingly dangerous. Yet the healer is not the shadowy Megaera.

He slumps back under the overhang, trying to sort out his confusion and to plan his next moves. At least the weather is bearable. There will be little enough to glean from this land, even though it is nearing harvest in Certis and Sarronnyn, and he has not even a knife, only a sleeveless tunic, faded trousers, and road boots. Not even a belt.

How can he escape the White Wizards? Any attempt to seize the winds will draw them to him. He studies the rocky slope below, the scattered pines and the scrub oak, then laughs harshly.

Patience. That is all he needs, that and the willingness to eat anything that is edible as he makes his way through the coming nights toward the plains of Certis. One way or another, he must find his way to Montgren.

He takes a deep breath, then another, and tries to relax until darkness comes, the time when the vulcrows cannot see quite so well.

XLIII

THE STOOPED FIGURE trudges, shuffles, and occasionally hobbles along the farm road. The rags that cover him are relatively clean. A cloth patch covers one eye, and a stout, if bent, walking stick rests in one square-fingered hand. Creslin asks himself again why it is taking so much longer to cross the plains of Certis the second time.

"Because you have no horse, no money . . ."

Why is he crossing the plains, heading eastward? Why is he traveling back in the general direction of the wizards, who clearly want him either dead or mindless?

"Because it feels right?" He talks to himself since there is no one else with whom he can talk. "Risking your neck feels right?"

The winds do not lead him to the White Wizards, but along the faintest of trails, too faint to be White or Black, a trail that partakes of both.

He remembers to shuffle as another wagon lurches toward him, and he holds out a supplicating hand. A copper bounces in his direction, but the man and woman on the wagon do not look at him. Creslin recovers the coin and tucks it away. He straightens and walks more steadily once the road is clear.

XLIV

"No . . ." A DARK-HAIRED woman staggers out through the side door but reaches only the second step before she is grasped from behind. Her already-ripped blouse gives way, revealing ample breasts and a bruised shoulder.

"You'll not spill good wine again!" The thin man with a scar across his cheek seizes the heavyset girl's bare shoulder and elbow, levering her toward the slop-filled gutter.

"I won't. I'll be careful. Please . . ."

Two bravos smirk as they watch the innkeeper. A capped maid standing on the doorstep across the road looks away and scurries inside.

"No! No!"

Clip . . . clippedy . . .

The innkeeper pauses as the horse draws near, then lifts his hand again at the serving girl.

The redheaded woman on the horse reins up. The innkeeper does not look at her, but his hand remains aloft.

"Please, mistress, save me . . ."

"Go ahead and save her," snaps the innkeeper. "She's a worthless slut. Throwing wine on paying customers. Good Suthyan wine at that."

The serving girl straightens. "They wanted more than wine . . ."

Two other mounts, carrying a pair of Spidlarian mercenaries, rein up, maintaining a good ten cubits' distance from the mounted woman.

"Why should I save you?" The redhead's voice is cool, almost deep.

The serving girl sways. "If your grace . . ." She shakes her head and looks down. Her eyes are red.

"So you will not beg." The redhead's voice remains distant.

"She's like that. Thinks she's above everyone," ventures the thin man. He does not release his hold on the girl's bruised shoulder.

"Why? Because she doesn't like being manhandled?" The redhead's voice sharpens.

"Customers expect friendly service."

The woman's eyes take in the dark bruises and the welt on the back of the uncovered shoulder, then move to the innkeeper. "And you expect her to provide *very* friendly service?"

"Business is business," responds the innkeeper, but his voice is cautious. "Besides, she was fine when she started."

The serving girl holds her head erect, looking at neither innkeeper nor horsewoman, but at the silent mercenaries in blue. Tears seep from her eyes; she makes no move, even with her free right hand, to blot or wipe them away.

"Let her go." The redhead's voice is level.

"Who will pay her indenture?" whines the innkeeper.

"That wasn't—" The dark-haired girl breaks off her outburst as the redhead's eyes focus on her.

"I don't believe that the Duke's laws permit the indenture of children for debts of the parents."

The innkeeper opens his mouth, then closes it.

"Even if the law is not always observed," continues the horsewoman. She reaches toward her belt and extracts a coin. "Here."

The innkeeper releases his captive to catch the spinning gold. "But—"

"It's more than you deserve."

The innkeeper looks at the hard-faced woman on the horse, then at the two bored mercenaries.

"Don't even think about it," warns the woman. "Cousin dear will have your head."

"Cousin . . . ." The innkeeper looks startled.

"Korweil. The Duke."

The thin man pales as his eyes flicker from the redhead to the mercenaries. The girl takes a step from him. She uses her freed hand to draw the ripped blouse over her shoulder and partly revealed left breast, but licks her lips nervously.

"Take her then, and be done with it."

"No."

The innkeeper backs up another step.

Light flares at the fingertips of the redhead. "Women are not things."

A fireball sears past the man's right ear.

"I trust you'll remember that." She laughs, a hard laugh, almost a bark, and the fire fades from her hands. Then she looks down at the girl. "You still want to be saved?"

The smallest of nods greets the question.

"Gorton. Help her mount behind me." The redhead watches as the innkeeper backs up the stairs.

The taller mercenary dismounts and lifts the short but stocky girl up behind the redhead.

"Put one arm around me, and hang on to the saddle rim there with the other. It's not perfect, but we don't have far to go."

"Your grace—" protests the girl.

"Just do it." The redhead flicks the reins.

The mercenaries follow, and the innkeeper glares from the doorway. The two bravos who have watched the entire proceeding shake their heads, but neither moves until the three horses have picked their way a good hundred cubits up the avenue and toward the walls of the Duke's keep.

The horsewoman asks, "What are you called?"

"Aldonya, your grace."

"Will you serve me, at least so long as I am at Vergren?"

"Yes, your grace."

"That will do." The redhead says nothing more as the horses walk up the sloping road to the keep.

XLV

"THERE'S NOT MUCH to go on," the military chief says.

"Enough. The Blacks helped him," snaps the High Wizard. "Who else could have?"

"Well, Gyretis says the only direct input was White."

"White? He is certain?"

"Is the noble Gyretis ever less than certain?"

"Hmmphh . . ." Jenred taps his fingers on the white

oak of the desk. "White . . . of course. White. Get detachments out to cover every main approach to Montgren."

"Montgren?"

"Don't you understand? White magic. Not anyone we know. Who else is left? The Tyrant couldn't do anything from Sarronnyn. Damn! She must be strong."

The other shakes his head. "No. That was the other thing. Gyretis said that whoever the White was, he—or she— didn't have the strength to break the barrier." He shifts his weight as he stands on the hard white granite. Marble is too soft for the workings of chaos.

"That means that some Black helped then, but was too clever to be detected. Damn them! What about the healers?"

"We don't know."

"Why not?"

"There was only one, and she's dead."

"Dead?"

The other shrugs. "That's what they say. The road wizard burned her body, as per your instructions."

"Idiots!" The High Wizard shakes his head. "That wasn't her body they burned. She got them to see something else. Demons only know where she is now, and this time they'll get away with it, unless those detachments find Creslin *alive*! Do you understand me?"

Hartor nods. "I understand. I don't know if it's possible. Especially if he avoids the roads."

"Do what you can." The High Wizard looks away, but his fingers continue tapping on the gold-sheened finish of the white oak. "Dead. Bah . . ."

XLVI

CRESLIN SITS UNDER the yellowing leaves of the scrub oak, slowly eating the last redberry he has pulled from a nearby bush.

Overhead, another vulcrow circles, and the white-clad road guards below show little signs of departing any time soon; it is almost as if they know he is somewhere close. But how?

The young man takes a deep breath, ignoring the soreness around one rib, resulting from a dive out of the way of a Certan cavalry officer with a bias against beggars, or apparent beggars. Creslin remembers the man's laugh, and his words: "Leave the roads for those who can use them!"

Through the yellow leaves, he watches as the vulcrow circles the end of the valley in a continuous slow spiral. Beyond the other end of the long valley, beyond the range of his vision, are the rolling hills that separate those gently climbing meadows from Fairhaven.

Could he find another road into Montgren? Probably. Would it be guarded as well? Probably.

Creslin? The voice is faint, so faint that he can barely hear the word.

He squirms around under the scrub oak, trying to find the speaker, but all he can hear is the rustle of leaves in the hot breeze of autumn.

Traaa . . .

The horn echoes from the road guards below. Several of them point uphill in his direction.

Creslin? He can feel no speaker nor see one, and the voice is so faint that he cannot tell for sure whether it belongs to a man or a woman. If he had to guess, he would say a woman, if only for the feel of his name.

Traaa . . . traaa . . . More riders point to the hillside, and the vulcrow banks in his direction.

Creslin peers overhead in time to see a wide-winged white bird vanish in the midst of a patch of clear blue. Megaera!

"Darkness . . ." he mumbles. "Now what?"

An unseen mist of white is beginning to climb up the hillside, and a dozen of the road soldiers are turning their mounts toward his scrub oak. If it weren't for the wizard . . .

Creslin shrugs. His legs ache; his stomach is filled with greenery and berries; and he has a walking stick and a belt knife that he scrounged in a town east of Jellico.

Ignoring the feeling that tells him he will pay dearly for the effort, he reaches for the winds, the upper winds that strike the Roof of the World. Under the trembling yellow oak leaves, his forehead breaks out in sweat.

. . . *wwwhhhsss* . . .

The winds sound as though they are hundreds of kays away, distant echoes in the skies.

"Find him! He's trying to call some magic!"

Creslin ignores the squeaky voice from below.

". . . more to your right! Toward those yellow leaves!"

The white mist surges uphill.

". . . can't see anything here."

". . . hope the frigger doesn't have a bow."

The roaring in Creslin's ears increases as the skies turn from mixed clouds into ever-darkening black swirls.

"Find him! Under the yellow trees!"

. . . *wwwhhstt* . . .

". . . which yellow trees? All the damned trees are yellow."

". . . that one! Over there!"

Darkness falls like night on the hillside with the screaming of the winter storms off the Roof of the World. Mixed ice and rain plummet from the towers of the sunset like frozen fire, and the winds . . .

. . . the winds lash the yellow leaves off the branches that shelter Creslin, off the scattered trees around the valley meadows. The winds scour the horsemen from their mounts with ice driven like arrows against armor and unprotected skin.

. . . *whhheeeEEEhhh* . . .

". . . demons . . . demons."

. . . *wwwwhhhEEEEeee* . . .

As the winds subside, the rains fall like the winter waves on the north coast of Spidlar, smashing against the sodden land, against the stripped trees.

On the hillside, a man staggers upright, wiping his forehead, which burns even under the cold torrents. He takes one step downhill, then another. He vomits the meager contents of his guts across a battered crawling evergreen.

Straightening, he staggers around a heap of white that was once man and horse; he slides then stumbles and lands farther downhill. Doggedly he picks himself up, totters onward toward the road below and the open pass into Montgren.

After what seems like a century, he lurches past another pair of white heaps. His head spins, but he stops and paws through a set of saddlebags, taking a small bag of provisions and a leather jacket. The whiteness of a blade twists at his stomach, and he leaves the weapon with its dead owner.

In time, his feet touch the hard clay that is already turning to ooze under the pounding of the skies.

"Megaera . . . why did you let them know? Why?"

He staggers on, lifting feet that weigh stones as the ice-rain falls around him. Though he notices not, little of the torrent strikes him, and after several years, or so it seems, he stands on the hard stones of the road through the hills.

The rain is endless—before him and behind him. His breath comes in gasps. With determination, he puts one foot in front of the other, ignoring the burning and the shuddering within as he steps toward Montgren . . . and Megaera.

XLVII

FROM HIS VANTAGE point on the narrow road that winds northeast toward Sligo, Klerris turns in the saddle to study the dark clouds to the north. The storm is only now beginning to subside after two days of pounding the high hills between Certis and Montgren. He shakes his head, then settles his eyes back on the winding ribbon of clay.

"Are you worried about the road guards finding us?" asks the woman with him. In the early morning chill that will soon be replaced by the warmth of the harvest season, she wears a faded green cloak thrown back over her shoulders. Her mount is a light-gray mare.

"No."

"Are you still worried about his escape?"

"It's not his escape. It's that." He points toward the storm on the horizon. "Do you know how high that has to be for us to see it? Do you have any idea of how much power he has? There's likely to be cold rain over most of Certis and Montgren for days yet."

"I said he was bright."

"Lydya, do you have any idea . . ." His tone is gentle.

"Klerris, you're going to have to stop taking the weight of the world on your shoulders. I can tell you that Creslin doesn't like playing with his abilities. If he created that storm, then he had a real need for it."

"That's only part of the worry. Not only could he destroy half of the world's climate, but none of the Whites will believe an untrained and unknown Black wields that kind of power."

"So?" She urges the horse forward alongside the Black Wizard.

"So Jenred will blame it on us, as well as blame us for Creslin's escape."

"That's why you put the road guards to sleep and burned the house. You told me that already. Jenred wants to blame you for something anyway."

"Too bad we had to use oil." Klerris shrugs as he looks northward again. "Better they think it's our doing than a Black conspiracy. Jenred would like nothing more than to have an excuse to turn on all the Blacks."

"Isn't that coming?"

"Sooner or later, but we really don't have any good defenses."

"Creslin does, clearly."

Klerris snorts. "He doesn't even know he's a Black, and he's tied to a Gray who thinks she's a White."

"Are you sure about that lifelink?"

"You told me."

They ride silently for a time.

"What next?" the healer asks.

"I'll have to do what I can with Creslin. You . . . Westwind, I think."

She shivers. "I hate the cold."

"I'm not exactly enthused about dealing with Creslin and Megaera. Do you want to try that?"

"I'll take the Marshall, thank you." She adds, "Cold or no cold."

XLVIII

CRESLIN SHOULD NOT be up, but he is tired of lying in the small cottage. Healing the sheep had been a mistake, with himself scarcely healed and certainly not knowing what he was doing.

Slowly he swings his feet off the cot and sits up, looking

toward the half-open window opposite the fireplace. The clear blue-green of the sky indicates that it is mid-afternoon, or later. He pulls on the shapeless trousers and heavy woolen shirt he has borrowed from the herder. Making his way outside, he heads to the fence that keeps the sheep out of the gardens.

He rests his right foot on the lower rail of the fence and crosses his arms on the topmost rail. His eyes take in the damp and heavy grass of the fall, grass with more than mere traces of brown, and the cream-colored, black-faced sheep that graze without noticing him.

To the west—beyond the rolling hills, beyond the fertile fields of Certis and the rivers that flood them before running to the Northern Ocean—lie the Easthorns, and the wizard's road that will allow the High Wizard to rule all of Candar, or at least all of Candar that lies east of the Westhorns.

"Your honor . . ."

Creslin wishes that the herders would not accord him rank. Certainly he has never claimed it, and he has only done what he could to help out while recovering from his travels and travails. In his weakened state, that has been little enough: sensing a diseased sheep or two, and actually healing one. That had been a mistake, since he had collapsed on the spot and had awakened back in the cottage.

"Yes, Mathilde?"

"There is a lady here to see you."

"What?" He turns from the fence to look past the barns, past the hilltop cottage with its heavy, gray-thatched roof, to where nearly a dozen armed soldiers sit astride chargers.

Overhead, he sees, briefly, a glittering white bird, which disappears as he watches. He walks downhill to the main path leading to both house and soldiers. With what Andre and his family have done for him, he cannot leave them to the soldiers. He gathers as much of the winds as he can, but his legs still shake and a stray breeze ruffles his hair.

"Wait for me, your honor."

He slows, looking at the small figure huddled inside the herder's heavy coat, realizing belatedly that the day must seem chill to Mathilde, despite the clear sky and warm sun. "Sorry." He channels some of the wind away from her, absently. "Did they say what they wanted?"

"Only the lady spoke. She asked for the master who had appeared from the west." The girl, after catching up with him, looks at him with an accusing stare. "You never said you were a master."

"I'm not." The tightness in his stomach betrays him, and he adds, "I don't like to think about it. Some people think I am."

Her short legs scurry to keep up with him as he strides through the high, damp grass. Shortly they come to the gentle incline leading to the house.

"I think you are. So does Papa. Mama doesn't know what the fuss is all about. She says that you're too gentle to harm a fly and that any fool can see that." An anxious glance crosses the thin face under the woolen cap. "Isn't that right?"

"I couldn't harm you or your family. Or anyone good," he adds.

"You hurt some bad people."

"Yes," he admits.

"I know it! You're a good master. That's what I told the lady."

Creslin does not sigh, torn between the child's faith and her damning honesty.

From the north, heavy clouds roil toward the hillside like chargers bound for battle. With each instant, they seem darker. He shifts his eyes to the troopers waiting by the house. All of them are mounted, save two, for there are two riderless horses. A woman is standing before Andre, and her voice carries toward the silver-haired man and the child.

". . . he walked out of the storm? And he was not wet?"

"Saving yer grace, that's true. But wounded and bleeding, and as hot as a kettle boiling, spewing words that made no sense."

The conversation stops as both the red-haired woman—her hair flows almost to her shoulders, though it is swept back with heavy combs—and Andre watch his approach.

"I found him, Papa," announces Mathilde.

Andre does not look him in the eye but stares at the damp clay by the feet of the lead chestnut.

Creslin catches the woman's deep green eyes for an instant, nods, then moves toward the shepherd. "Andre?" His voice is gentle. "Thank you for everything."

The shepherd still does not look up.

"I mean it. What will be, will be. Without you, I doubt that I'd be alive."

"Shepherd?" The voice of the redhead is commanding, although quiet.

Andre faces her.

"I mean him no harm," she says, "but he cannot remain here."

Creslin looks at the second empty saddle, wondering where the remaining soldier might be.

"Your honor?"

Creslin looks down at Mathilde.

"You won't forget us, will you?"

No, he will not forget this respite, nor the family's kindness. Nor the solemn, thin face and bright brown eyes. "I'll remember, Mathilde."

He straightens and turns toward the shepherd, who stiffens. Creslin ignores this and hugs the bearded man, briefly, but strongly enough to convey his thanks. "I meant it," he whispers as he steps back.

"Better man than me . . ." mumbles Andre.

Creslin looks toward the woman, who has remounted, then inclines his head toward the empty saddle. "Where is the other soldier?"

"Oh, no," she chuckles, and the sound is not quite music. "How else would you get to Vergren?"

"Lady—"

The flat voice of a man mounted on the far side of the woman grates on Creslin's sensibilities, and he steps forward to look at the speaker, a man with short silver-and-black hair and an aquiline nose.

"Wizard, just stay where you are," the man orders. "Look back."

Creslin turns and sees the pair of crossbows aimed at him. "Not exactly friendly," he observes.

"They're somewhat . . . overprotective," adds the woman.

Puzzlement shows on Creslin's face. "But—"

She laughs gently and turns to the man. "You see, Florin. I'm perfectly safe. Or I was until you decided to 'protect' me."

"I'll protect you as I see fit, as I have done at the Duke's command."

Creslin ignores the byplay. Instead, he looks at the horse, wondering which role to take, and finally he swings into the saddle. His legs protest, and he sways more than he would like, grasping the horse's mane with one hand to steady himself while the whirling in his head subsides. His abilities are still there, but not the strength.

"Are you all right?" asks the redhead.

"As long as we don't ride too far." He looks down at the herder girl. "Good-bye, Mathilde."

"Good-bye, your honor."

Her face is still turned toward the narrow lane long after the horses descend toward the main road; that he knows.

As he becomes more comfortable on the charger, far larger than the mountain ponies on which he learned to ride, even larger than the trader's gelding, he turns toward the redhead. She is the only woman in the troop, he has discovered. "Why did you come after me?"

The man glares at him, but Creslin watches the lady. She seems vaguely familiar, yet when he tries to dredge his memories, bright pin-lights flicker before his eyes.

"You really . . ." Her words drop off as she glances at Florin's dark countenance. "Perhaps you should tell us how you got here," she suggests, and her horse edges fractionally closer to his.

Creslin would shrug, but he needs his energy, particularly if the ride is going to be long, as he thinks it will be. "If I began with the beginning, I would run out of time before we reached the interesting parts."

The rain begins to fall in cold drops, but Creslin lets it strike him where it will, not wanting to spend effort in keeping it from him. Besides, compared to the blizzards of Westwind, the rain is not cold.

". . . too good a horseman for a wizard, if you ask me."

". . . riding without a jacket in this . . . doesn't even look cold."

Creslin ignores the whispers carried to him by the wind. "I left my homeland in the west—"

"Why?" Her question is direct but not cutting.

He shrugs, and his shoulder twinges. He purses his lips before he answers. "To avoid an arranged marriage."

"Was the idea so distasteful that you crossed the Easthorns?"

He does not correct her misperception of the distance he has traveled; instead, he concentrates on staying in the saddle, a problem he has not had since he first rode bareback. "Yes," he finally answers. "Customs there . . . are rather different . . . from here. Male initiative is . . . discouraged."

He has to concentrate on remaining in the saddle, using the chill of the rain on his face to contain the burning within. How many hills they climb and descend, he cannot say, nor whether he has said more than "yes" or "no" to the infrequent questions of the lady. All he knows is that the rain has begun to fall in heavy sheets and that the saddle is moving under him.

Then he knows not even that.

When he wakes for the first time, his eyes refuse to focus and the flames within him burn like the fires behind Fairhaven, like the sun on Freyja, like the rocks of the low desert behind the southern rim of the Easthorns.

"Easy, easy . . ." A liquid is spooned into his mouth before his thoughts reel back into darkness.

The second time he awakens, his eyes focus, if dimly, and he sees that the room is pitch-dark except for a low lamp on the wall. Again the liquid is spooned into his mouth before he relapses into darkness.

XLIX

CRESLIN'S EYES FINALLY open onto a dimness, verging on dark, in a high-ceilinged room lit by a single oil lamp mounted on a wood-paneled wall. His legs ache, and a muffled hammer pounds on his skull.

He lies back on the soft, cotton-covered pillows. His eyes glance from the heavy velvet hangings across the narrow casement window to a small table beneath the leaded panes. The dark gray outside indicates that it is past twilight. Two wooden armchairs, each upholstered in dark brocade, flank the table, on which rests a small brass oil lamp, unlit. The interior walls are paneled in a dark wood, but the outside wall is fitted stone.

The heavy iron-bound door whispers open on well-oiled hinges. Although the castle does not seem to be drafty or cold, the woman who enters the room wears a hooded cloak. Closing the door, she eases past the lamp on the wall, and her soundless steps carry her toward the high bed. Her cloak and the dim light shadow her features.

Still, Creslin's night sight is little diminished by his weakness. She is the same lady who retrieved him from Andre's lands, though now garbed in colors of black and white and gray.

"Good evening." He tries not to croak the words.

"I'm glad to see that you have finally returned to the land of the living." She slides the nearer chair from the table until it is beside the bed and sits down.

"That makes two of us, but which land of the living?"

"Oh, this is the castle of Vergren, ancestral hold of the Duke of Montgren, and you are his honored guest. As am I," she adds dryly.

"I'm afraid that I have not had the pleasure . . . except on our ride, and my thoughts were not the clearest then."

"We have met," she says, "but we were not properly introduced. You may have heard my name. But you have not introduced yourself, either."

Creslin shifts his weight, and sparks flash within his eyes. "I must question . . . whether doing so is wise."

She waits, her shadowed eyes on his face.

"Then, I do not see what difference it could make. My name is Creslin."

"No patronymic? No great and illustrious titles?"

He snorts, and fireflies of light blossom in his eyes at the exertion.

"You are weaker than you think," she confirms. "You're fortunate to be here. Few manage that sort of trip, and fewer still with such an illness."

Illness? Had his foot become reinfected in his flight from the wizards? What has he said? He had not mentioned his travels during the ride to the castle.

"I just wanted to see how you were coming along." She stands, extending a hand toward his face. Her fingers are warm, gentle against the damp heat of his fever for the moment they rest on his forehead.

Even so, even with the flicker of lights in his eyes, he notes the white scar that rings her wrist. Yet before he can utter another word, she is gone.

His eyes close, almost as quickly as the heavy door swings shut.

L

"WAIT?" ASKS THE Duke of Montgren. "How long must I wait? This is madness. Each day that he remains at Vergren, there is a greater chance that they will find him." He paces in a tight circle.

"There is no chance of that at all. The biggest risk to you is if he should be caught. And you can certainly ensure that. Just force him to leave before he regains his strength." Megaera leans back in the padded leather chair.

"Why did I—"

"Because, cousin dear, you just happen to need those horses that are arriving on the next coaster, and the western bows and cold steel shafts. You also need my dearest sister's protest to the High Wizard. You even benefit by the anger of the Marshall of Westwind."

"None of that will do me much good should the wizards find him here."

"You really don't think, do you?" Her lazy smile shows even, white teeth, and a flash in her eyes erases momentarily the tiredness. "They can't afford to invade you to find out whether he is here, not right now. You're safer while we're here than you will be later. He alone is probably worth several cavalry squads, assuming he can bear the weight of death."

"I just wish he were well and that you both were off doing whatever you're supposed to be doing." The Duke pauses. "What are you supposed to be doing?"

Her smile widens. "I don't know, dear cousin. Except that I'm unwelcome west of the Easthorns, and he doesn't seem to be welcome anywhere."

"Light!" The Duke closes his mouth, then opens it. "You aren't planning on . . . ."

"Staying?" The smile fades. "I had thought about it."

He looks at the coals on the grate. One flares into a white flash of light, then fades.

Her smile returns. "That really wouldn't be possible. Sister dear owns too many people in your retinue. And she wants us to create, shall we say . . . difficulties . . . for the wizards."

"You agree with her mad schemes?"

"Does it matter?" Megaera fingers a wrist but says nothing.

"I suppose not, not where Ryessa is concerned." He moves toward the corner desk that has dominated the study since before his grandfather's time. "But I wish Creslin were well."

"We're going to take a ride in the morning."

"Does he know how?"

"Only well enough that he rode ten kays while delirious and unconscious. Only well enough that he placed in the junior guard trials at Westwind."

"Ha! So Ryessa found someone strong enough to stand up to you, and with the talent as well."

"Do be so kind as to close your mouth, cousin dear. You don't have either the talent or the strength."

The Duke glares but slowly turns toward the dusty desk. Behind him, another coal on the grate pings.

LI

CRESLIN EASES HIS bare feet onto the heavy sheepskin covering the polished floor stones. Over by the window are the small table and two chairs, one of which he has used while eating the meals that have been regularly served to him for the past three days.

He has not seen the mysterious lady again. His only

visitors have been a solemn, white-haired healer and the shy young woman who brings his meals. Were it not for the near-luxurious shower and jakes in the adjoining room, he might have been imprisoned in some Western stronghold.

Laid neatly on the chair is a complete set of green leathers, cut and quilted in the style of the guards of Westwind. Their arrival in the hands of the serving girl had awakened him. The green leather is a shade brighter than that used on the Roof of the World. There is also a Westwind dagger, but no sword.

He stands, no longer dizzy as he has been for the previous days, but still aware of the weakness in his legs. For the first time, he realizes that the undergarments he wears are not his; they are of a softer fabric than the beaten linen of the guards.

The young, dark-haired and stocky girl enters through the heavy door, bearing a tray. She does not wear the green and gold of the Duke's household, but blue and cream. Creslin finds his mouth watering at the sight of the breads and the steam rising from the mug of tea.

"Good day," he ventures. "Who are you? You've been so kind . . ."

"Good day, ser. I am Aldonya." She sets the breakfast on the table, then looks at him, ignoring his state of undress. "The . . . her grace . . . would like to know if you are well enough for a ride this morning."

Creslin suppresses a smile. Why is the mysterious woman's name such a secret? Why does she remains hooded, and why is she always accompanied by guards? She cannot be the Duchess, for she wears no jewelry to signify that she is wed or affianced. The serving maid does not wear green and gold. The blue and cream are familiar, but he does not recall from where.

"I think so," he finally answers.

Aldonya nods and departs.

He remains a prisoner then, if a well-treated one about to partake of another solid breakfast. He debates between eating and dressing, but only momentarily. The memories of the wizards' gruel and the scraps and berries of his second trip eastward remain too fresh for him to pass up the tea, pearapples, and heated breads. In time, Creslin reflects, he may return to more casual eating habits. Perhaps.

The shakiness in his legs departs with the warmth of the tea and the first morsels of a honey roll. Hungry or not, he spaces his bites and forces himself to chew each mouthful slowly and evenly. Between bites, he looks through the leaded windowpanes at the clear blue-green sky above the heavy gray stonework facing his window. His quarters are surrounded by walls higher and thicker than the two-cubit-deep stonemasonry manifested in the window ledge before which the table rests.

While the serving girl did not mention an exact time, Creslin had heard the word "morning." He stands and makes his way to the washroom. Although the water coming from the tap is not ice-cold, neither is it particularly warm, and he hurries with his shaving and washing.

He dons the leathers, obviously sewn from measurements taken while he was ill, then gapes at the gray-leather boots beneath the chair: Westwind riding boots. He looks again, and smiles. The style is the same, but the waterproofing has not been applied and the toes are a touch too square.

Boots on, Creslin smoothes the coverlet on the bed before sitting down in one of the chairs. He waits for whatever might come next. He does not wait long, for the door opens almost immediately.

Aldonya stands there. Behind her are two guards, each wearing the same gold-and-green livery as those who had accompanied the mysterious lady on the ride from Andre's lands.

"Her ladyship is waiting for you. You are strong enough for a ride?"

"A short one, I suspect."

Creslin rises and follows her, ignoring the guards. The corridor is of solid stone, and windowless. Upon reaching the staircase, Aldonya does not hesitate, but continues downward. The guards remain at the top of the stairs.

Creslin nods to himself. This is the family wing of the castle, keep, whatever it is. Clearly, he is more than a prisoner, and just as clearly the Duke is not exactly happy about it. He hurries to catch up with Aldonya and succeeds just as they reach another heavy door.

"This is to the inside court. The Duke's stables are on the far side."

Before Aldonya can turn away, he touches her arm. "Who is she?"

"You don't know?"

"I feel that I ought to know, but I have yet to see her when I've been even halfway healthy. She seems to have been avoiding me."

"She does things for her own reasons, but she is good at heart."

"Good at heart?"

Aldonya stiffens.

"I don't really know her." Creslin wonders why he is trying to mollify the girl.

"Perhaps you should, ser . . ." The girl inclines her head, turns, and starts back up the stairs.

Creslin's mouth quirks. The girl is loyal, oddly loyal, to the mysterious woman, and she wears an unfamiliar livery, if it is livery at all. He reaches for the iron door handle. The door closes as quietly as it opens, and he steps onto the well-swept, flat stones of the inner courtyard. In the shadows where he pauses, the day is cool, cool enough to indicate that the summer and the warmth of the eastern harvest season have indeed fled. White, puffy clouds dot the sky. He is reminded yet again that he has lost more than half a year, although his memories of that time are present, in a way, as those of the struggling silver-top.

On the other side of the courtyard, less than thirty cubits away, stand two horses. The reins of the chestnut are held by a guard wearing the green and gold; he sits astride a black mare.

Silent steps carry Creslin toward the horses.

"Lord Creslin?"

He nods.

"Her . . . grace . . . awaits you outside the castle."

The black mare punctuates the statement by lifting her tail and dropping an offering onto the stones. Both the guard and Creslin ignore the impact as Creslin mounts the chestnut. Across the pommel of the cavalry saddle lies a Westward short sword and the shoulder harness Creslin favors. He loses no time in donning them. The guard's right hand touches his own belt-carried saber.

The two men ride through the archway leading into the main courtyard of the castle. As they near the gate, a guard on the wall gestures to a figure within the gate house.

The massive, iron-bound portal rumbles open. The sound of hooves echoes off the granite as the two riders pass under the stone arches and past the recently reinforced outer walls. Behind them, a guard again gestures and the gate rumbles closed. Iron-banded bars as thick as a man's waist drop back into place, and bolts slide into stone sockets.

Four mounted guards, plus the woman, wait beyond the end of the causeway. As Creslin approaches, the woman nudges her horse into motion along the ridge road that slowly drops away from the heights the castle commands.

All of the brush on the slopes has been cut back; tree stumps, some recently cut and as much as a cubit wide, spread across the slopes surrounding the gray granite walls of Vergren.

A light, cool breeze whips through Creslin's long hair. To his right, downhill nearly three kays, are the walls of a town. He wonders why the castle does not include the town itself, or at least border on it. Ahead of him, the lady continues to increase her mount's pace.

Instead of spurring the chestnut, he lets the horse drop to a walk. The air is crisp for the first time he can easily remember. He takes another deep breath, pleased to be again in the wind and the sunlight. His horse carries him down the long ridge road at an easy pace. By the time he reaches the first trees—a small grove bordering a stone-fenced field where black-faced sheep graze on browning grass—the lady is waiting for him. She has halted her mount apart from the guards, and the man who has followed Creslin joins the others.

Creslin reins up next to her. "Good day."

"You ride well." Her smile is polite, and her long red hair is bound back and partly covered with a blue silksheen scarf.

"I am somewhat out of practice."

"It doesn't show." She dismounts and leads her horse to a patch of grass underneath one of the tall oaks and loops the reins around a post protruding from the stone fence. She seats herself on a wide, flat stone.

Creslin follows her example with his mount but remains standing next to the fence. Even without nearing her, he can feel a thin line of . . . something . . . between them. He senses the flickering of unseen black-and-white flames that lick around her.

"Who are you?" he finally blurts out.

"Don't you know?"

"Why don't you just tell me? Why all these games? I know that you're a witch of sorts. Everyone edges away from you."

"I don't notice anyone exactly cosying up to you, Creslin." Her expression is wry as she shifts her weight on the stones of the wall.

"But the Duke? The guards?" He studies her eyes.

Her face is pale and serious. "The guards are there for me, as well as for you. The Duke is my cousin, and he sincerely wishes I were not here."

"Who are you?" he repeats.

"You know, whether you will admit it or not."

His eyes lock on the green eyes above the small, square jaw and the pale, freckled face.

"There is, for example, the rumor that the sole male heir to Westwind not only rejected his bride, the noted and most attractive sub-tyrant of Sarronnyn, but labored as a common prisoner on the great east-west highway." Her face grave, her green eyes glittering, the woman looks at him.

Creslin swallows, his heart beating faster.

"And further, this ingrate had the temerity to leap into a snowstorm to escape the fabled guards of Westwind. Then, I'm told, he let himself be taken by the White Wizards, lost his mind, yet walked through a storm and disappeared into the impassible Easthorns without even giving the High Wizard a chance to examine his body."

He laughs, recognizing at last the husky voice that does not quite match the fair complexion and freckles. Whether from relief or from joy, he knows not, but he laughs, and the notes of his laughter are golden, even against the chill wind. "You have me, lady. You have me." His laughter fades, for the glitter in her eyes is not laughter. "But what have you? A man who is less than a ruined heir? A man who must flee all Candar? A man who does nothing more than passably, except to escape from disaster after disaster? And not always then."

"Enough." She leans closer to him, her fire-red hair alive above the polished blue cotton of the light riding jacket. "I owe you something."

The words do not match the posture.

Crack! Creslin does not move—neither his eyes nor his face—as her white anger lashes across him, following her hand against his cheek.

He forces himself not to reach for the winds, though his teeth begin to grate. "I take it you believe that being the sub-Tyrant of Sarronnyn entitles you to abuse others."

"Very impressive." Her tone is only half-mocking.

"Megaera," he says slowly. "That must mean fury. Or senseless destruction."

"Don't you understand yet?"

"Understand what?" His voice is cold. "That I've been pushed, prodded, and manipulated across most of Candar? That I'm some sort of wizard that everyone wishes would disappear? That you're tied somehow to me, and that you think it's my fault? That you sought me out?"

"At least you're starting to think."

"Thought doesn't do much good, lady, when you have no choices."

This time she frowns.

"Megaera." He looks up at the guards, who have edged their mounts even farther from the two. "I'm not welcome on the Roof of the World. I'm not welcome anyplace where the White Wizards live, and I doubt that I'm welcome in Sarronnyn or Suthya . . . especially not now."

Her eyes rest on him without seeing him.

Wheee . . . eeah . . . The chestnut breaks the silence. A shadow passes over the hill as one of the puffy clouds covers the sun. He laughs harshly. "There you have it. You have me, and everyone else wishes I would disappear."

"No one has you. No one ever will."

"But you have me, lady, like it or not."

"You misunderstand, Creslin." Her voice is soft, softer than he had imagined it could be. "You have me—no matter what I do—just as I have you."

"And you hate it, and you hate me?"

"Yes."

He gazes at the cloud that has cast the shadow over them. Her mount flicks its tail at a horsefly.

"What a pair!" He looks toward the scattering of black-faced sheep on the far hillside, then toward the mounted guards, who shift their weight in their saddles, glancing from the two under the trees to each other and back again. "Let's return."

"Are you tired?"

"Yes," he admits. "Not that it should make any difference to you."

"What were you thinking?"

"Nothing useful." He mounts more carefully than normal, aware again of the lack of strength in his legs. "Just wondering what we can do."

The guards trail them back to Vergren.

LII

"YOU STILL DON'T understand, do you?" Megaera twists on the hard stone, curling one leather-trousered leg under her. She half-faces the east, where, beyond the three-kay spread of the cleared meadows, the broad walls of the town cast shadows across the buildings.

Creslin looks to his right, at the orange sun about to set behind the western hills, then turns back to Megaera. He tries not to frown, knowing it is futile this close to her. Yet, sensing the raging storm within her, he wonders if any answer is safe. "I don't think so."

She lifts her arms, letting the long cotton sleeves slide back to reveal her scarred wrists. "You've seen these before. Don't tell me you haven't."

"I won't." He could remove the scars, but there is no purpose in doing so until the mental scars that underlie them are gone.

"Iron, cold iron, every day since . . . since I stopped being a little girl. Do you know what it's like. Do you?"

"No."

"And then Ryessa, sister dear, and Dylyss exchange that cold iron for hot iron. Your blood for my chains, and my life is linked to yours. Do you know what it is like to sense your abilities and never be able to use them? At least not fully. Not without pain."

Not be able to use whose abilities? His or hers? "Go on."

"You don't really want to hear."

"Why do you—" He fixes his eyes on her. "I said to go on."

"No." She looks away. "I refuse to be humored, even by someone who is basically nice, if dense."

"Fine," snorts Creslin. "Then tell me why you showed that troop of wizards' road guards where I was. That almost killed me."

"What?"

"You know exactly what I mean. You and your damned white bird circled right overhead until that wizard could see me."

"Is that how it looks to you?" Megaera's voice carries a surprised lilt.

"Don't you know?"

"How would I know?" She lifts her arms again, letting the scars face Creslin. "How would I know? When every trip across the skies burns your skin and soul? When the only sunlight you see in days is through an iron-barred window? It's only in the last season that I could work without searing myself."

"You don't know? You don't see that damned bird when you reach for me?"

"Of course not, you idiot! Who would tell me? Are you strong enough to hold your hands across a red-hot grate to call your storms? And if you are, are you going to wonder what it looks like?"

A shadow appears on the stone pavement behind Megaera. Creslin watches as the dark countenance of Florin takes in the scene. The Duke's guard-master nods at him soundlessly and steps away, a faint smile on his normally immobile face.

"Don't you understand?" demands Megaera.

"What am I supposed to say? If I say I understand, you'll say I don't. If I admit I don't understand, then I'm damned, because no one can possibly understand your trials." Creslin swallows, but the words have been bottled up too long. "You're the one who insisted on branding yourself, on flinging yourself against cold iron. You had a choice. Not much of one, but you had it. There were times when you could have walked away, like at that banquet. What guard could have stopped you?" His words continue to rush out. "You didn't have to fight for every little step. You didn't have to prove yourself against the guards of Westwind. You didn't have to cross the Westhorns in winter and on foot. You didn't have your mind stolen by the White Wizards. Or your skull nearly split twice. I never did any damned fool things that threatened you. Your sister may have, and the Marshall may have, but I didn't. So stop laying all your troubles on me, as if somehow I caused them."

Megaera's mouth is wide open. "You . . . you still don't understand anything. Your mind—if you have one—is as closed as Westwind itself. You were trained as a warrior—who would stop you? You're one of the most powerful Storm Wizards born—who could stop you? The only chains you've ever had are those in your head, and you still wear them!" Now she is standing, and her eyes flash brighter than the sunset.

Creslin blinks. What chains?

"I had chains, and they couldn't hold me," she continues. "You have chains and you don't even know it. Light help me! You certainly won't." Reddish fire plays on her fingertips, then vanishes, and her face pales. "Damn you! Damn you!"

The footsteps of her riding boots echo on the stones long after she has fled from the parapets.

Chains? What are his chains? Or is Megaera just imagining something?

He lets his arms rest on the stone still warm from the day's sun. Megaera is telling the truth as she sees it, and that is more disturbing to him than the enmity of all the wizards of Fairhaven.

In time, he looks out upon the twilight, letting a few words slip out into the darkness.

> *. . . harp strings tell the story's old,*
> *from when the angels fled the fold,*
> *and yet you sing that truth is strong,*
> *when every note you strike is wrong.*
>
> *Should I trust what singing brings,*
> *when hatred hides in silvered strings?*

The song is wrong, the words not quite right, and he wishes he had his guitar. For all he knows, it rests somewhere in Sarronnyn.

LIII

CRESLIN KNOCKS ON the heavy door and waits. The note that had been handed to him by Aldonya at the noon meal is in his belt. Megaera had not been present. All the few neatly scripted words state is that he and she need to work together.

"Coming . . ."

Megaera's door is iron-bound, just as his is. Sometimes, the obvious constraints are easier to escape.

The heavy oak swings open, and Aldonya stands there. "Come in. Her grace will be here shortly. She is expecting you."

As he steps into the room, Creslin looks around. A closed door to his right leads, presumably, to a bedroom. A high-armed wooden couch and an armchair flank a low table on which rest two cups and a covered pot from which a wisp of steam drifts.

The wood paneling, brass wall lamps, small table, and matching chairs by the window are the same as in his room. The colors are different, for Megaera's spreads and hangings consist of blues and creams, unlike the greens and golds of his quarters.

Aldonya steps away from the closed door. "Would you like some hot tea?"

"No . . . no, thank you." He pauses. "Have you been with Megaera long?"

"No, your lordship. I . . . entered her service here."

"You were with the Duke's household?"

"No, ser. Her grace . . . found me herself." The girl's eyes do not quite meet his, and he wonders how much of the truth she is hiding.

"She is rather . . . striking."

"Yes, ser."

Again the words conceal more than they reveal, true as they sound.

"Good afternoon, Creslin."

Megaera's voice is not quite husky; its tones carry the sound he recalls from that night whose events may never have occurred. Could they have ever occurred as he recalls them? With Megaera's present attitude toward him?

She glides toward the window. The unlit lamp has been lifted onto the window seat, and a small mirror rests in the middle of the high octagonal table. Creslin follows, realizing for the first time how slender she is, with fine and delicate bones.

"Sit down. Whatever happens, you need to know a few things. You can go, Aldonya." The dismissal is soft, almost gentle, especially in contrast to the level tones she has directed at Creslin.

He steps toward the table, then sits down. The door closing is the only sound of the serving girl's departure.

Megaera sits down opposite Creslin, her back to the half-open window. "I'm sorry about the other day, but I still don't like you very much."

"I can't say that I understand, because you're not telling the truth, either to me or to yourself." He pauses, then adds quickly, "If it helps, you're probably right about me. I haven't thought a lot of things through."

"I attempt to apologize, and you attack me." Her eyes drop to the mirror on the table. "So tell me, Ser Storm Wizard, what I feel." The words are like blocks of ice.

"It wasn't meant as an attack. You don't know what you feel about me," he guesses and waits for her reaction. His guts remain calm, indicating that he, at least, believes what he says.

Megaera remains silent, her green eyes cool.

"You hate your sister," he tells her, "and you hate the fact that you're tied to me. You feel that you ought to hate me, but deep inside you don't. And you hate that, too." He raises his hand, in case her hand is headed for his cheek again.

"I owed you for one thing, Creslin. Hatred doesn't enter the picture."

"I did not say that you liked me. I did not say that you were secretly in love with me. I said that you did not hate me."

"I could easily hate you, especially for your arrogant assumptions."

"As you wish . . ." he sighs. "You had something you wanted to tell me?"

"Only because I wish to live, and that is clearly impossible if you do not. I have no desire to be mindless, or partly mindless, either."

"Why don't we just find a wizard who can undo this lifeline?" he suggests.

"Because it's too late. Sister dear was clever. I was imprisoned until you had returned to Westwind. Now— even by the time of the betrothal—breaking the tie would kill me. Sister had no idea of what you are, and she had to ensure that you remained alive to further her plans for using your mother's troops. What better way?"

Creslin shivers, but the tension between them has dropped.

"Do you recall how you felt when you were in the road camp?" Her voice is brisk again.

"No. I have two sets of memories, one without a past."

"They call it the White Prison. That's what the books say. Korweil's library is good, at least." She frowns before she continues. "But it's effective only with people who don't know what it is or how it works . . . or with someone who's been injured or hurt."

"I was naive." Creslin looks warily at the small mirror on the table.

The redhead shakes her shoulder-length hair, flowing free except for the combs above and behind her small, delicate ears. A brief smile touches her lips at his admission.

Creslin swallows as he looks at the creamy skin of her neck and the fine collar bones showing above the scoop-necked, pale green dress she wears. This is the first time he has seen her without a neck-high tunic, a riding jacket, or a full-closed cloak. He swallows again, and his heart beats faster.

"Stop it!" She is flushing.

"Oh . . ." Her reaction strikes him like the ice gales of the Roof of the World, cold enough to freeze him in his tracks.

The blush leaches from her cheeks.

"You feel everything I feel or think?"

She turns toward the leaded panes of the window. "No. Only . . . when you're near and you feel strongly. When you were working on the road . . . just the worst . . ." She looks away, although her hands and scarred wrists remain on the tabletop.

Creslin waits, trying not to gnaw his lips, trying to keep his hands still. Megaera is silent, not quite looking at him, but not overtly avoiding his glance.

"You said we still have to work together," he finally ventures.

"What do you think we should do?"

"Do?" Creslin wants to bite his tongue for the stupidity

of his words. "I'm not sure. I'd hoped to learn something in Fairhaven—"

"I trust you did learn something." Megaera's voice is dry.

"A great deal." He forces a laugh. "But not exactly what I had intended." He paused. "I can't return to Westwind. So . . . where can we go?"

"It's not where *we* can go. It's where you can go."

"That's not quite true. I suspect we could return to Sarronnyn. Or we could stay here. The Duke needs all the support he can find, whether he'll admit it or not."

"Do you honestly think we would be safe for long in either place?"

"Why not here?" asks Creslin.

"The Duke has no heirs. As a young man, he had the spotted fever," Megaera says flatly. "The Duchess died four years ago. She had no siblings."

Creslin nods. "So the wizards will wait for his death, but if you stayed, with a claim on the Duchy . . ."

"I'm glad I don't have to explain everything."

Creslin tries not to clench his jaw, merely tightening his lips. Finally he speaks to break the silence. "That leaves nowhere in Candar."

"You have moments of brilliance, best-betrothed. Especially when you note the obvious."

"Are we looking for a solution, or are you more interested in insulting me?" Even as he says the words, Creslin wishes he had not.

"Truth is not an insult, not unless you are looking for deception."

He wonders why he bothers. Then again, Megaera scarcely chose to be tied to him. "I know very little of human nature, of the intrigues of rulers, and . . . probably . . . little of women, at least of those not raised in Westwind. I know that, and you know that. I admit it. What good does it do to keep pointing it out to me? Does it make you feel superior?"

"Perhaps I am. In some ways," she adds almost hastily, a strained look on her face. "Damn you . . ." she whispers, refusing to look at him, her head bowed and her eyes fixed on the polished wood of the table.

Creslin shakes his head. In one moment Megaera is almost approachable, yet in the next . . . She is like two different people. Then he swallows, understanding finally. His eyes burn, and he tries to wall off his feelings, knowing that it is already too late, knowing that she feels what he feels almost as soon as he does.

"Stop it! I don't need your damned pity! Just go on being dense and stupid. It's easier that way." She has left the chair and turned her back to him, standing with her face toward the open leaded-glass windows.

The room is close, the air still, and Creslin touches the winds, bringing a breeze in through the narrow opening, watching as the air lifts strands of Megaera's red hair. She does not acknowledge his actions or his presence.

Feeling increasingly uncomfortable, he pushes back his chair and stands. He walks over to the couch, away from Megaera.

"How much longer can we stay here?" he asks.

Megaera does not answer him at first, keeping her eyes fixed on the hills beyond the outer wall and to the south—a better view than that in Creslin's room, which merely faces a corner tower of the outer wall.

"Korweil cannot force us to leave."

"Do you want to stay?"

"Where could you—we—go?"

"What about Recluce?" Creslin asks.

"That desolate island waste? Better that I stayed behind iron walls with sister dear."

Creslin shrugs. "Hamor?"

He senses that Hamor is no answer.

"Nordla?"

"That's as cold as Westwind, and they don't honor the Legend there."

"I don't think they do in Hamor, either. Not since the empire was founded."

"Damn you all . . ."

"Then I guess it has to be Recluce, at least for a while. Unless you want to risk staying here."

Megaera does not turn, nor does she speak.

"We should talk to the Duke after dinner." Creslin waits. "I will see you then." He moves toward the door, but Megaera still says nothing.

He closes the door and turns down the corridor toward his quarters, followed by another pair of armed guards.

LIV

DESPITE THE ELEVATED boots he wears, Korweil is considerably shorter than Creslin. The Duke's thin face appears pinched, and his deep-set eyes are bloodshot. "So you're the one who may bring the wizards down on me?" He stands by the massive desk designed for a far larger predecessor.

"I may be a convenient excuse. They will do what they will and give the most plausible reason available at the time."

"Excuses, excuses. At least Dylyss has taught you logic in addition to some reputedly fancy blade-work."

Creslin senses a tightness in Megaera, a mounting anger. The Duke is trying to push them. "You know, Megaera, I believe your cousin is attempting to get a reaction from us." His eyes flicker from her to the Duke. "Considering that you have few allies indeed, is a moment's satisfaction worth the trouble that provoking us might cause?"

"You're rather cool, Consort Creslin. And not terribly appreciative of one who has provided sanctuary for your recovery."

"I am deeply appreciative, my lord." Creslin's bow is not quite sardonic. "And I have come to discuss how best we might serve you in departing this sanctuary."

Megaera's eyes flash from one man to the other. "Might we be seated around the table, cousin?"

"Certainly, certainly." The Duke moves toward the nearest chair as if to offer it to Megaera. He stops short as Creslin's fingers curl around the high back.

Megaera steps around both of them and takes the Duke's chair. "If you two are ready . . ."

Creslin sits down in the chair he had thought to offer to Megaera and pulls it up to the circular table. Korweil steps behind one of the two remaining chairs and pours a glass of red wine from a green crystal decanter into a goblet.

"Would you like any?" He nods first to Megaera, then to Creslin.

"I think not, cousin."

"No, thank you."

"I see." The Duke sips from the goblet, then sets it before him and eases himself into a chair. "What do you have in mind, Megaera?"

"I'd be interested in your ideas, cousin."

The Duke shrugs. "Anywhere outside of Montgren that suits your fancy. Back to Sarronnyn, perhaps?"

"An amusing idea, but do you really think sister dear would like to see me back . . . unfettered?"

"Ah, yes. Ryessa might have some concerns about that." His fingers steeple. "Perhaps Suthya?"

Megaera's eyes fix upon the Duke.

"Ah. I see that might have some problems." His forehead shimmers in the lamplight. Korweil takes his handkerchief and wipes the dampness away. "Do you have any suggestions, oh vaunted Storm Wizard?"

"Just one. It might solve everyone's problem. Why don't you name Megaera regent of Recluce?"

"I . . . what?" the Duke sputters, choking on the wine.

"Name Megaera as viceroy of Recluce, as your regent of the isle."

Korweil wipes his face with the back of his sleeve, ignoring the napkin on the table and the handkerchief in his wide white belt. "It's more than ten times the size of Montgren, and I'm supposed to name her regent?"

Even Megaera's mouth is open.

"Yes."

"But . . . ?"

"She's your cousin. She is the sub-Tyrant of Sarronnyn. You cannot afford to hold the island, not with every man you have needed against the wizards, and I doubt that either Sarronnyn or Westwind would mind sending a small detachment to support your interests on Recluce, given Megaera as regent."

Korweil shakes his head. "No."

"Why not?" Creslin's tone is almost absentminded, as if Korweil's comments are irrelevant.

"Recluce is Montgren."

"They why isn't your keep there?"

"I prefer Montgren for its . . . more convenient . . . location."

"Practically next door to Fairhaven?"

Korweil wipes his forehead again.

"I think my dear cousin has forgotten how desolate most of Recluce is," Megaera observes.

The Duke continues mopping his forehead.

"Or how difficult it might be."

"Enough . . ." sighs Korweil. "Enough. Ryessa would like nothing better than for me to name you regent. Then when we're both out of the way, she can claim Montgren. Wouldn't that give the wizards fits?"

"Sister dear is smarter than that. She really hopes that, since my best-betrothed and I have nowhere to go, we might just ensure such a succession immediately. She has no interest in risking her troops this far from Sarronnyn." The corners of her mouth twitch halfway through her statement.

Creslin recognizes the gesture and wonders where Megaera is not telling the full truth.

Korweil looks back toward the entrance to the dining room, toward the pair of guards standing more than a dozen cubits away.

"Cousin," continues Megaera, "if we had any intention of doing away with you, you would already be dead."

"I still say 'No.' Your . . . friend's suggestion would create another land for the Legend-holders."

"That barren waste?" The words drop like cold hailstones on ice. "Who would want it?"

"My sire went to great lengths—"

"Korweil," interrupts Creslin, "if you want us out of Montgren, you have to come up with a place for us to go. Otherwise . . ."

The Duke wipes his forehead again. "So what can you do? Really do?"

Creslin grasps the breezes circling the courtyard outside and funnels them through the drawing room. A heavy parchment sheet starts to lift off the desk in the corner.

Creslin drops the winds.

"Good for cooling things off, I suppose," the Duke mutters.

"Cousin, don't be a fool. He has already killed a good score of the White Wizards' guards. And he did it when half out of his mind and with a split skull. He also, if you recall, disarmed the best duelist in Sarronnyn with three strokes."

"Megaera, your cousin clearly does not want you named as his regent. Nor does he offer any alternative. So I suggest that we return to our rooms and get a good night's sleep. Tonight, and every other night until the wizards come after us. Our being here gives them every excuse. And, of course, should anything happen to us, I'm certain that both the Marshall and the Tyrant would be more than a little displeased." He stands up.

Megaera looks at the Duke, then nods. Fires flare at her fingertips, then extinguish themselves.

The Duke's face appears even paler in the lamplight. Then suddenly he smiles. "All right. I'll name your child regent of Recluce."

This time Megaera pales. "You presume too much." The fires reappear.

The Duke swallows, looks from Megaera—standing with fire in her eyes and upon her hands—to Creslin. Finally he croaks out his response: "I don't trust you, Megaera. If I could, I'd make Creslin regent first, even if his mother is the iron bitch of all Candar."

Megaera lets the fires in her hands die, but not those in her eyes.

"The best I dare is to make you co-regents, contingent upon your marriage." The Duke tightens his lips and stands, looking straight at Megaera as if to dare her to do her worst.

This time Megaera looks away. Finally she speaks. "A formal marriage only, in your Temple, with only your household as witnesses."

Creslin opens his mouth, then shuts it. Marriage? That had never entered his mind. And to the one woman he fled the Roof of the World to avoid? Even, he is forced to add to himself, if he didn't realize who she was.

"Join the discomfort, young Creslin," rumbles the Duke. "The darkness help you both."

"Very humorous, cousin."

Creslin says nothing.

"When?" asks the Duke.

"Tonight is as good a time as any." The redhead's words are measured and drop like lead coins. "We'll leave tomorrow, or the day after, with the declaration of co-regency. We'll take your sloop, the one at Tyrhavven. We'll return it immediately after we land safely at Land's End, of course."

The Duke sighs, nodding slowly. "The documents will take a short while."

"Then I will change into something suitable for a formal

wedding." Her eyes flicker to Creslin. "If you could find something suitable for Creslin?"

"No," Creslin protests.

"You will not marry my cousin?" asks the Duke lazily.

"I'll marry her—in name only—but I'll wear what I am. Leathers and nothing more."

Korweil nods again. "I leave that to you and your bride. If this marriage is to take place, I need to find Shiffurth and several scribes. If you will excuse me . . ." He stands, bows, and turns.

Creslin looks at Megaera as Korweil leaves the study. "You and your regency," she says. The flames in her eyes have not died as she speaks.

"Do you have a better idea? I like the idea as little as you. Less perhaps."

"After those thoughts of yours? After you dragged me through the sewer of your mind? Deep inside, you're like every other man, protesting while hoping to get a woman into bed. This union is in name only, and for survival. I suggest that you do not forget it."

"How could I?" How indeed, thinks Creslin as he stares at the air currents that play around the lamp on the Duke's vacant desk. "How could I?"

LV

THE DUKE'S TEMPLE is little more than a long, narrow room under the Great Hall, although the walls are of light-paneled red oak and the floor of polished gray granite. Less than a score of men and women stand in a half-circle roughly ten steps back from the black wood of the Table. They stand, for there are no benches in the Temple of Order, just as there are no images.

Outside the open double door, Creslin shifts from one

foot to the other, wondering if his stubbornness in insisting on wearing the green leathers were wise.

Megaera is nowhere to be seen, although Aldonya has assured him that she will be arriving shortly. The serving girl's eyes had not met Creslin's, and an aura of sadness surrounds her as she repairs to the rear of the Temple.

"Nervous?" asks the Duke.

"In more ways than one." Creslin envies the serving girl. Megaera is at least kind to someone. He shifts from one booted foot to the other again.

"I offer you congratulations and condolences, Ser Storm Wizard. My cousin is a far greater storm than any you have called."

"I've begun to realize that."

"Realize what?" asks another voice throaty and feminine.

Creslin turns. "Oh . . ."

In blue and gold, Megaera stands there. The silver-haired man swallows once, twice, then nods.

"Thank you . . . best-betrothed." She smiles faintly but warmly. The smile is like sun after a storm, but it fades as Creslin watches.

"Do you have the documents?" Her voice is matter-of-fact.

"They're on the table, ready except for my signature and seal," affirms Korweil. "I will be more than happy to sign them before or after the ceremony."

"After will be soon enough," she tells him.

Creslin's lips tighten at the chill in her voice. How could he ever have considered this? He thinks again. What alternatives do they have? His eyes stray back to her, taking in the creamy, if lightly freckled, skin, the green eyes that can sparkle or storm, the strong, clean nose, the slender frame.

"Stop it . . . not a prize ewe . . ." Her voice is inaudible except to Creslin, and the words are as cold as ice.

He turns his eyes to the open double doors and to the black Table.

"Shall we begin?" asks the Duke.

Creslin turns to Megaera, who has stepped up beside him. "Best to get it over with," she says.

"You don't have to do this."

"I do if I want to survive." Her voice is barely more than a whisper. "Go on, cousin dear," she continues in a louder tone.

The Duke squares his shoulders and steps toward the black Table.

Megaera touches Creslin's arm. He extends his arm, but she does not take it as they move forward, past the men and women who have stood aside for them.

The Duke turns as he reaches the Table. Creslin and Megaera stop a pace or so before the Duke.

"In the name of order and under that ever-present chaos, which can only be postponed but never denied, we are gathered together to witness two souls who wish to strive to place a greater order on their unity." The Duke reads from the parchment easily, his voice deeper than when he talks privately with Megaera and Creslin.

". . . and will you strive to place understanding and order within your heart?"

"I will," answers Creslin.

"As I can," answers Megaera.

"Do you affirm your dedication to each other and to a higher order?"

Creslin swallows before responding, "I do."

Megaera's voice is so low as to be nearly indistinguishable. "If possible, darkness willing."

The Duke smothers a frown. "Then, in the presence of the order that must be created and recreated daily, and under the light of ever-present chaos, I affirm the bonds of this higher unity and the dedication of two souls unto order and unto each other."

Creslin realizes that he must make some gesture and that Megaera has not moved toward him.

"At least kiss her cheek," whispers the Duke.

That Creslin can do, and he does, gently, leaning toward her. But his lips come away damp from the tears that stream from her eyes.

". . . so beautiful"

". . . even his silver hair seems right."

Creslin ignores the whispers and offers his arm. This time Megaera takes it, and her head remains high as they walk back toward the doors, past those few individuals comprising the Duke's private household. Past the stocky serving maid in blue and cream, who weeps unrestrainedly, and not from happiness.

He presses his lips and keeps walking, ignoring the burning in his eyes.

LVI

"YOU SHOULD HAVE at least one maid, your grace," ventures the black-haired girl. "You are a sub-Tyrant and a regent."

"On my wedding trip?" The laugh that follows breaks between harshness and sorrow. "Do you think that best-betrothed would wish you looking on?"

The girl's eyes stray toward the saddlebags on the floor.

Megaera takes a last sip from the cup. "Why . . . why did I ever . . ." She pauses. "Aldonya . . ."

"Yes?"

"I have arranged it with Korweil and Helisse. You may remain in their service as long as you wish. It's not an indenture. You may leave at any time."

"Your grace is kind, but I would rather go with you."

"To Recluce? To that desert island?" Megaera's eyes rest

upon the gentle swelling of the girl's belly. "Recluce is no place to have a child."

"Your grace—"

"Aldonya, if you still feel this way, and if you and the child are healthy, and if I am still . . . able to help, then you may follow me to Recluce. Korweil will make the arrangements."

The faintest of smiles flits across the young woman's face. "You are kind. If only Creslin could see that."

"I'm not kind. He knows that. Sometimes I wish I were." Megaera raises her arms and lets the sleeves fall away from the white scars. "These don't let me forget. Being a woman and without power . . ."

The young woman smiles again. "I think he is good at heart. And he could love you."

"Probably, but good at heart isn't always good in word or deed." The redhead looks out the window into the early morning shadows cast by the castle's eastern walls. "Sister dear . . . she taught me that long ago."

Aldonya's smile fades as she notes the sadness in the redhead's eyes.

LVII

"HE'S IN THE Duke's keep at Vergren," Hartor tells the High Wizard.

"How do you know? Your usual sources?"

The heavy man grins across the table. "Gold sometimes works better than chaos or order. Korweil is as nervous as an unfledged vulcrow."

The High Wizard nods knowingly. "I assume that you're doing what you can to make the Duke even more nervous."

"We did make sure that he knows about the Marshall's

recall of her troops in Suthya. Pointing out that Westwind comes first, always."

"What about Creslin himself?"

"We've let it be known that he killed an entire bandit troop."

"Don't exaggerate, Hartor."

"Well . . ." temporizes the heavy man. "Only one of the seven escaped, and Creslin apparently killed Frosee personally and took his horse."

"You didn't ever mention that."

"We didn't know it until after he escaped."

"That brings up another question." The High Wizard frowns. "What about the troop on the way into Montgren?"

"Was that his doing?"

"Probably not. I doubt that he's mastered that level of work. It has to have been Klerris and that healer, Lydya. They got him out of the road camp. Both of them are gone, and Klerris fired his home—using oil, so there were some traces. Nothing useful, unfortunately, except some indications that they're headed west, back to the land of the precious Legend."

The heavy man inclines his head toward the mirror on the tabletop. "There's more here than your mirror shows. Are you sure that Klerris went west?"

"No. But there's nothing he can do here. Or in Montgren. Order has never been able to stand up to us in a direct battle."

"That may be." Hartor licks his lips briefly with a tongue too small for his broad face. "How long before we can move against the Blacks?"

The High Wizard smiles coldly. "I doubt that we'll need to. Most of them should leave of their own accord. Those who don't—"

"You're cold, Jenred. Cold as the poles."

Jenred nods vaguely, his mind still on the escaped heir of Westwind. "You'd better send a full White, somebody like Bortren, and two full troops from Certis."

"Creslin will be riding only with her and four second-rate Spidlarians."

"I can't believe that the White bitch hasn't taught him something, and he did destroy seven before he knew what he was doing . . . if you got the story right."

"I'll send Bortren. But that's a bit much, I think. Besides, where could they go anyway? To Recluce? To Hamor?"

"Recluce is no problem. Hamor might be. What if they put him in charge of their Legion training? Westwind has never let its training secrets be known. He went through all the courses."

"Hmmm . . ."

The two exchange glances. Finally Hartor sighs and stands. His lips clamped tight, the High Wizard stares into the blank whiteness of the mirror on the table before him.

LVIII

CRESLIN LOOKS TOWARD the pass, then back over his shoulder, although he has no need to do so since his senses show him the white mist that follows. Megaera shifts in her saddle. Behind them, the whiteness continues to pour from the road valley that twists its way back toward Fairhaven.

One of the four blue-vested mercenaries accompanying them also looks back at the white cloud, then forward at the dust cloud that represents a Certan force sent directly from Jellico, according to the Duke's spies.

Mixed with the white mist is the dust of a handful of horses, perhaps six or seven. One of the riders has to be a wizard of sorts.

"I can feel them," Megaera affirms.

"You can? I thought—"

"It's partly through you and partly on my own."

Creslin wonders how many of the talents that he and

Megaera possess are inborn and how many come from the knowledge that such powers are possible. Those in white behind him could inform him, but neither he nor Megaera would survive the informing. His left hand strays toward his shoulder, toward the short sword there in the shoulder harness.

"Ser . . . ?" asks the thin soldier who is the leader of the mercenary guards accompanying Megaera.

"Yes," she answers.

"We're not—"

"Hired for pitched battles. I know."

Creslin briefly seizes the winds and throws his senses ahead. Then he turns to Megaera. "There is a pile of broken boulders about a kay ahead and two hundred cubits north of the road. Can you use whatever you have to hold off that cavalry troop—if they get here?"

"And you're going to play hero and dispatch the wizard?"

Creslin tightens his lips. "I'm not a hero. I could use the winds and some fog to get us past the horsemen up ahead, but not with a wizard behind."

"And I'm not good enough to go with you?"

"No."

"You're being honest."

Creslin turns the chestnut back toward the white mist and the wizard that the whiteness contains. "I've never had much choice."

"One way or another, you'll be the death of me."

"We can discuss that later."

"If there is a later. Take care."

"Thank you. And there will be," he adds in affirmation as he nudges the chestnut toward the troop from Fairhaven, now less than two kays away. As he rides, he begins to gather the winds to him, especially the colder winds from high above, the winds that sweep to the west and dust the Roof of the World.

". . . just one rider."

". . . sent us after one man . . ."

Creslin narrows the distance between himself and the party from Fairhaven. Six white armored and white-clad road guards preceding the wizard reach for their blades.

"Here he comes!"

"Idiot!"

Creslin concentrates upon melding wind and water and the chill of a thunderstorm, trying to replicate the conditions he had created outside Perndor, although his sword finds its way to his hand as he bears down upon the White guards.

The blinding chill of a wall of ice-bolts lashes the three front riders, and his sword finds no resistance.

Essttt . . .

Fires flare around Creslin as he drives toward the fourth rider, but the winds carry him through the flames. His blade strikes once, and again.

"No . . . demon . . ."

Another flare of white sheets around him, around the shield of the winds he has woven, even while his sword sweeps under the fifth guard's arm and strikes.

"Uggmm . . ."

And the winds whip toward the White Wizard, where winds, fires, and cold iron meet. The iron triumphs.

Creslin reins up just in time to see the last guard spur his horse back toward Fairhaven . . . and to lean over himself.

"Uuugghhh . . ." His guts turn themselves inside out.

Wheee . . . eeee . . . The chestnut skitters, but Creslin ignores the mount as the tears stream from his eyes and he continues to puke from the saddle. Hammers pound through his skull, and he ignores the six bodies on the ground, three of them shrouded in slowly melting ice and three of them bearing dull red incisions. Overhead, the dark clouds mount.

Finally he straightens and turns the chestnut toward the pass from which the Certan cavalry is emerging. He still shivers by the time he nears the bouldered hillock where the mercenaries and Megaera wait.

Megaera glares at him. She is pale, he notes absently, and a few dunnish streaks dot the forelegs of the gray she rides.

"Sorry. I didn't expect that," he says.

Megaera makes no answer.

"Ser?" asks the head Spidlarian.

"You don't have to worry about the wizard. Or his troops."

The Spidlarian blanches.

The mounted troop, under the red-and-green banner of Certis, has reached the base of the hill on which the six wait.

"I think we need a storm," Creslin observes.

"You'll destroy the weather for months!" Megaera protests.

"Fine. Do you want to die right here? I can't take on twenty armed men."

"I count fifty."

"Shit . . ." murmurs the youngest mercenary under his breath.

"No battles," reminds the Spidlarian senior, his voice a shade more tense than before.

"Shut up." Creslin checks his blade to see if he has cleaned it before sheathing it. He does not remember doing so, but the steel is cold and blue and clean. He replaces the blade even as his eyes, and the feelings behind them, seek the winds again, although winds of a different pattern of twisted air and moisture than those before.

A trumpet echoes in the mid-morning air, rings in Creslin's ears, and vibrates copper-silver above the road less than a kay downhill, just before the squad leading the Certan horsemen.

Creslin swallows and grabs for the winds.

Whhssttt . . . weeehhsss . . .

His tunic threatens to tear away from his body.

". . . shit . . . *shit!*"

Creslin wonders if all mercenaries have such limited vocabularies as he wrestles with his soul and the lashes of the sky. Thick gray and swirling white clouds begin to build around them, and around the horsemen.

". . . wizardry . . ."

". . . didn't say an air wizard . . ."

Creslin touches Megaera's arm before their vision becomes nearly useless. "Rope. Twine."

"Hold hands, reins, something—"

"No! I can't!"

Creslin jerks back as one of the Spidlarians screams, claws at the cottony fog and spurs his mount toward the south, back toward the Vergren road.

Megaera reaches out, touches the wrist of the lead mercenary, tugs at his sleeve, and draws him and his mount closer. The other two mercenaries shiver in their saddles but follow Creslin, the redhead, and their leader.

"There's one! They're headed back!" a Certan horseman shouts.

The sound of hooves echo through the cottony fog.

"Watch it! Might be a trap!" another warns.

". . . damned wizards!"

Creslin leads the way downhill and to the north, farther away from the road, wondering why the one Spidlarian panicked. The fog is certainly no worse than many blizzards he has weathered, and far less cold.

". . . where are they?"

". . . can you hear them?"

". . . they're north . . ."

". . . I heard something over there . . ."

Slowly, slowly, his path guided by the winds and not by his eyes, Creslin picks his way around the fringe of the Cretan troop and toward the pass that cuts across the corner of Certis to the west before again twisting northward. He takes a deep breath, then reaches a bit farther, twisting and yanking even colder air into the clouds above, wincing as ice forms.

Threp . . . threp . . . threp . . . threp . . .

Most of the hailstones fall near the road.

". . . demons . . ."

". . . frigging captain. Ought to be here."

Through the gloom and fog, Creslin can sense Megaera's twisted smile even as he feels his legs shake, his eyes burn. He takes a deep breath, for they have not yet gone far enough.

A hand touches his wrist, and a sense of warmth flows into his body. It is Megaera, her mount's flank nearly touching the chestnut's. The weakness in his knees retreats, but they must continue to move onward. He releases the hail and takes another deep breath as he senses the walls of the pass begin to close on them.

"Where—" begins a mercenary.

"Shut up." The iron-edged whisper is the redhead's, not Creslin's, but it has no less power because of the sex of the speaker.

Another kay passes slowly, and Creslin releases more winds as they climb upward and out of the fog. He looks back. The pass, and the valley onto which it opens, remains swathed in white, almost as white as the faces of the three mercenaries.

"Oh . . ."

Creslin's body is nearly too tired to catch the redhead as she collapses across the neck of her mount. The two heavy packs behind her saddle hamper him as he tries to keep the horses together.

He swallows—realizing the cost of the warmth he had received—as he leans to support her partial weight, still attempting to keep the horses together for the moment and wishing that he knew how to return her favor.

She breathes, and he can only hope that her swoon is simple exhaustion. The Spidlarians help him move her in front of him, where he can hold her as they start downhill. His knees tremble, but he will not let her go, not when this may be one of the few times he can hold her.

He looks up and toward the lead mercenary. None of the three men meet his eyes, not even the one who takes the reins of Megaera's mount. The now-riderless horse looks like a packhorse, with clothes and other items stacked behind the saddle.

As the five horses head down toward the Sligo road, Creslin frowns. Why could he twist the winds the second time without the agony he felt after his first effort?

He looks up at the storm clouds marching in from the north, promising rain, cold rain, and takes a deep breath.

LIX

"He bested Bortren," Hartor says with disbelief.

"Bortren was a fool. He should have just helped the Certans. Still, it's hard to see how Creslin avoided two full troops on the Sligo road."

"Why don't you ask the guard who came back? This was your idea, and now we've got two monsters on the loose." He turns toward the doorway.

"Hartor."

The other stops. "Yes, Jenred?"

"It was my idea. We also lost only five men and one wizard, not an entire army. If Bortren had listened, we would have had no losses and a far less obstreperous viscount in Jellico. You will also note that the Duke did not provide Creslin and Megaera with his own guards."

Hartor's face remains impassive.

"Get the guard," Jenred orders. "Perhaps you should join the pursuit yourself to give greater importance to the effort."

"I might' . . . after you hear the guard."

Hartor leaves, and Jenred waits as a young road guard

trembles his way toward the table. The youth stops but does not look at the High Wizard.

"What happened?" Jenred demands.

"He . . . I don't know, but somehow . . . I mean . . . Jekko and Beran and the new guy, they turned to ice . . . and the wind near threw us right off our mounts." His voice is thin, stammering.

"What about the two others? And Bortren?"

"He killed them, with his sword. The wizard—our wizard, the one you called Bortren—he threw fire at the Storm Wizard, but it never even came close."

The thin wizard frowns. "Real fire?"

"I could feel the heat."

"Why did you . . . depart?"

"Because I was scared, Ser Wizard. Anything that kills five men and a wizard . . . I can't stop it."

"What happened after that?"

"The whole valley filled with fog. Then there was ice rain. They said it was there days later. I didn't stay."

"Well, you're honest. You've at least seen this . . . Storm Wizard. Tell Hartor you're going with the ship."

"Hartor, ser?"

"The big wizard who called you here. You'll be on the ship that sinks the Duke's schooner. You'll take a ship from Lydiar. That way we solve two problems."

"Yes, ser." The guard's voice is flat, resigned.

The thin man in white ignores the tone.

LX

THE THREE SPIDLARIAN mercenaries rein in at the seawall. Creslin follows their example, as does Megaera. Up the muddy road that leads to the rolling hills and the site of the attack by the Certan light horse, there are no horsemen, but there will be.

The cold rain beats around them, but not upon them. While the Spidlarians mumble, they do not protest the protection Creslin has afforded them. His senses expand to the cold sea breeze that flows in off the whitecaps beyond the too-short breakwater; it is almost a winter wind, carrying moisture barely warm enough to be rain and not ice.

Megaera shivers under a thin cloak, and her face is pale as she follows Creslin's eyes toward the pier.

Tyrhavven is a poor excuse for a harbor, large enough for only a few coasters and an occasional Hamorian trader, and nearly useless in the winters. While ice chokes the Spidlarian ports, Tyrhavven is south of the ice line, not far enough south for clear water, yet far enough that the ice floes and bergs could be avoided—if not for the combination of winds, tides, and waves.

Poor harbor or not, it is Montgren's sole outlet to the sea, and that only because of the treaty negotiated through the Tyrant of Sarronnyn.

Of the two ships moored at the pier, one is a sloop flying the Montgren banner, smaller than a coaster, her sails furled. The other is a two-masted war schooner bearing a white triangle within a black circle. A pair of guards in white-enameled copper breastplates flanks the gangway.

"Wonderful." Creslin's hand strays toward the sword in his shoulder harness, then drops. "Now what?"

"They won't do a thing here," observes Megaera.

"We just walk on board?"

"Why not?" She laughs. "It's better than sitting here and freezing."

"I don't think it's that simple."

"Of course it's not. Once we're on board, they'll send at least one assassin. If we clear the harbor, they'll follow, and when we're out of sight of witnesses, our ship will catch fire and sink. That's why cousin dear insisted on sending a messenger separately, and slightly later."

"If we don't make it, almost no one will know. Is that it?"

Megaera nods.

"We will make it."

"There are at least twenty White warriors on the ship, and another ship waits somewhere. They're expecting us."

"You took that—" he points to the Montgren sloop "—from Sarronnyn?"

"No. I bounced here on a Suthyan coaster. It was bigger, heavier, and slower. The Duke didn't want to risk one of his two ships. And of course sister dear did not press him."

"Let's go and visit."

Megaera shrugs. "I don't think it's a good idea."

"Do you have a better one?"

"After the way you treated the wizard's road guards and the Certan light-horse squad?"

"What was I supposed to do? The last time I visited Fairhaven wasn't especially healthful for me."

"You think it was much better for me?"

"You weren't out of your mind and hauling rocks with an infected foot and everyone hoping you'd die."

"No. I was just out of my mind, feeling every agony and wishing you'd get it over with."

"Ahem . . ." interrupts the thin-faced mercenary, lifting a document case bearing their warrants and right-of-passage.

Creslin looks back through the rain toward the hills. There is still no sign of the eventual pursuit. He gestures toward the document case. "Once you've delivered that and we're assured passage, your job is done."

"The lady is . . . our charge."

Creslin turns to Megaera. "Then let them go. They're your guards."

"Me? A mere woman? Compared to the great Storm Wizard?"

"You're the sub-Tyrant," Creslin reminds her.

A cough breaks the silence.

"Lady?"

"Go." Megaera's sigh has an edge to it.

Creslin ponders what he did wrong . . . again.

"Everything," she replies.

"Let's go talk to the captain."

"In a moment. Let the man do his work." Megaera dismounts and ties the horse to the railing. She glances up at Creslin, still on the chestnut he has ridden nearly three hundred kays over the past eight-day. Then she takes a comb and begins to repair the wind damage to her hair.

"What do we do with the horses?" Creslin slips off his mount, his eyes flicking to the rain-swept pier, where the mercenary has begun to board the sloop.

"They come. It won't be comfortable for them, but cousin has a set of stalls on the ship. On every trip, a pair is sent. He had hoped in time, to build up a full cavalry troop on Montgren." She laughs harshly. "It is rather difficult when you have only two small ships." The comb disappears.

"So why did he agree to naming us regents?"

"Why not? If we're powerful enough to survive and to hold Recluce, he couldn't stop us. And he needs the support of Sarronnyn." A ragged smile crosses her lips. "And he knows we're strong enough to cause the wizards more than a little trouble. It might cost him one ship. Already, he's doing well. How many troops and wizards have you destroyed?" She pauses. "For a Black Wizard, you're awfully creative at getting around the chaos limits."

"Chaos limits?"

"If you want to stay a Black, you can't use fire or anything else that breaks things apart. That's calling on chaos."

"Can't a great wizard do both?"

"Doing both calls for a Gray Wizard—part White, part Black. They say there have been only one or two Gray

Wizards ever. And not in years: One of the books I smuggled past sister dear said that trying to handle both order and chaos is the most dangerous of all because the guidelines change from situation to situation." She looks toward the pier. "We need to walk the horses down there."

Creslin follows her lead, his eyes taking in the mercenary and the man in green and gold standing on the deck and gesturing toward the Spidlarian. The captain's gestures are hardly encouraging.

The Spidlarian tenders the dispatch case, points toward Creslin and Megaera and bows, backing away politely.

The pier is short, and they arrive by the unguarded gangway as the mercenary steps back onto the pier.

"Our charge is done, ser, lady." He bows again.

Creslin returns the bow, then hands the man a gold. "I wish it could be more, but—"

With a lopsided smile, the mercenary takes the coin. "You've gotten us through, ser, when few could have. My life is worth a bit more than the gold, but I appreciate the thoughtfulness. Have a good voyage." He bows again, then strides back down the pier toward the horse being held by one of the other two Spidlarians.

"Synder!"

Creslin ignores the captain's bellow and looks at Megaera. "What about the horses?"

As he speaks, a youngster scuttles to the top of the gangway.

"Synder! Get the horses!"

"Yes, Captain."

The captain looks at the two on the pier. Creslin smiles, sensing the man's discomfort. "Let's go." Megaera shrugs but follows him up the unrailed gangplank.

"Name's Freigr. I'm the captain of the *Griffin*, subject to the Duke's orders, of course." The clean-shaven captain wears a green-and-gold surcoat, and flint-gray eyes inspect his passengers.

"Creslin, and this is Megaera, the sub-Tyrant of Sarronnyn."

"You claim no title, ser?" asks the captain with a half-smile.

"He's the consort of Westwind," explains Megaera, "but he claims that doesn't count as a title."

The captain nods. "According to this—" he raises the dispatch case "—you have been appointed the Duke's co-regents in Recluce, and I am requested to provide your transportation." His eyes wander toward the first horse being led on board. "You have other baggage?"

"Only what is packed on the horses."

"For regents, you travel light."

Creslin shrugs. "Most of my belongings either remained in Westwind or found their way into the hands of the White Wizards."

Megaera smiles brightly but adds nothing.

"The Duke's cabin is, of course, yours," Freigr says blandly, his right hand smoothing down his short-cut and thinning sandy hair. "But our fare will be rather simple."

Creslin grins. "I'm not used to rich food."

"At Westwind, I'd guess not. And your lady?"

Megaera's eyes flash and her lips tighten, but she says only, "I rather doubt that I will find it any problem. But . . . I am not exactly his lady, since he is from Westwind and I am from Sarronnyn."

The captain's eyebrows lift.

Creslin explains. "She is far more important than I, Captain. The Tyrant of Sarronnyn is her sister, and my sister will be the one to hold Westwind."

"Ah, I see, I think." Freigr turns momentarily. "Synder! Put the gray in the port stall. It's smaller."

Creslin tries to sense what Megaera is feeling, but she appears walled off behind a shield of gray—a whiteness shot through with black lines—that he can sense but not see.

"Yet the Duke named you co-regents."

"The Duke is an eastern male ruler." Megaera's voice is chill.

Freigr scratches the back of his head.

"Perhaps we could move our bags to the cabin," suggests Creslin.

"Ah, yes. That might be best." Freigr starts toward the single raised deck at the stern.

Creslin halts Synder and the gray horse in order to reclaim Megaera's belongings.

"Go ahead, ser. We'll bring them down," suggests Synder.

"Thank you." Creslin nods and rejoins the captain and Megaera. He has to lower his head as they enter the narrow passageway.

"The Duke's cabin is on this side, opposite mine. This is the mess room, and the galley's opposite."

The captain cannot stand upright, and Creslin's head touches the bracing beams of the ceiling as the three edge into the low-ceilinged space.

The Duke's cabin—less than eight cubits square—contains two bunks, one over the other, set against the forward bulkhead. The bunk frames are carved from red oak, and each bears an ornate green-and-gold coverlet. A built-in, shoulder-high chest is on the right-hand side of the bunks, and a narrow wardrobe is crowded between the bunks and the sloop's hull.

Creslin rubs his nose to stop the itching from the faint mustiness that pervades the cabin. A heavy circular table bolted to the deck and three wooden armchairs upholstered in green and gold fill most of the space. The carving on the chairs matches that on the bunks. An ornate chamber pot rests in one corner.

Two portholes offer the only light, although there is one unlit brass oil lamp hanging from the beam above the table.

"Not exactly the most suitable for a newly wed couple," apologizes the captain, "what with the separate bunks . . .

but a sight better than accommodations on most coasters."

"It's very nice," insists Megaera with an amused smile.

"Appreciate the hospitality," adds Creslin.

Heavy steps on the planks presage the arrival of two sailors bearing Creslin's pack and Megaera's baggage.

"Just set them down," Megaera says.

"Set them there," echoes Freigr. The captain waits until the two men depart. "Tide's not really a problem here, and the wind's right. We've got what we need; been waiting for the Duke's orders. So, if you'll excuse me, I'd like to—"

"That's fine. When do you expect we'll leave?"

"This afternoon, if I can drag three of the boys out of town. In the meantime, you might enjoy yourselves." Freigr smiles broadly at Creslin and closes the door.

"Enjoy ourselves! That . . . you . . . men!" Megaera unfastens her travel cloak with deliberation.

"I think he was assuming that we are . . . the usual . . . newly married—" Creslin finds that he is blushing.

"Stop it! It's bad enough that we had to get married to save your wretched neck."

"*My* wretched neck?"

"It was the only way to save mine, thanks to sister dear and your darling mother the Marshall. But it is your neck."

"You weren't exactly beloved in Sarronnyn."

Megaera begins to rummage through the topmost of her bags. Creslin reclaims his pack and places it on the top bunk.

"You could have asked," she says dourly.

Creslin picks up the pack. "Which one do you want?"

"The bottom is fine."

He grins.

"I don't need your crass comments." Fire glows at Megaera's fingertips.

"Never mind." Creslin places his pack back on the top bunk. "I'm going out on deck."

LXI

As THE SAILORS loosen the hawsers, Creslin watches the activities. Megaera has appeared, still gray but without the cloak now that the rain has lifted. Her face and hands are freshly clear of the grime of travel.

"Now what?" he asks.

"Next, I think . . ."

Creslin's attention drops away from Megaera's words as his eyes center on a wavering of the light; it resembles a snow mirage, or the summer heat mirages from the black stone roads leading to the Roof of the World. Although his eyes insist that nothing is there, the winds tell him that a man stands behind the twisted light, a man who has walked up the gangway just before it was hauled aboard. Creslin, short sword leaping into his hand, walks slowly toward the figure behind the light shield.

"Creslin?" Megaera's voice turns from conversational to sharp as she sees the sword, and her eyes widen as she senses what he senses.

The distortion vanishes, and a thin, black-haired man in black—black shirt, tunic, trousers, and faded black traveling cloak—stands on the deck, his empty hands palms up. On his back is a bulging pack of leather and canvas.

Creslin does not sheath the sword, but waits.

"My name is Klerris. I thought you might need some assistance, and you're going in a direction that might be beneficial."

Klerris? The name is vaguely familiar, but Creslin cannot place it.

"I'm generally thought of as a Black healer, and often I have helped with injuries to the road crews."

The healer who had helped restore Creslin's memory had

mentioned the name. "Where is she?" Slowly, he replaces the sword.

"Lydya? On her way to Westwind. The White Wizards are not exactly pleased with either of us at the moment."

Megaera glances from Klerris to Creslin and back again. "Would one of you mind explaining?"

As she speaks, the last of the lines is cast free; the *Griffin* swings away from the pier and, under partial sail, glides past the Fairhaven schooner and toward the open sea. On the war schooner, white-clad sailors are busily moving about, as if preparing to follow the *Griffin*.

"There was a healer at the road camp," answers Creslin slowly, studying the schooner; it bears the name *Lightning* on a plate above the stern. "She helped me get my memory back. She mentioned the name of Klerris."

"Does that make this man the same Klerris?" asks Megaera.

"Not necessarily," admits Creslin. "But I can't see any benefit to impersonating a Black Wizard, and he certainly isn't a White Wizard."

"Perhaps this would help," suggests Klerris, extending his hand. In it rests a heavy linked-gold chain. "Yours, I believe."

Creslin takes the chain, studies, it, notes the twist to the links. "Thank you."

"Lydya recovered it when you were brought into the camp. She thought you might need it."

"That's worth a fortune," Megaera notes coolly, "assuming it's real."

"Touch it. It's real." Creslin sways as the deck lurches.

Megaera's fingers brush the gold.

Outside the breakwater, the seas are heavier, but the sailors breaking out the full rigging of the sloop have no trouble with either footing or coordination.

"The first part of the trip is the roughest," offers Klerris.

"Oh?" Megaera's eyebrows rise. "You've made this voyage before?"

"Darkness, no. But the winds are higher north and west of the gulfs, and the northern seas harbor the storms."

Creslin steps to the rail and grasps the worn wood. His senses go out to the Fairhaven schooner, which glows with the whiteness he has come to associate with the White Wizards. Megaera is also correct in her estimations, for more than a score of the white-clad warriors ready their weapons.

Abruptly a white, shining mist envelops the schooner, invisible but seeming to bar Creslin from seeing anything beyond what his eyes could see from outside the *Lightning*.

"He's shielded their ship," Megaera notes.

"I discovered that."

"Could you enlighten me as to your companion?" The captain stands behind Klerris.

"Oh, this is Klerris," Creslin says.

Freigr inclines his head. "The passages didn't mention you."

"The Duke did not expect me."

Freigr shakes his head, then turns to Creslin. "The *Lightning* will be on our tail before long."

"Is she that fast?" asks Klerris.

"Not so fast as the *Griffin*."

Creslin looks at the captain. "You look like you have a question."

"Yes," Freigr says. "How do you propose to save us? The Duke's orders indicated that you would provide protection for the ship."

"You just said that your ship is faster than the schooner." It is clear to the silver-haired man that Freigr is considering his options.

Freigr smiles but only with his mouth. "I'm not worried about that schooner. I'm worried about the one that left the Great North Bay and will meet us in the gulf."

"Why?"

Freigr gestures toward the stern and the diminishing white triangle that is all they can see of the Fairhaven schooner. "That's the way they always do it. We all know about it." He shrugs. "But what can you do? The wizards talk. That schooner would be hard-pressed to take us, even if they caught us. The one in the bay will bear a full wizard, and generally a White one, in this sort of thing, is worth two Black ones." He nods to Klerris. "They must have guessed that you would be here, or they know."

"I'm a healer," Klerris admits. "Most uses of order aren't helpful in war. The lady will be of more use."

Freigr looks toward the bow, where Megaera's hair whips back over her shoulders. Spray sheets past the redhead as the *Griffin's* bow digs into a swell. Megaera regards the southeastern horizon without turning.

"I've got *three* of you on board?"

"Happily, yes," responds Klerris.

"Three?" mutters the captain. "If I ever get back to see Korweil . . . Three frigging wizards. There'll be at least two ships out of the Great North Bay, and me on a lousy sloop."

"How long?" asks Creslin tiredly.

"What?"

"How long before they arrive?"

"Not until the day after tomorrow at the earliest, perhaps even late the following day. It all depends on the winds in the gulf, and whether they have their own Air Wizard."

The ship lurches again, and Creslin finds that his stomach is not exactly where he thinks it is. His guts intend to turn themselves inside out. He refuses to give in to nausea and swallows, but the leaden feeling weighs at him. He can ride ill-mannered horses and ski ice-covered slopes . . . why should a simple ship leave him feeling sick?

Finally he hangs on to the railing, letting the cool wind bathe his flushed face.

"You all right?" asks the Black Wizard, stepping up beside him, carefully upwind.

"No."

"Can you listen to me?"

Another sheet of spray flies past. "I guess so."

"Then listen . . ." Klerris edges slightly farther toward the bow.

Creslin burps, hoping that will help. It does not. The bow dips into another swell, and his stomach tightens even more.

"Urrrppp . . ."

"That won't help. Are you sure that you can listen?"

"I'll try."

"The clouds, the winds, the rain . . . all of them are related. Every time you grasp for the high, cold winds, you change something. The storm you created to get to Mont- gren deprived the farmers of Kyphros of rain for more than two eight-days. The fog and thunderstorm you used to fight your way into Tyrhavven will probably bring a hard and early winter onto most of Sligo. The rain that kept falling while we left was your doing."

"My doing?"

"Don't you listen? When you pull the winds from one place, air from someplace else has to move."

"Ohhh?"

"Think of it this way," Klerris persists, his voice hard. "The air we breathe is just like the ocean. It's an ocean of air. Can you take a bucket of water out of the ocean without water pouring into the space you took it from?"

Creslin doesn't like thinking about an ocean of air. The ocean of water is giving him enough difficulty. "No," he finally admits.

"When you shift the winds, you shift the ocean of air. The more you change it, the more you stir things up."

"I was supposed to let them kill us?" Creslin forgets that his stomach is twisting.

"I never said that. That's your guilt, not mine."

"What do you want?"

"Your understanding, and to teach you how to use what you have."

"I'll think about it."

Klerris smiles softly, sadly. "As you wish." He turns and leaves Creslin at the railing.

Creslin, watching the swells, lets the cold salt air wash over him as the day begins to fade.

LXII

"KORWEIL DID THAT?" muses the Marshall, her voice calm as she looks up from the supply ledgers she is reviewing.

Llyse nods. "That's what the message said. It was a private ceremony, but the co-regency arrangement surprised me."

"What co-regency?"

"He named Creslin and Megaera co-regents of Recluce."

"He's a stubborn bastard, but not that devious." The Marshall marks the ledger page before closing the book. "Megaera, with those bracelets off, isn't about to submit to any man. At least that's what Ryessa indicated. But she never said why she felt Megaera was safe to unbind."

"Do you trust the Tyrant?" asks Llyse tentatively.

"No. But that kind of lie wouldn't benefit her. I suspect that somehow she linked her sister to Creslin, used some sort of magic tie. That forces the sub-tyrant to follow and preserve . . . Creslin." She shakes her head. "Creslin's gotten help from somewhere, probably from the eastern Blacks. But the co-regency thing—that has to be Creslin's doing. I only hope he knows the stakes he's playing for."

Llyse says nothing but waits. Outside the Black Tower windows, the winds howl and the snows fall.

The Marshall raises her eyebrows. "You have questions?"

"Creslin was never meant to go to Sarronnyn."

Dylyss turns and looks out through the frosted glass.

"Was he?" asks the Marshalle.

"No."

"I thought not. He was taught everything I was, but he was never told that, was he?"

The Marshall continues to regard the falling snow outside the Black Tower.

Llyse finally drops her eyes, bows, and leaves the room.

LXIII

CRESLIN IGNORES THE sniggers from the helmsman as he weaves his way aft. The passageway is dark, but even in his weakened condition, his senses guide him to the cabin doorway, where he fumbles before entering an even darker space. Megaera is breathing rhythmically in the lower bunk.

"Creslin?" Her voice is thick.

"Yes," he rasps.

"Go to sleep. Let your mind take care of your body. Good night . . ."

Creslin struggles out of his sword harness, then slumps into one of the chairs and pulls off his boots. He stands and shrugs off his tunic, shirt, and trousers. He folds them and lays them in the chair, then makes his way slowly to his bunk. Megaera has turned back the coverlet.

"Thank you," he mumbles.

"Easier that way. Go to sleep."

He puts one leg up and tries to lever himself over the high edge.

"Please. I'm not a ladder."

"Sorry."

Despite the faint mustiness of the cabin, the high-sided bunk is welcome. Creslin does not recall falling asleep, but when he opens his eyes, light is streaming through the portholes. Megaera still sleeps, her breathing regular.

Creslin sits up. *Clunk.* Rubbing his head, he reflects that the clearance is not much greater than that of a road-crew bunk, although the accoutrements at hand are far better. Easing himself to the deck, he avoids touching or waking the sleeping redhead.

Just as quietly, he begins to dress.

"You do have a nice body, I must admit."

Creslin blushes, pulls on his trousers, and sits down to retrieve his boots. "I tried not to wake you up."

Clunk. Creslin grins.

Megaera rubs her head with one hand while the other clutches the quilted coverlet over her shoulders. "It's not funny. That hurt."

"I know. I did the same thing."

"Oh."

Creslin, noting how fresh she looks despite the straying locks of red hair, fingers the stubble on his cheeks, wondering if he dares shaving on the moving deck. He swallows.

"Please . . ."

He looks away, concentrates on pulling on his boots.

"Thank you." She remains cocooned within the coverlet.

He picks up the razor, grabs at a thin green towel that is folded on the chest. "I'm going to find somewhere to shave and clean up."

Out in the passageway, wearing only trousers and boots, he lurches toward the deck, emerging into a clear and windy day.

Klerris stands at the bow, looking into the southeast.

Creslin finally sees what he seeks on the port side near the fantail. After taking care of the necessities, he looks for a way to shave. There is no fresh water, but two buckets hang from lanyards lashed to the railing. He lowers one of the buckets, raises it to the deck, and wets his face thoroughly. At least twice he cuts himself while shaving, and his face stings all over as he rinses away skin and whiskers.

Frowning, he lowers the bucket again, brings it up and

sets it on the rail. Then he concentrates. A small pile of white appears on the railing. He dips his finger into the bucket, tastes it, and grins. Then he strips off trousers and boots and uses the fresh water liberally to wash away as much of the travel grime as he can. The wind raises goose bumps on his damp skin, but they disappear as he dries himself and dresses.

Then he procures the other bucket and again obtains fresh water, letting the wind take the dried salt away before heading back to the cabin with the bucket in hand.

When he steps inside, pleased with his success in separating the salt from the water and displeased with the cuts on his chin, he finds Megaera dressed in faded-blue travel clothes and combing her hair.

Creslin searches for a place to put the bucket. "Fresh water," he points out.

"Thank you."

As he sets the bucket on the narrow chest, his eyes stray to the chamber pot, which has been moved slightly. "Do we . . . I need to empty . . ."

Megaera grins. "I can still manage some destruction. It's more convenient that way."

Creslin blushes again, then replaces his razor and finishes dressing. He looks at his sword but leaves it hanging in the harness on the hook by the chest. Then he adjusts his shirt and tunic.

"I removed the dirt and grime."

"Thank you."

At times she seems to be so warm, so friendly. He smoothes his clothes in place. "Biscuits and dried fruit for breakfast."

"Dried?"

"If you'd like some of it fresh, I might manage."

"Oh?"

"That's what landed me on the wizards' road."

A soft laugh greets his rueful statement.

"Seems stupid, with everything else I've done."

She nods toward the cabin door.

Creslin opens it, and they take the three or so steps to bring them into the mess room. Freigr is not there, but a man with an air of authority half rises from one of the two tables. At the other table sit three sailors.

"Gossel, first mate. Pleased to have you join us."

They sit down side by side, across from the brown-haired man with bushy hair caught in a ponytail. On the table are dried fruits, some hard yellow-cheese wedges, and even harder white biscuits. Two heavy brown pitchers sit in built-in holders in the middle of the table.

Gossel leans back and grabs two mugs from a railed shelf. "Here you be."

"Thank you." They speak together, then look at each other.

Creslin shakes his head. Megaera smiles faintly.

"Your pleasure . . ." Creslin gestures to the wooden platter of dried fruits.

"Could you actually . . . a fresh peach, I mean?"

"I can try."

Gossel's eyebrows knit as Creslin picks up a dried peach. The silver-haired man tried to recall the wondering sense he had felt about the cider. Suddenly a golden orb replaces the dried husk.

"Oh . . ."

He hands the peach to her, then wipes his forehead.

Gossel gulps. "Uh . . . never saw that before. The captain said that all of you are wizards . . ."

"I'm afraid so." Creslin fills the two mugs with whatever is in the pitcher and offers one to Megaera.

Two of the sailors rise quietly and slip past the table. One makes a protective gesture as he leaves the mess room. The third sailor shakes his head, grins, and helps himself to another round of cheese and biscuits.

"That's why the captain's got so much sail on, then," muses the mate. "The other wizard, guess he got the spare bunk in the captain's cabin. That doesn't happen often."

Creslin slowly chews the heavy biscuit, recalling the state of his stomach the day before. "You ever run into the White Wizards' ships before?"

The mate grimaces. "Once. That was when I first ran off to sea, crew on a Nordlan brig. The captain wouldn't pay their tax. They burned off the foremast, and the captain. The mate paid, but the owners had him hung. Claimed he supported piracy. Left Nordlan service soon as I could."

"How close did the wizards have to get?" Creslin sips the bitter and lukewarm tea.

"They came in right close, less than a cable—"

"Cable?"

"Cable's a little more than four hundred cubits. Anyways, we could see the White Wizard. He stood right up on the poop, next to the captain, and where he pointed, there was a fireball, the kind that burns."

"Did water stop the fire?"

"It would have, except that anyone who tried got fried with the next fireball."

Creslin nods.

"Need to be on deck," explains the mate as he rises. "Hoping you can help us through. Be nice to see those Whites get a dose of their own." He nods and ducks under the low doorway.

Creslin takes another biscuit. "I wish there were another way."

Megaera finishes the peach before answering. "Maybe there is."

"Such as?"

"Why can't we just avoid them? Use your power over the winds to speed us past them."

"I suppose we could . . ."

"You want to fight? Given your reactions, I don't think you enjoy destroying, do you?"

"No. But I'm missing something."

"Are you, or do you just . . . Never mind." She takes a sip from the heavy tumbler.

Creslin watches the remaining sailor finish off the cheese and fruit on the other table. Everyone just assumes that he will fight off the White Wizards as if it is the easiest thing in the world—except for Megaera, who insists that he doesn't have to fight at all. But Megaera believes in the Legend, claiming that all men want to do is to destroy. Is that what he really wants?

What is it that Heldra said so long ago during exercises? "If you lift a blade, you must kill or be killed. Kill cleanly and without regret."

Are the winds like blades?

Megaera looks up from the half-eaten peach. "Could you think about something else for a while?"

"Sorry. It's hard to always remember that . . ."

For a time there is silence as Creslin swallows another mouthful of tea, wondering what he can think about. He cannot think about how lovely she looked with her shoulders bare . . .

"Do you have to spoil a perfectly good morning?"

"What did I do?"

Megaera rises suddenly and is through the doorway before he has finished his question.

"That one's as hot as her hair." The remaining sailor grins at Creslin.

"Hotter, I think," Creslin mutters as he finishes his second biscuit. "And we're just beginning."

LXIV

How will he protect the *Griffin?*

A good strong rain, with lightning and thunder, will reduce the effectiveness of the wizards on board the three oncoming Fairhaven ships, but it will not stop the nearly five-score white-clad soldiers from boarding the *Griffin*.

And a more violent storm could be nearly as dangerous for the *Griffin* as for the wizards.

The green water streams below Creslin's feet, unseen.

Megaera can counter some chaos with destruction of her own. Creslin shivers, recalling how Megaera's being is now mixed with Black and White; then he shivers again at her reactions at breakfast on the first morning aboard the *Griffin*, and her refusal to even come close to him during the past two days. What does she want? A bloodless solution? When everyone is out for his and her blood?

The ship plows into a long swell, and Creslin's stomach lurches. Unlike the first day, his guts settle, albeit uneasily.

Ice? Enough ice to make a difference brings the same problem as a violent storm.

"Sail ahoy!"

The lookout's call reminds Creslin that he has but little time.

For the past two days, Klerris has been poking through the ship, mumbling to himself while strengthening the timbers—their joints and the masts—and even the cables and sails with an infusion of order. That infusion is strong enough that even the crew have comments on how much more solid the ship now seems to be.

"Figured it out yet, young fellow?" The wizard's voice is tired.

Creslin turns his eyes from the bow, where Megaera watches the faint dot of white on the horizon, to the black-clad man. Klerris's jet-black hair shows streaks of white, streaks that seem to have appeared overnight.

"You work this hard, and you show your age," the wizard responds to Creslin's appraisal.

"What would happen if we just avoided them?"

"The Whites, you mean?" Klerris pulls at his smooth-shaven chin. "Don't see how that's possible. We get around them and they'll head for Land's End. They have enough strength to take the town, even with the Duke's keep. Or they might simply wait and sink the *Griffin* if Captain Freigr tries to leave. They won't just let it drop, you know."

"Then the only way we can be safe is to sink all three of their ships. The High Wizard won't let that drop. How do we ever get out of this?"

Klerris grins. "You don't. Once you're a wizard, you're stuck with decisions like this for the rest of your life." His face sobers. "Of course, if you don't want to make decisions, you dither around until you or people around you get killed. That's been the problem with most of us Blacks. We don't like violence and killing. We really need a land based on order, somehow separate from the Whites and the conflicts over the Legend."

"That's fine," snorts Creslin, "but the lookouts have sighted the first of the wizard ships' sails, and I'm still trying to figure out how to get us out of this."

"You're a warrior. You'll find a way. You have an ocean of air and an ocean of water to work with."

"Thanks."

"My pleasure." Klerris turns and heads toward the bow.

Water? Creslin has never tried to deal with water, except to remove the salt from it. He sends down his senses, then recoils. The water is heavy, far too heavy and cold. But the air carries water, and that water has to come from somewhere. The winds pick it up from the rivers and lakes and oceans. He walks to the fantail, where he lowers a bucket, ignoring the curious looks from Gossel, who stands by the helmsman.

Setting the bucket on the railing, Creslin concentrates again. A small vortex appears over the bucket, and the water begins to swirl like a whirlpool. Creslin frowns, loses his concentration, and the vortex collapses. Still, something nags at his memory. He empties the bucket.

"Sail ahoy!" The second White schooner has appeared to the lookouts, and Creslin strides over to the mate.

"Aye, Ser Wizard?"

"What's the worst thing that could happen to a ship?"

"Fire."

"I mean something natural, like a storm, or ice, or . . ."

Gossel pauses. "I've heard tell, in southern seas, about waterspouts that could lift a whole ship high enough that she'd fall and break in two."

"Are there thunderstorms around when that happens?"

"Aye. Never happens without a thunderstorm."

Creslin nods absently and walks away.

". . . darkness help us if he calls a waterspout."

". . . light help us if he don't do something."

Freigr appears from below and heads toward Creslin, who stops the man's question with a cold glance and walks past him toward Klerris, who is conversing with Megaera.

Megaera starts to leave. "Just stay," Creslin says and feels for the winds. She raises her eyebrows. Klerris nods, and she waits.

"Do you see any way to save this ship and crew without destroying all three White ships?" Creslin asks Klerris.

"I do not know of a way. I do not know of a way to destroy them, either." His words are as formal as Creslin's.

"As a Black Wizard, would you judge those on board this ship of greater value than those on the White ships?"

"Wizards closing!" a lookout cries.

"Creslin, I can't answer that question. That involves the whole lifetimes of scores of people."

"I'll put it simply. Is this crew's survival worth the deaths of those on the White ships?"

"You can't balance lives that way," protests the older wizard.

"That's all I have to go on." Creslin takes a deep breath and calls forth to the cold upper winds, then begins to tease the warm currents above the water into a rising dance.

Rhhhssttt!

Megaera concentrates, and a small fireball swerves past the foresail. A second fireball follows.

Less than ten cables away, a White ship appears.

"Veiled approach . . ." mutters Klerris.

"Hard port! Sails!" bellows Freigr.

Creslin grabs the railing as the sloop heels.

Rhhssttt!

Sweat beads on Megaera's forehead.

Off the starboard bow, a darkness comprised of mist and swirling winds begins to solidify.

The *Griffin* shudders as the winds build.

Rhhhsttt! Rhhstt! Rhsssttt!

Fire clings to the foresail for a moment, but Klerris, sweating, murmurs something and the flame winks out.

"Dead ahead!"

Megaera looks up to see a black-green tower whirling, slowly and ponderously, toward the nearest White schooner.

The schooner turns toward the waterspout, as if to knife through it, or past it, but the water engulfs it in a tower now more than three times as broad as the schooner is long.

The second schooner turns south to take advantage of the wind. But the towering black-green spout swings south even more quickly.

Another fireball blazes through a corner of the sloop's sail. The loose canvas flails, but none of the crew moves, too intent on watching as the spout bears down on the fleeing schooner.

Klerris's forehead beads with sweat, and the flames on the canvas flicker out, leaving only a charred semicircle.

The schooner rises into the swirling darkness, then falls.

"Mother of darkness . . ." murmurs Klerris as he sees the white timbers, canvas, and debris strewn across the swells.

Creslin's eyes remain absent, unfocused, as the sloop eases back onto a southeasterly course.

In time, Klerris and Megaera watch as a distant darkness again turns, this time northwest and toward a fleeing dot of white, a dot that vanishes into that swirling darkness.

Creslin's eyes focus again. He grips the railing convulsively and pukes over the railing. Then his knees buckle. Klerris manages to catch him before his head cracks against the deck planks.

"Still overdoing it," says Megaera wearily.

"Did we give him any alternative?" Klerris asks softly as he lifts Creslin over his shoulder.

The crew looks away as the Black Wizard carries his burden to the Duke's cabin, Megaera following a step behind.

Freigr glances back at the debris, human and otherwise, that litters the swells behind the *Griffin*. Then he looks toward the Duke's cabin. The captain swallows once, twice.

LXV

CRESLIN WAKES WITH a start. "No. Nooooo . . ."

In the darkness, he jerks upright.

Clunk.

"Ooohh . . ."

"Idiot," observes Magaera unsympathetically from the lower bunk. She rises and pours a tumbler of juice, her movements in the darkness are sure as Creslin's.

"Idiot?" protests Creslin. "For what?"

"Nothing. Just for being you." Her voice is tired rather than harsh. She hands him the tumbler, careful not to touch his hands as she does.

He sips slowly for a time. "Thank you."

"For what? For calling you an idiot?"

"For the redberry. How late is it?"

"After midnight sometime. Klerris carried you in like a sack of grain."

Creslin takes another sip of the juice. He hears the sound of heavy rain on the planks overhead.

"How long has it been raining?"

"Ever since you tore those three ships apart."

Creslin rubs his forehead with his free hand. "You'd better take this."

"I'm not—" She reaches for the tumbler as she sees him sway, takes it from his limp hand and sets it on the table.

Then she touches his brow lightly, drawing her fingers away at the heat and dampness, wincing at the pain that lances at her as his barriers again dissolve.

Tears streak her cheeks. "Why? Damn you . . . sister dear. Damn you . . ." She rubs her forehead and pulls on a cloak before leaving the cabin and crossing the narrow space to the captain's cabin to get Klerris again.

LXVI

WHEN CRESLIN NEXT wakes, the interior of the cabin is light, as light as it can be with rain pounding outside on the planks. Hearing voices, he neither opens his eyes nor moves.

"He has no idea?" Megaera's whisper is strained.

Klerris says nothing, though Creslin gains the sense of a head shake.

"And I thought sister dear was cruel."

"Men are considered dispensable on the Roof of the World." Klerris pauses. "I do believe that our sleeping friend is about to rejoin us."

"How long?" croaks Creslin, realizing that his throat requires some lubrication. He eases himself into as much of a sitting position as he can, given the low ceiling above the top bunk.

"Just a full day," the Black Wizard answers.

"Thirsty . . . " Creslin tries to swallow.

Klerris supplies a tumbler of redberry, but the juice

contains something else; it is not bitter, not sweet, just an extra something.

"What's . . . in this?"

"Extra nourishment. Something healers use. You've asked too much of your body lately." The Black Wizard then adds, "And your mind. Now just keep drinking that."

Creslin sips slowly, feeling a trace less unsteady after the liquid eases down his throat. "How long before we reach Land's End?"

"Early tomorrow, according to Friegr."

"Friegr's a bit grouchy right now," adds Megaera with a trace of a smile.

"Why? The rain?" asks Creslin.

"That's part of it, but he's scared to death that you will die, and sort of hopes that you will. And he's angry because he feels that way," Klerris explains.

Creslin takes another sip. "I feel better," he announces. He stretches, as far as the confines of the bunk will permit. "And I'm stiff."

"No one's insisting that you stay in that bunk," replies Megaera.

Gingerly, Creslin extricates himself. He feels grimy all over. "I'm going to wash up."

"Are you up to it?"

"Probably not, but I'm not up to smelling like I do." He pulls off his shirt, boots, and trousers and stands there momentarily in his underdrawers before grabbing his razor and opening the door.

"I'm not—" The door closes before Megaera can finish her statement. "He's impossible."

"Just young," temporizes Klerris.

"He'll be impossible when he's older, too."

Klerris says nothing. Instead, he takes a sip from his tumbler and listens thoughtfully to the rain pelt on the planks overhead.

LXVII

THE GRIFFIN SAILS through long, even swells, gentle enough
that Creslin's stomach has no protests, smooth enough that
he actually has enjoyed a breakfast of pearapples and bread,
washed down with redberry. Overhead and behind the ship,
clouds linger, nearly black to the west, yet no longer
following the sloop.

Creslin stands at the railing. A smudge of darkness lies
off the starboard bow. Despite the clouds, the air is crisp,
and a hint of green emerges from the dark waters below. In
time, Klerris joins him.

Megaera stands a few cubits away, one hand lightly
resting on the battered wood of the rail, the other on a cable
that braces the foremast. She wears her faded gray travel
clothes, worn though they are, that bring out the fire of her
hair and the glint of her eyes.

Creslin avoids looking at her, knowing that if he looks
too long, she will sense what he feels. His eyes drift astern
to the western horizon. "The clouds aren't really following
any longer, like they did for an eight-day in Sligo, and in
Montgren. Why not?"

"Why don't you try to find out?" Klerris asks with an
amused smile.

"You don't make it easy, do you?"

"Does life?" Megaera's voice crosses the distance between them.

Creslin ignores her words and sends his senses out upon
the winds, aware of himself both on the gently pitching
deck of the Griffin and in the skies behind the ship. For the
first time, he looks at the winds themselves, not at the
ground or at distant scenes; looks not with his eyes, but with
his feelings, catching the snags and swirls, the heat and the

chill, the rushes upward and downward, and—far overhead—
the cold torrents that almost touch the Roof of the World day
in and day out.

How long he is gone, how long he is suspended between
two places, he does not know, only that when he stands
fully on the deck again, there are small patches of blue in
the overhead clouds.

"They're blocked," he announces before he realizes that
Klerris and Megaera no longer stand beside him but have
moved almost to the bowsprit, where they watch a dolphin
pacing the sloop.

With a sigh, the silver-haired man walks stiffly toward
them.

"Isn't she beautiful?" Megaera smiles as she watches the
dolphin give a last leap and dive beneath the dark green
water.

"Was it a female?"

"Who can tell?" Klerris says.

"It was a woman, " Megaera insists. "I could feel her
spirit."

"Then it was," Creslin agrees.

The redhead's smile lingers for a moment, but she says
nothing.

"What did you find out?" Klerris looks at Creslin.

"The southern winds are stronger. The low ones. Nothing
is stronger than the high torrents. Somehow, the way the
low winds come across the gulf . . . it has something to
do with the deserts on Recluce, especially the southern part
and the northern hills."

"Mountains and deserts always have a big impact on
winds and weather. So do the seas. It has to do with how
they affect the heat and the cold." Klerris looks toward the
south, where the smudge on the horizon that Creslin had
studied earlier has become the profile of a rocky coastline.

Creslin wishes that Klerris would say more, but the Black
Wizard has the habit of saying only what he wishes to say
and no more. It is probably a good habit to adopt, Creslin

thinks even as he wonders how the wizard can call the rocky peaks on the isle "mountains." Not when they are scarcely foothills to the Westhorns, or even to the Easthorns.

"You might remember that hot air rises and that cold air is heavier and stronger." Klerris heads back to the helm, where Freigr stands beside the helmsman.

Creslin is still shaking his head when Megaera speaks.

"You're not yet used to complexity."

Creslin opens his mouth, then shuts it. After a moment, he speaks. "You're right. But it seems too many people make things more complicated than they need to be."

"That's because most people aren't simple. Not once they have had to grow up."

Creslin takes a deep breath.

"You can be as stubborn as the mountains themselves, best-betrothed," Megaera tells him.

"We're married, according to the documents."

"Should I refer to you as 'husband-dearest' then?"

"If you must use a name, 'best-betrothed' is probably more accurate. For many reasons."

Megaera looks down at the dark water.

Creslin studies the coastline again, noting the barren rockiness. After a while he follows Megaera to the mess cabin, where they join half of the crew, seven men, in eating a highly-peppered stew accompanied by biscuits harder than any Creslin has ever gnawed.

"Won't be long now," affirms Freigr. "By midafternoon we should see Land's End."

"What is there to see?" asks Megaera.

A white-bearded sailor laughs harshly.

"A few fishing cots, a pier, and a breakwater too big for a fishing village, and the keep of the Duke's garrison. That's about it." Freigr crunches through a biscuit and slurps up another spoonful of stew. "But when I told that to the Duke, he sort of swallowed and turned red all over."

Megaera and Creslin smile, thinking of Korweil. Megaera purses her lips. "That doesn't sound like much, not after all the fuss he has made about it."

Creslin winces, but continues to eat silently.

"Well, there is the stable . . ."

Several of the sailors are grinning.

Megaera shakes her head, and her red hair brushes the shoulders of the gray travel tunic she wears.

Creslin gnaws on his third hard biscuit.

Klerris is grinning with the sailors.

"Now, the Duke has a map with lots of buildings on it . . ."

LXVIII

FROM BEYOND THE breakwater, Freigr's description of Land's End seems generous. No buildings can be seen on the rocky cliffs flanking the narrow inlet. The breakwater that comprises the eastern side of the harbor is little more than a pile of stones perhaps ten cubits wide and extending three to four cubits above the ocean's level. Even as Creslin and Megaera watch, some of the water's low swells slide over the rough-heaped stones.

From the flat ground behind the harbor, a pier protrudes. At the shore end of the pier there squats a small black-stone building. Behind that building, a gentle slope, surfaced in sand and stone, rises until it reaches an ever-steeper slope. The lower slope, showing a few bushes and trees at random, contains a scattering of perhaps a dozen small cots, or hovels. Tall grasses wave in the light breeze.

"Desolate indeed," murmurs Klerris.

A single road angles from the pier westward to the top of a rise. There the gray-black stones of a two-story building bear the gold-and-green banner of Montgren.

"Where will we stay? All I see is that second-rate keep on

the hill and some tumbledown fishing cots." Megaera
continues to study Land's End as the sailors scurry across
the deck and begin to work the sails.

"We'll have to build our own palace, " Creslin quips.

"You're serious, aren't you?"

"What else can we do?"

"I can help with the beams," offers Klerris. "The pines in
the canyons will have to do, though. There's nothing like
oak here. Not yet, anyway."

Creslin and Megaera turn.

"Blacks learn useful trades in addition to their wizardly
skills, " the black-haired man explains, "I do carpentry now
and again."

"Regents building their own palace . . . ridiculous,"
mumbles Megaera.

"Perhaps," offers Klerris, "But are there any alternatives?"

Once the *Griffin* is tied up in the deep water near the end
of the pier, out beyond a fishing boat so battered and
waterlogged that it looks ready to sink at any moment,
Freigr appears on deck in the gold-and-green coat that he
has not worn since leaving Tyrhavven. "Might as well get
this over." He lifts the leather dispatch case. "While we're
gone, Snyder will see that the horses are saddled and
off-loaded. He's done it often enough, darkness knows."

"What about our packs?" asks Creslin, checking his
shoulder harness and his replacement Westwind blade,
secured from the depths of the Duke's armory and sharpened.

"He'll take care of them also. Plus a few other supplies
we can spare, as suggested by . . ." The captain nods
toward the Black Wizard. "Shall we go? It's a steep walk."

"Ummm . . ." Megaera closes her mouth.

Creslin smothers a grin.

"Ah, here come some of the garrison."

On the end of the pier stand two soldiers, wearing
leathers and swords.

"They haven't learned that we never bring anything interesting." Freigr glances at Megaera. "This time, though—"

"I doubt that they will find me that interesting," suggests the redhead.

"Let's go," repeats Freigr.

On the open pier, the wind whips through Creslin's short hair and tosses Megaera's shoulder-length flames in every direction.

"Captain?" A black-haired soldier with a scraggly beard steps toward the group, lank locks falling across his forehead.

"Nothing new, except for this group, who are likely to be very interesting," Freigr tells the soldiers.

"Very interesting . . ." murmurs the blond, gray-eyed man at the edge of the pier, his hand on the hilt of his sword.

Freigr grins at him. "I'd be careful, Zarlen. All three of them are wizards, and Creslin, here, is reputed to know a little bit about blades."

Megaera lifts one hand, and a small flame dances on her fingertips. The dark-haired soldier steps back; the blond man smiles faintly. Creslin takes a deep breath but says nothing as the two soldiers turn to follow them.

"How many men are there in the keep?" Creslin asks as he and the captain lead the way up the sandy road.

"Not many more than a score. There were more, but the Duke took them back to Montgren." The sandy-haired captain glances back over his shoulder, then adds in a lower voice, "Mostly troublemakers left."

Creslin nods, glad of the sword across his back.

"Are you as good as they say with that blade?" Freigr asks.

Creslin debates an answer; then feeling the twisting in his guts as he thinks about a diplomatic reply, he responds as truthfully as he knows. "I'm probably not as good as the very best at Westwind."

"Good. That should be adequate. Find an excuse to

display that skill. It will save you a lot of trouble later." Freigr lengthens his stride toward the bleak, black-stone structure ahead.

The white-fir doors are plain, and stand open. Inside wait a lanky, brown-haired man in a gold-and-green surcoat, much like Freigr's, and a swarthy, short man. Each sports a well-trimmed beard; the tall man's beard is shot with threads of white, unlike his hair.

The *Griffin's* captain tenders the document case to the lanky man in the gold surcoat. "The Duke's latest proclamation, Hyel. It concerns . . . us all."

"Must be important, Captain, since you have brought it yourself."

"A second messenger will bring information."

"Very important, then." The narrow-faced, swarthy man to the right leans over to read the parchments held by the guard captain.

The two men behind Hyel and his assistant—the same two who had met the travelers at the pier—shuffle their feet while Hyel slowly puzzles through the documents.

As he waits, Creslin studies the long room that comprises the entire main floor of the building. The outside walls are of a native stone, almost black. The narrow windows are uncovered except for outside shutters, which are fastened open. The ceiling beams are rough-cut, and several of them still ooze sap.

Megaera looks at the four Duke's men, her eyes moving from Hyel and the narrow-faced man to the black-haired and short, bearded youngster on his left, and then to the blond, well-muscled giant on the right. Klerris appears to look nowhere, while Freigr shifts his weight from foot to foot.

"Fine documents they are," affirms Hyel, "and the Duke's seal is clear enough."

"Why would he even name a regency?" asks the narrow-faced man as he raises his eyes from the ornate script. "There's just us and a bunch of fisherfolk."

"That's simple, Joris." Hyel grins. "This here young wizard is the son of the Marshall of Westwind . . . you know, those women guards who chewed up the wizard's allies. And this young lady is the younger sister of the Tyrant of Sarronnyn. That makes her the Duke's cousin. I figure that the Duke needs more help, and a regency doesn't give away the isle. It's a sort of loan." He laughs.

"I don't like it much." Joris's dark-brown eyes flick from Creslin to Megaera.

"Welcome to the holding of Recluce. I am Hyel, guard captain and, until you arrived, the Duke's representative." Hyel bows so low, arm extended, that his long fingers almost touch the dusty planks. His smile shows strong, white, and uneven teeth. "I have mentioned Joris, and the other two are Thoirkel and Zarlen."

Creslin inclines his head. "Creslin. This is Megaera, sub-Tyrant of Sarronnyn and regent of Recluce."

Hyel merely nods without speaking.

"You claim no title?" Joris asks of Creslin.

"There are no titles in Westwind. I would not claim any if there were."

Hyel turns toward Klerris's black-robed figure, raising his eyebrows.

"Klerris, formerly of Fairhaven and still of the Black order."

"Damned wizard . . ." This time Zarlen speaks.

"That may be, but I am mostly a healer."

"Wouldn't hurt to have one," offers Thoirkel, speaking for the first time since greeting Freigr in the harbor.

"The real question is, where will you stay?" muses Hyel. "We are not suited . . . and little building is done . . . has been done—"

Creslin smiles. "I suspect that we may be able to adapt one of the empty fisher cots until we can build something."

"No masons or carpenters here . . . not now," observes Joris.

"We'll manage."

A look passes between Zarlen and Joris.

Creslin catches the look, and his guts tighten, but he smiles pleasantly. "It's been a long voyage. Perhaps one of you would be kind enough to spar a bit with me." He ignores Megaera's indrawn breath.

This time, Hyel and Zarlen exchange glances.

"Well, ummm . . . begging your pardon, ser, but that could cause—" Hyel begins.

"Nonsense," insists Creslin heartily. "This is such a small community that if I stand on position, I shall have no exercise at all, except for lifting stones and hewing timbers."

"But . . . blades?"

"Creslin . . ." Megaera's voice is low.

"This is really uncalled for, " Joris interjects.

Creslin shrugs. "Then perhaps a friendly wrestling match—"

"Still . . ." Joris shakes his head. "What earthly reason—"

"Because, if you will, I stand for the Duke." Creslin's voice turns as cold as the winter storms, and coldness radiates from him.

Even Klerris steps back.

Zarlen grins as he looks at the redhead, ignoring the byplay between the officers and Creslin.

"Surely, we have a few wooden blades," interposes Hyel, sweat beading his forehead as he compares Zarlen's height and muscles to Creslin's and notes the head's difference between the two.

"A pair, I think," adds Joris with a resigned shrug. "I'll get them."

Creslin almost grins as Megaera's body relaxes fractionally. But her eyes flare as they rest on Creslin. He tries not to swallow, knowing what he must do and knowing that Megaera will scarcely be pleased.

"You think this . . . exercise is necessary?" temporizes Hyel.

"Unfortunately, yes," says Creslin.

Zarlen looks down at Creslin, then at Megaera, and smiles faintly. Thoirkel looks from Zarlen to Creslin, not quite shaking his head. Hyel looks over the parchments still in his hand, as if to extract some meaning from between the scripted lines.

Klerris lays a hand on Megaera's sleeve, which she starts to shake off, then stops as she looks into the wizard's eyes.

"Here we are," announces Joris jovially, returning with two white-oak wands with sword grips and hilts. He offers them to Creslin, who takes the slightly shorter one. Zarlen nods as he receives the other.

Without speaking, Hyel, Joris, and Thoirkel step back to the eastern wall of the keep. Megaera and Klerris remain by the doorway.

Zarlen smiles at Megaera, then leads with the white-oak wand.

Creslin waits. Zarlen's wand weaves toward him.

Creslin moves his own blade and deflects the bigger man's attack once, twice, and again. His blade is seemingly independent of his eyes. He has scarcely moved as Zarlen has brought bone-crushing force against him, yet none of the man's strokes even graze him.

"A dancer, are you?"

Zarlen's oak wand moves faster, yet Creslin remains untouched. Then, like lightning, Creslin's wand slashes.

Cluunk.

Zarlen shakes his wrist, where a red welt already rises, looks at his empty hand, and at the white-oak wand on the stones. His eyes flame as he glares at Creslin.

"Berserker . . ."

The whisper comes from Klerris, but Creslin's short blade is already out even as Zarlen drives his blued steel toward him with impossible speed. Impossible speed or not, Creslin is not where the blade is when it strikes, and the short sword flashes twice.

Zarlen's eyes glaze as he looks down at his blade on the

stones, just before his knees buckle. Creslin waits only long enough to ensure that the man is dead before cleaning his blade on Zarlen's tunic.

Hyel's mouth is wide open. Joris is pale, as is Megaera.

Creslin looks at Hyel, then at the body. "I'm sorry that was necessary, but . . . " He shrugs. "He'd already planned to kill me and have his way with my wife."

Hyel closes his mouth and looks toward Thoirkel.

The dark-haired young soldier looks from Creslin to Hyel and back again. Finally he moistens his lips. "Ah . . ."

Creslin waits, as does Hyel.

"Ah . . . Zarlen said . . . no wizard could stand 'gainst cold steel. No woman, witch or not, neither."

"He was wrong in both cases, apparently," Creslin observes mildly.

Hyel nods to Thoirkel and to the body. The young soldier begins to drag the heavy corpse toward the back doorway of the long room.

"What are you?" asks Joris.

Creslin looks from Klerris to Megaera. Klerris shrugs. Megaera looks away, but Creslin nearly winces at the flames in her eyes before her head turns. He looks back to Joris and Hyel.

"I'm one of your regents." He pauses. "I was the consort-assign of Westwind. I'm the only man ever trained by the Westwind arms-master, and I walked the Westhorns in the dead of winter to escape marrying the woman I married. I'm told that I'm also a Storm Wizard, and the Duke named both of us regents of Recluce, to hold and strengthen the land for him as we can." He bows slightly. "Does that help?"

"Shit . . ." Only Creslin hears the inaudible murmur from Thoirkel.

Joris looks at Klerris. "How good a Storm Wizard is he?"

"Better than any I've ever known; he was born to it."

Creslin looks at Klerris. Even Megaera looks up.

"Does the Duke know all this?" asks Hyel tiredly.

"Why do you think we're here?" Megaera says with near-equal fatigue in her voice. "Do you really think the Duke liked the idea of having two wizards from Westwind and Sarronnyn under his roof?"

"I think you'd better take the cot I've been using, at least until we can get something . . . more suitable," suggests the guard captain.

Joris nods. "I'll show you to it, since I am certain that the captain and Hyel have some cargo to discuss."

"The horses?" Creslin asks, looking at Freigr.

"I'll find you later, and you can walk back with me to get them, if that's all right."

Creslin nods, and the three wizards follow the swarthy man through the still-open doorway.

LXIX

"The storms were unusually severe, Jenred, even for winter in the gulf."

"Severe enough to sink three schooners and leave the Duke's sloop untouched?" asks the High Wizard sardonically.

"Klerris was on board the sloop," offers another voice.

"What about the other healer?"

"And I suppose a pair of master healers could suddenly learn to build storms that severe?" Jenred's voice has become louder. "Don't give me another excuse, like 'the White bitch helped him.' She's there only because she has no choice."

The chamber becomes silent.

Finally a voice from the last row speaks, tiredly. "You've disagreed with everyone. What do you suggest?"

Jenred smiles, a cold, white smile. "Nothing."

"What—"

"Let the Duke get away with this?"

"The Legend-holders will . . ."

The High Wizard Waits quietly until the tumult subsides. "Let us consider the situation. After a generation of hard work, subterfuge, and treachery, the Blacks within Fairhaven and Candar have raised a worthy champion. That champion has fled to a huge and worthless isle off Candar. He is tied to a White witch, and he wants little to do with the continent. He also owes something to the Duke of Montgren.

"From his isle, Creslin could clearly destroy any fleet sent against him. He can also protect the Duke's two ships and a few others, but no more. He has no gold, or not much, and few allegiances.

"We leave the Duke's ships alone, and any few ships that Creslin might purchase or build. We sink any others from Candar that approach Recluce. In the meantime, we can always encourage the eastern continents to attack. It would cost us very little, and it would keep Recluce busy. At the same time, we will finish the great highway and consolidate White rule. After a while, Creslin will die, and Recluce will wither away."

"But the Blacks will flock to Recluce," protests another member of the White Council.

"What about Nordla and Hamor?"

"So? How will the Blacks get there? It will take years, and they will be weaker, and we will be the stronger." Jenred snorts. "As for the Nordlans and Hamorians, the only reason they would help Creslin would be for gold or goods, and he has no gold, and the isle produces no goods of note . . . even assuming that he had enough people to gather them."

"What about the western kingdoms?"

"Have they helped their supposed ally, the Duke? Will they send troops to Recluce?"

"The Marshall will have to send some."

"Fine. She cannot afford more than a small detachment.

Nor can the Tyrant. That just makes them weaker, since we have no interest in taking that wasteland anyway." Jenred smiles. "Think about it, friends. Think long about it."

LXX

ALONE IN THE single-room cot, after Joris's quick apology for its inadequacy and equally quick departure with Klerris, who is insisting on looking at another nearby empty cot, Creslin turns toward Megaera.

"You're nothing but a demon-driven killer," she says.

Creslin steps back.

"Don't worry, Creslin. I dare not hurt you, not unless I want to die, and that's the last thing I want. I wouldn't give sister dear the pleasure. Nor my dear cousin. And I certainly wouldn't wish to disgrace my best-betrothed husband."

"What—"

"Of course you don't understand. You were born in the Legend, and you don't understand. That's because you're a man. Give a man great power and he does great wrong. Sword and storm. So you killed that poor man. He couldn't have touched you."

"You're wrong."

"You provoked him so that you could kill him. Do you deny that?"

"No. But you're wrong."

"Do tell me, best-betrothed. Tell me how you are different from other men. Lie like every man."

Creslin sighs.

"Do we now have sighs of regret? Or of exasperation?"

"Are you going to listen, or is your mind made up?"

"He's dead, isn't he?"

"Megaera!" Creslin rolls her name off his tongue, and the sound booms like thunder, yet echoes like lightning. "This is a prison garrison. Every man in that keep has killed at least one person. Not in battle, but in cold blood. The Duke took the salvageable men back to defend Montgren. Zarlen would have kept up his provocation until I killed him or he killed me. You're right. I did challenge him. I did it in plain sight so that every other guard understands that attacking me or lusting for you is death." Creslin's eyes are like the ice of the Roof of the World.

"I am from Westwind, and I am of Westwind. And I do believe in the Legend. But I do kill. As little as possible, strange as it seems. The Legend of Ryba does not forbid violence or death, only senseless violence and death. You seem to have forgotten the difference. You also seem to forget that I also die, in a way, whenever someone dies in a storm I have created. In that way, I'm selfish. If Zarlen had forced me to use the winds against him, I would die again, and I've felt enough deaths."

Megaera's eyes remain bright, and dust streaks her cheeks. "Dead is still dead."

"I know. But I'm tired of reacting. If I had thought things through, half of the destruction I've caused with my creative and orderly powers would not have happened. This time I could see the whole chain of deaths—revenge, lust, and anger—stretched out." His eyes rake hers. "And I didn't notice you doing much to discourage that attention."

"You still don't understand. Not me, not women, and not life."

"I'm getting the horses. I expect you to be here when I get back."

"Where else could I go, O best-betrothed?"

He steps outside; she watches.

"Where else could I go, O best-betrothed?" The words ring in his ears as he closes the battered door behind him. Where else can either of them go?

"Are you all right?" asks Klerris, who stands outside an even more dilapidated stone cot less than twenty cubits away.

Creslin shakes his head, then looks down toward the pier and the breakwater, toward the *Griffin* and the horses he must reclaim.

The older wizard smiles wryly and crosses the sandy, stony ground that separates them. "After all the years, I still can't claim to understand Lydya."

"All the years . . ." muses Creslin. "All the years . . ." His eyes shift from the harbor below to Klerris. "Is Lydya as old as you are?"

Klerris gives a sheepish smile that makes him seem momentarily boyish. "Well, she has a bit better control of internal order than I do. She's . . . somewhat older."

Creslin lets his senses drift around the man, but the words ring true, and Klerris stands calmly waiting with the unvarying *solidness* that Creslin has come to associate with order. "Besides live forever and heal people, what else can you do?"

Klerris purses his lips. "Except for weather control—and very few, if any, of us can match your raw power—order magic is mostly limited to healing and strengthening things. There are some illusions we can create that don't involve chaos, like disappearing. We can put people to sleep without hurting them, unless they fall. And we're generally good with plants."

"Plants?"

Klerris points to a scraggly blue flower that droops from a thorn vine twining from half a dozen heaped rocks a cubit or so from Creslin's right foot. "Watch closely. It's not really obvious, but . . ."

A certain sense of power flows from Klerris toward the tiny blue flower . . . and slowly, at the deliberate pace of drops falling from a roof corner to a rain barrel long after the storm, the petals firm, the stem strengthens, and the color brightens.

"Now, Lydya and Marin, they can actually take a pearapple seedling and make it so the fruit will be sweeter or tarter, larger or smaller." He shrugs. "But most people aren't interested in growing plants or miracles that take years for the results to show."

"I suppose not. Magic is supposed to create instant results."

Klerris grins, boyishly again. "Magic itself is quick. It's the results that take time to become obvious. And unlike the skills of our friends, the White Wizards, our skills create results that are rather hard to undo."

Creslin can sense Megaera staring through the narrow window. Freigr walks down the dusty hillside road, and both horses are now tethered on the pier.

"I'll have to think about that." Creslin takes a deep breath. "In the meantime, I need to reclaim some horses. I think the good captain wants off Recluce."

LXXI

THE CENTER OF the white-misted mirror displays a black keep upon a black cliff. The black walls shimmer, as if they are not quite real.

Before the mirror, the High Wizard's lips move, but his words are not audible. Then he frowns, and only the ceiling reflects in the silver of the mirror. He walks toward the single narrow window in the stone wall.

Thrap!

"Come in."

Hartor edges through the door to the small chamber. "You heard?"

"Bah. I felt it. Who couldn't? The whole world screamed. I didn't want to bring it up in council." The High Wizard gestures to the chair closest to the door, then eases himself into a straight-backed seat.

Hartor sits down and looks at the blank mirror. "Do you have something in mind?"

Jenred nods slowly, his lips turning in an expression of disgust. "Yes. Leaving him alone."

"You were the one who claimed—"

"It doesn't matter what I claimed. I was wrong about his powers. But I wasn't wrong about his inclinations."

"So how do we deal with him?"

"Let the envoy from Hamor know that Creslin has on the island the treasures of Heaven, stolen from Westwind. Let the Westwind spies know that Hamor is thinking of attacking Recluce."

"Oh. Will it work?"

"Use a Compulsion on the Hamorians. No one will check there. They don't believe in magic."

"Any special images?"

"You might try the idea of the lances of winter. You know, from the Legend."

"Did they ever really exist?"

"Who knows?" Jenred shrugs. "They'd certainly like something like that. So they might be bold enough to attack Land's End. The Marshall might send a few troops, and anything she sends there won't come back."

"Can you be sure of that?"

Jenred nods. "Creslin's just the type that people follow."

"Doesn't that mean he'll be a danger?"

"No. Not to us. In a generation or two, they'll damn us for being short-sighted, but we can't afford to lose any more wizards and allies. So do what you can with Hamor. You might even let the Nordlans know first."

LXXII

CLICK . . .

The redheaded woman glances up, pausing briefly from her exercise routine, and extends her senses beyond the room into the morning air.

A chipmunk has dislodged a pebble and is skittering under the stone that serves as the doorstep to the cot. She smiles as her senses follow the hurrying rodent. Then the smile fades. "Back to work, Megaera. Back to work. He isn't the only one who can be as tough as green oak," she mutters to herself.

Sweat streaks down her flushed face, and her muscles burn, but she continues until she can no longer force her body into the proper patterns. Then she straightens and begins to take deep breaths, walking slowly around the narrow space she has created by shoving the heavy table and the chairs into a corner.

In a few moments she is to meet with Klerris for her lessons in the basic theory that her co-regent appears to spurn.

As she cools after having rearranged the cot again, she wets a worn towel with water from a pitcher and dabs herself into a more presentable state. ". . . really need to learn Klerris's tricks for removing dirt and grime from myself, not just from clothes . . ." she murmurs.

Then she combs her hair and uses two combs to hold her tresses away from her face, adjusts her faded gray work trousers and shirt, and steps out of the cot. She pauses.

Something, someone, waits around the corner of the small structure.

Fire? She shakes her head, then quickly lifts the heavy black stone that serves as a doorstop. She senses the lustful anticipation of the man who, knife in hand, waits for her to step on the path that will carry her past the corner of the cot toward the keep. Her stomach turns in response to his cold hatred.

Megaera eases forward, the small boulder held high, noting with her mind where the man stands. Finally she scuffs her foot and whistles softly, oh so softly, and casts an image on the path where he expects her to be.

A bearded figure lurches forward, grasping—

She brings the rock down with all of her strength and steps back.

Megaera looks at the semiconscious man who struggles to rise, to grasp the knife, the lust-hate still welling up within him. Deliberately she kicks the knife clear and again hoists the heavy rock. This time her aim is more accurate, and the bearded figure lies sprawled motionless on the clay. The thorough combination of human evil and chaos that writhes within the man—even though he is unconscious, dying—beats at her.

She swallows, forcing the bile back down her throat, but she does not hesitate. Creslin has taught her the value of swiftness, taught her well, and she reaches for the knife.

Should she take his manhood as well? That would be too gruesome . . . and also just plain disgusting. Instead, she slits his throat, easily, for the knife is sharp indeed, and he would have died from the fractured skull in any case. Healing was out of the question, at least for someone like the now-dead trooper.

After replacing the doorstop and thrusting the knife in her belt, she drags the body the few dozen paces to the keep. Then she checks her hair and garments to make sure that she appears more composed than she feels.

Thrap! Thrap!

Joris steps out, followed by Creslin and Hyel.

"What—"

"Light!"

Of the three, Creslin alone says nothing and just looks at her, his green eyes as blank as the heavy swells of the sea.

Her eyes fix Hyel, and she wills them to burn. "I don't appreciate your troopers attempting rape. I trust I won't be required to take care of your failures in discipline again. Next time I won't be kind enough to use cold steel." At her last statement, her stomach twists and she wants to damn Creslin for betraying her with his squeamish order.

Instead, she ignores his faint smile, though she would

like to lash out at him for understanding what is happening to her.

She watches Hyel, keeping him pinned with her eyes until he looks down, even though he stands a head taller.

"Yes, Regent . . ." the guard captain finally whispers.

"I leave the body and other disciplinary arrangements to you. Good day." She forces a cheerful smile and is gratified by the pallor on the faces of Hyel and Joris.

Creslin, still silent, seems to give a nod of approval, and she wants to strike him with every trail of chaos fire that she can seize. What is he turning her into? Why doesn't he understand? Will he ever understand? Knowing that he will not, she turns with careful and measured steps toward the more dilapidated cot downhill, which Klerris has begun to clean and otherwise restore.

She lets her senses gather while trying to ignore the mutters behind her.

". . . skull's caved in, and his throat's cut."

". . . must have hands like steel."

". . . how you live with her—"

"No, she permits me to live with her."

Creslin's cool comment, true as it is, chills her. Cannot he see what he has done to her? Done to the powers for which she has sacrificed so much for so long in order to learn? She tightens her lips and maintains her even steps toward the cot, ignoring the burning in her eyes and the tightness of her stomach.

LXXIII

AS THE REDHEAD'S angry departure leaves the three men and the body alone on the steps to the keep, Hyel shakes his head. "Never . . . asked to accept so much—"

Creslin snorts loudly.

"You find this—" Joris gestures at the body "—amusing, Lord Creslin?"

"No. He got what he deserved. Maybe not even that. Megaera's opposed to unnecessary violence." Creslin's voice sounds weary, even to himself.

"He was tired of living without women. Can you blame him for that? Isn't this sort of death a bit much?"

Creslin wants to shake his head. Is attempted rape enough to condemn someone to death? Then again, he himself has killed to forestall murder. He answers the dark-haired man slowly. "There will be women here before long. And, yes, I can blame your man. If not just for trying to violate a woman against her will, then for gross stupidity. Anyone who attacks a wizard should be prepared for the worst. Megaera is a White Wizard, and she could have burned him on the spot." He pauses but sees that Joris is not satisfied. "Sometime, when she is preoccupied, look at the scars upon her wrists. Those come from practicing her art when bound with cold iron."

Joris shivers. "She is that strong?"

Creslin sighs. "We may be young and untried in many ways, guardsmen, but do you think truly that the Duke would entrust Recluce to us just so he could buy a few blades and supplies?"

Joris clears his throat. "You mentioned women?"

Creslin nods. "Women, supplies . . ."

"How do you propose to pay for supplies, Lord Creslin?" asks Hyel sardonically. "With dried fish? That is all that is in your treasury."

"Some of it will be a gift of sorts. Some," Creslin shrugs, thinking of the gold chain that Lydya had recovered and Klerris has presented to him, "I'll have to pay for."

"You have high plans for this desert island."

Creslin is tired of the veiled warnings and cautions, of the skepticism, and of Hyel's doubting tones. His eyes flash, and he turns full on the tall man. For a moment he says nothing, and when he speaks, his voice is soft. "You doubted my skills until I murdered your tool. You doubt my co-regent's abilities until she leaves a corpse at your feet. Will you then continue to doubt? Or must I leave you as a corpse before you will dream again?"

"Hyel does not attempt to meet Creslin's eyes. "No one yet has succeeded in Recluce . . . my lord."

"I am scarcely no one, Hyel." Creslin laughs harshly. "And Megaera is certainly more than no one." He nods to both of the men. "I would like parchments and quills in the cot shortly. I trust that you will think about my words, deeply."

His first steps follow those of Megaera, but he has no interest in finding her quite yet. For all that he has said in her defense, Joris's question still rings in his head. Should a man die for lusting after what he cannot have? Is the act of forcing such lust upon another enough to justify murder? Yet what choice did Megaera have? And what is the difference between one death and another? She has said it: "Dead is dead."

He stretches his legs, then lets his booted feet carry him uphill and along the trail toward the eastern cliffs.

How is he that much different from the nameless guard? Certainly he has thought about forcing his attentions on Megaera. How thin is the line between thought and action?

Behind him, two men watch him and his shadow for a time, their eyes falling occasionally to the corpse at their feet.

LXXIV

"CAN YOU INSTILL order in plants?" Creslin studies the drawing that Klerris has set before him. "Isn't that what you did with that blue flower the other day?"

"Order? Blue flower?" Klerris smoothes the paper into

place over a set of drawings that show the needed expansions to the keep. The Black Wizard places small stones on the coarse paper to hold down the corners against the stiff breeze that gusts in through the single window.

"To make them grow healthier. Or to determine which plants will produce the most fruit, the sturdiest grain . . . that sort of thing."

"Oh, that. I can strengthen them. Certainly Lydya can do more. I suppose I could too. Why?"

"We're getting additional people. People need food."

"Creslin," Klerris says slowly, "it's too dry here to grow much of anything, even if the winter is mild, without cold rain or snow."

"You're speaking of the regular kind of plants."

"Ah . . ." Megaera interrupts.

Creslin looks up from the table, the only steady table in Recluce, he suspects, borrowed from Hyel for the needs of the co-regency. The table and three chairs fill nearly all of the cot's floor space.

"The plans for the . . . residence . . ." Megaera reminds the young Storm Wizard. "Unless you want to risk dying in your sleep sooner or later."

"Oh." Creslin looks down at the paper before him. "What's this big room?"

"Dining hall. You'll have to entertain," Klerris explains.

"This?" asks Megaera.

"An extra bedroom," Klerris admits.

Megaera's eyes flash. "We agreed that Creslin and I will have separate bedrooms and that guests will be housed in adjoining guest houses, to be built later."

"Then it must be a private study," Klerris adds mildly.

"Then call it that. I'll certainly need one," Megaera says.

"This will take some work—"

"You're going to have to use the troops."

"Not until after the keep is expanded."

"You're right about that," Megaera agrees while her eyes again study the rough plan on the table.

"What about clearing away the dirt and rock?" Creslin asks.

"I can do that," Megaera notes.

Klerris nods. "Do you want to?"

"I'd better do it now, hadn't I?" The redhead's voice is flat, distant.

The room is silent for a time before she speaks again. "Why can Creslin use his powers to kill people and still be a Black or a Gray Wizard? I thought that all destruction was linked to chaos." Megaera's green eyes fix on the slight black-haired man.

"It's not *what* magic is used for; it's what kind of power is used." Klerris's voice slips into the well-worn grooves of a teacher who has explained repeatedly. "Order magic is involved with the ordering of things, sometimes rearranging, sometimes building. Chaos work breaks the bonds between things, destroys them, if you will, through fire or collapse." He looks at Creslin. "How have you used your powers to kill?"

Creslin leans back in his chair, nearly unbalancing himself at the directness of the question. "I always called the winds."

"What did you ask of them?"

"To build a storm, sometimes with hail or freezing rain."

The Black Wizard looks at Megaera. "Do you see?"

"But that's not fair! That means that an evil man can use order to kill and destroy."

"Within limits . . . if he is a very strong wizard, and if he plans ahead well."

"Would you explain that?" Creslin asks. Although he knows the answer, he wants Megaera to hear it from someone else.

Klerris shrugs. "Take Creslin. If ten armed men jump from behind that door at him, he has virtually no chance to use magic. You generally can't call a storm that quickly, and you can't count on being able to do it in all weather conditions . . . not easily. A White Wizard with equal strength could fry all ten of those men in an eye-blink."

Megaera muses for a moment. "But why can't a wizard do both White and Black magic then? You say that it's the kind of magic, not the use to which it is put that matters."

Klerris laughs. "It's hard to be two things at once. For example, while you can for a while both love and hate Creslin, harboring both feelings over time will tear you apart inside. That's why people end up either loving or hating something or someone about whom they feel strongly. The same is true of magic. Some are called to order, some to chaos, and some can choose. I've known of only one Gray Wizard, and she died very young. It's theoretically possible, but I doubt that many could manage it." He smiles sadly. "You also have to be sane to use order. Not loving, not necessarily compassionate, but sane."

"But it's not fair."

Klerris understands the thought behind her words. "You are not called to chaos, thankfully. You can choose. Creslin has no such choice."

"What do you mean?"

"Why do you think Creslin doesn't like to use his powers to kill?"

"He gets sick." She grimaces. "I know that too well, but I don't understand how a man can lose his guts if he calls a storm to kill but remain perfectly calm if he uses a blade."

"I don't," Creslin responds. "But the reaction isn't nearly so great with the blade. You don't feel what I feel when I use a blade because it's shadowed with your own anger." His stomach remains quiet, reassuring him of the truth of his statement.

"But why?" persists the redhead.

"Because," answers the Black Wizard, "death is a form of chaos, and order that causes death creates stresses of a logical nature within the magician. That's why Black magicians move away from the violent uses of order as they grow older. A young, healthy person can take that stress for a while, but not forever."

"So . . ." Megaera sighs. "How do I learn order?"

Klerris shrugs. "I wish I could give you an easy answer. There are less than a handful of people who have made that transition. None would share the particulars, but the first step is to renounce all uses of chaos, even the silly little things like finger-fire."

"I have to give up . . ." She shakes her head. "I don't know."

Neither man says anything, nor do Klerris or Megaera appear to notice the dampness on Creslin's cheeks as he looks away and out through the small window, the one that shows the hillside to the north where the existing keep will be expanded.

He swallows but says nothing as his hand reaches out and pins down the nearest corner of the paper. Although he could still the breeze, the coolness is welcome.

"Hyel won't like his troops being used as builders," Klerris adds.

Creslin looks at the rough plans on the table again. "We don't have much choice. Neither does he."

"Are you going to tell him that?"

"Who else?"

"Of course," adds Megaera. "Another chance for best-betrothed to establish his authority."

"Don't you think that is a little unfair?" asks Klerris.

"Yes. But most men are unfair by nature."

Klerris begins to roll up the plans.

After a time, Creslin frowns, his eyes still focused elsewhere. "We need trees, too. Can you get seedlings?"

"Trees?"

The silver-haired man with the sun-tinged skin and the recently calloused hands nods. "They use aqueducts in Sarronnyn to bring the water from the mountains."

"Creslin . . ."

"He's off somewhere," Megaera interjects from the other

side of the table, her eyes turning from Creslin and out through the narrow window on the wave-tossed winter sea beyond the breakwater.

LXXV

"You want them . . . us . . . to act like common laborers?" The garrison commander's voice is not quite disrespectful.

"No. I want them to earn their pay." Creslin adds, "They just might survive that way."

Hyel's hand goes to his sword. "Even you wouldn't—"

"How do your men like eating fish every day? Or having just enough dried fruit to keep them barely healthy? Eating lime rinds to ensure that their teeth stay firm?"

The grim expression on the lanky guard captain's face is replaced with one of puzzlement. "They don't. But what—"

"It's clear enough. Fairhaven isn't likely to want to lose any more ships. They won't touch the Duke's ships, either one of them. And they won't touch the ships that carry refugees from Candar or anywhere else. But they will make it known that any ship trading with Recluce cannot trade with Fairhaven, and who besides a few smugglers will risk losing the White Wizards' gold for our few coppers? Yet I wouldn't be surprised if we had five hundred more souls here in Land's End in less than a year. We need a larger keep for the soldiers, and one with separate quarters for female guards—"

"Women?" Hyel's tone turns colder than the troubled northern seas beyond the breakwater.

"I expect a detachment of Westwind guards," Creslin notes coolly. "And perhaps one from Sarronnyn. They'll have some consorts and children, but not enough. That might provide a bit of interest for you and your men, assuming they don't mind meeting women who are likely to be their betters with blades."

Hyel's eyes flicker from Creslin to Megaera, who has remained slightly behind Creslin's shoulder, almost as if in a shadow of her own making. "Do you think this is wise, lady?"

Megaera shrugs. "Wisdom comes after survival, Guard Captain. Without . . . the Storm Wizard here, and the troops he is calling in, you would be dead in less than a season."

Hyel takes a deep breath. "This all . . . will take some getting used to."

"You'd better start quickly," observes Megaera tartly. "Zarlen wouldn't have lasted against a Westwind guard much longer than he did against Creslin."

"But my men, building quarters—"

"Don't worry. The newer guards will have plenty of building projects as well. We need an inn by the harbor."

"An inn?" Both Megaera and Hyel look at Creslin.

"Why not?" Creslin grins. "We will have visitors. We might as well separate them from their coins legitimately. And a public room, controlled by a few trustworthy guards, might be worthwhile for everyone."

"Couldn't some of the guards start on that now?" asks Hyel.

Creslin purses his lips, frowns, then shrugs. "I don't see why not, but first we'll need to see if Klerris can draw up some rough plans."

"Does it have to be all that big?" Megaera asks. "Couldn't you plan it so that we could build it bigger later?"

"Well, the public room . . ."

Hyel nods. "Better to build that pretty big to begin with."

Creslin clears his throat. "There's one other thing."

The half-smile fades from Hyel's face. "Yes?"

"I'm going to spend part of each morning training your

men and part of the morning teaching you the conditioning routines."

"If you're replacing us with—"

"Hyel," snaps Creslin, "I'm not replacing anyone. Before this is over, we're going to need every single person on this isle who can wield a blade. Besides, I don't want to see another Westwind, where all of the arms are controlled by women. And Megaera doesn't want to see someplace like Montgren or Fairhaven, where women are regarded as inferiors. But the only way there's likely to be equality around here is if your men are actually good enough to command respect." Creslin stares at the tall man.

Hyel takes a half-step backward.

"That includes you as well," Creslin adds. "I'll be here early tomorrow to tell your men what I just told you."

"I would appreciate that." Hyel wipes his forehead.

Creslin nods and turns, walking toward the open doorway.

Megaera smiles brightly, falsely, at Hyel, who retreats another half-step.

Outside, Megaera steps up beside Creslin. "Best-betrothed, how are you going to do all of this?"

Creslin smiles. "I'm not. You're the co-regent. I thought that you could supervise either the harbor projects or those here at the keep. Klerris is going to work on the orchards and the plants, but I want him to teach both of us how."

She shakes her head, and the flame-red strands fly out against the wind. "You intend to build a kingdom overnight to challenge Fairhaven?"

"No. Recluce won't challenge any country. We just won't be challenged."

"You mean that. You really mean that." Megaera ponders for a moment, glancing from the empty pier to the small keep and the small cot they so uneasily share. When she looks up, she sees that Creslin's quick strides have taken him toward the gnarled orchard on the hillside above the keep.

A faint smile crosses her lips.

Below, in the harbor, a fishing boat beats in toward the pier, and sea gulls circle the single mast, hoping for an easy meal. Two women push a cart down the dusty road to off-load the fish for gutting and drying on the hillside frames under the old nets that hold off the birds, or most of them.

Megaera looks back toward the hillside where Creslin stands by the wall next to the orchard of gnarled pearapples. She shakes her head again, but this time the gesture holds a wistful sadness.

LXXVI

THE HEALER STANDS before the Marshall, her faded-green travel clothes still slightly damp from the melted snow.

"You asked to see me?" The Marshall's flint-blue eyes take in the slightly built, dark-haired woman.

"Yes, Dylyss, I did. I've come to collect for Creslin."

"Your name?"

"I'm known as Lydya. Werlynn was . . . from my family."

The Marshall does not reply immediately, nor do her eyes leave the healer. "You're not just a healer."

"No. I never said I was."

The Marshall's lips quirk. "What are you collecting?"

"Seeds, cheese, weapons—and the detachment you promised Korweil. The new regents of Recluce would appreciate the aid."

"Creslin didn't send you?"

"No."

"The seeds . . . we have some in trade from Suthya. They'll do us little enough good. And there's always extra

cheese. Older weapons? There are some we could spare."
The Marshall pauses.

"And guards?"

"I'll ask for volunteers. The other kind wouldn't do him
any good, would they?"

Lydya smiles faintly. "No. And losing those volunteers
will help you as well."

"Tell me, healer . . . what is she like?"

Lydya shakes her head. "That, Marshall, I do not know.
Only that you and Ryessa will create the greatest good and
the greatest evil that Candar will ever know."

"That's what Werlynn said."

"I know."

"Will you stay a time?"

"Only until all things are gathered. I have to collect from
Ryessa."

LXXVII

"But I'm a White." Megaera glances at the gnarled
pearapple tree beyond the tumbled stone wall. A gust of
wind whips sandy dust across her boots, for the road they
stand on is little more than a trail.

"Names do not matter," Klerris observes mildly. "You
have the ability, although it will be harder for you.
Whatever you do, do not try to remove disorder."

"What? But isn't that the purpose?"

"It is," responds the Black Wizard, picking up a stone
and absently replacing it on the wall, "but you cannot
remove disorder through the power of disorder, at least not
until you are *very* accomplished. How can you stop killing
with more killing?"

"You can reduce it," offers Creslin, scuffing his boots in
the hard red clay.

"True." Klerris smiles in the afternoon sunlight. "If you kill those who kill hundreds, the killing will be reduced, but your potential for destruction is that much greater. That is why Megaera so fears your blade, not because you can kill, but because even without using your powers for order, you become a White force of destruction."

"I've felt that way, but I didn't know why, exactly," admits the redhead.

"Now you know." Klerris points to the pearapple tree. "Look at the tree with your senses . . ."

Creslin complies, seeing the faint underlying blackness of order and the red-tinged white streaks of chaos.

"But why can't I just remove the white?" asks Megaera. Klerris sighs. "Go ahead."

Creslin holds his breath as Megaera, though not moving from her stance behind the wall, seems to enfold the tree.

She withdraws, and the whiteness is indeed gone, with only the faint blackness remaining. "See? I did it!"

"Yes, you did." Klerris's voice is neutral.

Creslin watches the gnarled tree, watches as the remaining blackness stretches as if to cover the space the whiteness has departed, watches as the blackness thins . . . and vanishes.

Crackkkkk . . .

The tree splits,, but even before the trunk fully cracks, a sense of dryness emanates from the winter-bare branches.

"It will take a few weeks to fall over, but this tree is dead," Klerris says.

"But why?" protests Megaera. "You knew that would happen! You let me kill that tree."

"Because," Klerris explains in his patient teaching voice, "both order and chaos are energy. If anything living has too much chaos as part of its being, removal of the chaos lowers the vital force below the minimum for life. A good chaos-healer can cure some sicknesses, but it is always a risky process, especially with the cases of sickness where chaos actually changes the body."

"Is anything all chaos?" Creslin looks beyond Klerris at the next gnarled tree.

"Darkness, no. Nothing living, anyway. It takes order to hold a body together. That's why most of the Whites die young, except for the body-stealers." The Black Wizard straightens and points to the now-dead tree. "Consider that an object lesson. You can usually defeat chaos only by strengthening order. You especially, Megaera, need to keep that in mind."

But the redhead is looking at the ground, her lips pursed tightly, her hands clasped behind her.

LXXVIII

CRESLIN DEMONSTRATES AGAIN, his white-oak wand arcing in slow motion.

Thoirkel, the black-haired soldier with the scraggly beard who had first met Creslin on the pier, follows the maneuver slowly, trying to duplicate the ease displayed by the silver-haired man.

Creslin stops him halfway through. "Your wrist . . ."

Thoirkel steps back and begins anew.

This time Creslin does not watch the maneuver fully but concentrates on the man himself, looking at the order and chaos warring within Thoirkel. Then he reaches out, and as Klerris has taught him to do with the plants and the mountain sheep, strengthens the order within the soldier.

"Oh . . ." Thoirkel staggers, shakes his head, and lowers the wand. He brushes his lank black locks off his forehead, then looks down at the white-oak wand in his hand.

"You'll be all right, but you need more practice." Creslin nods to the next man. "You are?"

"Narran, ser."

Like Thoirkel, threads of white and black intertwine within the soldier; unlike Thoirkel, the white threads are strong in themselves. Creslin sighs silently, hoping that not many of the men are as chaos-dominated as Narran. He raises his wand again.

LXXIX

CRESLIN SLOWS HIS steps by the orchard that he and Klerris have reclaimed. The pearapples are just beginning to bloom, earlier than in the lands of Candar. And, too, the frosts will be later on Recluce than in Candar.

Megaera's footsteps scrunch in the sandy clay of the road as she struggles to catch up with him.

He drops into a walk along the low stone wall separating the trail that will one day be a real road from the orchard. Farther south, along the eastern shore, the trail rises to the top of the black cliffs, to the site he and Klerris have picked out for the holding, and where Megaera has cleared the ground to bare rock and he has begun the stonework.

"You do . . . this . . . for . . . pleasure?" the red-head pants, sweat rolling down her face. Her thick hair is twisted into a bun at the back of her head. "With . . . boots . . . on?"

"Hardly for pleasure. It's to make me a more efficient killing machine. You don't fight when wearing sandals or going barefoot." He smiles sardonically, setting his hand on the stone, then removing it from the sun-warmed heat. "You ready for the next part?"

"Next part?"

"The rest of the hill?"

"Not . . . yet . . ." Her breath is more regular now, but Creslin avoids looking at her, for even when she is disheveled and sweaty, he will find her desirable, and that desire will bring both of them pain.

Instead, his eyes travel across the gnarled trees that have begun to show new life, his senses reaching out to strengthen the flow within them. Beyond the trees, he sees the tan wool of one of the few mountain sheep that he and Klerris have coaxed out of the hills and into the regenerating greenery above Land's End.

Some of the green is from the makeshift aqueduct and some from the tougher grasses that Klerris has coaxed into covering the clayey soil.

"What are you looking at?"

"The sheep."

"Sometimes you're like two different people. Working with stone and plants and animals, you can be so . . ."

Creslin takes a deep breath, not wanting to deal with the question she has raised. "Ready?"

"No. But I'll follow you. Anything you can do . . . I'll learn." She wipes her forehead with her upper arm and takes another deep breath.

Creslin begins to jog along the short flat before the trail turns and heads upward and due south behind the rock jumbles that build to the high, black stone cliffs.

Behind him, Megaera's lighter boots echo his steps.

On the winds, he can hear her murmurs between her gasping breaths. "Westwind . . . bitches can . . . I . . . can . . ."

He would smile, except that he has felt the cold fury of that steel will of hers. He forces his pace into regularity, trying instead to think about the other provisions that must be made: provisions for hay, for vegetables, for some sort of cows to provide milk and cheese. And trees. Klerris keeps telling him that trees, rain, and time, plus some order magic, could turn Recluce into a garden.

In the meantime, Klerris is working with Hyel. The guards are also learning stonework and expanding the keep, particularly the guard quarters in process. Except for a few, who would rather garden.

Creslin begins to pant halfway up the slope, and his legs begin to burn.

"Finally . . . bastard's hurting . . ."

The glee in Megaera's mutterings forces him to pick up his legs, to deny the fatigue, and to push the last hundred cubits uphill.

"Whoooff . . ."

He slows, looking over his shoulder to see the redhead stumble, then wobble back upright. Quickly he turns his head and drops into a walk. A walk for the last kay will supply enough conditioning. He realizes, as he has for the past eight-day, how much work it will be to regain his former shape, and how much more tiring it is to be active in the moderate heat of Recluce than in the chill of Westwind.

The chill. Whatever happens, he will always miss the clean cold of the Roof of the World.

By the time he is within a half kay of the partly built stone shell of what will be the co-regents' dwelling, carefully planned with separate bedrooms, Megaera has caught up with him.

Creslin walks straight past the stonework, past the raised-stone cistern that he, Klerris, Joris, and several guards completed even before the foundation stones were laid. At the edge of the cliff where, before too long, there will be a stone-paved terrace and a stone wall, he pauses and looks down at the long swells of the dark green water.

Behind him, Megaera splashes her sweaty, dusty face with cool water. He waits until she is finished, then walks back and follows her example, enjoying the coolness of the water from the stone basin fed by the cistern. Klerris had located the spring, and had shown both Megaera and Creslin the tracing of order lines. Megaera, somewhat surprised, had had no problem at all.

"You're not necessarily White," Klerris had said.

But she had pointedly ignored his words. Creslin shakes

his head at the recollection, then splashes more water across his brow. The dripping locks over his ears remind him that his hair has again grown too long.

There is so much to do, for he has no doubt that the White Wizards will provide yet another challenge.

After wiping his face on the shoulder of the worn shirt he uses for exercise and stonework, he takes a last swallow of water from cupped hands and straightens. Should he cut stone, or should he mortar?

Megaera is surveying the low line of stones that will become the northern wall of the structure. "For a warrior and a wizard, you do good stonework." Her voice is light.

"We try to please." He steps toward the pile of rough-cut stone, each stone carried nearly a quarter kay from the jumble to the south. Soon he will have to carry stone again before either cutting or mortaring further.

Finally he picks up an odd-sized chunk, letting his senses enfold it as he carries it over to the waist-high block dragged nearly a kay by three horses to serve as a cutting table. He searches for the order lines, the places of weakness, the stresses, then tries to visualize what the finished stone might look like.

Like so . . . or if he strikes it there . . . He lifts the heavy iron mallet and the order-hardened wedge. *Clung . . . clung . . .*

Megaera has disappeared into the rock jumble, and in time she returns staggering under the weight of a large black stone, which she deposits near the cut pile.

Creslin wipes his forehead and sets another cut stone in the row. While his abilities and strengths are improving, the house still appears like an endless undertaking.

Clung . . .

More cut stones appear, but as they do, so do more rough stones arrive from Megaera. Creslin pauses, taking a deep breath and setting down the mallet. Megaera looks at him, then plops herself on a low wall that has been mortared and long since order-set.

"Why do you drive yourself so hard?" he asks.

She looks up slowly. "Am I that different from you? How many people insist on running up desert hills in boots to cut stone? How many people work at everything from developing water systems to gardening from dawn until after dusk?"

"Do I have a choice?"

"Do I?"

He looks away from the piercing green eyes, away from the reddened but still creamy and freckled skin, and his fingers tighten around the wedge he holds before he sets it next to the mallet. His eyes drift back to her. A stray breeze caresses her forehead.

"Stop that . . . please," she says.

"That wasn't me."

"I'm sorry. I shouldn't have blamed you." Her tone is soft.

"Sometimes it is me. But not now."

"Why do you like me?" Her eyes look out on the dull dark green of the sea below the cliffs.

"If I have to explain . . ." He sighs, knowing that she will persist. "You're honest, and you hate scheming. When you weren't so tormented, you could laugh at the absurdity of things. I know you still could, if it weren't for me."

"It's not you. It's being tied to you." She shifts her weight, but her green eyes remain fixed on the stillness of the sea.

"If you weren't tied—"

"Creslin, somewhere inside that driven killer is a sweet man, but you know there's too much blood and tears tying us. Even the greatest order-master born couldn't break the tie. Only my death will do that, and I'm too young to consider it."

In time he sighs and picks up the mallet. She stretches, rises, and heads back for another stone.

LXXX

CRESLIN SHAKES HIS head, realizing from the light that it is well past dawn, well past the time he should have risen.

Thrap!

Megaera? Where is she?

He sits upright, looking from the low pallet on the stone floor toward the closed door between their unfinished rooms. Only the two bedrooms at the seaward end of the holding are done, and the partial roof would let in rain, should it ever fall on the northern end of the desolate island. Through the unglassed and unshuttered window, he can see the high, hazy gray clouds that promise yet another hot and rainless day.

"Put on your leathers, Creslin." Klerris's voice penetrates the closed door to the hallway.

The silver-haired man stretches and stumbles to the door, opening it. "Where's Megaera?"

"Outside in the washroom." As usual, the Black Wizard's faded robes are dustless and clean.

"Why are you here so early?" Creslin wears only ragged undershorts. He looks back at the pegs in the stone alcove that will be a closet someday.

"To tell you that your ship's coming in."

"I don't have a ship." The co-regent of Recluce struggles toward the outside washroom. A shave will make him presentable, and the cold shower might restore some of his energy.

"It's a Suthyan coaster flying the banner of Westwind. She'll make Land's End by mid-morning." Klerris looks happier and more alive than Creslin can recall; the Black Wizard matches the younger man's steps.

"All right. Just let me gather myself together."

"Not that much to gather together . . ."

He ignored Megaera's whispered mumblings from behind the shower screen and begins to shave. Before he has finished, the redhead, her hair wet and plastered away from her face, has retreated, wrapped in a damp robe that barely conceals her shapely thighs.

"I'd appreciate it if you'd stop that, too . . ."

The shower is stone-cold—the sun-warmed water has already been used by Megaera—and Creslin shivers through it, too tired to feel virtuous.

"You're pushing yourself too hard." Klerris turns and studies the sky to the east, above the sea.

"Why not? At least I can collapse and not dream. At least I can point to another field, another orchard, another line of dressed and mortared stone. Even to another tiny bit of understanding the great and massive forces of order."

"You need to talk to Lydya."

"All right, I'll talk to Lydya. Where is she?"

"On the ship. How do you think I knew when the ship's coming in?"

"Hadn't thought about it." Creslin gathers up his razor and shorts, wraps his single threadbare towel around his midsection, and marches back toward his near-empty bed chamber.

Shortly Klerris provides each of them with pearapples and bread, which Creslin eats while sitting on the only completed terrace wall, the waist-high barrier that will flank the walkway to the guest house that may never be built.

Megaera eats as silently as Creslin, taking slow, small bites.

He does not look at her, for he can no longer afford such glances, not when each glance reminds them both of how lovely he finds her.

The walk down toward the pier is equally silent, although Klerris points out the sails of the coaster from the hillside. "We should make it to the pier before she clears the breakwater."

Creslin watches as an escort boat is dropped and precedes the ship toward the pier. The Suthyan coaster—its three masts making it the largest ship Creslin has ever seen—waddles across the harbor in the light wind, winching itself along on the escort's cable made fast to the heavy stone bollard on the pier.

Creslin lifts his senses into the winds, searching the seas out beyond the small harbor, but finds no other ships, no feeling of the chaos-white that marks the wizards of Fairhaven.

As he returns to full possession of his body, the coaster eases up to dock. Two seamen leap ashore with a second mooring line.

The three wizards walk toward the gangway that is being lowered. At the end of the pier, armed, stands a squad from the keep, led by Joris.

Creslin finds himself leading the way.

A balding man in a worn gold vest thrown over a sailor's blue trousers and shirt greets Creslin and Megaera. "The co-regents? You look just like the sketches, except younger. There's a lot here, and we'd like to get it off-loaded. This harbor's small for us, and the winds tell that the storms will be sweeping in 'fore long. Not before tonight, you understand, but it's going to take some time—"

"What do you need from us?"

"Your seal, something, on the ladings once we get everything off. Maybe your clerk could do it for you. Understand the business of ruling—"

"We're shorter on clerks than on regents at the moment. Once you unload, we'll handle your documents."

Before Creslin completes his sentence, the nervous captain is halfway back aboard his ship, and a muscular, black-haired woman, with a familiar smile that he cannot place, has stepped before them.

"Guard Captain Shierra, Regent Creslin, Regent Megaera." The inclination of her head is as much a salute as either is likely to get.

"Did you have any trouble with the wizards?" Creslin asks.

"No. But then," the woman's face crinkles into a smile, and she gestures to the mid-mast, "we insisted that the captain fly our banner. One war schooner did follow us. It left halfway across the gulf."

Creslin's eyes note the crossed black-and-silver lightnings on the azure, and he returns the smile. "You seem to have a full group."

"Two and a half squads, actually."

"There are your quarters, rough as they are. We'll discuss other needs once you look things over." Creslin gestures up toward the newly completed walls of the addition to the keep. "We might as well get whatever you brought offloaded."

"Some horses or carts would help. The . . . healer . . . was apparently quite persuasive. We brought field rations sufficient for nearly a season, medicines, seeds, and enough weapons—older, but serviceable—for another two squads."

Creslin keeps his lips closed, but Megaera smiles as she senses his amazement.

"The healer also purchased a range of woodworking and stone-handling tools in Suthya. The forward hold is half-filled with surplus timber owed the Marshall; it was unsuitable for cold weather, or so the Marshalle claimed when she sent the voucher."

"Now that is true wizardry." Creslin finally laughs.

Shierra shares the laugh for a moment, then turns toward the guards lining the deck. "Let's off-load!"

Creslin looks beyond the guards, in full war packs, beyond the consorts and the handful of children, less than a half-dozen, and sees the figure in green he has half-expected. Klerris stands on the coaster's deck embracing Lydya, and Creslin's eyes burn for an instant. He shakes his head, returning his attention to the guard captain, whose back remains turned to him and who reminds him of someone.

"That's more than statecraft or duty, Creslin." Megaera has moved close to his shoulder. "Maybe it's the only way your mother the Marshall can declare her love."

Creslin says nothing. What can he say? Instead, he swallows and watches as the two Black Wizards separate, wearing near-matching smiles. Klerris and Lydya do not hold hands, although they might as well, for the closeness between them is obvious.

His heart pounds, and somehow he almost wishes that he were Klerris, and he wonders if no matter what he does, or what he becomes, Megaera will always be forever beyond his reach.

The forward hatch cover is coming off, and two sailors are beginning to rig a pulley attached to a geared hand winch.

"Megaera, would you like to escort Guard Captain Shierra?" His question is not rhetorical, for he is not certain whether he or she would be better in dealing with the Westwind contingent.

"I think that might be best, since she would prefer to deal with women and since the captain clearly prefers not to . . . although—" and her momentary smile is like the clear noonday sun "—we could make them both uneasy."

Creslin smiles, without strain for one of the few times in recent days. "We could . . . but then I'd have to explain how a mere man managed to escape from Westwind, and you'd have to fry something or other to assure the captain that you meant business."

"I'll take the Westwind troops."

Creslin wonders, once again, what he has said to upset her.

"A woman can be competent without using force or wizardry." Megaera looks past him and toward the pier, where the Westwind captain is marshaling her guards.

"I didn't mean it that way," Creslin apologizes.

"Oh . . . best-betrothed . . ." She shakes her head.

Creslin feels like shaking his head, too. Instead, he waits for the two Black Wizards who are making their way off the ship. Lydya is carrying a black leather case that appears familiar.

"Creslin, I'd like you to—" Klerris begins.

"We've met," Creslin interrupts gently. "Lydya is the one to whom I owe my life, and perhaps more." He bows, the first bow he has made since he has left Westwind, but the Healer Wizard deserves that respect. He straightens to find her blushing, to find Klerris with a bemused expression.

"That's quite an honor, Creslin, from a . . . regent yet." Lydya's tone reveals thoughtfulness, and something else.

"It is a signal honor, indeed. There may be hope for him yet." Megaera's words are not quite humorous, nor yet etched in acid.

"Lydya, might I present you to my co-regent, Megaera, also sub-Tyrant of Sarronnyn?"

"I am pleased to meet you, Megaera. The Tyrant seemed most helpful."

"Sister dear? She did? And how did she manifest her graciousness?"

"With a pledge of grains and olives, and some timber . . . to be sent after the fall harvests."

"I will look forward to that shipment with pleasure."

Creslin nods. So will he, although both he and Megaera understand the timing of the pledge. If they survive the wizards and whatever other hazards await them in the summer and early fall, such a shipment will be more than worth it to Ryessa.

"I must be going, Lydya, to deal with the arrangements for the Westwind guards," Megaera says. "I look forward to talking with you later."

As Megaera makes her way toward Shierra, who still appears familiar to Creslin, Lydya bends down and picks up the black leather case she has carried. "This is from the Marshalle."

Creslin frowns, wondering what Llyse could possibly have sent. As he takes the case, he suddenly knows. His guitar. But why?

"There's a note inside."

Creslin decides not to look for the note while still on the pier. Then he sees the captain looking toward him. "It appears that I have a few more duties."

"If you wish, Lydya and I can take the guitar back to the keep," Klerris offers.

"Most appreciated—"

"Regent Creslin? Regent Creslin?"

Creslin smiles at the healer and at the Black Wizard, then turns toward the nervous ship captain, who bears a stack of parchment in his hands.

LXXXI

"YOU'VE MADE A good start with the physical conditioning. But . . ." Megaera raises her eyebrows, waiting for the guard captain's next words "whether you can master a lifetime of training in a season or two is another question."

Megaera shakes her head slowly. "There's no choice."

"Creslin's not that hard, is he? My sister felt that he was a good man at heart."

"It's not that at all. Against him, I need no defenses. Besides, from what I've seen, I'm not sure that I'd ever prevail by force of arms." She lifts the white-oak wand. "Where do we begin?"

The guard captain raises her eyebrows in response. "At the beginning, with the way you hold a blade."

The redhead smiles faintly but allows her fingers to be repositioned.

". . . and in the way you stand . . ."

The sorenesses she will receive cannot be as bad as the burning that has created the scars across her wrists. At least that is what she hopes.

"You may regret this, lady . . ."

She may indeed, but the time for regrets is past. Instead, she concentrates on how the older woman places the blade within her fingers, on how she should grip and wield the weapon.

LXXXII

THE MAN WEARS gray leather trousers and a faded green shirt with sleeves trimmed short above the elbows. For a long time he stands at the end of the pier studying the long, slow swells out beyond the breakwater, watching as a few higher waves surge white over the rocks. The pier is shadowed by the western hills, by the shadows just preceding sunset.

He turns westward, where the high, hazy clouds begin to glisten orange and pink to herald the sun's disappearance into the sea beyond the western slopes. With a last look at the skies, at the towers of the sunset, he turns.

His scuffed boots carry him from the pier toward the half-built inn, where the walls and the roof are in place for the public room. The walls for the guests' sleeping quarters lag behind, partly by design and partly because the troopers have diminished enthusiasm for the section of less immediacy to them. Strangely, some of the Westwind detachment have begun to help with the co-regents' holding on the cliff, so much so that they have completed the exterior and interior walls, doing more in a few eight-days than Creslin had done in nearly a season.

Those working on the keep with Megaera have accomplished even more, and whatever Megaera is doing—

beyond her determination to master a blade—she is developing a increasing bond with the guards. Creslin shakes his head.

Two fishermen are folding nets left out earlier to dry as he leaves the end of the pier. "Evenin', ser," the gray-haired one offers, barely looking up from the cording.

"Good evening," Creslin returns with a smile. "Are you heading out early in the morning?"

"Always early . . . leastwise if you want to catch anything."

The other fisherman, younger and darker, with a welt across one shoulder, nods his bearded face but says nothing as Creslin continues toward the building under construction.

". . . new regent, hear tell, him and the redheaded woman."

". . . witches, both of them."

". . . better a witch who's here to look after . . ."

"Maybe . . ."

Creslin hopes that he can fulfill the faith of the one and gain the confidence of the other. He pauses by the unfinished inn, glancing at the nearly completed split-stone roof tiling over one end. Then he makes his way between the piles of rough-cut stone. Inside the public room, the hearth is completed, and the stone flooring slabs have been set but not grouted. The windows have, as of yet, neither shutters nor glass, but neither are necessary in the heat of the summer to come.

Klerris feels that a cloudy glass can be made from the sand of the beaches that lie beyond the low hills to the east of Land's End. The glass will make the inn and the keep more livable year 'round.

Erecting three buildings, trying to grow a few crops, and encouraging a few old orchards are taking most of Creslin's time, time that isn't spent in trying to get back into shape and in talking with Shierra, Hyel, Megaera, Lydya, and Klerris in figuring out what else he should be doing.

With a deep breath, he steps out into the shadows and

starts uphill toward the cool, black-stone house of the co-regents. He thinks again about the short note from Llyse, the note whose words could mean anything . . . or nothing. The words he has shared with no one are burned into his thoughts:

Creslin—

Some things cannot be won with cold steel or black storms. This might prove helpful. We are well, but I still listen in the night for the words you are not here to sing. If the angels are merciful, we will send another shipment in the fall, after the winter stores are reckoned.

—Llyse

"Some things cannot be won with cold steel . . ." he murmurs. "Like Megaera?"

Now that he thinks about it, he has never even mentioned to Megaera that he plays the guitar and sings. But . . . he really has never played, except in the privacy of his room at Westwind. And for Lorcas, the trader's daughter, who insisted that a princess was waiting for him. His lips twist. Waiting, yes, but not exactly as Lorcas pictured.

A time will come when he needs the guitar. He has needed every other skill or understanding he has obtained. Why should music, no matter how private, be any different?

Something deep-toned sounds in the darkness by the road, then falls silent as his footsteps echo.

In the near hush of twilight, the murmur of the surf drifts up the cliffs' facade from the narrow beaches under the black-rock walls of the eastern side of Recluce. Creslin stops and listens, but there is only the sound of the waves on the sand.

Ahead he sees the glimmer of a lamp, perhaps of two

lamps. Megaera is in the house. He takes a deep breath and strides forward until his boots scrape in the darkness on the black stone of the terrace.

"Megaera?" He opens the main door into the roofed, but otherwise unfinished Great Room. There is no answer as he eases the door back into place behind him. Crossing the unlighted room, he steps onto the stones of the corridor leading to their bedrooms. He stops at her door.

"Megaera?"

"Come on in."

The redhead sits cross-legged on the quilt covering her pallet. Also in her room are a small stool and a narrow, ladder-backed chair. A single bronze lamp, cleaned and polished, throws light across the spotless stone tiles and the woven grass rug that covers the space between the chair and the pallet.

Creslin eases onto the small but sturdy stool. "How was your day?"

"A bit wearying." She wears a robe that he has not seen before; it is buttoned to her neck and has voluminous sleeves that cover her arms, even down to her wrists. "When you have to make charcoal before you can even start—"

"For the glass?"

Megaera nods. "It works, but it's slow. Once we get the furnace working, some of the guards can take over. What about you?"

"We could use the glass. The public room's done, and most of the kitchen. Not the lodgings or the entry hall." Even as he responds to her question, he wonders what she is hiding. "What else have you been working on with Shierra?"

"Not much. I'm trying to learn how the guards operate, how I can help."

Creslin grins. "What are you hiding?"

"Damn you! Damn your puking guts, and damn your order-infested honesty! I hate you! Get out of here!"

"What did I do?"

"It's not what you did. It's what you are, sitting there and looking so smug. You're so twisted that you don't even know you're dishonest. Now get out of my sight."

The silver-haired man retreats, closing the door behind him. He hears the bolt shoot into place as he enters his own room, empty except for the unlit lamp and the pallet with the plain quilt.

In the darkness, he stands by the window for a long time, listening to the sound of the surf and the whisper of the sea breeze long after the light in the adjoining room has been snuffed, long after clouds have covered the diamond-sparked band of sky that contains the north star—supposedly Heaven itself.

In time, he sleeps . . . but not well.

LXXXIII

MEGAERA BENDS, ANGLES her wand and lets the junior guard's practice wand slip by, then follows with a quick thrust.

"Oooffff . . ."

"The thrust was adequate, but you let down at the end and you didn't recover," states the senior duty guard. "You're not supposed to be dueling. You're fighting to kill and to keep from being killed."

The redhead wipes her forehead, then glances around the Westwind guards' practice yard. No one else has even looked directly at her. Three other pairs of guards continue to practice. The rest of the detachment is working with stone or timber to turn the rough-built keep addition into more livable quarters, except for the three working at the cliff house with Creslin.

Why they feel so constrained to help him, she does not know. She tightens her lips and grips the practice wand.

"Don't grip so tightly that your fingers are white," adds the guard.

Megaera forces her hand to relax. Before long, she is due to meet with Klerris and Lydya to work on the glass problem.

"Try it again," suggests the guard. "Remember, there's always someone else waiting to strike." She nods sharply and walks to the next pair, studying them for a time before speaking. "Hold it. You're both going to get killed . . ."

Megaera takes a deep breath, then resumes her position, signifying with a quick nod that she is again ready. If Klerris is correct, the blade will be her only reliable defense before long.

Her shoulders already ache, and her arms bear more bruises than she would have believed possible. But she always wears long sleeves, and she will until her arms are not purple from shoulder to wrist.

". . . Westwind guards . . . aren't . . . the only deadly fighters . . ." The words hiss under her breath as she parries, giving ground.

"Ooooffff . . ."

This time she is the recipient.

"Are you all right, lady?" asks the junior guard, barely old enough to have been allowed to choose the detachment.

"I'm fine. Let's try again."

She should be leaving, but there is never enough time for everything, and she wonders how Creslin has managed to juggle so many projects. But she owes him, owes him so much for his pigheadedness and his failure to understand.

"Damn you . . ." The words hiss under her breath again as her sword wand weaves her defense, as she imagines that he is the junior guard, as her wand moves even faster. She ignores the twisting in her stomach.

LXXXIV

THE LATE-AFTERNOON sun breaks through the clouds above the northwestern seas and pours through the narrow window in the old part of the main keep.

"The public-room idea isn't working." Hyel frowns. "My men sit on one side and her guards glare at them from the other. The only people who like it are the fisherwives who pour. That's because everyone drinks more when they don't talk. And we don't have enough to drink, either, by the way."

"Have your men . . . I don't know. We may be dry for a while, but the orchards are going to produce more than enough to ferment something drinkable." Creslin thinks about other fruits and grains. "We might be able to do something with those purple berries that grow on the cliffs. Isn't there somebody who's making his own alcohol in the keep?"

"Several," admits Hyel. "But would you want to drink it?"

"Put them on half-duty if they'll gather the berries and use them for something. Let either Megaera, Klerris, or me look at the casks or barrels or whatever they put it in before anyone drinks it."

Now he is worrying not only about quarters, and the lack of sanitary facilities in the expanded keep, the lack of bedding, the lack of—He even has to suggest a brewery! He shrugs. Megaera is working with Shierra on refitting and further expanding the keep, using the green timbers from Suthya and the tools brought by Lydya. Where additional linens will come from, who knows?

All of the useless things about running a keep, all of Galen's chatterings, and all of the studies about commodities and supplies that had so bored him—these have become treasures as he flails through his days. These, and Megaera's commonsense approach.

"Do we need it?" she asks. "How soon?" He doubts that he has heard those questions less than a score of times. Yet she is right. What do they need, and when do they need it?

Creslin wants everything done now, and with everything to be done now, who has time for wizardry? The order-strengthening he has learned is wonderful for encouraging plant growth, but he cannot encourage what is not growing. So he has managed to dragoon some of the more venturesome consorts, a handful of the remaining fisherwomen, and two disabled fishermen into plowing and sowing the few abandoned fields on the lower plateau to the north side of Land's End. Lydya has located another spring or two, and the would-be farmers have rebuilt the ditching.

He rubs his sore shoulders. Someday he may get back to finishing his and Megaera's house, now nothing more than two half-finished bedrooms and four enclosed and unfinished rooms: the dining room, the common room, the so-called study, and the kitchen.

"That might do it . . . for now," Hyel says tiredly. "But that won't solve the hostility. They still drink and stare at each other."

"What about a minstrel?"

"Who would come here? At least now?"

The silver-haired man nods, thinking of his sister's note. "Perhaps there is a solution. We can at least try."

"What—"

"I'll meet you at the public room after the evening meal."

The tall man stands with a puzzled look on his face.

Creslin smiles. "It either works, or it doesn't." Then he departs, heading uphill toward the black stone house that still remains unfinished and alone upon the cliffs overlooking the eastern shores of Recluce.

When he reaches the door, he calls. "Megaera!" But

there is no answer, and he senses no one in or around the dwelling or on the terrace.

After fetching the guitar, he sits on the wall, the low sun at his back, and lets his fingers find the strings and the tones. Despite the calluses on his hands, his fingertips are no longer as tough as they once were. So he puts the guitar back into the black leather case, and thinks. Thinks about the songs he once sang, the few he has composed, and the many he has learned, left to him by another silver-haired man.

As he reflects, the sun drops behind the hills at his back, but Megaera has not shown up, not that he would expect her now that she has begun to identify with the Westwind guards. Most nights she sleeps in her room, but that is all; she takes her meals in the keep with Shierra, or spends time talking to Lydya.

As twilight nears, Creslin picks up the guitar and walks down to the town and makes his way to the public room at the half-finished inn.

Hyel is waiting. "What is that?"

"A guitar. Someone once told me that sometimes music helps."

Hyel follows the younger man through the open door at the western, and mostly completed, end of the inn. The windows have neither glass nor shutters, although Klerris has been working with Megaera and a small furnace and has promised that rough and cloudy glass will be on hand before long.

As he stands inside the too-large room, Creslin waits a moment for his eyes to adjust to the dimness. Only half a dozen small lamps—borrowed, he suspects, from the keep—light the walls, and a faint odor tells him that they are fueled with some type of fish oil.

He drags a wobbly table—another of Klerris's efforts, he suspects—to a point directly before the doors, then turns to Hyel. "Find me a stool of some sort, if you can."

The guard captain shakes his head but makes his way toward the small doorway that leads to what will be a kitchen but serves now only to store their limited stock of beverages, plus too-old cheese and crumbling biscuits.

". . . what's *he* doing here?"

"First . . . she starts coming with the bitches . . . now he's sitting apart from anyone . . ."

Creslin ignores the whispers and looks into the center of the Westwind contingent, toward a halo of flame-red hair. Megaera looks away, her eyes cool, yet puzzled.

"This is the best I can do . . ." Hyel sets a rough-sawn, four-legged stool by the table.

"That's fine." Creslin carries it into the empty space between the tables, perhaps six cubits across. Then he returns to the small table and takes the guitar from its case and carries it to the stool, where he seats himself.

The whispers and mumbles die away.

Creslin lets his fingers caress the strings of the guitar, wishing that he had practiced more, but who has had time for practice? Finally he settles himself on the stool and looks out to the rough tables . . . to the Westwind detachment sitting on the near-windowless shoreward side, and to the Montgren keep soldiers gathered at the four trestle-style tables before the unshuttered open windows that carry in the chill breeze, salt, and the odor of fish from the harbor.

He smiles raggedly. No one smiles back, not even Megaera, who is seated next to Shierra. "I don't know too many songs that don't favor one group or another. So enjoy the ones you like, and ignore the ones you don't," he announces quietly. His fingers touch the strings.

> *Up on the mountain*
> *where the men dare not go,*
> *the angels set guards there*
> *in the ice and the snow.*
> *The guards they are women,*
> *with blades out of steel,*
> *and their hearts they are colder*
> *than any ice you can feel.*

Up on the mountain
where the trees do not grow,
the sun seldom shines
nor the rivers do flow.
From out of the Westhorns,
guards march from the stone.
Their blades are the fires,
that slice to the bone.

They'll cut you and leave you
all bleeding and cold,
and no one will find you,
till the mountains grow old.
The rocks they will splinter,
and the snows will fall deep,
and the guards of the mountains
will hold to their keep.

Their castle will stand, dear,
till the whole world is white,
till the Legend's forgotten,
with the demons of light.
Till my songs have been buried
in the depths of the nights,
and all the young men shun
the mountain's chill heights.

Up on the mountain
where the men dare not go,
the angels set guards there
in the ice and the snow.
And there they will stay, dear,
till the whole world is white,
till the Legend's forgotten,
with the demons of light.

Till my songs have been buried
in the depths of the night,
and none of the young men
seek out that cold height;
and none of the young men
seek out that cold height.

There is silence as Creslin finishes the song. Not muttering, just silence. The notes had been silver, with only a few traces of copper.

Rather than talk, he touches the strings and begins again.

. . . white was the color of my love,
as bright and white as a dove,
and white as he, as fair as she,
who sundered my love from me . . .

He pauses after finishing, stretching fingers that are already sore from lack of practice and hoping that he has recalled truly the words.

"Another one . . ."

The request is whispered, but the whisper carries even against the rustling of the breeze. He shrugs, resettling himself on the stool.

. . . sing a song of gold coins,
a pack filled up with songbirds,
a minstrel lusting after love,
and yelling out some loving words . . .

Finally a few faces smile as he finishes the silly song he learned so long ago, but the Westwind guards seem a bit chill. Creslin thinks, then takes a deep breath and begins, picking through the words.

Ask not what a man is,
that he scramble after flattery as he can,

or that he bend his soul to a woman's wish . . .
after all, he is but a man.

As not what a man might be,
that he carry a blade like a fan,
and sees only what his ladies wish him to see . . .
after all, he is but a man . . .

He exaggerates the phrases and is rewarded with sardonic smiles from the Montgren soldiers and a chuckle or two from the older Westwind guards.

His fingers are sore, and he needs at least another song or two. But he stands for a moment, looking around for something to drink, and Megaera brings him a small cup of redberry. She is so pale as to be nearly white.

"Are you all right?" he asks.

"Fine, thank you. I thought you might need this." She steps away and resumes her place beside Shierra.

He takes a swallow, aware of the continuing quietness, before finally setting down the empty cup by the stool and touching the strings again.

. . . from the skies of long-lost Heaven . . .
to the heights of Westwind keep,
we will hold our blades in order,
and never let our honor sleep!

He almost loses the melody as the guards finally begin to sing, and more voices join in as he continues playing.

At the end, he turns toward the Montgren group. "I'd sing your songs, too, but I must confess that I had to leave the Duchy before I learned any of them. Someone . . . anyone . . . who can work out the melody with me?"

Slowly a dark-haired man stands; it is Thoirkel. "Ser, I don't know as I can sing much . . ."

A snicker comes from his companions.

". . . but I do know the words to a few songs."

Creslin glances at the Westwind faces, conscious that the cold hostility has somewhat relaxed. Creating some sort of unity among the two groups is going to be a long, tough job.

> . . . *the Duke he went a-hunting,*
> *a-hunting he did go* . . .

Thoirkel's voice warbles off-key and off-tempo, but Creslin can pick up the basic melody and words, and before long stronger voices rise up in chorus.

At the end of two more songs, Creslin stands, shaking his hands. His fingers are not quite bloody. "I'll surrender the guitar to anyone . . ."

For a moment, he is afraid that no one will take it; then a slender Westwind guard steps forward. He hands the instrument to her and walks toward the small, empty table set between the two groups.

The guard has a fair voice and a good sense of the guitar, and she begins with an old ballad.

Creslin holds his cup up, and one of the women fills it with redberry. Then he fumbles, realizing that he has no coins with him.

"I think you need not pay at your own tavern, ser," suggests the woman with a smile. "Especially after such a lovely performance."

Two chairs slide into place to his right, and Megaera and Shierra sit down. As he looks up, Megaera beckons to Hyel, who immediately picks up his chair and crosses the five cubits. He sets down the straight-backed and armless chair, roughed out of the castoffs from the building timbers, and sits to Creslin's left.

"I didn't know you could sing." Megaera's statement is an accusation.

"I never had a chance until now, and you never seemed

to be interested," Creslin says absently, still watching the guard on the stool.

"Fiera said that the hall guards used to sneak up outside his door when he practiced," adds Shierra, her voice warmer than Creslin has ever heard it.

He tries to keep his mouth from opening. Fiera? Shierra? Are they related? Is that why the older woman appears familiar? "Fiera?" he finally asks. "Is she your—?"

"My youngest sister. She talked a lot about you, probably too much."

"How is she?"

Megaera stiffens, but Creslin ignores it for the moment.

"She went with the detachment to Sarronnyn. She'll be rotated back later in the year sometime."

"Where did the guitar come from?" asks Hyel.

"It was mine. I left it . . . behind. Lydya—the healer—brought it. My sister, Llyse, thought I might like to have it."

"You've never played in public?" Shierra smiles, as if she knows the answer.

"No. I was scared to do it, but sometimes music helps. The second song, the white-as-a-dove one, probably saved me from the White Wizards."

"You didn't exactly sound scared." Megaera's voice remains cool.

"That wouldn't have helped much," he responds slowly. "Besides, no one born in Westwind shows fear. Not if they can help it."

Megaera looks to the guard captain.

Shierra nods slowly. "Feeling afraid is acceptable, but letting it affect your actions is not. That's one of the reasons the guards are often more effective than men. Men too often conceal their fear in brashness or in unwise attacks. The guards are trained to recognize their fears and set them aside."

Hyel raises his eyebrows at the comment about male brashness, then takes a long pull from his earthen mug.

At the other tables, both men and women are clapping in time to the driving beat of a marching song.

LXXXV

CRESLIN STANDS UP. His fingers still hurt, and his muscles ache. He forces a smile. "I'm going to get some sleep."

A glance passes between Lydya and Klerris, but Hyel begins to talk.

". . . hope you'll play again for us. That really was a treat, and just about everyone liked it."

Creslin picks up the guitar case and shrugs his shoulders in an effort to relax them. As he checks the fastenings before lifting the case, the tenderness of his fingers reminds him again of how little he has played recently.

While the Westwind guards and the Montgren troopers are not sitting at the same tables, neither are they glaring at each other and muttering. Creslin hopes that in time some of the consorts and the attached guards will join the singles.

"I do hope you will play again," seconds Shierra.

"I need to talk to you." Megaera's words are low and tired.

"Now?"

"When you get to the house will be fine. I won't be long." She remains pallid. Creslin notes her color and cannot help but worry that she is pushing herself too hard.

"Stop it. Please . . ."

He stops. She starts toward him, but Klerris steps up to her. "A moment, lady?"

"Oh . . . can it wait until tomorrow?"

"I think not."

Creslin sighs as he steps away, glad to let Klerris take the brunt of Megaera's sharp words but feeling guilty all the same. As he makes his way out of the public room and past the two outside lamps, he is conscious of Lydya moving toward him.

"Creslin . . ."

"Yes?"

"Would you mind if I walked with you for part of the way? There are a few things I think you ought to know."

He does not like the sound of Lydya's words, but he shrugs and is reminded of how sore his shoulders are. Farmwork has been even harder than stonework was. "No. Come along. Where else have I failed?"

"Failed?"

"You and Klerris talk to me these days only to point out where I've made another mistake."

"Unless it's serious, you don't really take time to listen." Her voice is half-humorous, half-chiding, as she matches her steps with his and they start up the hill road.

"I guess I deserve that. What now?"

"Megaera," the healer states. "You really upset her tonight. Again."

"Again? Everything I do upsets her! If I talk to her, it upsets her. If I don't, it upsets her."

"Creslin."

The soft tone chills him, and he answers warily. "Yes?"

"Megaera is your wife."

"In name, perhaps. Not in much else."

"Have you ever really asked why?"

"No, because that's clearly the way she wants it."

"Have you ever told her that you love her?"

"Do I?"

Lydya snorts.

"All right. But it's hopeless. I look at her and I can't help wanting her. She senses that as soon as I look, and she slices me apart."

"That's right. Do you remember how you felt every time you had to walk down the Great Hall at Westwind?"

Creslin swallows.

"Now . . . you didn't even know what the guards were

feeling. You just heard the words. How would you have felt if you could have known every thought behind those words?"

The healer's tone is as cold as the northern stars, and as distant, yet as close as a blade in his guts. He can say nothing, for his eyes begin to burn, although his feet do not stumble.

"Your wife, and she is your wife in the unfortunate and old sense of the word because of Ryessa's meddling, has heard only a few warm words from you. You have never courted her, and you lust after her all the time. That's going to make her feel close to you? That's going to show her you love her?"

Creslin winces, but the healer's words continue, like the ice-winds that he has called before from the Roof of the World.

". . . every chance you get, you show yet another skill. Tonight was especially painful. You sang love songs and hate songs, funny songs and war songs, and your soul was out there, open and exposed. You risked your soul for people you scarcely know and owe little enough to. Yet you have never sung to the woman you say you love. How do you think she feels about that?"

"Not very good."

"You're right." Lydya's voice softens. "What's worse is that if you come to her in guilt tonight, she'll take your head off, and you'll deserve it."

"What am I supposed to do? Besides think?"

"You'll listen to every nasty word she says, and you will think about them, and you will not say anything nasty in return. You will not act superior. You will not act guilty, and you will not try to make amends, whatever they may be, tonight. You will tell her, however it seems fitting, that you honestly did not understand all that she felt and that you will try to make up for it by treating her as a friend in the days ahead."

"I don't know if I can . . ."

"If you can't, you'll both die before the end of the summer." Lydya stops. "Good night, Creslin."

Her retreating steps are so silent that they are lost behind the chirring of the insects in the rocks that line the road combined with the gentle hissing of the waves upon the sand.

He stands there, listening for either Lydya's footsteps or the oncoming footsteps of a red-haired woman. He hears neither. So he turns back to the south and walks slowly uphill. Since he reaches the black stones of the house first, he lights the lamps, one in his room and, in turn, one in hers.

Then he stands by his window, leaving the door ajar and waiting. The night air is cool, but not so cool as even the warmest of summer nights on the Roof of the World, that simple castle that had seemed so complex while he had dwelt there.

The lamps continue to burn, but Megaera does not appear. Has she decided to spend another night with the Westwind guards? Has he appeared that uncaring?

He walks back to the terrace, letting his senses flow to the winds and through the light sea breeze that flows off the ocean and up the cliffs. How long he floats there, he does not know. He only knows that when he senses her coming, he drops back into himself and crosses the terrace toward the Great Room.

He reaches the door and opens it as her hand reaches for the crude handle. "Good evening. I wanted to make sure you got back safely."

"Who would trouble me?"

"No one, I suppose. I just needed to say something. We didn't really talk, and you said you wanted to."

"It doesn't matter. You haven't listened before. Why would you listen now?"

"I'm listening now." He eases the door shut behind her. The light streaming down the corridor from her room and across the dusty stone floor is enough for him to see by.

"It's easier to listen, I suppose, after yet another conquest." Her eyes dart to his right, as if she wants to step around him.

"It wasn't meant that way."

"You never mean anything the way it turns out. You just act, and damn how anyone else feels. Or you feel without thinking about how your feelings make other people feel." Her eyes rest directly on him, cold, yet burning.

"You're right," he admits. "I still act before I think things out."

"I'm supposed to be wed to you, best-betrothed, and I didn't even know that you can sing love songs that wring women's hearts. Or marching songs. You never bothered to tell me."

He swallows instead of pointing out that she has seldom given him enough time to tell her many things. "I suppose I didn't. Perhaps I was afraid that you would criticize me for that, too."

"Criticize the great Creslin? Heaven forbid."

"I didn't realize that you felt that way. You know what I feel. I don't know the same about you."

"Whatever you've been doing tonight, you ought to keep doing—for several years." She starts to step around him.

He holds up a hand, but does not touch her.

She stops. "Well?"

"We can't keep going like this, Megaera."

"I've only been telling you that since the day after you woke up in cousin dear's castle."

"So . . . I'm slow."

"I'm tired. It's been a long day. All my days have been long lately. What do you have in mind? Throwing me into bed and calling it love and thinking it will solve everything?" Her lips quirk angrily.

Creslin lets his breath out slowly. "No. Something . . . like friendship. Like not finding the cruelest possible words whenever we're angry. Like thinking about how my actions affect you . . ."

She shakes her head. "I just don't know. Right now you feel that way. But will you feel like that tomorrow? Or the next day?"

He shrugs. "I don't know. But could we try?"

"You try. I'll see. Good night."

He let her step around him.

"Good night."

For a time he stands in the dimness of the unfinished Great Room, the coolness of the sea breeze flowing over him. Then he returns to his room and peels off his clothes, snuffs the lamp, and stretches out on the pallet that is marginally softer than the stone flooring on which it rests.

As he listens to the unseen insects and frogs, as he wonders how he will learn to consider his actions before he acts, his eyes grow heavy.

Good night, Megaera, he thinks.

Does she hear his wish? He turns over on his stomach and tries to ignore the tightness within him. Dead before fall? He squeezes his eyelids together, then tries to relax.

LXXXVI

CRESLIN WAKES EARLY, not long after the sun has cleared the swells of the Eastern Ocean. There is time for some stonework before he and Megaera head to the keep to meet with Shierra, Hyel, Klerris, and Lydya.

"The unofficial High Council of Recluce . . ." he murmurs.

On his feet, he pulls on the old fishing trousers he has scrounged, work boots, and the tattered, short-sleeved green shirt.

In the recently walled room that will some day be the kitchen, he retrieves some stale bread. A fuller repast will have to wait until they reach the keep. He chews the tough crust and walks to the cistern, where he fills a mug with cool water. Although the air is still brisk and damp coming in off the ocean, the cloudless day promises to be hot.

Because Megaera is probably still asleep, he does not work with the mallet and chisel but carries rough stones from the jumble, stacking them by the stone that serves as his trimming block. After having made a dozen trips, he stops and wipes his forehead. The day may be the hottest yet of the early summer, and it is far from even mid-morning.

"You're up early." The redhead leans out of the open window. Her hair is tousled, and she wears a faded blue robe.

"I tried to be quiet."

"I appreciate the thought. Someday, if I can ever wake before you do, I'll demonstrate a comparison between real quietness and what you call quietness."

"If you ever make it up that early . . ."

"Some of us have no desire to greet the sun. Aren't we supposed to meet with everyone this morning?"

"I'll get washed up in a moment." As Megaera's head disappears back into her room, he puts a stone on the block and raises the heavy hammer.

Clung . . .

He stops with one stone. As he lifts and fits it so that there is less than a hairline crack between it and the one below, he wishes again that he were better with creative chores, like woodworking and stonemasonry, rather than expert with the ethereal and the deadly, such as music and blades and bows. After removing the stone and setting it down until he is ready to mortar, he picks up the tools and puts them away.

By the time he reaches the washroom, the wash stones are wet and Megaera has already finished. He hurries through a cold and quick shower and—naked and carrying his work clothes—dashes for his room.

His hair is still wet when he joins her on the terrace. "You run more gracefully without clothes," she tells him.

"What can I say? Do I get to see whether you do?"

"After last night?"

He wonders whether this is the time for an apology but seeing that she still smiles, he decides against seriousness. "I thought I'd ask."

"At least you're asking now."

"It seems like a better idea."

"We'd better go."

For the first fifty paces, neither says anything. Creslin just enjoys the sun and the peacefulness. They cross the crest of the hill overlooking the harbor. Only one damaged fishing boat remains in the water.

"It's too bad this place is nothing but starving fishermen and disgraced courtiers."

Creslin laughs. "I can't fish, nor was I ever very good with the polite phrases. Disgraced? I suppose so."

"You seem . . . resigned, calmer." She looks evenly at the man who is scarcely taller than she, although he is becoming ever more solid with maturity and the heavy stonework he does. "As if you decided—What are you going to do?" Her eyes flick from the road out toward the waves of the north of the town below, then to the silver hair above the gray-green eyes.

"I told you last night. Try to work at being your friend."

"I mean about Recluce."

"We'll try to build it into something, at least into a place for people—"

"Like us?"

"That was the general idea."

"Do you think it's really possible? Not just a dream?"

"Somehow . . . yes. In the morning, anyway. By nighttime, it seems a lot harder and more distant."

She says nothing, withdrawing into herself, and Creslin wonders what touchiness his words have rubbed against. But he walks beside her and they do not argue, nor is there a wall between them. Not this morning, at least.

LXXXVII

THE EVENING IS warm, purple-clear in the moments after true twilight. Creslin stands behind the completed stone wall that marks the end of the terrace and looks down the thirty cubits or so of hillside leading to the sheer cliff overhanging the white beaches below. While he cannot see the sands, he can sense, through the winds and the scents, their presence.

The swells of the Eastern Ocean are flatter and lower than usual, with the foaming of the breakers on the sands barely audible in the near-silent evening. Behind him, the Black Holding is black; no lamps are lit, for neither Creslin nor Megaera needs them, and no one else is present.

In the near-darkness, he clears his throat and begins to sing softly.

> *. . . they'll cut you and leave you*
> *all bleeding and cold,*
> *and no one will find you,*
> *till the mountains grow old.*

> *The rocks they will splinter,*
> *and the snows will fall deep,*
> *and the guards of the mountains*
> *will hold to their keep . . .*

He stops and turns. Megaera stands at the far end of the terrace. "Go ahead. I want to hear you sing."

"You sure?"

"I wouldn't be here if I weren't."

Creslin has his doubts, but he buries them, coughs softly, and returns to the song.

> . . . till my songs have been buried
> in the depths of the night,
> and none of the young men
> seek out that cold height;
> and none of the young men
> seek out that cold height.

"Do you know any happy songs?" Soft as it is, her husky voice carries across the stones from the side wall where she has seated herself.

"Not many, but I'll try."

Pursing his lips, he casts back into his memories, trying to recall a cheerful melody. He runs his left hand through his ragged and short hair, wondering if he should get his guitar. He decides against it, clears his throat once more, softly, before humming a bar or two, trying to touch the right key, the hint of silver that is his to reach. He looks to the south, not quite at Megaera but not exactly away from her either.

> . . . catch a falling fire; hold it to the skies;
> never let it die away.
> For love may come and fill your empty eyes
> with the light of more than day . . .

When he finishes, his eyes flicker to his right. Megaera has not moved, nor does she say anything. Creslin hums again and tries to search out another song.

> . . . I would not live without you,
> like aching souls I know,
> like older men with hearts of stone,
> who chose to live alone . . .
>
> I would not love without you,
> like empty homes I've seen . . .

"That's too sad."

"Sorry."

"Don't apologize. Could you sing something happier?"

"I don't know many happy ones. Let me think."

The stars begin to glitter as the last hints of twilight dissipate in the western horizon. The song frames in his mind, and as trite as the words are, they say what he has wanted to say, what he has avoided saying.

> *You are the fire of my nights,*
> *the light of my days,*
> *and the end of my wand'ring ways.*
> *You are . . . you are . . . you are*
> *the sun in the skies.*

When he finishes, he does not sing another song but walks slowly toward where Megaera sits in the darkness. He perches on the flat stones of the wall, leaving several cubits of space between them.

"You sang that like you meant it." Her voice barely rises above the swishing of the surf below the terrace. The breeze is soft but brisk and cool off the ocean.

"I did."

"I know, and it hurts."

"Hurts?"

"Hurts. I can feel the longing there. No one . . ." She stops, then starts again. "Sometimes you can be so gentle . . . and I think . . . it could work out. It really could, and then . . ." She shakes her head, and her hair sparkles like flame in the darkness.

Creslin notes that faint huskiness in her voice, the slight poised tilt to her head, and holds them within himself.

"You know," she continues, "you once spoke about seeing songs, or notes, shining silver in the air. For the first time, tonight, when you sang, I saw the words glistening there. They glistened silver."

"I've tried to make the gold; only one person I knew could sing gold."

"Your father?"

"Werlynn." In the cooling night, he still prefers not to look directly at her.

"You don't call either parent mother or father. Why not?"

"I didn't understand that he was my father until long after he was dead. The Marshall never treated me like her son, so I didn't really understand that she was my mother until I was old enough for her to forbid me to call her mother."

"You don't think of her as your mother, do you?"

"No."

"I wish she could have heard you sing. I wish . . ."

Creslin waits, even though the stone is hard under him.

"Wishes just don't come true," Megaera finally goes on. "No matter how hard you wish, life doesn't work that way. And if you wish someone would do something and they don't, it spoils everything if you have to tell them what you really want."

"It does," he agrees, wishing that Megaera could come to love him, wishing that he could understand why she continually pushes him away, when he knows somehow that she is drawn to him.

"I am drawn to you, but that doesn't change anything."

As she answers his feelings, he swallows. So close to her, he has few secrets. "Why not?" he asks, reaching out and touching, barely touching, her hand.

"Because I did not choose you. Because we never had the freedom to decide."

He looks past her toward the southwest, where the stars glitter coldly above the hills. "Will it always come to this?" he asks.

"Yes."

His fingers tighten ever so tightly around her hand. "Doesn't it matter that I love you?" He does not look at her as they sit so close, yet so far apart, and he tries to think of the cold stars in the cold sky.

Yet the stars do burn in the sky, and Megaera burns like a black flame that he cannot, dare not, touch. Instead, he slides a trace closer, continuing to hold her slender fingers. "I don't think you want to find out whether we might be meant for each other," he ventures.

"You might be right. But don't push me."

Don't push her? When has he ever pushed her? His feelings are so strong that he has to bite his lips, swallow his words.

"Everything you've done pushes me. You got me to marry you when even sister dear couldn't manage it. You got me to come to the most desolate spot on the earth, and you've forced me to give up what little I had that was superior to you." She withdraws her hand from his, deftly but abruptly. "And now you're angry because I'm upset about being pushed around."

He stands, only to find that she has risen simultaneously. "I'm angry, but that doesn't mean I don't love you."

"I know you love me. But you're so practical that you'll just destroy me without even thinking twice." She turns and walks toward the seaward end of the terrace. "You'd be sorry afterward, but then it would be rather late."

"I'm not sure I understand. How could I destroy you? I don't push you. I let you make your own choices. If you want to learn blade-work from Shierra, that's fine. Or order-mastery from Lydya—"

"You're right. You don't understand! I tried to let you know who and what I was . . . just once . . . and all I got was uncontrolled lust. Do you remember that inn in the Westhorns? Both my mind and my soul were blistered by that, and you still don't even know what you did. That was from hundreds of kays away. After that, I'm supposed to trust you?"

"That was different. I didn't even know who you were."

"Wonderful! You raped me in your mind, and it was all right because you didn't know who I was?"

"That's not it at all. And you know it's not."

He swallows as she runs across the stones toward her doorway.

. . . never understand . . .

The fragment of thought, or is it feeling, twists in his thoughts as the surf hisses against the sands below. Standing alone in the star-drenched night, Creslin again recalls the healer's words: "If you can't, you'll both die before the end of the summer."

Light! How can he be a friend to a woman who invariably attacks him whenever they are close? How can he court a lady who rejects every word that might have a sensual overtone? Why does she hold him responsible for thoughts and reactions that arose from ignorance? Why doesn't she hear what he means, what he feels?

The stars glitter coldly, and the wind off the Eastern Ocean reminds him once more of Freyja, and of the Westhorns he will never see again. But the winds are warm, and they do not comfort him, and the Black Holding behind him is lightless.

Shhhsss . . . ssshhhh . . .

The seas beat on the sands, and the sands throw back the sea.

LXXXVIII

"THE LAST ITEM is the taxation notice from Montgren." Shierra glances around the table.

Hyel nods warily, his gesture a mere acknowledgment. As usual, only one of the two older Black Wizards is present. Lydya's nod is perfunctory. Creslin glances at

Megaera. To him, she seems paler than normal, and her jaw is set. Outside the sun beats through the clear sky.

Shierra's eyes reach Creslin. "Is this some sort of joke?" he asks.

"I don't think so," Megaera answers. "It's just about what cousin dear would let himself get pushed into by Helisse or Florin."

"What does it say?" asks Hyel.

"That the quarterly assessment is fifty gold pence."

"Has the Duke sent an assessment before?" Creslin turns toward Hyel.

"No," admits the brown-haired man. "He's usually had to send coins to cover the supply costs, along with the pay chest."

"Could it be a trick?" asks Shierra. "Something from Fairhaven?"

"It's his signature, and it arrived in the pouch with the confirmation of the regency." Hyel shrugs, his eyes looking down at the battered table.

Creslin frowns. "The ship was a Suthyan coaster, wasn't it?"

"Yes . . . the *Swift Serpent*."

"I see what you mean," Megaera interrupts. "If cousin dear sent it through Suthyan channels, it should have arrived with the Westwind detachment."

"That's not certain." Hyel's fingers drum on the wood before him.

"It really doesn't matter," Creslin says slowly.

The others look at him.

"First, we don't have fifty golds. Second, there was no agreement for tax collection. Third, whom would we tax? And fourth, what can the Duke do to enforce it?"

"Are you talking about rebellion?" asks Hyel.

"Who said anything about rebellion?" Creslin sighs. "To begin with, we're not quite certain whether it was even the Duke who sent the notice, or if he even knew what it was he signed. More important from a practical sense, you cannot collect taxes when the people you would tax have nothing of value. What do we have? A mostly built inn that has collected perhaps twenty golds in total. A score of fishermen who probably don't net thirty golds in dried fish during the year. And three-score soldiers and guards we can barely pay, even with the last pay chest from the Duke. Unless we can develop greater trade, become self-sufficient, or find some other way of raising money, in less than a year we'll be begging at someone's doorstep."

"There are some possibilities . . ." suggests Lydya. "Most of the pepper in Candar comes from Hamor. Rosemary and brinn come from Astran. Winterspice comes from Nordla."

"Pepper?" asks Shierra.

"Are you saying that you can grow those here?" Megaera interjects just as Hyel opens his mouth.

"Yes. We've already started the brinn and the winterspice. The pepper takes longer . . ."

Creslin listens as Lydya explains the spice values, the time necessary for growth, and the likely trade patterns.

"Smugglers," Hyel adds when Lydya halts.

"Or Suthyans under Sarronnese trade flags," Megaera says.

Creslin reflects on Derrild, the trader, and the question of timing. Recluce is far closer than the great eastern and southern continents, therefore able to allow for smaller shipments of shorter duration, and from less affluent traders. "What grows in Candar that the eastern powers would prefer to have?"

No one answers.

"What about black wool?"

"You can't manage that as quickly," Lydya observes.

"No," he agrees. "But how long can we use spices? How many people use them? Everyone needs cloth."

Megaera smiles. "You want to use order to develop products no one else can sell?"

"Why not?"

"Can we do it?"

Creslin turns to Lydya. "Some of the mountain sheep have black patches."

"It will take several years," she points out.

"Start when you can, then. Does anyone disagree?"

Megaera frowns. Hyel shrugs, and Shierra nods slowly.

"Is there anything else we need to talk about?" Creslin asks.

Silence settles around the table.

"Then until we have something new to discuss, let's get back to the things we're working on." The silver-haired man stands up, and the others follow his example.

Creslin eases around the table to Lydya. "I didn't mean to push you on the wool."

The healer's eyes settle on him. "You didn't mean harm, but you did mean to push a little, I think."

Creslin flushes and finds himself feeling sheepish. "You're right. I worry about how much time we have."

"So does Klerris." She smiles for an instant. "While most people are not that eager to leave Candar, there are some who can help a great deal."

The Blacks?" asks Megaera, who has joined them.

"The council is forcing us from Candar. We're too cautious, too concerned about the misuse of chaos, and too worried about the order-chaos balance."

"Balance?" Megaera's question is tentative.

"Klerris thinks that Creslin is a creation of the balance, that too much chaos necessitates a greater focus on order. Theoretically, the opposite would be possible, of course. If, for example, Recluce became a home to order, too much emphasis on order could create an imbalance and empower a few great Chaos Wizards." She shakes her head. "That's just speculation. We really don't know."

Megaera wears a faraway expression, her eyes unfocused as if she looks into a distant future. She shivers minutely; then her eyes focus on Creslin.

Creslin wants to avoid the chill in those green eyes, and he looks instead at Lydya. "I guess I do push too much."

Megaera nods.

"You wouldn't be here if you didn't," Lydya says, "but there comes a time to let events take their own pace. Now, if you don't mind, I need to go make sure that Klerris isn't getting too impatient." She grins, turns, and moves down the sun-splashed steps.

Looking back into the dimness of the main floor of the keep, Creslin sees that Shierra and Hyel remain in conversation. He steps into the sunlight, then wishes he had not as the heat strikes him almost like a hammer.

"Sometimes . . ." Megaera's voice is low.

"Sometimes what?" His eyes sweep the harbor and the pier, empty except for the half-sunken fishing boat that has not budged since they arrived.

"You are so perceptive and so dense."

"I admit it. There's a lot I don't understand."

"There you go again! Poor little Creslin! 'I don't understand anything. Just help me out.' But a little while ago you manipulated an entire meeting. You're determined to turn this . . . desert into a place more powerful than Fairhaven in the years to come." Her words bite like a blizzard, despite the glare and heat that surround them.

"You want Recluce to remain a desert? I thought—"

"That's not it at all. I agree with your goals. There has to be someplace for people like us, for people like Lydya and Klerris. But you never ask anyone about anything. You just do things and then expect everyone to follow along. I'm not your camp follower! I may have to act like a guardian angel, but that's not because I long for either your body or your soul."

"But you stayed beside me . . ." Creslin's now-tanned forehead knits in puzzlement.

"It was easier for both of us."

She is not telling the whole truth, as shown from her shift in position and her obviously suppressed feeling of discomfort.

"Why do you lie about it?"

"Damn you! You think you know everything! A kind word, some consideration, and you think I'm ready to jump into your bed."

"I didn't even think that, and you know it." Creslin is tired, physically tired from farm work and from trying to regain his former conditioning, and mentally tired from being on edge each and every day, from not knowing when Megaera's words will turn acid.

"You're ignoring what I said about pushing me and everyone else around. Just like always. Just like every man. When it's convenient, you feel sympathy and understanding, and when it's not—oh, I'm sorry about that, you say, and you're not." Megaera raises her hand until her fingers touch the hilt of the blade she has taken to wearing.

Creslin stiffens as he notes that she has no difficulty in holding the cold steel and that the aura of white that has suffused her is now almost entirely gone . . . and that she radiates mostly the blackness of a Lydya, though thin, white flames flicker around her occasionally.

"You're not even listening, like always . . ."

"I was listening, but I was thinking of how much you've changed."

"Of how much you have changed me, you mean."

"That's not what I said."

"That's what you meant." The redhead's hand slides away from the blade.

Creslin looks up into the east, where a line of clouds dots the horizon out over the dark green sea.

"Until you listen, really listen, nothing will change." Megaera's steps scuff the stones.

Creslin takes another deep breath, watching as the slender redhead turns toward the new practice yard of the guards.

To the east, the clouds mount as the sun crosses into the western sky.

LXXXIX

AFTER BREAKING THE plain wax seal, Megaera reads the lines: "As written by Helisse, for Aldonya, faithful retainer of Megaera, sub-Tyrant of Sarronnyn, and Regent of Recluce . . ."

The redhead wonders whose idea the titles were—Helisse's through irony, or Aldonya's through devotion?

. . . though the birth was not easy, we have a daughter, and I have named her Lynnya, in your honor, and would beseech you, should anything happen to me, for unexpected things can happen to new mothers, that you would make sure that she does not have to submit her future to those she does not know.

In less than five more eight-days, according to the midwives, we will be able to travel, and there will be a ship leaving near that time. Helisse says that we can take it. That is, if we are both well.

Lynnya is a beautiful girl, and she will have red hair. I think it will be darker than yours.

We look forward to seeing you and serving you.

At the bottom, another line is appended: "They are both doing well. —Helisse."

Megaera Lynnya purses her lips, then walks toward the darkening window, blinking back the wetness in her eyes.

For a long time she listens to the surf, clutching the folded parchment to her breast.

XC

The way is the way,
as the west mountains are.
The way is the way,
as solid as the sunset towers,
and the southern seas.

The way is the way,
as all life is sorrow.
The way is the way,
as all sorrow is joy.

THE WAY IS the way. The silver-haired man ponders the words, stepping into the shadows that had not existed until he had thought of sorrow. As he walks from the shadows into the sunlight, his eyes narrow against the glare, and dust puffs from under his feet.

He lifts another stone, setting it on the cutting bench with a delicacy one would not guess at from the muscles in his arms and the calluses on his hands.

The stonework for the terrace walls is completed, and now he works on the unfinished portions of the guest houses. All of what he has done has been completed between dawns and breakfasts, or between dinners and restless sleeps. Then, what else can he do? Since that night on the terrace, Megaera has become even less approachable.

She will be returning to the Black Holding shortly from her morning run, which now exceeds his in length. He has watched her practice against Shierra, and her blade-work will soon surpass that of most of the senior guards.

The hammer strikes the stone perfectly, and the rock shears away. He sings softly—the words are for his ears alone—and his hands are gentle upon the stone, using only the precise amount of force necessary with the order-hardened chisel and mallet.

"The way is the way . . ." he hums under his breath.

He finally puts down the tools and walks toward the cistern and outdoor washroom. The echoes of his feet are lost against the faint roar of the sea below the terrace.

As he shaves, he asks himself if what he plans is fair.

No, it is not fair. Have they any other options? None that he can see, and those suggested by Lydya and Klerris have failed. For he will not be merely Megaera's friend for life, not when her soul is burned upon his. Nor will he spend the rest of his life forever on guard against her tongue and his emotions.

The cold water cools his thoughts. By the time he is dressed, he is calm enough that he will not radiate unrest until Megaera is within cubits of him. He walks across the terrace to watch the summer sun sparkle on the morning sea and waits for her. Shortly thereafter, Klerris will arrive. Even Klerris does not know exactly why Creslin has requested his presence.

". . . All sorrow is joy . . ." He hopes so. But he shivers, thinking about what must be done. Can he do otherwise?

Perhaps, but what? He has listened to Lydya; he has listened to Megaera. Klerris has offered no answers, saying that answers have no meaning unless they are found by whoever asks the questions.

The faint sound of running boots alerts Creslin that Megaera is nearing the holding. He remains by the seaward wall of the terrace, even after she has gone to the wash-house.

Only after she appears on the edge of the terrace, as if to ask whether he intends to walk back to the keep, does he turn. Though his tanned skin is smooth and unlined, a darkness dwells behind his eyes, as if he were older, far older, than he looks.

"You're worried," she announces, her hand resting on the hilt of her blade.

He still prefers the shoulder harness but wears no blade much of the time, unlike Megaera, who wears hers everywhere, except when she sleeps or runs.

"You're right," he agrees. "This can't go on."

She frowns. "Things are going well. The spices are ready for harvest, the traders have finished their warehouse—"

"I meant you and me."

"You're pushing again."

"I've made some decisions." He turns, steps forward, takes her arm as if to escort her.

"I don't need help."

He says nothing, catching her chin with his right hand and turning her face toward his.

She tries to step back, but suddenly his muscles are like iron bands holding her in place. "You can't force . . ." One hand starts to draw the Westwind short sword.

His free hand clamps over hers. "I know." Inexorably he forces her head back to meet his eyes.

Her booted foot slams against his.

Creslin staggers but holds the pain and concentrates on reaching her soul.

"No . . . no!"

But it is too late, and she slumps in his arms.

Creslin holds her for a moment, tears streaming from his own eyes as he watches her chest rise and fall. Her body feels so light with her spirit sleeping, but he carries her into her room and lays her on the bed.

Then he paces by the window until Klerris arrives. Lydya, although she was not invited, follows the Black Wizard in.

"Don't do it. Another life-link will kill her, and yourself," she pleads.

Creslin looks at her and opens his soul as much as he can. "I have not touched her, ever, except once in mind when I knew nothing. I have tried to be a friend. I have tried to court her, to sing to her, and to be gentle. The situation is no better, and perhaps worse, than in the beginning. My death will kill her . . . and continuing in this way will only lead to both of us hating each other. Tell me that things will be better."

Lydya finally looks away. Klerris waits for them to finish their argument.

Creslin tries again. "Can you tell me that things will get better?"

"No, I cannot promise you that."

"Can you tell me that letting me know her as she knows me will make things worse?"

"What you plan will either kill you both within days or . . ."

"Or?"

"I don't know. No one has ever tried a double link."

"Tell me I'm wrong."

Lydya looks at Creslin, and her eyes are clear and deep. "You're using violence to equalize violence. Because the evil done first was so great, this may be the only answer. That does not make it right."

"I've been a tool of the Blacks, of my father, of the Marshall. Don't I have the right to try for happiness and love?" His voice is ragged.

"Patience does not always work for the young." Klerris's voice is slow and calm.

"Or for men," adds Lydya wryly.

The silence in the room draws out. Lydya and Klerris look from Creslin to each other. Finally Lydya shrugs. "It will be quicker this way."

"Quicker?"

"You're already starting to develop a link to Megaera.

Doing what you want to do will hasten and deepen the process, but it may not change anything. Do you still want to?"

Why hadn't he considered the feelings, the occasional strong thoughts that had not been his?

"Are you sure that you want to do this?" the man in black asks Creslin. "As you know from her reactions, the results can be rather severe."

"No, I can't say that I *want* to do it," answers the silver-haired man. "It's just that things will get worse if I don't."

Klerris shakes his head. "You're young. There are worse things than having someone forced to watch out for you."

"Not many," answers Creslin, baring his arm. "Not when that someone is Megaera."

Lydya smiles sadly. "You don't know what's in store for you. But the shock just *might* lead to some understanding."

Klerris shakes his head, but opens the small case he has brought with him. "I do not envy you, Creslin. She is extraordinarily strong-willed."

Creslin can say nothing, nor can he speak through the tears that flow.

XCI

"YOU ARE A demon-damned fool! You've probably just killed us both." Megaera is flushed. While the afternoon is hot and cloudless, the sweat upon her forehead is not from the sun's rays.

. . . *damned oversexed, thin-brained lusting animal* . . .

"You couldn't wait! You couldn't be patient! You couldn't learn more about me! No, like all men, just when you think they might have some understanding, they start thinking with their glands." She takes a quick breath, ignoring the breeze with which Creslin cools the terrace. "What I don't understand is why Lydya even considered this idiocy."

"Because . . ." Creslin stumbles ". . . she said that it was already happening one way or another, and . . ." He has to change what he was about to say. ". . . and I think she felt that if the process was too drawn out, neither one of us could possibly survive it."

"Happening already?"

"Yes. Sometimes I can hear what you think, at least when you're really angry."

"What?"

"You just thought that I was an oversexed, underbrained, lusting animal."

"Thin-brained!" she snaps.

"Fine. Thin-brained. It's the same thing."

"I'm leaving."

"Where are you going?"

"For now, I'll stay with Shierra." She steps back toward the room that has been hers. "No, you don't have to worry about my leaving Recluce. Not yet, at least."

. . . not until the next time . . .

Creslin shrugs, although the words and thoughts go through him like a short sword, and he has to swallow. Again she is giving him no chance at all.

"I've given you more than enough chances, and you twist each one around to suit yourself."

"That's not true. Not quite true," he amends.

"True enough."

He feels the discomfort, although it is not his, and shakes his head.

"You . . . you don't understand at all!" Megaera shouts. "Now even my feelings are yours!"

"Mine have been yours, and you've certainly been kind enough to use them against me when it suits your purpose."

. . . damn you! Can't keep anything . . . how could he have stood it for so long?

"Damn you . . ." The words are more sob than curse. Her hand touches the blade hilt. "You come after me . . . now . . ."

. . . and . . . kill us both . . .

Creslin stands helplessly as she backs away, her hand still on the blade, before she disappears into her room.

There on the terrace, caught between the sun and the surf, between the past he did not create and the future he cannot foresee, he waits and watches until a flame-haired woman in blue marches north and westward, back to the keep, back to another outpost of Westwind.

XCII

WITHIN THE WHITE mist of the mirror on the table rears a forest of masts upon the dark green swells of the Eastern Ocean.

The High Wizard nods. "Soon . . ."

"Soon what?" Hartor watches the images in the glass.

"Soon we will cloak their fleet from both eyes and magic."

"Jenred, do you really think that Creslin could not penetrate the cloak?"

The thin wizard smiles, only with his mouth. His reddish-brown eyes glitter. "Of course he could . . . if he bothered to look. But he's not in the habit, and those who would look for him do not have the ability."

"What about the Westwind detachment? Why did you let it land?"

"If we had attacked it, he would have been alerted."

"I don't know. I don't like the idea of a Westwind detachment on Recluce. And how would he have known?"

"From Klerris. His Black bitch was on the coaster."

Hartor asks, "Won't the Westwind group make a difference if . . . when the Hamorians storm Land's End?"

"So? We can't lose. Either the Marshall loses troops or the Hamorians do. Creslin is destroyed, or the Hamorians discover that they have another enemy among the western continents."

"Fine. What if Creslin wins? What about Montgren?"

Jenred snorts. "What about it? Neither Creslin nor that bitch Megaera will ever claim it, and Sarronnyn can't. The Duke has no heirs. We've seen to that. It will be ours, without even a battle. Korweil can't live that much longer."

"I wish I were as certain as you."

Jenred shifts his eyes to the mirror, and to the ships that fill the glass. More than enough to take Land's End. More than enough.

XCIII

"ARE YOU SURE you don't want to try to break your blood-link to her?"

The two men look out over the dark gray cliffs onto the low, sweeping swells of the black-green northern sea. Only an occasional wash of white breaks across the crests of the slow-moving waves. Despite the high clouds, no rain has fallen, and the powdery red dust has drifted from the road onto the black stones of the terrace and over the uncut stones stacked beside the terrace where Creslin still works in the early mornings.

Now the guards are beginning the mortar work on the second guest house, using the stones he has cut, and Klerris has brought up enough timbers for the guest-house roof.

"What good would that do? Lydya said that the linkage would develop anyway." Creslin leans down and picks up the short-handled stone sledge. Even though the essentials of the Black Holding proper are finished, the windows need glass and the kitchen is only a shell. In the interim, Creslin still putters with the stones for the walkways for the second and third guest houses. Someone will use them, he hopes.

"It might buy you some time."

"Has that done us any good?" He cannot just stand and wait. Despite Megaera's insistence on patience, the more he senses of her feelings, the clearer it is that patience is only an excuse for her not to face her feelings about him, and his feelings for her.

He lusts after her. He cannot lie about that, either to her or to himself. He also loves her, independent of lust, because of the other things that she is: determined, intelligent, incisive, and when she is not threatened, kind and considerate.

"I still doubt the wisdom of the whole double linkage," Klerris adds.

"There wasn't a choice."

Klerris frowns.

"Lydya was right. I was already sensing Megaera's feelings and thoughts. For better or worse, we're linked. Right now, if she stays in the keep and I stay here, we have only the strongest of thoughts and feelings, but before long it won't matter."

"What are you going to do?"

"Wait until the link gets stronger." Creslin pauses. "In the meantime, we might think about a good stream and a waterwheel."

"A waterwheel?" The Black Wizard shakes his head. "I don't think you understand. In a few days, if she has a mind to, Megaera could kill you both. That could be exactly what she's waiting for."

The silver-haired man listens, but his hands wield the hammer and order-sharpened wedge, trimming the black stone before him. For an instant, he can sense salt spray and hear the raucous call of a sea gull. Is that an illusion? He thinks not.

"Would she be that desperate?"

Klerris shrugs. "What woman wants her feelings known?"

"Do you think I have exactly enjoyed her knowing every strong emotion I feel?"

The Black Wizard laughs. "Women have always known what men feel, even without magic."

"You're talking about eastern women, about those who no longer follow the Legend."

"Creslin, all women—except the warrior guards of Westwind, and I suspect that they just do not find it convenient to mention their abilities—all women can read men better than most men can read women."

Clung . . . clung . . .

"Why should that make a difference? It's probably due as much to practice as to an inborn talent."

The older man shakes his head. "What will you do?"

"Wait until the link is stronger. Then we'll see."

"Lydya's worried."

"So am I. So am I." His hands trim the stones automatically, only his senses pointing the weaknesses and sheer lines in the hard black stone.

XCIV

"Now what?" asks Thoirkel, placing another rock on the field wall.

Locked into the soil and the order lines within and around the small section of field, Creslin does not hear him. The not-quite-stifling heat has begun to create wavering heat lines above the walls and the clay road.

"Now what?" repeats the dark-haired man, who is now as clean-shaven as Creslin.

Creslin returns to himself and wipes his forehead. The plateau gets hot earlier in the day than the town and stays hot longer, but Klerris has noted that the soil is far more fertile here. Creslin doesn't need the Black Wizard to tell him that, since the town is built on rock, sand, and red clay so hard that even few weeds appear on the hillside or the flat behind the pier.

Creslin has been merely repeating the painstaking process that Klerris has taught him, strengthening the right worms, grubs, and beetles, ignoring those that are not helpful, and infusing order into the shoots that will become dry maize. Between the liberal application of order and the not-so-liberal application of spring water and limited rain, the maize—destined, if it survives the hazards of Recluce, to become flour for bread and pasta—shows healthy growth, far healthier than that in more temperate lands. Creslin wipes his sweating forehead again.

"Ser! Ser!" A figure sprints from the northern edge of the field.

Creslin straightens at the urgency behind the voice and moves toward the running man. "What is it?"

"Raiders! Pirates! Sails, lots of them!"

"Damn . . . damn . . . damn . . ." Creslin sends his senses to the winds, reaching toward the northern sea, where a forest of masts sweeps shoreward. No White-pulsed energies lurk beneath the sails or within the hulls, but the masses of archers and armed men speak loudly enough.

The co-regent of Recluce scoops up his shoulder harness and adjusts it as he strides eastward, already searching the skies, grasping for the winds. His feet carry him toward the road leading to Land's End. Thoirkel trots beside him.

From the keep, a horn calls—a Westwind trumpet.

Creslin attempts to twist the high winds lower, to call for the cold torrents that sweep toward the Roof of the World.

warships . . . Creslin? . . .

He pauses at the edge of the plateau. A dozen ships creep on partly furled sails toward the harbor. The lead ship has already slipped past the breakwater, out of the sullen, dark green swells and into more sheltered water, and two boats are being lowered.

"Darkness . . ." he mutters, still working to channel the winds toward Land's end, realizing the truth of Klerris's example all too well. Yes, he will have winds, but already he can tell that they will not arrive before the first two ships reach the pier. Perhaps not even then. His feet bear him downhill as his mind struggles with the elements and the winds.

A squad of Westwind guards races for the pier, and Creslin turns cold as he sees a flash of flame-red hair near the lead.

. . . *show you, best-beloved* . . .

His soul twists the skies, and he rips winds by their roots from their icy heights. Yet, as fast as the high winds speed, as quickly as the darkness builds to the west, the lead ships, and the boats filled with armed men, move more quickly, now nearly touching the pier.

As he hurries downhill, Creslin does not run, for even he knows that arriving at a dead sprint and exhausted will do no one any good, especially himself. But his heart pounds as he thinks of Megaera. He forces his thoughts elsewhere, coldly studying the scene unfolding below.

A second squad of Westwind guards and the duty detachment of the Montgren troopers have started downhill from the keep.

The third and fourth ships are sailing past the harbor and to the east, toward the flat beaches where boats may also land. Even if the guards can hold the harbor, they will soon face attack from behind, although it will not be instantly, since it will take some time for the beach-landing troops to cross the soft sand and climb the low but rocky hill that shelters the town.

Arrows have begun to fly from the inshore vessels, vessels that fly the orange sunburst of Hamor.

Creslin pushes and twists the great winds, those on which

he had never called. They strike back, and he sprawls onto the dust of the road.

Thoirkel lifts him to his feet, the dark-haired man looking back toward the west. At least one Westwind guard lies flat on the pier stones, an arrow through her neck.

A gray haze covers the sun, and the darkness towers in the western skies as Creslin unsheathes his blade. He holds it loosely as he steps toward the storm of steel and shafts boiling up around the pier.

He continues downhill, his eyes on the harbor, his sense in the skies. Thoirkel is still there, with a blade that has appeared from somewhere.

. . . now . . . thrust . . .

By the time they are halfway to the fighting, boats are carrying troops onto the eastern beaches, and the end of the pier is held by the attackers.

"Aeeeiii . . ."

"Bitches . . ."

The sounds of swords and voices echo off the cots and rocks, and Creslin looks for the redness that is Megaera and sees none, but neither has he felt the pain he knows he will feel if she is injured.

Lightning forks from the sky and toward the seas, narrowly missing the tall ship that stands farthest seaward.

Arrows continue to arch into the air and sleet down upon those who struggle on the stones of the pier, but some now fly from the shoreward end of the pier onto the two Hamorian ships within the harbor.

RRhhhssttt . . .

. . . aeeeiiieeee . . .

Creslin staggers at the white flame that sears him as Megaera releases the firebolt. Fire sheets from the pier, and the foresails of the lead schooner burst into flames.

Creslin strides forward onto the pier, wrenching winds, wrenching at all he can grasp in the skies above.

Thurrummm . . . thrum . . . crackkk!

The tall ship shudders as lightnings flash upon it and the

winds howl, and as the mist and swirling tempests solidify into a funnel of blackness.

"Ooofff . . ." Thoirkel pushes Creslin aside as a bronze-faced man appearing from nowhere swings an ax toward the regent. A pair of swords stops the Hamorian.

Though Megaera has said nothing, the white agony of her use of chaos burns Creslin as though he had stood in the flame himself. He staggers before he remembers that he has a blade and lets his body react, even as his thoughts twist the black tower of water toward the next Hamorian ship.

The lead schooner at the pier is shrouded in fire, and her masts and timbers begin to burn.

Double lightning forks from the swirling darkness to the north and west, shivering another Hamorian vessel, which one Creslin is not quite sure as he struggles with blade and winds.

The two ships flanking the debris that had been a tall ship try to turn from the waterspout, but the waters swallow them in a tower that rears like a wall between the harbor and the north.

". . . light!"

". . . get the redhead and the silver-head!"

Creslin's blade snakes out and drops another Hamorian as his thoughts twist the darkness upon the ships beyond the breakwater, knowing that he dare not bring that much water within the small harbor.

"Around the regents . . . *now!*"

Creslin finds himself side to side with another fighter, one with red hair, and he almost lowers his blade in relief. "Get the other ships!" Megaera hisses.

. . . *idiot* . . .

Creslin swallows as he recalls those off the eastern beaches, as he pulls the waterspout around the point and toward the three ships. Only those three and the two schooners within the harbor remain afloat.

"Hit the center. That's where they are!"

"Ooo . . ." Creslin winces. Flame seems to sheet

through his right shoulder, but he continues to concentrate on the winds, bringing them and the entire wall of water down upon the Hamorian vessels off the beach.

Ruuu . . . swwussshhhHHH!

Creslin's teeth grind under the impact of Megaera's pain and his own. Yet, off the eastern beaches, only debris and bodies float. The sands are scoured clean by the mast-high wave that has ripped men, weapons, and vegetation alike off the low hill that protects Land's End from the stones and the waves—and that has driven one nearly mastless hull hard upon the sand.

Creslin's guts are in his throat, and he pukes over the man felled before him by Megaera's blade before she follows his example.

"Damn your weak guts . . ."

. . . puking . . . weak-kneed . . . bastard . . .

"Shut up . . ." he mumbles, lifting his blade.

There is no further use for the blade, for all of the Hamorians on the pier are fallen. Perhaps a score have dived into the debris-laden waters to swim out toward the second ship, which has slipped her cables and turns toward the seas.

The lead schooner flares brightly, burning so hot that steam rises where the waters from the sky pelt her. The few Hamorians remaining in the water try to swim beyond the heat.

Hard rain swirls around Creslin, and his right arm lies leaden at his side. He swallows, knowing that he is not finished. Taking a deep breath, he regathers the winds, waiting only until the last Hamorian ship clears the rocks of the breakwater. Then he calls, ignoring the white stars before his eyes. Willing away the agony in his arm and shoulders, he summons the high winds and the cold.

He watches until he is certain that only timbers and debris dot the heavy swells; then he turns to Megaera, who looks at him white-faced, blood smeared across her gray tunic and leathers.

He cannot hold the image, cannot speak, and finds himself sinking to the slippery and bloody stones underfoot, knowing that Megaera is sinking with him.

XCV

CRESLIN'S ARM AND shoulder burn, not with the flame of suns, but with the heat of well-banked coals. When he tries to open his eyes, miniature fires flicker across the dark ceiling. A cool cloth is pressed over his forehead, and the fires retreat.

He dozes, and sees that the room is darker when he again awakes.

A shadowy figure steps toward him. "Ser?"

". . . think I'm here . . ."

"The healer said you should drink this."

A cup is placed before his lips, and he sips. Lifting his head sends a wave of heat through his right shoulder and down his arm. He forces himself to keep on sipping until some of the liquid spills out of his mouth and the cup is withdrawn.

He sinks back on the pillow, trying to puzzle out where he is. The room is small, and the guard who presented the cup is female. So he must be in the newer keep section of the Westwind guards.

A small lamp, its wick low, hangs from a bracket on the stone wall just beside the open door, where a pair of guards stand. Outside, the sky is the purple of twilight, and the dampness of rain fills the air. The thunder is distant, as if coming in over the northern sea.

He dozes, but not for long. When he wakes, Lydya has returned, and the sound of the rain continues.

"Megaera?"

"Better than you, but she's at the Black Holding. The

distance helps some, although the link is too strong for her to escape it, no matter where you are."

Creslin lies motionless for a time on the narrow bed. Lydya offers him the cup.

"Uggghh. That's bitter . . ."

"You need it."

". . . drinking it. Don't have to like it."

When she withdraws the cup, he sinks back, but not into sleep.

"I didn't handle this one very well," he mutters, low enough that the guards by the doorway cannot hear.

Her lips quirk. "Since you're both considered great heroes, I doubt that anyone will question your judgment at this point. They just look at the sky."

"What happened?"

"You saw it all. After you destroyed the Hamorian ships, and the guards and troopers mopped up the stragglers, there wasn't much left."

"How many guards, troopers, did we lose?"

"Despite all the blood and arrows, less than a score."

Creslin shakes his head, and bright stars flash in front of his eyes. A score is far too many to have lost. If only he had been watching the seas, many of those deaths could have been avoided.

"You cannot redo the past."

". . . hard not to think about that." Creslin tries to moisten too-dry lips. He wants to shake his head again but remembers the dizziness, and the stars in his eyes. "Stupid . . . so stupid . . ."

"What? Being human? Or trying to do everything yourself?" For the first time, the healer's voice is tart. "You can't do it all. Neither of you can, even together. Megaera's almost as bad as you are. But you can think about that later. In the meantime, take another sip of this."

He complies, then lets his head fall back on the pillows. "How is she?" Lydya never really answered his question.

"She took several gashes, but no arrows. She also had to fight the shock of your wound."

"Damning my weak guts . . . the whole way . . ." he murmurs as he drifts back into the darkness of sleep.

He wakes with the light, and Westwind guards still remain posted outside his doorway. He no longer sees stars or fires when he moves his head, and his shoulder is only fevered rather than fired. The dressing has been changed.

He tries to moisten dry and cracked lips. Finally he croaks, "Anything to drink around here?"

"Yes, sir. The healer left something for you." The slender guard, no more than just past junior training, carries the mug to the narrow bed. The contents are not quite as vile as swamp water or as salty as the sea, but the bitterness makes raw ale taste like fine wine by comparison.

"Uggghhh . . ." He swallows it all, slowly, holding the mug as the dark-haired young guard retreats, an opaque expression on her face.

Whatever the potion is, it helps, for in time he can sit up. The rain continues, although the skies are not so dark as before. After a while he leans back and dozes once more.

When he wakes, before he can speak, another guard, gray-haired, is offering him more of Lydya's concoction. He drinks. It still tastes worse than sour swamp water. "How long has it been?"

"Since the battle? Four days, more or less."

Creslin wonders how Megaera is faring and if the Black Holding is even habitable in the continual rain. Gingerly, he moves the fingers of his right hand. The motion sends a twinge to his shoulder, and he purses his lips. If only he had thought ahead; one more Westwind blade hadn't really been needed on the pier. If anything, he had probably just been in the way. Yet how could he have stood back and let others fight for him?

"How are you doing?"

Creslin's eyes focus on Hyel as the tall man slouches into the room.

"About as well as . . ." He breaks off the confession. There is no sense in publicly confessing stupidity. Lydya has hinted as much. ". . . as anyone who takes an arrow in the shoulder deserves, I guess. Sorry to leave you and Shierra to clean up the mess."

Hyel grins ruefully. "It has been interesting. I didn't really believe you until I saw those guards fight." He shakes his head. "The men who are left think you're an angel returned—"

"That's a bit much."

Hyel shakes his head. "No, it's not. They watched you kill half a dozen men and call in storms that destroyed eleven ships, and the storms still rage. And the co-regent . . . she fired one ship and a score of Hamorian marines. She even killed some with her own blade."

Creslin wants to change the subject. "What about the survivors? Were there any?"

"Shierra and I decided, subject to your approval, ser, to use them on stonework and farming until they can be ransomed, at least once the rain stops. There aren't many—perhaps a score and a half, most of them from the ship you drove onto the beach. But splitting them up into smaller groups makes sense. Klerris managed to get enough glass made to put windows in your rooms in the Black Holding. Once the weather clears, we want to finish the rest of the building and all of the guest houses. Then the inn." Hyel grins shyly. "I think we will have a few visitors from here on in."

"I suppose so. You'd better see if you can get Shierra or one of the senior guards to offer blade-training to your troopers."

"Well . . . with the rain . . . I mean . . . it's something we can do in the main room . . . a little. We've already started . . . after they saw—"

The silver-haired man represses a grin. "Shierra's probably much better at instruction."

"She says that you're one of the few Westwind masterlades, but no one was ever allowed to tell you so." The lanky man's voice drops almost to a whisper. "Ser, is it true that you escaped a White Wizard's road camp?"

Creslin is beginning to feel tired again and leans back into the pillows. "Yes, but I had help."

"Still . . . no wonder they wanted you prisoner."

Creslin looks out the narrow window. Is the sky lighter? He hopes so.

Hyel straightens. "I think it's time to go."

Creslin turns his head at the other's tone, understanding the meaning in it as he sees the flash of red in the doorway. "We'll talk more later."

Hyel grins, then lets his face become respectful as he turns. "Good evening, Regent Megaera." He inclines his head.

"Good evening, Hyel. You can certainly stay."

Creslin savors the sound of her slightly husky voice, glad for the moment that she is there.

"Thanking you, Regent, but there are duty rosters to be checked."

"Well, go ahead and check them." Megaera perches carefully on the stool near the foot of the bed. Her eyes are unreadable in the dimness of the twilight. "It's about time you woke up."

"Guess I overdid everything."

. . . overdid? . . .

Her eyes flicker toward the window. "Including the storms. No one has ever seen so much rain, and Klerris says that it's likely to go on for a few more days."

Creslin shrugs. "Oooo . . ." His shoulder indicates that the gesture was unwise. "I wasn't thinking about having to stop them at the time. I was more worried about not letting any of the Hamorians escape."

She smiles. "Most of them don't want to go back."

Creslin wills himself not to move, realizing that she will feel the pain as well as he. "Why not?"

"Do you know what the emperor does to failed soldiers?"

"Oh."

"And besides, they figure they're safe here."

Creslin snorts. "Until the White Wizards dream up something else. Or Hamor does."

"They won't. Not so long as you live, great Storm Wizard. Who wants to lose a whole fleet or an army for a mostly worthless giant desert isle?"

"It won't be worthless before long."

"It's not now, best-betrothed." She sits silently on the stool as the night descends.

The two guards have stepped out into the corridor, and the door has been closed, although Creslin cannot say exactly when. The rain continues to fall, but not in the pelting fury that he sensed earlier.

"What are we going to do?" she finally asks.

"Can't we learn to . . . live . . . with each other?"

"You? Me?" She laughs, hard and cold. "When I must preserve you, when I cannot stop knowing how you feel . . ."

. . . still changes nothing . . .

"Do we have any choice?" he asks.

Megaera does not answer, although she sits across from him on the stool until he can no longer remain awake.

XCVI

THE SMALL ROOM on the top floor is brightly lit by four mirror-backed, white-brass lamps. Outside the narrow casement windows, the rain continues to fall, as it has for the past eight-days.

"If this keeps up much longer, there won't be a crop left to save anywhere in East Candar, Jenred," complains the heavy White Wizard. "And the Hamorian envoy has protested that you used wizardry to trick him into reporting Cres.in's theft of the Westwind treasures."

"They don't really believe that, do they?"

"I don't think the emperor of Hamor is exactly pleased with the total loss of twelve ships." Hartor shifts uneasily in the chair, and his eyes flicker toward the half-ajar doorway.

"Oh, well. It was worth a try," notes the thin man in white, lifting his head as if to sense something in the air. He frowns, looking again at the rain outside. "Creslin is strong. I have to grant him that."

"Strong! That's like saying the winters in Westwind are cold."

"So . . ." rejoins Jenred, still puzzled, still looking for something—for an odor or for a whispered word he cannot make out. "It doesn't affect us. He's not leaving Recluce, and he certainly gives Hamor something else to worry about."

"Jenred," Hartor says slowly, "why couldn't you just have left Creslin alone? Let him wander through Fairhaven untouched? He would have wandered off somewhere and settled down, perhaps taught as a Black."

"It wasn't possible."

"I thought it was. So did the council."

"Thought what?" The thin wizard's eyes swivel from the rain to the doorway and back again.

'That you were still after Werlynn, the only man who ever escaped you. Hatred makes for bad policy, Jenred. We can't keep on making decisions based on hatred."

Jenred struggles to his feet but topples as the black sleep closes around him.

Hartor takes a deep breath and bends over the sleeping form, removing the amulet and chain of office. He looks from the former High Wizard to the dark clouds and the rain. Then he eases the amulet and the golden links into place around his own neck as the White guards enter with the chains of cold iron.

XCVII

CRESLIN STANDS ON the hillside east of Land's End, overlooking the Eastern Ocean. Below, the waves ebb and foam
around the beached hull of the Hamorian ship.

Megaera is somewhere away from the shore. He has a
sense of walls surrounding her—possibly the keep's. His
eyes drift back to the hull, the sole remnant of the Hamorian
raiders. Then he shakes his head ruefully, and with a soft
laugh, he turns, walking briskly toward Klerris and Lydya's
cot.

Lydya is there. Klerris is not. Lydya escorts him to the
newly built covered porch and motions to a wooden chair.
She perches on the half-wall, her face solemn. "How are
you?"

"All right so far. Megaera's still spending nights at the
keep."

"Did you expect anything less?"

"I could hope."

Lydya's eyes are level with his. "That's not why you're
here."

"No. I want Klerris to build a ship. Rebuild one,
actually."

"He might like that. He's enjoyed the building projects a
great deal more than he's enjoyed the plants. What are you
planning on rebuilding? Fishing boats?"

"The Hamorian war schooner on the eastern beach."

"Can it be done?"

Creslin shrugs. "I certainly hope so. We need our own
ships. When you think about the markup on goods—"

"That's a big job."

"We could use the prisoners for it. Some of them might
even want to crew it."

"Crew what?" interrupts another voice. Klerris stands in the recently created doorway leading from the main room of the cot.

Creslin repeats his idea. As he does so, Lydya slips back into the cot, leaving the two men alone on the porch.

"I don't know," muses Klerris.

"We have to," insists Creslin. "I'll talk to Hyel and Shierra about using the prisoners for it. Besides, the boat is sitting on sand, not on rock. I think that we could dig around it enough to right it." His eyes flicker over the mage's shoulder as he sees Lydya leave the cot and turn downhill, toward the inn and a cot where Megaera and a small crew labors over the glassmaking.

Klerris smiles. "Someday . . . someday you may undertake something that absolutely cannot be done."

"I already have." Creslin pauses. "Megaera. But I have to keep on as if things will work out."

"Did you tell Lydya that?"

"No."

"You should have."

"Why?"

Klerris shakes his head. "Never mind. Are you going to talk to Hyel now?"

"Why not?"

"I'll come with you. That way, he'll believe we're both crazy."

XCVIII

THE WOMAN IN black leathers stands in the late-afternoon sun, watching as the peak that is Freyja turns into a glistening sword raised against the towers of the sunset. Her black hair is uncovered in the chill wind that passes for a summer breeze on the Roof of the World.

Beside her stands another woman, younger, in green leathers, still holding a dispatch case.

"They've already begun to change the world . . ." muses the black-haired woman.

"Begun?" asks the silver-haired Marshalle.

"Begun," confirms the Marshall. "No one else could do it besides those two. In that, Ryessa was right." She shrugs. "But they're still fighting each other."

"The dispatch doesn't—"

"Unless Creslin is more understanding than I was, he'll destroy both of them."

"I can't believe that."

"Believe it or not. He has that much power." The Marshall remains studying the ice needle until it is cloaked in the early moonlight.

XCIX

SAND AND SEA and birds, and a black boulder rising above the surf—how many hundreds of places are there with such a combination? Creslin does not know exactly, but one of them is where Megaera is.

With the briefest of head shakes, he places the hammer and chisel in the chest, which he stores in the third guest house. He has waited and waited, and knows that further waiting will solve nothing. He pauses, reflecting that he has felt that way before and it has always led to pain.

This time he shrugs—with sadness—and heads for the washroom.

"You have to be clean?"

How else? He laughs bitterly as the cold water flows over him and as he uses the harsh soap to scrub away stone grit, sweat, and dirt. Little enough governing or wizardry has he done while he has recovered, and only a trace of stonework, and too much thinking. Still, the captives from Hamor have completed the walls along the walkways, as well as the interior walls and roofs of all three guest houses. The Black Holding is coming to resemble the plans that Klerris had once laid out on the keep table. The only problem is that the two people for whom it has been built are unable to live anywhere close to each other.

Creslin steps away from the cold water and snaps the tap closed. As he dries himself with the worn and frayed towel he has carted across Candar and beyond, his lips twist into a wry smile. He has a title he never wanted, a land to build that he never asked for, and he loves a woman for whom he walked the winter snows of Westhorns to escape marrying. Yet he married her for convenience.

And for lust, he reminds himself. He cannot deny how much he wants Megaera. He rips his thoughts away from images of the red-haired lady before too-graphic fantasies appear in his mind.

Lust or not, the time has come for the two of them to resolve their destiny. "Resolve our destiny?" he thinks. "How pretentious!" He snorts as he pulls on his trousers.

After donning the short-sleeved shirt and his boots, his hair still damp, he begins to walk down the dusty road. He hopes that one day the road will be a highway stretching from one end of Recluce to the other. For the wizards are right about one thing. Good highways knit people and trade together. But that will come later, assuming that Megaera will accept him. If Megaera will ever accept him.

He continues walking, his thoughts searching the winds before him. The first beach he checks has birds and sands, but neither the black boulder nor Megaera. The second has a black boulder and birds, but no Megaera.

Five more beaches and six kays later, as he scrambles down a skree of rock, he sees pale gray on a pale black boulder, pale gray surmounted by flame-red hair.

"Megaera . . ." His heart pounds faster.

Damn you . . . best-betrothed . . .

His feet slip under the impact of the unspoken words, but he recovers with only the faintest of staggers, hitting the slanted sands under the eastern cliffs at a half-run, his booted feet digging into the softer sand above where the gentle waves cascade in.

A coolness flows within him, the cool, shivering feel of fear. Creslin slows to a walk. Fear? Not his fear, but why fear?

. . . because you are stronger than I am, except in will . . . because I will always be forced to submit. My body cannot bear . . . just as your soul cannot . . .

The fragments of thoughts cascade through his head. His steps hesitate, more than necessary on the soft and shifting sand above the waterline. The white water foams in to within cubits of his feet. Overhead, the hazy, high clouds turn the sun shrouded-gold, and the damp breeze from the sea seems suddenly chill. He stops before the bleached black boulder.

"Megaera?"

"Yes, best-betrothed?"

"Why . . . why do you . . . avoid . . . ?"

. . . to save my soul . . . myself . . .

"The correct word is flee," she says.

What answers does he have? All he knows is that he has always loved the lady.

. . . Love? You don't know love, just lust . . .

"Always lusted after the lady," she corrects him, still sitting on the far end of the gray stone.

"Not just lust . . . not just that." The calmness within his soul reassures him.

Why . . . love? How can you call that . . . love?
"You're lying to yourself. What you feel isn't love," she insists. Yet she is shaken by his coolness.

"Perhaps you don't know love, either," he suggests.

. . . don't know . . . what it's like . . . you have no idea . . .

"I know what I know." Creslin's heart pounds, even while his words are spoken quietly.

You know nothing . . . "Perhaps you should see what it feels like." Megaera's eyes fix on him.

"What what feels like?"

. . . *your* . . . *love.* "What you call love." Megaera smiles.

Can she never love him? He watches as she lifts one hand theatrically. Fire flares at her fingertips.

Flames leap along his forearms—or are they Megaera's forearms?—and sweat beads on his forehead. His/her stomach turns at the order/chaos conflict, as if he had told an untruth.

"Come now, best-betrothed. That's nothing like cold iron." Megaera's voice is hard, and both of her arms lift.

Yet the ugly internal twisting tells him that she is lying.

. . . *nothing at all like fighting cold iron* . . . *RRHHHssssstt!*

Fire slashes into the blue-green of the sky.

Creslin stands immobile on the rocky beach, looking at the redhead, his muscles convulsed and knotted like the bark of a gnarled oak.

"You didn't spend a lifetime bound against such pain, O husband dear . . ." *Damn you, sister dear . . . and you, unwitting tool. If . . .*

Sensing the pain beneath the pain, Creslin forces his lungs to breathe and takes a step toward the end of the rock where Megaera sits. Once more that fire-white, almost lost within the blackness that enfolds Megaera, jets toward the clear eastern sky.

Again Creslin's muscles knot with the internal flame that runs through his blood like acid. His guts turn, and he burns from sole to crown. But he takes another step forward. Megaera must feel the pain even more than he does, and how she has borne such agony for so long . . . how?

Not easily, best-betrothed . . .

The white flame, jetting into the sky, still burns both of

them, and he sways, but breathes, and takes another step—another step toward the fires of the demons of light.

"Do you still love me, O best-betrothed?" *How can you call . . . this love?*

"Yes." The words rasp from his hoarse throat as he reaches the midpoint of the seaward side of the boulder.

Megaera sits on the landward and northern end, another five cubits from him, another five long steps.

"Then know the measure of . . . my love . . . for you." *Love is . . . pain . . . sorrow . . .*

He takes another two steps before he feels the gathering of whiteness that precedes the flames. If he must walk the fires of damnation—

RHHHHHSSSssttt!

. . . never . . . not ever . . . love like that. "Such a lovely . . . thought . . ." Megaera's voice is ragged.

Creslin can feel her unsteadiness, can sense the feeling of loss. He forces himself to take another step.

RRRhhhsttt!

Fires course through his arteries, through his arms and legs, and his eyes see only flares of energy. His arm breaks his fall against the boulder, and the sheer physical pain is almost a relief. A hissing escapes his lips. But he steps to within an arm's length of where she sits.

Her legs are pressed against the pale gray stone, the once-black stone now bleached by sun and sea until it no longer matches the black of the cliff from which time and the sea have riven it.

"Look . . . at your . . . arms."

Creslin does not look, knowing that they must be as red as though he had thrust them into a hearth. Instead, he lurches forward and grasps her elbows, fumbling but dragging her arms down until his fingers twine around her wrists.

RHHHsstt!

. . . save me . . .

Someone moans, but Creslin cannot tell which of them it

is. He wraps his arms around Megaera. She slides off the boulder, and he staggers backward in the sand that captures his boots. His heels dig in with the force of his and her weight.

"*Sssss . . .*"

A different kind of pain lances through his shoulder where her teeth bite into the muscle. He twists his body to escape.

"You . . . bound me . . . like no one . . . ever bound . . ." Her knee jabs into his thigh, seeking his groin and barely missing as he moves.

. . . not be a slave . . . not even to you . . .

"I bound . . . myself . . . same way." His gasping words match hers.

"Different. You chose . . . I didn't." *That was different. You chose to bind yourself to me. I didn't choose to be bound to you.*

Ice runs through his veins as the words chill him, words both spoken and echoing through his brain, and he drops away from her. He steps back, staggering, then stands beside the sea-smoothed gray boulder.

"You chose to bind yourself to me. I didn't choose to be bound to you." The words spin through his thoughts. *You chose . . . I didn't. You chose . . . I didn't . . .*

The waves ebb and flow. White birds wheel on wing tip as they cut the air above Creslin, and the sea pours across the sands, slipping around his boots.

He cannot see for the burning in his eyes, for the tears that streak his face. He cannot speak, for there are no words left to say. For Megaera is right. Megaera is right.

. . . right, right, right . . .

Binding himself to her was yet another act of violence, another kind of rape, an invasion of her innermost feelings.

His feet drag as he stumbles to the other end of the rock. He cannot see, but he does not need to. He has nowhere to go. Seabirds dive into the foam down the beach from where he stands frozen, and the sea whispers onto the sands.

Megaera is right, and he has no words, and no answers.

Go . . . don't know what I want. Don't want you to stay . . . don't want you to go . . . damn you . . . damn you!

Creslin cannot speak, nor can he leave. Nor can he see beyond the blurriness that clouds his eyes.

Even as she has fought him, she has never struck at him other than to escape, as might a caged animal or a prisoner lash out. The flames were thrown to punish herself, and the physical struggle was but to escape, not to attack.

He swallows, looking out at the sullen swells, knowing that he will never again see the ice spire that is Freyja, save in his mind, nor touch the woman he has loved too well and never touched, yet assaulted all too familiarly.

White water foams in, flowing toward his boots, not quite reaching him, just as he has never quite reached understanding—or Megaera. Above, the gold-shrouded sun seems to retreat into the hazy, high clouds. The cool flow of air off the water does nothing to calm the burning of his arms and soul.

He does not look at Megaera, who stares as though frozen at the sea.

In time, Creslin begins to sing, for what else is there? He can say nothing, nor can he hold her, nor can he take back the pain that he has inflicted on her. Yet he must do something, and the song is old.

. . . down by the seashore, where the waters foam white,
hang your head over; hear the wind's flight.
The east wind loves sunshine,
and the west wind loves night.
The north blows alone, dear,
and I fear the light.
You've taken my heart, dear,
beyond the winds' night.
The fires you have kindled
last longer than light.

*. . . last longer than light, dear, when the waters foam
white;*
hang your head over; hear the wind's flight.
The fires you have kindled
will last out my night.
Soon I will die, dear,
on the mountains' cold height.
The steel wind blows truth, dear,
beyond my blade's might.
*. . . beyond my blade's might, dear, where the waters
foam white;*
hang your head over; hear the wind's flight.

I told you the truth, dear,
right from the start.
I wanted your love, dear,
with all of my heart.
Sometimes you hurt me,
and sometimes we fought,
but now that you've left me,
my life's been for naught.
*My life's been for naught, dear, when the waters foam
white;*
so hand your head over, and hear the wind's flight.
So hang your head over, and hear the wind's flight.

After the song, Creslin is silent. His hands remain knotted
around the bleached gray stone.

How long he stands there, he does not know, and though
the clouds thicken above, he has not called the winds. Nor
has Megaera, although he knows now that she could, for
she knows all that he knows, and more.

"No . . . there is one thing I don't know." Her voice is
soft, but he does not move.

Finally he swallows. He does not ask the question,
hoping only that she will answer.

"Why you never struck back at me."

"Because . . ." *Because you love me . . .*

He nods. Impossibly, unwisely, he loves Megaera. And he can never touch her, never even hold her.

"You may hold me, best-beloved."

. . . best-beloved . . .

Creslin is not aware that she has moved until she stands beside him.

Why?

Because you love me. And because I could love no other. Sister dear, damn and praise her soul, was right.

"You deserve to love someone, not just to be loved." The words are hard, for he knows that he may be pushing her away, but he must be fair, no matter what it may cost. Especially now, for he has not been fair, though he thought he had been.

"Hold me. Please." *. . . always fight you . . . but you know that already. Hold me . . .*

He turns toward her, and there is a lump in his throat. He cannot see past the rekindled burning in his eyes.

"Are you sure?"

This time she is the one to say nothing, but her arms go around his neck, and her head is on his shoulder, and her silent sobs rack them both.

So hard to love . . . "Just keep . . . holding me." The words come like sobs themselves. *. . . keep holding me . . .*

"Always . . ."

Always . . .

The sea hisses, and the waves ebb and flow.

In time, a man and a woman walk northeast along the white beach toward the towers of the sunset. Neither speaks as they are enfolded in the blackness that only they and few others can see. A single ray of sunlight strikes the sand before them, then retreats from their oncoming steps.

The storms in the western sky dwarf the towers of the sunset. Holding those towers in their place, the storms form a black arch toward which the two walk, soul in soul, hand in hand.

III.

ORDER-MASTER

C

CRESLIN TRUDGES UP the sandy slope under the makeshift yoke balanced by a bucket of saltwater at each end. This is his second trip, though the sun has barely cleared the Eastern Ocean.

He eases the yoke down until the buckets rest on the black stone pavement and stands by one bucket, concentrating. The water swirls, and a pile of dirty white grains appears on the stones beside the wooden bucket. After repeating the process with the second bucket, Creslin pours the now-fresh water into the stone tank and replaces the cover.

"Creslin?" *Creslin . . . you idiot . . .*

He sets the yoke and buckets inside the storage alcove and walks to the terrace, where Megaera waits, wearing a faded thin shift.

"You know, that's not exactly effective."

"Oh?" He wipes his forehead, looking over her shoulder. Heat waves, like half-visible black snakes, already undulate over the browned hills to the west of the Black Holding.

Megaera smiles. "Can't you let someone else carry the water?"

"Habit . . ."

"But you're the only one who can separate the salt out."

"You can, and so can Klerris and Lydya."

"Fine." Exasperation edges her voice. "It's work desalting the water. That's something only a few of us can do. Can't you understand? Let somebody else do the manual work. You have to do the things that only you can do."

"Like rule?"

"That was unfair, best-beloved."

"You're right. But in some ways, I'm not cut out to be a ruler, to watch other people work. It's hard to sit here and watch the sun burn everything up. It's hard to wait for ships to arrive—"

"That's not what I said." *Idiot!*

A white flamelet sparks from the unseen blackness that now enfolds her, a stubborn remnant of chaos triggered by anger. "You equate manual effort with work. They're not the same. You know that. Being a ruler means working with your mind, not with your body. You can do it. But whenever you get frustrated, you start going back to the physical."

"But I'm not frustrated," he mock-pleads.

"You are frustrated. You just said so."

"All right. I am frustrated. The inn is almost finished, but we have no visitors to use it. The crops are in the fields, but we don't have enough water and they're dying. The pearapples are dropping fruit because they're too dry. I'm tired of eating fish, and so is everyone else. Lydya tells me that we won't have any spices until fall, if then. If I carry water, at least there is some result. What am I supposed to do? Wait until the sun bakes us into cinders?"

"You're the one who brought us here."

Creslin glances from the browning hills to the almost unnoticeable swells of the Eastern Ocean. In every direction he looks, he can see heat waves forming, dancing across hilltops and dusty, sandy ground, across the dry, green brush that is all that seems to thrive in the heat, and even across the beaches that contain the Eastern Ocean. Overhead, the sun blisters its way through a cloudless sky.

"You're right. I'll just bring enough water for us from now on."

"I can carry some water."

He returns her smile.

"And you should eat before you wash up."

He turns his hands upward in mock helplessness but

walks up onto the stones of the terrace and sits on the wall.
A loaf of brown bread and two pearapples rest on a plate on
the wall between them. So do two mugs of redberry.

"You planned this," he comments.

"You need something before you go to work on the
ship."

"Ship?"

"You said you were going to meet that Hamorian . . ."

"Oh . . ."

"Don't tell me you forgot?"

Creslin nods, sheepishly.

Megaera grins. "I don't believe it. You actually forgot."

He breaks off a corner of the tough, hard bread, scattering
dark crumbs across the black stone. Bread in hand, he sips
the redberry. "What are you doing today?"

"We're going to try for glass for goblets. That's harder
than what we did for windows, but Lydya says there's a
market for goblets in Nordla."

He crunches the dry bread, sipping from the mug to help
moisten both crust and mouth.

"As you have pointed out, best-beloved, we need as
many markets as we can develop."

"We also need ships in which to carry the goods," he
mumbles through another mouthful of hard bread.

Megaera nods.

When he has finished eating, he stands, bends over, and
reaches for the platter.

"I'll take it. You need to get to the wreck."

"Ship . . . I hope."

"Whatever." She stands, gives him a quick hug and
breaks away before he can prolong the gesture, scooping up
the platter and mugs as she leaves. She stops by the
doorway. "Will you be at the keep later?"

"If you will be." He tries to leer at her.

Megaera shakes her head. *Beast . . .*

Not quite certain of the tone of that thought, Creslin

shrugs, but she has gone inside. He heads for the wash-house.

Before long he is on the beach where the Hamorian ship rests; he is accompanied by a stocky man in shorts and a sleeveless tunic.

"She's wedged pretty tight, ser."

Creslin walks up from the water's edge, his eyes traveling the schooner's hull planks, until he reaches the bow, half-buried in the soft white sand. "How deep is the keel, or whatever it's called?"

Byrem frowns. "Maybe four, five cubits."

Creslin shakes his head.

"That's the easy part, ser. Stem's narrow, and she's not weighted fore. Most of the weight's midships." The Hamorian wipes his forehead. "Couldn't you call a storm, get her off the same way . . . same way she got here?"

"If I call a storm, the waves will just push the ship farther onto the beach, no matter which way the winds blow, unless . . ." Creslin walks back down toward the water's edge, using the back of his forearm to blot away the sweat that threatens to run into his eyes.

The stern remains in the water, although the depth around the rudder is less than two cubits. He looks at the rudder, then pulls off his boots and wades into the warm, gently lapping water. After a time of tracing the hull lines, he splashes from the water toward the small bronzed man.

"Byrem . . . are there any usable sails?"

"There's an old mainsail in the locker, and some topsails. The mainsail probably won't last long in a blow. The others probably wouldn't—you can't sail her off sand, can you?"

Creslin shakes his head. "No. But I have an idea. When is the tide going to be at high?"

"That's only a half a cubit difference."

Creslin waits.

"Around midday. That's if the storms don't change things. Tides don't matter as much as the high storms."

"Do we want storms or not?"

Byrem frowns, then looks at Creslin. "I don't think so. You'd get too much chop coming onshore. Quiet noon would be the best time to pull her off. There's no place to anchor a pulley or a pivot. That'd make it easier to pull her."

"We'll work out something." Creslin steps into the narrow shadow cast by the ship and begins to brush the sand off his bare feet. "Something . . ."

CI

THE HEAVYSET WHITE Wizard fingers the chain and amulet around his neck, then releases them and studies the mirror on the table, which shows browning meadows, dusty, drooping trees, and an empty road leading to a black keep.

"Jenred was too pessimistic. He forgot about the summer."

"Perhaps, Hartor. Perhaps. But Creslin is a Storm Wizard. What if he brings rain to Recluce?" The white-haired but young-faced man sitting in the second chair watches as the mirror blanks.

"He probably could," admits the High Wizard. "But one rainstorm will buy only a few eight-days and will just make things worse. The one that destroyed the Hamorian raiders encouraged Recluce's fields and orchards to leaf out too much for the hot weather that followed. Now look at them."

"What if he decides to do more than that?"

"Gyretis, do you think he could actually change the world's weather? That's a bit much even for Creslin."

"With Klerris and Lydya advising him, and by drawing on . . . his mate . . ."

"I see that her conversion doesn't set well with you, either."

"I didn't think it was possible," Gyretis responds, "but

that's not the question. He's continually done more than we thought possible. What happens if he does it again?"

Hartor frowns. "If he sends rain to Recluce, it's going to be hotter and drier elsewhere in Candar."

Gyretis stands. "You've inherited this mess, but you'd better not make the same mistakes Jenred did. The council won't be nearly so understanding."

"I know, I know. I just have to figure out how to isolate them on Recluce, even if he does get his rain."

Gyretis pauses by the tower door. "You don't want to try a direct attack?"

"Would you?"

"Hardly, unless things change. But that's your job . . . to figure out how to change things. Good day."

The latest of the High Wizards walks toward the window, noting absently that the walls again show the stress of the forces swirling within the tower. Time for the Blacks, one of those left, to reorder the stones once again.

That will be simple enough compared to his problem: How can he remove Creslin's ties to Westwind and Sarronnyn, and to Montgren as well? Without the support of those lands, Creslin will have a hard time just to survive. Hartor frowns again, his fingers stroking the amulet all the while.

CII

"THE MAIN TIMBERS are as strong as I can make them. So is the sail, but there's only so much I can do there."

"That's all I can ask." Creslin walks down the powdery sand in the mid-morning glare. Not for the first time, he wishes for the chill of the Westhorns, or even for the temperate clime of Montgren.

Klerris matches him stride for stride.

The beached schooner now rests in a small lake surrounded by piles of sand. Nearly two-score men, most of them Hamorian prisoners, stand on the sand. Two hawsers are connected midships, one on each side of the ship, and stretch across the water in which the schooner rests.

Byrem, still wearing ragged shorts and tunic, steps forward. "She's wobbly on the sand but still hard aground. It'd be dangerous to dig more."

"We'll just have to try." Creslin lets his senses enfold the schooner. Can he and the winds even nudge that solidity?

"Let us know." Byrem glances from the two wizards to the men standing by the hawsers.

"How tough is that sail?" Creslin asks.

"She'll take a strong, steady blow. Shifting winds, gusts—things like that will rip her pretty quick."

Creslin reaches for the skies, trying to bring down the trade winds, not the ice winds of winter, which lurk even higher in blue-green depths overhead.

"Get your men ready. He's starting to call the winds." Klerris gestures toward Creslin.

"Take up the lines. The lines!" Byrem's tenor voice rises over the soft sounds of the low surf.

Before long, the gray canvas is billowing seaward, but the schooner does not move.

"Heave now . . . heave now . . ."

The ship remains mired in the sand-circled water.

Creslin takes a deep breath and draws in more of the higher winds, twisting them into a directed force that is becoming a small storm. He tries to focus them on the single square of canvas.

"Heave . . . heave . . ." Byrem leads the chant.

Backs bend, muscles tighten, and the wind rises.

". . . heave . . . heave . . ."

The ship wobbles in the sand, leaning to the left as the patched mainsail's taut curve strains seaward.

Whhupppp . . . creaakkkk . . .

". . . heave . . . heave . . ."

Another shiver grips the hull, and the water around the schooner rises into a chop.

Standing beside Creslin, Klerris concentrates, and a darkness wells from him.

". . . heave . . ." Byrem's voice is a lash across the men on the ropes.

Whuuppp . . . cracckkk. Even as the large sail splits with a thunderclap, the schooner gives a last shudder and slides seaward, seemingly gaining speed as she enters the Eastern Ocean.

A cheer rises from the Hamorians and the keep troopers.

Klerris staggers. Creslin puts out an arm. "What did you do?"

"Just added a little slipperiness to the sand."

"I should have thought of that."

"You can't think of everything, young Creslin," snaps the Black mage. "Leave me some pride."

"Sorry. I didn't mean it that way." Creslin wipes his forehead, although the wind has dried most of the sweat there and the dry clouds block the worst of the heat. The thundercaps are already beginning to break, and there is no rain.

Both wizards turn and watch as Byrem continues to bark orders from the helm of the schooner wallowing seaward on her two remaining small sails.

CIII

CRESLIN LOOKS OUT from the terrace across the flatness of the Eastern Ocean, dull in the gray light before dawn. In the motionless air, he can smell his own sweat from the restless, hot night.

Megaera sleeps, for now; the gray sky turns pink, and Creslin thinks about the dried-up and drying springs, and about what Klerris once tried to teach him about the weather.

Megaera finds him still on the terrace wall long after the sun has cleared the sullen dark green of the ocean. Her hands touch his bare shoulders, and her lips the back of his neck.

"Thank you."

"No thanks, best-beloved. You just sat here so you wouldn't wake me, didn't you?"

Creslin nods as she sits beside him in the familiar faded and thin blue shift. "I hoped that one of us could sleep."

"The hot weather's hard on you."

"I miss the Roof of the World a lot more when it gets this hot."

"Lydya thinks it will get hotter."

"I can hardly wait." He turns, easing an arm around her waist and squeezing, then releasing. The soft scent of Megaera fills him for an instant, and his eyes water.

". . . flattering me . . . it's morning, and I'm just as sweaty as you are . . ."

But her hand takes his, and they watch the ocean for a time.

Finally, he speaks again. "We can't survive if this keeps up."

"The heat?"

"It's the dryness. There's another score or more of refugees camped by the keep. This bunch is from Lydya. One of us is going to have to desalt more water. The pearapples are turning brown."

"Lydya says that's because the water for the fields used to flow under the orchards."

"No matter what we try, we get stopped by the lack of water. We need food. If we irrigate the fields, the orchards die. And with all the new people, we can't buy enough food." Half of the heavy links on his gold chain are already gone, and it is but early summer.

"You have something in mind?"

"Changing the weather."

"That's not a good idea." . . . *terrible idea!*

He rubs his forehead at the violence of her thoughts, and she blushes as she feels his discomfort. "I'm sorry. This still takes getting used to," she explains.

"Not all of it," he says, thinking of one aspect of the night before, flushing as he does.

Her embarrassment matches his. Then they laugh—together.

"Sometimes . . ."

". . . you . . ."

A few moments later, Megaera speaks. "Will you at least talk to Klerris before you try anything with the weather?"

"I will." He can feel her start to stand. "Let's get dressed."

"Do you want to talk to him this morning?" she asks.

"Why not? If I'm right, we should get started. If I'm not, somehow, I need—we need—to look for another answer."

In time, somewhat cleaner from the water that Creslin has lugged up once again from the beach, they make their way to a small cot in Land's End. Both are sweat-streaked and dusty by the time they arrive.

"So much for cleanliness. We ought to think about adding a stable," Megaera suggests.

"It's hard to stay clean when it's either too hot or too cold." Creslin glances at the cot door. "Klerris is expecting us."

The Black mage stands in the doorway of the one-time fisher's cot that has been expanded into a comfortable bungalow, with even a covered porch to catch the cooler breezes off the harbor. "You're here early. Shierra and Hyel weren't expecting you until later."

"We're here for a different reason. I want to talk to you about changing the weather. Megaera feels that no matter how bad things are, trying to make Recluce wetter on a permanent basis would just make things worse."

Klerris motions them toward the porch. "That's really

almost a theoretical question, and I thought you weren't fond of theory."

"Theoretical?"

"Well," Klerris smiles, "until you appeared, no one was ever strong enough to think about it. So why didn't you just go ahead and do it?"

"Megaera convinced me otherwise." Creslin steps out onto the porch and stands facing the light sea breeze.

Megaera glances from him to Klerris and back. "There's something he's not telling us." Her right eyebrow lifts for an instant.

"I'm sure there is." Klerris wanders to the corner of the porch, then turns. "Since you are here, you obviously have a reason—"

. . . *doesn't he always?*

"You're both right," Creslin tells them. "We need cool weather, and we need rain. I can call the ice winds, but I feel that to get them here—now—would bring so much destruction that the orchards and crops would be ribbons before the kind of rain we need would fall."

. . . *at least he asked* . . .

"Would you please—?"

This time Megaera is the one to blush. "Sorry. I still forget."

"That's because you use force in the wrong places." Klerris takes one of the rough wooden chairs. "Sit down. This is going to take a while."

Megaera eases into one of the chairs, while Creslin sits on the stone wall at the back of the porch, where he can see Klerris, Megaera, and the harbor—vacant once more except for the waterlogged fishing boat.

"Think of a lever," Klerris says. "If your lever is short and you have a boulder to move, it takes a lot of force on the lever, and the movement, if it happens at all, happens right then. A longer lever takes much less force, but you have to move the lever farther. Working with weather is similar if you think of the lever's length and movement as distance and time. When you built the storm that destroyed the Hamorian raiders, you used brute force immediately—"

"I didn't have much choice."

"Don't be quite so sensitive." Klerris shakes his head. "That isn't the point. Had you been able to predict when the Hamorians were about to arrive, you could have reached farther away, days earlier, and shifted a few winds slightly in order to create a storm front that would have been much easier to tap—"

"But how do you know which winds to change and how?"

"If," Klerris takes a deep breath, "you wish to listen, I would be happy to explain. You may recall, I wanted to tell you this some time ago, but you didn't seem interested."

"I was seasick at the time," Creslin answers dryly.

Megaera looks at him.

"Sorry . . . you're right. I could have asked later."

"Before we get started, and this will take some time, would you like something to drink?"

Creslin nods and stands. "Where—"

"I'll get it," Megaera interrupts. "You can tell Creslin the background information you've already told me."

Creslin does not sigh. Once again Megaera has shown that he needs to think ahead more clearly. He takes the other chair, sits down, and turns toward Klerris.

CIV

"You'll take care of the details?" asks the Duke as the black-haired woman lifts the cup to his lips. He struggles upright against the pillows.

"Of course, of course." The woman touches his feverish brow with her free hand. "I know how you worry."

". . . feels good . . ." he mumbles between sips.

"Drink some more. It's good for you."

"Tastes terrible . . . hand feels good."

Helisse lifts the cup from his lips, suppressing a frown.

"Can't keep going like this. Every time it's worse. Don't know what I'd do without you." The words are followed by a ragged series of gasps. "So hot . . . so dry . . ."

"They say that's because of the Black magic on Recluce. They've stolen the rain." Helisse sets the cup on the table next to the high bed.

"Don't believe it," gasps the Duke. "Year started hot. More rain when Creslin was here . . . any time last year. Make sure the pay chest goes on the next shipment."

"I understand, dear man. I understand." Helisse lays a hand on his sweating forehead again. "But you need to rest."

"Rest, rest. It's all I do."

After a time, Helisse removes her hand. A shimmer of reddish-white lingers at her fingertips. His eyes closed, the Duke coughs raggedly.

"Sleep softly, dear man. Sleep softly."

She turns to the girl seated on the stool by the window. "Call for me if he needs anything. They know where to find me."

"Yes, mistress."

The Duke coughs again, but Helisse does not turn as she departs his sickroom, only nodding at the pair of guards in the corridor outside.

CV

FROM THE TERRACE southward, the dry plateau stretches into the dusty horizon. Before long, heat devils will appear. Out on the Eastern Ocean, its swells low and flat, the water barely laps at the beaches below the terrace.

Creslin glances at the buckets and the yoke. Today will be another long day of desalting water for the keep and the handful of refugees at Land's End. Should he even bother to wash up? Megaera has said that he should not do so much manual labor, and lugging water is certainly a labor.

"Creslin?" Megaera's voice is soft as she stands in the morning light just outside the doorway from the hallway, barefoot and in her thin shift.

He wonders what she wants.

"Is it that obvious?" She twists her face into a grimace. . . . *damn you* . . . But the feeling is not edged, only regretful.

"Sorry," he says.

"The *Griffin* will land tomorrow."

"And?"

"Aldonya and Lynnya will be on board."

"You want them to stay here?"

"I promised."

"Which guest house?"

"You don't—thank you."

The arms around him are more than worth the inconvenience that may follow. He slips an arm inside the shift and around her naked back.

"Creslin . . ." *No! Not now* . . .

With a last squeeze and more than a slight wandering of his hand, he releases her.

"You—" . . . *take too many liberties . . . always have* . . . "—always have one thing on your mind."

"Not always. Just when I'm around you."

She shakes her head and straightens her shift, not meeting his eyes.

"Anyway . . ." Creslin says to break the silence and to change the unspoken subject on his mind, ". . . I know that you've worried about Aldonya."

"She'll be pleased." Megaera's smile lifts some of his fear.

"I know she'll be pleased to see you . . . she's very loyal. But will she be pleased to see me?"

"Of course. She once told me that you're good at heart."

"But do you believe her?"

"Of course not. You still haven't changed *that* much, best-beloved."

Beneath the banter, the anxieties bounce back and forth.

Why does she still . . .

. . . can't he see?

. . . never meant that, and she knows it . . . love her . . . never hurt . . .

Creslin wipes his suddenly damp forehead, swallowing, looking down at the terrace stones, concentrating on their shape, pushing away mental images of Megaera.

"Best-beloved?"

He looks up.

Tears streak her cheeks, a hint of the fine red dust that settles everywhere muddying her clear skin. "I didn't mean . . . just hold me."

Creslin wraps his arms around her and does not think. Nor does she. In this, or in much else, they can scarcely deceive each other.

She lets him be the one to break away. "I'm going to get some water, just for us," he tells her.

"What are you doing today?"

"Looking for another well. Klerris says there's water somewhere beyond the high fields." He shrugs. "It's better than watching the island dry up and blow away. How about you?"

"More blade practice, then some glasswork. Avalari's done a goblet, and it's pretty good. I still can't get the mixtures right all the time. Some of the glass cracks."

"But—"

"I know. I could bind it with order, but that's not the point."

Creslin agrees. Neither of them can do everything, but it's hard for them to realize it sometimes. He crosses the terrace and hoists the yoke. "I'll be back as soon as I can."

CVI

CRESLIN SQUINTS AGAINST the glare of the sun. Behind him, on the eastern side of the pier, is tied the newly named *Dawnstar*, her masts still bare of canvas. A half-dozen men work on the former Hamorian war schooner. At the shore end of the pier, a wagon and a cart wait. A few steps from him stands a squad—half trooper, half guard—waiting to help off-load the sloop.

"She's heavy," offers Creslin as he watches the *Griffin* wallow toward the pier.

"She is not," counters Megaera, her eyes on the dark-haired woman standing by the railing, an infant in a cradle-pack on her back.

"I meant the ship."

"Sometimes you're just too serious." Megaera grins at him.

He shakes his head, then grins back at her. They wait as the *Griffin* is moored to the stone bollard.

Freigr acknowledges their presence on the pier with a half-salute, but he remains by the helm as the sail is furled and the gangway lowered.

Aldonya is the first off the sloop, nearly running down the plank despite the child on her back. She kneels at Megaera's feet. "Your grace . . ."

Taking her hand, Megaera helps her rise.

". . . it is so good to be here!" Aldonya breathes.

Creslin and Megaera consider the black-walled keep, the heat-browned hills, and the heat waves that ripple off the hillside, then look at each other before looking back at Aldonya.

Megaera raises an eyebrow. "I appreciate the sentiment, Aldonya, but this is not exactly paradise."

"Oh, but it is, your grace. Living in Montgren was—but I should not complain, the Duke was so kind, when he was not ill."

"Go on," Creslin prompts gently.

"Waaaa . . ."

Aldonya slips out of the harness and cradles the red-haired infant, rocking her. "Now, now . . . we're home. No more traveling, little Lynnya. No more traveling . . ."

Megaera smiles, and her smile warms Creslin. Then she flushes as she feels his pleasure. "You're impossible," she whispers.

Aldonya looks up from the wide-eyed baby. "I told you that he's good at heart."

Megaera flushes even redder.

"About Montgren . . ." Creslin prompts, as much to rescue Megaera as to hear what Aldonya had begun to say.

"Oh . . . it was like living under a storm. I mean—" her shoulders shrug even as she opens her blouse and lifts the child to her breast "—there is a storm coming, and there will be trouble, and everyone knows this, and no one will say anything. It was so sad, and I am so glad to be here."

As she talks, Synder leads a chestnut mare off the *Griffin.* The squad forms a chain up the gangplank and onto the ship. A heavy cask is passed along the chain and set upon the pier stones, then another cask, and a third.

"It is good to see that you are happy. Lynnya and I will be happy with you."

"Do you have any baggage?" Creslin asks.

"Oh . . . I forgot. Many things." Aldonya grins at them. "Perhaps some . . . anyway . . ."

"Your graces?" interrupts Freigr, standing halfway down the gangway.

"Why don't you talk to Freigr?" Megaera suggests.

"You'll take care of Aldonya?" asks Creslin.

"I'll see you at the keep later, after she's settled." Megaera pauses. "I arranged for the horses. We do need some stalls or a stable at the holding."

"With Aldonya . . . I suppose so."

"The Hamorian stoneworkers are through with the addition to the inn."

"Fine. See if Klerris . . . someone . . . will rough out plans for the stable."

"You can still walk to the keep if you want the exercise."

. . . *stiff-necked* . . .

He supposes he is, but he turns, and after easing past the guards and troopers still unloading the *Griffin*, he steps aboard the ship.

"Greetings."

"Same to you, your grace." Freigr is standing by the helm.

Creslin waves away the honorific.

Freigr looks across the pier at the bare-masted schooner. "You've done a good job with her."

"I can't say that I've had much to do with it. Byrem—he used to be a Nordlan mate, before the Hamorians captured him—has been handling the *Dawnstar*'s refitting. He tells us what he needs, and I try to figure out how to get it." Creslin eyes the *Griffin*'s captain. "You interested in recruiting?"

"Don't you have enough here, with the Hamorians and some of the refugees?"

"Close enough, if either you or Gossel want to captain her, assuming that Korweil won't mind. But that's not the problem."

"Korweil doesn't own either one of us." Freigr laughs. "You keep thinking about the problems that haven't reached you. Most of them won't."

"If we get another ship, we'll need a crew."

"You haven't finished that one."

Creslin looks at the *Dawnstar*. "If we're going to make it here on Recluce, we'll need more ships. I'll have to figure out a way to get them, even if it means stealing them from the White Wizards."

"That won't exactly make them happy."

"Has anything? Do you really think they'll let us build up Recluce without trying something else?"

Freigr pulls at his chin. "Can't say as I'd thought about it one way or another. After you did in the Hamorians, do you think they'd want to risk any of their own ships?"

Creslin steps to the railing, looking northward into the nearly flat green sea. "They don't have to. We can't grow enough food yet, and it will be a few years before we have enough sheep. Already you can't supply what we need, and Korweil won't let the *Hypogrif* cross the northern waters."

"I wouldn't either," snorts Freigr. "Not enough freeboard, or a solid enough keel. She'd go over in any sort of blow."

"I'm paying twice what I should—"

"About the dried—I meant to . . ."

Creslin groans. "The mutton was from the Duke, right?"

"But the dried fruit came all the way from Kyphros. You insisted that the fruit was important."

"You couldn't find any fruit from anyplace closer than Kyphros?"

"Lucky to find that. It's been a dry year everywhere."

"How much did it cost?"

Freigr doesn't look at Creslin; instead, he digs out a slip of parchment. "I did the best I could."

"I'll have the payment for you later today." Creslin swallows. More of the heavy gold links will go. Some of the fruit he can trade for fish or sea ducks. He looks at the *Dawnstar*, then at Freigr. "We need that canvas."

"It should be ready by the next trip. But they want the gold in advance."

"In advance?"

The *Griffin*'s master shrugs. "You know how many I had to talk to before anyone would agree to it."

"You're saying that you won't get sails for the *Dawnstar* unless I show gold in advance." The graying master looks at the smooth planks underfoot. "I'd never make a free trader, but even Gossel couldn't get around it. And he was raised to it."

"Nothing's ever as easy as you think it will be."

"No, it's not. And it always takes longer." Then Freigr smiles. "At least you have a proper inn now. You going to sing tonight?"

"Somehow I'm not much in the mood for singing."

"Too bad. You'd have made it with the best of the minstre.s, and you'd probably be happier."

"Could be," admits the co-regent of Recluce. He straightens. "What else do I have to find a way to pay you for?"

"Well, there are the tools . . ."

CVII

"THERE WASN'T A pay chest." Hyel looks around the table. "And there was another taxation notice."

"It came on the *Griffin*," Creslin explains. "But the notice doesn't change anything. What do we have to pay it with? Was there anything else? Any letters for Megaera or me?"

Hyel shakes his head. "The notice was addressed to you as regents."

"Korweil . . . even given . . . I can't believe it," murmurs Megaera.

Klerris glances from one regent to the other, purses his lips, then waits.

"What about the cargo?" asks Shierra.

"It's paid for," Creslin snaps. Paid for with gold links and his remaining coins—except for the Duke's mutton and the salted beef, the last of the provisions sent by Llyse.

"Did you have to pay, since the ship is Korweil's?" Shierra's question is blunt.

"Freigr's acting as a consignment agent. Even if the Duke made good the loss, would we get another shipment? Would anyone else trade with us?"

"Oh."

"Exactly. Until the *Dawnstar* is finished, and until the *Griffin* brings the canvas—that should be on the next trip—our choices are limited."

"Limited?"

"The traders know we don't have ships and that most Candarians won't trade with us. We don't buy enough to make it worthwhile for the Nordlans or the Bristans to make a special run—"

"So they're gouging the darkness out of us?" assesses Hyel.

"That's why we need the *Dawnstar*, and a few others as well."

"We can't pay for one ship, let alone others."

"We can't afford not to," snaps Creslin. "Sorry," he adds as a faint aching echoes across his skull and as Megaera rubs her forehead. Even his righteous frustration can hurt both of them.

"How do you plan to get more ships?" asks Lydya.

"I don't know."

Both Megaera's sharp look and the tightness in his guts bear witness to the lie, but no one presses him. Still, he stands. "I'm heading out beyond the high fields. I need to see if we can find another spring."

"What are we going to do about the pay chest we don't have?"

"I'll tell everyone the truth—that they won't get paid, that we've been abandoned by Korweil. If they trust us, I'll promise to make it up them when we can. Those who don't—" Creslin shrugs "—they can leave or go try to live off the land."

"That's not much of a choice," presses Hyel.

"I don't have any better to offer. I've spent almost

everything I have on food and supplies. And I certainly didn't eat it all personally."

"That's a little harsh." Megaera's voice is sharp.

Creslin winces, not at the words, but at the feelings beneath them. He continues to stand, although he does not step toward the doorway.

"Especially since they wouldn't be in this mess—"

Creslin focuses on Hyel, and the thin officer breaks off his statement. "You are right," Creslin agrees. They wouldn't be in this mess now. It would have happened a year from now, and they'd all be dead for certain."

"You don't know that for sure," Hyel retorts.

Creslin turns and leaves the room, his ears ringing. His steps are quick as he takes the steps down to the main floor of the keep two at a time. Trying to ignore the sadness and anger that Megaera feels, he mounts the mare and urges her toward the high fields and the spring he will—must—find.

"Damned fools. As if there were ever easy answers . . ." But his guts twist as he rides.

CVIII

"The second tax notice went as scheduled, and we have the pay chest." Gyretis smiles happily. "It's nice when you can even make a profit on an operation."

"Don't be so quick to rejoice," warns the High Wizard. "What if Creslin or Megaera find out?"

"How? They can't return. They're bound to blame Korweil, and Korweil will resent them—"

"That's one possibility."

"What are you going to do if Creslin changes the weather?"

"*When* he changes the weather?"

"You think he will?"

"He has to, and someone is far-sensing on all the high winds. I'd guess it won't be long."

"Then what?"

The High Wizard spreads his hands, looking at the blank mirror on the table, then out the tower window. "We see how the disruption can be used. I have some ideas. It has already been a dry summer, and if the rains go to Recluce . . ."

"Then what?"

"We'll see. We'll see." Hartor fingers the chain and amulet he wears around his neck.

CIX

CRESLIN CHEWS THE fish methodically, grateful for the sauce with which Aldonya has basted the dark meat. Fish is still fish. A deep pull of warm water follows. He looks at the unnamed roots lying on his plate beside a heap of fish bones, then across the battered wooden table at Megaera.

Aldonya, sitting in a chair at the foot of the table and feeding Lynnya, also looks up.

Megaera meets Creslin's eyes, but shrugs.

"What are they?" he asks.

"Quilla roots," answers Aldonya. "You should try them."

"Quilla roots?"

"I dug them myself. They come from the prickly long-leaved cactus. One of the fisherwomen told me about them. They're almost like yams."

Creslin looks at the pale green cylinders on his plate, then at Megaera, who has not touched hers either.

"Shush, you two. You would attack the world, and you hesitate at a mere root?" Aldonya rocks the red-haired infant, who, wide-eyed, stares at her mother. "Little Lynnya, would you believe it of these two brave warriors? If you grow up to be a magician or a warrior, will you spurn good food because it's different?"

Creslin winces, then cannot help grinning. After another swallow of water, he uses his knife to cut a small portion of the quilla, which he pops into his mouth. He forces himself to bite into the crunchy green. "Ummm . . . that's not too bad."

"You see, Lynnya? Your mother knows what she is doing . . ."

Megaera hastily follows Creslin's example.

"Aren't there a lot of these in the high valley down the road?" Creslin asks.

"I would think so." Aldonya shifts Lynnya from one breast to the other.

Creslin shakes his head. "We should have asked the local fishing people. What else did we miss?"

Megaera continues crunching the quilla root, finally swallowing. "It's chewy."

"Tomorrow we're having a new kind of seaweed," announces Aldonya.

"Then, again . . ." mumbles Creslin.

"It's really not bad, best-beloved."

"The seaweed is good. I tried it," adds Aldonya.

Seaweed, and cactus roots? Creslin takes another bite of the quilla, chewing thoroughly.

CX

CRESLIN WIPES HIS sweating forehead and stretches out on the pallet, wondering how long his efforts will take.

"You're still going to do it, aren't you?" . . . *beloved idiot* . . . Megaera stands in the doorway.

He sits up. "I didn't expect you back so soon."

She laughs softly. "You found me from kays away, and you can't tell when I'm entering the holding?"

"That's different."

"Because you're trying to hide the fact that you're going to try to switch the weather?"

"Yes."

"Fine. I can't keep you from it, nor can Klerris and Lydia. But do you really understand what you're going to do?" *How can you understand?*

"Probably not."

"Thousands are going to starve because their crops will be either parched or flooded by your meddling. At least one or two rulers will lose their heads or their kingdoms or both, and the White Wizards, who will love the chaos you're going to create, will end up stronger than ever. Do you still want to do it?"

"Do I have any choice? If I do nothing, Recluce will fail. Korweil has cut us off, and what can I do about that? Threaten to destroy him? That won't bring back the pay chest."

"It could be Helisse who did that."

"Does it make any difference? How would I accuse her from fifteen hundred kays away?"

"It's not *that* far."

"All right, but it might as well be. Helisse is all he has left. Even if he believes me, he won't last long if she dies."

"I wondered about her. That was one reason I was glad to have Aldonya with me."

"Where is she?"

"At the keep, silly." . . . *likes privacy sometimes, too* . . .

Creslin flushes again. "Anyway, if I do nothing, the White Wizards will still get stronger, and they'll still take over Montgren when Korweil dies. And Ryessa will still probably embark on some conquest, but she'll avoid Fairhaven. Westwind will eventually fall, because it will be caught between two absolute empires that will grind it to pieces."

"So much for belief in the Legend."

"That was unfair."

Megaera swallows. "I'm sorry."

He smiles faintly. "No matter what I do, it's going to be wrong. But I can't wait any longer." He reaches into a pouch by the pallet. "Here."

She takes the five heavy gold links.

"That's what's left. That's all," he tells her.

"The last Suthyan coaster's supplies . . . did they cost that much?"

"Yes, between the coaster and the refitting supplies that Freigr brought for the *Dawnstar*. I had to pay for the canvas in advance, and it will be an eight-day yet before it's delivered."

"That's unreasonable! You could have destroyed the whole Suthyan ship for that extortion." . . . *thieves! White-hearted merchants* . . .

Creslin rubs his forehead at the violence of her thoughts, then holds up a hand. "I could have. But that was the only ship arriving in I don't know how many eight-days besides the *Griffin*. If I ruined her, who else would risk both the White Wizards' anger and mine?"

"Damn sister dear! Where is her promised support?"

Creslin waits. It's clear that they cannot count on Ryessa.

"I know . . . but it's hard. I remember when we played "Hide and Seek" in the courtyards and she promised we'd always be sisters, no matter what happened."

"You are. She's just doing what she thinks is best for Sarronnyn."

"Would an occasional cargo of hard cheese or old grain hurt anyone?" Finally she shrugs and sits down next to him. "Before we do this . . ."

"What?"

Her lips still surprise him as they meet his, but his hands are gentle on her skin.

. . . best-beloved . . .

. . . Megaera . . .

Later, far later than Creslin had intended, his arms still around her, her scent still around him, he kisses her neck, slowly, then finds her mouth again.

"Mmmm . . ."

Megaera eases away from him. He lets her go but studies her body, drinking in the fire of her hair, the luminescence of her skin, the fine bones; he marvels again that she is there.

"You're impossible." Her voice is throaty.

He listens to every nuance, letting her words die before speaking. "I've always felt this way about you."

"Not in Sarronnyn."

"I enjoyed your sense of humor, even when I didn't know who you were."

She smiles. "That was a big point in your favor." She reaches for the clothes she has discarded. "We, unfortunately, have a job to do."

. . . why?

"Because . . . well, because—" Megaera blushes. *. . . I love you, and . . .* "—I wanted you to know that before the real troubles begin."

"You think it's going to be that bad?"

"No." Her face is suddenly somber. "It will be worse."

Creslin shivers despite the heat and reaches for his undergarments. They dress silently.

"My pallet is bigger," Megaera says as Creslin pulls on his trousers. She blushes again. "That's not . . ."

"I know." He follows her into her room, and they lie down side by side.

"Hold my hand," she says. "That way . . ." *. . . if you need the help . . .*

His eyes burn for a moment.

"Don't get sentimental now," she warns.

Creslin pushes away the thought and casts his mind toward the high winds of the far north, toward the nodes of those winds, toward the patterns that rule the world's rains.

The high winds, the great winds, are like rivers of steel, throwing Creslin back toward the south, shaking his senses as a waterspout smashes a ship. He can scarcely sense where he is, tossed and tumbled as he is above the northern seas.

. . . little changes . . .

The warmth that comes with the thought is enough, and he no longer seeks to bend those high, steel torrents; instead, he looks inside, behind, with a nudge here—

—and there . . .

—and there.

The winds twist, howl silently, and lash at the changes and the makers of those changes. Winds the world over shiver and wail as the high winds shift.

At last Creslin returns to Recluce . . . and he lapses into a stupor that is half-sleep, half-coma. Twilight is almost night when he wakes, lifts his head, and puts it down with a gasp.

. . . Creslin . . .

He squeezes her hand silently, holding himself motionless lest he trigger another stab of pain.

Later yet, he turns.

Megaera's eyes are open. "Are you all right?"

He rubs his forehead. "Yes, I think so." His neck is sore.

"So is mine."

After a moment, he adds, "Thank you. It wouldn't . . . have worked . . . without you."

Her hand reaches for his, and they lie together in the darkness, hearing the distant wail of the high winds, listening to the shifting storms . . . and dreading the deaths to come.

CXI

"HE'S DONE SOMETHING," observes the young-faced White Wizard. "I felt it."

"Who didn't?" Hartor ponders for a moment. "It wasn't just Creslin. There was a certain . . . delicacy . . . there. Not the kind of brute force—"

"There was plenty of force. Enough to shift the winds in their courses."

Hartor rubs his square jaw with his thumb. "I don't like the feel of it. There was more there than a wind shift."

"You're right. But it plays into your hands."

"So tell me, good Gyretis." Hartor glances at the blank mirror on the table.

"What's Creslin's biggest problem?"

Hartor waves at the young wizard. "Stop the guessing games. Just tell me and be done with it."

Gyretis shrugs. "Food and water. He's not wealthy. We shut off Korweil's coins, and even Westwind isn't sending a lot of either coin or supplies. Recluce is already too dry, and he just couldn't wait any longer."

"Great . . ."

"It is. You've already observed that the summer has been dry. What happens when there are no rains in Montgren? Or when the summer rains don't reach the fields of Kyphros? Or the Westhorns, and Westwind, are no longer buried in snow rods deep for most of the year?"

"It's going to change a lot of things."

"Exactly. I think that now is the time to let all Candar know, quietly of course, that those renegade Blacks on Recluce are going to starve thousands."

"We can't exactly post signs or hire criers to shout the story on every corner," snorts Hartor.

"Rumor is more effective, and more believable."

Hartor smiles. "So we tell a few people, carefully chosen, and insist that they keep it quiet?"

Gyretis nods.

"And then we make a few more plans . . ."

CXII

CRESLIN STANDS ON the hill crest, at the top of the narrow road he hopes someday will be a grand highway, looking northward beyond the harbor, looking out over the northern waters.

Megaera stands at his shoulder. Both still wear their exercise clothes: sleeveless tunic, trousers, and boots. Both sweat in the late-afternoon heat.

Behind them, the stonework continues on the small structure that will be a stable. Unlike the holding itself, Creslin has not touched a single stone for the stable, leaving that work to the Hamorians, most of whom no longer even regard themselves as prisoners.

Creslin wipes the perspiration off his forehead. But the dampness returns almost as quickly as it is removed, despite the dry air around them.

"I think I can feel it," Megaera offers.

Creslin nods, his senses halfway out to the winds, out toward the dark clouds that roll toward Recluce from the northwest.

Directly beyond the harbor, the ocean is flat, a prairie of sullen green swells that barely move. Farther north, white-caps are forming under the wind that precedes the storms. The horizon is dark with clouds, low and roiling.

Barely audible, distant thunder whispers southward toward the couple on the hill's crest.

. . . *mighty storm* . . . *best-beloved* . . .

"You were there. Nothing else worked." He pauses. "If it's too much, maybe we can work with Klerris to shift some of the winds."

"Don't do anything yet. The patterns have to sort themselves out first."

"How long will it take?"

"Two or three eight-days."

"Well," he laughs. "We could probably use that much rain. It's been dry for too long."

"You might regret those words."

"I might. Let's walk back."

Turning away, they stride through the heat toward the cooler walls of the Black Holding, past the unfinished walls of the stable, ignoring the sound of steel on stone and waiting for the promised coolness of the storms to come.

CXIII

HE WAVES TO Narran. "Over here!" The rain seeps through Creslin's hair and down his neck as he levers the heavy stone into place.

While the foundation of the wall has been replaced, doing so has required carrying rougher boulders from the hillside, since some of the original stones have been buried in mud and clay or carried so far downhill that finding them, let alone retrieving them, is an impossibility.

Narran staggers through the mud with another boulder.

"There." Creslin points.

Into the gap in the wall goes the stone, and the wiry trooper turns back uphill.

Heading toward the rocky hillside from which the water pours, Creslin steps over the diversion ditch that he, Narran, and Perrta have completed to keep the runoff from again undercutting the wall.

Carrying a stone on each hip, the stocky Perrta passes Creslin without speaking. A gust of wind whips the trooper's oiled-leather parka half open, and he twists as if to keep the jacket from being blown off his back.

Following Narran, Creslin plods toward the rocky outcropping another fifty cubits uphill, his boots squelching through the red mud that had been unyielding clay less than an eight-day earlier.

Creslin retrieves two boulders, squarish but smaller than those lugged earlier by Perrta, and carries them through the mud to the wall, where he wedges them into place, adjusting one of the stones brought by Narran.

Another trip and the last gap in the upper field wall—and the cause of further field erosion—has been repaired.

"That's it. Let's head back."

Narran glances from Creslin to the gray rain clouds and back. Creslin ignores the look and steps eastward toward the path that winds down to the keep. Rain continues to soak his short hair and to dribble inside his jacket and tunic. Too tired to redirect it away from himself, he methodically puts one foot in front of the other until he is within the keep.

"You look like something dragged from a swamp." Hyel tosses a ragged towel at Creslin. "Did you have to handle the repairs personally?"

"Yes. I caused this mess, remember? If I just sent people out, how would they take it?"

"They'd do it."

Creslin wipes his face and hands. "I'm heading back to the holding. There's not much more that has to be done, and besides, I'm not up to stonework in both the rain and the dark."

"No one asked you to do it in the rain." Shierra steps into the room that she and Hyel have come to share as joint commanders of the small, would-be army of Recluce.

"You sound like Megaera."

Shierra laughs. "At least you listen to her."

"I didn't want the fields we still have to be washed away in the rain. Why is that so hard to understand?"

Hyel and Shierra exchange glances. "Well . . ." begins the brown-haired man, "it's just that you ask so much of yourself. If you occasionally asked, rather than led by grueling example . . . anyway, would you think about it?"

Shierra nods.

"Since you two seem to agree, I guess I do have to think about it." He folds the towel and lays it on the clammy stone of the windowsill. "And I'm going home."

Hyel and Shierra look at each other again. Shierra suppresses a smile.

With his muscles aching and his damp clothes cool on his body, Creslin sees no humor in the situation. "I'll see you tomorrow."

"Vola is saddled and ready," Shierra adds, stepping farther into the room and beside Hyel.

"Thank you." Creslin nods and departs.

A young black-haired guard turns over the black's reins to Creslin. "Good evening, Regent Creslin."

"Good evening."

Outside the stable, the rain pelts at him more heavily than earlier, although the water feels somewhat warmer. The road from the keep is firm as far as the upper end of Land's End, where he reaches the muddy way uphill to the holding and the drainage ditch that has become a fast-flowing stream.

Spewing toward the town below, the miniature torrent beside the road has deepened from a mere depression into a jagged cut two cubits wide and nearly as deep. Ignoring the water that now flows from his hair across his face and down his neck, Creslin nudges the mare toward the Black Holding.

Even his oiled jacket is sodden by the time he ducks under the still-green wooden beam framing the doorway. Although Klerris had order-strengthened the wood, some of the green timber will shrink and crack. But there is neither time nor coin for seasoned woods.

Outside, the water continues to cascade from the dark gray clouds. Dismounting, Creslin pulls off the oiled-leather jacket and hangs it over a stall wall. Vola shakes, and water sprays across him.

". . . getting to you . . ." He loosens the saddle, removes and racks it, and reaches for the brush.

"Why?" he asks himself. Why does his meddling with the weather always yield such absolute results? Recluce scarcely needs all the rain it has had in the last eight-day. ". . . tried to be careful . . ." he mutters.

He brushes the mare, casting his senses beyond the stable. Megaera, Aldonya, and Lynnya are in the kitchen, as well as someone else: Lydya. For a moment, blackness wavers before him, and he reaches out and touches the wall to steady himself. Then he resumes his currying.

Finally he puts up the brush, adds some grain to the feed trough, and closes the stall door. After picking up his leather jacket, he walks out of the stable and along the slippery black stones of the walkway and into the front entryway. He stamps his feet, trying to remove excess water and mud.

The jacket goes on a peg in the open closet, next to Megaera's jacket, also damp. A small puddle remains on the stone floor underneath. After looking at his sodden boots, he pulls them off, nearly crashing into the wall twice. Then, barefoot, he pads across the Great Room and into the warm kitchen. "Greetings."

"Greetings, Creslin." Standing at one side of the small but heavy stone oven that Aldonya has obtained from somewhere, Lydya holds a steaming cup in both hands. Megaera cradles Lynnya, while Aldonya is slicing long green roots.

"Quilla again?"

"It is good for you. Even great wizards need to eat all the right foods." Aldonya gestures with the knife.

"You'd rather have the seaweed?" Megaera shifts Lynnya to her shoulder, patting the infant on the back as she does.

"If I have to choose between . . . between chewy roots and soggy . . ." Creslin shakes his head. "Anyway, I'm outnumbered."

"You just noticed, best-beloved?"

Creslin looks past Megaera and through the window to the darkness from which the rain continues to pour. Then he searches for a cup. "Do you think this is in time to save the orchards?"

"Pearapples can stand a lot of dry weather." Lydya takes a sip from her mug."

"Why don't you just sit down?" Megaera prods.

Creslin does, grateful for once for the warmth around him.

CXIV

THE MARSHALL READS the scroll upon the desk, then glances at the window, not even frosted over though it is early fall; in most years, the glass frosts well before the gathering in of the sheep and the reckonings of the winter stocks. She looks from the clear blue morning outside back to the scroll bearing the royal Suthyan seal over the signature of Weindre, Governess of Suthya. She picks up the document again. Finally she stands and walks to the door of her study.

"Get me the Marshalle and Aemris."

One of the guards departs.

The Marshall re-reads the scroll, frowns, and waits. Her eyes drift to the unseasonable warmth outside the gray granite walls. In time, she looks up to see Llyse and Aemris in the doorway.

She thrusts the scroll at Llyse. "Read this and tell me what you think."

They wait while Llyse reads the ornate lettering.

"It's a proposal to negotiate a permanent agreement for the use of the guards. Seems about standard. That business about the weather, though, is strange."

"Why? The weather is changing, at least for now."

"Do you really believe that rumor?"

The Marshall snorts. "Do you believe that Creslin destroyed a bandit troop single-handedly? Or that he sank an entire Hamorian fleet?"

"The bandit troop? He could have," offers Aemris.

"The ships? Yes." Both Llyse and Aemris speak simultaneously, then look at each other.

The Marshall takes back the scroll. "This is almost a veiled ultimatum. They're saying that Creslin—'your consort'—has created the disruptions that require greater protection of harvests and storehouses in the border regions between Sarronnyn and Analeria and Southwind, and they want us as the buffer. They'll pay us, of course."

"But not handsomely," comments Llyse.

"Well enough for us to go there and talk about it."

A moment of silence falls on the stone-walled room.

"I don't like it, but this summer's been as lean as any we've seen, and the winter doesn't look to be much better. And Weindre had something to do with the losses we took at Southwind."

"Why are you leaving the detachment there, then?"

"Do we have any better source of funds . . . now?"

Llyse shakes her head. "I don't like it."

"Neither do I. That's another reason to go to Suthya, with Heldra—"

"Heldra?"

The Marshall looks at Aemris. "Because, if anything happens to me—the Legend forbid—Llyse and Westwind will need you."

Llyse swallows. "Couldn't someone else go?"

"Weindre wouldn't talk to anyone else." Dylyss lifts the scroll. "That's clear enough."

CXV

"I TRIED TO be careful, and Megaera helped, but there's still too much rain headed this way."

"It's like . . . like cabinetry. You need a delicate but firm touch, and a lot of practice." Klerris looks out at the drizzle and draws his cloak closer.

"Fine, but we have more rain than we need, and half of Candar is ready to blow away. And the fishermen are complaining that there isn't enough sunlight to dry their catch. Not to mention the time we've spent repairing walls and keeping fields from being washed away. We've already lost a lot of the maize . . . just washed out." Creslin shakes his head in exasperation. "But I don't want to go back to where we started, or worse."

"Then it's going to take time."

"We don't have time. Rather, I'm not sure that Candar has time. According to Freigr, a lot of the meadows in Montgren have actually caught fire."

"That doesn't make sense. Peasants don't set their fields ablaze, and there haven't been any thunderstorms since you— Oh . . ."

"I'm sure they're blaming us. Me, actually. Or me and some renegade Blacks like you and Lydya."

"Patience would have helped, you know."

"I'm tired of hearing about patience, or time. I've never been allowed the luxury of either. Heaven knows I tried. We diverted water, and the streams dried up. I went out and found water—three springs in the hills beyond the fields. Fine. Two of them dried up within an eight-day. I spent half a day every day for eight-days on end desalting seawater, and it wasn't enough. If I hadn't changed the weather, half of the keep would be dying or dead, and everyone would be blaming me for that."

"That's an exaggeration."

"I don't think so." Creslin pauses to see if his stomach corrects him. It does not.

"You could be honestly mistaken. Being order-tied only means that you can't intentionally lie, not that you're infallible when you tell what you think is the truth." Klerris turns from the rain. "In any case, you've already changed the weather. Let's go in by the fire. I'll tell you what I know, and then we'll see what we can do."

Creslin lingers for a moment in the welcome coolness on the porch before following Klerris into the almost uncomfortable warmth of the cot's main room.

CXVI

"THERE'S SOMETHING WRONG here, Heldra." The Marshall pauses and adjusts her formal sword-belt, then steps briskly along the corridor toward the doorway of the grand dining hall.

"Couldn't it just be from the weather and the lost harvests?"

"Creslin is making things hard on everyone, us included." A low half-laugh follows. "Poor harvests mean less trade, and less money to pay for guards. Weindre talks about more money, but Suthya hasn't laid any coin on the table."

"They've always been tight."

"How well we know." The Marshall breaks off as she nears the entrance. Two guards and a page await them.

"The Marshall of Westwind! All hail the Marshall!" The page's voice is thin but clear and piercing.

The Marshall steps through the tapestried archway and up

toward the dais, Heldra close behind her, when a second page steps forward and murmurs a word to the training master, who pauses. Two paces, then three, open between the two women.

Hsttt . . . thunnk . . . thunk . . .

The crossbow quarrels sleet from the corner of the banquet hall like the briefest of thundershowers.

Heldra falls under the first of the quarrels, her body pitching on the polished stone floor.

"Darkness . . ."

The black-clad Marshall staggers before her legs buckle under her.

"Get the healer! Now!"

The Westwind guard in charge of the ceremonial squad ignores the cries and gestures toward the corner. The Suthyan nobility dive away from the grim faces and bare steel.

The guards charge the stairs, ignoring the crossbows dropped behind the stone-walled balcony normally reserved for the Suthyan house guards. The blond guard pushes them onward, toward the palace gates.

On the dais, the lone healer checks one body, then another, pausing at a third before shaking her head.

The Marshall lies facedown, three quarrels through her back and chest. Below her, Heldra's body bears but a pair, one through the neck.

CXVII

MEGAERA CUTS, DRIVING aside the other's blade. The guard staggers from the impact of the hard wooden rod.

"Good!" Shierra glances from the guard to the regent. "But you're still not recovering after the thrust. You're not fighting a duel. You leave the blade down like that and you'll be congratulating yourself while taking a gut shot. Get the blade back up. As for you, Pietra, you're holding the blade too low." Shierra steps forward and adjusts the angle of the wooden weapon. "Like this. You have it here, and you see how she beat past you?"

Pietra nods.

Megaera nods as well, finding her hand automatically repositioning her wand. Then she shakes her head and lowers it before wiping her forehead, damp from both the drizzle and her sweat. "That's all for now."

"Thank you, your grace." Pietra nods again.

"Thank you."

Megaera returns the wand to the rack, reclaims her blade, and walks quickly to the keep.

CXVIII

CRESLIN SITS IN the wooden chair that he has adopted for his vigils on the winds and casts his thoughts out to the west, toward Candar and Montgren. As usual since he has begun his vigils, there are no fleets in the waters around Recluce, only fishing boats and a three-masted bark headed back in the direction of Nordla.

The weather mage sends his perceptions across the winds to the west, toward the clear skies and drying lands, toward the unseen white miasma that cloaks both Fairhaven and Montgren.

Smoke puffs rise from valley after valley as tinder-dry meadows burn. Yet there are no soldiers in Montgren, only tiny points of whiteness that flicker in and out of existence. And none of those points of light appear near Vergren.

The soldiers will come later, much later.

Creslin stands and walks out of the study, down the short

hall, onto the terrace, and into the cold mist that blankets the afternoon.

Megaera is at the keep, finishing her blade practice. That he can sense. Should he see her first, or Klerris?

After strapping on his short sword, he looks for Aldonya, but she and Lynnya are not in the holding. He debates walking and decides that Vola would be quicker, even with time taken to saddle her. Besides the mount needs the exercise.

Vola's strides are quick and sure, each hoof leaving its mark in the damp red clay of the road with each step northward to the black-stoned keep that may represent the hope of order.

The hope of order? Pushing away the self-importance of the thought, he hurries through the cool dampness of the day. Overhead, gray clouds shift, but only a fine mist shrouds the town and harbor. The fishing boats are out, leaving only the *Dawnstar* and the waterlogged boat that never moves. Creslin reminds himself that he should do something about the abandoned boat.

Megaera stands in the doorway to the keep. Her lips are tight. "Have you looked at what we've wrought, best-beloved? Really looked?" Her face is pale, almost blank compared to the inner turmoil that tears at her.

"Should I?" He shakes his head at the flippant comment that was meant to disguise his feelings.

"Should you!" Then her voice drops, as she senses his pain and his reaction to her anguish. "I'm sorry. I didn't understand what you meant."

Creslin forces a smile. "I just meant—"

"I know."

"—that I didn't want to hurt you more."

"I'm stronger than that." She lifts a wrist, where a white scar remains. "And I want you to see and feel the chaos that you can create with pure order."

"That's why I came. I already have seen it. The wizards are burning Montgren."

Megaera raises her eyebrows. . . . *expected any less?*

"No. They're setting hundreds of little fires in dry fields, meadows, houses," he tells her.

"Anyone who can tell the difference would be identified as a Black mage, right?" she asks.

"Clever of them. I either change the weather back and bring on storms that will flatten and swamp anything that's unburned, or Montgren burns."

"Would you? Change the weather back?"

"I've been working with Klerris to make a new pattern, one with less rain here, more in Candar, but not as much as before. If I try to put out the fires . . . I don't think it will work." The cold steadiness of his stomach chills him as much as it confirms to both of them the truth of his statement . . . unless he is honestly mistaken, and that possibility worries him as well. Klerris is right, honesty is not infallibility.

Megaera looks at him. "They must have been waiting. They would have found some way to get at cousin dear."

"I expect so." Creslin is not thinking of Korweil but of Andre the shepherd and of his daughter Mathilde, who had insisted that Creslin was a "good master."

"That doesn't make it easier," she adds. . . . *so much death . . .*

"No. I'll talk to Klerris, but I wanted you to know." He has to ignore her feelings about death. "What are you working on? Right now, I mean."

"Besides riding the winds to look at Montgren? Besides watching the wizards use you to destroy Montgren? A trading plan for the *Dawnstar*."

"Perhaps the maiden voyage should be to the east, or as far west as Suthya."

"Suthya was the plan. How do we know that the Nordlans or the Hamorians wouldn't just seize her? In Candar, at least, they fear you. Even Fairhaven will grant you that."

Has it come so quickly to this? That for Recluse to

endure, he must be even more greatly feared than the White Wizards?

Megaera's smile is faint, but she reaches out and squeezes his hand. "We still need to finish the trading plan. Lydya has some ideas of what can be gathered. There's a shellfish that makes a purple dye—"

"The trading plan . . . first. I still need to talk to Klerris."

CXIX

A SLOOP WITH tattered sails beats northeast from Tyrhavven, trying to clear Cape Kherra before the war schooner, farther offshore, can intercept her.

Even with his senses so extended, Creslin can feel the whiteness of the war schooner, and he knows that there are but a handful of sloops that would risk the heavy seas. He shivers in his chair, nearly breaking his concentration, aware that he must do something to help the *Griffin*. He has never tried to focus the powers of the storms or winds at such a distance.

Recalling what Klerris mentioned about technique, he searches and searches . . . until he finds the gaps in the winds. While he cannot precisely judge distances with his mind, the wind sheers are close enough, for the schooner has not yet neared the *Griffin*. Creslin nudges, almost persuades, a further shift in the sheers, and withdraws.

He is gasping, nearly drained, his mind blank. Shortly he rises and walks to the kitchen, where he finds some cheese. He cuts a slab of black bread and trims the mold from it. Flour is in short enough supply as it is, and the continuing dampness is causing all the bread to mold. He rewraps the loaf and takes a bite of the bread and cheese.

He can see the changes that he and Klerris have worked

on, but once again, doing things delicately takes time, and the excess of moisture will not disappear immediately.

The pearapples, at least, have recovered and retained what fruit remains, and the spice crops are promising, except for the dark pepper. He takes another bite of bread and cheese.

"You must be hungry, your grace, to eat that." Aldonya stands in the doorway, carrying an openweave basket from which the odor of seaweed and fish emerge. On her back, Lynnya sleeps.

Creslin's mouth is full, and he shrugs, then swallows. "Sometimes the weather's hard work, Aldonya." He looks at the basket. "Fish tonight?"

"There's precious little else, your grace."

"Sorry." He takes another bite of bread and cheese, trying to ignore the taste of the bread. Lydya insists that the mold is not harmful, but the flavor is terrible. Still, he has bread, unlike most of those on Recluce.

"Will her grace be here for dinner?"

"I think so. Excuse me." Creslin remembers that he still has some work to do with the winds if the *Griffin* is to escape the Fairhaven schooner.

Aldonya shakes her head.

"Mmmmm . . ." Lynnya burbles.

Creslin smiles at the red-haired baby, but the smile fades as he reseats himself in the study, where he looks out the open windows to the cloud-swirled north.

The white war schooner has almost reached the *Griffin* by the time Creslin casts his senses to the winds and relocates the sloop. He edges the sheer between the two ships and watches the distance open between them as the schooner plows into a welter of chop and swirling head winds, while the *Griffin* clears the cape full before the wind.

Klerris and Megaera were right—again. If he can only plan ahead and use time to his advantage, even more is possible. He frowns. His success with the sloop ignores the chaos from which the *Griffin* flees.

Once again he quests toward Montgren, but he can sense nothing through the cloud of dense and dull whiteness that lies across the land. Fragments of fire, fear, and sickness escape the white gloom like arrows released at random. Vergren itself, Korweil's stronghold, smolders, but whether the fire is real or magic, Creslin cannot say. Nor, he suspects, does it matter.

When he stands, his head again is splitting, and at first he must steady himself on the chair. Not all of the pain is his, and he wonders if Megaera knows what he has discovered.

"Are you all right, your grace?" Aldonya stands in the doorway.

"No, but it will pass."

"Her grace is heading up the road, and I thought you might like to know." She departs. Lynnya is no longer with her, but sleeping in her cradle.

Creslin steps toward the terrace, where, for the moment, it is not raining. The late-afternoon clouds have thinned to a mere haze, and he eases himself onto the stone ledge.

Both the faint thud of hooves on the damp clay and the warmth that is Megaera flow toward him in the dampness before the twilight. He rises and walks toward the stable.

Vola lifts her head and whinnies as Creslin steps forward. He is uncertain of whether he should offer Megaera comfort or whether he is the one who needs the comfort.

"Does it matter?" Megaera offers him a lopsided smile and dismounts.

They hold each other, she still with the reins in her hands. Then she breaks away. "You're going to have to let me go, or I won't be responsible for the consequences."

He blushes. "I'll take care of Kasma."

"Thank you."

As Megaera scurries for the jakes, Creslin leads Kasma into her stall and begins to unsaddle her. Then he racks the saddle and removes the bridle. When he finishes, he walks around the holding to the terrace, where Megaera waits for him on the ledge, her trousered legs hanging over the edge above the slope leading to the cliff.

"Thank you again," she says.

He shrugs, seating himself next to her. "What does Shierra think?"

"She's worried, but Lydya thinks that the rain was soon enough for most of the pearapples to have some fruit, and the grasses on the plateau are already coming back. We can start grazing the horses there again in a day or so."

"But?"

"There still won't be enough food to get us through the winter, with nothing coming from Montgren."

"I'm sorry about Korweil . . ."

"Best-beloved, there wasn't much we could have changed."

He squeezes her hand. "If I'd only known more earlier."

"That's the story of life." She brushes a stray hair out of her eyes.

"The *Griffin*'s on the way. How Freigr got her clear, I don't know."

"You had something to do with that. I felt it."

"Oh, getting her away from the White war schooner, yes," Creslin agrees. "But how he managed to set sail—that took some doing. He'll have some supplies, knowing Freigr."

"Anything will help."

For a time, they sit quietly.

"Does Lydya know anything more about . . . about the Marshall?" asks Creslin.

"No. Just that Llyse has taken over. The traders didn't know anymore than that Westwind has a new Marshall."

"I should have felt . . . something."

Megaera touches his hand. "She didn't want you to be that close."

He looks into the darkness of the Eastern Ocean. "But . . . something . . . ?"

Mist settles on them, the faintest of drizzles as the overcast darkens into twilight.

"Dinner will be late," Megaera says.

"I suspected that. Lynnya was giving Aldonya fits."

"I offered to fix it, but Aldonya insisted that it was her job." Megaera smiles. "She threw me out."

"She does have definite ideas."

"So do you." She squeezes his hand for a moment.

Creslin's thoughts are still on the whiteness that blankets Montgren, and he returns the gesture absently. Megaera withdraws her hand but does not move, and the misty drizzle continues to bathe them.

"While we're waiting, could you . . . a song would be nice if . . ."

He clears his throat, moistens his lips, swallows.

. . . high upon highland, the brightest of days,
I thought of my lover, and his warm, loving ways . . .

The notes are cold copper, and his guts twist within him. He breaks off. "I don't . . . somehow . . ."

Her hand touches his. "Sorry. I didn't mean . . ."

"That's all right."

But the song that would not sing worries at him, and they are both glad when Aldonya appears in the doorway.

"You two will become sick, sitting there in the darkness and the rain. And how will the rest of us fare with our regents ill? Your dinner is ready." She gestures with a large wooden spoon, jabbing it at them as if it were a blade. "Come on."

Creslin and Megaera exchange grins as they turn and rise to walk across the terrace.

CXX

CRESLIN'S WHITE-OAK wand flashes, moving like the lightning that he has often called from the skies, and strikes.

"Oooff . . ." Shierra staggers back.

"Blackness," mumbles Hyel. "Are you all right?"

"I will be." She rubs her shoulder. "You're fast, Creslin. And strong. I could see the opening, but I couldn't get the wand there quick enough."

"I was lucky." Creslin sets his wand aside.

Shierra smiles, a smile that recalls Westwind and a kiss on the stones outside the Black Tower from another guard. "No. Luck has nothing to do with it. Your technique is sloppy around the edges, but unless you run into someone a lot faster, it won't matter. Or—"

"Unless I'm fighting more than one person," finishes Creslin. "That's what happened with the Hamorians."

"There's not much I can do about that, unless you want to try taking on two at once."

Creslin laughs. "How about you and Hyel?"

"Not now." She rubs her shoulder again. "I'm going to have the devil's bruise there anyway. Besides, it's starting to rain harder."

"Has it ever stopped?" Hyel glances up, and then at Creslin.

"I'm working on it. We just have to be careful." He grins ruefully. "Haven't you noticed that it doesn't pour any longer?"

"We only have endless mist." Hyel's tone is dour. "I think I liked the heat better."

Shierra completes racking the wand. Her eyes flash from Hyel to Creslin, and she smiles broadly.

"You two," complains Hyel. "You're from the coldest

spot in the world, and you've got no sympathy for anyone who likes heat."

"It's not that bad, dear man," Shierra says with a smile. Hyel blushes.

Creslin looks away, but he is pleased. "The *Griffin* will be landing in a bit. Are you coming?"

"Is there any need to? Won't Freigr be staying for a while?"

"This time . . . yes. He's likely to be here for some time, in fact."

"Is it that bad?" Shierra slips into the shoulder harness bearing her blade. "Already?"

"Sooner than I thought," admits Creslin.

"It's certain, then, about the Duke?"

"Nothing's certain, but I think so."

"Why didn't he come here to Recluce?"

"Vergren was his life." Creslin picks up his harness. The hilt of his short sword is cold to his touch, colder even than the mist that falls. "How could he give it up?"

"I don't know." Hyel looks down at the stones of the courtyard. "I used to think I understood things. Now—"

"It's not that bad," interrupts Shierra.

"I don't know," repeats Hyel, mechanically racking the practice wand and readjusting his sword-belt.

"I'll talk to you later," Creslin tells them, "after I see what shape Freigr and the *Griffin* are in. Don't forget to send a squad and some carts for off-loading."

"They'll be there."

Leaving Vola in the keeps' stable, Creslin stretches his legs toward the harbor and the expanded cot that has become Megaera's glassworks.

His eyes study the harbor, but he does not see the white sails of the approaching *Griffin*; only the *Dawnstar* and the sunken fishing boat are in view. He shakes his head. He had meant to discuss the relic with Shierra and Hyel. Sooner or later they will need the pier space.

Creslin stops outside the rough, clay-brick walls of the glassworks, then steps through the open doorway.

Her face smudged, Megaera does not look up from the stone-topped table where she studies a translucent blob. Beside the blob is a glass goblet, one of the products of her work with Avalari, an apprentice glassblower before his impression into the Hamorian fleet. Apprentice or not, the goblets are good, and in time their production will provide another trade item, assuming that Recluce lasts that long.

Megaera looks up at Creslin and smiles.

"You're not coming, are you?" he asks.

"What good would it do? You can deal with Freigr, and I'll see you both later."

He steps around the table, hoping for at least a quick kiss.

"You . . ." . . . *impossible . . . oversexed . . .*

He gets both the kiss and a full-bodied hug that leave his heart racing.

"Creslin . . ."

"I know." Another squeeze and a kiss and he is out into the gray afternoon. Before he has cleared the doorway, she is back at work with the mixtures of sand and chemicals that Klerris has laboriously provided.

As he reaches the foot of the pier, Creslin glances toward the point of white, still perhaps two kays seaward of the breakwater, barely visible through the haze that will again become drizzle.

He walks out on the pier, looking at the nearly refitted *Dawnstar*. Without Lydya's ability to mend wood, or Klerris's art of strengthening the timbers, rebuilding the Hamorian ship would not have been possible, not in just one summer. He smiles, though the smile fades quickly, for the *Dawnstar* still lacks adequate sails.

So they have waited for Freigr and the *Griffin* . . . and waited. It has been only three days since Creslin rescued her from the Fairhaven war schooner. Now he waits to confirm what he suspects but what the white mists have kept him from learning.

Montgren is quiet now, the whiteness subsided, but there are troops from Jellico, and even from Hydlen, camped throughout the gentle valleys that had once held little more than sheep. And Vergren alone still seethes with white.

In time, the sloop wallows up to the pier, half of her sails already furled by the time she passes the breakwater. By then, a group of guards and troopers has arrived and reported to Creslin. They stand a pace or so behind the silent regent.

As the lines are made firm and the gangway eased into place, Freigr finally looks out at the guards on the pier, then at Creslin. The captain's hair that had been sandy and silver is now mostly silver, and the clean-shaven chin is covered with a short and scruffy beard.

The *Griffin*, up close, bears its own scars: gouges in the once-smooth railings, patches on the single sail still unfurled, and an unseen and lingering sense of chaos.

As soon as lines are secured and the gangway settled, Creslin is across and onto the deck, where Freigr meets him, garbed in the green-and-gold surcoat worn over a graying black sweater. The crew, almost as scruffy as the captain, looks away from Creslin.

"That was your doing? To the war schooner, I mean?"

Creslin nods.

The flint-gray eyes are bloodshot. "I can't say that I want to be here, Creslin. Or should I say, Duke Creslin? Or will your co-regent wear the coronet?"

"I would claim no title, Freigr."

"No, you wouldn't. That I know. But can you afford not to?"

"How did it happen?"

Freigr shakes his head. "Who knows? Was it the plague? Or an assassin? All I know is that people were dying, mobs running through the streets threatening to stone anyone who was connected with the Black Wizards, and the messengers said that the keep had fallen to the mob."

"I take it that the White Wizards sent in the troops to restore order?"

"How—"

"I could see the troops after the magic cleared, but not how they got there. The keep itself is still clouded in White magic."

"It was magic?"

"Chaos magic of some sort. You can't use order-mastery for that."

"But they said that it was all your fault, changing the weather."

"The weather, yes." Creslin sighs. He glances again at the battered *Griffin*. "And I suppose the disasters that followed are my fault, although I didn't cause them."

"Cause . . . who can say?" Freigr looks at Creslin, the bloodshot eyes still flint-hard. "What do we do now?"

"You're welcome to become the flagship of Recluce."

"Do we have much choice?"

"No. You could command the *Dawnstar*." Creslin points to the nearly bare-masted ship across the pier.

"You've done a lot with her. We've got the sails. Plus some extra canvas. And as many provisions as we could bring." The seaman gestures at the barrels lashed across the forecastle, then pauses. "I'll have to think about it. Might be better to have Gossel as her master."

"It's your choice. Gossel could replace you here."

Freigr looks at the keep on the hill. "I don't know. I knew it was a bad omen, bringing three friggin' wizards here. Just didn't know how bad."

Creslin sees a woman peering from the hatchway leading to the mess.

Freigr's eyes follow his. "Synder's sister. Couldn't have more bad luck, so I let those who wanted to bring their women, sisters, whatever, do so. I figured you wouldn't mind, and I couldn't have done less."

"We're a bit crowded, but that's the best news you've brought." Creslin looks to the northern skies and the patches of blue between the puffy clouds. "That and the weather."

"I was glad for the rain."

"We've had a bit much, but I hope we've fixed that."

CXXI

THE SILVER-HAIRED woman looks from the singer back to the guard commander on her right. She ignores Krynalleen, the thin-faced arms-master who sits on her left.

"I don't like it, your grace," Aemris says. "The Tyrant didn't rebuild Nonotrer . . . before. Now there's even less of a threat."

"We should attack them? After losing two squads in Suthya?" Llyse sips from the black goblet. "And nearly another to the Analerian bandits? We're being bled dry."

"I never said that. But it bothers me."

"It bothers me, too. And that business of the footprints. There's at least a squad of invisible warriors somewhere above the high road."

"It bothers us all," puts in Krynalleen. "White devils."

"Wizards' business," snaps Aemris. "I've doubled the outriders. They can't spend the winter up here, not once the snows are deep. Then we'll get them."

"We don't have that much here to get anyone," Llyse comments, "not with the Sarronnese commitment. Not with the losses we took to Southwind. I'm not renewing—"

"You don't trust the Tyrant?"

"Trusting a woman who would abandon her own sister to the White devils isn't exactly the smartest thing to do. If we weren't so short of hard coin . . ."

"You did send supplies to the consort," Aemris reminds her.

Llyse's eyes flare, but her voice remains level. "Those

were things we couldn't turn into coin and couldn't use."
She pauses. "Anyway, see me in the morning."

Aemris looks toward the singer at the cleared end of the
dais.

"The man song . . . the man song . . ." cries a guard
from the middle tables.

With a shrug toward the high table, the minstrel slips off
the stool, sets down the guitar, and opens the pack behind
him. After a moment, he withdraws an object that he
unfolds into a long fan shaped as a sword. With a bow, he
begins.

> *Ask not what a man is,*
> *that he scramble after flattery as he can . . .*
> *. . . after all, he is but a man . . .*

As he sings, the minstrel, dressed in shimmering, skintight
tan trousers and a green silksheen shirt, prances toward the
high table, thrusting the fan suggestively.

". . . and, after all, he is but a man!"

The minstrel bows, accepting the applause, before setting
aside the comic fan and recovering his guitar. A single
whistle lingers after the clapping dies away. He sits down
on the stool, adjusts the tuning pegs, and lets his fingers
caress the strings. Finally he clears his throat softly.

> *. . . and in the summer, and under the trees,*
> *my love will lift you across the farthest seas . . .*

The applause is scattered, and he smiles wryly before
adjusting the guitar again and beginning a march. Immediately the younger guards pick up the rhythm with their
clapping.

> *. . . honor bright, honor bright . . .*
> *. . . from the mountain's height . . .*

After two more similar songs, the minstrel slides off the stool, holds up his hands, and bows. While the clapping fades, he sets aside his guitar and rummages in his pack for a moment before retrieving a package—almost a half a cubit on a side—that he carries toward the high table and the new Marshall.

Llyse stands for the minstrel. "It is good to see you again, Rokelle of Hydlen."

"I am honored, your grace." The figure is still slender, the voice still youthful, though the brown hair has thinned and the gray at his temples is more pronounced. The once-fine lines radiating from the flat brown eyes are heavier and deeper. "Especially that you would recall a mere traveling singer."

"Those who sing are always welcome." Her eyes narrow, but she steps forward.

"A token for you, Marshall of Westwind." The minstrel's voice is curiously dull behind the mellow tones as he holds the cloth-covered object as if to extend it to her.

"A rather large token." Llyse raises her eyebrows.

The minstrel inclines his head. "I thought you might find it of interest." Easing his burden onto the table, he lifts the cloth.

"Oh . . ."

Aemris leans forward. On the table is a model of Westwind itself, its heavy walls and towers captured in metal, except that in the central courtyard there is a large candle.

"If you will permit me . . ." The minstrel uses a sliver of wood to transfer the flame from the table lamp to the candle.

In the glow from the taper, the small castle seems to glitter, though the walls are clearly solid, if somewhat sketchily etched in the hammered metal.

"Tin?" asks Aemris.

"Alas, Guard Commander, I do not know. The space between the metal is filled with a plaster, I think." He laughs, an empty sound. "I could not have carried this were it solid metal." He coughs and looks toward the pitcher on the table.

"Your pardon, Rokelle. You entertain us and bring a gift, and we keep you standing and thirsty." Llyse nods, and the serving boy pours a goblet and sets it before the empty chair between the guard commander and the arms-master. "Please join us."

"I would indeed be honored." He eases himself into the chair and reaches for the goblet. "Singing's a thirsty business even when you're appreciated."

Llyse frowns again, and her eyes flicker from the minstrel to the candle-lit model of Westwind and back to the minstrel. "What news might you bring?"

"There is always news, your grace. Where might I begin? Perhaps with the Black Wizards . . ."

. . . sssss . . .

Llyse's eyes turn to the candle within the miniature castle; it flares brighter and hisses before subsiding.

". . . say the fires that are sweeping Montgren come from the renegade Blacks of Recluce, though that I would not know . . . and the orchards of Kyphros are dying, Weindre's daughter has pledged fealty to the Tyrant."

"We'd heard that."

Rokelle takes a deep pull from the goblet before continuing. "The Whites have pledged to aid both Hydlen and Kyphros."

"I wonder how much it will cost us all," murmurs Krynalleen into her goblet.

Llyse's brow remains knotted, although her eyes stay on the minstrel. Her lips purse, and she clears her throat, as if to speak.

CrracccKKK!

A flare of fire, like the impact of lightning, shatters the table and throws instantly charred bodies across the hall, flattening the guards at the lower tables.

Even before the echo has died, another gout of white fire

flares across the Great Hall, turning the two tables holding the senior guards into another instant bonfire. In the wavering heat, a hooded figure is outlined momentarily before beginning to fade.

A single blond guard sees the fire that issues from the near-invisible hooded figure, and almost faster than thought, she draws and throws her cold iron blade.

"Ooofff . . ."

Another smaller fire flares.

Overhead, the roof creaks as two beams smolder, and from the distance, the sound of blade against blade echoes in the late-summer evening.

The blond guard retrieves a blade from an unmoving figure. "Quarters! Quarters, damn you!"

Tra-tra!

The watch trumpet echoes from the Black Tower, even as a healer's face turns white over the four crumpled and blackened figures on the dais, even as the blond warrior rallies the remaining guards.

CXXII

CRESLIN CRUNCHES THROUGH the crisp green root on his plate, swallowing the last hard bits. "It's really not bad."

"Not if you like edible shells. You must have teeth like iron." A pair of quilla roots remains on Megaera's plate.

"You should eat them, your grace." Aldonya peers from the kitchen at the redhead. "They help keep the skin soft and clear."

"I've done well enough so far in life."

"They are tasty," Creslin adds.

"Stop it. Both of you. I'm not going to eat the rest of them, and nothing you say will change that," Megaera protests.

"Nothing?"

"Wait until she carries a child, your grace. Then listen to what she says."

"Stop it, you two," Megaera orders again. "I refuse to eat something that sounds like shells when you chew it and tastes like the proverbial wizard's brews."

"If you say—" A white, soundless thunderbolt flares within Creslin's brain, and he shudders, putting both hands on the table to steady himself. He shudders again, looking at nothing.

. . . *best-beloved* . . . Megaera has turned faintly green. "What . . ."

The white emptiness turns within him, and he knows. How he knows, he does not know. But the awful sureness of the knowledge cuts like the dullest of swords.

"Llyse . . ." He shakes his head, and his eyes burn. "Llyse." Slowly he pushes back his chair and stands, almost unseeing as he walks toward the door to the terrace and the mist that is not quite heavy enough to fall like rain.

Megaera follows, and Aldonya watches for a moment, until the redhead has left the dining room. Then she shakes her head. "Wizards . . . but still, they should eat." She begins to gather the remnants of the dinner that will not be completed, her ears alert for the sound of a child who is due to wake.

Outside, Megaera stands beside Creslin and slips her hand around his. For the first time she can remember, his fingers are colder than hers.

"She's dead."

"Do you know what happened?"

"Just that she's gone."

"Do you . . ."

"White . . . it's all white. They're both gone. Gone." Creslin's eyes are dry, dry like the desert, like Recluce before the rains, and his guts are lead-tight and heavy within him.

She takes both of his hands.

"That's another I owe them," he says.

"You can't look at it like that."

"Probably not, but I do." . . . *Llyse* . . . *Llyse* . . . He wishes that tears would come, but his eyes are dry and they ache, and his hands are cold in Megaera's.

As the mist chills the terrace, as the swells of the Eastern Ocean wash upon the sands below, the warmth flows from her hands into his.

CXXIII

"AT LEAST WESTWIND'S no longer a problem." Hartor fingers the chain around his neck, his eyes darting to the mirror.

"Was it worth it? They still managed to get Jeick, and you had to sacrifice your tame minstrel. That doesn't even count the men the remaining guards slaughtered," Gyretis points out.

"That leaves Creslin with no support from Candar. Ryessa won't support her sister. Montgren is ours, and Westwind's deserted." The High Wizard smiles tightly.

"What about the guards? There are still three squads and their kept men and children marching across the Westhorns."

"Three squads? With camp followers? Let them march. What can they do? Where can they go?"

"To Recluce, I'd guess. You've probably given Creslin the beginnings of an army even more dangerous than the guards . . . and bearing even more hatred."

"We destroyed the guards, Gyretis."

The thin wizard purses his lips. "I think you went too far. Ryessa will probably regarrison Westwind, and I'd rather have had a young Marshall there than Ryessa. The remaining guards, assuming they reach Recluce, would join the ancient devils to strike back at you."

"Not if they starve first. Creslin can't feed what he's got, and he doesn't have ships, tools, money, or weapons. What can he do? Create a few more storms? What good will that do?"

"I don't know. But Jenred thought he had everything figured out, too." Gyretis shakes his head. "There must be something about that amulet."

"What did you say?"

"Nothing." The young White Wizard smiles sadly. "Nothing."

CXXIV

VOLA'S HOOVES CLICK on the newly-laid entrance road to the keep, another project of the Hamorian stoneworkers. Despite the lack of coin, they keep working. Is life in Hamor that bad?

Creslin glances to the row of narrow and unfinished stone cots below the road. Despite the still-falling mist, the stoneworkers' hammers rise and fall, and their apprentices mix the crude mortar developed by Klerris from shells and sand and who knows what else. The next line of cots is theoretically for the consorts of both guards and troopers, though there are no consorts for the male troopers . . . yet. But the cots will ease the crowding in the keep.

Outside the stone bungalow that was once a cot and now hosts the two Black mages, Creslin dismounts and ties Vola loosely to the hitching rail he installed.

The neighboring cot, once deserted, boasts a new slate roof and glazed windows to shelter two stoneworkers who have already announced plans to find wives and stay on Recluce.

". . . more faith than I have, sometimes . . ." Creslin mutters to himself.

He walks to the doorway.

"Come out on the porch. Lydya's down at the inn." Klerris's voice carries from the porch.

Creslin shuts the door behind him and joins the Black mage. "I see that the stoneworkers have been busy." He gestures at the glistening slate roof of the nearest cot.

"They're going to build a place off the piers. A warehouse, they said."

"What?"

Klerris grins. "They have faith. Yord—he's the grizzled one—says that once you win, everyone will want to start trading and he'll be able to charge top gold for a ready trading office."

"Win? I can't even pay for supplies. The Duke's dead. The Marshall and Llyse are scarcely cold in the ground, and I still can't get the weather right."

"You're certain Korweil's dead?"

"Aren't you?"

Klerris sips from a tumbler of water and says nothing.

"We almost lost everything to the heat and drought, and now we're about to lose what's left to the rain, unless this works out." Creslin shakes his head. "Light! I can't even sing anymore." He pauses. "Why would I have trouble singing?"

"I know order, Creslin, not music." Klerris finishes the tumbler of water and sets it on the table before walking to the front of the porch.

"I don't think it's the music. I think it's me."

"I wouldn't be surprised." The Black mage does not face the regent. "Are either you or Megaera going to claim the title?"

"Korweil's? I certainly don't plan to. I'm not even related. I haven't mentioned it to Megaera."

"You haven't—" Klerris shakes his head. "Sometimes

you two amaze me. You share minds, almost, yet the most obvious issues—"

"We didn't discuss it, I think because we feel the same way. At least I think we do."

"Assuming the obvious can lead to trouble."

"Tell me about it." Creslin sets himself on the back half-wall of the porch. "But I don't intend to be a pretend duke of a Duchy swallowed by Fairhaven."

"It would make your claim here stronger."

Creslin snorts. "One way or another, it won't come to that."

"You're probably right. Who could contest you two?"

"Enough of titles that don't matter. I asked you about my trouble with singing. You said that you wouldn't be surprised at it." Creslin's eyes narrow.

"Why not?"

"I'd say that you're off balance. You've used order too creatively, and you're probably thinking of doing even worse."

"Worse?"

"Listen to your own words. You don't have enough coinage. You can expect no aid from Montgren or Westwind, and you don't want to count on Ryessa. Just what are you considering?"

"Nothing . . . Yet."

"Creslin, even you cannot go around evading the order-chaos balance forever. You're going to pay in one way or another. The fact that you have trouble with your music indicates that something's wrong."

"What am I supposed to do? Let everyone starve in an orderly fashion?"

"I told you in the beginning that I don't have all the answers. You asked me what I thought the problem was. I told you. You're the one who doesn't like the answer." Klerris's eyes are level with Creslin's.

"It's not a pleasant answer. You're saying that I have to choose between order and letting people starve."

"I said nothing of the sort. I said that you've been using order too dangerously. And the number of souls you've dispatched with that blade hasn't helped either." Klerris shrugs. "I understand your frustration. That's one reason the Blacks have nowhere to go. We can't handle that kind of conflict very well."

Creslin bounds to his feet. "Darkness! Just what I need. Now that I'm halfway there, you're saying that there's nothing you can do. If I use any more order, I'm courting danger. If I use my blade, that's dangerous. Just how am I supposed to get us out of this mess?"

"Preferably without more killing and violence," answers the mage dryly. "Me included."

"Sorry."

"You're not sorry. You're still angry at me because I don't have any magical answers. There aren't any."

Creslin understands that Klerris is telling the truth as he sees it, and his guts turn as he considers the mage. Finally he continues. "I came about the weather—"

"I don't think we need to do any more. Those last adjustments to the northern mid-winds seem to be holding . You'd know better than I would, of course."

"They're holding."

"We should have more sunny days as the summer ends."

"What about . . ."

Although they talk further about the weather, Creslin's stomach still churns, and his head aches when he leaves the cot.

Astride Vola and heading to meet Megaera at the public room of the inn, he surveys Land's End.

The keep is three times the size it had been when they arrived. All of the abandoned cots have been occupied and repaired, and several larger dwellings are being erected, although their construction—requiring stone, crude plaster, and pine timbers from the small stands of old pine nearly ten kays south—takes more time than it would in Montgren.

At the pier rides the *Dawnstar*, her canvas finally in

place. Freigr has said that the ship will sail in the next day
or so. The *Griffin* has already left for Renklaar, where
Gosssel claims to have both cargo and customers for the
small load of spices.

With a last look at the pier, Creslin vaults from the saddle
and leads Vola into the covered shed that serves as a stable
for the public room. He marches from the stable and
through the drizzle to the doorway of the inn.

Megaera has risen from a conversation with a guard to
meet him. "You're angry. I could feel you coming."

"You're right. I am."

"What did Klerris say to upset you?"

"Let's sit down and I'll tell you."

> . . . *if he had a mule, he'd give it to a fool,*
> *and if he had a knife, she'd not be his wife!*

The troopers and guards clustered around the circular
table laugh as the thin guard strikes the final chord. Several
of them glance up as Creslin and Megaera seat themselves
at a smaller table near the kitchen.

"Something to drink, your graces?"

The serving woman's polished tone tells Creslin how far
the tavern has come. "What is there?"

"Black lightning, wine, hard mead, and green juice."

"Green juice?" asks Megaera.

"It comes from wild green berries on the cliffs. It's very
sour, but some folks like it."

"Green juice," Creslin says.

Megaera suppresses a smile and nods. "I'll try it, tart as
it may be."

"Thank you, your graces."

"You're implying that I'm attracted to tartness?" Creslin
asks.

"It seems to have a fascination for most men," Megaera
observes.

He shakes his head, but he cannot hold back the twist to his lips.

Megaera's hand squeezes his, then releases it. "The public house was a good idea."

"One of those few that worked almost from the start."

"You did provide a little . . . help."

"There are times I wish I'd sung to someone else before then."

"Times?"

"All the time," Creslin admits. He takes a deep breath.

"You're still angry."

"I can't help it. Klerris gave me a lecture about my creative avoidance of the order-chaos balance—"

"Oh."

"I know. You've worried about it for a long time, but I kept asking for help. And he didn't have any ideas, except the same old bit about patience. What are we supposed to do? Let everyone starve? Beg the Whites to take us back? Eat quilla roots until we've uprooted every cactus on Recluce?"

Megaera grins briefly.

"It's all well and good to preach about absolute order, but it doesn't feed people, or pay for tools and weapons."

"That's why we're regents, best-loved." There is no irony in her voice.

Creslin turns and looks into her green eyes.

"Do you think your mother wanted to send you out alone?" She asks. "Or that Ryessa really liked putting me in irons?"

"I thought you hated her for that."

"I did. I do. Not for doing it, but for not caring. She felt that she had no choice, but she could have cared."

"Oh . . ."

"You see?"

Creslin sees, sees that he must do what he must, sees that he must never hide the pain from himself . . . or damn others for having no answers. Megaera's hand touches his briefly.

Creslin looks up at the guard on the stool as she eases into another song.

> *. . . holding to the blade,*
> *a-holding to the blade,*
> *He used it like a spade,*
> *A-holding to the blade . . .*

Although the notes are not quite silver, her voice is pleasant enough. Yet each note jars in Creslin's ears, echoes off-key through his skull.

"Are you all right? Megaera asks.

"I thought I was, but the singing . . ."

"Her notes are honest."

"I know."

Clunk.

Two heavy tumblers are set on the table by the serving woman, who does not even pause as she heads for the circular table around which nearly ten men and women sit. All of them are from the keep.

"We really need to think about some sort of common uniform," Creslin muses.

"That can wait."

"I know. I know." He takes a small sip of the nearly clear liquid.

"Oooo . . . " His lips pucker.

Megaera grins. "It can't be that tart."

"Try it."

He waits until her lips twist. "It can't be that tart," he echoes.

"Are you going to drink the rest of it?"

"Of course. We males have a fondness for tartness."

Megaera elbows him.

"Ooofff . . ."

"I still haven't forgotten."

He shakes his head, squinting, but the notes from the singer remain coppered silver, although honest. Yet the falseness echoes through his head. "Do you feel it?"

"Just through you."

They sip the green juice gingerly, listening to the singer.

In time, the guard strums a last chord, stands, and walks toward Creslin. She holds out the guitar. "Would you like to sing, your grace?"

Creslin smiles faintly. "I feel honored, but unfortunately I cannot. Not tonight. I wish I could." He does not know which is more disturbing—her look of disappointment or the calmness in his guts that indicates he is not lying to himself.

"Perhaps another time?"

"I would like that, but it may be a while."

The guard looks from Creslin to Megaera. The two women's eyes meet before the guard nods. "We all would like to hear you again . . . when it is possible, your grace."

"Thank you." Creslin's sip of the tart green juice turns into a gulp.

"Do you know what it is?" Megaera asks after the guard has returned to a table.

"Why the notes bother me? Klerris has to be right. But exactly how? No. My order balance is off."

"I gathered that."

"I just don't know. I haven't done much of anything lately, except to watch from the winds, and that shouldn't be a problem." He takes another sip and stares out through the cloudy glass of the window into the blackness of the night. "I just don't know."

He takes one more sip, the bitterness passing his lips and throat unnoticed. Megaera leaves her juice nearly untouched.

Another singer takes the guitar.

> . . . the Duke he went a-hunting,
> a-hunting he did go . . ."

Creslin waits through the song, sipping juice, his eyes focused somewhere beyond the night.

Finally he turns to Megaera. "It's time to go."

Silently she rises with him.

CXXV

WITH A SINGLE sail in place, the Sligan coaster edges through the heavy chop and past the breakwater. A crewman on the bowsprit tosses a light line to one of the guards standing pier watch by the deep-water bollard.

Below the Sligan ensign there flies another banner, one of crossed black and silver lightnings on the azure.

Why would a Sligan coaster be flying the Westwind banner? Creslin is practically running down the hill road now, his steps dodging the deeper puddles as he dashes through the light rain. He can think of only one answer, and it is not one he wishes to face.

Behind him, Hyel and Shierra exchange glances. "You'd better let Megaera know."

"She'll already know that he's upset," Shierra observes.

"But not necessarily why."

"You're right. We're going to have more guards, though. That's for certain."

"More—"

"Don't groan so loudly."

Hyel grins. "Are you coming?"

"I might as well."

They follow Creslin's steps in time to catch up with him before the coaster is fully secured at the deep-water end of the pier.

"Do you want to explain?" asks Hyel as he steps up beside Creslin.

Creslin points to the deck, where Westwind guards stand in loose order.

"I still—" Hyel begins.

"I see what you mean," interjects Shierra. "I hope they aren't all that's left."

"You think that's what it means?" Hyel asks Creslin.

"The Marshall's dead. Llyse is dead, and Ryessa has been moving troops eastward into the Westhorns. If Westwind still existed, there wouldn't be three squads coming to Recluce." Creslin's words are hard, solid.

The coaster is made fast as her heavyset captain gestures silent orders to a quick-moving crew. Several men glance sideways at the guards, moving around them as necessary.

As the gangway is swung into the stones, a blond guard marches down the planks. She steps past Hyel and halts before Shierra. "Squad Leader Fiera reporting."

The hardness of her voice tears at Creslin, and he swallows, waiting.

"Report." Shierra's voice is as hard as her sister's.

"Three full squads. Also ten walking wounded, five permanently disabled, and twenty consorts and children. Three deaths since embarkation in Rulyarth. We also bring some supplies, weapons, and tools . . . and what is left of the Westwind treasury."

"Report accepted, Squad Leader." Shierra turns. "May I present you to Regent Creslin? Squad Leader Fiera."

Creslin nods solemnly. "Honor bright, Squad Leader. You have paid a great price, and great is the honor you bestow upon us through your presence. Few have paid a higher price than you." He hates the formality of his speech but can offer her nothing besides the ritual, nothing to compare to her travails. At the same time, he remembers a single kiss beneath the tower called Black, and he swallows, for he knows one reason why he now possesses the guards and the Westwind treasury.

"Will you accept the presentation of your heritage, your

grace? For you are all that remains of the glory and power of Westwind."

"I can do no less, and I will accept it in the spirit in which it is offered." His eyes meet hers, and he lowers his voice. "But never would I have wished this. Even long ago, I wished otherwise." That is as much as he dares to voice on the pier, but it must be said.

"We know that, your grace." Fiera swallows. "By your leave, Regent?" Her face is tear-streaked.

"The keep is yours Squad Leader, as is all that we have. We are in your debt, in the angels, and in the Legend's."

"And we in yours, Regent." Tears continue to seep from the young, hard face, but the voice is like granite.

"Form up! On the pier!" snaps Shierra, her voice carrying to the coaster.

The guards file off the battered and damp-decked ship; the drizzle continues to blanket both ship and pier.

"What was all that about?" whispers Hyel to Creslin.

Creslin swallows and blots his forehead, and eyes, with the back of his hand. Finally he steps back to the other side of the pier, away from where Fiera and Shierra preside over the disembarkation of the Westwind guards. Hyel follows him.

For a time, Creslin looks out at the ocean, struggling to regain his composure. "That's . . . they're . . . all that's left . . ."

"Of what?" Hyel queries.

"Of Westwind." Creslin turns abruptly and steps back beside the two sisters, watching as the guards disembark and the crew begins the off-loading.

Several carts roll toward the pier, their passage clearly organized by Megaera, who will—must, unhappily—understand the lead in his heart.

CXXVI

SITTING IN THE wooden armchair with its back to the pair of bunks, Creslin studies the parchment sheets; Gossel studies Creslin; Megaera looks at neither.

Finally Creslin lifts his eyes. "You need ten golds. That's what you spent over the loss allowance."

"The ten golds—they aren't that important." Gossel clears his throat. "The holds were nearly always full. Most of the time, break-even is around half-full."

Creslin pushes the chair back and stands, ducking at the last minute to clear the low timber bracing the cabin's ceiling. "You brought back more than expected. And the lot of oak seedlings . . . Lydya is more than pleased with that."

"And I appreciate the cobalt," Megaera adds.

Gossel looks down at the inlaid crest on the table, the crest of a duchy that exists only in memory. "It isn't going to work, ser. Begging your pardon, it won't. Not unless things change." He takes a draft from the smudged goblet, then pours from the cloudy glass bottle that is from Megaera's glassworks.

"You seem to have thought this out." Megaera's voice is gentle. "Why do you feel that way?"

"It's like this, your grace. I know the traders, like the Ruziosis . . . Klyen and I served under his uncle. That was before Freigr offered me the number-one and when the Duke was talking about building a real merchant fleet. Anyways, Klyen middled for me in Renklaar—just this one time—because the Whites hadn't put out the word, but the declaration came out just after we loaded on everything but the trees. My boys had to load those themselves, even had to clean the pier, because it's like the theft decree—"

"Theft decree?"

Gossel glances at Megaera. "Lift a hand to help Recluce, like a thief, and you lose that hand. Doesn't matter what's right, but Klyen can't help again, leastwise not in Renklaar or anywhere east of the Westhorns. As for Nordla, the *Griffin*'s a good ship, but small to cross the entire Eastern Ocean, and . . ."

"How could we guarantee any protection?"

Gossel takes another sip from the goblet.

"So . . . we have to go at least as far as Southwind or Suthya to trade? Is that it?" asks Megaera.

"Yes, your grace. I don't know as that'd work . . . maybe for the *Dawnstar*. Freigr's got enough hold for the bulk stuff." Gossel takes another swallow from the goblet. "See, everyone wants the expensive stuff, but there's not much of it, and you try to sell it all at once and then the price drops. But ships come only every so often. That's how the trading houses work. They stock the spices and silks and jewels, but they sell only a bit at a time. Keeps the price up that way. With the decree, only the smugglers'd touch our stuff, and their rates are much lower . . . wouldn't even cover our costs."

"We didn't lose that much," Creslin points out.

"One ship in three is lost every couple of years."

"You're saying that we can trade for a little while, even through the smugglers, but that it will raise costs—"

"A lot. Do that, and you have to pay the crew bonus money. You also need to ship marines or some sort of guards. Otherwise, smugglers'll just take you, ship and all."

Creslin shakes his head. "Clever of the Whites. Just punish anyone who takes our goods. That kills legal trade, and the economics kill most of the smuggled stuff."

"I don't see why. Smuggling's been around for centuries," protests Megaera.

"What's smuggled, your grace? Weapons, drugs, jewels. Maybe art for a patron in Austra who isn't too picky, or sometimes some brandy or whiskey—distilled stuff, you know. We're buying weapons, and we don't have jewels, let alone art." Gossel lifts the goblet. "Now, if you could make a brandy out of this green-juice wine or whatever it is. But . . ." he shrugs . . . "we don't have much of the stuff the smugglers want."

"I see," Megaera says pensively.

Creslin sees too. "Let us think about it." He stands, reaching for his too-empty purse.

"No, ser. The coins are nothing. You made me a ship's master, and that's worth more than a few golds." Gossel squares his shoulders.

"That's why you're worried?" Megaera asks softly.

"Aye, your grace. The *Griffin*, small as she is—"

"We'll see what we can do." Megaera's eyes reach Creslin's, but only for a moment, as his anger and frustration wash over her. She stands up.

Gossel's head is down and he remains seated, still looking at the table, almost unaware that both regents are ready to leave.

"We will do something, Gossel." Creslin pauses. "And we appreciate the honesty and the fair warning."

They leave the cabin without further words. Gossel corks the bottle and racks it, then downs the last of the goblet.

As they cross the deck, Megaera looks at Creslin. "Why are you so angry? We've got trading crops. We'll even have some wool, and Avalari is beginning to turn out some decent goblets and other fancy glassware. Now that we can color some of it, it should sell well, certainly in Suthya, and perhaps even in South Kyphros. They don't pay much attention to the Whites there."

Creslin nods to the mate supervising the deck work, and both he and Megaera are rewarded with a casual salute. "Good day, your graces."

"Good day."

"Good day."

Creslin grins at their simultaneous responses, then sobers. "Fine, you're producing splendid goblets, and most of the fall spice crop will survive. We send it south and we get half of what it's worth. We try to send it east, and what's to keep the Hamorians from seizing the *Dawnstar*? It was theirs once, after all."

"You think they would?"

"I don't know. Can we afford to risk it now? We can last for a while, even though losing a few golds, as long as we get the goods . . . and as long as we don't lose a ship. Or too many crops. Or get too many more refugees." Creslin's footsteps echo on the stones of the pier.

"Did what Fiera brought help?" Megaera brushes her hair back over her right ear.

Creslin laughs harshly. "Help? We'd be at the edge without that chest. But what other miracles can we expect? And at what price?" He shakes his head. "She's sharp, sharper in some ways than Shierra."

"Oh . . . is that because you once loved her?" Megaera looks at the open window of the public room as they walk toward the stable, where Vola and Kasma wait.

"Some jealousy there? At least she has brains, unlike that perfumed fop Dreric."

"Best-beloved, I know what you felt toward Fiera. How could I not . . . on the pier?"

The combination of pain and anger stills his tongue more than the coldness of her words. "I'm sorry. It still hurts. She gave us everything, and . . . what can I return?"

"She knows that. And you did give her something. Everyone saw the grief and lost love on your face there on the pier. In time, that will help."

Their feet echo on the stones leading to the Inn stable.

"What I meant was that she saw, right at the time, that Westwind was doomed, and she moved everything she could." Creslin turns toward the stable door.

"Was it truly doomed?"

"Yes. What was left in the treasury, after they chartered the coaster and paid for all the cargo they brought wouldn't have been enough for the winter supplies. The Whites also killed most of the sheep, and you can't rebuild flocks in a year, the way you can with a bad field crop." He pauses in the open stable door.

"Sometimes . . ."

"Sometimes what?"

"Nothing." Megaera steps toward the stall and Kasma.

Creslin leads out the black and swings into the saddle. He does not need to wait, for Megaera has matched his actions, and they ride toward the keep.

His eyes traverse the town. Three or four more houses have sprung up on the hillside below the keep, and the warehouse promised by the two stonemasons rises perhaps two hundred cubits east of the inn.

At times, Land's End almost resembles a town.

CXXVII

"HALLO!" CRESLIN'S VOICE echoes through the still-empty public room.

"Hold to! Hold to!" grumbles a voice.

Despite the emptiness, the tables are clean and the stone floor has been freshly swept. Chairs and benches stand ready for the customers that the afternoon will bring, for there are no ships in the harbor, and no one from the town or the keep has time to while away in the earlier part of the day.

"We're not open—oh, your grace." The narrow-faced woman inclines her head to him.

"I know. I need to buy a bottle of that green-juice wine."

"That . . . ? Green juice?"

Creslin can't help smiling. "I want to see what can be done with it. The tartness has possibilities, I'm told."

"That swill? There be no understanding tastes, your

grace." The woman turns back into the kitchen with an iron key in her hand. "Be just a moment, your grace." After the rasping release of a heavy lock, a clanking of bottles, and the relocking of the storeroom, she returns and thrusts two bottles at him. "Two'd be strong enough for any lightning spell."

"Too strong, I suspect. What do I owe you?"

"Not a copper, your grace. Can't be charging the owner, now can we?"

"Thank you."

The woman is still shaking her head as Creslin departs.

Outside, he places a bottle in each empty saddlebag, then mounts and turns Vola toward the Black Holding.

The clouds to the east have begun to part, revealing clean, blue-green sky, almost as crystal as that viewed from the Roof of the World. Creslin swallows and continues uphill.

The holding is empty. He supposes that Aldonya and Lynnya are buying yet more fish for dinner and that Megaera is at the glassworks.

Once in the study, Creslin opens one of the bottles and pours the contents into four tumblers. After studying the first tumbler, he concentrates. Half of the liquid vanishes, and there is a small puddle on the stone floor.

"Oh . . . clean that up later," he mumbles. He sniffs the remainder of the liquid in the tumbler. "Not that much different." With even the smallest of sips, his eyes water at the sour bite of the distilled green-juice wine. "Whuuu . . ."

He tries again, with the second tumbler, and with the third and fourth. Then he walks out of the study and into the sunlight on the terrace. Some of the stones are still damp from the night's mists, but the heat of the early fall sun promises to dry them before long.

A raw alcoholic beverage he does have, but not one that most would drink, let alone pay for. Where does he go now? Aging is almost a function of chaos, not of order.

Below the terrace, the waves sweep across the beach at the base of the cliff, polishing the sands with their ceaseless ebb and flow.

Polishing? Creslin walks swiftly back into the study, where he concentrates on both order-distilling and polishing.

He pours the liquid from the tumblers back into the bottle. Perhaps two thirds of the bottle is filled with a translucent green fluid.

He resaddles Vola, and the single bottle goes back into a saddlebag, to be taken to the keep. Along the way, he makes several quick stops, arranging for a meeting.

Later, in the early afternoon, Shierra, Lydya, Megaera, Klerris, and Hyel sit around the table in the keep.

"You wanted us here," Megaera says. *For what . . . best-beloved?*

Creslin pours a small quantity from the bottle into several goblets and presses a goblet upon each. "Just taste this . . . carefully."

Megaera raises an eyebrow at her husband. Hyel frowns. Shierra looks from Hyel to Megaera. Lydya keeps her mouth still, but her eyes twinkle, while Klerris lifts his goblet without comment.

". . . strong."

"Pretty good . . . tangy."

"Smooth and bitter . . ."

"Decent brandy . . ."

"What is it?"

Creslin waits until the five have finished. "Polished green-juice brandy."

"I suspected so." Lydya nods.

"What have you got in mind?" Hyel asks.

"The other day there was something Gossel said," Creslin muses. "He was explaining that smugglers trade only certain things, like weapons, jewels, and distilled spirits. Then he sort of half-muttered that the green juice ought to make a decent brandy. So I tried it."

"Do you think we could make money on it?" Lydya asks.

"I don't know. But there are a lot of berries on the western cliffs. They grow anywhere, and it wouldn't take much effort to find out. The glassworks already makes some bottles. Would a colored one be much trouble?" He looks at Megaera.

"No. But would anyone buy it?"

Hyel laughs. "It's better than most of the good stuff out there. But you'd have to make a lot."

"Anyone mind if I try?"

"Hardly," Megaera finally says. "It is order-based and constructive."

Creslin swallows the implied reprimand.

"Is that all? asks Shierra.

"That's all."

Creslin watches for a moment as they look at each other, then turns and leaves, walking slowly down the stairs to the main floor, and out toward the stable.

Megaera catches up with him. "I'm sorry."

"It was stupid. I just thought it was a good idea."

"It is. It's simply that . . . I mean, how can we produce enough?"

"I should have thought about that. Fine. Say I can come up with a hundred bottles before winter, and that's a lot. Assume that they're good enough to fetch a silver apiece—even a gold. That's what? A hundred golds. What will the bottles cost? And everything else. A hundred golds would be nice, but they certainly won't solve our problems." Creslin eases the saddle onto the black.

"I still like the idea."

"Thank you. But it's not enough, and I should have known better."

"Are you going to do it?"

"Why not? Someday it might really lead to something, and it will give us a few coins in the meantime. Besides, I'd feel like a fool if I didn't carry it through now." He tightens the saddle. "I don't know. Sometimes it seems like nothing safe and orderly will save us."

"Don't say that."

"That's the way I feel. I thought that having a ship would help. We have two, and we can trade in maybe four places on the entire continent. I thought that having more people with more skills would help, and now that we have them, we can't find enough food to last the coming winter."

"You don't know that."

"I wish I didn't."

Creslin looks from Megaera's somber face to the open stable door and back again. "I'll see you tonight. I need to think."

"Tonight." . . . *best-beloved* . . .

Even her lingering farewell does not warm him as he rides southward past the Black Holding, on the road that he had hoped would one day be a grand highway from one end of the isle to the other.

The sun is low in the western sky, heralding the end of summer . . . and the darker days ahead.

CXXVIII

"I DON'T LIKE it." Hartor shakes his head. "Someone has been riding the winds around Lydiar, Tyrhavven, Renklaar, and even Hydolar."

"You think it's Creslin?" Gyretis leans back in the white-oak chair.

"Who else? It could be the White bitch—"

"She's not White anymore. Almost pure Black."

"That's not wonderful, either."

"So? What's the problem?" Gyretis shakes his head. "Half of Candar hates him, and the other half fears him. He has only two ships, and not a great deal of gold or coin. His crops were barely sufficient."

"The guard bitches brought him the remnants of the Westwind treasury." Hartor fingers the amulet he wears and walks to the window, where he glances across the white city.

"Fine. That will buy him another trader's cargo . . . or three. Several eight-days worth of food. It won't solve his problems."

"He's going to do something. Is that what you're saying?"

"I'm sure he is. But if we're careful, we can still come out stronger than before."

"Stop playing games. Just say what you have to say!" snaps the High Wizard.

"You're getting edgier than Jenred. Remind me never to consider taking a position of responsibility on the council." Gyretis straightens in the chair. "Look. In any fight, it really isn't who wins the battles that counts. It's what you have left when it's over. I don't think that Westwind ever lost a battle. The other thing is that you have to accept the fact that we probably can't destroy Recluce, at least not while Creslin's alive. So . . . we want to make sure that our losses are as small as possible and that Creslin can get as little help as possible, because it will take a long time, even now that he's ensured favorable weather for Recluce, to build up that island without the help of outside gold and resources."

"That's sound theory. Making it work could be difficult."

"Make Creslin use force to get what he needs, and make sure that someone else pays for our losses."

Hartor snorts. "That's easier said than done."

"He needs coin; he needs tools; he needs more food; he needs timber; and he needs skilled craftspeople. He doesn't have enough coin, and that means he's going to have to steal it, or steal something that he can turn into coin."

"And I suppose we should let him?"

"No. But I wouldn't try to anticipate where he might strike. He'll destroy whatever forces you send against him. Your best defense is to play the benevolent ruler. Help get Montgren back together. Send extra food. Blame the damage, again, on Creslin, that renegade Black who wants to build an empire. See if you can pay some of the Blacks to help restore the Kyphran orchards. And offer slightly higher prices for Hamorian and Nordlan traded goods . . . but only after delivery in Candar."

Hartor raises his eyebrows.

"That brings their goods here, leaves their ships on the seas. We have more than enough coin."

"There's never enough."

"Think about it." Gyretis stands. "It's your decision, not mine. You asked what I suggested. I told you."

CXXIX

"GIDMAN, I UNDERSTAND that the green juice is your concoction."

"Begging your pardon, ser, and it is, but only because there's no grapes here worthy of the name." The stocky and grizzled trooper glares at Creslin. "Nothing grows here that'd make a decent wine, except perhaps pearapple brandy."

"Maybe next year on the pearapples. Could you distill the green juice into a brandy?"

"Distill . . . greenberry? That swill's so tart it'd twist your guts inside out."

"I know that. But could you do it?"

"If someone could get me the tubing, and the time. But it'd taste like those lightning bolts raised by . . . the other regent, ser." Gidman licks his lips.

"What about aging? Would that mellow it?"

"Unless you have a secret bunch of casks, ser, we got nothing proper to age with. Aging mellows anything. It might turn that green lightning into simple poison."

"I take it you don't like it?"

"Some folks'll drink anything. Not me."

"I'll get you the tubing and the time, Gidman. And some more tubs. You start brewing as much of the green juice as you can. You turn it into green lightning, and I'll figure out how to make it drinkable."

"You do that, ser, and that's worth more than all the storms you called."

"Probably," sighs Creslin. "You're going to have to move. Hyel will tell you where to start, once we're set up."

"Begging your pardon again, ser. But you let me work it out with the masons and it'll happen faster, and it'll be what I need."

Creslin grins. "Fine. If they have problems, they can come to Hyel or to me. Will that be satisfactory?"

"Saving your grace, yes. 'Cept that stuff's still green swill."

Creslin is shaking his head as he climbs the stairs to Hyel and Shierra's office. Hyel is out, but Shierra stands as he enters.

"Gidman—the grizzled character who's making the green juice—is going to work out some deal with the stoneworkers to build a proper still, outside the keep. Would you let Hyel know that I said it was all right?" He turns to go.

"Creslin?" Shierra's voice is soft.

"Yes."

"We all know you're trying."

"Right now, trying doesn't count, does it?"

"Don't tell that to Fiera."

Creslin sighs and turns back to face her. "I suppose I deserved that. I can't ever repay her."

"No."

"What am I supposed to do? She brought those squads because . . . because . . ." He shakes his head.

"She wasn't sure you understood."

"What can I do? I still remember the one time we kissed. I wish I'd been smarter or braver or bolder. But then . . . everything would have turned out differently." He pauses. "So I owe her. We all do, but I owe her more than I can admit, and I don't even know how to repay it. There really isn't any way. Nothing I say—"

"You just have. In a way."

"I don't know. People want to see great deeds, and I'm trying to figure out how to pay for food two seasons from now, because what Fiera brought back won't last that long."

"There was quite a bit left in that strongbox."

"It's a trade-off. If we don't buy tools, and supplies like the metals for the glassworks, we'll never be able to support ourselves and we'll be starving two years from now. If we do spend the money on the future, we risk starving in the seasons ahead." Standing in the doorway, Creslin shrugs. "It's like juggling with sharp knives."

"Why the green-juice distillery?"

"I thought I'd explained that. No?" Creslin steps over to the window. "You can sell distilled spirits anywhere and at any time, usually without having to mark them down much, especially if the quality's good. Wool's the same way, especially if you're selling in Nordla. Right now we don't have any trading possibilities, not with the trade edict of the Whites."

"You're trying to develop hard-cash products."

"I thought I'd made that clear, but I guess not."

"Maybe I wasn't listening. Building a distillery didn't sound like it was going to solve our trade problems."

"It won't. But it might help for a little while."

"You just confused me again," admits the former guard leader.

"Our population's still small. The thirty or fifty golds we might net out of the distillery every season or so might buy enough food to make the difference. But what happens two years from now when we have another couple of thousand people here?"

"That won't happen."

Creslin catches her eyes. "We'll either have three thousand people or more on Recluce in two years or we'll be dead. We can't survive with fewer. We're getting a score every couple of eight-days already." He waits. "I need to be going. Will you tell Hyel about Gidman?"

"I'll tell him, along with the explanation. I'll also tell Fiera."

"How is she? I keep thinking about talking to her, but she didn't seem to want to face me. She avoids me even when I'm practicing."

"She feels like she failed, and nothing you say can help now. But she'll need to deal with it, and with you, sooner or later."

"I dreamed about her for a time, you know."

"I know. She knows, and so does Megaera. But that was in a different world."

Creslin nods, but the words, "That was in a different world," run through his head as he walks back down through the keep toward the stable. In less than two years, all Candar has been changed. Yet has it been only because of his and Megaera's actions?

He steps into the exercise yard, where he sees a familiar blond head duck back into the newly constructed guard quarters.

"Good day, your grace," offers a guard, saluting with a practice wand.

"Good day." His eyes linger on the empty doorway where Fiera had stood. Then he crosses the stones as though he walks alone through the high forests of the Westhorns, as though he scales the towers of the sunset against the demons of the light. The remaining guards draw back.

Even as he saddles Vola, the mare neither skitters nor whinnies, as though he is a storm that walks on two feet, bearing terrible lightnings poised like swords to fall from the Heavens.

By the time he reaches the Black Holding, he is silent, and Vola offers her opinion with a whickering as he unsaddles her.

"It's not that bad," he murmurs to the mare. "We only need to remake the rest of the world in a season." He slams the saddle on the rack and hangs the saddle blanket in place before dishing out one of the few remaining oatcakes into the manger. "Enjoy it. It may be your last for a long time."

He stops by the kitchen, since he can feel that Megaera is there, washing up.

"Begging your pardon, your grace, but is there anything you can do about the bread?" Aldonya looks up from a pot of soup on the stove and through the cloud of steam that fills the kitchen despite the two open windows.

"What about it?" he asks.

"There isn't any left, and no one seems to know when there will be more."

"I don't know either. The *Dawnstar* won't be back for at least another eight-day, and Freigr may not have been able to get flour, not with the drought in Candar. Lydya thinks that the first of our maize will be ready to harvest in two or three eight-days. But it needs to be dried before it can be ground into flour."

"We have not even maize flour? It will be a sad day when cornmeal is too dear for even the rich."

"We're scarcely rich, Aldonya."

"The fisherfolk think you are a great lord, and who am I to argue with those who toil on the great Eastern Ocean?"

Creslin snorts. "You know what we eat, and what I have to wear. Great lord?"

"They have even less, your grace."

"I know, I know."

"What do you know?" asks Megaera, her hair wrapped in a towel and her body garbed with the thin blue robe, clinging suggestively to her damp curves. Creslin cannot help but look longingly at her.

"Not that! It's been a long day," she says firmly. "Some idiot didn't . . . never mind. I don't want to get angry about it again. We lost an entire crucible of colored crystal." She adjusts the towel around her head. "Cleaning up after cleaning up. Now, best-beloved, what do you know?"

"Oh . . . about how little flour we have left, and how there's even less for the fisherfolk."

"They asked me, too." Her lips tighten. "When will the *Dawnstar*—"

"Not for at least another eight-day. There's no guarantee of what Freigr will be able to bring back."

"You two. You cannot worry over what you can do nothing about. You, your grace"—Aldonya gestures at Creslin—"you need to wash up. We have a good fish stew for dinner, and even some of the white seaweed."

"It's better than the brown."

Megaera raises her eyebrows.

"Would you prefer a desert of quilla roots?" he asks her.

"You . . ." She shakes her head. "I am dressing for dinner, and I expect you to be equally presentable, best-beloved."

After Megaera sweeps from the kitchen, Creslin, grinning, heads for the washhouse. He will worry about tomorrow when it arrives.

CXXX

"WE HAVE THEM now. Those few coins left from Westwind won't save them from slow starvation." A wide grin passes over the heavy wizard's face.

"You have them . . . now," agrees Gyretis.

"You think they can wiggle out of this one? How? They don't have that much coin. We're letting anyone go there who wants to, so they're getting more and more mouths to feed." Hartor licks his fleshy lips. "But he doesn't have enough gold for food, and we've bought up the prices. With the drought and the trade edict, they'll starve."

"What if they go east?"

"He has one ship that can cross the Eastern Ocean, and the emperor just might want to take it back if Creslin sends it there." Hartor fingers the amulet.

Gyretis stares at the mirror and its white mist, which clears and reveals a town built on a hillside. His eyes widen. "Look at this, Hartor."

"What about it?"

"It's a town. With new buildings, and a keep easily three times the size of the old Duke's keep. That all happened in less than a year."

"It will be deserted in less than another year."

The thin wizard releases his breath, and the vision in the mirror is replaced with swirling white. "I don't know. What if Ryessa decides to cause trouble?"

"What can she do?"

"Send them food and coins, for one thing."

"After what Creslin did to the weather, she can't send enough to make a difference."

"What if he builds more ships?"

"He can't build them in time."

"You seem to have an answer for everything. Just like Jenred," Gyretis says in a low voice.

"You're rather presumptuous today. In fact, you've become rather annoying recently. It's as if you were on Creslin's side."

Gyretis shrugs, trying to ignore the challenge in the heavy wizard's tone. "I was just offering some possibilities about what might happen."

"Bah. The coming small harvests, the economics, and the whole world are against Creslin. What can he do?"

Hartor pauses. "Now . . . what I should do with you is another question." He looks at the mirror.

The thin wizard lowers his head and makes no reply.

CXXXI

CRESLIN ALIGNS THE last stone, straightens, and steps back. The new and half-cubit-high wall encloses a square of three cubits on a side, the nearest edge perhaps a distance of five cubits from the southern terrace wall.

"Ought to leave enough room for growth," he mutters to himself.

He takes the spade and again mixes the dirt and other ingredients prescribed by Lydya. Once they are mixed to his satisfaction, he gently shovels the damp pile into the stone box. Then he plants the oak seedling in the center, carefully patting the soil in place.

Water from the bucket comes next, with more careful tamping of the soil. Finally he reaches out, and as Klerris has taught him, strengthens the internal order of the seedling.

"Not that I'll ever see you full grown," he thinks. "We plant trees for those who follow." Besides, he is merely making a personal gesture with the seedling. What counts more are the three small forests they have already planted in the lower hills to the south.

Creslin takes several trips to replace the tools and shovel in the third guest house, which still serves as storeroom and sometime-workroom. On the last trip, he returns with a broom and sweeps away the loose dirt from the stones. He carries the broom back to the storeroom.

"Your grace . . . I was wondering whether one of you had spirited this off for some wizardly task." Aldonya takes the broom.

. "Waa . . . daaa . . . gooo . . ." Lynnya lunges for the broom, nearly wresting herself from her mother's arms.

"Lynnya, how will we ever get the floors swept? I put you down and you crawl into everything . . ."

"I'll take her for a little bit." Creslin holds out his hands. "The *Dawnstar* won't reach the pier for a time yet."

"Your grace . . ."

"I think I can manage."

"Daaa gooo . . ." Lynnya twines pudgy fingers into the hair of his forearm and twists.

"Now . . . not that way." Creslin swings her up so she is looking over his shoulder.

The small hand waves, then seizes upon his hair.

"You little minx . . ." Creslin carries her back toward the terrace, wondering what ever possessed him to suggest baby-sitting for the little redhead, even for a short time.

Aldonya shakes her head, and watches as the wizard carries her daughter from the shadows of the covered walk into the morning light on the terrace. She watches for a moment longer, then lifts the broom.

Creslin sits down on the wall, holding Lynnya in his lap with an arm around her middle. The baby squirms and leans down toward the stones. "All right." He lowers her carefully to the terrace floor. She squirms again, one hand reaching for his boots. Inside, the vigorous swishing of the broom begins.

Lynnya reaches for a dead millipede, her chubby fingers closing on the small gray remnant.

"I don't think that's a good idea." Creslin disengages her fingers, sweeps her into the air and back onto his shoulder.

"Daaa! Gooo, ooooo . . ."

"I know you don't approve, but your mother doesn't want you eating bugs. Things aren't that bad. Not yet, anyway."

"Unmmm." A chubby fist goes against her mouth.

Creslin walks to the south side of the wall, looking at the oak seedling, its few leaves trembling in the breeze.

"Uuummm . . . da!"

"Oooww." He gently removes Lynnya's hand from his hair. A few silver strands float free in the wind. "You are a grabby child, aren't you?"

"Goo . . ."

"I'm not certain I believe it." Megaera stands on the terrace, grinning. "As much as I'd like to watch, I think you need to get ready. I can see the *Dawnstar*'s sails already."

"I said I'd hold—"

"I'll take her while you wash up . . . unless you want to look like a stonemason. What are you doing, anyway? All the stonework is finished, isn't it?"

He inclines his head as she approaches. "Just something for a little oak."

Megaera shakes her head as she extends her arms to take Lynnya. "Come on, little one. Your uncle can't stand to be idle for a moment, can he?"

"Uncle?"

"It's as accurate as any other description. And it's true that you don't relax."

Creslin refrains from comment, instead handing over one redhead to the other and retrieving a towel.

By the time he has washed and dressed, Megaera has returned Lynnya to her mother and is saddling Kasma. Creslin follows her example with Vola, and before long, they ride northward and down to the inn, where they will leave the horses.

The *Dawnstar* looks battered, whether from the trip or from other circumstances, Creslin can't tell.

"Freigr had a hard trip." Megaera edges toward the spot where Synder and another crewman lower the gangway onto the pier.

"Looks that way."

Freigr waits for them by the helm.

Creslin leans over the railing and looks down at the gouges on the *Dawnstar*'s fantail. "This because of your problems?"

"That was from the Devalonian catapult. Load of stones."

"Why—" asks Megaera.

"Because the Suthyan merchants guild embargoed us, and only a handful of the smaller traders would deal with me. They won't do it again."

"Why not?"

"Three of them were arrested. We left Armat in a hurry."

"Weindre's tied up with the Whites?"

"I should have guessed. Idiot," mutters Creslin.

Megaera and Freigr wait for him to explain.

"According to what Shierra found out from her sister, Weindre set up . . . the Marshall of Westwind. The Whites were behind the trap, and they were the ones who used those devil's explosions to kill Llyse and the senior guards."

"Well, that explains it, but explanations don't help. I'm sorry, your graces, but I got coin and not a lot of cargo. And unless we can figure out something else, we'll not get even that much again."

"What did you get?" asks Megaera.

"Wish I could have brought more of the staples." Freigr gestures at the barrels being lifted from the deck. "Mostly cornmeal and barley from a wet corner of Suthya. Still, only about fifty barrels. The White Wizards are buying up what they can."

"What are they doing with it?"

"Doling it out in Montgren, Kyphros, and Certis. According to the traders, every time they do, they tell how you destroyed the crops in revenge for the wizards' not accepting you and the Legend."

"What does sister dear say about this?" Megaera looks from the last of the barrels to Freigr.

"Sister dear?"

"Ryessa . . . Tyrant of Sarronnyn," Creslin explains.

"Nothing, except that Westwind was a stalking horse for the wizards."

"I suppose the White Wizards are claiming Westwind was going to unleash the Legend upon the innocent people of Candar?"

"Pretty much," admits Freigr.

"What else did you get?"

"Some gold. More than I'd like."

"Oh?" Megaera looks puzzled.

"They'll buy, but not sell?" Creslin asks.

"Some of them—those few I got to before the guild discovered who we were. I didn't exactly boast of our origins. We even flew the Montgren ensign. A lot of them had nothing to sell. There's not even the Kyphran dried fruit, and there's always dried fruit. I did pick up nearly a dozen barrels of oatcakes for the horses. Don't know whether you needed them, but they were cheap and I figured the barrels might be worth it alone.

"Then, I did pick up a couple of chunks of iron. Some cast-off timbers, mostly short birch, too brittle, and it rots too easily. Some odd lots of canvas—figured that would always come in useful. Plus another family, paid for passage in gold, Yerrtl's cousin. He's a cooper. Don't have any, but I warned him we didn't have much wood . . . said he could make baskets from rushes and seaweed, if need be. His daughter's already showing Black traits, and the Whites have been watching."

In the end, while the cargo is useful, Creslin knows there is not enough, particularly of flour and other staples.

As they walk back down the pier toward the inn and their mounts, Megaera brushes her hair back over her ears. "It could have been worse."

"Not much."

"Why are you always looking at the White side of things? Freigr did get us more staples, and forty-some barrels of cornmeal will last a little while."

"Not that long. You figure that a barrel of meal is maybe four hundred loaves, and we're running almost five hundred people now, or more. That's . . . what? Maybe a half-barrel a day, three to four eight-days' worth."

"It could be a lot worse, and it has been."

"I know. But sayings don't bring coins or food. And with no one trading with us, where do we go next? Your dear sister has yet to come up with the aid she pledged."

"You worried about housing, but we've managed," Megaera snaps back.

"What about food? We still don't have enough supplies to last the winter, and there's no coin to buy enough."

"Would you stop it!" Megaera gestures at the clear, greenish-blue sky and the bright noon sunlight. "It's a beautiful day, and there will always be problems. At least let's enjoy the respite. Everyone can stop worrying for a while about where the next meal—besides fish—will come from. And you can even have some barrels for your green brandy."

"Well—"

"Best-loved, I know that we have problems still. You know that. We can discuss them later. It's a beautiful day, and you are a good-looking man, if you'd stop being such a sourpuss."

Creslin laughs. It is a short laugh, but that does not matter after the full-bodied hug she gives him in the inn stable. He almost feels like singing as they mount and begin the short ride to the keep.

Above the road, past the inn and between two of the older and weathered fisher cots, a pit has been dug into the sand and lined with stone. A man and a woman struggle with a length of patched canvas that will serve as a roof. A barefoot boy wearing only a ragged shirt plays with two sticks. None of the three look up as the regents pass.

In the midday heat—reminiscent of the summer before the rains—Creslin wipes his forehead to keep the sweat from his eyes. When he looks up, a girl stands by the road, eyes cast down, hands extended.

"A coin, even a copper, noble ser . . . just a copper?"

Her brown hair is tangled and dusty. She, too, is barefoot on the hot, sandy clay, and wears a tattered shift with little beneath it. "Just a copper?"

Creslin has no coppers, only a few golds, and he turns toward Megaera.

"All right." She shrugs and fishes out a coin, lofting it toward the girl.

"Thank you, your grace."

"Where did she come from?" Creslin asks.

"I don't know. Did she hide away on the *Dawnstar*? Or on the last coaster, the one that dumped those people and no supplies?"

They ride in silence the rest of the way to the keep, but the images of the beggar girl and the near-naked boy remain with Creslin . . . and he again calculates how far forty barrels of meal will go.

CXXXII

"It's a mighty risk that I be taking to trade here, and what with the bonus I must needs pay my crew . . ." The muscular captain of the *Nightbreeze* lifts both shoulders, but his hand does not stray far from his sword-hilt, and his eyes rest on Creslin rather than Gossel.

"I can understand your concerns, Captain, but we can't afford to give away goods, not when we could make the trip to Brista and still do better, even paying our men a double-risk bonus." Gossel's voice is smooth. "And his grace, while he is a fair and just man, has been known to act against those who displease him mightily."

Creslin glances from the foredeck of the *Nightbreeze* to the masts of the *Griffin* on the far side of the pier. The *Dawnstar* is anchored off the Feyn River a good hundred kays south, where Lydya and a group of guards are gathering wild herbs and other edibles that the schooner can transport more easily than horses could haul across the rugged terrain.

Letting Gossel carry the negotiations for the moment, Creslin debates whether he should stir the breezes for effect, then drops the idea when he feels instant queasiness in his stomach. He decides it's best to save the dubious uses of order for times when more is at stake. Besides, the northwest sea breeze is fresh enough, heralding oncoming clouds and rain.

The smuggler offers; Gossel considers; Creslin looks displeased. Then, after a time, Gossel begins to offer those few goods that Recluce has produced, while the smuggler considers and Creslin still looks displeased.

In the end, the captains shake hands and Gossel and Creslin depart the deck of the *Nightbreeze* for the pier.

"You think that's the best we could have done?" Creslin stands on the pier watching as the *Griffin*'s crew begins to off-load the cargo from the *Nightbreeze* and to on-load the few goods purchased by the smuggler: a few cases of goblets, several small casks of purple dye extracted from shellfish, Lydya's spices, and a nearly dozen barrels of salted fish. The amount of fish is limited by the availability of barrels, not by lack of fish or salt.

"Did what I could." Gossel shrugs. "Maybe we could have gotten more for the goblets. His eye slit when he saw them, but we did well with the spices and the dyes, and a lot better with the fish than I'd have believed. The fish probably went for more because of the poor harvests and all the sheep they lost early in the summer."

"I appreciate it. You got a sight more than anyone else could have."

"Appreciate the trust, your grace."

"Will you need me for anything else?"

"I don't see as I would, ser."

"Thank you again. I'll check back later, but I want to see about some things at the keep."

Creslin has barely recovered Vola from the inn stable—after having peered in the windows and watched two of the serving women clean tables and prepare for the late-afternoon and evening business—and is riding toward the keep when a thin voice intrudes.

"A copper, your grace? The smallest of coins? My mother is wasting away and cannot feed us." The beggar is a dirty-faced boy wearing a sleeveless shirt and trousers so worn that the tatters barely cover his knees.

Creslin reins up, casts his thoughts around the area but senses nothing of whiteness or other power. "Where do you live?"

The child looks away.

"Where do you live?"

"In a cave . . ."

Either the boy is honest or Creslin is easily deceived, and he doesn't have time to sort out the truth. "Here." This time he has a copper.

"Thank you, your grace."

Creslin rides on, wondering whether he is supporting the beginning of a class of beggars or whether everyone is beginning to suffer. "Every town has beggars," he murmurs. But he is not convinced.

Then there is the business of the fish. Should the barrels that contain oatcake be used for salted fish or for aging the green-juice brandy? He needs to talk to Gidman, although the old Hamorian will insist on as many barrels as he can get.

A dull rumble of thunder interrupts Creslin's thoughts, and he flicks the reins to speed Vola's pace. Even as he does, the first rush of fine rain brushes across his face.

Megaera waits for him at the keep stable. "I was going to ride to the holding, but I thought I'd wait for you." She swings up onto Kasma. "What happened?"

Creslin looks at the misty gray overhead, then brushes the combination of mist and rain from his tunic.

"Gossel did the best he could, and I played the fair-minded but not terribly merciful Storm Wizard. We still paid too much, but what could we do? He had another fifty barrels of flour, half of it wheat, plus five barrels of dried fruits, hard yellow cheese, olives and olive oil . . . not to mention the caustic and a good hundred stones of iron ore. The high prices are what we have to expect." He edges the black around, heading back eastward on the road he and Vola have just climbed.

"See? It's not so bad. You worry too much."

"Even after what he paid us for the dyes, spices, goblets, and fish, we came out a good fifty golds on the short side. This kind of trading is going to wipe out what was left of the Westwind treasury before much longer."

"So why did you pay that much?"

"Because it's likely to cost less now than later. Remember . . . Montgren, Certis, and Kyphros will have no harvests to speak of this year. There's just not enough coin to stretch."

"If you're so concerned, why didn't you just take over the smuggler's ship?"

"I'm not interested in surviving at any cost. Besides, what good would it have done? His ship is smaller than the *Griffin*."

"Expediency again. Would you have thought about it if they'd brought in a ship the size of the *Dawnstar?*"

"Maybe . . . but it wouldn't solve the problem, and then not even the rest of the smugglers would trade with us."

"You've come a long way from the Westwind innocent . . . if you ever were."

"That was unfair." Creslin snaps the reins to direct Vola away from Megaera and toward Klerris and Lydya's cot, his guts churning and his eyes burning, whether from his pain and frustration or from hers, he cannot tell.

Then he reins up. What good will talking to the two Black mages do? They are even more constrained than he is.

Megaera eases up beside him again. "There's nowhere to escape ourselves, best-beloved."

At least she talks about both of them.

CXXXIII

"I'VE LOOKED AT all the possibilities," Creslin asserts. "Lydiar isn't well-guarded, and at times there are half a dozen oceangoing ships in her waters. If we use the weather, there's a chance that we can capture three or four of them."

"We have two ships already, and you said they would help. Now you're saying we need more. When will it stop?" Klerris speaks in a tired voice.

"We don't have any choice."

"Would you explain your logic, Creslin?"

Creslin first sips from the deep green crystal goblet produced by Megaera and Avalari. "We have only one true oceangoing ship. Everyone knows that we cannot afford to risk that ship. In addition, with more than one ship, we can keep a steadier flow of goods. Finally, if need be, we can use the ships as a lever—"

"How?"

"Piracy. With more than a single ship, we can tell Nordla, Austra, and the other traders that either they trade fair and square or we seize or sink their ships."

"And just how will you carry out that threat?"

"I don't want to. That's why I want the ships. but if we had to resort to piracy, I could ride the winds and see where their ships were. I could probably raise storms and run them aground . . . at least anywhere in eastern Candar."

"Could he?" Shierra looks to Lydya, who nods.

"This is not a good idea." Megaera's words are flat. *. . . idiotic, dangerous, and wrong . . .*

"We have no choice," Creslin repeats. "We either act before our position becomes clear and while we have some hope of surprise, or we act later and lose more troopers and guards."

"I don't know," Klerris muses.

"Fine. The fisherfolk were complaining about having no flour. We managed only enough to get us through the fall until harvest . . . from the *Dawnstar*'s last trip, and from what we could afford to buy from the smugglers. And what we can harvest won't last through midwinter, if that. For half the year, we were unable to pay our people. Freigr came back with less than half a cargo, and that was before everyone knew about the wizards' trade edict. We don't have enough food to last until spring, let alone until our next harvest, and while we could afford to buy food, no one will sell it except a few smugglers, and we can't afford to buy at their prices. So we steal either ships or money."

"It's a terrible idea," Megaera protests.

"You're right. You come up with a better one." Creslin stands, sets the goblet down and walks out.

The five still seated look across the table at each other.

"Sometimes . . . Do we really want to stoop to piracy and theft? Can we?" asks Lydya.

"No," answers Klerris. "We'll do nothing and starve. Or we'll let Creslin destroy himself to save us all."

"That's cruel."

"He offered a solution, and he asked a question. Do we have a better answer? One that allows us to survive?"

The five look at each other again, but no one speaks as the hooves of a single horse echo on the road.

After reaching the Black Holding and unsaddling Vola, Creslin sits on a shaded section of the terrace wall, listening to the low surf. In time, the shadows lengthen to cover the entire terrace, and still he sits there, staring sightlessly out across the Eastern Ocean toward distant Nordla, or even more distant Austra.

He does not look up at Megaera's approach, nor at her,

even when she sits on the ledge with her back to the cliff, facing him.

"We're not finished. Walking out didn't help anyone. Like always, you decided that the mighty Creslin was right, and darkness forbid that we should question you."

"I asked for any answer besides waiting to starve. Besides hoping that someone, somehow, will rescue us—like your dear sister. Do you really think she will?"

"She might."

"She bound you in iron, and she's going to provide you with enough supplies to raise a nation that just might threaten Sarronnyn?"

"What you're planning isn't right." Megaera's words are flat, evenly spaced. "You're using your abilities to pervert the whole spirit of order-mastery."

Creslin looks beyond the terrace, at the whitecaps of the Eastern Ocean that seem almost pink in the sunset. For a time, there is silence. "What would you have me do?"

"I don't think that piracy is exactly honorable."

"Honor is all well and good, but what would you have me do? The Blacks of Candar are being destroyed one way or another, year after year. Korweil is dead, and Westwind has fallen. Ryessa and Fairhaven have prospered, and we're struggling to stay alive. No one will help us, and the gold we have left, no one will take. Even if someone did, there isn't enough of it, and yet the people keep pouring in. Ships come, and they bring no cargo, only mouths to feed. What are we supposed to do? Sit here and starve?"

"You're not talking about taking food."

Creslin takes a deep breath, still not meeting her eyes, for he knows that there is truth in what she says. "I'm talking about taking one action. One action so that we don't have to keep begging and stealing. When we can, I'll even repay what we take."

"How will that help those whose lives are ruined?"

. . . how . . . how on earth . . .

Creslin shakes his head, feeling her pain and her helplessness. "What am I supposed to do? My mother was assassinated; my father and sister have been killed by the Whites. Montgren has been conquered, and your sister rejects both of us. And you tell me what I plan is wrong. I know it's wrong. But what else is there? Give me another answer.

"More than five hundred people have fled to Recluce in the past year. The rains saved a lot of crops and the pearapples, but how do we build a town with a few tools? Despite the new buildings, we still have people living in huts and in caves in the sand. We're even getting beggars. How can we build enough ships enabling us to trade so that we don't get fleeced on every item? How?"

This time Megaera winces and holds her head. "There aren't any answers, except—"

"I refuse to die honorably," he snaps. "And it's not fair to Hyel, Shierra . . . or Fiera."

The sun has dropped behind the western hills, and the whitecaps have faded to gray before he speaks again, his words a mere whisper above the evening breeze. "You think this is easy? No matter what happens—"

. . . *best beloved* . . .

Their hands and tears touch.

CXXXIV

"You're a Storm Wizard. Why did you have to wait for the fog? Why not just create fog or a storm?"

Heavy clouds loom in the sky to the west of the *Dawnstar*. Both the schooner and the *Griffin* seem ghostlike as they make their way southward through the light fog. Creslin continues to concentrate as he stands on the *Dawnstar*'s deck, his consciousness but half-present. "We waited until they didn't have any ships nearby, and so they wouldn't have any advance notice."

Freigr looks from the helmsman to Creslin.

Creslin dries his forehead. Not all of the moisture is from the fog. "I could create a storm, but if I do, it's like writing my name in fire across the sky for any wizard who's watching to see, and the White Wizards are certainly watching. If we wait for the right kind of winds—and I can see when they're developing—then I can change them into what I need at the last moment and no one will have any warning."

"But you called a waterspout when those ships came after us."

"I did." Creslin nods. "I barely managed to hang on to it long enough, and how many days was it before I could even walk again?"

The *Dawnstar*'s captain glances from the choppy water ahead back to Creslin. "I think I see that. Why won't the White Wizards just burn our troops once they land?"

"They'll try to. But it's hard to manage fire in the middle of a really violent storm, and you can't do it from a distance. So we only have to worry about the Whites who are in Lydiar right now." Creslin frowns. "I just hope there aren't too many of them."

The two ships ease southward through the thinning fog until the outline of the harbor appears.

Creslin concentrates, and to the south, the clouds billow, darkening into a blackness that turns midday into late twilight.

"How long?" whispers Thoirkel.

"Steady . . ." murmurs Freigr to the helmsman of the *Dawnstar*.

". . . can't see a thing . . ." The words drift from the forecastle, where the makeshift crew waits behind the armed squads.

Creslin pushes, twists, and pulls at the winds.

"Steady as she goes . . ."

Cracckkk! Thurrumm . . .

The hammers of the lightnings crashed against the wall keep above the harbor, each forked blast of energy echoing down the gentle slope to the harbor. Within the fog that shrouds them, the Recluce ships ease toward the trading piers as all eyes in Lydiar focus on the storms.

Creslin counts, once more, the hulls tied to the piers. Five, and he has barely enough bodies to crew them. He shakes his head.

"You all right, ser?" Thoirkel looks from his squad to Creslin. The black-haired soldier radiates disappointment at being held in reserve.

"Well enough." Well enough, considering that he is essentially perverting the Black order. Well enough, considering the creative use of destruction. Well enough, considering . . . "You'll have plenty to do," he adds.

"If you say so, ser."

Creslin twists the winds again, and another line of lightning hammers upon the towers of the newly built keep.

". . . darkness save them . . ."

"Look out for the ships!" The warning comes from the trading pier as the *Dawnstar* shivers into position, her crew leaping to the wooden pier and roping the schooner in. The raiding squads are already swarming across the gangways of the three-masted Hamorian brig and the Nordlan schooner.

"Pirates!"

"Get the bastards!"

The watchstanders on the traders yell their warnings, barely audible above the crash of thunder and the violence of the storm.

Thunk! Creslin's concentration on the winds breaks momentarily as an arrow vibrates in the railing beside him.

"Get the Storm Wizard!"

"Take over!" Creslin orders Thoirkel and the reserve squad. As he speaks, he edges behind the stern castle to his knees, putting the heavy timbers between himself and the archers on the Hamorian ship.

Thunk!

He edges farther sternward and attempts to hold the storm center above the White-held keep. Above him, Freigr and the helmsman drop behind the low timber shield that half-encircles the helm.

More yells, curses, and muffled sounds of combat echo along the pier as the squad assigned to the Hamorian ship overwhelms the handful of archers. Creslin eases forward to where he can see more clearly.

On the Nordlan ship, which had been essentially uncrewed, the prize crew is already beginning to make ready for departure. On both of the Lydian ships, the ship's crews—or some of them—appear to be working with the prize crews.

"Offf . . ."

. *Thunk, thunk, thunk!*

"Thanks . . ." Creslin looks up from the deck at the arrows and then at the concerned face of Thoirkel. He takes a breath and gathers himself back together.

"Best be careful, ser."

How can he be careful when his mind is split in so many directions? Still, he drops behind the superstructure as he again twists the storms. Rain lashes across his face, and intermittent sheets of water cascade along the pier.

No more arrows fall on the *Dawnstar*, and the *Griffin* has been tied alongside the Nordlan ship. Two squads race for the shops detailed on their maps. Another races for the grain warehouse.

Creslin takes a deep breath, then releases his hold on the warm winds that carry the fog, but he remains shielded by the stern castle. He can sense that a whiteness is moving toward the harbor.

"Thoirkel, you'd—"

Whhssttt!

A firebolt flares through the lower, unfurled sail of the *Dawnstar*.

Creslin touches his harness to ensure that his sword is in

place, then steps toward the railing. A small squad of White warriors has appeared on the avenue heading toward the pier. Behind them are two points of white that Creslin feels rather than sees.

"Let's go."

"Yes, ser!"

Creslin twists a small fragment of the nearest thunderstorm, directing it toward the head of the pier and the force there, even as he trots down the gangway. Somehow, Thoirkel is in front of him.

Another set of firebolts hisses past them.

Creslin pulls harder on the winds, and cold air rips through his hair. He stumbles but catches his balance, unsheathing his sword as they near the squad of White guards. Three more of Thoirkel's men charge in front of him.

"Oooo . . ."

One of the charging Recluce troopers staggers and collapses as a white firebolt turns him into a cinder.

Creslin yanks the forces of the winds into a funnel before him, hurling rocks of hail into the midst of the White guards.

"Get—"

"Kill the silver bastard!"

Creslin's sword flickers, almost automatically, as he forces the ice chunks against the White Wizards. A White guard staggers, then is hurled aside by Thoirkel.

Now the firebolts are directed upward, as if to melt the icy arrows flying into the rear of the White guards.

"That's it . . ." gasps Thoirkel.

A handful of White guards are scrambling uphill, up the avenue and away from the storm.

Creslin shakes himself and redirects his attention to the main storm, forcing himself to re-intensify the hammering lightnings.

Around him lie the bodies, the bodies that always seem to accumulate whenever he acts. He takes another deep breath, then looks at the black-haired squad leader. "Back to the pier."

"Yes, ser." Thoirkel turns. "Back to the head of the pier. We'll hold there."

Creslin watches as a heavy-laden cart rolls toward the pier, a single Recluce raider guiding the horse.

"The Nordlan ship!" Creslin snaps. "Last one on the left."

"Who—" The man stops as he sees the silver hair. "Yes, ser!"

Creslin moves behind Thoirkel's men and turns his attention from the storm to the ships along the pier. All five of them are being readied for sea.

Another cart rolls onto the pier, then another.

For a long time—Creslin is uncertain of how long, except that the fog has almost totally lifted, although the rain still lashes the port city—the carts roll onto the pier, and the cargoes are quickly stowed.

A flash of white grabs at Creslin's senses, and he probes farther uphill, toward the keep, where a point of white flickers and builds—from either one of the wizards who has escaped or from a third. With a deep breath, Creslin builds the storm cell just to the west of the keep, until it is darker than night, until the lightnings flash within. Then he releases his hold, while directing that force toward the keep.

Craacckkk!

Even Creslin pauses at the flare, and at the rending and crumbling of stone. Despite the downpour, the flames and smoke begin to grow and rise from the pile of shattered white stone above the harbor.

Creslin is no longer watching as once more his guts spill, although he has walked to the edge of the pier and manages to foul only the harbor. Blackness wavers before his eyes, as if he were blind. He takes a deep breath, then another.

"Gee-ah. Move, beast!"

Slowly he turns, feeling his way, using his senses to guide him along the edge of the pier toward the *Dawnstar*.

"You all right, ser?"

"Just hold the pier, Thoirkel. I won't be much more help."

"We'll scarce be needing more, I think."

". . . look at that!"

Though unseeing, Creslin needs no eyes to sense the destruction he has wrought, nor to know that Megaera must feel some of his discomfort. Step by step, he makes his way back along the pier and onto the *Dawnstar*, sensing, as he walks, how all has been seized; the horses being boarded in the makeshift stalls, the barrel upon barrel of grains and foodstuffs stored in the holds, the rest of the goods, seized under the cover of the storm, securely stowed away.

"You all right, your grace?" Freigr meets him at the *Dawnstar*'s railing.

"I've been better. How does it look?"

"The Nordlan schooner is pulling clear now, and Byrem is almost ready with the Hamorian."

"The Lydians?"

"Won't be too long."

Rubbing his splitting forehead, Creslin sinks into a heap on the ladder leading to the helm. "We may have to leave quickly. Can you pass the word to finish up?"

"Make ready for departure! Set sails!" Freigr orders.

"No one's headed to the harbor. You sure?"

"I'm sure. Remember, we still have to reach Land's End."

"That is that. But who would follow us on the high seas?"

"No one, I hope. Because there's not much else we can do."

Creslin sits sightlessly on the ladder as the seven ships glide northward on the dying winds of the storms he has built.

Few on the *Dawnstar* look at the exhausted man in green leathers, even after Cape Frentalia has become less than a dark smudge in the evening's distance.

CXXXV

MEGAERA SAYS NOTHING, but she doesn't have to.

Creslin can sense her churning feelings and disapproval, and has since long before his small fleet returned to Land's End. They sit at opposite sides of the table.

Lydya glances from Megaera's drawn face to Creslin's impassive one and back again. Hyel enters and sits down, followed by Shierra.

Creslin looks pointedly from Hyel to Shierra, who flushes before laying the ornate scroll on the table.

"The Suthyan brig that arrived yesterday carried an ultimatum, signed by both the emperor of Hamor, the Council of Nordla, and the Wizard's Council. We either return the ships and what we took or we face war with all three. Fairhaven also wants indemnification for the destruction you caused."

"What destruction?" Lydya's voice is strained.

"One of the storms pulverized the wizards' brand-new keep in Lydiar," Shierra explains.

"You can't keep doing this . . ." Hyel admonishes.

Megaera merely raises her eyebrows. "He will, at least until he's totally blind."

"It passed."

"This time. How long can you push the limits? Anyone else would be dead." . . . *and I don't want to die because you* . . .

"Important as that may be, Megaera," interjects Shierra, "we still have this ultimatum."

Hyel frowns, clears his throat, waiting until the room quiets. "Do we have a choice?"

"Of course we do. There's always a choice." Lydya shifts her weight in the wooden chair.

"Why are they doing this now?" asks Creslin.

"Best-beloved, you must be joking. You destroy their keep, ransack their port, steal ships from three nations, and . . ." She shakes her head.

"No, that's not what I meant. Why did they even bother with an ultimatum? They certainly haven't played this sort of official-message game before."

"They're desperate," offers Hyel. "That's all I can think of."

"How about scared?" Shierra snaps. "First Creslin sinks that Hamorian fleet. Then he develops an army, beefed up by the last of the Westwind guards, that's clearly superior to anything its size. Now, by seizing half a dozen ships, he has the beginning of a fleet. And because he can sink any other ship on the sea, who can refuse to trade with Recluce ships? The only way they can hope to stop you—" her eyes turns to the silver-haired regent "—is to destroy Recluce."

"But we're scarcely that kind of threat," observes Klerris mildly.

Megaera snorts.

Klerris raises his eyebrows. After a moment, he asks, "You feel that Recluce is that much of a threat? With all of perhaps a thousand souls on this huge and empty island? With little gold to speak of?"

"That's scarcely the question, Klerris, and you know it. It isn't what we are that counts. It's what the White Wizards persuade people that we are that matters. My best-beloved here has managed to whip half the world into fearing mighty Black Recluce. Yet they know in their minds that we aren't that strong. It becomes an easy decision to send aid to Fairhaven, especially now that the Whites have helped rebuild Montgren and are helping build dams in Kyphros, and are paying premium prices for Hydlen grain. Especially now that Ryessa has regarrisoned the ruins of Westwind. Do you want both a strong Sarronnyn, believing in the Legend, Heaven forbid, *and* fearing that destructive Black Wizard Creslin?" The redhead shrugs theatrically.

"There's more to it than that," observes Shierra.

"There's a great deal more." Creslin's voice is low, strained. "The ultimatum is to persuade Hamor and Nordla of how unreasonable we are, and to picture Recluce as a danger to the world."

"That's probably right," affirms Shierra. "And what do we do?"

"We send back our polite document stating that Recluce and all of eastern Candar has been the victim of assorted wizardly depredations, such as assassinations, conquest, and trade restrictions." Creslin adds after a pause, "Not that it will help right now."

"Now?"

"I see what he means." Shierra squares to face Megaera. "They've already decided what they'll do. This is but a justification. Any response of ours will be viewed as unreasonable. If we survive, however, Hamor and Nordla could always claim that they were misled by Fairhaven and use our document, which they will doubtless claim was withheld from them, to justify whatever they may later do—hopefully, trade with us."

"So we send the response just to Fairhaven?" Megaera asks.

"Hardly," Creslin replies. "We send it to each. They can certainly still claim they were misled. Truth isn't necessary for politicians."

. . . nor for you, best-beloved . . .

Both the sadness and the anguish cut Creslin like a blade.

"But can we afford a war?" asks Lydya, her face pale.

"No," Hyel says bluntly.

Megaera nods.

"That's not the question." Shierra glances from Hyel to Megaera. "Do we have any choice?"

"No."

"No."

All six look again at the heavy scroll before Shierra.

Outside, the rain begins to fall . . . again.

CXXXVI

"NOW THAT EVERYONE has finally agreed, what strategy would you suggest, cynical one?" Hartor fingers the amulet he wears, looking toward the clear, blue-green fall sky outside the white tower. "Keeping in mind that you will be taking personal charge of it."

Gyretis frowns. "Personal charge?"

"The strategy first," snaps Hartor.

The thin wizard swallows before he speaks. "Make one fleet obvious. Call it the vengeance fleet. Put our best vessels there. Then scatter the others into smaller groups—squadrons, whatever they're called—and have a White with each to conceal them."

Hartor fingers the amulet. "So we dispatch the vengeance fleet—we'll have to think of a better name than that—but more slowly, so that Creslin and his lady are focusing on it."

"Exactly."

"But how do you get anyone to attack Creslin personally?" ponders the High Wizard.

"Who says they have to?" Gyretis smiles. "If he has no troops left, does it matter?"

"It might work. I never liked the idea of going head to head with him." Hartor nods. "If our troops are with the vengeance fleet—let's call it the liberation fleet—and if he does manage to find and destroy the others . . ."

This time Gyretis nods. "We'll still be able to help our allies recover."

"I like that . . . helping them recover." Hartor glances toward the tower window. "This part of the strategy stays here, in this room. We'll let it be known that we're taking the risks by spearheading the obvious and great liberation fleet." A broad smile crosses his lips. "And you, of course, will show our faith in the success of this plan by accompanying one of the smaller fleets of our devoted allies."

"Is that really necessary?" Gyretis swallows again.

"It is your plan, and I do believe that you should be there to ensure its success. Or do you wish to reconsider your strategy?"

"Only the advisability of my being away from Fairhaven." Gyretis's eyes flicker toward the window, then back to the cold smile of the High Wizard.

"Under the circumstances, it might be best if you were with the fleets."

"Best for you?"

Fires dance at Hartor's fingertips. "You lack the proper respect, dear Gyretis. We'll discuss that respect *after* you return . . . or would you rather deal with it now?"

Gyretis stands. "I'd better see about transportation." He includes his head. "By your leave?"

Hartor nods.

The thin wizard stops in the half-open door. "I take it that Ryedel will be advising you?"

"Of course. He does have, at least, the proper respect."

CXXXVII

CRESLIN LOOKS FROM the terrace southward, noting the heat waves on the horizon and pondering their origin, for while the morning promises that the day will be warm, the raw heat of summer has long since passed. Could it be the great White fleet that has so recently left Lydiar?

"What is it?" asks Megaera.

There's something out there." He casts his thoughts to the south . . . and swallows as he recognizes the ships behind their visual shield. He tries to be careful, tries not to let his thoughts touch the shield before he withdraws.

"Ships. They're armed. See if you can find any more of them farther south. Don't let them sense you." His mouth tight, he casts himself to the winds.

Another small fleet lies less than twenty kays north of Land's End, and a third, behind the same kind of shield, beats upwind yet a dozen kays farther south along the eastern shore.

"There are nine ships, including a three-masted one, coming in toward the western beaches, the ones that link up with the valley," Megaera observes.

"They're not quite close enough—"

"It won't be long—"

They both hasten toward their rooms, and their blades.

How long it takes for them to dress and arm, Creslin does not know, but the nearest ships have scarcely moved from their position just below the horizon by the time the two regents are mounted and headed toward the keep.

"The horses make a difference," observes Megaera.

"I suppose so. Was the big fleet just a decoy?"

"It seems too large for that."

"Mop-up duty, perhaps. To turn whatever is left into a dutiful province of White Wizards."

"How about scorching whatever's left to make sure no one else gets similar ideas?"

"That sounds more like the wizards I met."

Neither says more as their mounts carry them down the damp clay of the road to Land's End. As they turn onto the rough stones of the road to the keep, a fisherwoman steps to the side of the pavement and turns her scarfed head away from them.

The duty guard at the keep is a thin-faced girl unknown to Creslin.

"Keren, get Shierra, Hyel, and the two wizards. Then sound the duty alarm."

"Yes, Regent Megaera." The guard is gone even before Creslin's boots have struck the sandy clay.

Hyel is pulling on a tunic as he stumbles into the room that has become their meeting place.

Shierra wears a faint smile, which fades as she sees Creslin's face. "I thought you said that the great White fleet was days away."

"It is," answers Megaera.

"But there are four smaller fleets almost offshore." Creslin steps up to the rough map of Recluce that Klerris has drawn on the inside white-plaster wall. "Here, here, here, and here." He looks toward the two military commanders. "They could land later today, and they are probably planning to."

"Can't you just destroy them?" asks Hyel.

"Why?" asks Megaera.

Lydya appears in the doorway, followed by Klerris. Both appear composed, unlike the regents and Shierra and Hyel.

"But—"

"That much destruction is dangerous," offers Klerris in his customary mild tone, "even if it uses order as a basis."

"Besides," adds Megaera, "why waste the ships?"

Creslin nods, understanding. "We just drive all of them onto the beach. That was how we got the *Dawnstar*." He pauses, wondering why he had not thought of such a simple expedient. Then he reflects. "But . . . that's going to be a mess. And what about the troops who survive? A lot of angry, armed men will be wandering around."

"I'm sure that Shierra and Hyel can take care of that," Megaera says.

Hyel straightens his tunic. "Maybe . . ."

"Do you have a better suggestion? There also might be more gold that way." Megaera's voice is reasonable. "And less loss of life."

"The less loss of life, the better." Lydya's voice is cool, as if she were discussing crops.

"In any case, we can scatter the ships. That way,"

Creslin explains, "the survivors will be strung out along the beaches."

"They're still not exactly going to welcome us. They've certainly been warned that we're devils and that they should fight to the death." Shierra looks at Creslin, her dark eyes probing. "How many ships are there?"

"Thirty, I'd guess. That doesn't include the big fleet."

"And how many soldiers on each?"

"It depends. At least two score, perhaps as many as five."

"Possibly two thousand armed men—and we're supposed to handle them with what? Three hundred? And that counts the Hamorians, and some refugees who have held a blade for perhaps a season." Shierra's voice is acid.

"Most of them won't make it," Creslin says coldly. "Just because the ships are grounded it doesn't mean that the troops will survive. Most of them can't swim."

"Fine," snaps Shierra. "You kill three quarters of them. That's still five hundred. And that's not even counting the biggest fleet."

"You've beaten those odds all too many times," Creslin says tiredly. He turns back to the map painted on the wall. "Here's where the ships are—"

"One other thing," Megaera interrupts. "If we take over the hidden fleets, there's no need to worry about the large fleet."

The others turn toward the redhead. Creslin lowers the hand with which he had begun to explain the locations of the fleets.

"Why not?"

". . . absurd . . ."

"It's simple enough," Megaera explains. "All of the wizards' ships, and those of their close Candarian allies, are there. The hidden fleets are ships from the Nordland Duchies, Brista, Hamor, Austra, and even Southwind. If they succeed, the White fleet will land and claim great honor. If they fail, the White Wizards will proclaim that we're the terrors of the world and make suitable excuses. But they'll still have their fleet."

Shierra nods slowly. "Are you sure?"

"Not completely. But they always try to get someone else to do the fighting."

". . . men . . ."

Creslin and Hyel ignore Shierra's low-voiced comment, while Klerris looks blandly at the map.

Creslin gestures toward the map again. "Here's about where the northernmost ships will land. I think you ought to put all your forces here, except for the reserves that are necessary here at the keep. The others can't march that fast over the sand anyway."

"More here, I think," Shierra says, stepping to the map. "Hyel will handle the reserves here, in case the White fleet changes its mind."

Hyel's mouth opens, then closes.

"Is there anything else you need to know?" Creslin asks.

"Don't be too charitable toward those soldiers." Shierra's voice is flat. "I don't care if they all drown."

Lydya raises her eyebrows as the former Westwind senior guard walks toward the doorway. Hyel shrugs and follows her.

"When do we start?" asks Megaera.

"Now," suggests Creslin. "We can bring the winds along gradually."

"Ahem . . ."

They look toward Klerris.

"Perhaps the porch at the cot . . ."

Megaera grins for an instant, and Creslin nods. Klerris is offering what protection he can against chaos.

"We'd better hurry."

Megaera nods.

Lydya has already left for the cot. The three hasten from the keep and through the sun-strewn morning. Creslin casts his thoughts toward the west and the high winds, trying to start the process while he walks.

Two wooden armchairs, with cushions, have been set out on the porch. On the table between the two is a clay pitcher of redberry and a plate on which hard biscuits, cheese, and sliced pearapples rest.

"You'd better eat something," suggests Lydya.

"Do we have time?"

"A little," affirms Klerris.

Creslin finishes two biscuits and a pearapple, washing them down with a tumbler of redberry. Megaera has but a biscuit and half a tumbler of the juice.

Lydya's eyes narrow fractionally as she looks at Megaera, who returns the look with a head shake.

. . . *no* . . .

"What?" Creslin asks, catching the redhead's eye.

"Later. It's not urgent. The ships are." She shifts her weight on the cushion. "You work on the ones farthest to the south."

Creslin nods, settling into the chair and sending his thoughts southward, tugging at the swirling forces that are the high winds. Then he swallows and reaches toward the farthest of the hidden fleets, seven narrow-beamed war schooners bearing the blue tower of the Bristan ensign.

His thoughts slip inside the shield raised by the White Wizard to guard against mere vision. As they do, the wavering barrier disappears and a white fog washes over the ships, leaving his mind blind to anything except the burning whiteness.

With a grim smile, he touches the winds, whipping them toward the half dozen or so vessels. To force the ships onto the eastern beaches, he does not need to see them. Beside him, he can feel Megaera's more gentle touch tapping his winds as she brings her forces against another shielded group.

Creslin tugs at the great winds, those on which he has not called since the destruction of the Hamorian fleet. Again they strike back, but this time, seated, he waits for the reaction to subside.

The too-familiar gray haze creeps across the late-morning sun, and twin towers of darkness loom in the skies, one somehow squatter than the other, and more elemental.

Creslin keeps his awareness well outside the white haze against which he flings the wind and sea that sweep the schooners inexorably shoreward, toward beaches suddenly surf-pounded, toward sands now as damp and hard as stone. By the time he withdraws, the shredded white haze is melting under the rain and only a handful of antlike figures struggle from the battered timbers and foaming waters.

Lydya presses a morsel of biscuit upon him, and a sip of redberry.

He glances over at the other chair. Sweat streams down Megaera's face, running over unseeing eyes, and her tension flows toward him. He turns away and flings himself at the second fleet; six broadbeamed brigs.

This time a ray of flame probes at his thoughts, lances toward him, yanks at his holds on the winds. His defenses flare, deflect the fires, and he regains his grip on the winds. But the flames lance again. With those flames, for an instant, comes the image of a thin, tormented face surrounded by chaos and fires. The wizard's face is all too human.

Creslin swallows and seizes his winds again. Flames lash against the clouds, angling the gales away from the ships, keeping the worst of the tempest from the white vessels.

Creslin slams the mid-winds toward the six ships.

The thin-faced Wizard's image stands between the winds and the attacking fleet, and each time that Creslin turns his forces to begin hurling the ships onto the sodden sands, the flames flash toward him and twist the winds with the scouring heat of the desert—or the demons' hell.

With a wrench, Creslin seizes the heart of his tallest storm, twisting the fires within and channeling them toward that ship from which the fires have flown. Lightning forks from the sky and toward the seas, narrowly missing the tall ship standing farthest seaward.

Flames lash back at him, flames stronger than any he has seen. He reaches for the strongest of the mighty high winds, wrestling them and their lightnings back down the path of flame.

Aaaeeeiii . . .

The White Wizard, the most powerful he has ever faced, is gone, and the white haze shreds. The winds blow unchecked.

Creslin is gasping, swallowing, as he sits in the chair.

Again Lydya offers him the redberry and he sips slowly, refusing to look at Megaera, feeling too strongly the strains and forces that rack her as she wrestles with the high winds. An edge of darkness pulls at him, but he resists, pushing it away . . . somehow.

Too soon he is back upon the winds, nudging, tugging, unleashing fire and ice, ice and fire, until another seven ships lie tossed across the rocky beaches well south of the Black Holding.

One tall ship remains, shuddering, trying to run for the high seas as the winds howl. But the whiteness holds tightly to the vessel, and the winds whip uselessly through bare masts.

Creslin seizes the heart of the winds, and as they howl, the mist and swirling vortex solidify into a funnel of blackness. That blackness strikes and then collapses across the storm-ripped sea where a ship had stood.

". . . ooo . . ."

. . . *hurts* . . .

Creslin's muscles clench under the impact of Megaera's pain even as he realizes that off the shores of Recluce, only debris and bodies float. The great White fleet has already begun to turn and to run for the safety of the stormy Northern Ocean.

Megaera is unconscious, and Lydya has stretched her out on a pallet brought from inside the cot.

"She'll be all right," the healer responds to Creslin's look.

Creslin's guts are in his throat, and he seizes the redberry, swallows it, then resettles himself.

"No!"

But the caution from the Black mage is lost as Creslin hurls himself across the skies toward the last great patch of whiteness. As his thoughts race northward, he regathers the storms and calls on all of the high winds, the great black-steel tides of the skies. Ignoring the flashing silver before his eyes, ignoring the fire that sears his limbs, ignoring the single image of the dying White Wizard—an image that he will hold forever—he turns the fury of the north upon the defenseless chips of wood on the sea below.

"Nooo . . ."

He disregards the plea, lashing the sea into a tempest from which none will emerge. Wielding the winds and the lightnings, he is the storm. Riding the black-steel tides of the high winds, he is the god of old Heaven . . .

. . . back . . . please . . . best-beloved . . .

Back?

. . . best-beloved . . .

He shudders, forcing himself out of the storm, out of the ordered focus of power, climbing span by span, cubit by cubit, southward through the clouds and ice rains.

His tattered thoughts find his body, and he rests in darkness. Finally he straightens in the chair and opens his eyes. But he sees nothing. He knows that Megaera is there, and two others. But there is only blackness.

He squints. Night? Hardly. He swallows. "Megaera . . ." His voice is tentative, not the voice of the lightnings and thunders he has been.

"Are you all right?"

The warmth in her words reassures him, and his hand reaches for hers.

"I can't see," he admits. "The blackness again."

Her fingers grip his, and the blackness dissolves into the piercing green eyes that search his face.

"You were gone so long." Tears cascade down her cheeks. "Too long. Don't ever—"

"I won't, I won't." He shakes his head. "Strange. I'm all right now. But I couldn't see. I knew you were there, but I couldn't see."

"I don't think you'd better do anything more with the storms. Not until you talk to Lydya." Her forehead wrinkles, and her eyes and her sense study him. "There's something . . ." She shakes her head.

Creslin forces a laugh. "I shouldn't have to do much more now. Not with the weather. Anyway, you can. Your touch is . . . more deft." He feels alone, and his hand squeezes hers.

"You're . . ." she begins. . . . *frightened . . . oh . . . best-beloved . . .*

Creslin does not have to provide the words to admit his fear—to acknowledge the chill created by that sudden blindness that can scarcely be an accident, not this second time—for Megaera understands, and her arms go around him. His eyes remain open, greedily drinking in the damp redness of her hair and the faded blue of the uniform tunic that encases her, even as his arms bind her to him.

CXXXVIII

"You'd both better drink something," suggests Lydya.

Megaera picks up one of the tumblers, and Creslin follows her example. He takes a deep swallow, ignoring the warmth of the bitter liquid that Lydya has provided. Perspiration drips from his short hair, dribbling behind his ears and down the back of his neck. He looks at Megaera.

Her hair is dark with sweat, matted against her skull. Both he and she stink of sweat, strain, and fear.

"Shierra took the eastern beaches. Klerris went with Hyel." Lydya's voice is flat.

Outside the porch, rain continues to fall, not quite in sheets. Creslin turns his head, looking northward, but the clouds are gray, not black, reassuring him that his efforts have not dislodged permanently the controls he and Megaera had placed upon the high winds. Even without straining, he can tell that the worst impacts of the great storm are flowing westward and mainly onto Sligo, Lydiar, and Fairhaven.

"What exactly did you do on that last trip?" asks Lydya. Her voice is neutral.

Megaera takes a deep sip from her tumbler. Creslin can feel her guts twisting, not from an order-chaos conflict, but from something more basic.

"Creslin?" asks the healer again.

"I'll be fine, best-beloved." Megaera's hand touches his.

For a moment after her hand lifts, he cannot see, although his eyes are open. He swallows, takes a deep breath, and the darkness passes.

"Oh . . . I built a storm," he tells Lydya.

"I had rather guessed that. For the bigger White fleet. Wasn't it leaving already?"

"Yes. I'd expected it to." He licks his lips. "But when I thought about it, it didn't seem like a good idea to let it go."

"It was a good idea to murder another four thousand people?"

Creslin takes a deep breath. "Yes. Even if you put it that way."

"Why?" *Why, best-beloved? So much death already . . . did you have to add . . .*

"Because," he says carefully, "it means that Recluce can survive even if we don't."

"So you murdered nearly ten thousand men to save a mere fifteen hundred?" the healer asks.

Creslin takes another sip from his tumbler. "Go back to Candar if that's what you want, Lydya. Wait while they slowly strangle the continent. Be happy with the lack of fighting as those who don't support the White Wizards vanish, or die. Then come back in a decade and tell me what you've learned."

"Best-beloved . . . that's harsh." Megaera's voice is hoarse, and her stomach churns.

Creslin pushes away the nausea that is hers but does not try to stand.

The healer forces a smile. "He's right. Megaera. But it doesn't make it easier."

Puzzlement wars with nausea, and nausea wins as Megaera staggers toward the bucket that stands in the corner. Creslin chokes back the bile in his own throat and manages somehow to keep down the contents of his near-empty stomach as he struggles beside Megaera.

"Just let me be . . . sick alone . . ."

"I can't, remember?"

Laughter mixes with queasiness when she finally lifts her head. "It's going to be an interesting nine months."

Creslin swallows. "That was the look . . ."

Lydya nods.

"You—we—still have some more work to do," reminds his co-regent. "Such as making sure that the few survivors of our efforts don't sink the glorious land of Recluce before it's even launched." She breaks off her words for another lurch to the bucket.

This time Creslin's weakened stomach fails to handle the strain, and he ends up emptying his guts over the edge of the porch. He shakes his head after rinsing out his mouth.

"It was your idea," she reminds him. "You had to feel what I felt."

"He would have anyway," reminds Lydya dryly.

Creslin is not listening as his thoughts skip along the eastern beaches, skirt the dissipating white fog, slip from one shattered hull to another and another, and from those to a schooner seemingly untouched save that it rests firmly on the soft white sands. Below the Feyn River estuary, timbers and sodden bodies bob in the heavy swells, and the whiteness of death seeps toward him. His thoughts hasten farther southward, noting in passing that a good dozen hulls appear sound enough to be reclaimed for trade or defense.

He also notes that more than a few armed groups have formed, especially on the sole western beach where Megaera attacked the main Nordlan fleet. He frowns, wondering if there are perhaps too many for the half-dozen squads that have become the army of Recluce. The invaders would certainly feel as though they had nothing to lose.

He straightens. "I think I'd better be going."

Megaera stiffens and reaches for her sword-belt. Unlike Creslin and the guards, she prefers the belt to a shoulder harness.

"Should you?" His stomach tightens as he asks.

"Does it matter, best-beloved?" Her voice is hard.

He bows his head and for a moment cannot see through the burning mist. Her hand, with a trembling warmth, touches his, and he swallows.

"Both of you, drink this."

"What—"

"You're each near the edge. This will help." The healer extends two small cups. Her face is drawn.

Creslin downs the liquid in a single swallow, wipes his mouth, and buckles his shoulder harness in place. "Klerris?"

Megaera, finishing her draught in two swallows, glances from face to face.

"Just go. They're on the western beach. That was the closest landing."

"Oh . . ." Megaera's soft exclamation rips through him.

"Success has other prices," he observes as he starts toward Vola, tethered to the railing below the porch.

Extending a hand to Megaera, he ignores Lydya's puzzlement even as Megaera ignores his gesture and swings into her own saddle fluidly and unaided. Creslin follows her but does not catch up to her until they are nearly halfway up the path toward the keep.

What can he say? Often enough he has done exactly what he planned, only to discover that the results created greater problems. Now Megaera has done the same. By ensuring that most of the ships she has beached are usable, all too many soldiers survive. Still, he had expected more understanding.

"Just stop gloating!"

He swallows. "Is there anyone left at the keep?"

"You told Thoirkel to stay."

"We'll take him and anyone else there."

"Fine."

Light rain continues to fall, its droplets far smaller and sparser that those that will scour eastern Candar.

Thoirkel is waiting. "Ser . . . ?"

"Round up anyone who can fight," snaps Creslin. Go to the western beach, the one below the second field."

"Yes, ser."

"Are there any mounts left?" asks Megaera.

"Just four. The others went with the eastern squads. They had farther to travel."

"Pick four guards—Westwind blades, if any are left— and have them come with us. Get the others to the beach as quickly as possible."

He guides the black under the overhang. There's no sense in staying in the gentle rain, and he doesn't feel like expending effort to direct the dampness away from himself.

Megaera eases the chestnut beside him. "Is this really a good idea?"

"Probably not. But Lydya knows they're in trouble, and I don't know what else to do. I'm not sure that I could even handle the winds, not from any distance."

"I couldn't."

"Each success costs more."

"When do we stop paying?"

"Never."

Neither speaks again until the four guards, each a Westwind blade, join them. Creslin urges the black forward. Megaera rides beside him, the guards two abreast behind them.

Through the mist that still descends, flowing out of the north, the six mounts carry them westward, past the lower fields, past the stone-lined ditches from the distant springs that now carry water to the keep and to the stone-paved reservoir that Klerris has added for the town.

They ride through the browning grass that fills the swale leading through the gap in the hills to the western beach. Creslin rises in the saddle, peering ahead.

All the way down the narrow trail, he surveys the battle on the white sands . . . except that it is scarcely a battle, with groups of Nordlans fighting guards and troopers. The Nordlans are larger in number. Splitting the Recluce forces had definitely not been a good idea, but Hyel or Shierra, or someone, had gone ahead while he and Megaera had still been destroying ships; they had probably thought that few survivors would escape, as was the case with the Hamorians.

Use of the winds—

"Don't even think about it," Megaera warns.

"Why not?"

"You couldn't even see after the last storm. I wasn't much better."

"Ser? Lady?"

". . . not a lady . . ." mutters Megaera under her breath.

"We'll take the nearest group," Creslin says, drawing the Westwind short sword from its harness. His heels touch Vola's flanks; the black snorts but picks up her feet into a quick trot, which is the most Creslin wants over the rough ground above the dunes, where a half-squad holds the high sand against twice as many Nordlans.

The six mounted riders bear down on the Nordlans from the side, the sands muffling their approach.

Creslin strikes first, his blade flashing, and a Nordlan falls.

"The regents! The regents!"

The cry echoes across the sands, foaming like the still-high surf, but Creslin ignores it, his blade working furiously.

A flash of fire sears his left arm, but the blade completes its short arc and reverses.

". . . the regents . . . the regents . . ."

Creslin wheels and cuts back across the dune, now merely hacking . . . but the hacking drops another man.

He pulls up as he realizes that no Nordlans stand on the high sand; only Hyel, Klerris, and their troopers are there.

A blond guard—the one who had suggested by use of their titles that action was necessary—is checking a narrow slash on one of Megaera's arms.

"All right . . ." pants the redhead. "Let's go!"

Creslin nods and urges Vola toward the largest group, fighting between the sand-mired stems of two Nordlan frigates. He feels the throbbing in Megaera's arm, but he raises his blade nonetheless as he guides the mount toward the right-hand end of the fighting, where the Recluce soldiers are falling back.

". . . the regents . . . regents . . ."

Almost in rhythm to the ragged chant, another man falls, and Creslin turns his horse.

Whpph . . .

A dart of red lashes his shoulder. His shoulder, not Megaera's. Even before the full pain of the arrow strikes, he looks up. Almost a dozen archers stand braced on the forward railing of the far Nordlan vessel, having appeared from seemingly nowhere.

"Get the guy in silver and the redhead!"

Another slash of agony scores Creslin's right arm, and he has to force his fingers to clutch his blade.

Megaera is weaponless, both of her arms burning.

Creslin grasps for the winds, seeing no choice. His blade

falls, and he wheels the black as he seizes the nearest high winds, bending them toward the archers, trying to grasp the water and ice, molding ice arrows.

Once again the winds howl.

"Get the silver-head!"

He ignores the cry but continues to ride across the dunes, sightless, letting the mare have her head and ducking low beside her neck, twisting the winds with what power remains to him.

Crackkk!

Lightning flares beside the archer-laden ship.

"Get him!"

Another line of flame scores his right thigh—or is it Megaera's?—as he grapples with the oncoming wind.

"Protect the regents!"

The panic in Hyel's voice spurs Creslin, and he wrenches at the higher winds, struggling, tugging, yanking . . .

Wheee . . . eeee . . . The black swerves, then stumbles, but Creslin's fire-scored arms hold tight.

The ice-rains lash the ships; the cold arrows of the storms drop the archers in a single line of death.

Creslin reins in the black, sitting erect in the darkness, waiting for whatever will come. Nothing does as the sounds of swords and shouts die away, nothing except the burning of wounds that are not his. The darkness remains.

"Ser?"

"Yes?" He can tell that the voice comes from below him, but he cannot feel the land.

"What should we do?"

"How many do we have left?"

"About half."

"And the Nordlans?"

"Ser . . . you killed all of them . . . and a few of ours."

Creslin's sightless eyes burn. Burn for his stupidity.

"Take the horses that are left. Find all of the Recluce troops. If they haven't gotten into fights, tell them not to.

Just wait until the land makes the Nordlans—and whoever else survived—surrender. It will, you know." Before the other can speak, he adds, "I should have thought of that earlier. Darkness, we've had enough trouble with the land." Waves of dizziness batter at him, and his left hand clutches the edge of the saddle.

"Ser . . ."

"Megaera? How is she?"

"The healer . . . she's looking at her. But ser . . . they're over there . . ."

"Oh . . ." Creslin tries to ease the black so that he at least appears to be looking in the right direction. He fights the darkness swimming before him, and he fights against the searing pains that score his shoulder, arms, and leg. He fights—and loses, even as his hands grasp for Vola's mane.

CXXXIX

"No ONE's EVER seen a storm like that," mumbles Ryedel, his thick lips barely moving.

"Tell me about it," snaps Hartor. "Hundreds of kays away, yet it ripped out the breakwater at Tyrhavven and turned the piers into so much kindling. Half of the waterfront at Renklaar is gone. Even the waterfront buildings at Lydiar—and that's inside the Great North Bay—were flattened."

"But none of it reached Recluce."

"Of course not. Creslin caused it. And that idiot Gyretis said that he didn't have that much power."

Ryedel spread his hands, his eyes not leaving the High Wizard's face. "Gyretis paid for it, didn't he?"

"I should have sent him to Recluce. He wanted Creslin to win."

There is no answer.

"How could anyone refuse to trade with Creslin now? Or attempt to cheat him?"

Ryedel looks toward the window.

"Can you honestly say that we're stronger now?"

"It depends on what you mean," ventures the younger wizard. "Hydlen has almost no ships left, nor do Certis and Austra. We're in a better position than anyone except Sarronnyn."

Hartor shakes his head. "So . . . now everyone will watch everything we do."

"And Ryessa," reminds Ryedel.

"Fine. At one stroke, Creslin turned Candar into a continent ruled in the west by the Legend, in the east by the Whites, and both have to bow to a damned island that perhaps has two thousand souls. Maybe he'll die young."

"It won't do much good unless his White witch does too, and unless they don't have a child. Even then, Gyretis . . . I mean, I wouldn't be too sure."

"What do you mean? Or what did our dear departed brother mean?"

"The rains stayed where Creslin put them, even after the great storm."

"Oh . . ."

"What he's done seems to stay done."

The High Wizard fingers the amulet. "I suppose things could be worse." He laughs harshly. "No one wants my job after all this."

Ryedel looks toward the window, then down at the stone floor.

Hartor shakes his head slowly. In the west, the clouds are breaking and the sunlight is cold, but the drought has passed. In time, he releases the amulet, but he does not turn from the window.

CXL

CRESLIN STRUGGLES INTO awareness, though not out of darkness. He opens his eyes, but he cannot see. Blackness enfolds him like the air he breathes; while not physically restricting him, it never leaves him.

A dry, soundless croak that is an attempt at Megaera's name emerges from his lips. He tries again. ". . . Megaera . . ."

A strong set of arms helps him into a half-sitting position, where he remains, propped up with pillows. "Drink this." A cup touches his lips, and a warm scent of broth drifts into his nostrils.

"Megaera?"

"Just drink this. You need to recover as quickly as possible."

Creslin swallows mechanically, knowing now from the still-throbbing wounds that are not his, and from the headache that is two in one, that she is the illest one. He swallows again, wondering what he can do.

"No!" Lydya commands.

He spills broth over his chest as he jumps at the steel in her voice. "Maybe later, when you're stronger, but it might kill you both now," she says.

"But . . ." he stutters ". . . if she . . ."

"Creslin," insists Lydya, "right now she's holding her own. If it gets desperate, I'll tell you. But the best thing you can do for the moment is to heal yourself and stop being a drain on her. She's been tied to you longer, and the flows still aren't quite equal." She pauses. His chest is blotted, and his chin. "You're strong enough to hold this and feed yourself."

He lifts his hands and finds the cup in them. "How did you know that was what I was thinking?"

"It didn't take much guessing. Not when you ripped apart a good chunk of the sky and nearly killed yourself in distorting the order-chaos balance to try to save her. Now when, unconscious, all you did was moan and apologize to her. Not when your first conscious word was her name."

"So stupid . . . again."

"No. This time it was my fault. I was worried about Klerris, and you wanted to help me. You weren't thinking. You don't think when those you care about are threatened. None of us do. I didn't either. Now drink some more. I promise you that if I need your help, I'll tell you."

"Promise?"

"I promise."

After finishing the broth, he lies back, but sleep does not find him, not immediately, not even in the darkness that could be full day. He can hear the distant surf beat upon the sand. That, and the small feelings he cannot place, tell him that he lies in his own room, but on a bed rather than on the pallet that he had used, and that the bed is not small.

He tries to lift his hand to feel the headboard behind him, but his arms tremble. The slightest effort to sense the room spins the darkness around him in waves. At least that is what it seems, although the blackness does not lift.

The dull, aching pains that are not his penetrate his arms, his leg, so much that his shoulder wound seems little more than a sting. He closes his eyes, but that fails to ease the burning in them.

Somehow he drifts back into sleep. When he wakes again, a cup is immediately pressed to his lips. "Drink this."

"Uhhh . . . wait."

He moistens his lips, then complies. The aching in his arms seems less painful . . . or is he more used to it? "Megaera?"

"She seems better," Klerris says.

"But not much?"

"Not as much as I'd like. Drink some more of this."

Creslin again complies. After he downs the cup of warm liquid, he clears his throat.

"You'll need more in a little while. You're weak and dehydrated."

"Dehydrated?"

"Not enough liquids. The body is mostly water, you may recall."

"Why can't I see?"

"I don't know. I can only guess. It's never happened before, and I'm really not prepared to speculate."

"Guess," commands Creslin.

"If you wish, your grace."

"Skip the titles."

"Then stop acting like a brass duke."

"Sorry."

"First, drink some more of this."

Creslin sips from the second cup, his hands now steady enough to hold it.

"This is only theory." Klerris pauses, coughs. "Somehow, you broke the order-chaos dichotomy. I don't think that it has ever been done in quite that way before."

"Order-chaos dichotomy?"

"You used a form of order to create destruction," continues Klerris as though he has not heard Creslin's question. "You may recall that I once pointed out to you that most Blacks found any physical destruction difficult as they grew older, even physical destruction that did not use magic. Well, you not only did the impossible, but you were slaying people with that deadly blade again when you did it."

Only the distant sound of the surf whispers into the room.

"And?" finally prompts Creslin, the word half question, half croak.

"You have too much basic order in your bones, and your mind just shut down what it thought necessary for your preservation. Then the basic order forces recoiled against you and Megaera and shredded your remaining defenses."

"What? You're telling me that my thoughts aren't my own?"

Klerris sighed. "I don't have an answer. I can only guess."

"How long will this blackness last?"

"I don't know. If you were a normal order-master, you'd already be dead. It could be for the rest of your life. Then again, you might get your sight back in . . . I don't know . . . a year, or it could be ten years. I just don't know. I'm amazed that either one of you is still alive."

"What about the raiders?"

"Shierra had more sense than we did. Your message was right. She just picked them off one by one until they gave up and surrendered. There are a few in the hills yet, but they're not likely to be a problem. The Nordlans and Austrans want to ransom theirs back. Shierra and Hyel set the ransom at the maximum." Klerris clears his throat again. "It appears as though the coinage problems, especially with what came off the grounded ships, have been more than solved. You and Megaera are rather wealthy now."

"We are?"

"You two as regents get twenty percent. Plus that, Shierra and Hyel insisted that you be reimbursed for all the food you bought personally. After Shierra told the troops that and paid them their back pay, they wanted to vote you and Megaera thirty percent, but Shierra and Hyel insisted that you wouldn't take it."

"Twenty's too much—"

"Don't be a damned fool. You can't afford to be poor. They'll expect you to do the same during the next drought, shortage, or whatever."

"Ummm . . ." Creslin's eyes begin to droop as he slips back into sleep.

CXLI

CRESLIN'S STEPS ARE even, if slow. His senses and his ears scan the hallway and as he opens the door and steps inside Megaera's room.

Her breathing is soft, and she lies motionless on the bed, so still that he cannot tell at first whether she is sleeping or resting quietly—not until he hears the rustle of soft cotton sheets.

"How—" he begins.

"Better." Her voice is a whisper, and the dull aches in her arms are echoed in his.

Creslin sits down on the stool beside her, and his right hand covers her while his left brushes back the damp hair he cannot see, resting on a forehead still too warm.

"Your hand . . . feels good . . ."

He swallows, feeling the dampness on his cheeks as for a moment he reflects, weighing the blackness within himself. Then he eases what strength he can to her, wishing that he were stronger but glad to spare some of the Black order, although not as much as she and their daughter may need. He realizes his hand is gripping hers so tightly that both are wet, and he relaxes his hold.

"Don't go."

"I'm not going anywhere." He squeezes her hand again, and the fingers of his left hand brush back her hair again and follow the line of her cheek. "Just holding too tight."

He tries to picture her face—the freckles, the fire of her hair—and for an instant the image forms, and is gone.

"What new . . . happened?" she asks.

"Shierra insisted that we send an offer to the three—Fairhaven, Nordla, and Hamor—suggesting that the wisest course was for them to recognize Recluce and our trading ships and for us to stop destroying their fleets."

"Ummm . . ." A sound of rustling and a pressure on his forearm tell Creslin that she has shifted her weight, although she still remains on her back, propped up by pillows.

"Nordla couldn't wait. They even sent their own proposed agreement. We haven't heard from Hamor or Fairhaven. Shierra, Hyel, and Lydya think they'll agree. Byrem already has four ships back afloat, and the Hydlen and Analieran prisoners are busy expanding the breakwater. The Nordlans are adding another pier, but they'll be gone in a few days. We agreed that they could have one ship back." He swallows, licks his lips, and shifts his hand so that it loosely holds her arm just above the waist.

". . . wise?"

"We'll still be able to salvage more than a dozen vessels, and we can't crew that many, can't even find many sailors for the next season. Besides, our quarrel's not really with Nordla."

At the sound of a footstep, Creslin looks up, his senses extended. The blackness identifies the newcomer. "Lydya?"

"I thought I'd find you here. Let me see."

Creslin's fingers tighten around Megaera's arm for an instant before releasing her. He stands and steps back toward the half-open window, letting the light but warm fall breeze flow around him while Lydya bends over Megaera, checking her arms and the deep slash in her thigh.

"You've had a little more help, I see." She turns to Creslin. "I just hope you could afford it."

"I gave only what you said I could."

"Not any more?"

"A little. I know my own limits."

Even Megaera laughs, but her hollow chuckle wrenches at his guts, and his eyes burn.

"Enough. You gave too much. There's such a thing as

emotional stability." Lydya's arm takes his above the elbow. "You need to rest in your own room. The last thing I need is for both of you to collapse." The healer smoothly but firmly draws Creslin out of the room and down the hallway.

She nearly throws him onto the bed before she begins to speak. "You're impossible! When you draw down your energies too low, you get overemotional, and that feeds right back to her. The last thing she needs to worry about is your worry for her."

"But—"

"But nothing. I know you have more strength than you need physically. But you're strung out emotionally and feel as guilty as light. Megaera will pull through, but it won't help if she's saddled with your guilt and sadness, or if she's reminded that you blinded yourself by trying to save her."

Creslin opens his mouth, but Lydya continues.

"Yes, I know it wasn't just to save her, but to save Klerris and Hyel and yourself as well—but that's the way she feels. And I can't help feeling that you did it to save Klerris. Do you understand?"

He nods.

"I need to get back to Megaera. Make sure that you *feel* cheerful and loving when you see her . . . and even when you don't. Do you understand?" she asks again.

"Yes, honored healer."

"Good!"

She leaves the door ajar. Quick steps take her back down the hallway and into Megaera's room. "Men!" The snort following the comment also carries.

Creslin slips off his boots and stretches out on the bed. Far sooner than he would have thought, his eyes close . . . although it is but early afternoon.

CXLII

CRESLIN KNEELS CAREFULLY, touches the damp ground around the seedling, then eases his fingers to the stalk that will become a great black oak . . . someday. For an instant, the calm of order flows from him to the small tree, to the handful of leaves that have not dropped but soon will, bolstering the plant against the coming winter.

Then he stands and makes his way back up to the terrace, feeling the dampness of the morning sea breeze on his cheeks, listening for the sound of surf upon sand, for the clop of Kasma's hooves on the road, or for the firm step of Megaera upon the stones leading from the stable. He will go to the keep later, but there is no need to hurry, not since his skills seem to be limited to thinking and deciding, and those can be practiced at the holding as well as at the keep.

The gentle hiss of the surf and the sounds of Aldonya in the kitchen surround him. No warmth falls upon his cheeks as he sits down on the terrace wall, for the clouds hide the sun, clouds that will bring the late fall rains.

A set of hooves echoes from the road, but the pattern is not that of Kasma, nor does he feel the closeness he would were the rider Megaera. He stands and walks toward the hitching rail outside the stable, where the rider will dismount.

"Regent Creslin?"

He struggles to identify the familiar-sounding voice of the man he cannot see; then, with a sigh, he uses his non-seeing senses to reach out on the air currents that dance around the holding. His head aches, for while his senses have returned, at least for those objects nearby, he remains sightless.

. . . must you . . .

Thoirkel waits for Creslin to speak. Creslin releases his tenuous hold on the air currents, and the aching stops. Though Megaera is at the keep, he can sense her relief.

"Yes, Thoirkel?"

"The guard commanders wanted you to know that two Sarronnese ships have docked at Land's End."

"What do they want? The Sarronnese, I mean."

"They would be honored if you or the co-regent would deign to see them. They did convey the goods promised last spring by the Tyrant . . . even more than that, and a chest of coins as a . . . belated marriage gift."

Creslin snorts. "I take it that the sub-Tyrant was not amused."

"Actually, your grace, she laughed. She said that it only took rearranging the known world to get Ryes—the Tyrant—to pay her debts."

"I'll see them, but not here. We'll both see them at the keep."

"But—"

"Her grace should certainly share in the bounty and gratitude of the Tyrant." Creslin turns toward the door that leads into the stable. Unseeing or not, his steps are sure, and saddling Vola takes him only slightly longer than in the past, although the chore requires greater concentration and leaves his head faintly throbbing.

Thoirkel waits, mounted, on the road outside the Black Holding. Farther downhill, the latest Hamorian prisoners work on the paving stones, transforming the former rutted trail into a true highway between Land's End and the holding.

Clink . . .

The sound of the stonecutter's hammer comes not from the road, but from farther south, where the first Hamorian stonemasons—no longer prisoners, but craftsmen of Recluce—work at constructing a smaller dwelling. It will house Hyel and Shierra. Hyel and Shierra? Creslin smiles.

Then again, who else does either one of them have? In their own way, they are as linked as he and Megaera are.

"How long since the Sarronnese docked?"

"Just a bit ago, ser. They haven't even begun to off-load when I left. Her grace insisted that I find you immediately."

"We'll need to find her."

Finding Megaera is not difficult, for she is standing inside the arched door to the keep.

"You were quick," she says.

"Blind doesn't mean slow. At least, not much slower. I can still sense where some things are, but it hurts to reach out more than a few cubits."

"I know."

"Sorry. Are we going onboard the Sarronnese ships? Or are your sister's envoys coming here?" He shifts his feet and turns toward her, as if he could see her.

"I thought we could let them see the keep, and then let them escort us to the ships."

As one, they turn back to Thoirkel. "Would you convey that invitation to the envoys?" Creslin asks.

"Yes, your graces. How . . . when?"

"Now is as good as any time."

Thoirkel bows and departs.

"You can handle the ship? I mean—" Megaera asks hesitantly.

"I can sense enough, and you can certainly stay by my side, playing the dutiful clinging eastern mate."

"I may stay by your side, but I will not cling."

Creslin grins.

"You . . . you said that just . . . just . . . Oh, you're still impossible."

"Blindness doesn't cure that," adds a new voice. Lydya climbs the steps to the old entryway where they stand. "I overheard the last bit. Where do you intend to receive the envoys?"

"I had thought that the six of us would see them in the room we usually meet in," Creslin tells her.

"Is it . . . suitable?"

"I don't know, and I'm hardly the one to ask."

"Oh, stop playing poor little blind, Creslin," she says, smiling faintly.

"That wasn't what I meant. I never thought about that room when I could see, and now I don't remember it too clearly."

"Oh . . ."

"It's amazing what you take for granted." Creslin's voice is unintentionally wry.

"I'll have the duty guards bring in several chairs and some refreshments, such as we have," Megaera offers.

"We've just fought a trade war. I'm sure that we won't be faulted if our table is scarcely up to your sister's standards. Besides, the burhka wasn't that good."

"Best-beloved . . ." Megaera sighs. "I'll be back in a moment."

Creslin listens as her steps carry her across the hard stone floor.

"Why do I know that you two will always bicker?" Lydya asks.

"Because neither of us wants to admit how dependent we are on the other."

There is silence. Then, "I'm sorry. I nodded, but you looked so attentive that I forgot you can't see."

"Thank you. It takes some getting used to. I doubt that I ever will. So often I feel awkward, and it's hard to forget that I could even see when there was no light at all." He licks his lips as the misty image of Megaera, beside him not so many nights earlier, flashes through his thoughts. "You never realize what you have."

"You still have much more than most." There is little sympathy in Lydya's soft voice.

"I suppose we should head up the stairs." Creslin's fingers brush the stone wall before he moves, and he can hear Megaera's voice when he is halfway up the stairs.

"Not those . . . the other set of chairs, from the other room. They are envoys, after all . . ."

Creslin grins as he makes his way toward the conference room.

Before long, the Sarronnese have arrived. "Might I present Frewya L'Arminz, honored advisor to the Tyrant of Sarronnyn and envoy to Recluce, and Lexxa Valhelba, also envoy to Recluce?" The youth's voice is clear.

The six from Recluce stand, and Creslin rises only fractionally after the others. Into the momentary silence, he speaks. "We are honored by your presence and wish you welcome, although—" he gestures around the room, "—our hospitality is by necessity far less impressive than that of Sarronnyn. Still, we welcome you in peace and friendship." He forces a grin. "And since that exhausts my poor supply of formality, for darkness' sake, let's sit down." He follows his own suggestion.

"We have some documents, your graces."

Creslin responds. "The sub-Tyrant is far more familiar with such than I."

"Perhaps before we continue," interjects Megaera, "we could offer some small refreshment." Even as she speaks, two guards enter, one bearing a tray with goblets and a decanter, and the other a larger tray with assorted cheeses and fruit.

The goblets are set out before those present and filled with a liquid that Creslin knows to be translucent green and to carry the taste of fire. His body does not rebel at handling trees or brandy—so those are the projects he has worked upon.

"A toast to our guests." Creslin raises his goblet, holds it high, casting his senses to Megaera and waiting until her goblet is lifted with his.

"To our guests," Megaera repeats.

The toast passes.

"This is . . . rather unique . . ." gasps Frewya after her first sip.

Creslin is glad that he is not sitting beside the woman. "Perhaps it would go better with burhka, but I regret that we cannot make that accommodation, although we would be more than happy to supply you with some of the green brandy to take back to Ryessa."

"My sister the Tyrant might well appreciate the uniqueness."

"If you could spare some . . ."

"We would be more than happy to."

"About the documents?" Megaera's voice is polite.

"Ah, yes, your grace. Her grace the Tyrant has entrusted us with a proposed agreement affirming the friendship of Saronnynn and Recluce, including other trade guarantees . . ."

Creslin sips the brandy as the deep voice of Frewya drones on.

". . . and, lastly, the cargoes of both the *Aldron* and the *Miratror* as a celebration to the union of your graces."

". . . since we're still alive," whispers Megaera.

". . . and would hope that you would grant us the favor of a brief tour of our vessels . . ."

". . . so everyone will know that we exist and are the devils of the Eastern Ocean . . ." whispers Megaera again.

"Stop it," Creslin admonishes. "Take what she has to offer with a smile."

"Oh, we will . . ."

"I beg your pardon, your grace."

"We were remarking upon the generosity of the Tyrant, Frewya." Creslin's voice is bland. "And we will take the agreements under consideration, though we certainly agree in principle, as you must know, with the need for free trade." He stands, knowing that Megaera will stand with him, if only to cut short the proliferation of flowery nothings. "We appreciate your undertaking this long and arduous journey. Knowing that you must indeed be tired, we would not wish to impose on your generosity further."

"Your grace, a last question. It has been rumored . . ."

Creslin cannot help but smile. "There have been so many rumors. Supposedly . . . but no matter. Let me dispel some of them. No, neither the sub-Tyrant nor I intend to claim Montgren, nor, as a matter of cold fact, could we, since it is held by the hard bronze-and-white magic of Fairhaven. Nor do we expect that further use of the storms will be necessary now that the right of Recluce to exist and to trade freely has been recognized." He shrugs in the direction of the two envoys. "Of course, we retain the right to do what we must should anyone move to——"

"Sarronnyn would certainly not infringe on those rights," emphasizes the deeper-voiced woman, "but that was not exactly the rumor."

Creslin reaches for the breezes—cooling the room is not against order, although later will pay for it with a headache—and wafts the winds through the room.

"Nor have I renounced the winds," he tells them.

"Ah . . . you make your point. However, there is one——"

"I have renounced the use of the blade, but there are many here who are equally capable——" Creslin nods toward Shierra "—such as those who received the same training as I and who have had far greater practice. Our recent experiences indicate that arms must be left to those who are true professionals."

"Do you have further questions?" Megaera's voice is like ice, despite the recently all-too-familiar churning that grips both her stomach and Creslin's.

"Ah . . . not about . . . rumors, your grace."

"We were asked, by the Tyrant, you understand," adds the second envoy, "to inquire about the possibility of obtaining an agreement for certain goods such as spices, and after our toast, I have come to believe that indeed she would be interested in your green brandy."

Creslin swallows a laugh and says politely, "We wish you well."

After the two envoys leave, Megaera turns to him. "You! You acted worse than Ryessa."

"I didn't notice you exactly shrinking away."

"For whatever reason," interjects Lydya, "your performance was successful in terrifying both of them."

"When do we visit the ships?"

"I would suggest immediately . . . unless you want to wait for several days," Hyel advises.

"Let's get it out of the way. They won't off-load unless we visit, and some of us are getting tired of cornmeal."

CXLIII

CRESLIN AND MEGAERA lead the way down the unrailed gangway. His steps are firm, although each one feels like an act of faith.

". . . doesn't act like he's blind . . ."

". . . quiet, idiot. He can hear the whispers of yesterday's gossip."

Creslin cannot resist. As he reaches the pier, he turns and calls toward the ship. "Not yesterday's gossip—just this afternoon's."

". . . ulp . . ."

". . . told you . . . ."

"Stop showing off," hisses Megaera.

Creslin edges to the eastern side of the old pier to avoid the cart and the guards who stand ready to begin the off-loading. "It was necessary, especially since someone has told them I'm blind. Either that, or it's painfully obvious."

"Mmmm . . . I understand, but I know you."

"Does it really matter, as long as they still believe I can hold the winds?"

"Probably not."

"Besides, you could call a storm, one big enough for now, if you had to."

"They don't know that, and I'm not sure that sister should."

"She knows already." Creslin steps past the horse harnessed to the cart. "The Whites know, and that's probably how she found out." He laughs as his steps carry him toward the inn and the horses. "Besides, it was clear enough that the cargoes were for you, not for me. Ryessa fears you far more than she does me."

"That's sad."

"I know."

"The cargoes are my wedding gifts and dowry, so to speak, only because she fears us."

Creslin can add nothing, and his head has begun to ache with the concentration required for maintaining his balance and for the occasional use of his order-sense in keeping himself oriented. He matches steps with Megaera but says nothing, even during the ride back to the keep.

The wind gusts in from the northwest now, chill, and even damper than earlier. Kasma's and Vola's hooves echo from the stone of the courtyard as they carry the two regents toward the stable.

Creslin leads the way, for by now he knows the stairs by feel and size.

The other four—Klerris, Lydya, Hyel, and Shierra—wait for them in the room that has become their council chamber.

"How did it go?" Shierra asks.

There is silence while the co-regents seat themselves at the table. Then Megaera answers. "They were quite deferential. Although they wanted to show us all they had brought, or at least some of it, we were most gracious and accepted it on faith."

"Which made them even more nervous, I suspect," adds Shierra.

"I had that impression."

"You've just added to the image of the mysterious and powerful regents of Recluce."

"None of this regent or Duke or Tyrant or what-have-you." Creslin shakes his head, and the blackness seems to swirl. "We've done much better as a council, anyway. And that's what we're to remain."

"But only because you've been in charge—" Shierra says.

"Crap! Anyone could have done better."

"I beg to differ." Creslin catches the edge in Klerris's voice and waits.

"I beg to differ," repeats the Black mage. "The idea of a council is fine, but only if you or Megaera lead it."

"Fine. Megaera can lead it. She's better suited to it than I am." Creslin pauses at the churning in his guts, swallows as he realizes that the feelings are not his, but Megaera's.

"I am sorry, best-beloved, but I disagree."

Creslin sets his jaw and waits. Megaera will speak as she wishes.

"Thank you," she begins. "First, like it or not, most of the world does not follow the Legend. Second, having a council composed half of women will do for Sarronnyn and Southwind. Third, you are the great and renowned Storm Wizard, he who has single-handedly destroyed most of the world's navies. Fourth, not having you as the head of the council would give rise to rumors that either you are not well or that the council is a charade."

"They'll say it's a farce if I am the head."

"They'll consider the council as at least an advisory body rather than a charade," observes Lydya.

"And it allows for continuity when . . ."

Creslin and Megaera nod together, leaving Klerris's statement uncompleted. Neither will survive the other. That is all too clear.

"So, best-beloved, you have to be the head of the council." Megaera smiles.

"Wonderful. And a blind man shall lead them."

"For a wizard, it doesn't matter, and you certainly don't act as though you're blind."

"Except that I'll never lift a blade again."

"I rather doubt you will have to." Lydya's voice is dry.

Creslin fights back a surge of nausea—Megaera's. Although the queasiness is diminishing, it is being supplanted by other equally disconcerting feelings, such as an awkwardness, and an increased urgency to relieve himself.

"Who will be on the council?" ventures Hyel.

"For now, the six of us. There could be others, but we'll choose them as their advice or knowledge become necessary."

"I think it's better with you running the council, best-beloved." . . . **at least in name** . . .

Creslin sighs. Some things will never change, whether he can see or not.

CXLIV

To THE EAST of the Black Holding, he can hear the gentle hiss of the Eastern Ocean upon the sands at the base of the cliff. The wind is gentle upon his face, soft still with the cool moisture of the night's rain.

His sharpened senses tell him where the wall is, although he cannot see it, and he seats himself on the stones he laid, his face warmed by the rising sun. He does not shift his still-sightless eyes toward the source of that warmth, but listens instead to the sea.

Keee-aaaaa . . .

His lips quirk at the sound of the sea gull circling somewhere above the beach, but he makes no sound . . . for Megaera still sleeps, and she needs that sleep, both for herself and for the daughter she carries.

The first sea gull is joined by another before both fly from earshot. The breeze fades away, as does the morning warmth, when the clouds from the west reach the eastern horizon.

Shortly the wind, cooler now but not chill, springs from behind him, heralding the cold rains that he knows will fall later in the day.

"Best-beloved?"

Megaera carries something as she steps carefully across the damp terrace stones, but his perceptions are not sharp enough to make out the large object.

"Are you all right?" he asks.

"A little tired, but Aldonya keeps telling me that's normal." She seats herself beside him, carefully setting the object on the stones on the side away from him.

"It's a lovely . . ." . . . **sorry . . . I'm stupid . . .**

"It's all right. Even I can tell that it's a lovely day. The air smells fresh, and I could even feel the sun before the clouds came." He shrugs.

"Would you do something for me?"

He frowns. "What? I can sense enough not to fall on my face, and I can dress myself . . ."

"Creslin . . ." . . . **no more self-pity . . .**

He cannot help but grin at the acerbic feel of the unspoken words, so like the lady he loves. "All right. No more self-pity. If I can avoid it."

"You can try." She extends something toward him.

The smooth feel of the guitar stuns him. "But—"

"You don't need to see what you play."

His fingers touch the strings. Why has he avoided the music?

"You had good reasons, but don't think about them. Just play and sing me a song. Any song." . . . **please . . .**

Her pain slashes like a knife, and his hands fumble with the neck of the instrument. After a moment, he swallows and lets his fingers find the notes.

. . . down by the seashore, where the waters foam white,
hang your head over; hear the wind's flight.
The east wind loves sunshine,
and the west wind loves night . . .

When he finishes, Megaera is silent, but the warmth within her is enough to encourage him to touch the strings again.

> *Ask not the song to be sung,*
> *or the bell to be rung,*
> *or if my tale is done . . .*
> *The answer is all—and none.*
> *The answer is all—and none . . .*

As his voice dies away and his fingers release the strings, the guest house appears before him for a moment, stark against white, puffy clouds and patches of blue-green sky. But it is only a moment before the blackness closes around him again. No towers of sunset, no great visions, just a stone guest house, clouds, and sky.

His eyes burn, and he sets the guitar gently on the wall. "Did I . . . ?"

Megaera's hand is on his wrist, warm, reassuring. "Best-beloved . . ."

He swallows.

"The notes—" she continues, . . . **were golden!**

Her arm goes around his shoulder, and for a time they sit silently.

Finally he asks again, "Was that a vision? I wish I'd been looking at you . . ."

"It wasn't a vision."

He takes a deep breath. "Lydya was right, wasn't she? About not being able to handle physical chaos? You asked a long time ago why I could use a blade to kill. Now I can't, can I?"

"No." Her voice is soft.

"And I never can again, can I? Even if I come to see? Or call the winds for anything but order."

"Lydya doesn't think so."

He laughs, a sound half-joyous, half-bitter. "So . . . to see you again, to escape darkness. Is that why you brought the guitar?"

She nods.

He reaches for the guitar again, but his hands do not touch the wood before Megaera speaks.

"Best-beloved—"

Her lips are upon his, awkward as the position is for her. Easing away from her, he stands, drawing her up to him. The clouds part, and the surf falls upon the sands, and the sun he cannot yet see falls upon the two who are three . . . and one.

PRIZE SURPRISE SWEEPSTAKES!

This month's prize:

A FABULOUS SHARP VIEWCAM!

This month, as a special surprise, we're giving away a Sharp ViewCam**, the big-screen camcorder that has revolutionized home videos!

This is the camcorder everyone's talking about! Sharp's new ViewCam has a big 3" full-color viewing screen with 180° swivel action that lets you control everything you record—and watch it at the same time! Features include a remote control (so you can get into the picture yourself), 8 power zoom, full-range auto focus, battery pack, recharger and more!

The next page contains two Entry Coupons (as does every book you received this shipment). Complete and return *all* the entry coupons; **the more times you enter, the better your chances of winning!**

Then keep your fingers crossed, because you'll find out by November 15, 1995 if you're the winner!

Remember: The more times you enter, the better your chances of winning!*

*NO PURCHASE OR OBLIGATION TO CONTINUE BEING A SUBSCRIBER NECESSARY TO ENTER. SEE THE BACK PAGE FOR ALTERNATE MEANS OF ENTRY, AND RULES.

**THE PROPRIETORS OF THE TRADEMARK ARE NOT ASSOCIATED WITH THIS PROMOTION.

PVC KAL

PRIZE SURPRISE
SWEEPSTAKES
OFFICIAL ENTRY COUPON

This entry must be received by: OCTOBER 30, 1995
This month's winner will be notified by: NOVEMBER 15, 1995

YES, I want to win the Sharp ViewCam! Please enter me in the drawing and let me know if I've won!

Name_____

Address _____ Apt. _____

City   State/Prov.   Zip/Postal Code

Account #_____

Return entry with invoice in reply envelope.

© 1995 HARLEQUIN ENTERPRISES LTD.   CVC KAL

PRIZE SURPRISE
SWEEPSTAKES
OFFICIAL ENTRY COUPON

This entry must be received by: OCTOBER 30, 1995
This month's winner will be notified by: NOVEMBER 15, 1995

YES, I want to win the Sharp ViewCam! Please enter me in the drawing and let me know if I've won!

Name_____

Address _____ Apt. _____

City   State/Prov.   Zip/Postal Code

Account #_____

Return entry with invoice in reply envelope.

© 1995 HARLEQUIN ENTERPRISES LTD.   CVC KAL

"Dammit, Pepper, this isn't how I wanted it,"

Jim growled. "I wanted...time with you. We don't have it. You're special. I...just wanted you to know that."

Stunned, Pepper stared up at him as the plane banked sharply. "Jim," she said brokenly, "there are so many—"

"Thirty seconds!" boomed the jumpmaster.

Jim cursed softly. It was too late. He saw the jumpmaster's grim face, watched the blinking red light that would soon turn green. The C-130 straightened into level flight, and the wind whipped against them. And Jim's mind reluctantly revolved forward to the mission at hand.

God willing, he and Pepper would find Laura Trayhern and get her—and themselves—out alive.

But so much could go wrong. So much...

The light flashed green.

The jumpmaster gave the signal.

Dear Reader,

There's a lot in store for you this month from Silhouette Special Edition! We begin, of course, with October's THAT SPECIAL WOMAN! title, *D Is for Dani's Baby*, by Lisa Jackson. It's another heartwarming and emotional installment in her LOVE LETTERS series. Don't miss it!

We haven't seen the last of Morgan Trayhern as Lindsay McKenna returns with a marvelous new series, MORGAN'S MERCENARIES: LOVE AND DANGER. You'll want to be there for every spine-tingling and passionately romantic tale, and it all starts with *Morgan's Wife*. And for those of you who have been eagerly following the delightful ALWAYS A BRIDESMAID! series, look no further, as Katie Jones is able to say she's *Finally a Bride*, by Sherryl Woods.

Also this month, it's city girl versus roguish rancher in *A Man and a Million*, by Jackie Merritt. A second chance at love—and a secret long kept—awaits in *This Child Is Mine*, by Trisha Alexander. And finally, October is Premiere month, and we're pleased to welcome new author Laurie Campbell and her story *And Father Makes Three*.

Next month we're beginning our celebration of Special Edition's 1000th book with some of your favorite authors! Don't miss books from Diana Palmer, Nora Roberts and Debbie Macomber—just to name a few! I know you'll enjoy the blockbuster months ahead. I hope you enjoy each and every story to come!

Sincerely,

Tara Gavin, Senior Editor

Please address questions and book requests to:
Silhouette Reader Service
U.S.: 3010 Walden Ave., P.O. Box 1325, Buffalo, NY 14269
Canadian: P.O. Box 609, Fort Erie, Ont. L2A 5X3

LINDSAY McKENNA

MORGAN'S WIFE

SPECIAL EDITION®

Published by Silhouette Books

America's Publisher of Contemporary Romance

To my long-lost Armenian uncle, John Vinton Cramer,
and his wonderful Armenian friends: Jack Harvey and
Bill Taylor, who all have motor oil for blood and a
Sprint race car engine for a heart!
and
To my long-lost Armenian cousins, Maryann and Martha.

 SILHOUETTE BOOKS

ISBN 0-373-09986-X

MORGAN'S WIFE

Books by Lindsay McKenna

Silhouette Special Edition

Captive of Fate #82
**Heart of the Eagle* #338
**A Measure of Love* #377
*Solitaire #397
Heart of the Tiger #434
†*A Question of Honor* #529
†*No Surrender* #535
†*Return of a Hero* #541
Come Gentle the Dawn #568
†*Dawn of Valor* #649
†*No Quarter Given* #667
+*The Gauntlet* #673
+*Under Fire* #679
‡*Ride the Tiger* #721
‡*One Man's War* #727
‡*Off Limits* #733
°*Heart of the Wolf* #818
°*The Rogue* #824
°*Commando* #830
†*Point of Departure* #853
***Shadows and Light* #878
***Dangerous Alliance* #884
**Countdown #890
‡‡*Morgan's Wife* #986

Silhouette Shadows

Hanger 13 #27

Silhouette Intimate Moments

Love Me Before Dawn #44

Silhouette Desire

Chase the Clouds #75
Wilderness Passion #134
Too Near the Fire #165
Texas Wildcat #184
Red Tail #208

Silhouette Books

Silhouette Christmas Stories 1990
"Always and Forever"

*Kincaid Trilogy
†Love and Glory Series
+Women of Glory Series
‡Moments of Glory Trilogy
°Morgan's Mercenaries
**Men of Courage
‡‡Morgan's Mercenaries: Love and Danger

LINDSAY McKENNA

spent three years serving her country as a meteorologist in the U.S. Navy, so much of her knowledge comes from direct experience. In addition, she spends a great deal of time researching each book, whether it be at the Pentagon or at military bases, extensively interviewing key personnel.

Lindsay is also a pilot. She and her husband of twenty-two years, both avid "rock hounds" and hikers, live in Arizona.

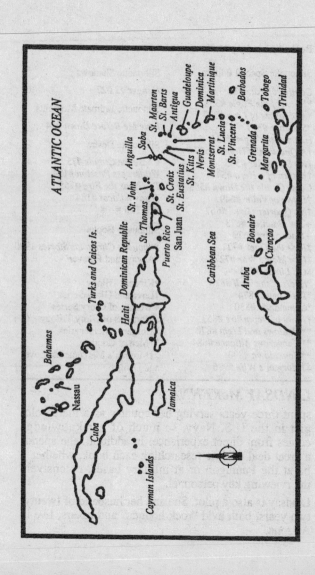

Prologue

"Are you about ready?" Morgan Trayhern poked his head into the bedroom and looked inquiringly at his wife.

Laura turned, the string of pearls Morgan had just given her as a seventh-wedding-anniversary present poised in her hands. She smiled softly, holding the luminescent necklace toward him.

"Will you? It's only fitting." As he stepped into the room, Laura's heart swelled with a fierce tide of love. How had seven years fled by? She watched his usually stoic features relax slightly as she laid the strand in his badly scarred hands. How much Morgan had suffered, Laura thought as she turned her back to him. He had come so far since they'd met on that fateful, rainy day at the Washington, D.C., airport.

She closed her eyes as Morgan leaned lightly against her back. He was wearing a suit in honor of the occasion—celebrating over dinner at a posh Alexandria restaurant. As he slipped the pearls around her neck, a tiny shiver of expectation accompanied his fingers' gentle path.

"Mmm . . ."

Morgan smiled slightly as he carefully worked the small gold clasp. Laura wore a camellia-scented perfume. Like her, the fragrance was heady, making his senses spin.

"Seven years," he murmured close to her ear as he slid his hands along the expanse of her shoulders. "Can you believe it? I can't." He never would. Laura was his bright, shining dream against the dark, nightmarish world that probably would never completely stop haunting him. Post-traumatic-stress disorder didn't necessarily go away with time—at least his hadn't. Laura had stood by him—and suffered with him—through the gut-wrenching flashbacks. Before Laura, Morgan never could have fathomed a person of such strength and courage that she'd *want* to remain at his side during those tortured times.

Responding to his gentle pressure, Laura leaned against him, feeling his warm breath on the side of her neck as he pressed a kiss against her temple. Her nostalgic glow gave way to more urgent feelings and she eased away just enough to turn in his arms and face him. Placing her hands on his broad shoulders, she smiled up into his serious gray eyes.

"I can."

With a sigh, he brushed a few wayward strands of hair back from Laura's cheek. She wore a simple ivory silk suit that showed off the pearls to perfection. Her blond hair fell in soft waves to her shoulders, arousing in him the urge to tunnel his fingers through its thick, silky mass. His mouth curved ruefully.

"I don't know. It hasn't exactly been heaven living with me, has it? More like a living hell at times."

The scar on Morgan's face from that long-ago hill in Vietnam presented a constant reminder to Laura of the deep, invisible scars he still carried in his heart and soul. She touched his other, recently shaved cheek. "No marriage is perfect, and neither are we. But these have been the best seven years of my life, darling. If I died right now, I'd be happy with exactly what I have here—with you." She glanced fondly toward the partially open door to the dimly lit hall. "We have two wonderful children, a boy who worships you and a baby girl who adores you just as I do." Her eyes filled with tears. "No, these years haven't been hell for me, they've been heaven."

Morgan felt the tension that inevitably gathered in his neck and shoulders with rising emotions. He cupped his wife's delicate face and looked deeply into her luminous blue eyes. "I still don't know how you can stand being around me sometimes, Laura. I guess I'll never understand it. But it doesn't matter. I love you with my life," he breathed against her mouth. He kissed her fully then, parting her lips, tasting the love she effortlessly gave to him. The emotional nourishment she provided was part of the miracle he realized his life to be. Laura was a beacon of strong, steady light for him and for their children. He hoped, as he kissed her, that he was imparting just how deep his love for her ran in him.

As he felt her lips meet and match his fervor, Morgan heard a distinct *click*. The marine part of him went on instant alert, though he was loath to break their molten embrace. A chill moved up his spine: another warning. One he couldn't ignore.

Breaking away from Laura, he gripped her shoulders, already turning toward the door leading to the beige-carpeted hall. "Stay here," he said in a low voice.

Laura gasped. Three men, dressed completely in black to the dark ski masks covering their heads, appeared soundlessly at the bedroom door. She didn't even have time to raise her hands to her mouth to scream as they drew their weapons. Morgan reacted instantly, thrusting himself in front of her. Too late!

The *pop* of the guns wasn't the sound of bullets. Laura felt a sting in her left shoulder, and everything became slow motion, like single frames of film passing before her. Two of the men fired at Morgan, and Laura saw two small darts strike him in his neck and chest.

She was disoriented by the intruders' eerie silence as a burning sensation spread rapidly through her, radiating from the area where the first dart had struck her. Looking down, she saw very little blood. Her vision blurred, and her knees suddenly turned to jelly. Morgan gave a strangulated cry, turning toward her, his eyes wide with warning and fear. At the sight of that fear she tasted abject terror.

How many times had Morgan worried about attack from any of the countless enemies he'd made running Perseus over the past seven years? Laura's breath was becoming chaotic, and she struggled for air. She staggered and fell to her knees, automatically reaching for the edge of the bed.

Morgan dropped suddenly and heavily, like a bull that had been shot in the head. He lay unmoving nearby, on his back, one arm extended toward her. Laura stared, feeling her mouth go dry. She looked up. All three intruders warily entered the room, their weapons still raised. A hundred questions swirled in her head as she fought the effects of the drug racing through her system.

She sagged to the floor, oddly conscious of the brush of the lavender carpet's nap against her hands, even as her terror mounted. Had they killed Morgan? Was she dying? Oh, God, no, the children! *The children!* The thought made Laura whimper, and with everything that remained of her rapidly dissolving strength, she tried to rise. But her weakened muscles would not cooperate, and darkness shadowed her blurred vision.

With a moan, she fell back toward the carpet and knew nothing more.

Chapter One

Jake Randolph looked grimly at the small contingent of Perseus mercenaries gathered around the oval oak table in what Morgan called the "War Room." Here, plans were laid for covert missions around the world. Jake clenched his jaw. "Morgan, Laura and their son, Jason, have been kidnapped," he said, his voice harsh in the room's tense silence.

Wolf Harding had just appeared in the doorway. "Who's behind it?" he growled.

Jake sighed wearily. "We don't have details yet—but we'll get to that in a minute." He'd been without sleep for forty hours. He'd just returned from a mission when the kidnapping occurred. Sean Killian and his wife, Susannah, arriving to baby-sit for Morgan and Laura, had discovered the Trayherns missing—except for their baby daughter, Katherine Alyssa.

"Son of a bitch," Wolf snarled as he stalked into the room. He'd just gotten off a flight from Montana. When he noticed that Morgan's faithful assistant, Marie Parker, was part of the group, he quickly apologized for his lapse of manners, then crossed to the coffee dispenser and poured himself a cup.

Jake looked at his watch. "Killian discovered them missing at 1900 yesterday evening." He picked up a plastic bag. "They were shot with tranquilizer darts." He looked toward Killian, who stood in the shadows, his back against the wall, his face unreadable, as always. "Tell them what you found."

Killian looked at his friends. He and Wolf and Jake had been on a number of mercenary missions over the years, and the two men were like brothers to him. "Their front door was standing partly open. I thought that was odd—especially in November—so I told Susannah to stay in the car until I could check it out. Inside, I saw nothing until I reached the master bedroom. There were a few drops of blood on the carpet, and that drug dart was under the bed." Killian scowled. "I checked the kids' rooms, and the boy, Jason, was gone. Katherine was still in her bed, asleep."

"Were there signs of a struggle?" Wolf demanded, taking a seat to Jake's left. Papers were scattered across the large, highly polished table. He noted the worry visible on Marie's usually calm features. He took a sip of the scalding coffee and grimaced.

"Very few," Killian answered abruptly, folding his arms across his chest. "Once I made sure the place was secure, I brought Susannah in and called here. Jake had just come in off a mission, and I told him what I'd found." Killian pointed to one of the many pieces of paper on the table. "Marie received this message on the Perseus fax at 2100, two hours after the kidnapping."

Wolf reached for the paper. He frowned as he read it aloud: "Don't try to find Morgan Trayhern and his family. They are scattered around the world. If you want to see any of them alive again, Perseus will stop its attacks against the Peruvian Cartel."

"Yeah, Wolf, our friends down south," Jake muttered. He eyed the Cherokee man, whose dark features had paled considerably. "I know the three of us have fond memories of Ramirez and his cocaine syndicate. Wolf had been captured, tortured and nearly killed under the drug lord's hand, and Killian had fared only slightly better.

"Son of a bitch . . ." Wolf darted another apologetic look at Marie. "I'm sorry," he rasped, suddenly getting to his feet, the paper clenched in his large fist.

"It's all right, Wolf," Marie whispered, dabbing her eyes. "What should we do, Jake? I don't know how to run Perseus without Morgan's input. I have no idea how to start a search for him, or if we should. Please, can you take over? At least for now?"

Jake looked at the other two men. Wolf had been out of the mercenary business for nearly a year, working a sapphire mine in Montana with his wife, Sarah. Killian, who now took only low-risk U.S. assignments, was out of the loop, too. Though Perseus employed nearly a hundred mercenaries, those teams were locked into missions that couldn't be aborted at a moment's notice. Grimly, Jake realized he was the only available player who was up-to-date on everything.

"Unless anyone has a problem with it, I'll run Perseus—until we can get Morgan back," he offered.

Killian eased away from the wall and sat down at the opposite end of the table, facing them. "We're going to need a lot of government interface on this. Have you contacted the CIA? The FBI? And what about the DEA? They know more about the Peruvian Cartel than we do."

"All of that's been initiated," Jake said. He took a long swig of coffee. His mouth tasted bitter, and his eyes smarted from lack of sleep. He'd already called Shah, his fiancée, in Oregon, to let her know what had happened. He should have been home by now. Instead, she was on a flight east to be with him. He wouldn't be going home now until Morgan and his family had been located and rescued.

"I've got Pentagon Intel specialists watching for messages of any kind. Part of the problem is satellite time. If we don't get it, we can't intercept potential messages between countries on satcom. It's pretty clear Ramirez is behind this, but that doesn't mean Morgan and his family are in Peru."

Killian looked at his watch. It was 1900 on Tuesday, November 22. Thanksgiving was two days away. "We need to do some long-range planning," he murmured, looking up at the weary group. "I think we should keep the local police out of this. We've already got every arm of the government involved at a high level. The Alexandria police won't add anything except potential media coverage that we certainly don't need. I say we keep this as undercover as possible. That way the cartel won't be able to anticipate our moves."

Jake rubbed his face. "Are we in agreement that we should try to locate and rescue Morgan and his family?"

Wolf nodded. "We don't have a choice. Killian and I know better than anyone what Ramirez is capable of. That bastard will torture Morgan to death an inch at a time. He's a murdering monster."

"And what about Laura?" Marie asked tearfully. "What will he do to her?" She gazed around at the set faces of the men, seeing the grim lines of their mouths. None of them would meet her eyes. "Oh, dear . . ."

"Look," Wolf said impatiently, standing again, "we can't afford to let our imaginations get the best of us. We need cold, clear-headed tactics." He nailed Killian with a searching look. "Will your wife take care of Katherine? She's Laura's cousin, right?"

"Yes. I'm sending Susannah home to Kentucky—to her parent's farm. She and Katherine will be safer there."

"Have Morgan's parents been contacted?"

"No," Jake said heavily. "I was waiting until we could get a group of us together to figure out our plan of attack. But they need to be called and informed now."

"I can do that," Marie volunteered, making a note on her pad.

"Fine. Wolf, your specialty is communications. I want you to be our liaison with the Pentagon. Killian, I need a lieutenant to talk things over with, someone to help me make final decisions."

"I'll hang around," Killian said dryly.

Jake smiled a little and rubbed his stubbled face. He needed a hot shower, a shave and some sleep. The first two he could get, but sleep would have to wait.

"First we'll try to intercept communications traffic and get a lead on where they've taken the family members," Wolf said, thinking out loud.

"From the message, it sounds like Ramirez has separated them," Jake said. "They could be anywhere in the world. Anywhere."

"It's like searching for three needles in a haystack," Wolf agreed unhappily, pacing the length of the room.

"I know." Jake moved his shoulders to release some of the tension that had accumulated there.

Killian looked at Jake. "Who's going after Ramirez and his goons?"

"I don't know yet," Jake admitted heavily. "We're short-handed. I'm going to go through the mission roster with Marie to try to cut loose some people to help us." He knew neither Wolf nor Killian would go. Wolf had quit the mercenary business almost a year ago, and he and Sarah were going to marry at Christmas. Killian was happily married and not about to risk everything—especially with Susannah four months pregnant. Jake didn't blame his friends for not volunteering for this kind of mission. If he took it, he knew Shah would raise all kinds of hell. Of late, they had grown inseparable, and Jake didn't want to risk their happiness on this level of danger.

Besides, the three of them had worked together for a long time, knew one another and how they thought. In a crisis like this, they'd be more useful in a behind-the-scenes overseeing role. "Somehow we'll find the teams," he muttered.

"Do you want me to contact Alyssa and Noah?" Marie asked.

"We'd better," Jake said ruefully. "If we don't, there will be hell to pay." Lieutenant Commander Alyssa Cantrell was Morgan's younger sister, a navy pilot. Jake had no idea where she and her husband, Clay, were stationed. He did know that Commander Noah Trayhern, Morgan's brother, was in the Coast Guard and, with his wife, Kit, lived in Miami, Florida. Noah and Morgan's parents, who lived nearby in Clearwater, would be easiest to reach. "Try to contact them through non-military channels if you can, Marie."

She rose, nodding, but gave him a questioning look.

"Ramirez has enough money to buy state-of-the-art tele-communications equipment that rivals anything the military has," Jake explained. "If we send these messages via the military, he might pick up on them and get an idea of our movements. I don't want him to know a damn thing if we can help it."

"I see," Marie acknowledged. She tried to smile, but failed. "I'll have dinner brought into the War Room for all of you."

Jake nodded. "Thanks, Marie." After she left, he turned to his comrades. "This is a hell of a bind."

Wolf stopped pacing, his hands on his hips. "Ramirez will kill them. It's only a matter of time."

"Yes," Killian agreed quietly. "He likes long, slow deaths. You know that, Wolf."

Harding nodded, his mouth a tight line. "I'm more worried about Laura. She's the one really at risk."

"Ramirez won't be easy on her," Killian agreed. "When I was first captured in Peru, I was taken to a different cell block from you, Wolf. Ramirez and his goons raped women prisoners as part of their torture to get them to talk. No, you're right—Laura has problems."

"And what the hell will they do with the boy?" Jake asked, his voice frustrated. "I mean, the kid's innocent."

Killian gave him a flat look. "In our business, no one's innocent."

"Why didn't they take Katherine?" Wolf wondered aloud.

"Probably because women are considered worthless—second-class citizens—in South America," Jake muttered. "She wasn't worth taking. You know how South American men think the world of their sons. Boys carry on the family name and honor. I'm sure that's why they took Jason."

"Do you think he's at risk?" Wolf asked.

"I don't know," Jake hedged. "Knowing Ramirez and his twisted mind, he'll probably stash the boy away somewhere and raise him in the cocaine empire. That's the way Ramirez is, you know. He'd think that was the ultimate revenge on Morgan—turn his son into a cocaine trafficker—or worse, a coke addict."

Wolf cursed and began pacing again. "There's no question we've got to get to them. The sooner, the better."

"First," Killian said, "we need a lucky break. Someone has to pick up communications between Ramirez and his world-wide cartel. We've got to get a clue to where they are."

"Our second problem is finding a team that can undertake the rescue once we do locate them," Jake reminded his friends.

"What do we have so far?" Jake demanded of his team. He was clean shaven, dressed in fresh clothes, and had even managed to snatch a little sleep. It was 2000 the next evening, and the three mercenaries were back in the War Room. Marie sat at the opposite end of the table from them, taking notes. A messy stack of papers still covered the shiny oval surface. On the wall, a map of the world had been pulled down for reference. Disposable cups littered the room, silent testimony to too many cups of coffee, and the burning stomachs and frayed nerves that went with them.

"The Pentagon is working double time on telecommunications," Killian reported. The Joint Chiefs of Staff have approved satellite telecommunication time for us. They've put a team of Intelligence people from the CIA on it, along with other military specialists. We're getting more help than I anticipated."

"Good," Jake grunted. "Wolf?"

"I'm getting help from the FBI and DEA. They're checking all flights from the East Coast to see if we can figure out how Morgan and his family were taken, and in what direction they went."

"Do you think there's a chance they're still in the U.S.?" Jake asked.

"No. The FBI thinks they're off U.S. soil."

Before Jake could speak, the door flew open. He reared back in surprise, automatically on guard. A Marine Corps officer, a lieutenant colonel, stood in the doorway, one hand on the knob, the other on the doorjamb. His face looked stormy; his eyes were narrowed in anger.

"Just what the hell has happened to Laura Trayhern?" he snapped, moving into the room and shutting the door behind him. "And what the hell are you doing about it?"

Jake stood. He'd been in the Marine Corps himself for many years before leaving to work for Perseus. The officer in front of him was in his middle thirties, lean as a cougar. Jake noted the gold parachute emblem above his dark green, wool shirt pocket and the full set of colorful ribbons denoting his time in service. The officer stood rigidly, his hands curled into fists at his sides, his eyes accusing as they swept the room, then settled on Jake.

"Who are you?" Jake demanded in a deep tone.

"I'm Colonel Jim Woodward, Intel, over at the Pentagon." He gave a disdainful look around the room again. "Where's Laura? What's happened to her?"

Jake held up his hand. "Calm down, Colonel Woodward. Are you part of the liaison the CIA put on telecommunications?"

"Yes," he said tightly, "I am. I've been pulled to oversee the operation. When I found out Laura was involved, I had to know a hell of a lot more than I was being told. That's why I'm here. I'm an old friend of hers, from before she married Morgan. Now will someone fill me in?"

Jake nodded. "Have a seat, Colonel."

Jim listened without interrupting. By the time Jake Randolph finished briefing him on the kidnapping, he couldn't seem to settle his rapid pulse or ignore the fact that his hands were sweating. Laura was in danger. His heart contracted at the thought. It was nearly impossible to keep his face carefully arranged. When Jake asked if they'd been able to intercept any likely communications yet, Jim stood.

Taking a piece of paper out of his breast pocket, he handed it to him. "I know where they've got Laura. We just picked up a sat-tel link off a small Caribbean island known as Nevis. It's a tiny spot in the Windward Islands, off the coast of South America. The message is cryptic, but we got a lead on the transmission."

Jake frowned as he studied the paper. "How do you figure this, Colonel?"

"I don't know who transmitted—yet. I've got the CIA working on that angle right now." Jim jabbed a finger toward the paper. "But it was transmitted from Nevis to someone in Dresden, Germany. It reads, 'The Tiger is caged.'"

"Why would that be Laura Trayhern?" Wolf demanded.

Jim held on to his disintegrating anger. "Before Morgan came into Laura's life, we had a relationship. I used to call her Tiger." He felt heat creeping into his cheeks. "It was a nickname I gave her because she was the only civilian woman writer working at the Pentagon archives." He felt foolish divulging the intimacy, but he had no choice.

"I don't know..." Killian began. "Isn't that a bit of a stretch?"

Woodward glared at the narrow-faced man sitting to Randolph's right. "Not when the CIA has already confirmed that Nevis is home to a world-class drug dealer by the name of Guillermo Garcia."

"Garcia," Harding growled. "Damn, he and Ramirez have been in cahoots for twenty years."

Jim smiled grimly. "I'm right and I know it. 'Tiger' is Laura."

"How would Garcia know that?" Jake demanded.

"He's probably drugged her and gotten a lot of personal info out of her," Killian interjected.

Just the thought of Laura being drugged, having her life bled out of her, made Jim sick to his stomach. "It's just a matter of time until I get more info pinpointing Garcia as her captor. I've already gotten permission to move one of our spy satellites to that part of the Caribbean. Right now—" he glanced at his watch"—a U-2 spy plane is in the air, on its way to take photo reconnaissance over the island. I guarantee you, with those photos, we can pick up a gnat's rear end at fifty yards. If my photo people see anything to suggest Laura being there, we'll have our proof."

Relieved, Jake nodded. "I'm damn glad you're heading up the Pentagon effort, Colonel Woodward. You obviously know what you're doing, and you've provided more information than any other source so far."

"Well," Jim rasped, "my association with Laura goes back a lot of years. She's a special woman...." He avoided Jake's probing gaze, cleared his throat, then looked back at him.

"What plans do you have for infiltrating that compound on Nevis, Mr. Randolph?"

Jake smiled for the first time, just a little. "We might be short on the information files, Colonel, but one thing Perseus does do well is mercenary work of any kind. This type of mission is right down our alley."

"I doubt it," Jim challenged. He focused on the men one by one. "I thought this situation through on the way here. The dossier on Garcia I've got coming over to you from the CIA is substantial. They've got a blueprint of his estate, which is behind an iron fence ten feet high. He's got guards and Doberman pinschers posted around his ten-acre kingdom. Nobody comes and goes from Nevis without him or his people knowing about it.

"If you sent one of your men to the island, they'd find out instantly. They'd tail him, and chances are, they'd take him out at first opportunity. You don't know what's involved here." He went over to the map and tapped the Caribbean area. "You need a HAHO," Jim said, using the military acronym for a high-altitude, high-opening parachute drop, "onto that island in the dead of night. And you'll need a specialist with maximum military parachute experience. Do you know how small Nevis is? It's not much of a target. But if you tried to parachute from a lower altitude, Garcia would spot you, and you'd be dead before you landed.

"Then *if* you get your man on the ground, he'll need jungle experience. Nevis is heavily wooded and, because it's so small Garcia's people will certainly spot you, if the locals don't. That is, unless you utilize maximum stealth technology."

"Hold it, Colonel," Jake said heavily. "We have those kind of people on our payroll. Morgan rarely hires anyone who's not ex-military. We've got ex-Delta Force and former Marine Recons. The problem is, we're stretched too thin. We don't have a team we can pull to take this assignment."

"You what?" Woodward's mouth fell open and he snapped it shut. "You don't have anyone assigned to fulfill this mission? It's a priority."

"Don't you think we're upset about it, too?" Jake retorted, his voice irritated. "Unfortunately, Colonel, this world of ours is full of trouble spots. Many of our teams are on dangerous missions. We can't just extricate them without jeopardizing their lives, or other people's lives, in the process. It doesn't make sense to lose two to six lives to save one." Jake tapped a bunch of computer printouts. "I've gone through our mission list twice. The teams with experience are in situations where they can't be pulled. The ones that can be pulled don't have the background you're talking about. I'm not about to put an inexperienced team into the type of situation you're painting for us. We don't throw our people's lives away like the military does."

Woodward smarted under the remark. He felt heat rising from his throat into his face. Whenever he got angry, his face turned red, and he knew it. "This is an unconscionable position. You've got three lives—one of them the man who owns this damn company—at stake, and you don't have anyone to run a rescue mission?"

"Back down," Wolf snarled, crossing his arms over his chest and returning Jim's glare. "We're doing what we can with the resources we have."

"I won't back down." Jim held his gaze for a long moment. "All right, then I'll volunteer for the mission."

Jake's brows knitted, and he studied Jim for a long moment before speaking. "This is personal, isn't it? Between you and Laura?"

"That's none of your business, Randolph. What is your business is that you've got someone to take this mission. I can get orders cut to allow me to do this. I'm a Recon. I'm HAHO qualified. I've been in more jungles than I care to think about. I've been in Panama, Grenada and other South American venues on deep undercover assignments." He stopped, his voice low and shaking with tightly held emotion.

Jake glanced around the table, assessing his team for some inkling of their thoughts. Killian stirred and placed his arms on the table, clasping his hands in front of him. He glanced up at Woodward.

"Laura is married to Morgan. They love each other," he said quietly.

Jim recoiled inwardly. "Don't insult me with facts I already know."

Killian held his stare. "Mercs who have an emotional involvement with the person they're trying to rescue don't live long."

"That may be your problem, Killian, but it's not mine."

With a shrug, Killian looked across the table at Wolf.

Wolf said, "You'll need a partner. We never go in alone. It's two or nothing. Do you have someone in mind who has the same qualifications?"

Jim hesitated. "Two?"

"Yes," Jake rasped, "two people on every mission. That's Morgan's law, and it's a good one. If one partner is injured, the other can always bring him out." He lowered his voice. "We have no time for heroics, Colonel. We work as a tightly knit unit and watch each other's backs. I know Recons. I used to be one. You don't go gallivanting off by yourselves, either. You have five men to a team and you know the value of working together."

"I don't disagree with you, but I can't honestly think of anyone who would volunteer for such a dangerous assignment. The one man who might be willing, a sergeant, is laid up in the hospital with a broken ankle right now."

Jake shook his head. "Colonel, this mission doesn't go down without two team members."

Wolf slowly unwound from his chair. He rubbed his temple and looked first at Woodward, then at Randolph. "I know someone who can do it. Her name is Pepper Sinclair. Her brother's a Navy Top Gun and a test pilot. She's a team leader for the National Forest Service's smoke jumpers. In fact, Pepper is in the Hotshots, the elite, highly trained group that goes into dangerous forest hot spots or wildfires. She's got over two thousand parachute drops and is ex-army." Wolf smiled a little. "Matter of fact, I've known her for nearly a year now, and her background is impressive. She was the only woman ever to complete Army Ranger training—but they wouldn't let her graduate because she was a woman."

Jake twisted to look in Wolf's direction. "What'd she do then?"

"She quit the army. She was an officer, and she resigned her commission in protest over their decision. Pepper went into the smoke jumpers because it was the most dangerous career she could find where nobody cared about her gender. She's got six years of military service behind her, and she was in Panama and Grenada, too, so she knows jungles. I think she's around thirty years old, and she's got a good head on her shoulders. Pepper doesn't go off half-cocked on anything." Wolf studied Woodward. "And in this case, that might be important, because, Colonel, I think you're in this way over your head emotionally. You're carrying a torch for Laura, whether she's married or not, and that's going to get you into trouble on this mission."

Jim opened his mouth to protest, but Harding went on.

"I know the question you're all wanting to ask. Would Pepper volunteer for something like this? I don't know, but I can sure call and ask. She's good friends with Sarah and me, and I think she'd be interested."

"She'll get good pay for it," Jake said hopefully, liking the suggestion.

Wolf's smile broadened a bit. "Pepper isn't turned on by money. She's a competitive person and she likes challenges."

"This is hardly a game!" Jim protested vehemently.

"Pepper doesn't play games, Colonel. What I'm saying is that she's as solid and trustworthy as they come. Hell, she leads a Hotshot team. You probably don't know a thing about smoke jumpers, but I can fill you in. You're a Recon, the best warrior the Marine Corps produces. Well, in the smoke-jumping world, Hotshots are the equivalent. We had a forest fire north of Phillipsburg, where we live, and I got to see Pepper and her crew up front. That fire was bearing down on our small mountain town, with seventy-mile-an-hour winds pushing the blaze.

"Of all the teams that could have been put on the line between that fire and our town, Pepper and her staff were chosen. She served as commander over ten Hotshot teams. I worked with her on tactics and strategies for the fire and I saw her parachute in with a team that I thought for sure would be burned alive. She went in there with her walkie-talkie—and with her people, who would go to hell and back for her—and she did the impossible. She got the fire to move, and Phillips-burg is still standing, thanks to her guts, intelligence and experience."

Jim sat down. "I'll be damned if I'm going in with a woman," he said harshly. "They aren't qualified for this kind of a drop."

"She's ex-army, ex-Ranger. Ranger training is similar to Recon," Wolf droned. "And you know that."

Jake nodded. "It's an excellent idea, Wolf. Can you call Pepper now and fill her in?"

"You bet." Wolf excused himself to make the call.

Woodward stood up. "You can't be serious about this, Randolph."

"I'm dead serious. You don't know Wolf, nor do you know his background and experience. If he says Pepper Sinclair can do it, I believe him." Jake held the officer's shocked stare. "I do know one thing for sure, however. If you take this mission, you're doing it the Perseus way, not the Marine Corps, John Wayne style. I've got three people I love very much on the line right now, and I'm not going to blow it by putting anything but two first-rate people on this mission. Do you understand that, Colonel? Because if you don't, or if you give me grief about it, I'll make a call to the JCS and tell them we don't want you. Do I make myself clear?"

Angrily, Jim moved around the table. "Don't threaten me, Randolph. I'm damn well capable of pulling off this mission *alone.*"

"It's not a threat, Colonel. It's a promise."

Was Randolph bluffing? Jim wasn't sure. As a matter of fact, he didn't like the loose way Perseus worked at all. This decision by committee wasn't in the least like the military. He rubbed his jaw as he assessed Randolph, who sat like a mountain in the chair at the other end of the table.

"Even you can see the folly of Harding's idea," Jim insisted.

"Really? What's that?"

"A *woman,*" Jim said in exasperation.

Jake grinned tiredly. "Colonel, one thing Morgan Trayhern has made very clear to everyone at Perseus is that in his opinion, women are just as good, and usually better, than any man at this work."

"That's ridiculous!"

"Not in our book." Jake tapped the table deliberately with his index finger. "And as long as Morgan is alive, we're running his company his way. You got that?"

Biting back the anger that warred with his fear for Laura, he sat down. "This woman could be killed."

"It's an equal-opportunity business, Colonel, just as women in the military can be killed as easily as men. Bullets don't consider gender."

Stymied, Woodward sat very still, evaluating his options. He knew no one was better qualified than he was to rescue Laura. But to have a woman—a civilian, of all things—along on such a dangerous mission was beyond his imagination. He wasn't usually so temperamental—but this was personal, just as they had accused him of earlier. Jim knew his emotional involvement could be a detriment to the mission. Somehow, he had to separate his feelings from the job to be done, and concentrate on surviving.

"I want your promise on one thing, Randolph," he insisted.

"What?"

"If this Pepper Sinclair is stupid enough to volunteer for this mission, I want the opportunity to put her through her paces. If she can't or refuses to do a HAHO, or in some way is not militarily qualified, I have veto power."

"With an attitude like yours, she's sure to fail whatever task you set her," Jake said tightly.

"Dammit, I have a right to protect myself in this mission. I don't care how glowing Harding's report is, if she can't stand the heat, she doesn't come with me."

Jake glared at him. "I propose an alternative plan, Colonel. If Pepper volunteers, you can set up the tests you need to feel comfortable, then you can both report back to me. I'll make the final decision."

In that moment, Jim disliked Randolph intensely. "I can set up the tests?"

"Any and all you want, understanding that we don't have much time. Once the CIA gets a fix and confirmation that Laura is on Nevis, we want to initiate the mission immediately."

Satisfied, Jim leaned back in the chair. "Fine. I'll bet you a hundred dollars right now that Ms. Sinclair is going to fail miserably at the tests I've got in mind."

Randolph smiled uneasily. "You're on, Colonel. A hundred bucks."

Jim crossed his arms, wondering about the outcome of Harding's phone call to Sinclair. He prayed she'd turn him down. What woman in her right mind would volunteer for a high-kill-ratio assignment like this? He didn't look too hard at his own answer to the same question.

Chapter Two

Tension thrummed through Jim Woodward as he stood waiting for Pepper Sinclair to walk through the partially opened door. It was 0700 on Wednesday, November 23, and she was due in from a red-eye flight from Butte, Montana, at any moment. Harding had gone to the airport to pick her up and would brief her on the way in, so she'd be up to speed by the time she reached the Perseus office.

Jim didn't want a woman with him on this mission; it was that simple. She could have taken first in Hawaii's grueling physical-endurance contest, the Iron Woman, and it wouldn't have mattered to him.

His sensitive hearing caught the sound of voices in the reception area, where Marie had her neatly organized office. Warm, husky laughter—distinctly feminine—drifted to where he stood. Jim tried to stay immune to that rolling, mellow sound, but it was impossible. It wasn't Marie's laughter, so it had to be Pepper Sinclair's. His mouth turned down. Why did she have to have such a provocative laugh?

He stood tensely, hearing Wolf's deep voice and Pepper's well-modulated one intermingle as they chatted amiably. He didn't know Harding well, but knew he wasn't the type of man to be chatty, so it must be Pepper's presence drawing him out.

Whatever Jim was prepared to see, it wasn't the physical reality of Pepper Sinclair as she followed Harding into the room. She was tall—probably close to six feet—medium-boned, with dark walnut-colored hair softly brushing her proudly held shoulders. More surprising, she was wearing a long red-and-yellow calico skirt that touched the tops of her comfortable, brown leather shoes. Her white blouse, with touches of lace around the throat, was partly hidden by a pale golden deerskin vest adorned with conchs. Long beaded earrings nearly touched her shoulders, giving her a somewhat Native American look, except for her pale, almost-translucent skin with a sprinkling of freckles across her nose.

Pepper's face was oval. Her nose had a slight bump and fine nostrils. Jim looked downward to lips curved in an impish smile, then his gaze moved back up—and into eyes as blue and clear as a Montana sky. His heart gave a hard thump, underscoring the impact of those eyes—the pupils edged in breathtaking turquoise, the frame of thick, dark lashes. Her dark brows were arched and full, offering a second frame for the magnificent eyes. Her cheeks were flushed, their rosy pink enhancing her classic bone structure.

But more than her striking and unexpectedly feminine looks, it was Pepper's direct, fearless gaze that caught Jim completely off guard. The look combined maturity with a woman's confidence—yet glinted with a girlish aspect that somehow strengthened its impact. Jim was chagrined to feel his palms growing damp. Meanwhile, his errant heart refused to slow its pounding beat.

Jim tried to suppress his reaction to Pepper. It didn't help that he'd expected a sturdy, mannish sort of woman with a tough, no-nonsense attitude—a hardened outer shell for this female smoke jumper who damn near walked on water, according to Harding. Jim's gaze ranged from her long, narrow hands to the graceful way she walked toward him, to those mesmerizing blue eyes. . . .

"Colonel Woodward? I'm Pepper Sinclair. Glad to meet you."

Her grip as she took his hand told Jim instantly that she wasn't as weak as she looked. Her firm, confident handshake, warm and dry, conveyed strength and capability. If it had been a man's handshake, he'd have been impressed. In a woman, he didn't know how to react.

"Ms. Sinclair," he said, hating the clipped abruptness in his tone as he stared challengingly at her.

"I'll leave you two to get acquainted," Wolf said dryly. He pointed to the counter on the left. "Pepper, if you want coffee, help yourself."

"You saved my life again, Wolf." Pepper laughed and waved to her friend as he stepped out of the room, closing the door quietly behind him. She shifted the strap of her deerskin purse off her shoulder and laid the bag on the oak table, then moved toward the coffee machine. The tension in the room was palpable, and she knew full well it was emanating from the marine standing rigidly next to the table, watching her every move like a predator ready to strike.

"I don't know about you, but four hours on the red-eye makes me thirsty as a horse." She glanced back over her shoulder at the officer, who was scowling heavily. "Coffee, Colonel?" she asked pleasantly. "Or would you prefer to take out your weapon of choice right now, shoot me and put yourself out of your misery?"

Shocked, Jim opened his mouth, then closed it. Her eyes were serious, but her voice dripped with honey and her mouth curved in a rueful smile. "I see Harding has been talking behind my back," he said finally.

"On the contrary," Pepper said smoothly, finding a clean white mug and pouring the fresh coffee into it, "Wolf was merely honest with me about potential problems and dangers. He did inform me that you were against using a woman on this mission."

Jim moved to the table, hating himself more as he snapped, "Ms. Sinclair, when it comes to life-and-death matters, all the cards get laid on the table. Nothing and no one is spared. And you're right—I don't want a woman on this mission."

Pepper turned. "I couldn't agree more with the truth of your first statement, Colonel. We're both in the business of life and death, aren't we?" She took a sip of coffee. Too bad Woodward was such a sourpuss, she thought. Because the man was undeniably a handsome devil, in a rugged kind of way. His green eyes were glittering like shards of ice in her direction right now, though, and his square face was set—like concrete. His black hair was militarily short and neat, and she liked his darkly tanned looks. Lines in a face told her much, and Woodward had his share. Creases at the corners of his eyes spoke of a great deal of time spent outdoors. The lines bracketing his mouth said something different, though. Lines of pain, possibly. But from what? Or who? His size, posture and attitude reminded her of their local college football captain. Fleetingly, Pepper wondered if Jim had played football in college. She smiled to herself and decided not to ask. Pulling back a chair, she smoothed her skirt and sat. Woodward stiffly took a seat opposite her, his hand folded in front of him, his knuckles white.

"We aren't in the same business, Ms. Sinclair. Not by a mile," he said tightly.

Pepper held his angry, defiant gaze. "Let's talk about your anger at the idea of a woman going on this mission with you, shall we?" she asked, her voice calm and steady. "I believe in gut-level honesty, so maybe that would be a good place to start in this messy little situation we seem to find ourselves in."

Jim reeled internally at her unexpected bluntness. Her quiet voice belied the strength of her demand. He grasped at a notepad with several items neatly printed on it and slid it around in front of him on the table, using the moment to collect his scattered thoughts. "I'm not angry at you," he said coldly. "I'm angry at the concept of Perseus installing a two-person team on this mission, when I feel I'd be more successful alone."

Pepper's smile was equally chilly. "Spoken like a politically correct officer in line to make general someday. Congratulations, Colonel Woodward. It's a great reply, but it's hardly complete and honest, don't you think?"

Under any other circumstances, Jim had to admit, he would have liked Pepper immediately. She wasn't conventionally beautiful. Her chin was stubborn and pronounced, and her aristocratic nose didn't match her full mouth, the corners of which always seemed to curve slightly upward. Her features were like puzzle pieces that shouldn't fit together, but somehow did, to create a whole more magical than the sum of its parts. A rebellious lock of hair fell across her broad brow, and she brushed it away, as if she'd made that effortless gesture unconsciously all her life. He bought more time by opening his briefcase and placing a couple of books on the table.

"Are you always this acerbic, or are you doing it as a special favor to me?" he asked finally, seeing the laughter flash in her eyes, though she didn't allow it to transfer to her mouth.

"I consider my answers honest," Pepper responded. "Maybe you're looking for political correctness or diplomacy. I'm neither of those, Colonel. I learned about both things early on as an army officer, but I'm a civilian now. I no longer have to play those word games with you or anyone else." She smiled slightly. "Thank goodness."

Jim found it difficult not to smile in response to the warmth shining from her eyes. In fact, he could feel her warmth—as real as if a beam of sunlight had suddenly struck him. Who was this woman? "It's not my nature to be base," he offered.

"Since when is honesty considered baseness, Colonel?"

His fingers tightened around the ballpoint pen in his hand. "If we're done sparring, can we get down to the business at hand?" he said through gritted teeth.

"Fine, let's do it." Pepper tried to feel anger toward Woodward, but it just wouldn't surface. He was obviously uncomfortable, backed into a corner of sorts and unhappy about her appearance on a mission he wanted to perform solo. She set the cup to one side and pulled out her own small notepad and a pen from her purse. "What's on your agenda, Colonel?"

"You. I told Jake Randolph I intend to put you through your paces. If you don't measure up to my high standards, you aren't going."

"I believe you agreed that Mr. Randolph will make the final decision," Pepper said smoothly, holding his glare. "Besides, what gives you the right to question my credentials while assuming yours are beyond question?"

"I'm a Recon Marine. My credentials *are* beyond question."

Pepper leaned back, slowly tapping the table with her index finger. "I'm a country girl, Colonel, and I've lived most of my life in Montana. Maybe we're kinda simple folk out that way, but you know what? We let people prove themselves through their acts. Your walk is your talk. I could understand your concern if I didn't have a military background. I could also understand it if I'd never jumped out of a plane with a parachute. But what I see going down here is a wounded male ego overreacting to the fact that I'm a woman. If I were a man, I think you'd drop this pretense. Back where I come from, that doesn't go down well. I'm a team leader for twenty smoke jumpers. I'm responsible for a lot of lives, and I've never lost one. I'm not about to start now with yours or my own. I found out a long time ago that ego and pride are expendable."

Her voice dropped slightly. "Colonel, I appreciate your concern about my qualifications, but it's not necessary. I probably have more time logged in parachute jumps than you do."

"All at low altitude."

"I took Ranger training. I've participated in HAHOs."

Frustrated, Jim said, "I'm not going to fire any more shots across your bow. We need to get down to business. I've outlined the next three days." He pushed the neatly printed paper toward her. "I'm going to test your map- and compass-reading ability. I've arranged for a HAHO and have preplanned the jump zone with the military boys at Andrews Air Force Base. It's set up and ready to go for tomorrow at 0700. The jump onto Nevis will be at night. But as much as I'd like to schedule day and night practice HAHOs, we just don't have the time. A day jump will have to do." Jim watched the soft fullness of Pepper's lips tighten a little as she carefully read his outline. Her fingers were slim with largish knuckles, her nails closely trimmed. There was no wasted motion about her, he had to admit, and in spite of himself, he savored her unique mix of serenity and efficiency.

"I feel like I'm back in Ranger training," Pepper said mildly, sliding his notes gently back across the table. If Woodward weren't so intent on making her dislike him, she thought, she might like to explore him personally, as a human being and a man. But the set of his square jaw warned her off. He was trying to intimidate her into quitting. Well, it wouldn't work. As the only female ever to go through Ranger training, she'd had plenty of experience with intimidation attempts by men far more dangerous to her than Woodward—but he didn't know that. "I'm assuming you'll be with me on these exercises? That you'll participate in the HAHO, too?"

"Of course."

Pepper grinned. "To watch me fail?"

"I expect you to."

"Colonel, you've just pushed a favorite button of mine—I love a good challenge. My whole life has been about dancing on the edge of a sword."

Jim almost smiled. Again that unsettling turquoise warmth from her eyes enveloped him, and he felt his heart beating harder in his chest. There was something arresting about Pepper that he couldn't quite put his finger on. At least, not yet.

"Tell me a little about yourself, Colonel. Personal stuff."

Her directness scuttled him. He eyed her. "Why is that important to the mission?"

"If I'm going to succeed at all your tests, I need to know more about my partner than his military title. I want to know something about the man." Her eyes narrowed briefly. "What makes you run, Jim Woodward?"

Jim pushed his chair away from the table and stood up. "You have a damn needling habit of being nosy, Ms. Sinclair."

"And you have a damn needling habit of questioning my credentials when what we really should be doing is planning how to save Laura Trayhern."

The set of her jaw, with her chin jutting out, challenged him, as did her incensed gaze. So she was angry, after all—but for the right reasons, Jim realized. "Believe me," he said, trying to hide his emotion in a gruff tone of voice, "no one wants to save Laura more than I do."

"I understand from Wolf that Laura is a personal friend of yours." Pepper watched his cheeks flame red and saw sudden shyness in that imperious gaze he was trying to control her with.

Maybe Woodward wasn't such a jerk, after all. For a moment, she'd glimpsed a real man behind that egotistical marine facade he was employing to try to scare her into quitting.

"Laura and I go back a long way," Jim muttered offensively, as he turned and walked to the window. In the distance he could see the Capitol and the Washington Monument outlined against the dawning colors of the horizon. "We met when I had my first tour at the Pentagon. Laura was—still is—a military-defense author. It's rare for a woman to find success in the field, and she's considered authoritative on a broad range of military subjects." His voice dropped. "She's an incredible woman...all that intelligence, that ability to comprehend..."

Pepper watched Jim Woodward's face soften tremendously—as if he'd forgotten she was in the room. The incredible tension around him dissolved as he spoke of Laura. "And she married Morgan Trayhern?" Pepper asked quietly.

He shrugged. "Morgan Trayhern crashed into our lives, and she ended up with him."

The sudden flatness of his tone belied his pain, his confusion over that issue, Pepper realized. No longer was he the tough marine officer; for a moment he was a human being struggling with unresolved emotions regarding a woman he loved.

"Are you presently in a relationship?"

Jim shook his head. "No, not a serious one."

"Any family?"

"Just my parents, until recently. They died in an auto accident a year ago." Jim turned. He felt oddly sad and didn't try to cover it up. Pepper's gaze was assessing, the warmth still there, continually surrounding him like sunlight. The genuine care and sincerity radiating from her was very real. Vaguely, he acknowledged that good leaders had that kind of charisma. Despite her almost-brutal honesty, Jim admired those qualities. He could understand now why men would work under her command without having male-female issues. Yes, she was personable and easy to talk to—too easy.

"I'm sorry to hear it," she murmured. No one deserved to have their parents ripped from them like that. Trying to establish a less-traumatic line of conversation, she asked, "Are you an only child?"

"Yes. And I was spoiled rotten."

"I have an older brother, Cam. He's married to a wonderful woman named Molly. They have three children now, and I like playing Auntie Pepper to all of them." She smiled fondly as she thought of her brother's family.

Jim tried to resist her husky voice, but it was like a soothing balm to the sadness he still held in his heart over the unexpected loss of his parents. It uplifted him, and he noticed the luminous quality that came to her eyes when she spoke about her brother. "He's the naval aviator?" he asked, remembering Harding's comments about a Top Gun brother.

"Yes. Molly used to be in the navy, too. They met at test-pilot school a number of years ago. She's such a homebody, a real hausfrau who enjoys being a mother and parent. Cam lost his first family in a freak airplane accident, so I'm really happy to see them together. I'm glad she decided to resign her commission and become a civilian."

"Surprising words from a gung ho career woman—or are you?"

"What do you think?" Pepper would play his game against himself. She wasn't about to become cannon fodder for him or any military man stuck in the "women should be barefoot and pregnant" mind-set.

Jim rubbed his jaw and held her gaze. "I don't know what to think about you—yet," he admitted. "I know what I thought you were, but my original assessment isn't turning out to be as accurate as I expected."

"I'm sure you expected me to come striding in here wearing men's clothes and acting like 'one of the boys.'" Pepper countered. "Well, I would have at one time, Colonel—back in my army days. I became that way to protect myself from the men who wanted to tear me down and make me quit." With a slight shrug, she added, "When I joined the Smokeys, I lost that facade. I discovered that the men and women who jumped into fires didn't care what gender I was so long as I could do the job. I was allowed to be myself, to flourish and grow into the woman you see now." Her smile was frank. "I think it's nice to be a woman and do a first-rate job, whether it's perceived as masculine or not. Don't you?''

"Touché."

"An honest answer. How refreshing, Colonel. Be careful, it could become a habit.''

Instead of being stung by her rejoinder, Jim laughed. And it felt damn good to laugh, as if an incredible weight he'd been carrying on his shoulders had slipped free for just a moment. That load had been there in some form ever since Laura had married Morgan, he realized. Getting up, he went over and poured himself a cup of coffee. Silence flowed back into the room, but the atmosphere was less tense than it had been.

"Since we're exploring each other," he said, coming back to the table, "tell me a little about yourself. Do you have a significant other?" He wondered what kind of man would be drawn to her.

Pepper slid her fingers quickly through some strands of hair. "No...not anymore."

Jim heard the pain underlying her soft answer. He also saw, for the first time, a look other than happiness in her eyes. Pepper had a real vulnerability to her, even if she held down a decidedly male career with success. In his experience, the military molded women into a male image in order to help them survive. The military was unforgiving if someone—man or woman—showed vulnerability of any kind, so he was fascinated by Pepper's ability to maintain that quality.

Pepper struggled with a sudden deluge of emotions that brought back her raw, unhealed past. She saw at least a shred of real concern mingled with the curiosity in Jim's eyes. Afraid to release that genie of past suffering from its well-stoppered bottle, she straightened her spine. "Since we've both laid our cards on the table, why don't we get down to the real business?" she said, her voice suddenly brisk. "What's on the agenda today? I'm sure you've got something up your sleeve."

Jim pulled himself from his reverie, realizing he was staring at her. Embarrassed by his own breach of officerlike etiquette, he murmured, "We're going over to my office at the Pentagon. My attaché called to say they've got reconnaissance photos of Nevis Island taken by a U-2 flyby."

With a shake of her head, Pepper got to her feet and slipped the purse strap onto her shoulder. "Amazing how all that old military lingo I thought I'd forgotten comes right back."

"Once in the military, always in the military," Jim said as he opened the door.

Pepper's smile was still laced with pain. "There are some parts of it I wish I could forget," she muttered, slipping by him and out the door. In the front office, she saw Wolf and Jake, their heads bowed together over some military information, talking in low tones. She went over to Wolf and touched his arm. The civilian clothes both men wore couldn't hide their military bearing.

"Wolf, I'm going with Colonel Woodward over to the Pentagon."

"Fine . . . we'll see you when you get back." Wolf gave her a brief, assessing look. So did Jake, who she'd met earlier.

Pepper smiled a little, reading his mind. "Everything went fine," she lied. Wolf had a habit of sticking up for friends rather boldly and sometimes to his regret. Not wanting Wolf to dislike Jim any more than he already did, she felt the white lie would help reduce office tension to below the boiling point. As she turned, she saw the oddest look in Woodward's gaze—an almost wistful expression combined with such heat that it threw her off guard.

Woodward didn't like her because she was a woman in a military man's slot. Okay, so why was that look so tough to decipher? Sighing at the knowledge that Woodward was something of an enigma to her, Pepper grabbed her Pendleton coat off the hook and followed him out of the Perseus office.

The late-November chill was matched by a gray sky that threatened the first snow of the year, and Pepper was glad to get into the heated Pentagon building. As she walked at Jim's side, she smiled to herself, once again surrounded by uniformed members of all four military branches walking the halls of this military icon. The tile floor was polished to perfection, and hundreds of pieces of artwork, depicting and honoring war from the ground, water and air, decorated the walls of the octagon-shaped building's outer ring.

Jim was aware of the stares Pepper was receiving from more than one gawking officer. He tried to ignore her natural grace—the way she moved was more like water flowing than like the steady, deliberate steps he took. Maybe it was that effortless ease, he decided sourly, that made nine out of ten officers do a double take. Disgruntled, he had to admit that any man worth his salt would certainly look at Pepper. An old saying came to his mind: "She was easy on the eyes." It was a decided compliment.

His office was tucked away, compared to many of the others. When they'd made their way in, Jim shut the door after Pepper. His natural inclination was to be a gentleman, to take her coat and hang it up for her. But a contrary part of him said, let her take care of herself. As he stood, debating which to do, Pepper crossed to the small closet, matter-of-factly hung up her coat and purse and turned toward him.

"What now?"

"This way," he muttered unhappily, preceding her into the interior office—his private space. His secretary had yet to come in, and with Thanksgiving tomorrow, many people in the Pentagon would be working only half a day, anyway.

Pepper stepped into Jim's small enclave and looked around at the officious degree certificates and awards hanging on the walls. She was impressed. Woodward was more than a Recon. He had a degree in engineering from Ohio State University and had graduated with honors. Curious, she moved to a wall hung with several framed color photos. Most were of him with graduating officers, but one exception drew her attention.

The photo showed a younger Jim Woodward, his arm around a much smaller, delicate-looking blond woman. Both were smiling, obviously happy, with champagne glasses lifted in a toast to the camera.

"Who's this?" Pepper asked, turning to him. Jim was behind his desk, riffling through a pile of papers that had been stacked there for his attention.

He looked up briefly. "Oh…that's Laura Bennett—I mean, Trayhern. Morgan's wife."

Pepper returned her attention to the picture. "How old is this photo?"

"Eight years." Frowning, Jim stopped reading the message in his hand and looked up. Pepper's profile was clean, even pretty. Her dark hair fell softly around her face, completely natural and untamed. He liked that about her—her utter naturalness, with no apology for the way she looked or dressed.

"What was the occasion?"

Jim set the paper aside. "It was taken down in the Pentagon archives. Laura had just sold a manuscript to a publisher. It was her first hardback book. I bought some champagne, and she and I and the people she worked closely with down there—who'd helped her bring the book to life—celebrated late one afternoon."

Smiling, Pepper nodded. "You both look very happy."

"We were...." Shaking his head, he muttered, "Come on, we're going to the photo lab. Those pictures of Garcia's fortress are available. Ready?"

"Sure." Pepper followed him out of the office. They walked, it seemed, forever, taking an elevator two floors down and into a more dimly lighted area. The photo laboratory had a small sign on its door. Jim ushered her in. The place smelled of chemicals. Without preamble, he led her into a smaller niche where several black-and-white photos lay on a hardwood table covered by thick glass. A naval-intelligence officer waited for them. She was dressed in a dark blue wool uniform with a white blouse and a black tie at the throat. Her black hair was neatly coiffed, barely touching the collar of her jacket.

Jim introduced Berenice Romero, a woman in her early thirties, to Pepper and immediately asked, "What have you got for us, Berenice?"

"Garcia's mansion, Colonel." Berenice smiled a hello at Pepper as she responded, then used a pencil to outline the shape of the main house and grounds on one of the photos. "This is his fortress. Garcia's got a ten-foot-high wrought-iron fence surrounding the main compound. Guards are posted every quarter mile, and Doberman pinschers walk the fence line, too. Take a look at this."

Leaning over the photo, Jim squinted through the film magnifier she handed to him. "Oh, yeah... big, black Dobermans. You can even see their teeth, can't you?" He smiled a little and handed the magnifier to Pepper, who also took a look. When she straightened, he said, "Still want to go, knowing those dogs are more than willing to rip us apart and call us breakfast?"

"Dogs like me."

"Those dogs don't like anybody."

Berenice chuckled. "Colonel, by accident, our flyby caught something else interesting." She brought out another picture and laid it on the table. "It's a jeep. I think you'll be interested to see who's in it."

Jim took the magnifier and leaned over the photo. He choked back a gasp. "Laura Trayhern . . ."

"Yes, sir." Berenice beamed triumphantly at Pepper. "We had no way to know for sure if Garcia had her, but for once we got lucky. I'm sure they didn't expect a flyby or they wouldn't have transported her during daylight in an open jeep like that."

Pepper nodded, noting the strained expression on Woodward's face as he handed her the magnifier. He had paled considerably, obviously shaken by the photo. She leaned over to study the minutely detailed photo, focusing on the jeep. Laura, her blond hair streaming behind her, sat in the passenger seat next to a driver dressed in battle fatigues. A handgun of some sort was pressed against the back of her neck by a soldier sitting directly behind her, and his hand gripped her shoulder.

"How awful for her," Pepper whispered as she returned the magnifier to Berenice. She glanced at Jim, who immediately turned and walked a few steps away. Sensing his anguish, Pepper said nothing more, but when he returned to the table, his eyes were suspiciously bright.

"We've got a mission report on Garcia for you, too," Berenice said, noting Woodward's reaction. "Come with me, sir."

Pepper remained at a distance as they moved to a small, comfortable office, where four steel gray chairs were arranged before a desk. Berenice moved behind the desk and sat down. She handed them each a sheaf of papers and gestured for them to sit.

"Guillermo Garcia is the top drug lord in the Windward Islands," she began. "This is a color photo of him. You can see he's short and overweight. His most distinguishing feature is his face, pockmarked with deep scars. He's fifty years old—an autocratic tyrant as murderous as his boss, Enrique Ramirez, of Lima, Peru.

"Garcia has been a pain in the neck to us since the early eighties. The FBI infiltrated his organization in Florida and Texas and managed to collar most of the U.S. bosses, but Colombia refused to extradite Garcia. However, it scared him enough that he moved his profitable operation from our country to the Caribbean. Now he's had ten years on Nevis to set up another empire, which has proven equally profitable."

"Berenice, do we have an operative there?" Jim fervently hoped so.

"No, sir, we don't."

"Damn," he muttered, then glanced apologetically at both women.

Nodding slightly, the lieutenant continued the briefing. "Garcia calls his fortress Plantation Paloma." Berenice looked at Pepper. "*Paloma* is spanish for *dove.*"

"Rather an irony, isn't it?" Pepper drawled.

"To say the least," she agreed. "Garcia is as cold-blooded a killer as Ramirez. All the bosses who work for Ramirez pattern themselves after him. When you make your jump, if Garcia discovers either of you, he'll kill you without question. Although we don't have an operative on Nevis right now, the CIA is working to come up with one. At one time we had an informant." She frowned. "She was a local Nevis woman, a laundress for Plantation Paloma. She was in Garcia's employ for five years, and we were able to gather a great deal of useful background information about his fortress from her. Unfortunately, Garcia somehow found out she was working for us."

"What did they do to her?" Pepper asked quietly.

Jim looked up. "You don't want to know."

"Don't protect me, Colonel. Just because I'm a woman doesn't mean I can't handle the gory details." Pepper looked at Berenice, who obviously agreed with her.

Stung, Jim nodded. "All right, give her the information, Lieutenant."

"Yes, sir. Garcia is known to use truth drugs on anyone he suspects isn't loyal to him. They shot the operative full of a

truth drug, and she spilled everything. After that, Garcia threw
her to his men, and she was gang-raped." Berenice sighed. "We
know because we found her body on the beach at the opposite
end of Nevis from the fortress. One of the locals found her
stripped of her clothes, and the CIA autopsied her body." The
distaste in Berenice's voice was obvious. "Garcia is a tor-
turer—an expert. He picked up his methods from Ramirez,
who's nothing short of a sadist." She handed Pepper a photo
from the file.

Pepper's stomach rolled as she stared at the photo of the
woman's body lying on a morgue slab.

"That's who we're going up against," Jim said in a steely
tone. He met Pepper's narrowed gaze. "And that's why I don't
want you along." He jabbed a finger at the offending photo.
"Now do you see why I'm against you coming on this mission?"

Bile coated Pepper's mouth as she laid the photo down and
pushed it slowly in Berenice's direction. The lieutenant picked
it up and slid it to the bottom of the file. Swallowing against a
dry throat, Pepper rasped, "Don't you think he'd do the same
thing to you, Colonel? What makes you think a murdering
bastard like that cares if you're a man or a woman?"

Jim scowled and leaned back. Pepper was right, but he had
hoped the photo and briefing session would discourage her.
"There's an old military saying—'Take no prisoners.' Garcia
doesn't. And you're right—he'll do the same to a man as he will
a woman."

Rubbing her brow, Pepper whispered, "My heart aches for
Laura Trayhern. I mean, what has Garcia done to her already? My God . . ."

Jim's heart lurched in his chest at her whispered words. He
saw tears in her eyes and felt unexpectedly touched by the depth
of her reaction to Laura's plight. He didn't think anyone else
had fully appreciated the terrible trouble Laura was in. As
Pepper wiped tears from her eyes, his heart swelled with an
unknown emotion. He dug in his back pocket for his handkerchief and handed it to her.

"Here . . ."

Pepper nodded, taking it from him. "Thank you." She dabbed at her eyes, not caring whether her companions approved of her nonmilitary emotional response. As an officer like Lieutenant Romero, she wouldn't have dared allow the tears to show. But as a civilian, Pepper wasn't about to apologize for wearing her emotions close to the surface. Not anymore.

As she dried her face, Pepper glanced at Woodward, expecting to see his face set with disapproval—just one more mark against her in his hard, military book of life. Instead, she saw a surprising softening in his glacial green eyes—and some unknown emotion touched her fleetingly.

Maybe, she thought as she refolded the handkerchief and handed it back to him, he lived vicariously through other people's emotions, unable to be in touch with his own or show them. Berenice Romero sat quietly, and Pepper saw dampness in her eyes, too.

"What an ugly little monster Garcia is," Pepper said, her voice tight with feelings. "All this does—" she pointed to the folder where the highly offensive photo now rested "—is make me that much more determined to get in there and rescue her."

Jim said nothing, but secretly he was thrilled by the determination in Pepper's tone. Her eyes, too, glinted with a new light. Gone was the warmth, replaced with a surprisingly steely anger. "You'll need more than desire fueled by anger on this mission," was all he said, as he pushed the handkerchief back into his pocket. "Please continue the briefing, Lieutenant."

"Yes, sir." Berenice cleared her throat and placed three more black-and-white photos before them. "Garcia's Dobermans not only patrol Plantation Paloma, they're trained to kill. They're also trained not to take any meat or other food that could be tainted with a drug to render them unconscious."

"Has the CIA come up with anything? A dart gun or something?"

"Pheromones, Colonel."

"Oh?"

Pepper leaned forward as Berenice showed them a photo of a small capsule containing a clear liquid.

"The CIA labs have developed a unique way to control the dogs—the hormones of a female Doberman in heat." She smiled a little. "All you have to do is create a diversionary trail with the hormones along the fence line, in the opposite direction of your entry point. The dogs will follow the scent. Garcia made a mistake in having only male guard dogs. They'll choose the female scent over their guard duties. Great idea, isn't it?"

Pepper grinned at the lieutenant. "I know this is a sexist comment, but isn't that just like a male?"

Both women laughed. Jim didn't think it was very funny but, reminding himself that women in the military took more than their share of sexist prejudice and harassing remarks, he gracefully allowed them their joke.

"Do we have a diagram of Garcia's plantation?" he asked.

The lieutenant became somber. "Yes, sir, we do." She handed each of them a detailed diagram. "Our operative, because she was a laundrywoman, was in every room of the plantation. Garcia's home is a two-story wooden structure, painted white. The upper floors include many guest rooms and his personal suite. The lower floors are mainly offices, with a telecommunications room, satellite feeds and anything else he needs to stay in touch with his people around the world. He also displays a multimillion-dollar collection of old-master paintings about the house."

"Has the CIA projected where they might be holding Laura?"

"She's probably being kept in one of the second-floor rooms in the right wing, where there are bars over the windows and a guard is posted."

Jim's stomach knotted. Unconsciously, his hand closed into a fist. The possibility that Laura had already been drugged to gain whatever information she had was a forgone conclusion. The Perseus team had assured him that Morgan never discussed business with her—to help prevent her from becoming a terrorist target. But... his mind railed against even thinking what other atrocities might have been done to her. Closing his eyes momentarily, he struggled with his anger—and his grief—

over Laura's situation. She didn't deserve any of this. If only she hadn't married Morgan...

With a sigh, he opened his eyes. Both women were watching him in the building silence. "What else, Berenice?" he asked in a strained tone.

"I've arranged an 0700 HAHO over the woodlands of Virginia for you. The C-130 will drop you from twenty thousand feet. Another team with a HumVee will monitor you from the drop zone." She pulled out photos of the landing area, which was covered with thick stands of oak, ash and beech trees. "We've tried to duplicate as closely as possible the landing zone chosen for you on Nevis. It's heavily wooded, so the potential for injury is high."

Pepper studied the photo carefully. "Looks just like the forests we chute into, Colonel, except that these aren't pine trees." She looked at him. "Are you used to landing in this kind of stuff?"

"No, I'm not," he admitted darkly.

"Welcome to a lot of getting hung up in trees, then." Pepper leaned back, feeling good about being able to contribute something from her area of expertise. "We have special chutes made so that we can pretty much zero in on which set of trees to land between. Of course, even if we're able to do that, we still get batted around by tree limbs. There isn't a time when we aren't bruised. At the worst, those limbs can act like spears, and gash an arm or leg."

Pepper tapped the photo on the table. "And even if you're lucky and experienced, and the wind is your friend that day, you still can get hung up fifty feet off the ground. Then you have to cut yourself loose and do a free-drop to the terrain below, which may or may not be rocky. Or if you manage to make the mark and go between the trees, you may not have the luxury of flexing your knees and bending and rolling when you hit the ground, the way parachutists are taught. Which leaves you open for at least a sprained ankle, and potentially a broken leg."

"Do you ever make a landing without some kind of injury?"

"Never," Pepper said matter-of-factly. "I work long hours with my team on precision landings, Colonel. We pick the most thickly wooded, steepest slopes, ones with boulders under the trees, to practice on, because, you have to understand, we may land within a mile of a roaring forest fire. The winds around a fire are very different, far more dangerous and unreliable, than those of a straightforward parachute drop like this HAHO. For this one, at least, we'll have weather information in advance. We'll know what the wind directions are and won't have to worry about vortex winds swirling at five thousand feet to throw us off course or into some trees."

As Jim listened to her husky urgent voice, a sense of admiration threaded through him. Pepper obviously knew her craft. And he didn't have much experience with heavy-tree landings. If anything, he could be the albatross on this trip.

"Colonel, I strongly suggest we wear support gear around our knees, elbows and ankles." Pepper held up her hands and gestured to her elbow. "We usually wear tight, hard elastic wraps around joints that are likely to be injured. I wear them especially tightly around my ankles. If I can't walk once I'm on the ground, I'm useless to my team."

Jim snorted. "We don't do that in the military, Ms. Sinclair. If you want to wear them, go ahead."

Pepper stared at him. "I can't believe you'd dismiss this safety feature so easily, Colonel. What if you hurt yourself on this HAHO exercise tomorrow morning? What good will you be to the mission then?"

Jim glared at her. "Give it a rest. I'm not going to impose my jumping habits on you, Ms. Sinclair, so don't shove your ideas down my throat."

"Good teamwork comes from working together, Colonel," Pepper said hotly. "Teamwork means sharing our experiences, deriving the best ideas from all parties concerned, then instituting them for everyone. Safety is my first and only consideration."

"Hitting the target accurately is mine. And you had better hope you hit it, too, or you aren't going on this mission." Jim rose, feeling the tension in himself, seeing the anger in Pepper's huge blue eyes as she slowly stood in turn. Tearing his gaze away, he looked down at the lieutenant.

"Thanks for the briefing, Berenice. You've done a good job, as usual."

"Thank you, sir."

Pepper moved to the door and opened it before Woodward could get there. She was stunned by his refusal to work together. Worried, she walked down the hall, making her way back to his office. She was too angry to walk back with him. His secretary was in his office this time—a woman with short blond hair and pretty blue eyes, dressed in a pale pink business suit. Nodding to her, Pepper went straight to the closet and got her coat. It crossed her mind that Woodward's secretary resembled Laura Trayhern somewhat—she had the same hair and eye color and was petite in build. As Pepper turned, shrugging into her coat, Woodward entered, his jaw set, his eyes grim.

"I'll get you a manual on HAHOs, then take you to another area to be fitted with gear," he said abruptly.

"Fine." Pepper's nostrils quivered with anger. What a bullheaded person he was turning out to be! Did she even want to try this mission with him? If he'd been one of her staff, she'd have kicked him out for lacking the team spirit that kept them successful and safe on the toughest jumps. She decided she would call Wolf later from her hotel room and talk more with him about the situation.

Vaguely, she heard Woodward talking to his secretary. His voice was no longer hard or clipped, but personable—even warm. She turned, realizing what a difference there was in his attitude toward her and toward his secretary. So he could be human, after all. He just didn't like her, didn't want her around and didn't believe she could contribute anything of value to the mission.

To hell with him. She stepped out into the hall to cool down. Arranging the deerskin purse on her right shoulder, she waited for Jim to reappear. When he did, she didn't want to admire him in his dark green wool uniform, the cap, with its shining, black patent leather bill, settled on his head. He was a stalwart warrior type, the epitome of the Marine Corps' finest, and he knew it. Pepper's anger dissolved as she appreciated him from a purely physical standpoint. The man was ruggedly handsome, there was no doubt, in a dangerous kind of way. Despite his stubbornness, Pepper found herself drawn to him—and then berated herself for allowing her feminine side to overlook the facts: the man was a danger to her—and to the mission.

Chapter Three

The chill in the C-130 as it leveled off at twenty-one thousand feet at 0630 the next morning sent a shiver through Pepper. It was below freezing. She stood, legs apart, balancing herself as the Air Force bird bobbed around in the choppy air, hitting continual pockets of turbulence. A yellow ribbon of color lay along the horizon in the clear, cloudless dawn. The high-pitched whine of the four turboprop engines and the cavernous expanse of the empty C-130 reverberated through her as they strained in the thin atmosphere en route to the drop zone. In fifteen minutes, the rear of the C-130 would yawn open, and she and Woodward would leap from the edge of the ramp into the sky, four miles above the earth.

She hadn't gotten much sleep last night. Instead she'd pored over the manual on the military parasail used in HAHOs, a specially made parachute that was wedge shaped, like an arrowhead. Although it was similar to the ones she used in smoke jumping, it had small differences, and that's what she had absorbed until three o'clock this morning, when she'd finally fallen asleep on the couch in her hotel room.

Glancing up, Pepper saw Jim standing about six feet from where she had anchored her booted feet on the metal grating. He was busy making last-minute checks on his gear, too. His attitude hadn't changed since yesterday, and in fact, she'd seen him give her a look of disdain when she'd pulled protective elastic coverings over her elbows, knees and ankles. Pepper didn't care. She had too much to lose by allowing him to push her into jumping without her safety gear. She hadn't done a high-altitude jump into a deciduous forest before, and she didn't want to take a chance that the limbs might not give way as easily as pines did—providing the potential for even more risk. Falling at fifty miles an hour and hitting a tree limb as thick as her arm would be enough to break bones.

Unlike her usual jumping gear, she'd been fitted with a walkie-talkie on her belt, the earphone snug on her head and the lip piece settled against her mouth so they could literally talk to each other during free-fall, if they wanted to. A tight cap imprisoned her hair, with a heavy, military-style helmet over it, strapped beneath her chin. She wore a number of bulky items, but she was used to carrying an ax and a shovel, as well as maps, compass, water, first-aid kit and other items, when she jumped into a fire situation. Woodward also had outfitted her with a specially made—to his specifications—Beretta pistol in a thigh holster. She carried eleven clips of ammunition for it, and an HK submachine gun with six hundred rounds and thirty magazines rested in her backpack. The equipment she carried today included everything they would jump with two days from now over Nevis. Today was Thanksgiving. A hell of a way to celebrate it, she thought.

Automatically, her fingers went to her chest, where the nylon straps bit into her green-and-tan-and-black uniform—"tiger" utilities, designed to blend in to the jungle environment. The knife—her own—she'd brought with her for emergency situations, such as to cut away shroud lines should her first parachute fail and the second one have to be deployed. The main chute was on her back, the reserve in front, and she'd personally packed them late yesterday evening.

Woodward had packed his own this morning on the floor of the hangar at Andrews Air Force Base, where they'd taken off from. Pepper had watched him off and on, becoming convinced that he did know what he was doing. After all, he'd informed her icily, he had made five hundred jumps. He was no novice. Still, with two thousand under her belt, she considered him less experienced and would keep an eye on him during the jump—just in case. Pepper smiled to herself, her hands ranging knowingly across her bulky gear. If Woodward knew what she was thinking, his male ego would surely smart under her decision. But out in the field, she was responsible for her people, and she always felt like a mother hen of sorts.

Jim watched Pepper covertly within the deep shadows of the C-130. The vibration of the deck beneath him moved through his booted feet and up his legs. He'd made hundreds of jumps from this type of plane, but he worried about Pepper and the fact that it had been five years since her last HAHO. He wrestled with telling her his concerns. His cool, professional attitude toward her wasn't really the way he wanted to treat her. Despite his anger yesterday, her eyes continued to hold that warmth toward him. Mentally, Jim kicked himself. Dammit, he liked Pepper. He wanted to call her by her first name, but something wouldn't let him. She probably realized it, since she always called him by his official title or last name. Seesawing from his chaotic emotions over Laura, Jim moved slowly toward Pepper.

Thanks to their headsets, he wouldn't have to yell above the din that always permeated the interiors of these cargo planes. Reaching out, he placed his hand on her upper arm.

"Are you checked out?"

Pepper nodded, wildly aware of his unanticipated touch. His grip on her arm was hard without hurting, and she could tell he was monitoring the amount of strength he used. Her skin tightened beneath his fingertips. "Everything's okay."

Jim felt the firm strength of her body. She was solid, and he was sure she was in top shape due to her job. Still, he longed to soften his hold on her arm and run his hand in an exploratory motion upward, across her shoulder. Why? He'd seen a shadow come to her eyes the moment he'd touched her. Did she consider his touch an invasion of her privacy? Forcing himself to drop his hand to his side, he said in a cold voice, "The jump master said ten minutes 'til they open the cargo-bay door for us. Remember, you jump first and I'll be ten seconds behind you.''

Pepper nodded, knowing he wanted to go second to watch her performance in the jump. "Fine," she said, striving to keep the irritation out of her voice.

"Once we hit the LZ," he said, using the common designation for landing zone, "you'll take the compass and map and get us out to the pick-up point where the HumVee team is waiting. It's a ten-mile hike.''

Pepper smiled grimly to herself. She knew Jim was not only testing her jumping ability, but checking out just what kind of shape she was in. She would have at least fifty pounds of weight on her back after the jump, and she was sure he didn't think she could go ten miles with it. Little did he realize she carried as much, sometimes more, into a smoke jump. Her team worked in shifts for almost twelve hours at a time, doing the grueling physical work of cutting fire breaks through stubborn brush. If only he knew that she was questioning *his* physical condition. Eight hours a day in a posh Pentagon office made for soft officers, not hard ones. She'd find out just what kind of shape Woodward was in—one way or another.

Exactly ten minutes later, a red light began to blink. Pepper moved to the starboard side, a bit ahead of Jim. Holding on to the cable above their heads she watched the maw of the C-130 slowly groan open. Whirring and grinding sounds clashed with the noise of the plane. Icy wind blasts began to buffet her body, pummeling her sporadically. As the ramp dropped, she saw the beauty of the night sky above them, a few stars still twinkling. Below them, dawn brushed across a thick carpet of barren, gray trees, which had already lost their leaves in fall's arrival. The hills of Virginia were rounded, but many were steep, and they'd been specially chosen because they resembled Nevis's volcanic terrain.

The jump master, a twenty-year veteran, stood opposite them. The wind whipped into the cargo entrance, striking Pepper heavily. She spread her legs a bit to take the invisible fists of air punching through the aircraft. The wind was biting, far below freezing. Although she wore black nylon gloves, she took them off at the last moment before she expected the light to flash green, indicating "jump." Jamming the gloves into a thigh pocket, she took a deep breath and felt her heart start a pounding but steady beat.

Pepper never tired of the adrenaline rush that accompanied such a jump. With it, all her senses became excruciatingly alive. She sensed movement behind her, knowing Jim also was getting ready for the jump. Fear struck at her, too. She hadn't made a jump this high in a long time. Talking to herself, telling herself it was the same as any other, she managed to dissolve some of the initial anxiety.

The light flashed green. The jump master gave her the hand signal.

It was like taking a long, summer walk down the sloping, greasy ramp of the C-130. Then Pepper took the leap, plummeting downward, keeping her hands, arms and legs tucked tightly against her body. The slipstream slammed into her as she tumbled clear of the aircraft. She gasped. It was icy cold. Her goggles protected her eyes from the tearing wind and enabled her to look around. She peered up to see the C-130 moving away from her, then glanced down at the luminous dials on her watch, counting ten seconds. Woodward had jumped, though she couldn't see him in his dark camouflage gear against the still-darkened sky.

Spreading out her arms and legs, she stopped her rocklike plummet. The wind beneath her became a cushion against her flattened body. Stabilizing, she checked the altimeter on her wrist, then glanced upward. At fifteen thousand feet, they were to meet and pull their chutes simultaneously.

Finally Pepper saw Woodward. He was coming rapidly toward her out of the darkness, his body like an arrow except for the hump on his back where he carried his weapons and gear. Bringing one hand in, she got ready to pull her rip cord. Woodward threw his arms and legs out, braking his plummet. When he was no more than twenty feet away, she saw him jerk his cord. To her horror, before she could pull her own, she saw his released chute begin to stream.

No! Pepper stopped herself from opening her chute and watched in dismay as Jim tried to open his by jerking on the shroud lines repeatedly. It wouldn't flare and catch the wind, and Pepper knew a parachute that streamed had little chance of opening. She saw him frantically take out his knife and cut away the shroud lines before he got tangled in them as he continued making slow, awkward spirals downward. Like Pepper's, his emergency chute was attached to his chest harness, and he quickly jerked it open. As she watched, the parasail started to open nicely, then developed a fold and crumpled. The horror on Woodward's face spurred Pepper into action.

Without thinking, she dove toward him. She'd have to be careful to avoid getting tangled in his reserve chute, and she made a sign for him to cut it away. She saw him shake his head as he frantically tore at the lines, trying to force the chute to open at least some of its cells, so it would catch the air and balloon out.

Fifteen thousand.

Pepper wanted to scream at him, but she didn't. She'd forgotten she had a mike and could speak to him.

Twelve thousand.

"Jim! Cut the chute away! I'll come in, and you grab my harness. I'll open my chute and we'll go down together."

She heard his heavy breathing, watched helplessly as he made large, corkscrews, fighting the chute all the time. Stubbornly, he jerked the lines again and again, trying to force the cells to open.

Ten thousand.

Pepper became alarmed. "Cut the chute!" she screamed.

He refused.

Eight thousand.

Breathing hard, Pepper again dove toward him. Dodging his chute, she made a grab for his shoulder harness. There! She slid her fingers strongly around the nylon straps. The thick material bit deeply into her hands and the two of them began to tumble slowly, like a huge, eight-legged spider in the sky.

"Cut the chute!" Pepper pleaded hoarsely, tightening her grip on his harness. She felt more than saw Jim hacking at the shrouds. He didn't think she could rescue him, much less hold on to him, but she'd proven him wrong.

Six thousand. It was now or never.

"Grab my harness front!" she screamed, and she jerked at
her rip cord. She felt his hands grab on to the crisscross of nylon over her chest. Her eyes trailed upward with the opening
chute, which streamed, then flared perfectly. Pepper had little
time to prepare for the opening. Woodward weighed more than
two hundred pounds with all his gear, and he had gripped her
harness with both hands, the front of his body pressed tightly
against hers.

The jerk was tremendous. Pepper groaned, but kept her
hands locked around Woodward's upper arms, knowing he
could easily lose his grip on her harness as the chute yanked
them upward. Her muscles screamed. She shut her eyes and
pulled hard. Fire seemed to roar through her body as every
muscle went rigid against the reverberation of their combined
weight.

Jim grunted as the pull of gravity fought the jerking, upward motion of the opening chute. It felt as if an invisible giant had gripped his legs and was pulling him downward with all
its might, almost forcing him to let go of Pepper's harness. His
gloved hands were sweaty and his fingers began to slip. He felt
Pepper's tight grip around his upper arms, but his fingers were
slipping even more. No! He gasped again, struggling. The terror of falling to his death tore through him. His grasp continued to weaken despite his panicky knowledge of what could
happen.

In that instant, his entire life began to flash before his widened eyes. He saw everything—things he hadn't remembered
since he was a young boy. He saw the death of his mother and
father. He saw himself on the deadly parachute drop into Panama City. Accompanying the inexorable vision of his life, he
felt every emotion with heart-stopping clarity. The replay was
pulverizing, and he gasped again, realizing he was going to die.

Somehow, Pepper must have sensed his situation. Jim was
amazed when she pulled him upward, with a strength few men
would have possessed. Adrenaline flashed through his body,
and he squeezed his eyes shut, pressing his face against her belly
region, her gear mashed against him, jabbing into his flesh. His
fingers stopped slipping. He crushed his helmet and goggles
against her, gasping for breath. Due to her one, upward mo-

tion, he was able to affix his fingers more tightly to her harness and prevent a fall to his death.

Breathing hard through her mouth, Pepper gave a quick, cursory glance around them. Thank God the chute was open and working perfectly. But where were they? She couldn't look at her compass or altimeter, since both were strapped to her wrists. She felt Jim clinging to her, their bodies fused together, their tangled legs dangling as they fell rapidly through the denser air nearer the ground. The parasail, without any pulling of shroud lines, drifted at the whim of the wind. The sky was getting lighter, though the sun wasn't up yet. Pepper could clearly see the woods below them, coming up fast. Too fast.

They were at three thousand feet, she estimated, and their rate of fall, because the chute was too small for their combined weight and gear, was a lot more rapid than it should be.

"Jim!" she gasped. "We're about three thousand. We're coming in too fast!"

He grimaced and felt a terrorizing weakness numb his arms. Did he have the strength to hold on until they landed? He didn't know.

"There's nothing we can do!' he rasped, trying to glance out of the corner of his eye. He dared not move. Dared not try to readjust his position. If Pepper's grip weren't so secure, he wasn't sure he could continue to hold himself in place, with the sixty pounds of weight on his back tugging him away from her and her lifesaving harness.

Gasping for breath, Pepper said in a hurried voice, "Okay, okay. We're about twenty-five hundred feet. We're heading into what appears to be a slight opening in the trees. Try and stay loose. Try not to tense up too much. We're gonna hit the limbs. Be flexible, but hang on."

It was frustrating not being able to see where they were going. Jim tried to steady his breathing. He felt Pepper flex her knees, a signal that they were close to the canopy. He could still die. They both could. The thought of Pepper being killed almost shattered him. What a brave, strong woman she was, he realized mere seconds before they smashed into the treetops at over eighty miles an hour.

The crunching and snapping began, and Jim felt the initial branches giving way beneath them. As they fell, the chute slowed their forward motion. Heavier, less-forgiving branches swatted at him, bruising the backs of his legs. He grunted as another smacked him hard across the shoulders. The pain was instantaneous and he almost let go. At once Pepper's hands tightened.

The sounds intensified as the crackling, popping branches stubbornly gave way. They were falling. Falling through space.

Jim hit the ground first, and Pepper's entire weight came down across his lower legs. Crying out in pain, he jerked his hands free of her harness and tried to cushion the force of his contact with the ground by rolling end over end, dirt and rocks flying up around him.

Pepper rolled headfirst across him and down a brush-covered gulch. She kept herself tucked as much as possible, her arms across her face to protect it, her legs drawn up. It was impossible to tuck as she wanted to, carrying so much weight. Finally, she hit a large bush and came to a sudden stop, landing flat on her back, the breath knocked out of her, her arms and legs sprawling outward.

Opening her eyes, Pepper took in the dawning sky above her and the many broken limbs where they had fallen through the thick, nearly impenetrable canopy. Panting for breath, she automatically went through a swift, physical check of herself. *Jim!* Her heart thudded powerfully in her chest. Was he alive? Dead? Suddenly, concern for him overwhelmed every other sense, avalanching through her with unexpected force and leaving her stunned as nothing had in the past six years.

Slowly, she forced herself to roll over and dizzily rise up on her hands and knees. Searching desperately she called out his name, her voice a terrified croak.

"Jim! Where are you? Answer me!" Pepper fumbled frantically with the harness straps, working quickly to free herself from the cumbersome pack.

"Dammit, answer me!" Her voice broke with emotion. What was going on? She never behaved like this in the field. Jerking the helmet off her head, she dropped it on the ground, her hair spilling around her face and shoulders as the cap came with it. Off came the goggles. Peering through the gray early-morning light, Pepper thought she saw a lump far below her on the brushy hill. "No..." she said in a half whisper. Breathing raggedly, she stumbled, fell, then made it to her feet. As she picked her way down the sharp incline, she saw the dark lump define itself into Woodward, lying in a ravine filled with dried leaves, rocks and small bushes. He was sprawled on his back, his left leg tucked up under his body, his arms thrown outward. His head was tipped back, mouth open.

Was he dead? Badly injured? Her mind spun with questions and ways to get help here as fast as possible. They had a radio. She could call for a rescue helicopter. Powerful emotions captured her, and tears flooded into her eyes. Arriving at his side and falling to her knees, she sought and found the jugular vein in his neck with shaking hands. A sob racked her body and she felt out of control, pulverized by these violent feelings toward him. It was crazy! She was crazy.

"Jim?" Her voice wobbled. Tears blurred her vision as she frantically searched his wan features, even as her fingers located a strong pulse. Thank God. Pepper saw his lashes flutter as she called his name again. Getting up, she moved to his left side, where his leg was folded beneath him.

"Don't move, Jim. Don't move," she crooned, placing her hands on his hip and knee. "You might have a broken leg. Just wake up easy. Easy..."

Pepper's husky voice entered Jim's burgeoning consciousness. He was aware first of her voice, then of those strong, sure hands on his left thigh. Groaning, he opened his eyes. Pepper was kneeling over him, her face drawn in tension, her tearful gaze fixed on him. Shaken by the change in her features, the panic in her eyes, he reached up for her.

"We made it," he mumbled. "We're alive...." A miracle in itself when he'd been so certain he was going to die. Struggling toward consciousness, he slid his hands over her shoulders. Life and death. How close they'd come to dying. Tears were rolling down Pepper's pale cheeks, and Jim dug his fingers into her shoulders as a fierce joy suddenly swept through him. Never had he needed someone as he needed her at this moment. His careening emotions had steamrollered his normal, controlled responses. A wild feeling thrummed through him and he pulled her down, crushing her to him as his arms slid across her back.

"You're alive, you're alive. . . ." he rasped, burying his face in her thick, silky hair. Jim groaned as he felt her surrender to his need to embrace her. He felt her sob once more, her cheek pressed against his. The dampness of the tears, the softness of her skin dizzied him, convinced him of the fact that they weren't dead. For one powerful heartbeat out of reality, Pepper clung to him, held him as tightly as he was holding her. She was warm. Alive. Moving his face away from her cheek, he released her and tunneled his fingers through her hair. As she eased away, her face bare inches from his, he drowned in the splendor of her anguished, sky blue eyes. And Jim saw desire there. Desire, heat and need. The realization tore at his disintegrating control and pummeled senses. He saw Pepper's lips part. The ache to kiss her was almost his undoing. As his fingers tightened against her face, he saw her eyes flare wide with shock.

Pepper gasped and placed her hand on his heaving chest, wildly aware of his strong, cool hands framing her face. What was wrong with her? She shouldn't be embracing him! What insane fear had made her lose her perspective? Her professionalism? She saw the burning hunger in his eyes for her alone. Shaken badly, she pulled out of his grasp, knowing that if she didn't, she was going to lean forward those final scant inches and bury her lips against his very male mouth.

Trembling violently, she sat back, perplexed. She tried to recover from her faux pas by examining his injury, but her face was burning with mortification. What was happening to her?

As he lay there, reorienting himself, Jim realized that if Pepper hadn't saved his sorry neck, he'd be dead. What had made him reach out and embrace her like that? Chaotic feelings sheared through him. And what the hell had prevented him from cutting those second shroud lines to release the reserve chute? Ashamed, he admitted the answer he already knew: he hadn't trusted Pepper to rescue him, because she was a woman.

"Your leg," she whispered tautly, giving him a quick glance. His cheeks were flushed, his look one of utter discomfort. Swallowing hard, she murmured, "How does it feel?"

"It hurts," he grunted, avoiding her darkened eyes, seeing the shame in them. "Look out, I'll try to move it."

Surprised, Pepper staggered to her feet. "Can you?"

"I think so. . . ." He grasped at any straw to lessen the tension, as if some invisible, throbbing sensation lingered palpably between them. Even if his leg was broken, it could refocus their attention on something other than their torrid, intimate embrace of moments ago. Jim sat up with difficulty, the pack he was wearing still weighing him down. Then, easing his body slightly to the right, he brought his left leg out and straightened it.

"You're lucky," Pepper said, a wobble of relief in her voice. She touched her damp cheek and wiped at the last of the tears. Inadvertently, she looked up at him. His gaze burned with an emotion that scorched her, and she looked away, shaken even further. "Brother, are you ever lucky. I thought you'd busted your femur in a compound fracture or something." She knelt at his side again. Whether she wanted to or not, she had to touch him. Resting her hands gently on his leg, she examined the length of it. Feelings she thought had died years ago swept through her as she explored his muscled limb. She felt a throbbing sensation seem to leap from him to the palm of her hand. Confused, she struggled to force the raw, newly awakened feelings aside.

Jim grimaced, fighting a hot awareness of her closeness—of her care. Her touch was galvanizing, and his skin tightened when she grazed him. Frantic to get himself back under control, he rasped, "I'm too hardheaded to break a leg. I should have had my head examined, though."

Surprised, Pepper looked up into his darkened eyes. "What do you mean?"

"You saved my neck despite my stupidity. Thanks." He held out his hand to her.

Stunned, Pepper slowly raised her own hand. Should she touch him again? Last time they'd ended in a torrid embrace. Shyly, she slid her fingers into his. There was nothing weak about his grip, and she gloried in its secure warmth. "You're welcome, Colonel Woodward," she said in a strained tone.

Jim didn't want to release her hand. He was entranced by the length and grace of her fingers, almost at odds with Pepper's obvious tough strength—both physically and mentally. If she hadn't had the presence of mind, as well as the experience and skill, to rescue his sorry butt from that situation, he wouldn't be here shaking her hand in a symbolic gesture of peace.

"Call me Jim," he said gruffly, reluctantly releasing her. The surprise that flared in her eyes astounded him. It was at that moment that he realized just how much of a bastard he'd been to her. Shame wound through him, and he forced himself to check out his left ankle instead of staring into Pepper's beautiful, vulnerable eyes.

Pepper watched him pull away the bloused material around his jump boot. *Call me Jim.* The husky inference in his voice had gone through her like hot sunlight on a cold winter's day. And the look in his eyes had stunned her—as if she were seeing his tough military facade melt before her eyes. The change was arresting, filled with promise. His mouth had lost its usual hard line, and his eyes had lost that icy glitter that warned her to back off. Most of all, Pepper was drawn to the tenor of his voice—strong yet decidedly gentle.

Shaken, she sat back, resting her hands tensely on her thighs as she tried to digest his change toward her. Finally, she forced herself to look around. "I have no idea where we are ... Jim," she admitted hesitantly.

He glanced up as he freed his ankle from the trouser material. "Let's worry about that later. Can you help me unlace this boot? I think I've sprained my ankle."

"Sure..." He was asking for her help. Pepper didn't quite know how to take this sudden attempt at teamwork. Was he feeling grateful because she'd saved his life? Would it last? Did it have anything to do with the sudden intimacy he'd established? Her hands trembled as she tried to untie the double knot on the boot.

"I'm still shaky." She laughed with sudden shyness.

"I'm shaking inside," he admitted, watching her slim fingers work out the tightly bound knots. Her hair fell in soft waves, and he had the maddening urge to reach out and thrust his fingers through that mass again. As he remembered its

softness, his hand lifted slightly, as if by its own accord. Jim
jerked it back. It was an idiotic urge. An insane one, he real
ized, chastising himself. Pepper's mouth was slightly open, re
vealing her full lower lip. The color was high in her cheeks, and
he could see she was shaken by the ordeal they'd survived. Or
was it by his unjustified embrace—his need to feel her strong
feminine body against him and prove he really was alive?

"I could have died," he croaked, the realization starting to
fully sink in.

Pepper glanced up at him. Jim's eyes were dark with the
harsh reality of his words. "I know. . . ." Her voice broke, and
she avoided his sudden, sharpened gaze.

Jim's heart began an erratic pounding in his chest. Sud
denly, he felt a trembling that seemed to start deep inside him
and spread outward. He had a wild urge to blather almost hys
terically. Fighting the feeling, he rasped, "I saw my whole life
flash before my eyes." He shook his head as Pepper began un
lacing the now-unknotted jump boot. "I've heard of guys see
ing it, like a movie in full living color, when they thought they
were going to die. But it's never happened to me. . . ."

Swallowing against a dry throat, Pepper nodded, her heart
still pounding wildly in her breast. Where Jim had gripped her
shoulder, her skin still tingled in memory. "We were lucky.
Hold on, I'm going to try to get this off you." She rose and
positioned herself at his feet, then carefully eased the boot of
his left foot. Pulling off his heavy cotton sock, she grimaced.
"You're right," she said, glancing up at him, "you've got a
dilly of a sprain." The skin around his ankle was already turn
ing bluish purple and swelling. Prodding the region gently with
her fingers, she felt a lot of heat coming from it.

Jim was fervently aware of Pepper's long, thin fingers mov
ing over his swollen ankle. Miraculously, wherever she touched
him, the pain momentarily ceased. "You look like you've done
this kind of thing before," he observed.

Pepper gave him a slight, one-cornered smile as she finally
managed to get some control over her rampant emotions. "Too
many times." Placing his foot on the ground beside her, she
slowly stood. "On myself and other members of my team.
Sprains are pretty common in our business."

Jim held her narrowed gaze. He was seeing the professional side of Pepper now, and he admired her coolness and common sense. "If I'd worn that ankle brace as you suggested, I might not have a sprain right now," he groused.

Pepper realized what it took Jim to admit his mistake and was grateful he'd abandoned his combative attitude. "It's a learning curve," she offered hoarsely, not wanting him to feel any worse than he did already. She wasn't one to rub salt in anyone's wounds. Good leaders didn't berate their people. Instead, she would try to support his decision to wear it next time. "I'm going back up the hill for my pack. I've got a first-aid kit with me. Just lie still" was all she said.

Jim lay back on the rough ground, feeling pretty damn humbled by Pepper and her forgiving attitude. She had every right to nail him with the fact that he'd not only refused to wear the joint and ankle braces but had openly challenged her idea. Angrily, he rubbed his face. What was the matter with him? He didn't normally act like such a jerk. Never with anyone under his command in a military situation. And why had he reached out and grabbed her? Held her in a hot, powerful embrace that had driven him to the edge of his control? He'd come so close to molding her parted, tear-stained lips against his mouth. So close. What the hell was happening to him? Looking up, he scowled at the horizon. The sun was rising, the sky turning a pale, translucent pink and yellow.

Pepper, he decided, was her own woman—and he wasn't used to dealing with a woman with such a high confidence level. He had some thinking to do about women, he conceded. He was just beginning to grasp the full weight of their potential. Pepper was a role model, a stunning example of what could be. Perhaps that was what made her different in his eyes, and explained his unexpected attraction to her. He had no direct experience with a woman like her—at once feminine and vulnerable, yet shored up by an incredible confidence that radiated from deep within her, translating into every action she took or decision she made.

Jim knew men like that. Hell, he was like that himself. A sour smile pulled at his mouth as he made the realization. If Pepper had been a man, he would never have questioned her experience. And he would have instantly reached out for help as he plummeted from the sky. With a shake of his head, he decided that once they got out of this mess and back to Perseus, he needed to sit down and have a long talk with her. First he would apologize for being such a jerk, as well as for his intimate behavior toward her, which was completely out of line—as sexist in its own way as his initial lack of trust had been.

Touching his ankle, which had quickly swollen to the size of a ripe cantaloupe, he wondered how he would be able to make the jump two days from now. He'd screwed himself up by rejecting Pepper's advice. Damn. He had a lot of ground to cover with her on their return to civilization.

"We're in luck," Pepper said as she approached Jim. She held out two small kits. "I not only brought my first-aid kit, but I packed my homeopathic kit, too." She saw him look up, felt his green gaze lock onto hers. For a moment she was speechless. The undiluted warmth in his eyes caught her off guard again. Slowly kneeling at his left side, Pepper fumbled with the first-aid kit, even as she fought the clamoring desire still burning within her. Heat stabbed at her cheeks, and she knew she was blushing.

"I'm in luck you were along," Jim stated. He saw Pepper's face flame red. The blush made her even more becoming, if that was possible. Her fingers worked the lock on the kit, as an ache built inside Jim's chest, and he fought another totally inappropriate urge to reach out and kiss her. The slightly curled length of her hair, now in disarray from the dampness of the cold November morning, enhanced her natural beauty.

Pepper made an effort to smile while avoiding his gaze. His eyes were like magnets, drawing hers, she decided as she opened the second kit. "We shared a close call. Stupid reactions always happen afterward," she stammered.

Jim nodded. "Yeah—stupid things..." Like grabbing her and wanting to kiss her until they breathed the same air. Stupid things like that. "I'm just glad we're alive," he told her unevenly. "Maybe that's why I grabbed you.... I don't know...."

Pepper felt the heat in her face intensify at his muttered apology. She refused to look up at him as she dug into her kit.

"That's all it was," she agreed breathlessly, "a close shave with death. Nothing more..." Wasn't it? Pepper was unsure. Her even, stable world seemed to be fragmenting before her very eyes. Hadn't she made decisions in the past to commit herself to her job, to her friends and her family—*not* to a personal relationship? Yes, absolutely. And in the six years since that decision, she'd made it stick. Ever since John's death. Until now. Pepper felt wary and shaken in a way she hadn't experienced before.

Jim frowned. Though his unexplained actions toward her were far from all right, she was kindly trying to provide a way out for him—despite her own discomfort. Now was not the time to examine his actions.

He watched as she drew out a small green tube and squeezed the clear, thick contents onto her fingers. "What's that?" he asked, making an effort to get their conversation onto something safe and impersonal.

"Arnica. It's a homeopathic remedy that I use for any kind of muscle sprains or strains." Pepper took in a ragged breath, relieved to be talking about anything other than their embrace. She gently slathered the ointment across his swollen skin and amended her earlier concerns: Jim was in tremendous shape—for an office type. "You must jog or something," she murmured, concentrating on covering the entire sprained area, "because if you didn't work out, you'd have broken something in that fall."

Jim glanced up at the thick trees on the hill above them. "Yeah... it was a hell of a fall, wasn't it?"

Her laughter was strained as she set the ointment tube aside and expertly wrapped his foot and ankle in an Ace bandage. "A hell of a fall," she agreed.

"How are you?" Jim realized he'd been remiss in asking after her condition. Had she sustained any injuries?

Panicked over his sudden interest, Pepper stammered, "A lot of bruises, but otherwise I'm okay." She looked up and brushed her hair aside. The concern on Jim's face tugged at her, and she felt her breath jam in her throat. Her heart pounded briefly, underscoring the look of care radiating from him. Again heat prickled her cheeks, and she quickly looked

away, her fingers trembling as she continued to wrap his ankle.

"You're blushing," he muttered, unwilling to acknowledge
his blame in her response.

"I haven't done that in years," Pepper said, frowning. Six
years, to be exact.

"It's becoming," he admitted gruffly. Shocked at the intimacy that seemed to continue to insinuate itself at the least
opportunity, Jim snapped his mouth shut.

"It's an embarrassing disease."

He cast desperately around for some impersonal comment,
but words he didn't intend to say tumbled out of his mouth.
"You're a woman who wears her heart on her sleeve." When
Pepper raised her chin and looked at him, he realized she was
so self-sufficient that few people probably ever considered she
might need a little care or a tender touch herself. He could give
her that, he realized suddenly. To cover up his error, he said,
"Recons take care of their own. You're no less important than
I am." He noticed a number of bloody scratches on the backs
of her hands. Without thinking, he reached down and captured her right hand. Gently, he laid his palm over it. "You're
hurt, too."

Stunned by his gesture, Pepper jerked away. "Oh...it's
nothing. Scratches are nothing...." Her heart was pounding.
She felt curiously exhilarated and at the same time wary. "I
guess I'm not used to my team making a big deal over something like this," she muttered. "During a fire there isn't time to
pay attention to minor injuries. We're always getting bruised,
scratched and cut. It's no big deal."

With a shake of his head, Jim said, "I guess I really didn't
realize the kind of danger you and your team jump into."

"Most people don't. Why should they? As far as I'm concerned, there are a lot of unsung heroines and heroes doing my
kind of work. We're rarely given media coverage, but our work
is intense and very dangerous." Pepper closed the first-aid kit.
"Of course, people in the military aren't acknowledged much,
either."

Jim nodded in agreement as Pepper took a small, amber vial
from the other kit and opened it. "Here, take these," she said.

Jim stared at the small, white pellets she placed in his open hand. "What are these?"

"They're sugar pellets that have been medicated with a high dose of Arnica. Just put them in your mouth and let them melt away." She smiled a little and closed the lid on the vial. "You'll see a miracle happen with that ankle of yours—the swelling should go down within the hour. Otherwise it will never be in good enough shape for a jump one day from now."

Jim wasn't about to argue with Pepper. He put the pellets in his mouth. They tasted like sugar, not medicine. Pepper rose, carried the kits back up the hill, then returned to Jim's side. In the meantime, he shrugged out of his pack.

She handed him the radio. "I think we need to call for backup. You're in no shape to walk ten miles."

"Roger that," he agreed sheepishly. He took the radio from her and made the call. He no longer questioned Pepper's abilities. She'd saved his life. She'd dealt with his injury with grace and without recriminations. Soon the helicopter would be hovering over the hill above them and they would be winched up on a cable, one at a time, since there was no appropriate landing area. But first Jim silently promised himself one thing. Tonight, at his condo, he and Pepper would have a long, serious talk. It was time.

Chapter Four

Pepper was unprepared for the flurry of activity that met them back at Perseus. The helicopter pilot had called in, alerting the team of their near disaster. As she entered the office, she was met by a number of people, some of whom she didn't know. Wolf and Killian guided Jim to another room, where Dr. Ann Parsons, the ex-Air Force flight surgeon who worked for Perseus, was waiting.

"Pepper," Wolf said as he came back out, "I want you to meet Morgan's brother, Commander Noah Trayhern, and his wife, Kit."

"Glad to meet you," Pepper said, extending her hand to a tall, spare officer with gray eyes. Noah Trayhern was dressed in his winter Coast Guard uniform, the dark blue wool a contrast to his tanned features and penetrating gaze. She liked his firm grip.

"Same here," Noah said with a tight smile.

Pepper extended her hand to the woman at his side. Kit Trayhern, tall as well, smiled warmly at her, offering an equally firm handshake. Her long, dark brown hair, alive with red highlights, was tied back with a red ribbon that matched the tasteful red suit she wore with a lacy white blouse.

Marie approached Pepper. "You look worn out. Are you all right, dear?"

"I'm okay." She looked down at her camouflage uniform and gave a slightly embarrassed laugh. "Dirty, bruised, but no worse for wear." She was acutely aware of Noah's assessing look, sure he was measuring her against what had happened and determining whether she had what it took to successfully complete the coming mission.

"Let me get you some coffee," Kit Trayhern offered. "You look like you could use a cup. Actually, from what we've heard, maybe you'd rather have a stiff drink."

Smiling sheepishly, Pepper nodded. "No thanks. If I drank alcohol, I'd probably ask for whiskey, straight up. Thanks, Mrs. Trayhern."

"Call me Kit. Come on, let's go into the War Room. Marie made a fresh pot when she heard you were coming in."

Pepper wondered how Jim was doing and wanted to find out, then thought better of it. She followed Kit into the Conference Room and gratefully sank onto a chair Noah pulled out for her. He closed the door, and he and Kit joined her at the table, coffee cups in hand.

"Can you tell us exactly what happened out there this morning?" Noah asked.

Without preamble, Pepper told them the story, leaving out only the fact that Jim had refused her help in the air and that he hadn't worn the safety bandages. She had no desire to embarrass him. On the flight in, she had sat next to him and had felt him withdrawing deep into himself. She'd wondered what he was thinking about, but then, the fact that they'd nearly died was enough to turn anyone inward for a while.

Kit sighed and smiled softly at Pepper. "We feel lucky to have you on this mission, Pepper. You've got the right stuff."

"Bruised but right," Pepper answered tiredly. She glanced at Noah. Did he feel the same way? The officer was somber, worry showing in his gray eyes.

"Have you heard the latest?" he asked.

"No. What?" Pepper sipped the hot coffee with relish.

"Wolf said still no communiqués have been intercepted to suggest where Jason or Morgan might be held. No more transmissions from Garcia, either. It's as if they know...."

"Darling," Kit whispered fervently, reaching across the table and touching his arm, "everyone's doing all they can."

"I know that," he said, scowling. He set the white mug on the highly polished table, sliding his long fingers around it. "I worry that if you go in to rescue Laura, they'll kill Jason and Morgan. We just don't know what they might do."

"Look," Kit said, removing her hand, her voice growing more adamant, "I know Garcia and Ramirez from my days as a detective in Miami. Laura isn't safe there. She's at serious risk. If we know where she is then Perseus needs to mount a mission as swiftly as possible to get her out."

Pepper saw Noah's face become rife with unspoken emotions, including obvious anguish. "I don't have a police background," she offered, "but from my days as an army officer, I know you don't avoid one objective because others might suffer. I'm sure Ramirez is expecting Perseus to back off. So we may have some element of surprise on our side."

Exhaling loudly, Noah stood, his dark brows drawn together. "We're dealing with the lives of my brother, his son and his wife." He looked down at Pepper. "Dammit, I wish I could go instead.... I wish—"

"Noah, please..." Kit said softly.

Pepper watched Morgan's younger brother struggle with barely contained emotions. She noted the glimmer of tears in his eyes, then he abruptly turned and walked deliberately to the other end of the room, his back to them.

"How much do you know about the Trayhern family?" Kit asked her.

"Only what Wolf told me on the way in from the airport the other day. I know Morgan has gone through hell regarding the Vietnam War and that he was used by the CIA against his will."

Kit nodded. "Then you realize how much trauma everyone's suffered." She rubbed her brow. "It's awful. I mean, this family has finally gotten back together. We have three beautiful children. Morgan's parents live in Clearwater, Florida, and we visit them all the time. Alyssa, Morgan's sister, is the youngest. She's married to Commander Clay Cantrell, and they're both pilots in the navy. They don't have any children, but they come and visit as often as they can, Pepper. We're very close-knit. Morgan's parents are in shock over the kidnapping. They're flying up this afternoon to Perseus, to meet you and Colonel Woodward, but it's a frightening situation for all of us. I'm an ex-cop, and I've had dealings with far too many drug dealers. They're the scum of the earth, as far as I'm concerned."

"Do you think Ramirez will try to attack you? Or Morgan's parents?"

Kit shrugged and looked at her husband, who stood silently, his profile silhouetted against the map on the wall. He was clearly suffering. "It's the right question to ask. That's why we've flown in with our entire family. Right now, Susannah Killian is playing baby-sitter not only to Morgan's Katherine, but to our children as well, at a hotel in Fairfax. Talking to Jake, I get the feeling they're worried about another hit from Ramirez. Anyone in the family could be vulnerable to attack. I think Jake wants all the Trayherns to go into hiding."

"It wouldn't be a bad idea right now," Pepper agreed slowly. "Especially if we hit Garcia and manage to take Laura away from him. I don't know how quickly or *if* he'll retaliate—or against whom."

"You can bet it will be our family," Noah growled, turning and walking slowly back toward them.

"Then you agree with Jake?" Kit asked.

"I do." The tall man picked up his coffee mug and took a swallow of the hot liquid. "I don't put anything beyond the realm of those murdering bastards."

Pepper could feel a number of new aches developing in her body. She needed to get out of this uncomfortable uniform, put arnica oil on her own minor injuries and take a long, hot bath. But she tabled her own discomfort for now because, by understanding some of the Trayhern family, she might be able to understand more about Laura and her potential actions or reactions—which could be important if they were able to get to her.

A knock on the door interrupted their conversation. Wolf poked his head in and looked at Pepper. "Colonel Woodward is asking for you. Got a minute?"

"Sure." Pepper excused herself and followed Wolf down the hall. Jake and Killian had just left the room where they'd taken Woodward earlier. The looks of relief on their faces told Pepper the good news. Trying to settle her suddenly pounding heart, she entered the room. Jim sat on a gurney, his left pant leg rolled up to just below his knee. The doctor, a woman in her early thirties, was just closing her black physician's bag.

"Pepper, I wanted you to meet Dr. Parsons," Jim said. He felt a tremendous rush of feelings as Pepper entered the room. Despite her disheveled state, she managed to look beautiful, he thought. "I told her you gave me those funny-looking sugar pills, and that they made the swelling go away on my sprain."

Pepper shook Dr. Parson's hand. "It's a homeopathic remedy, Doctor."

"Oh," Ann murmured thoughtfully. "That's a complementary form of medicine that's catching on here in the U.S., isn't it?"

"Sure is." Pepper noticed Jim's gaze on her and felt a little uneasy. "I've got a doctor friend in Anaconda, Montana, who teaches classes on homeopathy. I'd gone to her about three years ago with some pretty severe muscle strains from a bad jump. She used homeopathy on me, and I was back at work two days later. It made a believer out of me, so I took classes from her over the years, and I always carry a small kit of remedies with me no matter where I go."

Ann raised he eyebrows. "Sounds interesting. Maybe you could give me her name and phone number." She pointed to Jim's untaped ankle. "By rights it should look fat and purple by now, but there's no swelling. He told me how badly he'd injured it, and I just couldn't believe it."

With a laugh, Pepper said, "It was the size of a healthy cantaloupe out there at the LZ, Dr. Parsons. I gave him a high dose, and I knew it would take down the swelling."

"Good thing," Ann said, "otherwise Colonel Woodward would be grounded and someone else would be taking this mission." She smiled warmly. "Good job, Ms. Sinclair."

When the flight surgeon had left, Pepper turned to Jim. She examined his ankle closely. "Looks pretty good. Are you as impressed as Dr. Parsons is?"

"More impressed," he said quietly. He saw the strain in Pepper's face. "You look the way I feel," he commented.

"I'm getting a bit achy from my bruises and the letdown that always comes after a jump like that," Pepper said, standing awkwardly in front of him. Despite what they'd been through, Jim appeared relatively unfazed. His short, dark hair was plastered against his head, with several strands falling across his wrinkled brow. Some smudges of dirt trailed along his jaw, but otherwise he looked as good as new. The front of his uniform was open, revealing the strong column of his neck and some of the well-sprung dark hair on his chest. He was pulverizingly masculine, Pepper realized belatedly. She'd been so busy shielding herself from his attention that she hadn't noticed the details of him as a man—until now.

"I need to go back to my hotel room and clean up," she croaked.

"You should," he agreed, then added, "Later, will you come over to my condo?"

"What?" Startled, Pepper halted on her way to the open door. She had a great deal of studying to do today—manuals to read and details to memorize.

Jim opened his hands. "Tonight? About 1900, will you come over?" he repeated.

Her heart started a traitorous beating in her breast. "Well . . . I—"

He saw her hesitation. Saw the fear in her glorious blue eyes. "Please?" He said it softly, with just a slight, pleading edge. Pepper's face visibly relaxed and most of the wariness left her eyes.

"Sure . . ."

"It's personal," he admitted softly, then looked around the room. "I need to say some things to you in private, Pepper."

Swallowing convulsively, she nodded. "I'll be there. . . ."

Pepper's mouth was dry. It took a lot to make her nervous these days, but the possibility of intimacy—of the kind of unexpected feelings Jim had somehow managed to arouse in her in such a short time—had her running scared in a way that far surpassed the risk of jumping out of a plane into a raging fire. She knocked on the solid oak door of Jim's condominium. It was in a posh part of Georgetown—a redbrick building covered with dark green ivy that gave it an old, austere look. The building suited him, she thought. He was old-fashioned in many ways, clinging to certain traditions just as they ivy clung to the brick. The door opened, and Pepper's heart bounded once to underscore her surprise.

Jim wore civilian clothes, a pair of comfortable, navy blue chinos, a collegiate white shirt open at the collar and simple brown loafers. He looked approachable. Far too approachable, her heart warned. And when his mouth curved in a sincere welcome, Pepper became tongue-tied, which wasn't like her at all.

"Come on in," he invited, standing to one side and gesturing for her to enter. He wondered if he'd ever quit being surprised by her. She wore a long, dark green corduroy skirt and a soft mohair sweater of pale pink and green. Her hair, which had been matted and snarled after their ordeal this morning, glowed under the hall light, with golden strands sparkling among the dark brown ones. She wore no makeup, but she didn't need any. The flush of her cheeks emphasized the guarded look in her glorious blue eyes. Instead of shoes, she wore black suede boots and carried a purse to match. As she stepped inside, Jim inhaled the fragrance of her perfume; it reminded him of jasmine blooming in spring.

"Are you sure you're a smoke jumper?" he teased as he quietly shut the door.

Pepper smiled uneasily. "Are you sure you're a Recon Marine?" she countered.

"Touché." As he reached to help her off with her coat, his fingertips brushed her shoulders, and it was as if a shock ran through him. Jim felt a powerful desire overwhelm him. Never had he wanted to kiss a woman more than in this fleeting moment. It cost him every ounce of control to keep from doing exactly that. He hung Pepper's coat in the closet and motioned for her to follow him. "I guess neither of us look like our jobs, do we?"

"I make a point of not looking like my job. Otherwise I'd be a mess all the time," Pepper said in a strained voice, her skin tingling where he'd barely grazed her shoulders. She quickly looked around. The condominium was spacious and tastefully decorated. The ceilings were high, in keeping with the traditional style of older East Coast buildings, with ornate plaster patterns detailing the expanse. The hall was painted beige, the walls holding a number of original oil paintings, most of them landscapes. As she entered the living room, Pepper smiled to herself. A gray-and-white cat sat on the burgundy-striped sofa. The room was large, with a television in one corner, a stereo unit in another. A mahogany coffee table stood in front of the couch, with fresh fruit overflowing from a cut-glass bowl. The chairs, in shades of burgundy and navy, were complimented by a beige carpet.

"Did you decorate this?" she asked, impressed as she scanned the walls, where more pictures hung.

"I couldn't have in a million years," Jim admitted, stuffing his hands in the pockets of his chinos. If he didn't put them somewhere, he was going to touch her. He felt good as he saw the radiance in Pepper's face as she examined the room. She didn't miss much. With a chuckle, he added, "My only contribution to the interior designer's touches was this alley cat. Frank, meet Pepper. Pepper, this is Frank."

Pepper smiled and crossed the room, to gently stroke the large cat's scarred head. Both Frank's ears were partially gone. "Looks like he's been in more than a few fights."

Jim took his hands out of his pockets again, trying to contain his nervousness. "I found him on my porch one morning last winter," he said, coming around to the end of the couch, where Frank lay purring contentedly. "The garbage truck had hit him, and he crawled up on my stoop and waited for me to come home."

Pepper straightened and looked directly into Jim's eyes. "He must have known there was something special about you. That you'd take care of him. Cats have good instincts."

Ruefully, Jim held her warm, searching gaze. He didn't deserve Pepper's forgiveness for what had almost happened today, yet he knew he already had it. Could he have been as generous, if he'd been in her shoes? He doubted it. "It was a little rough at first, because he had a broken front leg, and he wasn't too happy about being incarcerated here, unable to go outside."

Pepper's mouth softened. She melted beneath his dark, hooded look. Again she saw a smoldering fire banked in his eyes—a fire that had something to do with her. Struggling to maintain an air of neutrality, she forced her voice to remain even as she said, "Well, it looks as if Frank has since made the adjustment from scrappy alley cat to fat cat."

"Yeah, he has. Come into the kitchen. I'm putting the final touches on our dinner." Jim forced himself to move, to break the almost-tangible connection that seemed to establish itself between them anytime they were together.

Pepper followed him at a distance, relieved to have his focus shift away from her. "Did you buy Chinese? Or stop at a local fast-food joint?" she teased. Jim walked with only a hint of a limp, she noticed. Silently, she gave thanks for her knowledge of homeopathy. Despite her confidence in her own abilities, Pepper knew she couldn't pull off such a mission without Jim's help and knowledge.

As they walked from the carpeted living room into any airy, light green kitchen with green-and-white polka-dotted curtains framing the window over the sink, Pepper smiled to herself. Jim might be like any other bachelor, but he didn't live like some of them did.

"A number of men on my team are single," she said, stopping a few feet from him, her hip against the kitchen counter, "and their apartments are in sorry shape compared to yours. I feel like I've stepped into *Better Homes and Gardens.*"

Jim pulled a bottle of chardonnay out of a bucket in the sink, where it had been chilling. "I hate to burst your bubble about me. Not that I haven't already, but this place was decorated this way before I bought it—from a general and his wife."

"Ohh . . ." Pepper met his sheepish smile and watched him pour the white wine into two crystal goblets.

Jim handed a glass to Pepper, his fingers barely meeting hers. For an instant, he saw surprise register in her eyes. She felt it, too, he thought. But just as quickly, he saw her hide her response. In that moment, her full vulnerability became excruciatingly apparent. Without thinking, he removed the glass from her hand and placed it on the counter.

"Come here," he rasped, stepping toward her and settling his hands on her shoulders.

Pepper's lips parted in surprise as she felt Jim's hands holding her. Shock turned to heat as she gazed wonderingly up into dark eyes that held her helplessly captive. *He was going to kiss her.* The thought was there, along with a rush of desire that made her move into his arms and lift her chin to meet his descending mouth. She had no time to analyze what was taking place, or why. She could only obey her heart, which cried out for closer contact with Jim, and personal consequences be damned.

As she felt herself enveloped in his powerful arms, her body coming to rest lightly against his as he drew her even more tightly against his hard, angular contours, a sigh of surrender broke from her. Pepper felt as if she were in a waking dream— a beautiful one filled with a raging desire that refused to be ignored. Her lashes swept downward, and she slid her arms around his neck, waiting. The instant his mouth captured hers in a demanding kiss, she responded with equal intensity. The heat of his mouth moving across hers, taking her, stamping her with his very male scent and taste, shattered every barrier she'd ever erected. His warm, uneven breath fell across her cheek as she opened her mouth even more to his deepening exploration. The slight prickle of his recently shaved face brushed hers. His hand moved upward, cupping her cheek, angling her mouth to an even more advantageous position, and she drowned in the splendor of his quest.

Lost in the molten power of his mouth, of his hard, straining body pressed to hers, Pepper felt a moan of pleasure coming from deep within her. A lightning heat swept through her, overriding her logical mind and connecting wildly with her heart—with a raw desire that was being born out of the fire of his searching, hungry kiss. Then, somewhere inside her, an

alarm went off, a warning so primal that Pepper pulled away
from the mouth that pleasured hers. That one movement broke
the dream. Her eyes flew open. She felt Jim ease his grip on her,
his eyes opening and focusing narrowly on her, like a predator
gauging its quarry. Panic spread through Pepper.

"No..." she pleaded brokenly, placing her hands flat against
his chest. "Oh, no..." The still-throbbing need within her belied the shattering knowledge that Jim should never have kissed
her. She shouldn't have kissed him. As Pepper stumbled out of
his embrace and gripped the back of a chair for support, she
stared up at his stormy face, met the burning gaze that clearly
said he wanted to claim her again. Her lips were still wet from
his kiss. Her body ached to complete what she knew they both
wanted. Shocked at how thoroughly her emotional barriers had
been lowered, she touched her brow, confused. How could she
have let this happen? She was as much at fault as Jim was. All
he'd done was brush her fingers when he'd handed her the glass
of wine. A small, grazing touch!

Shakily, Pepper stared at him in the building silence. His
chest was heaving, his breathing ragged. His hands were drawn
into fists at his sides. He looked as if he were fighting some inner demon to stop himself from moving the few feet to where
she stood. The hunger in his eyes was unmistakable. And how
badly she found herself wanting to walk right back into his
arms!

"Pepper," Jim rasped, opening his hands, "I'm sorry...."
And he was. Shaken by what had just occurred, he backed
away. His heart was pounding in his chest. He felt the tightness of his body screaming for relief, screaming to complete
what they'd started. The look in Pepper's eyes mingled fear,
accusation and sultry desire. She'd liked the kiss as much as he
had; he knew that. But her grip on the back of that chair spoke
of the depth of her devastation. Jim's mouth tingled in the aftermath of their fiery sharing. He could taste her on his lips. He
longed to taste her everywhere—and give her even more pleasure. As he studied her in the tense silence, he knew with every
particle of his being that he had given her pleasure. The
knowledge made his heart sing, lifting him in a sort of heady
euphoria he'd never realized existed.

"I think," he began in a strained voice, "that almost dying this morning is still with me." He wanted to take full responsibility for the kiss, even though she'd come willingly into his arms. "I'm sorry, Pepper. Really sorry..."

Trembling inwardly, she nodded and pressed her hand against her breasts, fighting for control of her frayed emotions. "I— yes, I think it was that...." she answered shakily. After all, there had to be some reason she'd done something so foolish!

"If you'll excuse me? I'll be back in a minute." Jim turned without waiting for her permission. If he didn't leave now, he feared he would walk right back over to her and take her. The vision of carrying her to his bedroom and making hot, hard love with her clamored in him. His leaving would break that damnable tension that seemed to stalk their interactions. And he'd take the opportunity to splash cold water on his face and get a grip on his unruly emotions.

When Jim had left the room, Pepper grabbed her glass from the counter and lowered herself to a chair. Her knees were shaking so badly she wanted to sit before she fell. In three gulps, she downed the wine. The alcohol took the edge off her frazzled emotions, soothing some of the shock out of her system, and Pepper was grateful to have time to pull herself together.

By the time Jim reappeared, nearly ten minutes later, he seemed back in control. No longer did she see undeniable hunger in his eyes. Instead, his mouth was an unhappy slash as he slowly walked to the sink and picked up his glass. Without a word, he drank the contents, then poured them both a second glass.

"I think," he began gruffly, "I owe you an apology for a lot of things regarding my behavior—"

"No," Pepper whispered. "It's all so crazy, Jim. I've had close calls before. I know what they do to me—to other people." She was blathering to cover her real feelings—her genuine need for him. It was totally inappropriate. Insane. "Stuff like this happens. Let's just chalk it up to the day, can we, and forget it?"

Working his mouth, Jim stared down at the wine in his glass. "Yeah—okay, you're right, of course." *Forget? How the hell could he forget her warm, flowing response to his kiss?* But she was right. Somehow, he had to put it behind him. Savagely, he reminded himself that Laura was the important one right now. At the thought of her, he felt his body shutting down, becoming less sensitized to Pepper's presence. Relief raced briefly through him.

Pepper took another gulp of wine. "It's already forgotten," she said, but her voice came out unexpectedly husky. *Liar.* Unwilling to analyze why she'd blindly walked into his arms in the face of everything she believed—no, *knew* to be true, she lifted her glass. "Let's toast to something. Anything."

Jim nodded. "Good idea." He frowned and thought for a moment, then touched the rim of his glass lightly against hers. "To a lady with more brains and courage than I gave her credit for." He lifted his glass, his gaze steady on her widening eyes. Taking a sip, he waited for her to drink. "Well?"

Pepper shrugged and tried to calm her alarm over his continued intimacy. "Bygones are bygones, Jim. It could just as easily have been me in trouble this morning." Her face serious, she lifted her glass to him, then took a small sip of the light, oak-flavored wine. The sincerity in his eyes and voice shook her, and she didn't want him to see the depth of her reactions to him. Casting around for some safer topic, she noticed a wonderful scent emanating from the oven. "Whatever you're cooking, it smells good," she said, forcing a cheerful smile. Right now, eating was the *last* thing on her mind.

Jim remained serious as he sat down opposite her. Something was driving him to remain intimate with Pepper. He ignored her attempt to lighten the mood. "I think you hold a lot of secrets," he said quietly, meeting her startled look. Setting his glass aside, he added, "I've had all day to think about you—us—and I've come to the conclusion that I know very little about you, Pepper." One corner of his mouth curved upward. "I do know that you're smart, gutsy and humble. You could have told Perseus about my attitude, the problems we had before and during the HAHO, but you didn't." He drilled her with a look. She colored fiercely. "Why? You had every right to."

Gazing down at her wineglass, Pepper murmured, "Look, I had that stuff pulled on me all the time in the army, Jim. It got worse when I demanded to take Ranger training. Every man there, almost without exception, was just waiting to gig me on something, to report me, to show my weaknesses to the world. I know what it's like to be singled out, to be the underdog." She gazed into his dark, somber eyes and saw another, hard-to-define emotion that set her heart to beating harder in her breast. "It would have been different if you hadn't realized your mistakes. But you did. Why pour salt in your wounds? I knew you were hurting." The larger, more encompassing truth was that she had been hurting for him, too.

"Maybe that's the difference between a woman being in charge and a man."

Relieved that the talk was turning more toward professional generalities, Pepper sighed inwardly. "There are many differences between the genders," she agreed slowly, tracing the rim of her glass with her fingertip. "I can tell you I don't treat my team of twenty the way I was treated in the army."

"Good leaders are rare, and you're one of them." Jim rubbed his jaw and said, "You made me feel ashamed of myself out there today, Pepper. It wasn't your fault. It was mine. I'd been a first-class jerk to you from the moment we met." He sighed, then smiled tentatively. "I wanted you to come over tonight so I could tell you that. To say I'm sorry and mean it. I didn't want to say it at Perseus, where we might get interrupted." He couldn't explain away their kiss, though, and he didn't even try.

Pepper felt the heat in her cheeks again, but this time she didn't care. The dark green warmth in Jim's eyes was sincere, blanketing her with a wonderful range of emotions that made her feel so incredibly alive. How long had it been since she'd felt that wonderful rush through her heart, which made her take a long, unsteady breath? Too long. "I knew you were sorry, Jim. Thanks for having me over, but it wasn't necessary."

He slowly got up and moved toward the kitchen cabinets. "I disagree. When I got home this afternoon after the debriefing,

I kept asking myself who *is* Pepper Sinclair? Where'd she get her nickname? Does she have another name? What about her personal life?'' He brought down two china plates edged with gold and placed them on the table.

When he turned and met her steady gaze, Jim saw real anguish, combined with fear. Why?

Pepper sat very still beneath Jim's heated inspection. She was seeing another surprising facet to this unusual man. His voice had gone low and husky, and her heart responded powerfully to his gentle inquisition. "I don't know that any of that matters," she said defensively.

"It matters to me," he said. Pulling out a drawer, he chose some flatware and brought it over to the table. "Rangers and Recons have a lot in common. They work as teams, and I know you understand the importance of that. You can't be on a team for any amount of time without getting to know your buddies, warts and all. There's a kind of unspoken marriage that happens—a personal closeness that binds the team together." He straightened and looked into her uncertain gaze. "You know what I'm talking about." And she did. He knew she understood very clearly what he was saying and what he was asking from her. But would Pepper drop that invisible wall between her professional life and let him in? Jim believed that sort of melding would be absolutely necessary if they were to survive the coming mission. But was she willing?

The silence in the kitchen seemed deafening to Pepper. She watched as Jim drew a Yankee pot roast, replete with potatoes and carrots, from the oven. He said nothing further as he proceeded to make a thick, brown gravy. Part of her wanted to bow to his request. It wasn't an extraordinary one, under the circumstances. At 0300 they would make a high-risk jump over the island in complete darkness—a jump that amounted to "out of the frying pan, into the fire," given what awaited them on the ground. Jim was right: they had to establish that bond now, no matter how painful it was to her.

Although dinner was delicious, Pepper ate little. She began to appreciate Jim's social abilities as an officer when he kept up a steady stream of polite small talk during the meal. Inside, she felt wary, knowing that after dinner the polite talk would turn serious—and personal. Her decision never to become personally involved with a man again was under assault. Pepper reminded herself what was really important in her life: her family, her friends and her team. The only thing she knew of that could stop her from accomplishing her goals was a romantic relationship. For that very reason, she had to fight her alarming attraction to Jim in order to maintain her promise to herself.

"Let's go in the living room and have dessert," Jim suggested. Pepper had barely eaten anything on her plate. He'd felt the unmistakable tension in the kitchen after he let it be known he wanted to get to know her, the woman, not the smoke jumper. Oddly, the shoe was on the other foot, he thought, frowning as he cut two slices of freshly made cherry pie. Placing them on dessert plates, he took them into the living room.

His pet had already made himself comfortable on Pepper's lap when he came in, and he chuckled.

"Frank's got an unerring instinct about people who love cats." Jim handed Pepper the pie, fork and paper napkin. Sitting down on the couch less than a foot from her and the contented alley cat, he noted Pepper's wary expression. Could he blame her? "It's a good thing you left the army," he said slowly.

"Oh?"

"You don't hide your emotions very well." He gestured to her eyes. "You broadcast everything in them."

With a groan of desperation, Pepper continued to stroke the cat, setting her pie aside on a nearby lamp table. She wondered if the animal had sensed her trepidation and come over to assuage it. Cats and dogs were psychic in that sense, and Pepper was grateful for Frank's comforting presence and the excuse to do something with her hands. Jim was too close, and she felt trapped. Clearing her throat, she said, "I did find it a minus in my work in the army, but it's been a plus in my job as a team leader with the smoke jumpers. Maybe because I've got five other women on my team, and we're used to looking into one another's eyes and reading how we're feeling or what we're saying, on almost a telepathic level. Over time, the men have learned to communicate the same way." With a shrug, she added, "My team functions as one body, one brain. They've

been with me two years or more...and we more or less grew up
together out there in those forest fires. They're like my extended family." Smiling a little, she noted, "They *are* my other
family."

"I see...." Jim noticed the softening in her eyes when she
spoke about her team. Without thinking, he reached out and
touched her hand—and saw the fear come back into her eyes.
"We've got less than nine hours to develop that level of communication, Pepper. The mission we're going on could easily
kill us. I want us to survive, and I know the mechanics of that
kind of survival." He moved his hand back to his lap. "We
need to talk about ourselves. Us."

Pepper's mouth went dry. Her skin tingled pleasantly where
Jim had so briefly touched her hand. Despite her fears, a part
of her wanted his continued touch. It had been so long. So
long... "It's hard for me to just sit down and talk about myself."

Wryly, Jim said, "I can tell. How about if I go first?"

Pepper met his gaze and felt a kind of warmth she'd never
encountered before. What magic was going on here? Was the
inner Jim Woodward really so different from his Marine Corps
image? "A-all right."

He set his dessert plate on the coffee table and placed his
hands on his thighs. "I was born in Maryland—very near Annapolis, as a matter of fact. My father owned his own soft-
ware company, and my mother enjoyed staying at home. I
wanted to become an engineer like my dad, so I went to Ohio
State, where they were known for excellence in that area. When
I graduated, my dad convinced me to put in six years as an officer. He said his six-year hitch in the corps had served him well
for the rest of his life.

"I agreed, and went into the Marine Corps, following his
footsteps." With a grin, Jim said, "It turned out to be a career. I like my work. I prefer field assignments to sitting behind some officious desk at the Pentagon, but this is what I
have to do right now to punch the ticket to get to general
someday. Well, that's pretty much my background." He
opened his hands and gave Pepper an encouraging smile. "How
about yours?"

Her hands stilled on the gray-and-white tomcat in her lap. "Well . . . I was born in Montana. Actually, Cam came first—my brother. Our dad was a silver miner near Anaconda."

"And your mother?" Jim was curious about Pepper's role model. He couldn't imagine her mother as a woman satisfied with being a housewife and parent only.

Pepper grinned. "She was a real hell-raiser, born way before her time. Mom is a CPA—that's how she met my dad. She worked for the silver company that gave Dad his paycheck. He found a mistake on his check one time and went into the front office to find out who'd made the error. Mom told me later the sparks flew."

"I'll bet they did." Jim chuckled. He watched the way Pepper's eyes and face became animated as she spoke of her family. How easy it was for her to plug into her emotions. He envied her that ability.

"My mother is also a horsewoman, and she rides to this day. She was twenty-nine years old when she met my father, so she already had a pretty independent life established."

"You're a real Montana gal, aren't you?" Jim observed.

"I'm a Westerner not only by birth, but by heart, too," Pepper answered. She petted the cat fondly. "My mom was born in Anaconda, so I guess it's in my genes. My dad is a real outdoorsman, and he taught us to fish and hunt at an early age. I couldn't enjoy killing those beautiful animals, so I quit hunting and fishing and stuck to horseback riding. Cam loved hunting, though, so he always went with Dad. I will say this—my father and brother hunted and used the food. They never killed for sheer sport."

Jim realised how important that was to Pepper, and he found himself mesmerized by the graceful way she used her hands to punctuate her statements. Finally, he was becoming privy to the woman inside the confident smoke jumper. "What made you go into the army?"

"Dad asked me the same thing," Pepper said wryly. "Mom thought it was a great idea. She said the military would teach me discipline and organization. She was right—it did. But it taught me a lot more. When the army wouldn't let me attend Ranger graduation after I was the top student in my training group, I resigned my commission. I went back to Montana to find my roots and see if I couldn't give back to the land that had bred me, in some way."

"Why?" Jim asked quietly.

Startled, Pepper glanced up at him. In the shadows of the large room, his high cheekbones and square jaw seemed emphasized. She felt herself automatically acquiescing to his reassuring steadiness. "I guess . . . well, I've never really thought about it, but I love the wide-open, blue sky, the miles and miles you can go without seeing another person. It's serene, but at the same time teeming with wildness and beauty."

"Sort of like you?"

Shaken badly by his insight, Pepper frowned. "I don't know about that."

"I think I do," Jim said, settling back more comfortably against the couch cushions. "It sounds like your mother and father really supported your being all you could be, not caring that you were a girl."

She nodded. "My parents have always been way ahead of their time, that's true. Cam and I were raised in a pretty evenhanded way in that sense. Not that I wanted to play football in high school or anything."

"But you didn't go out for cheerleader, either."

She laughed. "No, I didn't. I was with the band. I played saxophone for four years. And, since I had my own horse, Mom and I would compete in shows on weekends." Her hand stilled on the cat's back, and she said, "I had a happy childhood. I'm very close to my parents, and to Cam and his family."

Jim sensed the tension still stalking Pepper. "So how'd you get the name Pepper?" he teased, his mouth curving into a smile.

Flushing, she laughed. "Oh, that . . . well, I guess I was a pretty active baby. Mom told my father about five days after I was born that I was like a hot pepper bouncing around in the crib. I wouldn't lie still. I was always moving my legs or arms or rolling back and forth. So Pepper stuck."

"What's your given name?"

"Mary Susan." Pepper wrinkled her nose. "I can't imagine anyone calling me that, though. It sounds so foreign!"

Laughing, Jim shrugged. "It's not a bad name."

"I know," Pepper grumbled good-naturedly. "My mother named me Mary, after her mother, and my father named me after his mother, Susan. Go figure." Her laughter was husky. "However, I did know there was hell to pay whenever my mother or father used my given name instead of my nickname. That meant I was in *big* trouble."

Jim chuckled. Then he sobered a little and said in a quiet tone, "Cam's married, and it sounds as if you really dote on your family. How come you haven't married?"

It felt as if a spike had been driven through her heart. Pepper sat very still, wrestling with her unleashed emotions. Her hands rested on Frank, and she stared down at the animal. Finally, her tone strained, she said softly, "I was going to get married...but that was a long time ago. Or sometimes it seems like a long time ago. Then again, sometimes it seems like yesterday...."

Jim said nothing, holding his breath. He saw the anguish in Pepper's eyes and heard it clearly in her voice. Something tragic had occurred, there was no doubt. "Go on," he coaxed gently, "what happened?"

With a one-shouldered shrug, she whispered, "I met Captain John Freedman when I was in the army, six years ago. A lifetime ago..." Pepper raised her chin and stared blindly across the room, not really seeing it, lost in her past. "He was an incredible man. He didn't care if I was wearing a uniform. You know how a lot of men are—they see a woman in uniform and automatically write her off. Well, John didn't. I was wary of him, because I'd been hurt before by other officers, in a few attempts at relationships that ended badly. He was so patient. That was one of the many things I liked about him.

"John was a Ranger and head parachute instructor at the school. He taught me about parachuting, and pretty soon I was skydiving with him and his friends. I came to love jumping." She compressed her lips. "I came to love John." Pepper felt tears coming to her eyes and she self-consciously wiped them away. "He gloried in me, in who I was. I didn't have to play any games with him. I didn't have to fit into his idea of what a woman should be. He accepted me just as I was, without apology.

"We had known each other a good year, and we'd decided to get married. I wanted to marry a man who didn't hold a prejudice about women's roles. I knew..." Pepper swallowed against a lump forming in her throat. "I knew the kids we'd have would be raised in the same kind of environment Cam and I had been raised in. I was excited about life—about spending it with John and watching our kids unfold like unique flowers, watching them blossom...."

Pepper closed her eyes, pain making her voice hoarse. "Two days before the wedding, we went skiing with the army skydiving club. It was a celebration John's friends had arranged for us. He was a wonderful skier. He was good at anything he did, to tell you the truth. I'd skied all my life, being from Montana, and it was just one more thing we had in common." Pepper felt the lump in her throat hardening. Helplessly, she opened her eyes, her voice cracking. "He died on the slope that day in a freak accident. A broken neck. We—we were skiing together, and his left ski hit something under the snow. Later, we found out it was a rock. He fell and rolled. I went on, thinking he'd get right up again. When I looked back and saw him lying in the snow, I thought he was playing a joke on all of us, because he did that kind of thing." She stopped, struggling with her grief for a moment. "It was all so crazy. Crazy. I went back and saw his best friend, Steve, turn white with shock when he leaned down to see how he was. As I came up, Steve told me John was dead. I couldn't believe it. I stood there, frozen."

Pepper dragged her gaze to the ceiling and fought back tears. "I don't remember very much after that...." Anguish wrapped her in its persistent embrace. Pepper didn't tell Jim that since John's death, she'd made a decision never to fall in love again. She'd decided it simply wasn't worth the risk. She knew she couldn't survive a second such loss. The decision had been easy—born out of the fires of her grief. And she'd lived by her promise for six years, successfully sidestepping any romantic attachment—until now. Unable to explain why Jim touched her in that forbidden region of her heart, she felt confused and scared.

Jim groaned. Without thinking, he moved to her side and placed his arm around her tense shoulders. Her pain was mirrored in every aspect of her face and lovely, tear-filled eyes. He couldn't stand to see her suffer this way and wanted somehow, to soothe her. This time, his embrace wasn't one of passion, but one born of a need to help her. He saw the desolation in her eyes as she looked at him. "I'm sorry, Pepper. Really sorry."

She sat with her hands pressed to her face, bent over but not crying. He felt the grief in her taut muscles, in the way she held back the tears. Again following his instincts, he lightly caressed her thick, silky hair. He wanted to do more. Much more. Fighting to keep his touch light and comforting, he rasped, "At least you got to know what love is about. You had some time with him."

Pepper felt Jim's hand on her hair, appreciated the tenderness of his touch. She hadn't believed he was capable of such a thing. Blinking, she took in his serious, shadowed features through eyes filled with tears. Jim continued to surprise her with his humanity, his range of emotions and his willingness to share them with her. When he removed his arm from around her shoulders, she felt bereft. Alone. For a moment, she had experienced that wonderful sense of togetherness that only a man and a woman could forge between themselves. She and John had had that once.

She studied Jim in the silence, memorizing each nuance of his features, from his dark tormented eyes to his compressed lips and the softening lines in his face. She wanted to say, *Who are you? Why is there such a chasm between your officer image and this Jim Woodward? Which is the real man?* Whatever the truth, Pepper knew she didn't dare open up to him the way her wayward body and emotions were pleading for her to do. She couldn't afford the gift he was offering her. The price was too high, as she knew from bitter experience.

It took her long moments to pull back from her own grief and realize what Jim had just admitted to her. She saw the agony in his green eyes and found it unbelievable he'd never loved a woman.

"I don't understand," she said brokenly. "You must have loved before."

"Not like you have," he admitted, staring down at his clasped hands, resting between his thighs. "I envy what you had with John."

"You can't be serious. Surely there's been a woman in your life."

"Oh, there have been women, but not at the level of what you had with your fiancé." Jim saw such sadness in her expression at his words that it tore at him. In that moment, he realized Pepper had never truly gotten over John. He found himself unexpectedly wishing he could evoke that much emotion in her—and knowing it could never be.

It didn't make sense. Pepper sat silently for a long time. "You come across different than you really are," she said finally.

Jim angled a look in her direction. "What do you mean?"

"When I first met you, Jim, you were hard and cold. I didn't like you much." She lowered her lashes, her voice tight with hurt. "I know you didn't like me, either."

"And I was wrong," Jim rasped. "I'm sorry for hurting you, Pepper."

"I'm not asking for an apology. I know you've changed your mind." She grimaced. "It's just that I see such a difference in you now from when I met you. You're like two different people." She had to bite back the words: *And I like the man I'm with now.* But was he the real Jim? There wasn't time to analyze it, so she went on. "I know a lot of people wear a facade, a social mask. I have a friend like you. He's a pretty vulnerable man, but he protects his vulnerability by putting up this tough exterior. When Joe first joined our team, I had real problems with him, until a crisis occurred. Then he dropped those barriers, and I could reach inside and touch the real person. After that, we became good friends, and he never put up that barrier again toward any of us."

"Maybe I'm the same way," Jim murmured. "I don't know. I don't spend a lot of time analyzing myself." He shrugged. "Maybe I should."

"The military doesn't encourage that kind of thing," Pepper said with disgust. "They mold you into little mannequins trained to march, act and react the same way. I do understand how that can affect you, Jim. It's tough for me to believe you haven't ever fallen in love, though."

"Maybe I have and didn't realize it."

Pepper frowned, considering. She gave him an assessing look. "What about Laura Trayhern? When I was in your office, I noticed the picture of her was the only really personal one you had on the wall."

"Laura?" Jim straightened. "She's always been special to me."

"Yes, but did you date her before she married Morgan?"

"Oh, a few times." He stood up and jammed his hands in the pockets of his pants, frowning.

"You said she's special to you. In what way?"

With a shrug, Jim walked around the coffee table. "I don't know... I never thought much about it, to tell you the truth." He turned and gave her a slight smile. "Laura is... well, you know..."

"No, I don't know. Put it in words for me, Jim."

"She's just special." He frowned, thinking. "You want an example? Well, when she'd come into my office at the archives, I would feel better, happier. Not that Laura singled me out, or anything like that, for a long time. She was like this bright ray of sunshine down in that dark hole. Everyone in the archives responded to her.

"I admired Laura because she had beauty and brains—and she also had moxie. She was a go-getter, and she had the endurance to see whatever research project she was working through to the end. My office was at the entrance to the archives, and I enjoyed hearing her laugh whenever one of the staff told a joke. She was like a breath of fresh air in my life, that's all I can tell you."

"And how long did you know her?"

"Two years. Before Morgan turned up, I'd been taking Laura out some. They weren't official dates, but she'd happen to be leaving the archives at lunchtime when I was going, and I'd invite her along. Things like that." He shook his head, lost in memories. "She is just an incredible person, that's all." He omitted the fact that they'd kissed once—a kiss he recalled as vividly as if it had happened yesterday.

Pepper studied his expression, her heart squeezing with realization. Jim was in love with Laura. Didn't he know that?

Chapter Five

"Perhaps," Pepper ventured cautiously, "you care for her more than you realized."

Jim gawked at her. *"What?"* The word came out strangled, filled with shock.

"Maybe that's why this mission is so hard on you. I mean, it's understandable," she went on in a quiet voice.

"Wait a minute." He held up his hand. "You're wrong." But was she? Jim wasn't so sure anymore. He wanted to dismiss her words but an unexpected catch in his heart told him to look more closely at her observation.

"I don't think so," Pepper said, noting the confusion in his eyes. She did believe that Jim had never been consciously in touch with the fact that he loved Laura. She had met men like that before—so divorced from their feelings that they hadn't a clue about what was really happening deep within them. If Morgan hadn't come along so suddenly, Jim's love for Laura might well have surfaced in time. Not everyone closely tuned in to what their heart wanted—men and women included—and Pepper accepted that.

Sitting down on the couch again, Jim quickly reviewed hi[s]
past with Laura. "She's been married for seven years and I se[e]
her only infrequently at the Pentagon. She still comes by occasionally to use the archives, and we're still friends, but—" h[e]
looked up at Pepper "—that's all."

Pepper didn't believe him for a moment. His tone of voic[e]
changed every time he spoke Laura's name or shared something about the extraordinary woman. Why was *she* feelin[g]
suddenly bereft, then? Pepper didn't know. "At first I didn'[t]
realize I loved John, either. It just sort of grew out of ou[r]
friendship over a long period of time," she offered lamely
"Since he died, I've had a lot of time to think about our relationship." She opened her long, thin hands. "I was overly focused on my career—I wasn't looking for love or a relationship
I did plan to have a family, but much later, when I'd achieve[d]
my goals in the army."

Jim propped his elbows on his knees, with his chin resting i[n]
his clasped hands. "About the time I met Laura, I was in hig[h]
gear careerwise, too. It was my first assignment to the Pentagon, and I knew I was being watched closely by the upper ech-
elon. I was basically blind, deaf and dumb to anything outsid[e]
what was necessary to keep my career on the fast track." H[e]
gave Pepper a curious look, noting how the room's shadow[s]
softened her face, making her even more beautiful. She ha[d]
great depth, he was realizing, and from the grief still visible i[n]
her gaze, he began to understand what it had cost her to com[e]
clean with him about the love of her life.

"I've certainly never been in love to the depth you were wit[h]
John."

"It's been hell," Pepper admitted. "The experience taugh[t]
me a special sort of euphoria. But with him no longer aroun[d]
I've been lonely in a way I never knew could happen."

With a soft snort, Jim rose and put his hands in his pocket[s]
"My parents had the kind of love I want."

"Oh?" Pepper wondered if Jim was at all aware of his mag-
netism, of the way his natural strength and confidence cou[-]
pled with this surprising tender side acted as a beacon to he[r]
Surely other women had been privileged to know this side o[f]
him. If she believed what he was saying—that he had neve[r]

truly fallen in love—then she had to recognize the importance of this moment with him. If he didn't show this side of himself to others, why was he revealing it to her? Shaken by the possibilities, Pepper sat very still. It was automatic for her to embrace what was in her heart as well as what her mind told her; to separate them was folly. On the other hand, she had to be careful not to act on those feelings—if it might signal the risk of a potentially romantic relationship.

She knew it was often easier for men to separate their emotions from rational thought—and not even acknowledge the danger. From the moment she'd met Jim Woodward, he'd called to her heart—against her head's warnings—which could be why his aloofness and negativity toward her had cut so deeply, hurting her much more than it should have. She studied his thoughtful face and wondered again why he was revealing this very private side of himself to her. Could his love for Laura have forced him into the position? In her heart, Pepper had to believe he still loved the woman. It explained why he had barged into the Perseus offices and demanded to take the mission. And it also might explain his violent stand against Pepper coming along on the mission. Love made people do crazy things, she knew from experience. It wasn't out of the range of possibility that Jim subconsciously saw himself as the white knight coming to rescue the damsel he loved. And he didn't want any help in doing it, perhaps to prove to Laura once and for all that he was a man worth loving, a man willing to risk his life for her.

Jim continued thinking about his parents' marriage. "It was silly things, I guess," he said finally with a short laugh. Giving Pepper an embarrassed look, he pulled his hand out of his pocket and opened it. "Things like sharing a cup of coffee at the dinner table after we kids left to play. Sometimes my dad would take my mother's hand and stroll down the street in the evening, just before dark." His voice lowered with feeling. "I always knew they loved each other. My dad didn't show affection easily, but in those small ways, he showed he loved my mother very much."

"I think most men, even of this latest generation, are still struggling with showing their feelings."

"It seems to come so much more naturally to women," Jim agreed.

"It's natural because we were never taught, as boys are, that it's wrong to show our emotions. You men are the ones who get it in the neck, so to speak. You're taught it's not masculine to cry, to reach out, to touch and express. What a sad thing society has done to you. And everyone suffers for it."

With a grimace, he nodded. "I won't argue with you."

"Maybe that's why you were so slow to let Laura into your life," Pepper suggested gently.

"Maybe," Jim agreed, with a slight shake of his head. He held Pepper's velvet blue gaze. Did she realize how beautiful she was? He almost voiced his feeling, but thought better of it. Her dark hair was free and soft around her face, lighted with golden strands. He recalled touching that silken mass and found himself wanting to touch it—and her—again. Her mouth showed such vulnerability, its soft fullness always pulled into an expression that underscored how she was feeling. Jim liked discovering that about her. She might be a woman of extraordinary talents, but under it all, she was gloriously feminine and had never abandoned her heart or her feelings.

"You know," he murmured, "you're a lot like Laura, in some ways."

Pepper's chest squeezed in pain. She didn't want to be compared to her, because she knew she could never live up to the image Jim held of the other woman. "I don't think Laura and I share much in common."

His mouth curved ruefully. "More than you realize."

A warmth cascaded through Pepper as she stared up at him in surprise. Laura was ultrafeminine and delicate. In comparison, she was plain and gangly, far from the ethereal beauty Laura was. Her heart wanted to embrace Jim's statement, but her mind and the decision she'd made after John's death stopped her. She glanced down at her hands, at her practical, blunt-cut nails. She never wore fingernail polish or earrings. Nor did her job allow for dresses, perfume or many of the smaller appointments that, in her mind, made a woman feminine.

Jim saw her frown. "You both possess an inner strength. You're passionate about what you believe in. Laura was passionate about helping Morgan after she was injured and he rescued her. She saw *through* him, somehow, to the man beneath the armor." He shook his head. "I certainly didn't. When I met him for the first time, all I wanted to do was pick a fight with him." His voice grew gentler. "You both live, breathe and move through your emotional instincts." His mouthed twisted in a sad smile. "I find that commendable. Courageous." He touched his own chest. "If I tried that, I'd be laughed out of the corps."

"Laura put you in touch with your heart, maybe for the first time," Pepper pointed out, even though it was painful to admit that truth. She saw Jim's mouth curve more deeply in response.

"Yes, I guess she did. Laura always has had a way of making the men in her life take responsibility for how they felt— even when we didn't know what we were feeling in the first place." He eased onto an overstuffed chair opposite Pepper. Her long skirt added to her naturally graceful appearance, and he liked the way she slowly stroked Frank's gray-and-white fur. What would it be like to be stroked by those long, narrow hands—hands that had saved his life with their inherent strength just this morning?

Jim's mind gyrated forward to the mission. *Pepper could be killed.* The thought was pulverizing to him, and he stared at her hard, noting the shadows that lovingly emphasized her features. Her lashes, he realized, were thick and long, while her eyebrows reminded him of gently arched bird wings. The combination gave such startling definition to her soulful eyes that Jim felt as if he could get lost in them forever. Something was always going on in Pepper's eyes, in a way he'd never experienced with another woman. Her eyes broadcast her emotions so clearly that it aroused a powerful response in him.

For a split second out of time, he knew that Laura could die, too. The overwhelming emotions that came with that flash of awareness rocked through him, a vivid reminder of his own equally fragile hold on life. This mission could kill all of them.

Easily. He struggled internally to reject that knowledge, but his military mind and training coldly confirmed the possibility.

His focus returned to Pepper, who appeared lost in thought. She might never find love again, he realized sadly. Her heart was still in John Freedman's hands, even though he was dead. After this mission, provided they survived, Jim would never hear Pepper's husky laughter again or see that wonderful bevy of emotions mirrored in her eyes. She was rare, he realized—a rare woman who had the courage to make of her life exactly what she wanted. If life told her no, she went in another compatible direction, reweaving the fabric of her goals and continuing to move toward her heart's desire.

Looking back at himself, Jim gave an internal, derisive laugh. He'd merely had to punch the military system's ticket to get what he wanted. He'd never been told no, as Pepper had. All he'd had to do was play the game the way he was told, and the next rank would follow. Oddly, his successes didn't fill him with the kind of satisfaction he was sure Pepper experienced over her many battles, wins and losses. She might have had doors slammed in her face, but she'd never let it defeat her.

If there was anyone he'd choose for a mission this dangerous, he had to admit, it would be Pepper. She wasn't a killer, but that wasn't what was needed here. Her brains, flexibility and unique ability to turn a setback into a success would come in very handy. Jim knew he provided certain strengths to the mission, but Pepper's input and observations would be easily as valuable as his own.

But despite his discovered faith in her, he couldn't stop worrying about the chance of Pepper dying. His heart lurched violently in his chest at the thought. Much as he would like to deny it, the possibility was real. A maelstrom of feelings rose sharply in him, encircling his heart. Pepper was murmuring soothingly to the cat, her head bent over him, her mouth curved in a soft smile. For a moment, Jim enjoyed watching her, then, unexpectedly, Laura's face shimmered before him. Where had that come from?

Rubbing his chest, he rose suddenly. He excused himself abruptly and went into the kitchen, wrestling with a gamut of unexpected emotions. Placing his hands on the sink, he looked out the window over the sparkling neighborhood lights of Georgetown. The porcelain sink was cool against his damp palms. His heart wouldn't settle down. Maybe Pepper was right, after all, about his feelings for Laura. Did they go beyond mere loyalty and friendship? At the same time, his response to Pepper was new, something he'd never encountered—even with Laura. But maybe that was why he hadn't fallen in love during all these years—because his heart was still in Laura's hands. He frowned. The only way he could think to find out once and for all how he felt about Laura was to see her again. He knew it was wrong to love another man's wife—and he was very aware of how deeply Laura loved Morgan. He'd seen for himself the reality of what existed between the couple. So where did that leave him and this confusion of emotions squeezing at his heart?

Grimly, Jim studied his hands, still resting on the sink. Pepper's insight had blown the lid off something he'd been carrying around for years but had never realized until now. He'd never really considered his feelings for Laura. At first, he'd been too busy chasing his career up out of the depths of the archives. Then, when he'd realized Laura was drawn to Morgan, he'd slammed the lid down on whatever emotions he'd had.

With a shake of his head, he sighed. Morgan might already be dead. Laura could be a widow. Would he want to step in and try to start afresh with her? There were no easy answers. Yet his response to Pepper was wildly spontaneous and breathtaking, and Jim had never felt more uncertain in his life. What was real? What were mere idealistic dreams that would never be fulfilled?

The discovery of his chaotic feelings was painful, yet strangely euphoric. Somehow, subconsciously, he thought, he'd been looking all his life for a woman who possessed Pepper's unique combination of qualities. She was completely comfortable with who and what she was—and was not. No, she wasn't a magazine-model beauty. And maybe she wasn't beautiful in the same way Laura was, but that didn't matter. He pictured his mother. She'd been a strong, quiet woman with a deep passion for life—much like Pepper. Above all, Jim realized, he wanted people in his life who had commitment—as he did. Pepper's commitment to herself was mind-boggling in the sense of how much she'd accomplished in face of sometimes severe opposition. Fleetingly, he recalled that his mother, who'd had artistic leanings, had been refused schooling at a college where she'd wanted to take art courses, because her high school grades had been too low.

Closing his eyes, Jim went back to that time. He'd been ten years old, far too young to understand his mother's tears as she'd told his father that the college had turned her down. Jim recalled crying that evening in his bedroom, alone and unseen. He'd cried for his mother—for her dream being shattered by an unfeeling institution that looked at grades rather than the quality of her talent. From that day forward, he remembered, his mother had changed in subtle ways. She had never again tried to draw. She had put her box of paints away in the attic, never to retrieve them.

Releasing a ragged sigh, Jim opened his eyes and stared blindly out at the city lights. He felt anger at the insensitivity of the college's treatment of his mother. Pepper, too, had her passion for life, but she'd somehow managed to sidestep that awful trap of failure. He smiled at the thought. Pepper came from a younger generation of women, who had been told it was all right to fight back, to fight for their dreams.

A sizzling sort of electricity moved through him. It was a feeling he'd never experienced with Laura, and he knew it had to do with Pepper. He liked her more than a little, despite the small amount of time they'd shared. Their bonding had occurred through a life-and-death situation, Jim realized, and that kind of connection was soul deep, transcending time and space. He'd learned that in Desert Storm, Panama and Grenada, where he'd felt that same bonding with the marines he commanded.

Pepper, despite his poor treatment of her up to that point, had saved his miserable life out there in the sky. She'd reached beyond the hurt he'd delivered, wrapped her strong hands around his arms and held him. She hadn't let his pettiness stand in the way of risking her life to save his. Yet even as he savored his feelings for Pepper, Jim's heart cried out for Laura, for what might have been and could be in an uncertain future.

"Damn..." he rasped, straightening. He glanced toward the ~~li~~ving room. Turbulent emotions soared through him as he di~~ge~~sted what Pepper quickly was coming to mean to him. And ~~a~~t 0300 tomorrow morning, she could die. She could miss the ~~is~~land and, with sixty pounds of gear on her back, drown in the ~~o~~cean. She could hit a tree and be fatally gored. A bullet could ~~fi~~nd her, or one of those dogs could tear her apart. Worst of all, ~~sh~~e could fall into Garcia's hands as his prisoner. And Jim ~~k~~new what the drug lord did to women. Sickened, he turned, ~~h~~is stomach rolling with nausea. It was heinous enough that ~~G~~arcia had Laura; it was unthinkable that Pepper could fall ~~p~~rey to the sick bastard, too.

"Jim?"

Pepper's voice was soft. Questioning.

He turned abruptly on his heel. "I haven't been a very good ~~h~~ost," he said, more gruffly than he intended because she'd ~~su~~rprised him.

Reeling from the sudden hardness in Jim's tone, Pepper ~~s~~tepped back from the kitchen entrance. The old Jim Wood~~w~~ard—the hard, unfeeling marine she'd first met—was back. ~~P~~art of her was relieved. With Jim in this mode, it was easy to ~~re~~spond to him on a strictly professional basis. Anything be~~y~~ond that was too dangerous for her to contemplate, anyway, ~~s~~he reminded herself. Gathering her thoughts, she said, "I'm ~~ti~~red. I'm going to try to get some sleep before we meet over at ~~A~~ndrews at 0130."

Cursing himself, Jim started toward Pepper. He saw the ~~q~~uizzical look in her eyes—and the pain. He'd hurt her again. ~~S~~crambling for a way to apologize, but not knowing how to go ~~a~~bout it, he followed her to the door. He retrieved her coat ~~f~~rom the closet and helped her on with it.

"Thanks for dinner," Pepper said woodenly, suddenly ~~d~~rained by all the events of this very long day. She was an ~~e~~motional wreck. As she slung her purse over her shoulder, she ~~s~~aw anguish in Jim's eyes and had no idea what was going on ~~i~~nside of him. Had it been something she'd said? But what? She ~~h~~ad no idea.

"I'll see you later," Jim rasped, opening the door for her. It ~~w~~as the last thing he wanted to do—let Pepper out of his sight.

He was consumed by gnawing hunger to ask her a hundred different questions about herself, about her growing-up years and her family.

Stung by Jim's inexplicable withdrawal, Pepper stepped out onto the sidewalk leading to the curb, where her rental car was parked. The November air was icy cold—but nothing like the chill that enveloped her insides. As she pulled on her gloves and walked quickly to the car, her chest began to ache. Dammit, she liked Jim! At least her silly heart did, she chided herself, as she slid onto the cold vinyl seat and shut the door. The street was well lighted and lined with trees, their bare branches lifting skyward into the darkness. Wind stirred the dried leaves along the curb and sidewalk.

Pepper started the car and drove slowly down the street. Why had Jim left her alone in the living room so long? She grimaced. Even if it had been something she'd said or done, he hadn't needed to disappear like that. He was a mature adult. He at least could have stayed and made small talk. The Marine Corps drilled officers on small talk for social occasions, Pepper knew, but Jim hadn't been willing to do even that much. Frowning, she made a turn that would take her to her nearby hotel.

Why had he turned so gruff? He'd been accessible, then ten minutes later, he'd been closed off. Perhaps, she ruminated, he had got in touch with the fact that he still loved Laura Trayhern. Bothered, Pepper wondered how or if that knowledge would affect his performance on the mission. It had to affect him. Whether he wanted to believe it or not, he was human and dammit, he had feelings.

Angered, Pepper drove to the hotel and went directly to her room. After a long, hot shower, she slipped into her cozy flannel nightgown, which fell to her ankles. Going to bed was the easy part. Going to sleep was another story. Her mind swung from the manuals to the HAHO, to Jim and John. Every time her heart touched on Jim, she became a mass of vibrant feelings. Frustrated, Pepper got up and started to read another manual to distract herself from the thought of Jim Woodward, but even that didn't work. Finally, she started pacing her hotel room.

Jim still loved Laura; Pepper was sure of it. Desperately, despite her roiling response to the idea, she wanted it to be true. She couldn't dare risk true love again, so it was just as well that Jim was otherwise involved. As the clock ticked toward one a.m., she tiredly rubbed her smarting eyes. She should have tried to sleep, not think. Her mind was spinning with data to remember—radio codes, satcom codes, what to do if they got separated. What to do if she was captured. That last thought scared the hell out of her. Pepper didn't want to die. At the last moment, she wrote a letter to her parents—just in case. Then she wrote a letter to Jim, too. She tucked both of them away in her purse, which she would be leaving behind at Perseus, along with the rest of her luggage. If she died, her personal effects would be gone through and the letters delivered.

The seriousness of the mission impinged upon her more than ever as she slowly pulled off her nightgown and began to dress in striped utilities that the Marine Corps had provided. She could die tonight—in a variety of ways. Even so, Pepper found herself repulsed at having to carry weapons. She didn't want to kill anyone. It simply wasn't in her. And she might have to. She pulled on thick, dark green socks as she explored her feelings. Even as a child, she hadn't wanted to shoot deer or catch trout with sharp hooks. Some of her passion for smoke jumping came from her role in stopping the destructive fires that inevitably killed the wildlife in their paths.

Pepper knew she'd be hard-pressed to squeeze a trigger to kill someone. She didn't doubt Jim would do it—probably because his survival instincts were more sharply honed. But despite her hitch in the army and getting through Ranger school, she was less than sure about her ability to take a life—even in her own defense. Pepper shook her head. Why was she taking this mission? Wolf had told her about Laura and Morgan. She liked Wolf and knew he was a man of honor. If he wanted her help, she didn't question it. Wolf was like part of her extended family, and if he needed her, she'd be there.

Pepper decided that her morals and values were terribly confused. On one hand, she'd dive into life-threatening danger at the blink of an eye, yet she was loath to pull a trigger to kill another person—even one intent on killing her. Go figure.

Well, it was too late to change her mind, although these weren't really second thoughts. Her heart centered on Jim, and Pepper knew unequivocally that she was a balance to him and the skills he brought to the mission. He wasn't a killer, either, but he would kill in self-defense—although she believed that if he had to, he'd regret it.

As she pulled her thick, shoulder-length hair up and back into a ponytail, Pepper looked at herself in the bathroom mirror. What a contrast, she thought. Her big, blue eyes didn't seem suited to the military uniform she wore. She looked vulnerable, not tough and soldierly. Maybe that was what Jim was concerned about.

Sighing, she realized that she had no answers to the various dilemmas she faced. A part of her liked Jim and was glad to be there for him on this mission. Another part was willing to do what was necessary to rescue Laura Trayhern. And part of her didn't want to go at all—because of Jim, who stirred the coals of life brightly within her. Somehow the danger he presented to her very soul seemed to outweigh the many external threats.

By the time Pepper arrived at Andrews Air Force Base, she was a mass of nerves. Wolf drove her there, his face set and hard. He said little on the way, and as Pepper stepped out of the vehicle and toward a small office inside a hangar, the tension was electric. There, squinting in the bright lights, an Air Force team met her and began helping her into her parachuting gear. Pepper felt as if she were in a surreal movie. Where was Jim? Four people worked with her, saying little, the strain obvious in all of their faces. In half an hour, she and Jim would board the C-130 that would take them across the Gulf of Mexico to the Caribbean for the drop.

Wolf remained nearby, and Pepper felt reassured by his presence. The pack she would carry on her back was loaded with ammunition and weapons. Pepper made sure that her knife was situated, as always, on the front of her harness, with easy access, though she hoped this time she wouldn't be cutting away shroud lines.

The door opened. Jim, already in his tiger utilities, appeared in the doorway. His face was grim, his eyes hard. Pepper swallowed convulsively, suddenly wondering if she really ought to go on this mission. She could die. Jim could die. The thoughts shook her, and as she held Jim's glittering gaze, Pepper *felt* his raw, boiling emotions. Though he hadn't said or done anything, she experienced his feelings as if they were her own. What was going on? Had she suddenly become psychic?

Pepper acknowledged that during critical fire situations, her intuitive abilities were nearly clairvoyant, probably because of the adrenaline, which automatically heightened everyone's senses. She watched Jim skirt her to talk in low tones to Wolf, who stood, arms crossed, listening intently.

Jim was ignoring her—again. She felt hurt as well as relief wind through her as she turned toward the two men. Her talk with Jim earlier tonight—their unexpected intimacy—had been wrong, she realized, as she followed the jump master out to a waiting vehicle that would take them to the C-130 warming up on the runway.

"Pepper?" Wolf reached out, his hand wrapping around her arm to halt her forward progress.

They stood on the tarmac, the light from the hangar casting eerie shadows across the huge base. Pepper looked up into Wolf's face and saw the worry in his eyes. "I'll be fine, Wolf. Stop worrying." She gripped his hand.

"Just be careful," he growled. "Sarah won't forgive me if you don't come back."

She nodded somberly. "I know." Sarah was her best friend, and Pepper knew how much Wolf loved her. "I'll be back."

He reluctantly released her hand. "I'll be praying."

Pepper smiled weakly and waved goodbye to him and to the uniformed men and women standing around him. She found herself walking next to Jim, who seemed to appear out of the darkness. His profile was sharp. His eyes revealed nothing. Most of all, she saw the forbidding set of his mouth—a single line. Swallowing against a dry throat, Pepper climbed into the vehicle. The doors slammed and they lurched forward, gears grinding.

Darkness closed in around them, except for the dull glow of the dashboard lights. Pepper sat in the back seat, alone. She felt horribly deserted. If only Jim hadn't retreated so far inside himself. She knew that certain members of her team reacted like that before a jump. Still, she wished for some friendly sign from him, some humanity.

The C-130's engines were whining, the four turboprops spinning and invisible in the night. Jim and Pepper boarded through the rear ramp, and she hauled her gear on board, taking a seat next to the jump master, a grizzled-looking sergeant in his mid-forties. The load master, a woman sergeant, gave the signal, and the ramp began to come up, the sound of clashing metal echoing through the cargo plane's cavernous hull. Soon the inside of the aircraft was dark, the gloom broken only by a few small lights.

Jim had sat opposite Pepper, on the other side of the aircraft. He wouldn't look at her, she noticed. Instead, he fiddled with his pack, going through last-minute checks on various items. His movements were sure, brisk and economical. He knew what he was doing. He'd done this many times before—and she hadn't.

Squelching the urge to go over her own pack again, Pepper sat quietly. The C-130's engine whined at a much-higher pitch, and the aircraft began trundling awkwardly down the runway toward the takeoff point. The vibrations went through her, launching the faint smell of hot oil and metal. The human element was lacking in this mission, she realized. The weapons were cold steel. The plane was metal. Even the air crew with the C-130 seemed stoic and robotlike. At the moment only Pepper and her rising internal panic seemed frighteningly soft and human.

Her palms were wet, and she rubbed them against the fabric on her thighs. Her heart wouldn't settle down. Every time she thought of the coming HAHO, and all the possible problems, she broke out in a sweat. This time, if Jim's chute didn't open, she wouldn't see it. The darkness would mask the view of a partner plummeting to certain death. So many harrowing possibilities ran through Pepper's head. What she wanted, what she needed, was Jim's closeness. She tried to reassure herself that her need to be close to Jim and feel his touch was a normal desire she always had before a risky jump—a way to know she was connected to the rest of her team. Still, her stomach tightened, and an odd tingling at the base of her spine as she looked at his strong, reclining figure, scared her more than she wanted to admit. Maybe she should be thankful Jim had shut himself off from her, she thought suddenly, dashing fiercely at unexpected tears that threatened to spill from her eyes. She was alone in this mission, as she ultimately was in life. She had her family and friends and that was enough—more than enough. She sat up a little straighter in her seat.

As the C-130 rumbled through the air toward Nevis, Pepper thought about her past. While the hours passed, she was able to review her entire life to date—the good experiences and the bad. All of them had been instructive in some way, and she was grateful to realize that. As she continued to sit on the vibrating seat, tired but wide awake, her hands in her lap, she was glad she'd left her parents that letter.

And Jim . . . She stole a glance through the gloom. He was lying down, his back to her, curled up on some nylon seats across the aisle. Pepper admired the possibility that he might be able to sleep so close to a jump. She couldn't. She thought again of their dinner together and realized just how much she'd come to like him. That brief moment where he'd been human, warm, even tender with her, had shown her the real man beneath his harsh military facade. Her heart cried out at the injustice of it all. But he was in love with Laura. That's why he'd separated from her, kept his distance. His mind and heart were focused on Laura's rescue—not on what might be frightening Pepper, what her needs might be.

Pepper understood those things without bitterness. Surely she was old enough, wise enough, to allow people to be themselves. Although she might not agree with Jim's behavior, especially under the circumstances, she wasn't going to try to change it—or him. But didn't he realize she was scared, too? That she might need a brief touch on the shoulder, a slight smile or sign from him? Wolf had given her that before they'd left. But then, Wolf was different from Jim. He'd been through the fires of hell with Sarah, Pepper knew, and she had brought him out of his own closed world.

Feeling sad as never before, Pepper decided she would lie down, too. She stretched out on a row of uncomfortable nylon seats, her arm beneath her cheek, and closed her eyes. Exhaustion swept over her. Too much had happened too quickly. As much as her mind counseled against it, her heart ached with the pain of Jim's reproach. Her feelings toward him were good and true and strong—yet he pushed those genuine emotions away. *Because he loved Laura.*

Pepper shifted, trying to shut out the overwhelming noise of a C-130 in flight, and to ignore the bone-jarring vibrations. She could die, and Jim would never know what lay in her heart. Tears matted her lashes, and she struggled to hold them back. Even as she fought her rampant emotions, she fell into a deep, exhausted sleep.

Chapter Six

A hand gripped Jim's shoulder. Instantly, he was awake. The jump master leaned over and said, "It's time to get ready, sir."

Shaking off the much-needed sleep, Jim nodded and moved into a sitting position on the nylon seats. Removing the black covering from his watch, he saw that it was 0200. They'd be over the target in an hour.

Automatically, his gaze ranged through the gloom. The jump master must have sensed his worry, because he leaned down again. "She's been sleeping almost as long as you have, sir. Shall I wake her?"

"No, I'll do it."

"Yes, sir."

Jim took the can that contained the colors they would use to darken their faces before the jump. His heart twisted in his chest as he drew closer to where Pepper slept. Her long body was tucked along four of the nylon seats, her hand beneath her cheek. She looked angelic, her lips softly parted, her hair in mild disarray around her serene face. He felt guilty at the

thought after his concerted effort to remain apart from her
during the flight.

As he knelt down, one hand gripping the nylon for support
as the aircraft bumped along, he had a wild, nearly uncontain-
able urge to reach out and touch her hair. The only thing that
stopped him was the fact that the jump master was probably
watching him. Instead, Jim settled his hand firmly on her
shoulder and squeezed just enough to waken her.

Pepper felt a strong, warm hand on her shoulder. Her eyes
flew open. She blinked, thinking she was dreaming. Jim was
kneeling over her, a concerned, unguarded look on his face. His
eyes were shadowed, but they burned with a fire she felt go
through her as surely as morning sunlight after a cold Montana night. No longer was he hard and unapproachable. No,
this man was the one she was helplessly drawn to, against her
better judgment.

She savored the feel of his hand on her shoulder and the
strength and care it conveyed. When Pepper realized she hadn't
moved, but had only stared up into his eyes like a child for that
long, undiluted moment, she made an effort to sit up. Her hair
fell in tangles about her face, and she used her fingers to tame
it into some semblance of order. Jim's nearness was agony. He
had removed his hand, but not himself. Why not?

Confused, she looked at him.

"It's time to get ready," he said. He handed her the can
containing black, green and tan coloring agents. "Cover your
face, neck, hands and lower arms," he explained, then forced
himself to get up before he did something crazy like kiss her
senseless.

As he rose to his feet, Jim knew he should return to his side
of the aircraft, but he couldn't do it. Instead, he settled a chair
away from Pepper and used her open tin to start camouflaging
his own face. Covertly, he watched as she slowly applied the
greasepaint to her lovely features. When they jumped, they
would be completely invisible to anyone on the ground.

As he sat, absorbing the din and heavy vibration of the aircraft, Jim was surprised at how much Pepper meant to him. It
was all so crazy, he decided in frustration. He continued ap-
plying the greasepaint to the exposed skin of his hands and

forearms, wishing himself anywhere but here. Without question, he wanted to rescue Laura, but his heart longed for anything but the danger he knew they would be parachuting into. He'd had no time to talk to Pepper, to share his chaotic feelings, which were as surprising to him as he was sure they would be to her. Just as their kiss had been. . . .

With a slight shake of his head, he finished smearing on the agent, feeling completely at loose ends. One part of him, the warrior, was focused on the mission to rescue Laura. But the man in him was torn between Laura and Pepper. Pepper was like a delicious, mysterious flower that had yet to open in his presence—a rare, beautiful orchid hidden deep in the jungles of the Amazon, waiting to be discovered, to be touched, to be loved.

Loved? Jim got to his feet, unable to stand being so near her. He was going to end up doing something foolish and embarrassing if he didn't move. Such a large part of him wanted to get to know her—all of her, on all levels. As he made his way back across the belly of the aircraft to the seats against the other wall, Jim realized he had to rise above his personal dilemma and focus on the mission. He needed to rescue Laura and find out just what she really meant to him.

No woman in his life had stunned him as Pepper had. Not that she'd meant to. No, he'd seen with painful clarity just how much she'd loved Captain John Freedman. He couldn't talk openly to people. He didn't possess those magical qualities that held Pepper in thrall.

Sitting down, his mouth grim, he began putting on his gear, plus the elastic joint protectors Pepper had brought along for them, with the help of the load master. Angrily, Jim forced his focus to the business at hand, but every once in a while he stole a look across the aircraft to where Pepper was being helped with her own gear. He saw the strain on her face and the fear in her eyes. That was a healthy sign. Beneath his own emotional state, he felt that same fear and trepidation. But his mind and heart were centered on Laura and Pepper.

Life was so screwed up, he decided disgustedly as he shrugged on the sixty-pound pack containing his two parachutes and everything else he'd need for the mission. Pepper had walked into his life, sent him reeling emotionally, but her heart was still trapped in the past—just as his apparently was. He had no time to savor her and discover her. Instead, they had a mission staring them in the face, and either, or both of them could die at any point. Never had Jim felt the surge of anger he felt now. How unfair life was. How damned unfair to all of them.

Compressing his lips, he thanked the load master and adjusted his headset.

"Pepper?" he said, trying it out.

Instantly, her head jerked up. "Yes?"

"You hear me okay?" Jim was barely whispering into the mike placed against his lips. Her husky voice sent a wave of need through him, one so excruciating that he had to take a deep breath to steady himself.

"Y-yes. Fine."

Jim heard the fear in her voice. Without thinking, he crossed the cargo plane to her side. The jump master had finished helping her on with her pack and had gone to his position near the ramp.

Reaching out, Jim slipped his hand around Pepper's upper arm, his eyes meeting her shadowed gaze. "Are you okay?"

She drew in a ragged breath. "Scared to death, if you want the truth. I mean, I'm nervous about the jump, but I'm more scared of what waits for us on the ground."

He gave her a tight smile. "It's healthy to be scared. It will keep you alive."

Pepper gazed up at Jim's dark features, at his eyes, glittering with some unknown emotion. "You look like we're going for a stroll in the park," she observed, trying for levity. His hand hadn't left her arm, and she desperately wanted to move closer to him. Did Jim realize the strength and confidence he exuded? How it helped her steady her own frayed emotions?

"I'm scared to death, too," he rasped, meeting and holding her gaze. Pepper had tucked her glorious hair beneath a helmet, black knit cap and positioned the headset over it. Her once-tan skin was streaked black, green and brown.

"I'm glad to hear it. My knees are feeling weak. I'm shaking."

"It's okay," he soothed, losing the hardness he wanted to keep between them. If Pepper realized how much he ached to have her, to discover her as the wonderful, unique woman she was, Jim knew she would retreat permanently from him. He squeezed her arm and found himself wanting to slip his around her shoulder to reassure her.

With a nervous laugh, she said, "I haven't been this scared in a long time. Maybe on my first jump into a fire with my team, but not since." She felt bereft when Jim removed his hand. To her surprise, though, he didn't move away, instead remained only inches from her, as if to shield her with his tall, stalwart body.

"Fifteen minutes," the jump master informed them.

"Roger." Jim checked the altimeter on his right wrist and the watch on his left. "Is all your equipment in working order?"

"Yes." Swallowing hard and suddenly very thirsty, Pepper bit back the rest of what she wanted to say. She felt like babbling nervously to bleed off the fear that crouched in her chest and knotted her stomach. She could die in the jump. She could miss the island and drown. She could be gored by a tree limb.... Sitting down awkwardly with her pack, she fumbled with her bootlaces, tying them into double knots. Jim stayed close, and stymied, she wondered why. Was he worried she wouldn't or couldn't fulfill the mission now that she'd admitted her fear?

Her three-hour nap had left her feeling groggy. If only they'd had another day or two to rest up before the mission. Pepper felt strung out emotionally, uncertain about how Jim saw her, or even if he trusted her at all with this mission. The urge to turn, slip her hands around his broad, capable shoulders and press herself against him was very real. Too real. She told herself she was human, seeking comfort from an understandably scary situation. It was normal to find solace with another person. But why Jim? His heart was held captive by Laura Trayhern, whether she knew it or not. His love was bound up in the past.

"Five minutes," the load master said, hitting the switch that caused the giant ramp to open. Grinding sounds filled the cargo bay.

Pepper tried to still her pounding heart, without success. She got up and walked across the deck, with Jim at her side. Her mind whirled with a litany of what needed to be done and in what order. Everything hinged on her parasail opening without a hitch, and she worried about Jim's jump. This time if something went wrong they wouldn't be able to help each other. Although they would be in radio contact via their walkie-talkies, silence was a must. In fact, until they were established on the island and sure they hadn't been spotted, hand signals would be their only means of communication, for fear of someone overhearing them or discovering their position.

Jim gripped Pepper's arm, when the ramp opened fully and a gusting wind began to tear through the cargo bay. At twenty thousand feet, the air was freezing cold. He felt the aircraft begin to bank, bringing them east of their target, Nevis.

"One minute," the jump master warned.

Jim's fingers dug into Pepper's arm. "Listen," he rasped, his face very close to hers. "I want you to be careful. No heroics, okay?"

Startled, Pepper felt his warm breath on her face as she was pulled against him. She opened her mouth to reply, caught up in the fierce, burning light in his dark green eyes.

"Dammit, Pepper, this isn't how I wanted it. I wanted time . . . time with you. We don't have it. You're special. I just wanted you to know that. . . ."

Stunned, she stared up at his grim features. One of her hands was resting against the pack on his chest, and she swayed slightly off-balance as the plane tilted. She felt his hand tighten on her arm to steady her. Somewhere in her mind she realized that Jim could have held her at arm's length and helped her regain her balance, but he hadn't. He wanted her close, as close as they could get under the circumstances. The helmet on his head, the tight chin strap, the greasepaint and the darkness combined to give his face a dangerous look. She felt his eyes burning into her, touching her heart, her soul. Not believing what she'd just heard, she said brokenly, "There are so many ghosts from the past, Jim. . . ."

"Thirty seconds," boomed the jump master.

Cursing softly, Jim released Pepper and moved ahead of her.
t was too late to talk. He saw the jump master's grim face and
watched the blinking red light that would turn green any moment now. The C-130 suddenly straightened out into level flight
after the deep, tight turn. Wind whipped against him. Fortu-
nately, his goggles protected his eyes. His mind revolved forward to the mission at hand. God willing, they'd find Laura
and get her out alive.

So much could go wrong. So much.

The light flashed green.

The jump master gave the signal.

Jim moved down the ramp and leapt off its lip. Almost instantly he was hit by the power of the slipstream. He groaned
and righted himself in the icy night air. Twisting to look upward, he heard the plane but couldn't see if Pepper had jumped
yet. But he didn't have time to worry. Watching his altimeter,
he pulled the cord when he reached ten thousand feet. The
parasail opened flawlessly, jerking him upward as his gear
sagged down, tugging mercilessly at his body.

Where was Pepper? All he could see under the quarter moon
was the glinting of light on the smooth water of the Caribbean
below. A few stars twinkled. He didn't have time to look
around. Checking his compass, he pulled at the lines, directing his parasail in a slightly more westerly direction. The winds
weren't cooperating; in their briefing earlier, the weather fore-
caster had warned them of this. Where the hell was Pepper?
Again Jim twisted his head, but was unable to locate her.

He was panting hard, his breath coming in rasps. If he could
just steady his breathing, he might be able to hear her. Wrestling with his chute in the uncooperative winds, he saw Nevis
coming up. The dormant volcano sat on the western end of the
island, near Plantation Paloma. In fact, Garcia had built his
fortress at the bottom of its velvety green slopes. Again Jim
checked his compass and made another adjustment. If he
wasn't careful, he'd overshoot the whole damned island.

At five thousand feet, he was drifting silently toward the
northern coast. He could see the white beaches now, and the
black glint of the water. The iciness had changed to warmth,
and he felt a trickle of sweat down his rib cage. It was hurri-

cane season, so the humidity was high. He would feel his parasail slowing in the heavy wet air as he came closer and closer to
the island. Making some last-minute adjustments on the lines,
he aimed for their agreed-on LZ—a small clearing about half
a mile inland that had been photographed by the U-2 flyby.

Where was Pepper? Jim couldn't look for her now. He could
only pray she was somewhere nearby, probably five thousand
feet above him, coming down safely. The wind was fickle. He
bobbled. Yanking the lines, he steered the parasail farther in
land. Two thousand feet. The trees formed a thick, continuous canopy. Automatically, he bent his knees and forced his
lower body to relax. If he hit the LZ, he would have a clearing
about the size of a football field in which to land.

Another gust of warm wind coming in off the ocean hit him
and spun him around. Damn! Gritting his teeth, Jim saw the
canopy flashing beneath his boots. One more yank. There! The
meadow opened up beneath him. Instantly, he prepared to
land. On the very best of days, he was able to land on his feet.
But the sixty pounds of gear was pulling him off-balance.
Rather than risk a broken ankle, he pulled the parasail around
at the last possible moment to face the wind. There was lift
about fifty feet above the ground, then, gently, he was eased
downward.

It was a nearly perfect textbook landing. His feet hit the wet
grass and he bent his knees, absorbing the shock. The parasail
fell to the earth, and he quickly jerked it toward him. Breath
ing hard, Jim looked around for Pepper. Anxiously, he
searched the sky. All too aware of the wind gusting off the
ocean, he narrowed his eyes against the dark sky.

The sudden breaking of tree limbs made him freeze. To the
left! Jim jerked around, dropping his chute and kneeling. The
crash continued, a crescendo of snapping branches. Pepper had
landed in the trees! Quickly releasing his harness, he dragged
everything under the jungly growth at the edge of the meadow.
He pulled off his helmet and substituted a utility cap in the
same camouflage colors as his uniform. The submachine gun
was in his hands as he raced quietly along the edge of the
meadow toward Pepper, a hundred questions racing through his
mind as he hurried toward the sounds.

Voice communication was impossible; he couldn't risk it. ooking up, he finally spotted her. She was hanging about forty et above the ground, dangling at the end of her lines from a ige rubber tree. He could hear her ragged breathing. With- it a sound, he set his weapon aside and began to climb the e's gnarled expanse. As he drew closer he could see that pper was tangled in her lines, so she couldn't just cut herself ee and drop. Damn.

Pepper tried to steady her breathing and avoid making any ore noise than she already had. When she saw Jim climbing e tree toward her, she nearly cried out. Biting her lower lip, e waited silently. He was like a dark panther scaling the rooth-barked tree almost effortlessly. Pepper knew she was trouble. The shroud lines had somehow become wrapped ound her neck and arms. If she tried to cut loose, she might rrote herself. Worse, the branches above her, supporting her r the moment, were not stout. She was hanging tenuously at st.

She knew enough not to move. But had Jim ever cut some- ie out of a tree before? she wondered. In smoke jumping it is a common procedure, but she wasn't sure if he'd had the perience. She saw him study the situation. Their eyes met and grinned a little. A flood of feelings tunneled through her. She ed to smile back but didn't succeed. Knowing she shouldn't eak radio silence, Pepper merely waited, watching as he oved gingerly out on a limb above her. Good, he knew he had cut the lines tangled around her neck and arms first.

Relief sped through her as the lines were shorn and fell past r. Just as she reached for her own knife to cut the remaining nes and fall, Pepper heard a loud crack. She jerked her gaze oward as the limb Jim had crawled out on broke beneath his eight. With a gasp, she watched in horror as it tore from the ink behind him. He had no time to prepare for the fall. A cry caped Pepper as he fell past her, and hit the ground, hard.

Rapidly, she unhooked her heavy pack and let it drop first. ien she grasped her knife and began cutting her lines, one by e. Hanging precariously, she bent her knees, preparing for e coming fall. Jim had crawled off to one side. She could ake him out in the dim moonlight, his back against the trunk of the tree. Dropping, she hit the ground, her bent knees taking the shock. She rolled, absorbing more of the shock, an dried leaves and dirt flew up around her.

Gasping for breath, Pepper scrambled to her feet and hurried back to Jim, falling to her knees at his side. She saw th grimace of pain in his face and followed his gaze to his lowe right arm, which he held tightly against him. Even in the dark ness, she could see blood oozing through his uniform.

"I cut it," Jim rasped, throwing his head back, the pai flaring up his arm and into his shoulder. To hell with commu nications blackout. He had to talk to Pepper.

Gently, she eased his hand away from the wound. Jim sleeve had been ripped open. Pulling it aside, she gasped. "It deep."

"Tell me about it," he groaned softly. Looking around, h said, "Do what you have to do. We have to get out of here."

Pepper felt guilty. If she hadn't landed in the canopy instea of the LZ, Jim wouldn't be injured. Compressing her lips, sh shoved herself to her feet and went to retrieve her pack. He fingers were already bloody, a sign that his wound was bleed ing heavily. Locating her first-aid kits, she took them back him.

"Take this," she said in a wobbly voice, putting several whi homeopathic pills directly into his mouth. "It's arnica—goo for sprains as well as hemorrhage." Setting the kit aside, sh drew out more items.

"I cut it on that damn branch I was on," he muttered an grily.

"I know . . . I'm sorry, Jim."

He held her guilt-ridden gaze. "You couldn't help it. Th wind was all over the place." He stopped, a wave of pa flooding him. Finally, he gasped, "I'm just glad you're okay."

"I'm fine . . . fine. . . ." Pepper quickly dumped the conten of the bottle directly into his wound. It was too dark to se much of anything. All she could do was disinfect the gash, the wrap it in a dressing and an Ace bandage. "I can't do muc until it's lighter."

"I know. Just wrap it tight. We've got to move."

Nodding, she worked quickly. Though her fingers trembled, she was fast. In no time Jim was pulling down his torn sleeve. She helped him stand. He wavered for a moment, caught himself and straightened.

Anxiously, he searched her drawn face. "No injuries?"

"No..."

He reached out, unthinking, and brushed her cheek. "I was worried...."

The brief caress sent her heart skittering wildly. Shaken by his unexpected tenderness, Pepper pulled away. "Let me put my pack on and we can go."

"I'll bury the chutes and other gear." Jim tested his right arm. To his dismay, it hurt even to pick them up. The injury held far greater ramifications than he wanted to admit. Without his right arm, he was damn near useless.

By the time Pepper had situated her heavy pack, Jim had dug a shallow hole and laid the equipment in them. She noticed he wasn't using his right arm, instead pulling leaves and debris across them with his left hand. Helping him finish the job, she knelt next to him.

"The arm is bad, isn't it?"

"Yes." Grimly, he caught and held her gaze. "Listen, I'll take point. Whatever happens, we can't engage anyone in a firefight. Do you understand? I can't even count on using my fingers to pull the trigger." He looked with disgust at his right arm. "Maybe it's just as well," he muttered. "We'll do what Recons do—be quiet and not engage the enemy." He drilled her with a hard look. "Do you think you can do that?"

"I don't want to kill anyone, Jim. I never did. It's fine with me."

With an abrupt nod, he forced himself to his feet. Luckily, he hadn't lost too much blood before Pepper wrapped up his wound. He knew enough about anatomy to realize that his luck could have been worse—an artery could have been torn open and he could have bled to death. And he knew what the jungle environment with its high humidity and decaying bacteria would do to a wound like this. Once the sun came up, he'd have Pepper sew up the wound and give him a shot of antibiotics from the supply of medications they carried in their first-aid pack. Infection in the jungle was the surest killer of all, and those antibiotics could be the only thing ensuring he finish this mission. And he was going to finish it.

Pepper allowed Jim to take the lead. They walked quietly but quickly toward the unseen volcano. The surrounding trees were mostly coconut palms. According to the LZ information, they'd landed in a coconut plantation. The soil was tilled, dry and easy to navigate beneath the arms of the flowing palm trees, which rattled in the gusting winds. Pepper's heart settled down and her senses took over. Although she carried a submachine gun, she didn't want any part of using it. In the distance, a dog barked once. They froze and waited. No more barking. Jim moved on, more shadow than human being.

Pepper's throat felt like sandpaper by the end of the first hour's hike. Jim had kept up a fast, steady pace, and where they could, they trotted. Her shoulders ached from lugging the gear, and she was glad when Jim gave the hand signal to stop and rest. They were out of the plantation now and into the jungle itself, which was more tangled and harder to navigate. Twisted roots kept tripping her up, and she'd fallen too many times to count. Her shins were bruised and sore.

Pepper eased to her knees and unsnapped the pack. It fell behind her, and she wanted to groan with the pure pleasure of getting rid of the thing, but didn't dare. Worried about Jim, she turned and devoted her attention to him as he came and sat down next to her. The dawn light finally allowed her to get a good look at his injury for the first time.

"Well?" he demanded, watching her face closely for reaction. He knew it was bad.

"It's deep," she said in a choked voice. She laid his hand on her thigh and opened the first-aid kit. "The bleeding's stopped. That's good."

"I got lucky on that, at least," Jim agreed. Pepper's face was glistening with sweat, and a few dark brown curls had escaped from beneath her knit cap. Though her long fingers barely grazed the skin around his wound, he felt their warmth, with a tingling sensation that momentarily eased some of the throbbing pain. He concentrated on her lips—that full, lower lip—remembering what it was like to kiss her. Remembering her passion and generosity.... The loss of blood was making him light-headed. For a moment Jim allowed himself the indulgence of really looking at Pepper. She was beautiful....

"Did anyone ever tell you that you have a beautiful mouth?" he asked almost dreamily.

Stunned, she gazed at him. His face was sweaty, his mouth grim from the pain she knew he was feeling. "What? Oh...no, they haven't." She felt heat sweep across her cheeks, and she avoided his burning, intense stare. Taking out some surgically clean gauze that had been soaked in disinfectant, she steeled herself to begin scrubbing out the wound. In the light, she could see it was free of splinters or debris, but it had to be as clean as possible before she taped him up.

Jim leaned back against a tree trunk, honing in on Pepper's face. Anger sizzled through him. Well, what was wrong with the perfect Captain John Freedman that he'd never noticed Pepper's lovely mouth?

She began to scrub. "I'm sorry...."

His mouth tightened and he stiffened against the pain. "Somehow, I think I have this coming. I was such a bastard to you earlier," he groaned.

Pepper shook her head and bit down hard on her lip. She knew how much pain Jim was in as she continued to cleanse the wound. "It's the mission." And his love for Laura Trayhern.

Fire leapt up his arm, and Jim felt sweat pop out across his face and under his arms in reaction. He shut his eyes tightly, fighting off a dizzying faintness. "I was thinking about you," he gasped. His lips lifted away from his gritted teeth. He fought swirling dizziness—and more pain. Finally, it was over.

Pepper watched Jim worriedly. He lay in a prone position now, sweating heavily and breathing raggedly. His eyes were tightly shut. She couldn't blame him. Pulling the antibiotic syringe out of the pack, she gave him the shot in his upper right arm, above the injury. Much of what she did in fire-fighting situations was coming back to her, and she was grateful for her paramedic training.

Glancing around, she saw hundreds of trees, mostly rubber trees and palms of all sorts, silhouetted against the coming dawn. Odors of decay mingled with the salty smell of the ocean

and some unidentifiable, exotic floral fragrances. Focusing on
Jim's wound, Pepper located the surgical strips that would pull
the edges of the wound together. At least he wouldn't have to
be stitched up.

"This is going to hurt," she warned in a low voice. She used
one hand to pull the wound together, and instantly he became
rigid, his entire body convulsing. Hating to hurt him, she
quickly taped the adhesive across the wound, closing it. In a
matter of a minute, she'd completed her task. Breathing shakily, she began to rewrap the wound in clean gauze to protect it.

Jim wiped sweat from his eyes. He felt awkward using his left
hand, but he'd better get used to it—it was the only one in
working order. Concentrating on Pepper, he absorbed her clean
profile as she worked over him. Her touch was exquisitely gentle, and in his hazy, shorted-out state he wondered if she made
love with that same kind of touch. It was a crazy thought in an
even crazier situation, he told himself harshly.

"I wish," he rasped unsteadily, throwing his arm across his
eyes as she worked, "that we were anyplace but here right
now."

Pepper smiled grimly and glanced at his face. His mouth was
a line of pain. "That makes two of us." She completed the
bandaging and stretched an Ace elastic around the gauze to
further protect it.

"I keep seeing us talking over a candlelit dinner. I know some
good restaurants in D.C. You'd like them, too. Quiet places.
Intimate. Where good conversation can go on and on...."

Pepper felt mild shock over his rambling. Was Jim out of his
head? Impossible. But his words were disjointed, ragged
sounding, filled with fervency. Was he teasing her? Her heart
said no, her head said yes. She remained kneeling beside him,
more uncertain of herself than she'd ever been in her life.

Chapter Seven

"We've lost the time advantage," Jim said when she sat back, the bandaging of his arm completed.

"What should we do?"

Jim looked up through the canopy of palm fronds and heavy rubber-tree leaves. Daylight was already upon them. In another half hour the sun would be up. He didn't want Pepper to feel bad that her getting snagged in a tree had wrecked their initial timing. Being injured was something he hadn't counted on, either.

He slowly sat up, his back against the tree for support, and rested his right arm across his belly. Pepper remained kneeling and alert, slowly perusing the area with her sharpened gaze. There was little to be wary of now. But as they neared Garcia's fortress, her watchfulness would pay off.

"I worked out two plans with Jake," he said quietly. "The first involved striking before dawn, but that opportunity's gone. The second is to hit them tomorrow at 0300. Noah Trayhern is sitting off the coast of Nevis, on a Coast Guard cruiser with a helicopter platform. If we get to Laura and can spring her, we're to meet at the beach south of Garcia's fortress. I showed it to you on the map.''

Pepper nodded. ''If I hadn't blown it by getting hung up in the tree, we might be there now.''

Jim sat up, reached out with his left hand and gripped her arm. ''Things happen, Pepper. Let it go.''

She shrugged. ''At least our chutes opened this time.''

He breathed deeply. ''Yes, there's plenty to be grateful for.''

''Do you really think you can continue the mission with that arm, Jim?''

It was a fair question. He held her worried gaze. ''We don't have a choice. You can't do this alone, and I'm not going to call in air support for further medical help. No, we'll do it. We're just going to have to be particularly careful—and quiet.'' He scowled. ''But if we get in a firefight, I'm going to be next to useless.''

Feeling bad for him, Pepper said, ''I don't want to kill anyone. I have real issues over that, Jim.''

''Fine time to tell me.''

She saw his mouth quirk. ''Seven years ago, when I was young and wild and going through Ranger school, I thought I was capable of killing. At least I convinced myself I could do it.'' Pepper shook her head. ''I'm older now, and looking back, I'm glad they didn't graduate me. I liked the army for its discipline and organization, but I found those same elements in smoke jumping.''

''The best of both worlds without lifting a weapon.'' Jim removed his hand from her arm. The intimacy between them was strong and good. If Pepper minded his touch, it didn't show this time. Instead, she had opened up, and was talking with gut-level honesty. ''We have no backup if we get in trouble.'' He tapped the walkie-talkie strapped to his waist. ''But we can change channels and call for Noah to send the Coast Guard helicopter in.''

''They don't carry weapons, either.''

''No, not on the chopper.'' Jim was worried, but he didn't voice the fact. It was one thing on a Recon mission planned to be exactly that. But this mission had too much chance of human contact, and weapons might well be used. He held her clear blue gaze.

"Would you use your weapon to defend?"

"In a heartbeat."

"Good."

"I'm not a pacifist, Jim. I just don't want to kill if I don't have to." She added more softly, "I know if I do, it will haunt me the rest of my life."

He understood only too well. "It's all right," he said gently. "I still get nightmares from what I did in Desert Storm and Panama."

Without thinking, Pepper reached out, her hand covering his injured one. "Somehow I knew you'd understand."

The tremble in her husky voice sent a sheet of longing through Jim. But it was the wrong place, the wrong time. "Help me up. We'll go slowly and take our time circling the volcano to reach Garcia's fortress. We can use the daylight to time the guards and observe the routine."

Somehow, Pepper thought this might end up being a better plan, after all. Knowing the guard's coming and goings and getting a direct feel for the place would help them tomorrow, when they made their raid into the plantation itself. She got to her feet and leaned over, offering Jim her hand. His grip was strong and steady as he heaved himself to his feet with her help.

She watched him for signs of dizziness but saw none. When she'd fashioned a sling for him to rest his right arm in, he went over to his pack.

"There's no sense in me carrying all this weight," he said, bending over it and fumbling with the straps. A left-hander he was not.

Pepper crouched next to him and opened the pack.

"Thanks," he rasped, offering her a crooked smile.

"I'll be your hands on this trip," she joked weakly, as she spread out the items from the pack so he could choose what to take and what to discard. He kept his handgun and its ammunition. At his request, Pepper dug a hole deep enough to bury the items he didn't need. It took nearly half an hour to repack the contents, then he hoisted the pack onto his shoulders.

Pepper opted to continue carrying the full weight of her own pack. If they got into trouble, she could still use the submachine gun to spray the area and protect them.

As the first streaming rays of the sun shot across the ocean and touched the island, Jim and Pepper began heading toward the fortress. He took the lead, since he was more familiar with jungle trekking. Mainly, they had to be careful not to step on branches that could crack or snap, since the sound carried too far for comfort.

Birds had been calling since dawn. As Pepper followed about fifty feet behind Jim, she noticed how he moved not in a straight line, but in one that took advantage of the brush and taller bushes in the area as protection from curious eyes. She could smell smoke from a wood fire in the breeze drifting toward them. Dogs barked now and then, and once she heard children laughing in the distance.

Because they were skirting the volcano, there were few homes, just thick brush that made for slow going. Every once in a while Jim stopped, consulted his compass and map, then moved on. Pepper worried that his arm must be hurting terribly, but she knew he wouldn't complain. Still, she watched him for signs of weakening or fever. The antibiotics should hold him, unless she hadn't cleaned out his wound well enough, which was always a possibility.

Near 0800, Jim stopped. He'd found a fairly thick grove of rubber trees that provided excellent cover, so he dropped his pack and sat down. He watched as Pepper silently came into the circle of trees. Her face had a sheen of sweat from the high humidity coming off the ocean. He was sweating heavily, too, as evidenced by the dark splotches on his utilities.

Taking out the canteen, Jim awkwardly opened it and drank deeply. Pepper joined him, sitting not more than a foot away after placing her pack next to his. He capped his canteen and watched her drink from her own. She had such a long, slender neck. The greasepaint they wore had streaked off with her sweat. It didn't matter now, anyway. Jim looked around, satisfied that they were fairly safe from natives who might inadvertently discover them. They were miles from any of the dirt or asphalt roads that lined the coast.

Another sound caught his ears and he looked skyward. A helicopter. Pepper was watching the sky intently, too. They knew that Garcia had a helicopter. The *whapping* sounds grew closer. The aircraft was coming in from the west and heading south—toward the fortress. Jim barely glimpsed it as it skimmed by, nearly at treetop level.

Pepper stood, straining to catch sight of the aircraft. "It's a blue-and-white Bell," she reported.

"That's Garcia's," Jim said. He gestured for her to sit down near him. "Let's eat."

Pepper wasn't really hungry. The excitement and danger levels were too high for her to be in touch with something as basic as the need for food. The chance to be near Jim was enough, however, and she sat down next to him, her legs crossed. He handed her an MRE—one of the military's ready-to-eat meals that needed only to be reconstituted with water. She watched in distaste as he showed her what to do.

"At least out on the fire line we get real food," she grumbled.

He laughed softly. "Yeah, MRE's are the pits. I prefer the C-rations we had before they instituted this new stuff." Glancing at Pepper, he saw that some of the fear had left her eyes. Sobering, he asked, "Are you settling into the routine?"

She nodded and picked at her mushy MRE. "Yes, I am." She wrinkled her nose as she tasted the fare. "It tastes like cardboard."

Chuckling quietly, Jim agreed. He tried to ignore the pain in his arm by concentrating on Pepper—which was easy to do. Despite their circumstances, her vibrant inner beauty shone through. Several more curls had escaped from beneath her black knit cap. "You're the first woman I've seen wear Recon gear and look damn good in it."

Pepper's heart thumped once to underscore his huskily spoken words. She glanced up and nearly melted beneath his burning green gaze. Feeling suddenly shaky, she tried to concentrate on eating the unpalatable food. "Sure," she joked, "my face is streaked with that awful stuff, my hair desperately needs to be washed and I stink—some pinup poster I am,

Woodward. Maybe you've been out in this jungle a little too long, huh?''

He grinned and spooned some more rehydrated fruit into his mouth. ''Do you always parry a compliment, Ms. Sinclair?''

''Probably,'' she admitted, chewing thoughtfully. ''It comes from my hitch in the army. Sexual harassment was everywhere. I got so I hated it, and most of the time I wouldn't take it.''

''I don't blame you,'' he answered. ''No one should be subjected to that kind of humiliation.''

''Usually, marines are the worst harassers.'' She watched him laugh at her with his eyes. For the moment, Pepper felt safe and she relaxed for the first time. Was it Jim? His confident presence? The fact that he'd done this before, and if he was relaxed, she could be, too? Or was it that lazy, warm smile he gave her that automatically made her feel boneless in such a wonderful, thrilling way? Did he realize what his heated look did to her? She was sure he didn't. After all, his heart had already been given to Laura Trayhern. Pepper had no chance with him. Though she knew she should be relieved, a ribbon of sadness wound through her at the thought.

Jim finished his MRE, dug a hole and buried the remains. ''Marines are diehards,'' he finally admitted. ''And you're right—they are pretty macho.''

''The Tailhook scandal proved that.'' And the navy and its stonewalling admirals were no less guilty, she thought to herself.

Jim nodded. He couldn't argue the point. Half the aviators at the Tailhook convention had been marine pilots, and word was out that one of the worst suites at the symposium had been a Marine Corps one. Glancing around, keying his hearing, he reassured himself that everything was normal. The birds were singing, a sign that all was as it should be. If they were to stop singing suddenly, he and Pepper would go on alert.

He lay down carefully, using his pack as a pillow. ''Let's rest awhile. We've got three more miles to the fortress.''

''Is your arm hurting you?''

"A little," he lied. It was burning, as if on fire. He saw Pepper's eyes change and grow shadowed with worry. "Are you always like this?" he asked.

"Like what?" she asked, leaning against the tree inches from Jim's shoulder.

"A mother hen."

Grinning, she said, "I get accused of that all the time by my team. I guess I am."

"Worrywart is probably closer to the truth," he said, looking up at her. He watched as Pepper removed the black knit cap. Her hair was a mass of curls from the humidity. With her slender fingers, she began to ease them into some semblance of order, and he longed to stroke the dark, wavy strands. She replaced the headset, settling the mike close to her lips, but she left the cap off. He couldn't blame her. The humidity was making him sweat like a racehorse.

Something drove him to get to know her better. He knew he wasn't going to get many chances, and he wanted to take advantage of everyone of them. "Tell me about your growing-up years. Were you a hell-raiser like your mom—a wild woman?"

Laughing softly, Pepper shared a warm look with him. This was the man she wanted to know, and it sent an ache straight to her heart. His green eyes were dark with an emotion she was afraid to define. His mouth was curved recklessly, giving him a boyish look.

"I was no 'wild woman,' as you put it." Tipping her head back against the trunk of the rubber tree, Pepper closed her eyes, suddenly happier than she could recall being in a long time. "Cam, my older brother, might disagree with me, but I never saw myself that way. As I said, we lived in Montana, so we did grow up in the wilds, in that sense. I spent every spare minute hiking and learning about nature."

"Tell me about it?"

Embarrassed, she shrugged. "I was just a kid with a high sense of curiosity, that was all. I used to hunt red asparagus berries every fall, collect them and make necklaces out of them. Later, I'd dry and shellac them and give them as Christmas gifts to my friends at school. Or I'd go out with my mother with my

flower book and try to identify the different wildflowers that
grew around our place, then press and save them.''

"So you were a wood nymph." Jim closed his eyes, imagining Pepper as a youngster. "You must have been a pretty little
girl.''

Pepper rolled her eyes. "No, I wasn't. In fact, I felt awful
sometimes because my nose grew larger than the rest of my
face, or my lips did. You know how some kids go through that
awkward period? Well, I was worse than most. When I was
fourteen, I looked in the mirror one day and started to cry. My
mom came into my room and found me." Her voice went soft.
"My mother, bless her heart, just put her arm around me. I
blubbered about how ugly I was, and she said that each part of
me was beautiful in its own right, and that one day soon I'd
grow into all of them. She assured me I was just going through
a gangly stage.''

Jim opened his eyes. "Your mother is special—like you," he
murmured.

Flushing, Pepper said, "I don't know about me, but yes, my
mom is special. Cam and I were really lucky. Hearing all the
horror stories nowadays really makes me appreciate my parents. I know we weren't perfect kids, and I'm sure we caused
them some anxious times, but out in Montana, at least we
didn't have problems with drugs and gangs like the big cities do.
Anaconda is a relatively small town—a silver- and copper-
mining community.''

"I think some of the old-fashioned Western morals and values are still alive and well up there, don't you?''

Pepper was grateful for his grasp of her world. "Yes, that's
why I love living there," she said, smiling as a vision of her
home flashed before her.

"Western people seem different from Eastern types," Jim
offered. "I grew up in Maryland, in a suburb a stone's throw
from Annapolis. It wasn't the wide open spaces, but we still
learned serious values, it being an Academy community.''

"You were lucky," Pepper said. She smiled at him, loving the
ease of conversation now that the barriers between them were
down.

"Tell me," he said, catching her dreamy gaze, "what are your dreams?"

"What?"

"Your dreams. You've got to have some. What are they?"

Frowning, Pepper ruminated. She drew up her knees and rested her arms around them. "You'll die laughing, Woodward, if I tell you."

"No, I won't. Come on, what are they?"

She moved uncomfortably. "They're nothing special. . . ."

"So? I'd like to hear what's in your heart."

Pepper tore her gaze from his. Her mouth was getting dry again. She wanted to blurt, *"You're* in my heart, but I know I can't have you." Bowing her head, she said instead, "I have a very common dream, Jim, but it seems to have been taken from me." She swallowed against the lump forming in her throat. "Despite my choice of careers, I wanted to find a man who loved me as much as I loved him—one who'd love Montana's mountains and plains as I do. I dreamed of having his babies and of teaching our children, as my parents taught me. I would close my eyes and picture those kids as if they were real—and me showing them the red berries of the asparagus in the autumn, or hunting fresh-water mussel shells along a trout creek. Little things . . . important things."

Jim eased into a sitting position. He saw the tears in Pepper's eyes. What remained unsaid was that John Freedman had been the man meant to fulfill those dreams. "You'd make a good mother," he said in a low voice filled with emotion. "You're like a kid yourself in some ways." He smiled a little. "That's one of the many things I've come to like about you, Pepper—you're completely adult when you have to be, but there's also a kid inside you that never grew up. I think that's great."

Shaken by the grittiness of Jim's voice, Pepper stared at him. He was so close, mere inches away, and she could feel the heat throbbing between them. The burning look in his eyes rushed through her, making her aware of herself as a woman in every way. The thought that Jim would be a wonderful father himself flashed through her head, and Pepper quickly looked away, afraid he might see a yearning in her eyes. If he did, she'd be mortified. Still, she longed to reach out and tenderly touch his face, though the shadow of his growing beard and the streaked remains of his camouflage paint made him look even more dangerous. What would it be like to kiss his firm mouth again—to feel his powerful form against her heat and need? She ached to reach out and slide her hand across his chest, to absorb his strength. His wonderful half smile tore through her, beckoning to her, and Pepper literally had to stop herself from leaning forward . . . to meet his mouth and melt against him.

Was she going crazy because of the pressure they were under? Pepper sighed and tried to get a handle on her escaping emotions. Sitting here talking with Jim was opening up her heart in a way she'd thought would never happen again. Clearing her throat, she said, "Fair's fair. Tell me about your dreams."

He chuckled. "They're as pedestrian as yours, Pepper. I want a woman who will love me, warts and all. I want a couple of kids, too. I dream of finding a woman who likes to laugh, who can find humor in even the worst situation. I grew up in a pretty somber family, and I'm afraid I was the joker—the guy who was always playing tricks and then catching hell for it."

Pepper's eyes rounded. "You?"

"Yeah, sure. Why not?"

His grin was devilish, and in that moment, Pepper caught a glimpse of the original Jim Woodward—before the Marine Corps had shaped him to meet their exacting standards. "So, you're a joker?"

"Every chance I get." With a laugh, he said, "Not that I get much chance at the Pentagon. It's one place where you have to watch your every move. There's always someone with a lot more rank watching you—ready to mark you down."

"So when you have a field command, you're different?"

"You bet I am," he exclaimed. Looking up at her he found his gaze caught by her parted lips. Damn, but he wanted to kiss her again. Jim knew she was a woman very much in touch with her needs. She lived too close to nature not to be in tune with herself on those levels. What was it he could see in her eyes? Desire? Longing? Or was that just wishful thinking on his part?

Hope coursed through him as his gaze continued to probe hers. She was a woman of incredible strengths and courage—the kind of woman he'd been looking for all his life, he thought suddenly. The discovery sent a sheet of heat through him, radiating from his heart. Pepper was as natural as the timeless cycles of the seasons. She had no pretenses; what you saw was what you got.

But even as those thoughts crowded into his mind and heart, reality drenched him. They were sitting in a jungle on foreign soil. Interlopers. The government of Nevis would not be informed of their mission until after Laura was rescued—if she could be rescued. And what made him think he would survive this mission? Or that Pepper would? The threat of death was strong. Jim knew Garcia's guards would kill without a second thought; they'd pull the trigger first and ask questions later. He also was positive that Garcia was on alert, knowing full well that Perseus would attempt to rescue Laura.

"When I was a little girl," Pepper said softly, her voice sounding as if it came from far away, "I used to sit by the trout stream on our property. I had a favorite rock that was large, round and flat. I'd sit there, shaded by the trees and brush, and watch the rainbow and cutthroat trout flash by in the water. I loved the rainbow trout, because when the sunlight caught them, they really lived up to their name. I'd just sit and watch, my legs crossed, my elbows on my knees and my chin cupped in my hands.

"I'd wonder what my life was going to be like after I grew up. What I'd be someday. I used to daydream for hours, trying to imagine myself as an adult and what I'd look like. Then—" her mouth curved gently "—I imagined my children. I saw the color of their hair, their faces, the color of their eyes. I imagined each of their personalities and how much fun I would have with them.

"I saw this two-story white house with a green roof and a white picket fence around it, too." She laughed a little. "Actually, it was an exact replica of my folks' place. Every summer Cam and I would get out there and paint that picket fence. And we'd help dad on the roof when it needed new shingles. Mom would plant bright red geraniums, and I always thought it looked like Christmas in summer with the house's green trim and the red flowers.

"I guess I'm really pretty simple, Jim. I don't want much. I don't need much. I just needed a man who would love me and respect me for what I was—and what I wasn't. I wanted him to be as excited as I was about bringing a bunch of mop-haired children into the world, growing with them and loving them." She turned, gazing down at Jim's thoughtful expression. "Sometimes there's an ache in my heart when I remember those dreams," she admitted. "I'm old enough now to realize it won't happen that way."

Jim slowly sat up and faced Pepper. He slid his left hand over hers and held it gently. "Don't ever stop dreaming, sweetheart. They're good dreams. Dreams that deserve to be lived out."

The tingling heat that spread from her hand up her arm set her heart pounding. Looking deep into Jim's darkened eyes, Pepper saw the desire burning there. His hand was at once strong and gentle as he held hers. Perhaps it was the roughened quality of his voice that tore at her the most, making her long for what she knew could never be hers.

Without thinking, she found herself leaning toward him. And almost simultaneously, she saw Jim coming forward to meet her. His grip on her hand tightened, her breath snagged as he bent his head and she drowned in his suddenly stormy green eyes. Her eyelashes swept downward. Never had Pepper wanted so badly to be kissed. Her lips parting, she raised her hand to his shoulder and tilted her chin just enough to meet his descending mouth.

Pepper's world spun dizzily as Jim's lips touched, met and claimed hers with a strength that threw her off guard. His mouth was molten, searching. With a small groan, she submitted to his quest, molding herself against him. She felt the prickle of his beard against her cheek and absorbed the plundering strength of his mouth as she was swept into a river of fire, no longer aware of anything but him—his masculinity, his power.

His mouth moved effortlessly across hers, seeking, tasting and deepening its exploration of her as a woman. She felt his agged breath against her cheek, pressed herself to his broad chest, her hand sliding up and around his neck. She could feel his heart pounding as hard as hers was, and their breathing seemed to synchronize magically as she opened her mouth to his onslaught. The fragrance of the island flowers and their own natural scents enhanced the euphoria that flowed through her. She felt Jim release her hand, and in the next instant felt his palm against her cheek, tilting her head back even farther, tasting her deeply.

A knot of heat unfolded within Pepper, spreading through her lower body, crying for fulfillment. As Jim's fingers tunneled through the damp, curly hair at her temple, she felt tears of joy coming to her closed eyes. His mouth was at once cajoling and tender now as the overwhelming power of his kiss gentled, and she felt his tongue trace the outline of her lower lip, awakening an ache of pure longing. Never had she been kissed like this, and hungrily she absorbed the amazing sensations his touch evoked.

His hand moved away from her jaw, skimming the slenderness of her neck, sending prickles of fire racing through her. A softened moan was torn from her as his hand ranged farther, finding and cupping the round ripeness of her breast. Despite the rough utilities she wore, she felt his fingers caress her as through the finest silk. Her skin tightened to a painful intensity, and Pepper pressed herself shamelessly forward into his open hand. Her breathing became chaotic as his searching fingers slipped beneath the fabric. Her own fingers opening and closing spasmodically against his taut shoulders, she felt the delicious sensations as he grazed her breast, his thumb feathering across her hardened nipple and sending a keening need through her.

Pepper became lost in a host of plunging, deepening responses as she felt him shift her, bring her more fully into his arms, his hand tugging impatiently at her clothing, to open it more and expose her breasts. His mouth remained strongly on hers, taking even as she gave as never before with her breath, her body, her heart. Somewhere in her spinning senses, she realized this fire that burned so hotly out of control was more powerful and threatening than any forest fire she'd faced. The

white-hot need consumed her as his hand fully captured he
breast, his touch tentative, as if she were some priceless, frag
ile treasure. A treasure to cherish. . . .

An overwhelming fear slammed into Pepper. What was sh
doing? Why was she allowing Jim to touch her, to take her? He
emotions cartwheeled as her reawakened mind screamed tha
he loved Laura, not her. Tearing her mouth from his, she pulle
away. How desperately she wanted to stay in his arms, to con
tinue accepting his caresses. She opened her eyes and looked u
into his stormy, slitted ones, which now studied her with blaz
ing passion. That stare made her freeze with the realization tha
his hunger equaled her own—only she was the one runnin
away. What was she running from? Bitterly, Pepper admitte
she knew the answer to that one. Every particle of her bein
screamed out for the feel of Jim's mouth on hers, for his hand
roving across her, inciting her, teasing her, fulfilling her. He
gaze clung to his mouth—to that powerful male mouth that ha
made her lose all sense of time, direction and rational sense
Her world had narrowed to the breaths of air they'd shared, hi
mouth conquering hers, his hands scorching her, awakening he
to a frenzied awareness of her needs as a woman. Never ha
Pepper felt like this. John's touches and kisses paled in com
parison. Frightened by that knowledge, she simply stared at Jir
in the drawn silence.

Shaken, Jim sat back, breathing hard. What the hell had h
just done? Fear, curiosity and desire were mirrored in Pep
per's widened, lustrous eyes as she stared at him, her lips glis
tening and well kissed. He raised his left hand and wiped hi
mouth with the back of it. How could he have allowed his de
sire for Pepper to overwhelm any rational thought? He'd nearl
taken her. He'd come so close. The painful knotting sensatio
in his lower body cleared his mind. He had to think! They wer
on a dangerous mission. What business did he have puttin
them in jeopardy by kissing her, allowing his emotions to tak
over? None. Absolutely none. But no one compared to Pep
per, he admitted at the same time. No one. She'd met him o
equal ground in a way that had been startling as well as grati
fying. Her strength seemed to emanate from an endless well o
femininity he'd never realized existed.

Unexpected tears slipped from beneath Pepper's lashes. Blinking, she continued to look dazedly up at him. His own eyes burned with a newfound tenderness as he lifted his hand, stopped its motion toward her, then hesitantly stroked her cheek with trembling fingers.

"Tears?" he rasped, as he touched their silvery path down her cheeks. Why was she crying? Had he hurt her in his overwhelming desire to take her?

With a choking sound, Pepper eased back and wiped them away. "It's nothing...." she answered in a hoarse whisper.

Jim looked at her intently. "Sure it is, sweetheart. What is it? What made you cry?"

Still dizzied by his branding kiss and the fire his touch had brought to a blaze within her, Pepper tried to look away from the desire she continued to read in his eyes. If only that desire were really for her. She certainly didn't hold any ill will for Laura. The woman probably didn't even realize Jim still carried a torch for her. Despite the passion in Jim's kiss, Pepper couldn't help but believe he'd kissed her in lieu of Laura. Her mind whirling with the tortured observations, Pepper finally tore her gaze from his. How could she tell him her tears were due to the realization that he could never love her—that his heart had already been captured?

She turned away. She had to lie, and she hated herself for it. The truth was she'd enjoyed their exploration of each other. "Don't mind me," she said, her voice strained. "I cry over everything. If you don't believe me, ask my team. I cry when someone gets hurt. I cry at weddings. I cry when babies are born. It's just me, Jim, that's all."

Jim frowned, feeling real frustration. Pepper had turned away, so he could barely see her face. She was embarrassed. Why? Because he'd kissed her? Cursing silently, he admitted that he'd overstepped his bounds. And what a hell of a situation to be in. He could still taste her on his lips. The kiss had been fusing, stirring the deepest parts of himself to such vibrant, throbbing life that he'd barely been in control of his actions.

Jim knew Pepper hadn't answered him honestly about her tears, but he didn't know what to do about it. This mission was all tangled up with Laura, and his heart told him to back off to have patience and wait. In time, Pepper's reason for tear would be revealed. A part of him still wanted to take her her and now, knowing she was capable of loving him as hotly as h wanted to love her.

What was wrong with him? He'd lost his focus. His reality With a shake of his head, he reminded himself that that wa how powerfully Pepper influenced him by her simple, quie presence. He would never forget the word pictures she'd painte for him of her dreams as a little girl. More than anything, h wanted to ask her about those children she'd dreamed of s vividly. What color was their hair? Were there any with greer eyes like his own? Or black hair? The ache in his throat inten sified, and he turned toward Pepper, wanting to speak.

The sad line of her mouth stopped him. She was sitting apar from him, her arms again wrapped tightly around her drawn up knees. Her tears were gone, and Jim wondered what it ha taken for her to jam them back inside. He hadn't realized hov easily touched Pepper was until now, and it was an exquisit discovery.

"If we were home, back at my condo," he said, his voic rough with emotion as he caught her startled gaze, "you and would have a long, heart-to-heart talk. Your tears aren' something to be ignored, Pepper. I care enough for you to wan to know what brought them on...."

Chapter Eight

The inky night gave Pepper some relief. After Jim's hot, startling kiss, she had withdrawn deeply into herself. How was she going to manage to stay at arm's length from him? She'd done it with every other man since John had died. How had Jim so easily scaled her barriers? She was thoroughly confused. What did it mean, that he could kiss her like that? She still had no doubts that he loved Laura. She'd seen his eyes take on the darkness of worry as the daylight had waned. Of course, she was worried for Laura, too. She didn't wish for any woman to be in Garcia's clutches. But Jim's responses had once again grown cooler, more disconnected.

As she knelt in the jungle overlooking the fortress, the darkness complete, Pepper knew she had to shove her vibrant feelings toward Jim aside once and for all. The sadness she felt at the thought of never truly getting to know him brought tears to her eyes, but she fought them back. If they could reach Laura and release her, Pepper knew Jim would gravitate back to the woman without question. And whatever wonderful things had sprung up between him and Pepper on this mission would dis-

solve into the halls of his memory. But she was afraid she
wouldn't so easily be able to relegate her recent emotions to the
past tense, no matter what she did.

From where they knelt, their packs propped nearby so they'd
be unhampered, Pepper and Jim timed the movements of the
guards. Luckily, they were upwind of these men and the large,
savage-looking Doberman pinschers that walked at their sides
on long, thick leather leashes. The map of Garcia's plantation
was firmly etched in Pepper's mind. In another few minutes,
she would begin spreading the pheromone substance along the
wrought-iron fence, away from the area where they wanted to
breach it. Luckily the ten-foot barrier was just that. Garcia had
put up an ornate fence, seemingly more for show than for actual protection, Pepper thought. There were no spikes or con-
certina wire, atop it, of the type that could easily cut an intruder
to the bone.

Her eyes were well adjusted to the darkness, only vaguely
brightened here and there by the quarter moon's light. It was
perfect—enough light to work in, but not enough to give them
away. Still, they'd reapplied their greasepaint to make sure no
hint of pale skin might reflect the watery moonlight. As much
as Pepper tried to ignore Jim's powerful presence, she couldn't.
She felt his tension and tasted her own. Soon they would scale
the fence, with only side arms and knives to protect them.
Pepper shivered. She hoped she didn't have to use either one.
Right now, her entire focus had to be on getting to the white
plantation house with its dark red trim. The red-tile, Spanish-
style roof gave it an odd look as far as Pepper was concerned,
creating a sort of hybrid between Spanish and Southern-
plantation design. Four huge white columns supported a
wooden porch roof and every twenty minutes a heavyset guard
with a Doberman passed by the south doors, where she and Jim
planned to enter.

The night was warm and humid, and the stars had long since
disappeared under approaching clouds. Pepper remembered the
chance of a hurricane building south of the Windward Islands. She wondered if it would rain. The air seemed heavy,
almost pregnant with moisture. Rain would be something they
hadn't counted on, but it was a natural defense for any in-

truder, hiding noise and wiping out scents and footprints. Pepper almost wished it would start raining now.

Jim glanced over at Pepper. She was still and alert, her eyes intent on the fence line. His heart felt as if it were on fire with the need to talk at length with her. Their kiss had rocked his world—his soul. How badly he wanted to impart that to her, but he'd watched her retreat within herself. And he knew why: Captain John Freedman. Though he'd tried to initiate some talk, he had been cut off when some locals had come by, fishing lines in hand, heading for a nearby creek to catch some fish.

Jim had been frustrated, as the rest of their day had been devoted to getting to Garcia's fortress without detection, then to timing the guards' movements. Using long-range binoculars, they'd sat for hours marking down the times and memorizing them. In a way, he was glad they'd had a chance to acquaint themselves with the way Garcia's world ebbed and flowed. It would definitely work to their advantage.

Jim's mind swung to Laura, then back to dwell momentarily on his kiss with Pepper. He'd seen the desire in her wonderful blue eyes—and the tears. Why tears? That had eaten at him nonstop all day. He swore to himself that once they were safe, he would corral Pepper on that very subject, and they would have a long, in-depth talk, whether she liked it or not. Did she think he was one of those men who took and ran? he wondered with disgust, then caught himself. After all, wasn't he? Right now he wasn't at all sure of what might exist between him and Laura.

Scowling at his own confusion, he looked down at the dials of his watch. It was 0200. Time to spread the pheromone. Pepper had volunteered to do it. He would stay, watch and, if necessary, speak to her in a low tone through the headset to alert her of any unanticipated guard activity. So far, everything on the plantation seemed to occur in twenty-minute increments, and Pepper would use that time gap to spread the pheromones away from the area where they wanted to climb the fence. Jim wondered how his arm would handle the physical demands to come. At least Pepper had done a good job of binding the wound tightly so it wouldn't break open and start bleeding.

Jim gave Pepper a hand signal. She nodded, her mouth a tight line as she slowly rose and straightened. With her camouflage utilities and greasepaint, she blended perfectly into the surrounding jungle. The pheromones, Jim knew, were in unbreakable vials in the cartridge belt around her waist.

At the last second, as Pepper carefully stepped by Jim, she felt his hand grip hers. Halting, she stared down at him, shocked by his action. His hand was strong, grasping hers almost painfully. She met his burning, narrowed gaze and swallowed convulsively. She couldn't deny the look in his eyes or the expression on his face. Verbal communication was out at this point, except in dire emergency. But everything about Jim's expression said, "Be careful." Pepper nodded and tried to smile, but didn't succeed. Instantly, he released her hand, a satisfied look replacing his searching one.

Her heart pounding hard, Pepper made her way down the easy slope. Though shaken by Jim's unexpected touch, she tried to shove the feeling aside and concentrate on each step she took. Luckily, the brush and trees had been cleared away from the fence, so it was easy to move along it once she arrived at the bottom of the slope. Digging into her cartridge pouch, as quietly as she could, she took out the first container. Moving quickly, avoiding a few small branches, she began spreading the pheromone, placing a drop here and a drop there in an unmistakable path. She knew she had twenty minutes to cover the fence line up to its northernmost point.

Trying to control her ragged breathing, her eyes riveted on each place she set her boots, Pepper continued distributing the scent. Soon she knew she was out of sight of Jim, but somehow she could feel his presence as surely as if he was at her side. It was an incredible feeling, one that gave her confidence to rival her fear, though she knew that one misstep could bring the guards' fire. She could die here.

Jim waited anxiously, his only contact with Pepper the sound of her soft breathing via the headset. He had worried that she might break a branch and cause a snapping sound, but she didn't. An incredible sense of relief overwhelmed him when he saw her move like a shadow back to his position. Sweat glistened on her brow. The humidity was near saturation, and rain was imminent.

Reaching out, Jim gripped Pepper's arm and offered a tight, swift smile to convey his relief, and his pride in her efforts. She reached out, briefly touching his shoulder in acknowledgment, then moved to his side, waiting.

The guard appeared, right on time. Pepper watched with fascination as the Doberman with him picked up the scent of the pheromone. Instantly the big black-and-brown male lunged sharply against his leash—in the direction of the pheromone. Pepper felt like a statue, watching with her eyes, controlling her breathing, not moving a muscle. The guard and his dog headed north. Pepper could see the quizzical look on the guard's face but was relieved to observe he was willing to let the dog follow the scent.

Five minutes passed, and Jim gave the hand signal to move out. The fence was their next challenge, but with Jim at her side, Pepper felt a bizarre sense of confidence. They moved slowly, deliberately, their eyes and ears keyed. A breeze startled the palms, which began to clack noisily. The unexpected sound made Pepper's pulse jump, and she touched her chest in reaction. Jim moved ahead, a mere shadow in the night. She admired his stealth as he approached the fence. But would he be able to scale it with his injured arm?

Despite the fence's imposing height, Pepper saw Jim grab the solid iron bars and hoist himself upward. He groaned softly and stopped. Pepper moved into position beneath his feet, bending over so her back became a platform. When his boots made contact, she grabbed a bar to steady herself. She heard Jim choke back a sharp sound as he made a final lunge, pushing hard against her back. She glanced up to see that he'd made it up and over the fence. Getting down would be easier than hoisting himself up.

As Jim eased himself to the ground, Pepper could see the pain in every line of his face. Her gaze automatically went to his arm, covered by the torn sleeve of his utilities. Had the wound opened? If it had, the bleeding could begin again, and the scent of blood might alert one of the dogs. As she worried, Jim gave her the hand signal to scale the fence.

Pepper found the iron barrier fairly easy to climb, so she concentrated on remaining noiseless. Jim's hands wrapped firmly around her waist as she slid down on his side of the fence. But as soon as her feet touched the ground, he eased his hands away, and she felt bereft. Did he realize just how much she needed his touch? Pepper glanced up at his shadowed face and found care and anxiety in his eyes. For her? She doubted it, knowing how he felt about Laura, who could soon be within reach.

Pepper and Jim remained close together as they headed into the heavy jungle cover, making their way along the quarter-mile route to the plantation. Luckily, although street lamps lined the white gravel road leading to the house, few lights were placed elsewhere. Jim thought Garcia's arrogance might have given him an exaggerated sense of safety, so that he hadn't lighted up his house. Lucky for them.

Jim's every sense was excruciatingly heightened as he led Pepper through the maze of brush and trees toward the house. The breeze began again, rattling the hundreds of swaying palms growing among the rubber trees. He tensed as he spotted a guard moving slowly past the front of the plantation. Feeling Pepper's light touch on his shoulder, he glanced to his left and saw her glistening features and the fear in her eyes. He understood that fear. They had exactly half an hour to slip inside that house, locate Laura and get her out.

So many questions reeled through Jim's mind. What if Garcia had forced Laura to sleep with him? Then the drug lord would have to be disabled. A blinding, hot anger rose in Jim, and he knew without a doubt he could happily take out the bastard with a shot to the head, if he'd touched Laura.

A sharp, cracking sound emanated from the right. Jim froze, his hand automatically going to his Beretta. The wind had risen, gusting sharply, and the smell of rain surrounded them. He watched as the guard halted, turned and looked in their direction. A limb of a rubber tree fell with a *thunk* no more than a hundred feet from their position. Jim's heart rate skyrocketed, but he didn't move a muscle. The guard started toward them.

Pepper's eyes rounded as she saw the guard move. Oh, no! Luckily, the wind was still in their favor, so the dog with him wouldn't scent them. A second strong gust of wind made another branch crack and give way—on the other side of the house. The guard stopped and looked in that direction. With a shrug, he pulled his guard dog back and continued his normal path around the house.

Pepper closed her eyes, pressing her hand against her heart, which felt like a drum threatening to beat right out of her chest. She felt Jim relax and glanced at him. He was wiping sweat from his upper lip, his eyes remaining narrowed and watchful. She felt suddenly shaky and realized it was the aftermath of an adrenaline surge. Locking her knees, she stood very still, concentrating on not making a sound.

They moved closer. The southern entrance to the plantation was supposed to lead to the kitchen. They moved to that side of the house, protected by the darkness, and moved swiftly toward the door. The information they had from the CIA mole laundress had indicated that the kitchen entrance was the only one with no laser beams or warning device attached to it, because of heavy traffic in and out that door during the day and into the evening.

Let it still be so, Pepper prayed. She saw Jim reach out, his gloved hand almost caressing the brass knob. Tensing, she waited. Her breath jammed. Her eyes narrowed. Jim slowly twisted the knob. The door opened! Pepper expelled her breath in a relieved sigh.

Miraculously, she found herself inside the darkened kitchen with Jim, who shut the door as quietly as he'd opened it. Looking around, she realized the room was set up like a restaurant kitchen, with huge pots and pans hanging over commercial appliances. Everything was stainless steel, clean and glinting dully in the pale moonlight. Trying to steady her breathing, Pepper followed Jim across the tiled expanse. So far, so good.

Their plan was to take the kitchen stairs to the second floor sleeping area. But were guards stationed inside the house? They didn't know. Pepper watched as Jim drew his Beretta and held it ready in his left hand. Their weapons had muzzle suppres-

sors and silencers, so if they did have to fire, there'd be less
chance of detection.

She drew her own weapon, locked and loaded it, and held it
ready in an upraised position in her right hand. The door leading out of the kitchen revealed a sliver of dimly lighted, carpeted hallway. Seeing no one, Jim pushed on the door. It
squeaked. Pepper froze. Jim eased it open just enough for them
to slip through. Watching the hall, the silence in the house
deafening, Pepper moved toward the stairs.

Luckily, they were carpeted, too, but the two of them climbed
slowly, listening for telltale creaks. At the top, they faced another door. This time Pepper took out a small can of oil and
applied it to the hinges. As she stuffed the container back into
her web gear, Jim nodded his agreement. He got down on one
knee and slowly eased the door open. The expanse of carpeted
hall, lined with valuable paintings, was blessedly empty.

In his mind, Jim visualized the blueprint of the second floor.
As he moved soundlessly through the doorway, pressing his
back against the opposite wall, his gun held ready, he knew that
the second door was the one they'd tagged as most likely to be
Laura's room. What if it wasn't? What if— He savagely
stopped himself. First things first. Try the second door, the
prison room.

Pepper joined him, and they inched toward the door. Once
there, Jim tried the knob. It was locked. Sweat poured down his
body. Outside, he heard the wind rising and the first pings of
rain on the roof tiles. Good, it would provide excellent cover—
if they could find Laura and escape. His breathing was chaotic
as he bent down and, ignoring the pain in his arm, jimmied the
lock. He heard a distinct click and froze. The sound might
waken whoever was inside. He prayed it was Laura.

Pepper swallowed hard against a dry throat. Raising her
weapon, she watched Jim straighten. His gloved hand moved
to the knob. He twisted it. The door opened! Her heart rate
skyrocketing, she kept her focus on the door. Would it creak?
Awaken the person inside? Give their position away? Her hands
tightened around the butt of her weapon.

The door swung open easily. Moonlight streamed into the
room, and Jim saw filmy curtains over windows covered by

bars. He slipped into the chamber, every muscle in his body rigid with anticipation. Pepper entered behind him quietly closing the door. Straining to see, he spotted a canopied bed to the right, and his breath caught. Someone was in the bed, all but a twisted sheet thrown aside against the muggy night.

Pepper remained at the door as a guard, watching him move soundlessly toward the bed and its occupant.

Jim moved slowly up beside the bed. His eyes widened. A lock of blond hair spilled across the sheet. It had to be Laura! He'd recognize that color anywhere. Holstering his weapon, he leaned closer. It was Laura! She lay with her back to them, curled tightly, the sheet up over her shoulders. How beautiful and untouched she looked, Jim thought as he swiftly placed one hand on her shoulder and the other across her mouth.

Laura jerked. Her eyes flew open. Instantly, she convulsed, terror in her expression.

"Ssh! Laura, it's Jim Woodward!" he hissed, his mouth close to her face. She struggled momentarily and he saw the horror in her eyes, felt dreadfully sorry he had to waken her like this. It took a moment for his words to filter through her panic. Then she stopped struggling. The sheet had fallen away, revealing her slender form covered by a long, pink-silk nightgown. Easing his hand from her mouth, he smiled a little.

"Are you okay?" Jim wasn't sure she was. Her eyes didn't look quite right, he thought, and her skin felt clammy.

Laura sat up, fear etched in her expression. She looked at Jim and then toward Pepper, in shadows near the door. Automatically, her hand went to her lips.

"Jim? Is it you?" Her voice trembled. "Oh, God, am I hallucinating again?"

He grinned tightly. "It's me, Tiger. And we're no hallucination. This is real. We're real. We've come to get you out of here." He touched her tousled hair, then her cheek, with trembling fingers. His heart flared with anguish. "Are you okay? Are you hurt?"

Tears welled up in Laura's eyes and streamed down her cheeks. "Jim, it's really you," she quavered. Awkwardly, she threw her arms around his shoulders.

Groaning, he held her momentarily. They didn't have time for this. "Laura, listen to me," he urged in a low, ragged tone, "you've got to get dressed." His eyes darted to his watch. "We've got twelve minutes before the guard comes around again. Can you walk? Are you hurt?" he repeated.

Laura sniffed, fighting tears. "Y-yes, I'll live." She climbed out of bed, obviously shaken and uncoordinated.

"Get some clothes on," Jim coaxed. He watched her closely. Something was wrong with her. He saw it in the jerky way she opened the drawer, in the terror-filled look in her eyes. The moonlight illuminated bruises on her arms and around her throat. Just what the hell had happened to her? He stopped the questions before he could voice them. Glancing at Pepper, he motioned her over.

Pepper moved swiftly to Jim's side, holstering her weapon.

"Help her get dressed. I'll stand guard at the door," he ordered gruffly.

She nodded. For the first time, she got to meet the woman Jim loved without question. Laura was petite in comparison to her, and Pepper quickly saw how Jim could fall in love with her. In person, Laura Trayhern was beautiful in a delicate, almost-fragile way. Her blond hair, disheveled but still lovely, fell around her face, and her cheeks were flushed pink. But the woman was so obviously shaken that the slacks she'd retrieved from the dresser fell to the floor.

Pepper quickly retrieved them and handed them to her.

"Thanks," Laura quavered.

Holding her finger to her lips to warn her not to speak, Pepper saw the woman nod shakily that she understood the silent command. Pepper forced herself to listen for other sounds. The rain was pinging sharply against the windows of the room now, and the wind continued to rise. Good. All of that was to their advantage. Laura was trying to hurry, but she fumbled with her clothes. Pepper grabbed a green tank top, helped Laura pull off the silk gown and threw it aside. Completely naked, Laura reached for the slacks.

Pepper glanced over her shoulder. Jim wasn't looking. All his attention was on the door and the dangerous possibilities on the other side of it. Returning her attention to Laura, Pepper again could see why Jim would like her. Despite having had two children, the woman was in wonderful shape. Climbing into the slacks, Laura took the tank top from Pepper, pulled on a pair of cotton socks and slid into a sensible pair of leather shoes that Pepper had found in the walk-in closet.

Jim glanced at them. Nine minutes; it was going to be close. Maybe too close. As he opened the door, he felt Laura come up behind him, her hand tentatively touching his shoulder. Pepper would bring up the rear. Opening the door, he looked both ways. Nothing. He moved in one swift motion across the hall to the stairway door. Laura followed unsteadily. Shoving that door open, Jim moved sideways, and Laura joined him in the stairwell. Pepper? He anxiously looked back toward the hall. She was locking the door. *Hurry!* he urged silently.

Pepper turned on her heel and moved quickly to the door he held open for her. She saw the anxiety in Jim's eyes, and her gaze automatically went to Laura, who stood with her arms wrapped protectively around herself. She was physically trembling, and she didn't look very steady on her legs. There was more light here, and Pepper could see an oddly waxen quality to her skin, and dark, almost-purple circles beneath her lovely eyes. What kind of torture had she endured? Pepper found her anger surging as she reached out and slid her arm around Laura in support as they made their way down the stairs.

After checking the downstairs hall, they slipped back into the kitchen. Eight minutes. Again Jim took the lead, opening the door to the yard. A gust of wind almost ripped it out of his hand. Cursing inwardly, he used his body to hold it in place, after making sure no guards were around. With his injured arm, he signaled Pepper sharply to come on through.

The rain was falling with stinging force, the wind gusting and ebbing. Pepper kept an arm around Laura as she watched Jim move rapidly toward the rear of the house. Seven more minutes before the guard came by. Breathing rapidly through her mouth, she felt Laura sag against her suddenly. Alarmed, she turned and saw that the woman was semiconscious. With a strangled sound, Pepper again holstered her weapon and grabbed Laura's right arm, pulling it up over her shoulders. She

moved her own left arm snugly around her small waist an
hitched the woman close against her.

Jim signaled for them to follow him. Luckily, Laura was
featherweight, Pepper thought as she half dragged, half car
ried her across the lawn to the jungle. Once under cover of th
trees, she relaxed a little. Still, Laura's feet were dragging
making noise.

Jim turned at the sound and realized Laura had fainted
Pepper was practically dragging her. Damn! Was Laur
drugged? Hurt? Moving back to them, he quickly examine
her, discovering several needle marks on both of her arms
Alarm soared through him.

"She's been drugged," he rasped, his voice shaking wit
fury.

"I'll carry her."

Jim was about to protest, but realized it would be stupid n
to agree to Pepper's plan. Laura probably weighed less than
hundred and ten pounds soaking wet, but he couldn't carry he
with his injured arm. He nodded brusquely, signalling that he'
help Pepper lift her over her shoulders in a fireman's-carry po
sition.

Pepper lowered herself to one knee, knowing that that pos
tion was the easiest and safest way to carry a person, putting th
bulk of their weight across the strength of the carrier's shou
ders. But how long could she actually carry Laura? she wor
dered. There was a vast difference between lugging sixty-poun
packs and hefting a live human weighing more than a hundre
pounds. Still, she had no choice. She was grateful when Ji
helped maneuver Laura's limp body expertly across her shou
ders. Now it was up to her.

The wind was strong, slapping at them, and rain slashed
Pepper's face as she slowly got to her feet. Time was of the e
sence. She knew that a Coast Guard helicopter, flown by
woman lieutenant commander named Storm Gallagher, woul
meet them on the beach at exactly 0400. It was now 0325. The
had to hurry. They hadn't counted on Laura being injured.

As Pepper began to walk with her burden, Jim stayed next
her. The wind and rain covered her mistakes as she move
awkwardly forward. The cold rain fell in sheets, and Peppe

shivered despite the heat she was generating with the effort of carrying Laura. Rain dribbled down her face, blinding her, and if it hadn't been for Jim's guiding hand gripping her elbow, Pepper knew she would have fallen.

The fence! Pepper was never so glad to see anything in her life. As they lowered her to the ground, Laura became semiconscious again. Jim moved around and took her in his arms.

"Laura!" he growled. "Laura, wake up!"

Pepper knelt nearby, seeing the anxiety and care burning in Jim's eyes as he spoke. He touched Laura gently, almost like a lover, and it hurt Pepper to her soul. She had been right, after all. Jim loved Laura—still. Pepper tasted salt and realized it was her own tears.

Laura sat up, encircled by Jim's arms. "I'm so groggy," she whispered, touching her brow. "I—I'm sorry. I can hardly think, hardly walk...."

"I know, Tiger, I know. Look, we need you awake. We have to climb this fence. We can help, but you've got to help us, too. Do you think you can do it?"

Laura shivered. "I'm so cold, Jim. And I'm dizzy."

"I understand, honey. But you have to help us. Can you?"

She nodded, her hair tangled and dripping around her face. "I'll try, Jim...."

"That's my Tiger," he said, hoisting her to her feet. She was none too steady, but Pepper was there, helping keep her upright. Jim led Laura to the fence and turned to Pepper.

"Let me use your back to get up there. Once I'm on top, help push Laura, and I'll pull her up and over." He grimaced. "Somehow."

Pepper nodded. She made Laura lean against the fence for support as she waited for Jim to get started up the fence. Once he did, she moved into place beneath him. His muddy, booted feet struck her back, but she stayed steady. With one leap, he made it to the top of the fence, and Pepper was glad for her height. She was able not only to maneuver Laura onto the wrought-iron fence, but to push her upward. Jim caught Laura's outstretched arms, and Pepper knew what it cost him in terms of pain to gently lower her to the ground on the other side.

Laura managed to stand when her feet hit earth, and Jim slipped off the top, leaping down beside her. Pepper was next. The wrought iron was slippery from the rain. She knew any minute now the guard could return and catch them. Grunting, she hoisted herself up the fence, her arm and shoulder muscles straining.

A howling bark broke through the rain and wind. Pepper gasped. She heard Jim curse solidly. Scrambling, jerking a glance to her left, she saw the guard—and the dog. The Doberman had been released and was hurtling toward her! Anxiety shot through her. She saw Jim push Laura to the ground and pull out his weapon.

Just as she clambered to the top, gunfire ripped through the dark night. A bullet struck the iron inches from her, and sparks flew in all directions. She saw Jim returning fire, but knew he couldn't aim left-handed, so could offer only temporary cover at best. She had to get off the fence! Adrenaline pumping, Pepper had no choice but to leap. More bullets whined around her. Shoving off, she bent her legs. She hit the muddy ground off-balance. The soil gave way. Tucking, she rolled several times to minimize the force of her landing.

Jim fired again and again keeping the guard pinned down. The Doberman leapt out, snarling, its white fangs bared as it tried to bite at them through the fence. Jerking around, Jim saw Pepper slowly getting to her feet.

"Grab Laura! We've got to make a run for it!"

Pepper spun drunkenly toward them, the carpet of dead leaves turning slippery beneath her boots. She grabbed at Laura, who was already heading toward her. Their hands met, and Pepper shoved her ahead, using her own body as a protective shield for the woman. Her breath came in gulps as they scrambled into the dense, surrounding brush. *Jim!*

Pepper turned momentarily. The firing had stopped. He was hurrying toward them. Good, he wasn't wounded! So many thoughts and feelings careened through Pepper as they climbed the slope of the hill. On the other side was the beach where Commander Gallagher would be picking them up. What time was it? Pepper didn't take even a second to look.

In moments, Jim joined them, gasping loudly from the exertion. He grabbed Laura's other arm, and together they propelled her quickly up the hill. Jim's muscles burned from the exertion. Worriedly, he watched Laura. They were moving too fast for her. Her legs were like rubber. She kept falling, and they could do little more than drag her upright between them. At the crest of the hill he slid his left arm around Laura's waist, and told Pepper to do the same with her right. Together, they could hold Laura firmly enough to prevent her from falling down the slope.

The wind continued gusting, but the rain had stopped. Jim looked back. He thought he heard voices, shouting. He knew the guard had radio communications and was sure the entire fortress was now awake. It wouldn't be long before they were found. They had to hurry! Through the darkness of the trees, he could see the white sand beach. But where was the helicopter?

His mind reeling, Jim realized that if that Coast Guard helicopter didn't arrive exactly on time, they could all be dead. It wouldn't take Garcia long to discover where they were. He heard Laura gasping for breath. Glancing left, he looked at her. She was semiconscious again. Damn! Pepper's face was glistening, her mouth set, her eyes narrowed on their objective. Pride exploded through him for Pepper. What a courageous woman she was. In that moment, he felt such deep, startling emotion that it brought tears to his eyes.

Pepper kept her head, staying cool and calm under some terrible circumstances. Jim expected such a response from himself and from other men under his command, but he realized belatedly that there were women with those necessary ingredients, too. With a shake of his head, he realized how much Pepper was broadening him, awakening him to the huge potential women possessed. Laura's courage was no less impressive, though it came in a different form. She was drugged, maybe beaten, yet she wasn't crying out or hysterical. No, in her own way, she, too, had that bone-deep courage. He felt proud of both of them.

"Look!" Pepper cried, realizing too late that she'd broken the communications silence. Out at sea, she saw the red and green, blinking lights of an aircraft rapidly approaching.

Grinning, Jim nodded. He gave Laura a reassuring squeeze. The slope leveled out, and they hit the white beach at a jog. The sand was thick, sucking, and it slowed them down. But the knowledge that the Dolphin helicopter bearing the white-and-orange colors of the Coast Guard was landing made him dig in and work harder. Pepper did the same.

The wash from the blades kicked up sand everywhere. Bowing his head against its fury, Jim dragged Laura forward. Never had an aircraft looked so good. The door slid open, and a crew member reached toward them. Jim saw the helmeted heads of the two pilots in front. Turning, he released Laura into the capable hands of Dr. Ann Parsons, dressed in a bright orange Coast Guard flight uniform. He glanced back toward the hill. Still no sign of Garcia or his men.

Turning, Jim focused on Pepper, who had helped Laura into the helicopter.

"Get in," he ordered.

She nodded, climbing in swiftly.

Jim was the last to board. As soon as the door was shut and locked, the chopper lifted off smoothly, heading skyward, away from Nevis Island. The cabin lights flashed on and Jim blinked in the sudden brightness.

To his alarm, he saw Dr. Parsons, a helmet on her head, talking rapidly to the pilots. He looked down. Laura was unconscious. Pepper's eyes were wide with fear. Jim frowned. What was going on? He wasn't hooked on the cabin intercom with the pilots and the doctor. His confusion turned to terror as he saw Parsons lift Laura's neck and tip her head back so that she could breathe properly.

"Something's wrong!" Pepper cried.

Jim managed to turn around in the small area. He threw off his own headset and grabbed a pair of headphones patched into the cabin intercom. He moved around until he was on the other side of Laura, opposite the physician.

"What's going on?" he demanded.

Parsons gave him a swift look as she placed her hands on Laura's chest. "She stopped breathing. Do you know CPR?"

Shocked, Jim stared. Laura's face was waxen, her lips parted, her skin so translucent he could see the small veins showing in her eyelids. "I—yes..." *Oh, God, no!* His mind spun as he took a position near her head, ready to breathe life-giving air into her body.

"She's been drugged!" he told the doctor, as she started to press hard and fast on Laura's chest.

"Probably cocaine," Parsons snapped. She turned to the pilots. "Tell them to stand by. I've got a woman with a drug overdose coming in. She's stopped breathing."

"Roger, Doctor," Command Gallagher replied calmly. "We'll alert the *Falcon.*"

Jim bent over, breathing into Laura's slack lips. Of all people, she couldn't die. She just couldn't! Tears leaked into his eyes, ran down his cheeks as he coordinated the CPR with Dr. Parsons. He'd never expected this. Laura couldn't die!

Pepper remained out of the way, an unwilling witness. The vibration of the helicopter warred with her feelings. Jim was crying. In that moment, with Laura's life hanging by a precarious thread, Pepper was stunned by the depth of his emotions. The way he cradled Laura's head, the gentleness of his touch, the wildness in his eyes all confirmed his love for her.

Exhausted and anxious, Pepper could do nothing. She felt ridiculously helpless, but CPR didn't require a third person. Below, the dark ocean kept disappearing behind wispy, low-lying clouds. In the distance, she briefly spotted the lights of a huge Coast Guard cruiser. She prayed for Laura's life. The woman didn't deserve what had happened to her. She looked so fragile, so broken lying on the helicopter's cold, metal deck, her life in the hands of a man who loved her unequivocally, and a doctor whose expression told Pepper she wasn't about to lose her patient.

Chapter Nine

When they'd landed safely on the *Falcon*, Pepper stayed out of the way. She crowded tightly against the bulkhead, allowing a medical team to take Laura off the helicopter. Dawn was barely breaking, a silvery ribbon along the horizon for as far as she could see. Lights flooded the aircraft, making Pepper squint as she crawled out after the others. One of the pilots slid open the small window.

"Hold on, I'll take you down below. They've got officers' quarters waiting for you."

Pepper nodded. The pilot was a woman, and Pepper smiled to herself. It was good to have women in all phases of military life. She watched her disembark after shutting down the aircraft, then followed her across the deck.

Pepper felt incredibly tired and drained. All she wanted was a hot shower and sleep. Her heart was on Laura, though. Would they get her breathing again? Would she live?

"I'm Pepper Sinclair," she said, extending her hand to the woman pilot.

"Storm Gallagher. You look like hell."

"I've been through it."

Gallagher laughed huskily. "Yeah, I know. We monitored your transmissions on the way in. I'll bet Garcia's fit to be tied right now. Serve the bastard right. If that Dolphin I flew came with bombs, I'd dearly love to drop them on him. Come on, we'll go into this hatch."

Pepper followed blindly, barely noticing the activity around her. The roll and pitch of the *Falcon* tipped her off-balance more than once. Waves from the passing storm were three to four feet in height and the sky above them continued to threaten. No sooner had they ducked inside the hatch than the rain began again.

"Where are they taking Laura Trayhern?" she asked as they made their way down a narrow passageway.

"Sick bay. We've got a Coast Guard physician on board in addition to Dr. Parsons. Good thing that woman is an emergency-room specialist. Why do you think Laura stopped breathing?"

Pepper halted when the pilot did in front of a dark brown, mahogany door. "I think she'd been shot up with a drug. Probably cocaine, since that's what Garcia traffics." With a shake of her head, she added, "If she was, I don't know how she managed to get dressed and make it as far as she did before she fainted on us."

Storm nodded gravely. "Adrenaline does wonders."

"You're right." Pepper smiled tiredly at the woman and held out her hand. "Thanks."

Gallagher grinned and shook it firmly. "Any time. I'll let Colonel Woodward know we've taken care of you. I sure hope Mrs. Trayhern makes it. Helluva break. If you get hungry, the chow hall is on Deck Three, just below us."

Pepper nodded, watching Storm move briskly down the narrow passageway. Opening the door to her quarters, Pepper prayed they could get Laura to breathe on her own. An awful feeling in the pit of her stomach refused to leave. Quietly, she closed the door behind her and looked around. The quarters were small, spare but clean. A set of lockers lined the bulkhead, and another door led to the head, where she was sure a shower was located.

With tired movements, Pepper climbed out of her muddy, rain-soaked gear, leaving it in a heap by the door. Every muscle in her body cried out for sleep. Moving slowly, she found the shower stall and turned on the faucets. In no time, steam rolled through the small area and she gratefully stepped in. The water pummeled her, heating her chilled, shaking body, rinsing off the last of the greasepaint from her face.

Pepper recalled how wonderful a shower always felt after she'd been out for days at at time fighting a forest fire. There was nothing like it. This time, instead of cool water, however, she wanted it as hot as she could stand it. The washcloth lathered with soap scrubbed away at the sweat, the mud and the dirt. Her hair became squeaky clean, hanging limply around her face. Finally, she shut off the faucets. The towel was large and thick. Pepper realized her movements were becoming jerky from letdown. The feeling was familiar—she'd experienced it many times after coming out of a raging forest fire where her life had been in jeopardy.

She dragged herself from the bathroom to the small bunk that served as a bed and pulled back the sheet and light blue spread. The rolling of the ship was lulling her now. With a groan, she towel-dried her hair, lacking the strength even to comb out the tangled strands.

Lying down on her side, Pepper pulled the covers tightly across her shoulders. She could no longer hear the rain, only some distant sounds of the large engines that powered the ship. Her last thoughts as she drifted off to sleep were of Jim and the stark terror carved into his features as he bent over Laura on the deck of the helicopter. His eyes had telegraphed a burning anguish—something she'd never seen in them before. Only true love could wrench such emotion from such a controlled man, Pepper suspected. As sleep closed in on her, she said a prayer for Laura's life.

Jim struggled with bone-deep exhaustion coupled with a drowning array of emotions. He sat alone with Laura, his hand on hers. She was waxen and unmoving, but she was alive, thank God. Dr. Parsons had undoubtedly saved her life in the very room where he now sat. Laura's hand felt cold, and he gath

red up her limp fingers, hoping his body heat would somehow transfer itself to her.

His mind was spongy, his feelings clamoring to be acknowledged. As he stared down at Laura's serene features, Jim realized the depth of his caring for and loyalty to her once and for
all. But she was a friend, not a lover. Rubbing his face harshly,
he wearily took in a breath of air. Maybe he'd underestimated
his long-ago feelings for Laura—and maybe he had still been
carrying something of a torch when this mission had started.
But looking at her now, Jim knew for certain that he didn't love
her in the romantic way he'd wondered about.

New feelings crowded his heart now, and they were vibrant
and stunning as he sat, pondering them in the silence. Before,
Jim had attributed them to Laura, thinking they'd been triggered by her unexpected kidnapping. But now he knew differently. The feelings in his heart had been aroused by Pepper
walking into his life.

"You've done all you can," Ann Parsons said wearily,
touching his sagging shoulder.

Jim stirred. He straightened a little in the chair and removed
his hand from Laura's. Parsons' touch reminded him how exhausted he was. His gaze had never left Laura, who was finally breathing on her own again. The two doctors had battled
nearly fifteen minutes to get her heart started.

"I'd rather stay, Doctor."

Ann shook her head. "There's nothing else to be done. We
have her on an IV, Colonel. Her heart is working well. Dr.
Thompson and I will watch her like hawks, believe me. You
need to rest. You look like you're about to fall down."

Wasn't that the truth? "Will she stop breathing again?" he
asked.

"I hope not. But we have no way of knowing how much of
whatever drug was shot into her. The ship has a small lab, and
they're testing her blood right now. I'll know more shortly."

Anger surged through Jim, despite his exhaustion. "I don't
know how she managed to get up and dress herself." He
searched the doctor's blue eyes.

"I don't, either. Sometimes when your life is in danger, you
can override a drug reaction for a while. Laura did. She wanted

to escape, to live." Ann shook her head and rubbed her brow. "There are at least five needle tracks in her arms. Garcia must have had her on drugs from the time he captured her."

Jim clenched his fists. Laura still looked wan, but her skin was no longer gray. Even her hair looked washed out beneath the fluorescent lights of the sick bay. Dr. Thompson, a Coast Guard physician in his late thirties, tended Laura, ever watchful. Jim turned his attention back to Ann.

"Thanks for saving her life, Doctor. I'm glad as hell you were out there to meet us."

She nodded. "You weren't too shabby in the clutch, either, Colonel. Come on, I'll show you to your quarters. They're right next to the ones Pepper was assigned, on Deck Two."

Pepper. Jim halted. He scowled and followed the doctor out of sick bay and down a series of passageways that led to a stairway that would take them topside.

"Does anyone know how she is?" he asked as they climbed the stairs. The ship was rolling fairly heavily now, and he had to grip both railings.

"No. I think I'll check on her," Ann said as they made it to the second deck.

Jim glanced out the hatchway window. The rain was coming down in torrents, and the once-azure Caribbean had turned steely gray, with small whitecaps. He drew abreast of the doctor, who was still dressed in the bright, red-orange flight suit.

"Let me check on her, Doctor."

"No problem. If she needs any medical attention, though, call me?"

"I will." Jim saw her point to a door.

"This is yours for the duration of the trip, Colonel. Pepper's cabin is next door."

"Thanks." He watched the doctor move off and saw Commander Noah Trayhern appear at the other end of the passageway. Since he was captain, he had to stay on the bridge, though Jim was sure he wanted to be down in sick bay watching over Laura. He saw the doctor stop and begin to talk with him.

Still worried about Laura, Jim opened the door to his quarters. As he shed his clothes and took a scaldingly hot shower, he felt the last of the adrenaline ebbing away. He dried off and dropped the towel on the bunk. Someone had left him a one-piece, dark blue Coast Guard uniform, and he climbed into it. First he wanted to look in on Pepper, then he'd go get something to eat, check on Laura, then hit the sack.

Stepping back out into the passageway, Jim felt the ship rolling and balanced himself by placing his hands along the bulkhead as he walked. Stopping at the door to Pepper's cabin, he knocked loudly enough for her to hear, but got no answer. He waited. He knocked again. Nothing. Worried, he opened the door and stepped inside. His mouth stretched into a tender line as he saw Pepper in her bunk, sleeping deeply.

His heart started a slow pounding as he shut the door and made his way over to her. Jim lowered himself to one knee, steadying himself with a hand on the edge of the bunk. How fragile she looked in sleep. Her face was pale, much paler than it should be, he thought. All the usual pink had been washed out of her freckled cheeks. And the darkness beneath her thick, lowered eyelashes was obvious. He lifted his other hand and lightly touched her tangled hair. How he wished he could be here when she woke up, to take a brush and smooth those strong, silken strands.

A sudden memory of their heated kisses flowed through him, momentarily easing his various aches and pains. Barely touching Pepper's hair, careful not to waken her, Jim smiled. She lay on her left side, her knees drawn up, the blanket and sheet tightly wrapped around her. The desire to slide into the bunk with her was almost overwhelming. Right now, he needed Pepper more than he ever could have imagined possible.

Allowing his hand to fall back to his side, Jim slowly got to his feet, convinced Pepper was fine. All she needed was eight to twelve hours of uninterrupted sleep, and she'd be in good shape. Before he left, he picked up her dirty gear and took it with him.

Pepper awoke slowly. Where was she? The sounds were strange. The motion was, too, until she groggily remembered she was on the Coast Guard ship. As she slowly sat up, every muscle in her body screamed in protest. Shoving her hair back out of her eyes, she sat there, assimilating her surroundings. The gentle rocking motion was comforting. As she came fully awake, the memories—the danger—all flooded back.

How was Laura? The question spurred her out of bed. She located a Coast Guard uniform in the locker and put it on. Luckily, she also found the toiletry articles she needed, and quickly combed her tangled hair into some semblance of respectability and brushed her teeth. Pepper didn't look too closely at herself in the mirror. But what she saw, she didn't like. Her skin looked pasty, and dark circles lay under her eyes. Well, didn't she always look like this coming off a five- or ten-day fire?

Her heart moved back to Jim, and the pain nearly overwhelmed her. She had to find out how Laura was. Her stomach growled ominously. Looking around, she found a clock on the desk that was bolted to the deck. Six p.m. Impossible! They had landed on the ship at 0500. Had she slept that long?

Getting directions from a crew member outside her quarters, Pepper headed directly to sick bay. Looking out the round hatch windows, she noted it was dusk. The sky was clear, the ocean smooth as glass. She ignored the dramatic red sunset as she moved stiffly down the stairs that would take her to the lower deck. She prayed Laura wasn't dead.

Pepper entered sick bay, a large room in comparison to her quarters, and a corpsman on duty greeted her.

"Mrs. Trayhern? Is she alive?" she blurted.

"Yes, ma'am."

Relief flooded through her. "Thank God," she whispered, touching her heart. "May I see her?"

"Colonel Woodward is with her right now, ma'am. It's a pretty small area, so it gets a little crowded in there."

Pepper hesitated. Her heart bled at the information. Jim was with Laura. What else had she expected? "Oh, okay..." She felt a sense of anguish, mingled with an odd relief. Why? Was she glad that Jim loved Laura? It was just as well he did love her, she told herself sternly. She must have been crazy, allowing herself to get so emotionally caught up with him in the first place. It had to have been the heat of the mission that had allowed her carefully constructed walls to fall into such shambles—that had allowed her to actually consider the possibility of her relationship with Jim going beyond the professional experience they'd shared. Now it was time to get back to reality, before she lost her heart for good. Pepper frowned, hoping it wasn't too late already.... John's unexpected death had taught her the hard way that her heart could never withstand such pain again. Never again would she surrender to such overwhelming emotion without the balance of rationality.

But why had it been so easy to say no and not get involved romantically with men until now? Pepper had no answers. The corpsman was looking at her strangely, so she tried to appear more alert.

"Dr. Parsons doesn't want Mrs. Trayhern to have too many visitors right now," the corpsman continued placatingly. "Perhaps if you went to the galley for dinner and came back after that?"

"Sure." Pepper's hunger was gone. Tears flooded her eyes and she swallowed. Jim was with Laura. As she quietly shut the sick-bay door, she wanted to sob, but didn't. Why was there so much pain in that realization? After all, John had been her life. Her soul. Her only experience with love.

"How're you feeling, Tiger?" Jim smiled and reached out to grip Laura's hand, which lay across her blanketed body. She looked very weak, her skin still translucent, her eyes cloudy.

"Jim . . . it's so good to see you." Laura cleared her throat, her voice raspy. She tried to squeeze his hand but couldn't muster the strength.

He leaned over and placed a chaste kiss on her brow. "I gotta tell you, you look a little better now than when we found you at the plantation."

"Plantation?"

"Yeah. You remember, don't you? Garcia kidnapped you?"

"Wait . . ."

Mentally, Jim kicked himself. Dr. Parsons had warned him about hitting Laura with too much information too soon. Sometimes cocaine—which they had verified through lab tests was in her bloodstream—could wipe out certain events in a person's memory. He squeezed her hand. "Let me begin at the beginning," he told her quietly. "Stop me if I give you too much information too fast, okay?"

Laura felt chilled. Desperately, she looked up into Jim's face. "I haven't seen you for such a long time. The last time I remember was when we had lunch in Fairfax, at the Bicycle Club."

Relief raced through him. "Yes, that's right, Tiger, we did." He sat down on a chair and faced her. "Do you recall anything of the last couple days, Laura?"

"I . . ." She touched her head. The IV in her arm made it difficult to move. She looked around the room and then back at him. "Something terrible happened, didn't it?" Her voice was tremulous.

Jim stroked her hand in an effort to soothe her. He heard a noise behind him and looked around. Commander Noah Trayhern stood there. He was tired, his face lined with worry and his gray eyes burning with concern. Nodding to him, Jim turned and watched Laura carefully. Would she remember Morgan's brother?

"Laura, how are you?" Noah came around to the other side of the bed. He touched her shoulder and looked at her closely.

"Noah." Laura managed a weak smile. "What are you doing here?"

Noah traded a glance of alarm with Jim.

"Her memory will come back," Jim assured him. "As the drug wears off, everything will come back, from what Dr. Parsons said."

"I see." Noah looked down at Laura. "How are you feeling?"

"Awful. I'm cold."

Jim released her hand. "Let me go ask the corpsman where I can get another blanket for you."

"Thanks," Noah said, his voice filled with raw emotion.

Jim returned a few minutes later with two more blankets. The corpsman had assured him that the chills Laura was experiencing would eventually go away. Together, Jim and Noah tucked the warming covers around her. He was relieved to see some of the cloudiness leaving her eyes. How terrible it would be if the drug erased her memory completely. Laura still hadn't remembered that Morgan and Jason had been kidnapped.

Jim felt he should leave. Laura had an established rapport with Noah; he was much more present in her life than Jim was. Besides, it was obvious Noah was upset over the events. Jim moved to the side of the bed.

"Listen, I'm going to grab some chow, Laura. You're in good hands here with Noah. I'll come back later, and we'll talk, okay?"

Sleepily, she nodded. "Sure. Thanks..."

Jim smiled. "See you later, Tiger." As he left sick bay, he wondered if Pepper had slept off the worst of the mission. He'd gotten some solid sleep, but his worry over Laura's condition had forced him up after six hours.

Going down to the galley, he was surprised to spot Pepper there. She was sitting alone at one of the bolted-down tables, a tray before her with a little food on it. She didn't see him. She seemed immersed in looking down at the coffee cup she held between her thin hands. Jim's heart thumped hard to underscore the vibrant feelings she brought out in him. Her hair was combed, softly framing her face. Color was back in her cheeks, and he breathed a sigh of relief. He went through the chow line, loading his tray with food.

"How are you?"

Pepper's head snapped up. Jim's voice was low, intimate. Her eyes widened as she saw him sit down opposite her. His smile was warm, and his eyes burned with that same caring light.

"Jim..."

"Didn't expect to see me?" he teased, cutting up a pork chop.

"Well—I..."

"How are you feeling?" He saw Pepper's cheeks flush red. She couldn't quite hold his gaze, and he wondered why. Her hands fluttered nervously over the coffee cup.

"Like something the cat dragged in," she muttered under her breath.

He pointed toward her tray with his knife. "Have you eaten anything?"

"No...not much."

Between bites of food, he asked, "is this the way you are after coming off a forest fire?"

Touched by his insight, Pepper dabbled with her meat disinterestedly. She should eat, she knew, but her stomach was tied in a terrible knot of grief. Jim looked unscathed by the mission. His hair was clean and combed, his face freshly shaven. His eyes glinted with their usual intelligence.

"Oh...I'm usually worthless for about two days when we come in from a fire," she admitted finally.

"I never realized the demands on you," he murmured. Why was Pepper so nervous? Her fingers trembled when she picked up her spoon and ate a bit of the canned peaches on her tray. Growing serious, he said in a low tone, "You're an incredible woman. I want you to know that, Pepper." They had shared so much in such a short amount of time. Those kisses that had nearly led him into making love to her still burned brightly in his memory, and his body responded to the thought. Now that he'd freed himself of confusion about his feelings for Laura, his uncertainty about Pepper had cleared up. A desperation to let her know how much she meant to him made him hope for an opportunity to talk with her honestly about so many things.

Pepper shrugged, not daring to meet his eyes. His voice, low and gritty, shone through her like blazing sunlight. "We both pulled our share of the load." She glanced up. "How's your arm?"

"Fine. Once Dr. Parsons got Laura stabilized, she checked it out and gave your work her seal of approval."

"How is Laura?" Pepper picked up her coffee, sipping it, and met his eyes for the first time.

"She's going to make it, thank God." Jim frowned. "The only problem is she doesn't remember anything about the kidnapping. Nothing." With a shake of his head, he muttered, "Noah's down there with her now. I think he'll probably break the news to her about Morgan and Jason."

"At least she's going to live. That's everything. I don't know Noah that well, but he seems so gentle. He's probably the right person to break it to her." Sighing, Pepper looked around the

room. It was beginning to fill up with off-duty crew. The noise
level rose, the laughter in direct opposition to how she felt.

"No disagreement there." Jim saw the shadows in Pepper's
eyes but wrote them off as being due to the mission. "You still
haven't said how you are."

With a shrug, she took a bite of the chicken on her tray.
"Okay."

"I'm discovering that you tend to use that word as a cover-
up."

Pepper stared at him. His voice was low with concern. When
she looked into his eyes, she was instantly wrapped in that incredible warmth he exuded. Her heart squeezed with such pain
that she felt the sting of tears in her eyes. Instantly, she forced
them back.

"Well?" Jim prodded.

"I'm just a little sore, that's all," she hedged, her voice
huskier than usual. "And tired. I'll be glad to get home."

Jim scowled. "Home meaning Montana?" He wanted time
with her, dammit.

"Yes. It's snowing there now. It's a beautiful time of year up
in the mountains."

"I see. . . ."

"I imagine Laura's going to need a lot of emotional support
and help from friends and family to get through all of this,"
Pepper said. "I'm glad she has you."

"Yes, she's going to need help." Dammit! Jim dawdled over
his dessert of baked apple with vanilla sauce. So much had
happened that he hadn't thought much beyond Laura's unexpected health problem. Pepper was right; she would need
friends and family now more than ever, and he had every intention of being there in that capacity for her. Worse, Pepper
would be leaving.

"What are your plans for returning to Montana?" he demanded.

Pepper heard the slight edge of anger in Jim's voice. Why?
"When we get to D.C., Marie will put me on the next plane
out."

With her simple words, Jim lost his considerable appetite.
The last thing he wanted was for Pepper to leave, but even if she

stayed, he'd be too busy to spend much time with her, between
his job at the Pentagon and remaining in Laura's life until her
husband and son were found. *If* they could be found, he reminded himself grimly. There was no telling what Laura's
freedom would mean to Morgan's situation. The drug lord
could kill him outright. There were so many unknowns. And no
answers.

Looking up, he met and held Pepper's luminous gaze. She
looked as if she were going to cry. Frustration ate at him. Those
tears again. And again, this wasn't the time or place to ask
about them. Damn. "So what does a smoke jumper do during
winter? There can't be many fires."

"As a Hotshot team, we're always on standby. Sometimes we
get calls from the Southwest—California and Arizona in particular—and we go fight a fire for them." Pepper set her tray
aside and grabbed the heavy white mug that contained the last
of her coffee.

"What else do you do?"

"We repair our equipment, I put my team through training
seminars and, in general, we rest up. There's a lot to do in other
ways, believe me. We aren't sitting in Montana twiddling our
thumbs."

He grinned a little. "I know you ski."

"Yes, mostly cross-country, anymore." She stopped for a
long moment, recalling that it had been a good two years after
John's death before she'd put on a pair of downhill skis.

Sliding his own tray aside, Jim sipped at his coffee, deep in
thought. "Do you realize we missed Thanksgiving?"

"I know . . . it's one of my favorite holidays."

"Oh?"

"Yes." She gazed down at her cup. "I always go home for
it—to Anaconda."

"Family means a lot to you, doesn't it?"

Pepper lifted her head. "Sure. Doesn't it to everyone?"

He shrugged. "Nowadays, I think a lot of people have lost
their sense of family togetherness. Not that it's anyone's fault.
It just happened."

"I'll probably make up for my absence by taking a few days
off when I get back and going home to see my parents."

"They can't know anything about this mission. What will ou tell them?"

"A white lie. I'll tell them a friend of mine got into trouble n the East Coast and I flew back to help her."

"That's painless," Jim conceded. He ached to have long, xploring conversations with Pepper. "So what are your other avorite holidays?"

She roused herself, trying to fight her inner pain. "Christ-nas. I love it. I go home then, too. My grandparents live in Billings, and as old as they are, they drive over for the week if here's no blizzard in progress. Cam and Molly and their kids ome home, too. We have a great time. I just love seeing the ids, playing with them, building snowmen and stuff like that."

The warmth in Pepper's eyes made Jim want to rail against ife in general. Her voice had such a velvet quality to it, and her ove for her family touched his heart as few things ever did. He aw new life in her eyes, and he longed to share that with her. f only he could. If only...

"Well, we're due in Miami in two days," he said in a low voice. "I hope we get to share more times like this, Pepper."

Startled, she sat up. "Like what?"

"Talking with you." He frowned. Why did she look incred-lous, as if she didn't really believe him? Was the ghost of John Freedman still standing between them? Probably. Jim no longer ared. One way or another, he was going to replace that ghost rom her past.

Nervously, Pepper stood up. "If you'll excuse me, I want to o see Laura, if I can."

He nodded. "Okay. I'll see you later."

Laura was sleeping when Pepper stopped to see her. Too estless to go back to her cabin, Pepper went up to the bridge, where she found Noah Trayhern. Though Noah wore the same dark blue uniform as everyone else, it was obvious he was in harge. His carriage, his low, commanding voice and the way he crew members on the bridge responded showed that. Pep-er liked the officer. He was easygoing yet firm. She liked to hink she was that way with her team, too. It was obvious

Noah's crew not only respected him, but liked him—a ra[
combination.

When he spotted her, Noah stood up and offered her hi
captain's chair, with the best view on the ship. Huge window
framed the entire area, giving everyone good visibility. "Hav
a seat."

"Thanks." Pepper slid into the chair. From here, she coul
see the dark expanse of the Caribbean. Above, thousands o
stars seemed quilted into the velvety sky.

"How about a cup of fresh coffee?" Noah suggested, ges
turing to one of the crew to get it for them.

Pepper nodded. "Thanks, I could use it. I came up here t
find out how Laura is doing. Colonel Woodward said you wer
just with her."

Rubbing his jaw, the officer leaned against the console an
faced her. "She's making good progress physically. Her mem
ory is spotty, though. I just had a talk with Dr. Parsons, an
she said that gradually Laura should remember everything."

Pepper took the white mug offered to her, with thanks. Noa
took the other proffered mug and sipped the coffee thought
fully. "I'm just glad the worst is over for her," she said.

"In one way it is, and in another way it isn't," Noah mur
mured. "Dr. Parsons examined her thoroughly and told m
Laura had been raped."

Stunned, Pepper sat very still, the mug resting in her hands
"Oh, God, no..."

Grimly, Noah rasped, "If I *ever* get my hands on Garcia, he'
a dead man."

Shaken, she whispered, "That's terrible. She's already go
her own private hell she's going to have to deal with."

"Yes, and I just talked to Perseus. They still don't have a lin
on where Morgan or Jason are." Frustration was evident in hi
voice. "I'm having a tough time with this whole situation.
knew Morgan going into a security business like this woul
make him enemies, but I never envisioned it turning into suc
a can of worms."

"At least," Pepper said hesitantly, "Laura has her family—
and Jim."

"Yes, she's got that," he admitted. "I'd like to stay behind
and be with her, but I can't. I have a Coast Guard ship to run.
I wish I could...."

Reaching out, she touched his broad shoulder. "You've done
more than most people could have already, Noah."

He took her hand and squeezed it warmly. "Without you,
this mission wouldn't have been a success. Jim told me what
happened, how he injured his arm too badly to be of much
help." He looked straight into her eyes. "I'm just glad you were
in place, Pepper. I have to admit, I had my doubts about your
qualifications, but you've convinced me. Jim's right—you're
the very special woman. One hell of a role model, to boot."

Pepper felt heat spread across her face, and she knew she was
blushing. Noah's hand was warm and strong. She released it
and said, "Jim is giving me too much credit. Without his experience, I wouldn't have been able to pull this mission off,
Noah."

The captain cocked his head and studied her in the building
silence. "No, I don't think he has. I think Jim sees you very
clearly. I don't think you always see yourself and how much
you accomplish on a daily basis as a smoke jumper."

"Maybe not," Pepper hedged, unaccustomed to all this
praise. "I have a job I love. It combines everything I ever
learned in life, and I can use it all."

"I know what you mean," he murmured, satisfaction in his
tone. "I love what I do in the Coast Guard, too."

"From what I can see, you've got the best of all worlds. You
have a wonderful wife who obviously adores you, kids and a
great job."

He laughed a little. "I do. I'll be the first to admit it. Kit is
something special to me. She's my life, my soul...." He gave
her an embarrassed look. "Kit and I met at a real bad time in
her life. I fell in love with her immediately, but she was gun-shy
of me."

Pepper nodded. "You're a lot like Colonel Woodward,
though."

"Oh?"

"He has that same warmth, that humanity about him that
you have."

"I guess he does, only he hides it a lot better than I do.
Noah chuckled.

Pepper became glum. Somehow, for the next two days, sh
was going to have to hide how she really felt about Jim. If on
she could get off the ship earlier. She knew she had to fill out
report at Perseus, but after that, she was free to resume her li
as it had been before—without Jim.

"Noah?"

"Yes?"

"Is there any way to get off the *Falcon* earlier than two day
from now?"

Chapter Ten

"Laura? I'm Pepper Sinclair...." Pepper extended her hand to the woman who lay on the hospital bed, covered with blankets. Laura's eyes were half-open, red-rimmed. It was 0700, and Pepper wanted to talk to Laura before catching a flight to Miami with Commander Gallagher. Her heart went out to the pale woman, her skin still translucent. But it was her eyes that most touched Pepper's heart. They were filled with tears. As their hands connected, she felt Laura's cool, damp one weakly wrap about hers.

"Hi..." Laura whispered. "I'm so glad to finally meet you. Jim and Noah have had nothing but praise for you...for helping me, for saving my life. Thank you...."

Pepper squeezed her hand gently and released it. She watched as Laura shakily raised her other hand and brushed the tears away. "I'm glad I was able to help, Laura." She moved uneasily. "I'm sorry, I've come at a bad time."

With a half smile quirking one corner of her mouth, Laura whispered, "No, you didn't. It's just the memories...."

"They're starting to return," Pepper said empathetically. She saw the terror in Laura's blue eyes and wanted to help, but didn't know how. Helplessness seized her. "I just wanted to touch base with you. I'm hopping a flight in a few minutes. I guess I just wanted to wish you the best in an awful situation."

Laura closed her eyes and sniffed. "Thank you, Pepper. Wh-when things are better, I want to spend some time with you. I—I don't really remember very much about your rescuing me."

"You don't have to," Pepper whispered unsteadily, her throat closing with tears. The woman's husband and son were still missing, yet she was attempting, despite her own pain and horror, to keep up a conversation. How unselfish she was. Touched beyond words, Pepper gripped her hand gently once again. "Just get well. Maybe in six months or so, when things have settled down, I'll call you and we'll talk."

Laura opened her eyes. "I'd like that, Pepper."

Releasing her hand, Pepper moved away from the bed. "Goodbye," she quavered, and she turned on her heel, fighting her own tears. Outside sick bay, she halted in the passageway. Quickly wiping the moisture from her eyes, she glanced around, relieved that no one had seen her crying. Her last—and worst—visit was going to be with Jim. He didn't know she had managed to wrangle a lift on Storm's helicopter, which would be leaving shortly. When she'd gotten up earlier, Jim had still been asleep in his quarters.

A part of her didn't want to face him and hoped, as she climbed the ladder between decks, that he would still be sleeping. That was the coward in her talking, Pepper thought, as she moved down the passageway. Of course, part of her very much wanted to see Jim. But what was the use? He'd spent every waking moment in sick bay with Laura. And Pepper couldn't blame him. Laura was a beautiful person—from the heart outward.

Her hands suddenly damp, Pepper stopped outside Jim's cabin and knocked. No answer. Again she knocked. Still no answer. She had no idea what time he'd gone to bed last night. For all she knew, he may have spent half the night with Laura. If so, he'd be sleeping deeply now.

She took a deep, shaky breath. Going to her own quarters, she quickly penned him a note. Fighting back tears for herself—for a future she'd unwillingly gotten a brief glimpse of before knowing with jarring reality that it would never be hers—Pepper finished writing her goodbye. She folded the paper and gently pushed it beneath Jim's door. When he woke up, he'd find it.

Outside, she could hear the helicopter warming up, the blades *whapping* in the early morning air. Hurrying forward with her small duffel bag, she left the main deck of the Coast Guard cutter. She'd seen Noah already and thanked him for his help and hospitality. As she moved outside to the damp, almost-cool morning, Pepper saw the pale pink horizon dotted with a few puffy clouds, but she was in so much personal pain that the beauty of it didn't really register on her senses.

A crew member opened the Dolphin helicopter door, and Pepper climbed on board. She found a place to sit on the cool metal deck behind the two pilots, then leaned against the bulkhead and closed her eyes. She didn't want to say goodbye to Jim. The burning sensation around her heart moved up her throat, and Pepper's hand came up to cover the area. Choking back a sob, she heard the engine of the Dolphin deepen. In moments, the helicopter broke contact with the deck of the cutter, and they were airborne.

Jim stumbled to his feet, his eyes bleary and slightly puffy. What time was it? He glanced down at his watch as he moved toward the head. It was 1000. He'd overslept. With a shake of his head, he twisted the knobs on the shower to get the water running. He'd been up with Laura until almost three this morning. The memories had started to come back, and she had verged on hysteria. There'd been no way he was going to leave her to battle her demons alone.

Jim didn't feel at all good this morning. He needed a long, uninterrupted sleep to recover from the grueling pounding he'd put himself through on this mission. After a hot shower, he shaved and dressed in a clean, dark blue Coast Guard uniform. His heart cried out for Pepper—for her nearness. Because of Laura's continuing crisis, they hadn't had the time together he'd hoped for. If Dr. Parsons hadn't given Laura a tranquilizer at 0300, Jim knew he'd have been up all night instead of just half. He and Noah had arranged to take turns with her as she regained her tortured memories, but the captain had more-immediate responsibilities, so Jim had shouldered most of the load of remaining with her.

Not that he minded, but his heart was torn. He knew the time he spent with Laura now would ultimately help stabilize her and help her cope. Last night, she had recalled the rape with vivid clarity, and he'd cried with her and held her, wanting so much to protect her from that pain but not being able to. Soon enough she would remember the kidnapping—and the fact that Jason and Morgan were still missing. He wasn't sure which would be more devastating to her.

Grimly, he glanced in the mirror long enough to comb his short, dark hair. There were circles under his eyes, which were bloodshot from too little sleep. He looked like hell. He felt like hell. What he really needed was Pepper's company. She had been like a serene angel through all of this. More than once he'd seen her with Noah. She was an easy person to talk to, Jim realized. And in her own way, he acknowledged, she was there for Laura and him—only at a distance.

He made up his bunk and turned to go out into the passageway. First he would get some chow, then he'd visit Noah and, finally, go see Laura. A flash of white on the deck caught his attention as he opened the door. It was a folded piece of stationery. He leaned down and picked it up.

Standing half in his quarters and half in the busy passageway, Jim opened the paper. He frowned and his eyes narrowed as he read the message:

Dear Jim:
By the time you get this, I'll be gone. I knocked twice on your door this morning, but I guess you were sleeping pretty hard. I'm hopping an early flight to the mainland this morning. I wanted to say goodbye, but I guess this note will do.

I don't feel my presence on the cutter is necessary. I'm

pretty wrung out by the mission, and right now home looks good to me. It's a place to heal. To forget. Goodbye...

Pepper

"Damn!" He folded the note, turned on his heel and hurried up to the bridge. Noah was standing at the window with a pair of binoculars when Jim opened the hatch door to the area.

"Where's Pepper?" he demanded, slightly out of breath.

Noah lowered the binoculars and looked at him. "She left at 0700 this morning with Commander Gallagher." Glancing at his watch, he said, "They'll arrive at the Miami Coast Guard station after a refueling stop in the Bahamas."

His heart beating frantically in his chest, Jim stood, feeling a terrible pain in his gut. A bitter taste filled his mouth. "Did you see her this morning?" he asked, his voice strained.

Noah placed the binoculars on the console. "Yes." He searched Jim's face carefully. "Pepper finally did get a chance to introduce herself to Laura this morning before she left."

"Why did she leave?"

Noah shrugged and returned his attention to the islands in the distance. "She said she felt useless around here and that it was best if she went home early."

With a shake of his head, Jim crossed his arms against his chest. "I should have spent more time with her...."

Noah cocked his head. "Is there something between you two? Not that it's my business, but—"

"Yes," Jim admitted abruptly, "there is." Or more accurately, should be. "She shouldn't have run...."

"Pepper didn't say much, but as she walked out to the helo deck, she looked pretty upset."

Jim compressed his lips. "How upset?"

"She looked as if she was crying, but I couldn't really be sure," Noah said quietly.

Jim took in a ragged breath. "I've really screwed up."

"Reading between the lines," Noah volunteered as he sat down in the captain's chair, facing Jim, "I think Pepper feels you care a lot for Laura."

"Of course I do," Jim rasped. "She's been a friend for more than seven years."

Holding up his hand, the officer said, "That's not what I mean. Pepper said something odd to me when we were eating dinner in the galley last night." He frowned. "She said she understood why you could love someone like Laura, even if it was at a distance."

Suddenly the conversation they'd had back at his condominium deluged Jim. He was thunderstruck. "Pepper must think I'm still carrying a torch for Laura!" What a fool he'd been. And of course, it would look that way to her. After all, he'd spent every possible minute at Laura's side, helping her cope, being there to support her through her horrible trials. Why hadn't he realized Pepper might see his attention toward Laura differently?

"I guess," he said, pain in his tone, "Pepper could interpret my time with Laura that way."

"Very easily," Noah said. "I didn't help things, either. I told her how close you two were." With a grimace, he added, "I probably helped nail your coffin closed on that one without ever realizing it. I'm sorry."

Frustration ate at Jim. He was even more torn now. "Laura needs continued support. I can't just pick up and leave, even if I want to." He was talking out loud, more to himself than to Noah. "Pepper will probably skip Perseus, grab a flight out of Miami International and go straight home. At lunch yesterday, I could see how much she wanted to get back there. When she spoke about snow in the Rocky Mountains, she got tears in her eyes. And she's looking forward to spending Christmas with her family in Anaconda."

Jim wanted to cry himself. Pepper had completely misinterpreted his relationship with Laura. Hadn't his hot, branding kiss on the island told her something? His touching her intimately, almost loving her? Had it meant so little to her? No, Jim cautioned himself, he couldn't be angry with Pepper. She might have thought the kiss and his intimacy were due to nothing more than the intensity of the moment. What she didn't know—and what he hadn't ever communicated to her—was that he didn't take what they'd so explosively shared at all lightly. For him, it had been a promise of a future exploration of their relationship. But obviously Pepper didn't know that.

"I just talked to Dr. Parsons," Noah said, interrupting Jim's tortured thoughts. "She gave Laura a mild tranquilizer and is down there with her now." His eyes showed agony. "We've all focused so much on Laura that I think we forgot to check how Pepper was feeling. That was a rough mission, and I'm sure she still has a lot of emotional baggage to sort out from it. I know when my wife, Kit, was an undercover cop, she would go through hell after a dangerous bust. It was important for me to be there for her through those times." He sighed. "I'm afraid Pepper needed us, but we weren't there for her."

"I wasn't there for her," Jim agreed guiltily, a lump in his throat. "You're right—Pepper needed care, too, and I didn't give it to her."

"It wasn't anyone's fault," Noah said, placing his hand on Jim's slumped shoulder. "The situation was unique. I don't think any of us could have done much differently even if we'd been aware."

"We could have done a lot more. *I* could have." Jim felt such a bitter sense of loss that he wanted to sob. Had he lost Pepper entirely? Was there any hope for them? Her note hadn't been signed. "Your friend" or "Love." But what did he expect? He'd practically ignored her since they'd completed the mission. The mistake he'd made was in thinking that their kiss had sealed a promise for their future.

With a shake of his head, Noah murmured. "Ever since this kidnapping, the whole Trayhern family has been in a state of shock. We've been running around like a bunch of lemmings." Scratching his head, he said, "I think we've got to get a handle on our emotions, whether we want to or not. I know my parents are beside themselves over what's happened. My sister, Alyssa, and her husband, Clay, are coming in off a top-secret assignment and they're waiting to hear if Perseus or the Pentagon can get a lead on Jason or Morgan. They're going to take thirty days' leave to be here and help out."

"That's good," Jim said sincerely. But it didn't solve his problem. They had another day-and-a-half sail before they reached Miami. Then he would fly north with Laura and Dr. Parsons. "What are you going to do with Laura once she's home?"

"I've been in contact with a rape-crisis center in D.C., and have been referred to a woman psychologist who will work with her. Killian definitely thinks Laura and her daughter shouldn't go home until after we've located Jason and Morgan."

"Good idea," Jim said. "Ramirez and Garcia could strike again, to get even with us for rescuing her."

"You'd better believe it." Grimly, his eyes narrowed, Noah scanned the nearly smooth expanse of blue-green water. "Garcia and Ramirez have been albatrosses around our family's neck for a long time. Now it's coming down to the wire. It's them or us." His mouth flattened. "And I'll be damned if the Trayhern family will pay the price again, to this country or otherwise. We've lost so much. We got it back when Morgan returned to us but now it's been taken away again in a different way."

Jim felt the deep emotion behind Noah's softly spoken words. He saw the anguish in the officer's expression. No one was more aware of the Trayhern history than he, because of Laura's involvement. No, of all people, this family didn't deserve to suffer this kind of attack. "As soon as we get Laura established, I'll be back at the Pentagon," he offered. "Maybe, with some luck, we'll pick up more satellite transmissions."

Noah brightened slightly. "You were responsible for this one, and it turned out to be a good lead." He ran a hand through his close-cropped hair and, shifting gears, said, "It's none of my business, but what are you going to do about Pepper?"

Jim exhaled. "Wait, I guess. I can't just drop everything and go to her. I was lucky to get leave for this mission. My superiors aren't about to let me go again so soon. Besides, I want to try to locate Jason and Morgan. I think I can do it, given some time."

"Maybe," Noah said, "time is what Pepper needs right now, anyway. She needs to get some distance on what happened. Hopefully, she'll realize why you had to spend so much time with Laura. It wasn't love but loyalty."

"I hope," Jim whispered, "she sees exactly that, but I'm not counting on it."

"Go get some chow," Noah urged.

Jim didn't feel like eating, but he knew he had to. Leaving the bridge, he headed for the cutter's bottom deck, but his mind and heart were on Pepper. How was she feeling? What was she feeling? Had he made up this idea of something strong growing between them?

Noah was right, Jim decided. Time could be his friend. But it could be his enemy, too. Somehow, he had to figure out a way to let Pepper know she was part of his life. Some kind of foundation had to be laid so she understood that his kiss had been the seal of a new relationship—not something taken from her in a stolen moment.

"Hey, Pepper!" Joe Conway stood at the door to the cavernous structure where they laid out and folded the smoke-jumping parachutes.

Pepper raised her head. She was at one of the tables, refolding one of her chutes. It was lunchtime and the rest of her team was over at the chow hall. Their smoke-jumping facility was a few miles outside Phillipsburg, next to the small airport there.

Joe looked at her expectantly. "What?" she asked shortly.

"You aren't going to believe it, but in the middle of this snowstorm, a florist truck pulled up. Phillipsburg doesn't have a florist, so this guy must have come all the way from Anaconda, the poor bastard. Bad day to be driving." He flashed her a happy smile and opened the door with a flourish.

Frowning, Pepper saw a man bundled in a heavy wool coat and hat carrying a large, long box under his right arm. He was an older gentleman, with silver in his hair. He removed his hat and thanked Joe for opening the door. Then Joe, her second in command, pointed at her. Joe was tall, brash and only twenty-eight, full of Irish blarney right up to his dancing green eyes and black hair. Was this a trick? He'd been known to pull plenty of practical jokes, especially at this time of year, when things slowed down and got a little too boring around the camp to suit him.

The older man stepped up to her, his hat in one hand, the mysterious box in the other. He smiled, his brown eyes crinkling with warmth as he nodded at her. "Are you Ms. Sinclair?"

"Yes." Pepper watched him break into a wide smile.

"I got this special order at our shop in Anaconda." Chuck
ling, he said, "I gotta tell you, the roads are pretty slick ou
there. That snow's fallin' faster than the plows can remove it.'
He offered her the large box. "These are for you."

Though completely puzzled and still wary of a trick, Peppe
accepted the box and thanked him. When he'd left, Joe wan
dered over.

"What's inside?" He peered at the box, placing his hand
behind his back.

"I don't know." Pepper took a pair of scissors and cut on
of the tight plastic straps that held the box together.

Joe raised his thick, black eyebrows. "Secret admirer, huh
I knew something special was going on while you were myste
riously gone that week."

"Quit," Pepper ordered, as she snipped the rest of the strap:

Chuckling, Joe shoved his hands in the pockets of his Levi
and rocked back on the heels of his jump boots. "You wer
awful down and quiet when you got back." He gestured to th
box. "Must have met some dark, mysterious stranger whe
ever you were and fallen in love with him. Maybe that's wh
you were so hang-dog lookin', huh?" His eyes glinted wit
teasing.

Pepper held on to her irritation. Sometimes Joe could mak
her split her sides with laughter. But today wasn't one of tho:
days. This first week back home had been a special and une:
pected kind of hell for her. She had tried to forget Jim's ki:
and his words, which haunted her dreams each night. The
were torrid dreams, unfulfilled dreams that made her wake wi
an ache in her lower body. Shooting Joe a dirty look, s
growled, "For once your Irish blarney is totally wrong." Se
ting the scissors aside, she opened the box. Her eyes widene
The fragrance of roses wafted upward, and she inhaled deeply

"Hmm," Joe murmured, leaning over, "looks like th
Irishman is right—again. Too bad I didn't put money on a be
I could've taken you for a real ride on this one, Sinclair. R
and yellow roses. I'll bet there are two dozen in there."

"Get out of here," Pepper said lightly, matching his teasin
tone. Her heart was pounding, not from Joe's prophecy, b

from her overwhelming surprise at the gift. Her instincts told her it was from Jim. But was it? Or was it her silly heart in overdrive again, creating wishful, idealistic dreams that would never come true? Pepper saw Joe's mouth draw into a beatific smile of righteous pride. "You're such a know-it-all, Conway," she said dryly, waving her hand at him to leave.

Laughing heartily, he gently patted her shoulder. "Okay, boss, I'll leave you to savor the roses alone." He walked a few feet, then turned around. "By the way, who's the lucky guy? Does the team know him?"

Heat stung Pepper's cheeks. "None of your business, nosy. Why don't you go eat?" She put the top back on the box and went to her office. Joe was like a younger brother to her, but at times he was too curious and got under her skin. He had been especially curious about where she'd gone for a week and what had happened. Of course, Pepper hadn't told anyone, nor would she. As far as her smoke-jumping team was concerned, she'd taken a week's leave to go back East to visit an old friend, and that was all.

Joe raised his hand. "I hear ya, boss. Okay, I'm gone. I'll eat an extra piece of apple pie for you. I hear Sally made us some. Bless her good Catholic heart. Too bad she's not Irish, but I love her anyway. Catch ya later...."

The door closed.

Pepper shook her head. "You're such a pain in the neck sometimes," she muttered, gently touching the roses. Opening the crinkly paper wider she discovered a pristine white envelope among the blossoms.

The past seven days had been bone-achingly lonely for Pepper. None of her friends, though glad to see her, had succeeded in filling the empty cavity in her heart that they'd once satisfied so easily. If only Jim hadn't branded her with that all-consuming kiss. Somehow he'd touched the depths of her soul and reminded her just what was missing in her life—a man she could love forever. But the price was too high, and Pepper knew it.

Her fingers trembled as she eased the envelope open. Inside was a small white card, which read: *From the heart, Jim Woodward*. Pepper stared at it for a long time, digesting his

sentiment. It was vague, but at the same time, it wasn't. Nee-
dled, she forced herself to count the roses. Joe was right—there
were twenty-four in all. Half were red, the others a buttery yellow. Their fragrance was heady, and Pepper suddenly laughed
at the ridiculousness of it all. Here she was, tucked away in
some of the most beautiful back country of the Rockies. There
were near-blizzard conditions outside, with the temperature in
the teens and the evergreens coated with a thick blanket of
white snow. And she had two dozen roses. Beautiful, wonderful fragrant roses from a man she'd never dreamed she'd hear
from again.

Pepper stopped at the Phillipsburg post office, part of her
evening routine after getting off work. She expected very little
mail—maybe some catalogs and certainly the perennial bills,
but no personal correspondence. To her surprise, a long, busi-
ness-size envelope lay in her box, thick and heavy. She stood in
her colorful Pendleton jacket, a knit cap on her head and her
gloves tucked under her arm as she examined the piece of mail.
It bore no return address, just her name and address. The
postmark, however, was from Washington, D.C. Her heart
began a slow pounding of anticipation—and fear.

First the roses, which were out in her truck even now, with
the heater running so they wouldn't freeze in this terrible
snowstorm. Now a mysterious letter. Pepper jammed the envelope into the large pocket of her jacket, pulled up her collar
and put her gloves back on. She would wait until she got home
to read it. There was no doubt in her mind that it was from Jim.

As she drove slowly down Main Street, the town already
wreathed in near darkness at four-thirty in the afternoon, Pepper tried to contain her wild imagination. She concentrated on
driving, careful not to slide off into the ditch as she left the
center of town behind. Two miles down the road, she turned
left. A mile farther along the rutted, fir tree-lined road, now
coated with ice, she was home. Pepper had built the cedar-log
cabin herself over three years' time, with a lot of help from her
smoke-jumper friends and her family. It had been a weekend
project, and many memories of laughter and sharing had
worked their way into her home as a result.

The cedar logs were barely visible in her headlights as she pulled into her driveway. Getting out, she tramped through the snow, the wind howling around her as she opened the garage door. Once she'd driven inside, Pepper shut off the engine, got out and shut the door behind her. She felt like a kid at Christmas with the huge box of roses under her arm and the letter in her pocket. Nudging off her boots at the door to the service porch connected to the garage, she went inside.

Her cabin was cool, so she laid everything on the kitchen table and went on into the living room. After making a fire in her Earth Stove, the environmentally benign wood-burning stove she'd installed for heating, she got up, dusted off her hands and went back to the kitchen. First she took the roses out of their box and arranged them in the largest glass vase she had. Inhaling their fragrance, she carried them into the living room and set them on the cedar coffee table.

Standing by the stove, feeling the first tendrils of heat from the newly made fire, Pepper carefully opened the thick envelope. Her heart thumped as she unfolded several handwritten pages. Jim's name, address and phone number were in the upper-left hand corner of the first page. Trying to still her pounding heart, she began to read the letter with an unexpected hunger:

Dear Pepper,

By now, you've got the roses I sent you. It's the least I could do, under the circumstances. When I found your note under my door on the cutter, it jolted me out of my narrow focus. I talked to Noah, and he told me you'd left. To say I was unhappy about your leaving the ship doesn't begin to describe how I felt.

There was so much going down after the mission that I lost my sense of balance. Laura's health, her nearly dying, scared the hell out of me. I was so worried about her that I forgot to think of you and how you might be feeling. I know you weren't wounded in the action, and you came through it with flying colors, but that doesn't matter. I should have paid more attention to your needs, whatever they might have been.

We went through a lot, you and I, in a very short, intense amount of time. And I went from almost disliking you to feelings that I can't begin to explain in the confines of this letter, Pepper. But first I want to say I'm sorry for ignoring you on the cutter. Looking back on it, I should have known better. I know what combat does to a person, and about the necessary letdown period afterward. You took the high ground, and whatever you were feeling, you didn't tell me.

I wish you had. I wish . . . so much. To say I'm feeling a little guilty is an understatement. We almost died on that island. If it hadn't been for your bravery and levelheadedness, we would never have gotten Laura out safely. And yet you kept to yourself. I asked Noah if you'd talked to him, and he said no. I'm sorry I wasn't there for you, Pepper. I should have been.

The roses are a way of apologizing to you. I wasn't a very good team member for you. Experiences like this bond people for life, and I felt that bonding with you on that island. I dropped the ball when Laura stopped breathing. So the yellow roses are asking you to forgive my all-too-human failings.

The red roses are to ask if there is a future for us. I know I have no right to ask that of you, but I meant what I said on the island. When I kissed you, you cried, and I never found out what those tears were about. I guess it was the wrong place and the wrong time.

I'm pretty busy here at the Pentagon right now. We still haven't got a lead on Jason or Morgan—yet. I'm spending about sixteen hours a day working with the communications people, trying to ferret out something in all that worldwide traffic via satellite. When I'm not working, I'm exhausted and inevitably, you come to mind. Our conversations are like water to me, Pepper. I'm thirsty to hear what is in your mind and heart. I felt cheated when you left, but I don't blame you for going. I think I understand why you did. Or at least I hope I do.

Some night, if you don't mind, I'd like to call you. But it's your decision, not mine, to make. I've enclosed a self-addressed, stamped envelope. If you want me to call, just mail it back to me. I can't make up for what wasn't given to you, Pepper. Maybe, if you're willing, we can talk. I'd like that very much. I hope to hear from you. Take care.

                                                                    Jim

Pepper released a small, shaky sigh. Jim's writing was far from legible, but she realized how he must have labored over the letter. There wasn't a single ink smudge, and she smiled a little. Once an officer, always an officer. The fact that he'd handwritten it instead of using a computer meant a lot to her. Fingering the return envelope, she wondered if she wanted to talk to him. After all, what was there to talk about? He loved Laura, not her. He spoke of the future, but what kind of future could there be for them?

Unhappily, she moved away from the stove and gently laid the letter on the coffee table, next to the roses. Her heart wouldn't seem to settle down, nor would her flights of imagination. Looking out her front windows, she saw the snow thickening and blowing even harder. How lonely she'd felt until Jim's letter had come. But were his gifts nothing more than a request for atonement?

Turning, Pepper went to her bedroom to shed her dark green trousers and long-sleeved, tan blouse. She'd worn the official Forest Service uniform all day; now she wanted to relax in a far more feminine velour lounger of pale pink. Still, the cabin felt terribly empty, and as Pepper undressed, trading her uniform for civilian clothes, she wondered what it would be like if Jim were here, in her home. The mere thought made her shaky, her feelings raw and clamoring. She had to admit she wasn't sure she could control herself if he was here and kissed her as he had on the island—touched her as he'd touched her then.

With a shake of her head, Pepper wondered if she was getting winter fever early. Tomorrow she might mail back the envelope, but she was still uncertain. It would be a crazy move if she did. A desperate one.

Chapter Eleven

It was Friday night, and Pepper was wrestling with a ton of
paperwork, mostly supply orders to replace equipment lost or
damaged during the past year's fires. A headache lapped at her
right temple and across her forehead, and she rubbed the area
as she concentrated on filling out the government paperwork.

Her office was in a small niche within the parachute facility.
It was six o'clock, a good hour past quitting time, and her mind
strayed, as it so often did, to Jim. She felt nervous and edgy.
Telling herself she was chasing a pipe dream, she'd given in and
sent the envelope back four days ago, after three long weeks of
resisting.

Closing her eyes, she rested her hand against her brow and
sighed softly. Her emotions seesawed among euphoria, anger,
helplessness and absolute fear. She'd never had this chaotic
experience before, so she didn't know how to cope with it. It
must be romantic love, she decided—the very kind of love
Pepper had made her life-altering decision *not* to experience
again after John died. Never again could she risk the pain that
came from losing the one she loved. It just wasn't worth it. He

parents had a wonderful marriage—one they worked on continually. Neither of them took it or the other for granted. That was the kind of love Pepper had expected to share with John, but fate had decided otherwise. Now, at thirty, she had to remember why she'd made her decision not to get involved again.

Her office door was open just enough so she could hear the comings and goings of her team. Everyone had left right at five tonight. After all, it was the week before Christmas, and there were parties to attend, gifts to be bought and wrapped, places to go, people to see. Glumly, Pepper opened her eyes and frowned down at the piles of paperwork. The only person she wanted to see was Jim.

Out in the main room the outside door quietly opened and closed. But peering into the shadowy depths, Pepper saw no one. Her imagination?

"Stop it," she muttered, irritated with herself and her unrequited longing. "You are such a stupid idealist. The sooner you get this paperwork done, the sooner you can go home." Home to an empty cabin. Home to the silence. Loneliness gnawed at Pepper as if it had carved a wide swath through her center.

A noise, the sound of footsteps, caught her attention. Frowning, Pepper put her pen aside. Someone *had* come in the door at the other end of the facility. It was fairly dark, save for the emergency lights at the exits, and she didn't want whoever it was stumbling and breaking an ankle. The building was a huge Quonset hut from the Korean War era, made of corrugated aluminum. The floor was concrete, and the whole structure was large and empty, save for the area where parachutes were folded, hung and repaired.

Easing out of her squeaky leather chair, Pepper crossed to her office door and pushed it all the way open, sending a wide path of light into the gloomy building. She saw a shadow—a man, she thought—halfway to her office. Who was it? Pepper could recognize most of her crew by physical build, but this wasn't one of them. Still, there was something oddly familiar about this man, though she couldn't place him. Leaving her office, she moved down the wall to the main electricity supply. She flipped several switches and turned around to face her visitor.

Pepper's mouth dropped open. Her heart slammed against her ribs.

"Jim!" His name echoed oddly through the building.

Jim halted about fifty feet from her and gave her a strained, slight smile. "I'll give you this," he said, embarrassed, "you made me use all of my Recon training to find you." Looking around, his mouth stretching into a wider smile, he moved his gaze back to her shocked features. "This is one hell of a hole in the wall."

She could only stare. Had she gone crazy? Was this some kind of waking dream? Jim Woodward stood before her, a huge pot of bright red poinsettias in his hands. He wore comfortable-looking, dark blue chinos, leather hiking boots and a bright red flannel shirt beneath a well-worn leather jacket. How handsome he looked. How much she'd missed him. Pepper swallowed convulsively, meeting and drowning in his amused green gaze.

"Wh-what are you doing here?" Her voice cracked. Her palms were damp. Her heart was pounding so hard it made her voice wobble off-key. She saw Jim's mouth work into a tense line. Internally, she went on guard. Anger slammed through her, and on its heels, euphoria. Hunger for him, for the feel of his mouth on hers, flowed over her. How badly she wanted to fly into his arms and welcome him back into her life, like a thrilled and trusting child. But she was no longer a child, no trusting of Jim—or herself.

"I got the envelope back," Jim said simply, slowly approaching Pepper. Despite the mannish Forest Service uniform she had to wear, he thought she looked incredibly feminine. Her dark hair was longer now, touching her shoulders and falling in soft folds around her face. He saw the shock, the denial, in her eyes. Was she glad to see him? He wasn't sure. He'd risked everything by coming to visit. An impending avalanche of fear was poised over his desire for her. Time hadn't dulled his need of her. Like a knife twisting hotly through his lower body, he hungered to kiss her soft mouth, to again slide his hand around the small, firm breast that fit so wonderfully in his palm.

Halting, he lifted the poinsettias. "I decided that what we had to talk about should be said in person, not via a long-distance phone call. Here, these are for you," he murmured. "It's Christmas, and I wanted to bring you something...." Holding the potted plant toward her, he wondered if Pepper was going to take it or not. Her face was devoid of color. Her cheeks, ordinarily pink, looked wan. As he eased out of the shadows, he saw stress around her eyes and mouth that hadn't been there before. Anger flashed in her eyes—toward him. Was the mission the reason for her gaunt appearance and the stress plainly etched in her lovely features?

He held the poinsettias between them. *Please, take them. Take them.* Inwardly, Jim believed that by accepting his small gift Pepper would also at some level be accepting him—even if it was a tentative truce. Rapidly changing emotions flashed through her eyes as she slowly looked down at the flowers and then up at him.

"Christmas—" Pepper choked. She felt justified rage. Jim loved Laura. So what was he doing here? "That's right, it's Christmastime, isn't it?" The poinsettias were large and healthy looking, the flowers bright red among the green foliage. They were beautiful.

"As a holiday, it's kind of hard to forget," he teased huskily. Were those tears in her eyes? The anger in them came and went along with a flash of desire—aimed directly at him. Jim's heart squeezed at the anguish in Pepper's eyes as she wavered, not sure if she should accept the flowers. Her gaze snapped back to his, her eyes wide and incredibly blue, the pupils large and black, belying the gamut of emotions she was feeling.

Jim stood patiently, knowing full well that Pepper could tell him to do an about-face and walk out of her life—forever. The thought was devastating, and every fiber of his being yearned to step forward, set the flowers aside and take Pepper into his arms, kissing her until she melted like hot butter, silkily permeating his body and soul.

Pepper wavered. "I—I just can't believe you're here." Her voice came out tinged with indignation, but her heart cried out for him, for his wildly sensual kisses, the unbridled passion they'd shared on the island.

"I can't, either."

She saw the irony in his eyes and heard it in his voice. It hur
to blurt out the question, but it had to be asked. "Why—wh
are you here?"

"I couldn't not be here," Jim answered honestly. A little o
the anger in her eyes became banked and he saw the desir
again, for just a fleeting moment, before distrust replaced it
She still thinks I love Laura. The realization was devastating
He lifted the poinsettias a little higher. "Please take these
There are no strings attached, Pepper."

"I don't believe it," she rattled defensively. Oh, why did sh
ache for him like this? Need him so much? She couldn't eve
think of entering a romantic triangle. It was Jim and Laura, no
she and Jim. Loneliness was better than heart-shattering pain

Jim squelched his impatience. Pepper was right; there wer
strings attached to his gift of flowers. His lower body ached fo
relief—ached to love her fully. Wildly. With absolute aban
don. As he stood, watching her distrust of him grow, Jim knev
Pepper was above all a natural woman. She brought out ever
primal feeling and need he possessed. Right now, he felt mor
animal than human, longing to obey the impulse to claim he
make her his. The desire ate away at his considerable contro
like acid. Clearing his throat, he rasped, "The only thing at
tached to this gift is a dinner invitation." It wasn't a lie, but i
wasn't the full truth, either.

"Dinner? That's all?" Pepper hated the waspish sound o
her voice and saw the effect it had on Jim. Hurt showed briefl
in his eyes before he covered it up with false cheer.

"That's it. Dinner." He urged her silently to take the flow
ers. If only she would give him a chance....

Robotlike, Pepper reached out and took the plant. The po
was large, and the colorful petals brushed her jaw and shoul
ders. "This is heavy!"

"I know."

Nervously, voice wispy and strained, Pepper suggested
"Let's take them to my office?"

Jim gestured toward the lighted area. "After you." He saw
that the venetian blinds had been pulled to give her some pri
vacy from the rest of the facility. Her personal space was smal

and cramped, typical of a government-run office, he thought. Several dark green, metal filing cabinets stood at one end. Even her desk was a military-issue gray metal. Opposite it, against the other end wall, was a twin-size bed stalked with several fluffy pillows and covered by an old but much-loved quilt. Jim studied the bed darkly. Pepper probably used it during the summer, when fires were frequent. He could imagine her falling exhausted onto it for a quick nap between fire calls, inundated by the demands on her time in her responsible position as team leader.

The bed appeared startlingly feminine in the confines of the otherwise stark office. The very real desire to reach out, take her hand and pull her over to that bed and love her was nearly Jim's undoing. No one would come into the facility at this time of night, he thought. And the blinds had been drawn for privacy. All he had to do was shut the door, turn out the light and— Savagely he squelched his imaginings. Somehow he had to get control over his emotions. Jim noticed a small group of photos on the wall next to her desk and walked toward them, eager to discover who Pepper was—all of her facets, not just those he'd seen on the mission.

The fluorescent lights were harsh. Pepper nervously placed the plant on top of one of the file cabinets and rubbed her damp hands down the thighs of her trousers. She turned around to face Jim. He had a slight frown on his broad forehead as he studied her bed at the other end of the office. The lightning-bolt realization that all she had to do was take a few steps, reach out and tug him toward the bed shot through her. She could love him until her bruised and aching heart and lonely soul were satisfied. The idea nearly unstrung her and she gasped internally at her unbidden thoughts. Curling her fingers reflexively against her palms, she throttled the desire to reach out toward Jim. How wonderful he looked! Pepper stifled the urge to simply walk forward and throw herself into his arms. His presence was overwhelming to her heightened senses.

"You've got a real government cubbyhole here," Jim said, moving toward her desk and taking a quick, perusing look at the framed photos on the wall. One of them was of Pepper with her family. She stood next to a man who, Jim decided, was probably her brother, Cam. They looked very much alike. The proud, older woman at the end was as tall as Pepper. No question this was her mother—and no question that Pepper took after her strongly. Her dark-haired, tall and heavily muscled father stood at the other end of the group. It looked like a happy family. Jim's mouth pulled into a gentle smile.

"Nice family picture." He straightened and turned toward her. Trying to quell his own nervousness, he realized his voice was strained. Hell, he was scared to death. It was a kind of fear he'd never experienced before—not even in combat. It was the fear of being told to leave Pepper's life—once and for all.

Pepper managed a one-shouldered shrug. "Thanks."

"Going home for Christmas?" Jim didn't know where to start. Something warned him he couldn't be totally honest about his reasons for being here with her—yet.

"Uh...yes. Home. For Christmas. Sure..." Pepper's throat ached with tension, and she battled her tears. She stood helplessly, unsure what to do with her hands. Finally, she crossed her arms over her breasts. The words begged to be asked: *Why was Jim really here?* Too much of a coward to press the issue, she cast about for another topic.

"How's Laura doing?"

Jim pushed his hands into the pockets of his leather jacket. Small talk. He wanted to do away with it. He wanted to get to the bottom line. The bed behind him beckoned. His imagination was running away with him. Pepper belonged in his arms. Her mouth belonged on his. Compressing his lips, he said, "Surviving. Right now, she's hidden at a condominium that only a few people know about." He shrugged. "The fewer who know, the less chance of slipping up and letting the bad guys find her."

"I see. Yes, that's a good idea."

Jim looked around, desperate. "Susannah Killian, her cousin, is staying with her and helping her with her baby daughter, Katherine. Right now, Laura's mainly trying to recover. She's under the care of a great woman therapist who has plenty of rape-counseling experience." He shrugged, his voice becoming hoarse. "I guess it's the best we can all do for her, right now. I wish we could do more, but healing has to take place from within."

Pepper heard the frayed emotions in Jim's deepening voice and saw the distraught look in his eyes. There was no denying he was suffering for Laura, for her pain. "Rape is murder," Pepper whispered. "My homeopathic-doctor friend, Michaela Ryan, was raped when she was in her early twenties, back at medical school. Even now I see how it affects her. She's lost a piece of herself as a human being, as a woman, and I don't think she'll ever get it back."

Jim scuffed his hiking boot against the drab gray concrete of her office floor and frowned, looking down at it. "Yeah . . . that's what I was afraid of. . . ."

"Michaela survives okay," Pepper murmured. "I guess. . . ."

Looking up into her grave features, he murmured, "That's what Laura's doing right now—surviving. She's hanging on to hope." He shrugged and added, "At least we've got a lead on Jason."

"Really?" Hope rose in Pepper's heart, and she saw a ruddy flush appear on Jim's cheeks. "You found him, didn't you?"

"Sorta."

"You're too humble."

He grinned sheepishly. "Maybe . . ."

His smile flowed through her, hot and claiming. It was the first time she'd seen Jim smile like that—a little-boy, embarrassed smile that endeared him to her and momentarily washed away her anger, even as it increased her need of him. "Tell me how it happened."

He took his hands out of his pockets and unzipped his coat, suddenly very warm. But this heat had nothing to do with the temperature inside the facility—it was from being close to Pepper. Did she have any idea how powerfully she affected him? Wrestling with those thoughts, Jim tried to keep the small talk on track. He knew it was a good way for them to adjust to being in each other's presence again. "I worked closely with the CIA on this one, and we got Interpol help, too. Actually, Killian made a lot of the deductions."

Pepper knew Jim well enough to realize he was acting like any good leader—giving his subordinates the lion's share of the praise. "So where is Jason?"

"Maui, Hawaii, we think. It's not confirmed yet, but all the indications are there."

Pepper gawked. "Maui?"

"Yes." Jim shrugged. "It threw me, too, until I contacted the FBI and we started interfacing directly with Interpol." His voice deepened. "Damned if we didn't find out that Garcia flew from Nevis to his *other* home, on Maui. The bastard escaped the Nevis police after we rescued Laura, and went there. It blew me away that Garcia possibly had two of the Trayherns."

"Do you think Morgan's there, too?"

"I don't know. There are two merc teams coming in right now. One had his partner die on him, and the other's partner suffered a heart attack. The upshot is, Jake is teaming an ex-Israeli army officer named Sabra Jacobs with an ex-marine helicopter pilot, Craig Talbot."

"Sounds like a good match."

With a grimace, Jim said, "Actually, Jake says these two don't get along at all. But he doesn't have a choice. They don't have their regular partners, and he doesn't have another option right now. They've got to move fast on this, because if Garcia thinks we know about Maui, we're sure he'll move Jason somewhere else, and it could take months to pick up another solid lead."

With a shake of her head, Pepper murmured, "I'm glad we could do what we did. I don't envy Sabra or Craig. One mission like that is plenty for me."

Jim attempted a smile. "No, you're not a mercenary at heart." Then he amended his statement. "You're a warrior when it comes to a cause that means a lot to you, though."

Heat flooded her cheeks, and Pepper looked away from his intense gaze. "Yes…I guess." She managed a strangled sound. "I always said I was Don Quixote—tilting at the windmills in life." Wasn't *that* the truth? She'd fallen for John, given her heart, her soul, and look what it had gotten her.

Jim forced himself to move forward, closer to Pepper. She looked excruciatingly uncomfortable, and he had no desire to add more agony to her life than he already had. "Lady, you're the last person I'd accuse of such a thing. You're a passionate person, someone who embraces what she believes fully." He forcefully kept his hands at his sides, fearful that if he didn't, he'd reach out and put them on her slumped shoulders.

"Sure," Pepper said a little breathlessly, her pulse leaping as Jim came within a few feet of where she stood. "It's called being a right-brained woman." She couldn't help herself; automatically, she tensed as Jim took another step toward her. Why didn't he realize it was torture to be with him and not to reach out and touch him?

"No apologies are needed."

Pepper sobered and cast about for some sane response. "I'm not giving any. I like being a woman, and I like thinking and feeling like one." She glanced around her office. "I might be in a man's career, but I don't allow it to affect me as a woman." She tapped her chest. "I work strictly off my feelings, gut and intuition. It's saved lives."

Jim nodded. "I like your fire, your belief in yourself." How he wanted to experience that fire again firsthand. She might be cool and calm on the outside, but he'd acknowledged the inner heat that burned deep within her. His aching need of her grew at the thought.

"My confidence was earned the hard way, believe me," Pepper said with more than a little fervency. Taking a step away from him, she said, "Let's go to dinner."

Jim glanced at his watch. "I haven't eaten since noon, East Coast time. I don't know anything about the local eateries, but I bet you do." His breath became suspended, because Pepper's face softened for a moment, and he saw her without that mask of anger and distrust she'd been wearing. The expression on her face confused him. For a split second, he saw hope in her flawless blue eyes, followed by fear, then something else he couldn't quite define. Realizing he was holding his breath, he made a conscious effort to expel it.

"Well—uh—sure . . . if you want," Pepper responded hesitantly.

He'd never wanted anything more, he thought as a surge of joy tunneled through him. He had a tough time keeping a neutral look on his face as she acquiesced to his invitation, even if less than wholeheartedly. "Besides," he murmured, eyeing her desk with a teasing tone, "it looks like you need a break from all this government red tape."

Pepper groaned in response, then laughed. Suddenly, she felt free, euphoric. Going to her desk, she opened the bottom drawer and pulled out her dark brown elkskin knapsack, which doubled as a purse. They were having dinner, she admonished herself. That was all. A one-shot deal. "You ought to know," she countered. "You're in the military paper machine. I'm at the opposite end of the spectrum, but a government-run agency is a government-run agency."

Jim stepped aside, realizing Pepper needed to keep a safe distance from him. Did she have any of the urge to embrace him and kiss him that he felt for her? He wasn't at all sure, but his head cautioned him to proceed slowly, to feel his way intuitively with her. When she straightened and slung one strap of the knapsack over the Pendleton coat she'd donned, he smiled warmly at her.

Pepper felt the hot sunlight of Jim's smile—and the promise that came with it. Again, desire burned in his eyes. For her? Why? He loved Laura. She stepped past him and turned off the light, then closed and locked her office door behind them.

"If you're expecting a five-star restaurant out here, you'll be disappointed," she said as she switched off the main lights to the facility and the place was bathed in gloom once more. She took the lead, knowing the way to the door by heart.

"You choose," Jim told her. Their voices carried eerily through the structure. Pepper opened the door. As the last to leave, it was her responsibility to lock up. The air outside was freezing, their breath visible as they walked through the snow to the parking lot behind the building. Above, the night sky was dotted with thousands of sparkling stars. Pepper felt Jim come abreast of her, his shoulder sometimes brushing hers as they walked carefully along the snow-packed trail to the asphalt lot. A few street lamps lighted the way.

"Man, it's cold here," Jim said, pulling the collar of his leather jacket up around his neck.

Pepper nodded. With her heavy coat, she wore a warm knit cap and a pair of elkskin gloves lined with sheepskin. "Your D.C. gear won't keep you warm in Montana," she agreed. Her heart kept up its rapid beat. She felt like she was floating! All her awareness was focused on Jim, on the fact he was here— with her. As much as she wanted to let down her barriers, Pepper knew she didn't dare. She kept reminding herself of her own past pain, of Jim's involvement with Laura. Two good reasons to keep him at bay.

Giving him a quick, nervous glance, she reveled in the shadowed contours of his strong face. How desperately she wanted to explore it, to explore him. But there was no hope for them, she reminded herself for what felt like the millionth time.

Jim smiled warmly at Pepper, reading a mix of fear and confusion in her darkened eyes. They made it to the parking lot. The only two cars in it were parked side by side. "I can't think of a better place to be right now," he said. Pepper drove a Jeep, he noted, smiling to himself. The vehicle was obviously old, with a lot of dents and in need of a paint job. He had no doubts that on her days off, she blazed trails in the wilderness of the Montana Rockies, hence the less than mint condition of her intrepid vehicle.

Pepper dug into her knapsack for her keys. Her fingers were trembling—Jim's unsettling effect on her. She saw that his rental car was new and fairly clean, considering he'd driven from Anaconda. It made her wince at her beloved Jeep, which looked like a nag next to the thoroughbred of a car he had rented. Oh, well. He might as well know the real her. *Why?* The word haunted her. Turning at the door to her Jeep, she said, "There's a diner in town. It isn't much to look at, sort of like my Jeep here, but it serves great home-cooked food. Mandy, the owner, makes the best apple pie I've ever tasted. It's even better than my mom's, and hers is great."

Jim said, "Sold. I'm a sucker for a home-cooked meal."

"Spoken like a true military type. Home-cookin' is hard to get a hold of in the service."

Jim fished the keys from his pocket, momentarily lost in the laughter he saw flash in Pepper's eyes. How desperately he wanted to know this. Pepper, so comfortable in these giant mountains in their winter raiment and this sleepy town nestled deep in the valley.

"Just follow me. It isn't far," she called, sliding onto the cold seat of her Jeep.

Jim liked the old diner. It was straight out of the Depression era, with a mustard yellow interior, its chrome tables topped by red Formica. The place was filled at this time of night, mostly with locals who had been out getting firewood, hunters and townspeople. He noticed a Non Smoking sign on the door, and praised the owner for her courage in putting it up. Inside, he saw many Pendleton coats, red-and-black checked flannel shirts, knit caps and jeans.

As they walked down the aisle between the booths, Pepper was greeted warmly by the locals. There was no question that she was well liked, Jim thought, as he ambled behind her. Noticing the way just about every head in the place followed them to a corner booth, he smiled to himself. By the way he was dressed and his unfamiliar face, they all knew he was an outsider.

Sitting down across from Pepper, he murmured wryly, "Nothing like sticking out like a sore thumb, eh?"

She shed her coat, cap and gloves. "Don't take it personally. Usually, by this time of year, the tourists have left, and it's just us locals. When we see a dude from the East come in, it's a novelty, that's all."

The waitress, dressed in a white uniform with a black apron, smiled as she handed them menus and automatically filled their cups with coffee.

Pepper saw the look on Jim's face. "Around here, real men and women drink coffee."

"I see." He met her gaze which alternated between warmth one moment and wariness the next. "I'd really get talked about if I ordered hot tea with lemon, wouldn't I?"

She laughed heartily, holding his gaze. How wonderful his sense of humor was. Pepper realized how much she didn't know about Jim—and how much she wanted to know. Joy flowed through her, hot and sweet. Did she dare hope? Dare dream?

"You're really funny."

"Thank you, I'll take that as a compliment." Jim took a sip of coffee. "Whew, this is strong stuff."

Pepper said, "We have a saying about Mandy's coffee—actually, I guess it's a military saying. 'If you put a spoon in the center of the mug, it will stand at attention and salute you back.'"

"That's powerful coffee," Jim agreed, amused. Pepper's eyes cleared of wariness and her cheeks once again blossomed with their familiar pink, making her look excruciatingly lovely. He had to force himself to stop staring into her sky blue eyes. Did she realize how beautiful she was? How he wanted to tell her exactly that! Even more, he wanted to show her. The waitress returned, and Pepper ordered without even looking at the menu, so Jim surmised she was a regular here. He chose a T-bone steak with all the trimmings.

Trying to quell her nervousness, Pepper cleared her dry throat and asked, "How long will you be here?"

Jim became serious, his smile dissolving. He felt renewed tension radiating from Pepper, and he lifted his heavy white coffee mug in both hands. The old jukebox in the corner was playing a romantic song from the sixties, a slow song—one of his favorites. "Well, I got an open-ended return ticket." His throat ached with tension.

"Oh."

He looked up through his lashes. "Really, it depends upon you."

Pepper sat very still. Her heart pulsed powerfully. "With Christmas coming, I imagine you'll want to be home," she murmured nervously.

Shrugging, Jim said, "Home is where the heart is." He looked around the diner and then back at her, his expression growing tender. "I know you go home for Christmas to visit your folks."

"Yes . . ." Pepper stared down at her coffee mug, her hands clasped in her lap beneath the table. She began perspiring as her mind leapt to a number of responses, none of them seeming appropriate. Out of sheer desperation, she whispered, "The roses you sent were beautiful, Jim. I didn't really thank you for them."

He smiled tentatively, watching her closely. "I wanted to le
you know, in some way, how I felt about you. About us..."
Pepper, he was discovering, wouldn't look him in the eye whe
she was nervous. Instead, she stared down or past him. Thi
woman warrior, who had more courage and guts than most o
the men he knew, was wonderfully vulnerable in a way tha
made him want to protect her. There was nothing hard or im
placable about Pepper. She was right—she had clung to he
femininity and not allowed the male world to strip her of it, a
it had so many other women who'd been in the military. Sud
denly the love he held for her seemed so incalculably deep an
moving that he knew he'd never be able to put it into words. H
could only show her—if she would allow him that privilege.

Pepper sat very still, absorbing the huskiness of Jim's voice
the seeming sincerity behind his words. This was not the place
with all the locals who knew her around, to start a highly emo
tional, personal conversation with Jim. It would have to wait
she realized sadly. When they were done with dinner, she woul
suggest they go back to her office and talk. It was all they ha
left between them, she realized lamely. Honest talk. Forcing
pain-filled smile, she made herself look at him. Inevitably, he
heart melted, and a little more of her fear with it. Jim's gaz
was so direct—fearlessly burning with a warmth that left he
breathless and feeling incredibly beautiful.

"I—they were nice. I mean, they were more than nice. I wa
so surprised," she stammered, opening her hands. "That wa
only the third time in my life I ever got roses, and I've neve
gotten that many." She touched her brow and smiled apolo
getically. "They really were beautiful, Jim. I was just over
whelmed by them, by your gesture."

"I hoped," he said in a low voice, leaning slightly forward
"that it would act as a door to forgiveness."

Tilting her head, Pepper said, "Forgiveness?" She shrugged
"What do you mean?"

"In my letter," Jim said, holding her startled look, "I sai
how I'd neglected you when we got off the island. Lookin
back on it, Pepper, I realize I really screwed up. I was overl
focused on Laura and her problems."

Shaking her head, Pepper whispered, "Listen, Laura stopped breathing. I'd say you should be concerned. I know I was. I felt helpless. It was a terrible feeling to be sitting on the deck of that chopper, knowing I couldn't do a thing." Frustration ate at her. "I've done CPR before, and I knew how you were feeling. Laura means ... a lot to you. I know that." Without thinking, she reached out and briefly touched the hand wrapped around his coffee cup. "And I don't blame you, Jim. Even if you didn't know Laura, you'd probably have reacted the same way. I'm aware of how deeply you care for people."

Pepper was internally aghast that she'd touched Jim, and she quickly withdrew her hand. What on earth was she thinking? Right now she was reacting without thinking—the worst possible thing she could do. Not only that, but in touching him she'd discovered, to her dismay, that she only wanted to touch him more. She wanted to lay her hand on his arm, slide it up beneath the sleeve of his shirt and feel the wiry quality of his dark, springy hair. Wanted to feel the latent strength of his muscles leap and harden beneath her exploration.

The briefest touch of her hand sent a tingle of need flying through Jim, igniting the fire deep within him to a flame that burned with a powerful hunger he couldn't fulfill except with Pepper. "A fault of mine at times," he murmured wryly, holding her warm gaze.

Pepper's fingertips still tingled from her imprudent touch. How strong Jim was, in ways she presently was not. "Never a fault," she rattled, her emotions very close to the surface. "There aren't a whole lot of people out there who take commitment for what it really means anymore—for sticking with a person through thick and thin." With a shake of her head, she rasped, "No, I like your loyalty to people. Your commitment to them, no matter what."

"I wanted to get out here to see you much sooner," Jim admitted, "but I couldn't. Part of it was that Laura needed me, and I was damn well determined to hunt down some or the rest of her family before I left Washington."

"I would have expected nothing less of you, Jim. In some ways, we're alike," she murmured as the waitress brought their salads and a small loaf of hot bread. Pepper was absolutely not hungry for the usually appetizing food. The only hunger she had was for Jim—to love him, hold him and become one with him. Forcing her mind away from her unruly yearning, she whispered unsteadily, "People count with me. I want to make a difference in their lives as much as I do in my own."

"It's called unselfishness—a commodity too long lost in our society, particularly in the past decade," he said wryly. Jim didn't want to eat; he wanted to talk, to explore Pepper—to spend the rest of his life discovering all her wonderful facets. But he forced himself to pick at the salad, occasionally glancing at her. Pepper wasn't eating very much, either, and he struggled to contain his impatience. Timing was everything. He would have to wait until later.

Chapter Twelve

After dinner, Jim knew it was time to get down to serious business with Pepper. Now or never, he thought. Neither of them had eaten very much. As they approached Pepper's Jeep, he reached out, wrapping his fingers around her arm and gently drawing her to a halt. She turned, startled, her eyes searching his.

"We need some privacy so we can have a talk, Pepper."

Gulping, Pepper was wildly aware of his monitored strength on her arm. He was so close—inches away. His breath came out in white wisps as he spoke in a low tone to her. The shadows and light carved his face, accenting its strength as well as its tenderness, from the way the corners of his mouth were flexed to the burning quality in the depth of his serious eyes.

"Okay," she said, a little breathless. "How about my office?" That was safe, neutral territory, she thought.

Jim forced himself to withdraw his hand from her arm. "How about your home, if that's okay with you?" He didn't want to risk interruption once they started to discuss everything. Her silence told him a great deal. She didn't want him there.

Pepper's pulse was fluttering wildly at Jim's softly spoken request. The desire to reach up and slide her arms around his shoulders, to melt against him and feel that strong mouth on her own was nearly her undoing. *Home*. Her home. Her empty, lifeless home, where she'd felt so alone since returning from the mission. Her hands fluttering over the knapsack as she dug for her keys, she said, "Just follow me. It isn't far from town."

Jim nodded. He ached to touch her fiery red cheek, to smooth a strand of precocious hair away from her brow. Pepper was shaken by his request, he could see. But no more shaken than he was by fear over what was to come.

Pepper's cabin was warm, the fire in the stove sending an orangy glow through the living room. Jim fought himself—his need to reach out and touch Pepper. They had gone directly from the garage into the warmth of her living quarters. Pepper stood apart from him, nervously tugging the knit cap off her glorious hair, which tumbled in a shiny cascade about her tense features. Her hands were trembling, he noticed. As she tried to undo the buttons on her coat, his mouth went dry.

"Here, let me help..." he murmured thickly, stepping forward, his hands closing over hers.

Pepper gasped at his sudden, unexpected move. Jim's hands were strong, warm and cherishing on her cold ones. Her head snapped up. Her heart slammed into her ribs. Lost in the darkness of his predatory gaze, she parted her lips breathlessly beneath his tense, silent scrutiny. In less than a heartbeat, she whispered his name. It came out broken, pleading. The look in his eyes changed, grew narrower. Intent.

Without thinking, throwing all caution to the wind, Pepper raised her hands and settled them about his strong shoulders. Instantly, she felt Jim's arms wrap about her like tight bands, drawing her hard against him. The air rushed out of her lungs. She tipped her chin upward. He called her name—a low growl that jagged through her like lightning. His mouth claimed hers hotly, conquering her weak protest. The taste of him, the power of him combined to overwhelm her as she opened her lips far-her to drink deeply of his offering. Time dissolved and only his sandpapery skin against her cheek, his mouth taking hers, his ragged breath against her face existed.

Pepper's hands ranged awkwardly across his jacket, finding the opening and moving up across his shirt. She felt the immense breadth of his chest, his muscles bunching and tightening under the skimming touch of her eager, exploring hands. Sagging against him, she returned the raw desire of his mouth against hers, tasting him, sliding her tongue across his. Unable to get enough of him, she pushed the leather jacket off his shoulders, vaguely hearing it drop to the cedar floor at their feet. His hand moved downward, pinning her hips against him in a grinding motion meant to convey his need of her. Instantly, heat exploded within her, and her knees weakened as his fingers curved over her, capturing her even more tightly against him.

Jim tore his mouth from hers. Nothing mattered but now. Right now. To hell with all the reasons—the barriers that stood in their way. This was real. This was what they both needed. Wanted. His arms tightly holding, he lifted her effortlessly. Looking around, he spotted a hallway and carried her down it until he found her bedroom.

Fragments of light stole into the darkened expanse. It was enough. He took her quickly to the bed and laid her on it, continuing to undress her. Off came her coat, which dropped to the floor beside the old brass bed frame. The sultry look in Pepper's half-closed eyes told him everything he needed to know. Thinking was no longer possible. Driven by something so primal he could no longer control it or himself, he tugged impatiently at the buttons on her blouse until it opened to reveal the pale pink silk of her bra. His eyes narrowed upon her breasts, which were rising and falling in ragged timing with his own harsh breathing. As Pepper's hands moved upward, pushing his shirt off his shoulders, Jim growled. He was more animal than man—and more ravenous than he'd ever been.

Each heartbeat, each touch burned like a brand through Pepper's skin as Jim's hands ranged up and down her rib cage. His mouth claimed hers again, and she took his weight as her slacks and panties were pushed aside. Each movement of his

mouth drove her deeper and deeper into the fire. The agony in
her lower body was like a conflagration. As his fingers tunneled through her hair, her hands slid down to his pants, tugging and pulling at his belt.

Jim froze as Pepper's hand brushed his hardness, his zipper
opening easily beneath her trembling fingers. Moving to one
side, he pushed his chinos off along with his shorts. He soared
inwardly at the sensuous look in her eyes. Never had two people been so meant for each other, he realized as he leaned down,
again capturing her soft, glistening mouth.

As he eased down upon her, she arched her hips upward. Air
hissed between Jim's clenched teeth as she brazenly brushed
against his hardness. She was like velvet, giving and teasing. He
slid one hand beneath her hips and felt her breath hitch as he
eased his knee between her strong thighs. The look in her eyes
was molten, expectant. Her lips parted in a silent welcome.
There was such overwhelming urgency that he couldn't wait.
Wouldn't wait. Neither would she. Just as he tried to counter
the flowing forces careening through him, to ease into her, she
thrust upward, taking him, consuming him.

A startled cry of joy burst from Pepper's lips as she felt him
plunge into her, filling her. Tipping her head back, she closed
her eyes, his name an answered prayer on her lips. Unable to
catch her breath, she felt his hand center on her lower back,
bring her up hard against him as he rocked deeply into her. A
rippling, melting sensation emanated from her core outward.
She was dissolving beneath his capturing motion. Each movement was unrelenting, deeper and more consuming than the
last. She gripped his shoulders, her fingers opening and closing spasmodically against his skin. The sense of oneness, of
flesh meeting and being forged in the fire of something over-
whelmingly beautiful and cleansing, tunneled through her.
Each rocking movement brought her higher and higher, closer
and closer to that ragged cliff of unequaled sensation. As he
molded his mouth to her, drinking of her, the movement of his
hips thrusting against her triggered an avalanche of molten lava
pulsing through her lower body. Her lashes dropped and she
surrendered fully to his hands, his mouth, his exquisite body
fused with hers, and an intense pleasure swirled through her.

Jim felt the hot, cascading explosion surround him, and moments later he froze against Pepper, their hips locked in a primal union as he spilled richly into her silken depths. His fists locked on either side of her head, his body straining against hers. With each pulsing release, the heat tripled. He felt as if he were being consumed in the white-hot core of a fire, and the only thing that existed in his universe was her.

The moments strung tautly together. Pepper moaned and became limp in Jim's arms. She felt his mouth on her cheek, kissing her lashes, her nose and her parted lips. The smell of him, the dampness of his strong body sliding against hers, were all precious to her. Forgotten sensations from so long ago had been brought to new and vibrant life. She felt his hand move shakily across her hair and she opened her eyes. Pepper drowned in the darkness of his gaze, gleaming with a fiercely tender light. Even now, spent by the explosiveness of their lovemaking, she began to realize just how deeply she touched him. As his hand skimmed her breast, feathering across her hardening nipple, she gasped with pleasure.

He smiled and leaned down, capturing the peak between his lips, suckling her. The sensation was throbbing. Electric. How easily he brought her to ripe awareness of her need of him again. Pepper reached up with her hand, sliding her fingers through his short, dark hair. As he eased his lips from her breast, his eyes glittered with triumph and satiation. Words were too primitive for what she was feeling toward him. How could she have ever thought they weren't meant for each other?

Jim captured Pepper's hand, opening her palm and kissing the center of it, then slowly licking it with his tongue. He felt her move. He smiled inwardly. Pepper was as wild and natural as the earth that had bred her. She was more than a woman of the soil; she was like the majestic mountains that encircled this small town—outwardly beautiful and tranquil, with a roaring volcano of potential beneath that exterior raiment.

Exhaustion ate at Jim, and he slowly eased out of her—the last thing he wanted to do right now. If he hadn't been so tired, he'd have started loving her all over again, but he knew the limits of his body. Without a word, he pulled back the thick, downy quilt, the smooth cotton sheet and eased her beneath them. Pepper's eyes were nearly closed. He understood that she needed sleep, too. Slipping beneath the covers, he contented himself with drawing her into his arms. Gratified as she moved her length against him, he sighed.

"Let's sleep, sweetheart," he murmured near her ear as she settled her head against his shoulder. "We can talk in the morning...."

Pepper nodded, unable to speak. Right now she felt so weak and sated that all she wanted was Jim's continued nearness, the scent of him, the touch of him. Nothing else mattered. As she spiraled downward into a deep, healing sleep, she realized that she'd broken her word to herself: she'd sworn after John's death never to love again. Now she'd not only done that, but she'd loved a man who loved another.

It was all too complicated, and her heart felt satisfied regardless of what the halls of her mind whispered. Right now, only the moment meant anything. Tomorrow would come soon enough.

Jim awoke slowly. For a brief moment, he was lost, until awakened enough to realize he was at Pepper's home in Montana. Opening his eyes, he searched for her warmth. She was gone.... Instantly, he sat up, the covers pooling around his waist. Blinking away sleep, he looked around. The clock on the pine dresser read ten a.m. Ten! Throwing the covers aside, he located his chinos and pulled them on. Keying his hearing, he recognized the soft crackling of the wood stove in the living room. Classical music—Mozart, he realized—played in the background. The floor was cool beneath his bare feet as he launched himself upward.

Pushing several strands of hair off his forehead, he hurried into the hall toward the living room. He came to a halt at the door. Dressed in an old pair of jeans and a bright red sweater, Pepper was curled up on the couch near the fire, a book in hand. As if sensing his presence, she lifted her head. His heart thumped in his chest as he anxiously searched her eyes. She had such serenity, yet he found a mass of emotions in the depths of her thoughtful eyes. He didn't care if he wasn't fully dressed. What mattered was her—and them.

"Good morning," Pepper whispered, slowly closing the book and setting it aside. How wonderful Jim looked clothed only in the body-hugging chinos. His chest was broad and covered with thick dark hair that emphasized his powerful masculinity. She had loved that wonderful body last night, and the memory sent such a warming sensation through her that she could barely hold Jim's devouring gaze. Still, she saw anxiety in his eyes—and worry? About what? Her? Them? Pepper felt so tentative and uncertain. She sat up, her hands clasped in her lap.

Jim walked over to her, his gaze never leaving hers. When he sat down, his knee rested against her leg. He reached out and gripped her hands. "It is," he said huskily, his voice still filled with sleep.

"You look worried," she observed.

"You weren't in my arms when I woke up." He gave her a partial smile and looked down at her long, spare hands—hands that had loved him last night. Hands that he wanted loving him always. "Last night," he began with an effort, "wasn't planned, Pepper. I swear it...." He held her wavering gaze. It was important that she believe him, he thought, recalling their "no strings attached" conversation back at her office.

Bowing her head, she managed a painful smile. His hands were warm and tender over hers. "I—I know, Jim."

Relief cascaded through him. "Thank God...."

Risking everything, Pepper raised her head and met his searching eyes. "I thought we might go for a snow picnic this morning. A kind of brunch in the snow." She smiled a little wistfully and pointed out the picture window of her cabin. "It stopped snowing last night and the temperature has risen. I've already packed us a thermos of hot chocolate, made some scrambled-egg sandwiches and fried some bacon."

He studied her in the strained silence. Her cheeks were flushed, and her voice wavered with uncertainty. Jim felt her pain. Gripping her hands surely in his, he rasped, "That sounds great. Let me grab a quick shower, a shave and a change of clothes?"

"Sure...."

* * *

Pepper had two sets of skis waiting for them in the garage
After helping Jim into his, she easily attached hers to her boots
Jim carried the knapsack containing their brunch, while she le
them out into the crisp air and across the deep, white snow. I
was nearly noon, and the sun peeked out from behind grayis
clouds that hung low around the tops of the mighty mountain
surrounding Phillipsburg. The dark green forest contraste
sharply with the pristine snow. Every once in a while, Jim no
ticed a patch of brilliant blue sky, quickly swallowed up by th
swift-moving clouds. But his heart was centered only on Pep
per, who moved with such abandoned grace, gliding easily o
her skis as she led them deep into the forest.

It was as if she telepathically knew they had to talk, but ha
chosen the time and place herself. Jim was content with he
decision. He knew Pepper had done it to shore herself u
against whatever he might say to her. She was noticeably ten
tative, the wariness observable in her eyes. How badly h
wanted to ease her inner pain, but he didn't know how. Mayb
after they'd shared an intimate lunch in surroundings tha
nurtured her, he could finally communicate with her.

A blue jay screeched suddenly above them, startled by thei
silent approach, sending snow flying off the branch where i
had been sitting. The powdery flakes fell around them lik
stardust thrown by an invisible magician. Jim laughed at th
beauty of the sunlight striking the tiny particles, which spar
kled around them like miniature rainbows. He saw the appre
ciation in Pepper's eyes, too, and began to realize humbly jus
how much she was a part of this forest. She was, for the in
stant they watched the jay take flight, a child in awe, innocen
and filled with the rapture of life. A fierce tidal wave of love
flowed through him, and he fought the urge to reach thos
precious inches with his gloved hand and caress her fiery cheek
Her red cap emphasized her large eyes, and the dark curls es
caping from beneath it shouted of her femininity.

"It isn't far," she whispered, smiling at him. How changed
Jim's face had become, Pepper realized in that moment. Gone
was the eternal stress she'd seen around his mouth and eyes
before and during the mission. Gone was the tight line of his

mouth. When he smiled, her heart mushroomed with a joy so fierce that Pepper thought she might faint from it. Her, of all people! The tough fire fighter! She laughed at herself, at the momentary appreciation they shared of their surroundings—and each other. Sadness ate at the foundation of her happiness, though, and not wanting to spoil the moment for Jim, she turned away and continued on up the gentle slope of the hill to her favorite spot.

At least a dozen huge cedar trees made a semicircle at the top of the hill, providing a secure nook against the wind, although the breeze was light now anyway. Pepper removed her skis and, with Jim's help, laid a dark blue, plastic-backed blanket on the snow. The sunlight shone strongly now, reflecting brightly off the limitless white expanse. Most of the clouds had moved away toward the east. Pepper felt a contentment here on this knoll as she helped Jim spread out their brunch on the blanket. Finally, she sat down, and he sat less than a foot away, facing her.

"This is incredible," he confided quietly, in awe of the beauty that surrounded them.

Pepper poured some hot chocolate and offered it to him. "Isn't it?"

"You're beautiful," he whispered, taking the cup from her. He saw her blush and look away as she poured herself some in turn.

Pepper set her cup aside and offered him one of the scrambled-egg sandwiches she'd made. "Last night," she began awkwardly, "was beautiful." And it had been. His nearness was pulverizing. Did Jim realize the overwhelming effect he had on her? Was he torturing her on purpose? Reminding her she was a woman with fiery needs that matched his own?

Pepper didn't believe he knew her feelings toward him. Yes, they'd shared wild, hungry passion, but sex didn't necessarily equate with love. How could he know what lay in her heart? He loved Laura with a blind certainty that everyone could see—everyone except him. What did he want to talk about? She nibbled at her sandwich, not really tasting it.

Jim took a deep breath, watching Pepper's lips purse as she stared down at her sandwich. Why did this have to be so painful to both of them? He laughed at himself and considered the

question. If he didn't have so much at stake, if he didn't care
as deeply as he did, he'd be able to cope much more easily with
the potential pain of a rebuff.

As he exhaled, he spoke. "I've had more than enough time
to think about you since we got back from Nevis."

Pepper turned her head just enough to meet and hold his serious, darkened gaze. A lump jammed her throat, and it was
impossible to make a sound. Her heart was hammering.

Jim saw the wariness come to her eyes—along with unshed
tears. Damn, those tears! He couldn't stand to see them, and
automatically he put his hands on her slumped shoulder and
forced her to look up at him. "Sweetheart, don't cry...please.
Tears tear the hell out of me," he rasped unsteadily.

His voice tugged at Pepper's heart, unraveling her emotions. His hands had fallen gently upon her and his eyes burned
with a tenderness she'd never believed existed in any man—but
obviously it existed in Jim. Her lips parted, and a choking sob
escaped. Tears burned in her eyes, and she felt his fingers
tighten against her jacket. Anguish was in his voice and in the
way his mouth twisted with her pain. She felt foolish, as if she
couldn't control her feelings in his presence.

"What are those tears about?" he demanded huskily,
reaching up and using his thumbs to remove them from her
now-pale cheeks. "Pepper? Talk to me. When I kissed you on
Nevis, you cried, too. It wasn't the time or place to ask why, but
it's bothered the hell out of me. Why are you crying?"

Pepper felt her defenses crumbling. "I—I can't...it's too
late," she said in a choked voice.

"Too late?" Jim demanded, his hands upon her shoulders.
"What are you talking about?"

The intensity of his gaze held hers relentlessly. Jim was going to make her say it. Never had she felt so foolish. So helpless. "I—I didn't want to have feelings for you, Jim. A-after
John died, I went into a horrible nosedive. Shock, I guess. I
went around like a zombie, not feeling anything. My friends
couldn't help me, my family—no one could help. For over a
year, I felt numb to living." She looked up and blinked away
the tears as she gestured to the huge cedar trees. "See how
beautiful these trees are? After John died, I came up here and

couldn't feel anything. Before that, I would feel my heart open, like a flower. I could sit up here, no matter how badly life had treated me, and feel at peace. Feel whole.''

Pepper sighed and shook her head. ''When I came home after John's funeral, I came up here. I stood in this grove and I felt nothing. It scared me. After that—'' she frowned, avoiding his sharpened gaze ''—I plunged into the darkest barrel in the world. The doctors said it was depression. I called it a living hell.'' She touched her breast over her heart. ''Jim, I can't even begin to tell you how awful that year was. Finally, slowly, I began to come out of it. And as I did, I felt pain like I'd never felt before. I never knew that kind of pain existed. Every time I thought of John, of what we'd shared—what we'd planned to share—I felt this knife twisting in my heart. It literally took my breath away. I'd start hyperventilating.''

Pepper put the sandwich aside and gave him a sad look. ''I had been such an active, outgoing person before that, Jim. But suddenly I had no energy, no will to live. It affected my work, my interactions with team members—my family and my friends. It took nearly two years for me to climb out of that hole.'' She took a deep, ragged breath and looked up at the trees clothed in snow. ''I was so afraid of ever feeling that way again that I decided to shut off the possibility of romantic love. I moved my commitment to my job, my family and my friends instead.'' Shaking her head, Pepper whispered, ''I'd learned that love was the one thing that could bring me down—could break me and stop me from living and meeting the goals I'd set for myself. I made friends of any men who wanted to date me. I steered clear of entanglements.'' She lifted her head and stared at him. ''I was successful at it. I had managed to control my life so it wouldn't ever hurt me that way again.''

''I . . .'' Jim allowed his hand to drop from her shoulder, digesting her pain and the intimacy of her admission. ''Love can be hell,'' he admitted somberly.

''To say the least,'' she said brokenly.

''That's why I see so much fear in your eyes?''

''Partly,'' Pepper admitted rawly. ''I never expected to kiss you, if you want the truth.''

He smiled deprecatingly. "I didn't, either. But I'm not sorr
that it happened, Pepper." When her head snapped up and he
eyes widened, he added, "Not ever."

"I—" she struggled visibly with the admission. "—I though
we kissed after you almost fell to your death in that jump be
cause we were happy we'd both survived it."

"And the island?" he asked quietly. "What did you writ
that off to?"

Wearily, she said, "I wrote it off to the stress we were under
that we could be killed at any moment. I felt guilty for having
caused you to be injured in the first place. Guilt and worry—'

"I didn't write either of those kisses off," Jim said soberly.

Pepper stared at him, the silence brittle. "Why?" she fi
nally forced herself to ask.

Jim felt her tension, saw the grief and terror in her eyes. Now
that he was beginning to understand what was behind Pep
per's wariness, he rasped, "A certain woman walked into my
life and made me rethink what I wanted out of it."

Tears stung her eyes. Her voice cracked. "Y-you love
Laura...." There, it was finally out. The truth.

Jim stared down at her for a very long, painful minute. His
hands tightened considerably.

Pepper saw the darkness in his eyes, but her tears wouldn'
stop. Frustrated, she swiped at them with both hands. "I said
you love Laura. There's no room in your life for anyone else,
Jim!"

Jim assimilated her heated, anguished words. The suffering
in her face tore at him. Her lower lip trembled as the tears
streamed down her cheeks. With a groan, he called her name
and moved closer before she could escape. His hands closed
around her upper arms.

"I'll admit my understanding of my feelings for Laura were
confused. My emotions ran deeper than I realized. I had fallen
for her a long time ago, Pepper, before Morgan entered her life
The truth is I was far more interested in a possible relationship
with her than she ever was with me. I was being an idealist
about it, putting her on some kind of pedestal—and that was
my fault, not hers. When Morgan came into her life, I was bit

er for a long time. After a year or so, I got over it, or at least I thought I had."

Pepper met his suffering eyes. "And when Laura was kidnapped?"

His mouth went grim. "It raised a lot of unresolved feelings I'd buried inside, Pepper. When you and I kissed up on that ridge after I damn near died in that jump, I got even more confused. I liked you, but my worry for Laura and the stuff I hadn't worked through about her was clouding how I saw you." He eased his hands from her shoulders. "I don't love Laura. Yes, she's a good friend who deserves my loyalty, but I never truly loved her." He gently smoothed back several tendrils that clung to her damp cheeks.

Jim's hands were warm, strong and dry against Pepper's face, and she wanted so badly to fall into his arms and be held. Fighting it with the last of her emotional strength, she met his confused gaze. "Back in your condominium I saw how much you cared for her. I challenged you on your feelings for her, but you wouldn't admit anything."

"Yes, I recall now what I said when we had our talk." Frustration cracked his voice. "Sweetheart, that was a long time ago. I no more love Laura now than she loves me. She loves Morgan with every breath she takes. I've never seen two people more in love, more committed, than they are to each other." He touched her wrinkled forehead and her cheek. "I don't love her, Pepper. Please, you've got to believe me. I know I screwed up with you. Badly. So much happened so fast. We had a mission to concentrate on." He pursed his lips, holding her lustrous gaze and seeing some of the pain dissolve from her eyes.

She nodded. "Yes, there was a lot going on," she conceded.

He raised his hands and followed the curve of her soft, dark hair with them. "I knew we'd come to some impasse between us. I felt it before and especially after the mission. Is that why you left the Coast Guard cutter early? You couldn't stand being around me because you thought I was in love with Laura?"

Miserably, Pepper nodded. Each caressing touch he bestowed eased a bit more of her pain. She absorbed his gentleness like a desert plant too long without water. How she thirsted for his touch! The feeling was startling, heated. "I know she

almost died," she whispered unsteadily, "and I didn't blam
you for devoting your attention to her. It wasn't Laura's fault
I've never blamed either of you. Sometimes love happens lik
that. It's no one's fault."

Making a frustrated sound, Jim pulled Pepper into his arms
At first she stiffened, but then, in increments, he began to fee
her surrender. "Sweetheart, from the moment I set eyes on you
I knew you were special. I admit," Jim said harshly, burying hi
face against her hair, "that I was a royal bastard at first. Yes
I was upset that Laura had been kidnapped. She's been m
friend for many years, and I like her, but that's all. I respec
Morgan. I sure as hell don't wish that man any more pain tha
he's already suffered at the hands of our government. Yes,
was upset when Laura first fell for him. But I'm not an obses
sive person, Pepper." Jim eased her away from him just enoug
to place his finger beneath her chin and make her look into hi
eyes. She had to understand his sincerity on the most basi
level.

"When I finally understood that Laura loved Morgan a
much as he obviously loved her, I backed off. Maybe I was a bi
of a burr under their collective saddle for a while, but after
realized what was going down, I let her go."

Pepper drank in his dark, intense gaze. He was so close. S
wonderfully close. She could feel the hard beat of his hea
against her breast. His arms were strong, supporting, and fo
the first time in a long time, she allowed her full weight to lea
against him. His gaze was probing, and she felt his frustra
tion.

"Laura is like a ghost from your past," she whispered.

"Yes," Jim rasped, "and I've been battling your ghost, too."
Pepper frowned. "What are you talking about?"

"Captain John Freedman," he said, scowling. "I've watche
your face change every time you talk about him, Pepper. I saw
your eyes fill with tears, heard your voice go soft. What els
could I think? Hell, it took every ounce of courage I possess t
get up the gumption to fly out here and face you. I felt Freed
man still had a claim on your heart."

"He doesn't . . . not any longer. I—I thought Laura claime
yours," Pepper admitted, embarrassed.

"No more," Jim whispered, touching her cheek. "There's a beautiful, strong, confident woman I'm holding in my arms this very moment. She's the one who holds my heart in her hands."

Pepper reached up, her fingers sliding along the strong line of his jaw. "John is gone," she whispered unsteadily. "And yes, I mourned for him." She squeezed her eyes shut against the pain. "I knew that because I was so different—because I refused to be anyone but myself—I would scare most men away, Jim." She allowed her hand to rest on his freshly shaved cheek and opened her eyes. "John was the only man who loved me just the way I was. He loved my confidence, the job I did in the army, my talents and skills. He loved me. He didn't try to pigeonhole me into what women are supposed to do by society's standards. He didn't care. He loved me for walking my own path in life, and I loved him for allowing me to be myself. There just aren't that many men out there who are confident enough in their own masculinity to let women be all they can be."

Jim smiled tenderly and brushed her tears away with his fingertips. "I understand," he whispered. "You're a new breed of woman, Pepper. You've been lucky enough to have parents who supported you regardless of gender, and you've been lucky to be born at a time in history where women are grudgingly being allowed to develop fully. That's one of the things that drew me to Laura. She's a lot like you, you know."

Pepper gave him a confused look. "I don't see much similarity between us."

He smiled a little and caressed her damp cheek. "That's because you don't really know Laura. She's held down a man's job in the defense industry for years. She's a noted specialist on defense issues. And like you, she never abandoned her femininity to become 'one of the boys.' Beyond that, Laura is opinionated, stubborn and knows what she knows—just like you."

"I don't think I'm opinionated or stubborn. If I were a man, you'd say I know my own mind and know what I stand for."

Jim grinned a little, feeling some of the tension drain from her, even as it drained away from him. He saw a spark of defiance flare in her eyes along with desire—for him he hoped.

"You're right," he amended. "You see, I'm still learning to give ground gracefully to women in general. I'm not as liberated or ahead of my time as John was." He held her gaze. "I wish I were, Pepper. But I'm beginning to understand what kind of raw, continual courage it takes to stay strong within yourself. Laura was the first woman to make me aware of that. Now you. I've been watching her gather up the shattered pieces of herself, not knowing whether she'll ever see her son or husband again, and she's fighting to heal herself despite that ongoing trauma. She has guts." Jim leaned down, his mouth barely brushing her tear-stained lips. "Like you," he whispered against them.

Pepper moaned as Jim's strong lips brushed hers. Without thinking, she found her arms sliding around his broad shoulders, feeling the latent power of his muscles beneath his jacket, discovering the power of his mouth as he pinned her against him. He eased her down on the blanket, the sun warm upon them, and a heated bolt of lightning seemed to plunge through her as his mouth moved confidently across hers, igniting a fire of such burning need that it turned her knees to jelly. His mouth was at once ravishing and tender, and she felt his ragged breath chase across her cheek as he deepened his kiss, taking her completely.

Pepper was lost to everything except Jim and his mouth covering hers. Their hearts clamored in unison, their bodies stretching and reaching toward each other, crying for closeness. As Pepper surrendered against Jim, her breasts pressing into his chest and the points of their hips grinding together as their thighs fused, she moaned in pure joy. The joy of celebration. Jim didn't love Laura! He was here to see her and only her. Her arms tightened around his neck, and she felt him tremble with barely contained need.

"Love me...." she whispered, dragging her mouth from his. Breathing unevenly, she unzipped his jacket. The day was perfect, the sky a dark, clear blue, and the world seemed to be holding its breath. She felt Jim open her jacket and ease it off her. The jackets became pillows as they stretched out on the blanket. Pepper's emotions were alive, illuminating her as if some golden light had been switched on within her very soul.

She turned and, with shaking fingers, began to unbutton Jim's shirt. He smiled down at her. It was a very male smile, filled with incredible tenderness as he in turn, slowly unbuttoned her blouse.

Both articles fell to one side, and Jim's fingers lingered against Pepper's warm satiny skin, tracing the outline of her collarbones. She didn't have an ounce of fat on her, just solid, firm muscle shouting of a woman who was strong on so many levels that his heart nearly burst with need. She was his equal in every way, and he savored the discovery as he unbuttoned her slacks. Kneeling over her, he allowed his hands to slide down the length of her firm, long thighs and calves. Helping Pepper out of the slacks, he slowly stood.

The smile on her mouth was dessert in itself for him, as was her look of devilry combined with desire. He admired her boldness and relaxed as she got to her knees, reached up and unbuttoned his Levi's. Her hands were warm and followed the lines of his hardened thighs as she slowly, tortuously, slid his jeans downward. Jim sucked in a deep breath as her hands lingered against the bulging hardness displayed beneath the denim. She caressed him, then pulled the Levi's lower. Jim tunneled his fingers through her hair, gently gripping it for a moment as she returned to caress him again. Heat burned through him, and he nearly lifted her off her feet after he was rid of his clothes. The chill of the air was sharp, contrasting to the heat of Pepper's hands on his skin.

The look in her eyes set him on fire. He knelt down, capturing her mouth, ravishing her soft lips, pressing her hard against him as his fingers sought and found the hooks of her bra and released them. The silky fabric fell away, and Jim broke the kiss, breathing hard. Pepper was so perfect, her breasts small, proud and begging to be seduced—by him.

He felt her hands slide beneath his white T-shirt and slowly push the cotton fabric upward. He surrendered, allowing her to undress him. A look of pleasure entered her eyes as she ran her artistic fingers through the dark hair of his chest. Every touch was like a feathery brand. Groaning, Jim pulled her against him, feeling the soft brush of her breasts. As he slid his hands along her supple spine, he was again aware of how firm and muscular she was.

Laying her back on the blanket, he moved his hands down over her hips. Her belly was softly rounded, ripe for carrying babies, he thought hazily as he teased her silky panties away from her long, coltish legs. She lay before him naked, vulnerable. As he joined her on the blanket, he drew her into his arms.

Pepper inhaled sharply as Jim's hand moved provocatively up her rib cage, caressing, exploring. The hair of his chest teased her nipples, and they hardened. She waited in near frustration as his fingers moved slowly around her breast, shaping it, savoring the feel of her. He leaned down, his mouth capturing the hardened peak, and the warmth and moistness sent a shattering heat streaking through her. In that moment, her world revolved around his strong touch, the power of his body and the trembling control he barely held over it.

She arched against him, begging him to enter her. His smile was primal, as before, but the look in his burning eyes said not yet. She wasn't helpless. He could clearly see that she longed to please him as much as he was pleasing her. Reaching down, sliding her hands along his narrow flanks, she caressed him. A groan ripped from him, and he stiffened against her. She smiled at him this time, and he met her mouth with a growing intensity. Their breath mingled, and she welcomed his weight as he settled above her.

Pepper wasn't disappointed. Jim thrust hard and deep into her, and her wet heat met his plunge as he buried himself in her. A moan of pleasure rippled from her throat, and she threw her head back, feeling his arm slide beneath her neck, bringing her more tightly against him. The rhythm was wild, unfettered. Devouring. She matched him thrust for thrust, moving with him, engaging his powerful movements with her own totally feminine response. Their bodies grew hot and slick, the friction burning them up, consuming them as their mouths clung to each other with frenzied abandon.

Pepper's world shifted, then tilted as he slid his hand beneath her hips, bringing her into irrevocable union with him. Her cry of release was caught and drowned in his mouth as she surrendered herself to him. Seconds later, he stiffened against her, nearly crushing her, squeezing her breath from her as he held her to his trembling, damp body. Moments—golden, heated—spun by, entwining them as tightly as her arms were locked around his narrow waist.

Wordlessly, Jim loosened his grip on her and framed her face, now damp and flushed, as he once again claimed her soft, well-kissed mouth. Her sweetness flowed through him. Tenderly easing his mouth from hers, he brought her down on the blanket. When her fearless blue eyes met his, he smiled gently, still feeling her heat, her tightness—not wanting to give up this sense of oneness he'd never before experienced.

"I dreamed of you every night," Jim whispered, nuzzling her cheek, trailing a series of small kisses downward until he found her warm, beckoning mouth. "Like this. Like now," he uttered, his voice rough with emotion.

Pepper moved sinuously against him, absorbing Jim, reveling in his strength and incredible tenderness. Closing her eyes, she was content to lie against him, their legs tangled, their arms around each other. Fire and ice. The glittering snow surrounded them in its cold beauty while the heat of their recent lovemaking kept them warm. Slowly, ever so slowly, their ragged breathing calmed, as did their heartbeats. Pepper was amazed by their union, which had flown far beyond the physical. Jim filled her with his strength and masculinity in a way she'd never encountered in her life. It was as if she were embracing the sun itself, piercing and brilliant with life.

As he caressed her hair, gently stroking her, Pepper surrendered to him by resting her cheek against his rock-hard chest. The black mat of hair tickled her nose, and she smiled softly. Sliding her hand across his powerful muscles, she whispered, "I never knew this existed. . . ."

Jim smiled tenderly, and he leaned over and caressed her smooth, unmarred brow as he repeated, "I dreamed of this. But I never believed it would happen, either, sweetheart," he admitted. His eyes darkened with haunting memories as he slid his fingers across the warm velvet of her flushed cheek. Her lashes fluttered open to reveal drowsy, fulfilled blue eyes. His smile deepened. "I want to cherish you, Mary Susan Sinclair."

The words, spoken huskily and with such hope, roused Pepper from the golden cocoon she was lying in. Lifting her chin, she drowned in his stormy gaze, which was alive with something she wanted to call love but didn't dare. Her lips parted, and she started to say something, but the words jammed in her throat. His eyes, so steady and intense, held hers, waiting for her answer.

Her heartbeat thumped in response to the magnitude of his statement. What was Jim saying? Did he want to spend the rest of his life with her? Was she imagining this? Had love, an emotion she'd denied herself for so long, made her hear things that hadn't really been said? His smile grew tender, and he moved within her, underscoring how much she wanted him all over again.

He had captured her wrists above the tangle of her curls, his fingers heated against her cool skin. With each slow thrust, she moaned, and the heat fanned out deeply within her.

Words were useless, and Pepper cried out with pleasure as Jim leaned down, capturing her hardening nipple. Arching against him, drawing him deeply into her, she felt his fingers in her hair, pulling her against him until her cheek rested against his damp shoulder. Did she want to spend the rest of her life with him? Yes, a thousand times, yes! Pepper lifted her chin, seeking Jim's mouth, striving to meet and match his power. She wasn't disappointed because in a heartbeat his mouth was plundering her, ravaging her, teasing her, testing her and taking her where she'd never been before.

Each touch trailed liquid fire down her body. Each motion was powerful, riveting. Pepper met his narrowed gaze, recognizing the look of a hunter. She was his quarry—but at the same time she was a hunter, too. Every plane of his body was hard as steel, trembling with bare control as he surged into her, making her his all over again.

Exhaustion lapped at Pepper as they fell into each other's embrace. The minutes fled by, and she was content to remain in his arms. Finally she felt Jim sit up and gather the warm, thick jackets over them. Snuggling against his damp body, she burrowed her face against his neck, her arms around him. Pepper felt his arms tighten, felt his mouth upon her cheek, his warm breath reassuring. Winter's chill would drive them indoors soon enough. But now Pepper would be content simply to go home and spend time with Jim, alone and uninterrupted.

Jim quietly entered the bedroom, a cup of hot tea in hand. It was nearly two in the afternoon. He and Pepper had happily fallen back into bed once they'd returned to her cabin, and had slept like two innocent children in each other's arms. He'd awakened half an hour ago and made them tea. Pepper's cabin radiated with wood-fire warmth, and he smiled tenderly as he eased himself down on the bed next to her sleeping form. Without him at her side, she slept on her stomach, one hand beneath her cheek, the other beneath the goose-down pillow. Sometime after he'd got up to go to the kitchen, the colorful down comforter had fallen to one side.

Now Jim lightly touched Pepper's back, feeling the delicious curve of her spine. He was happy when she didn't stir. He didn't want to wake her; he just wanted to spend this time absorbing another new facet of her. Her hair, once sleek, was curled in disarray around her sleeping features. Her lips were parted, shouting of her vulnerability. Her cheeks had their usual flush, emphasizing her beautiful English complexion.

Frowning, he allowed his hand to come to rest on her satiny shoulder. How many loads had she carried on these proud shoulders? Did she want to assume the load of a relationship—with him? When he'd asked her the question, he'd seen surprise in her eyes, followed by another, unknown emotion. Why hadn't Pepper responded to his question? Perhaps he'd asked too much too soon. By the very fact that she'd loved him twice already, she was showing her courage to reach out and try to love again. He had to be content with that for now. Jim hadn't even guessed at the magnitude of the wall she had erected after John's death. If he had known, he wondered if he'd have been willing to take the chances he had so far with her. Sometimes not knowing could prove to be an advantage, he thought wryly. Moving his fingers gently across her shoulder blade, he again realized just what incredible physical shape

Pepper was in—as she had to be to do the demanding work of fighting fires.

A serenity washed over him as he sat on the bed, his hand lightly resting on Pepper's shoulder. He sipped at the lemon-flavored tea he'd brewed. Out in the living room, the soft snap of the fire enhanced his tranquillity. Leaning over, he nudged a curl back from Pepper's temple, and she stirred. Damn, he hadn't meant to wake her. He saw her lashes slowly rise, revealing drowsy blue eyes.

"Jim . . . ?"

"Everything's okay," he said quietly, keeping his hand on her shoulder. She started to rise, but he applied just enough pressure to let her know he wanted her to go back to sleep.

Rubbing her face, Pepper smiled softly. "What time is it?" How dangerous-looking Jim was, she thought sleepily, dressed only in faded Levi's, his chest dark with hair and his shoulders thrown back with natural pride. Her body responded automatically to his quiet presence. His hand was warm against her. The intimacy he'd established with her was powerful.

"Fourteen hundred hours." He grimaced. "My military background is showing again, isn't it?" And he chuckled.

Pepper laughed softly and slowly sat up, the quilt spilling around her waist. She felt no embarrassment as she watched his eyes narrow with appreciation of her.

"I remember my mother making me read the Greek myths when I was nine or so," Jim said as he handed Pepper the cup of tea and rose from the bed. He walked to the closet, found a pink velour robe and brought it back to her. Trading the tea for the robe, he said, "One particular myth involved Diana, the Huntress. She captured my imagination because she did everything the boys did—but did it better. She was an athlete—a prototype, I think now, looking back on it, for the women of today." He enjoyed watching Pepper rise slowly from the bed and slip into the robe.

Placing the tea on the dresser, he went over to her. "You're a modern-day Diana."

It was so easy for Pepper to open her arms and receive him. "I'm not interested in being anyone's role model, thank you very much. I know what I enjoy doing, and that's all that counts. Personally, I just couldn't handle doing an eight-hour-a-day desk job."

Jim leaned down and captured her mouth, sharing her warmth and vulnerability. Then, easing away, he smiled at her. "I didn't mean to wake you."

Pepper smiled and touched his hair. It was thick and silky. "When the man of my dreams wakes me up, why should I mind?"

"I got thirsty," he said, gesturing to the tea. "Want some?"

"At this hour, it's better than coffee."

"Come on," he murmured. Slipping his arm around her waist, he walked her out to the kitchen, where he made her sit down while he brewed another cup.

Pepper propped her elbows on the table and rested her chin in her hands. "Do you realize how delicious you look right now?" she asked huskily.

Jim glanced over his shoulder at her as he stood at the sink, refilling the old copper teakettle. "No." He grinned and looked down at his bare feet sticking out from beneath his Levi's. "Somehow, I don't think this uniform of the day would make it most places."

"It only has to make it here."

Jim's heart mushroomed with joy at her heartfelt comment as he set the kettle on the stove. He realized that, in his sleepy state, he'd zipped up his jeans, but neglected to button them, leaving his navel revealed. "There's a difference between you and Diana," he teased mischievously, buttoning up. "She was a virgin and refused to let any man touch her."

"I wouldn't like to be Diana," Pepper said decidedly.

Sauntering over to her, Jim stood behind her and placed his hands on her shoulders. "No," he rasped, "I wouldn't like it, either."

Leaning back against him, Pepper gazed up into his shadowed face, its strong planes accentuated by a slight growth of beard. "Am I dreaming? Are you really here? Is this real?" she asked, only half joking.

Jim heard the quaver in Pepper's voice. He squeezed her shoulders and came around and knelt at her side. Facing her, he slid one hand behind her waist and held her hands with his other one. "I'm real. This is real. What we have is real," he said quietly, holding her luminous gaze.

"I'm scared, Jim. Scared as hell."

"I know you are. So am I."

"I worry...." Pepper shrugged. "I mean...I've never felt like I do when I'm with you."

He cocked his head. "What do you mean?" He ran his thumb across the top of her clasped hands. Her skin was firm and soft. Inviting. An ache began building in him again, her mere closeness fueling his desire.

"Something about you touches me so deeply—on such a primal level—that I stand in awe of it," Pepper admitted shakily. "John never touched me in the same way. It was different. With you, I feel your intensity, and you arouse an answering intensity in me. This may sound silly—maybe you'll laugh—but I feel as if you're my wolf mate—the one my soul has been searching for all these years." She gave him a shy look and realized from his expression that he wasn't taking her words lightly.

"Wolves mate for life." He pursed his lips, then lifted her hand and placed a small kiss on it. Raising his chin, he held her gaze. "I think we deserve to spend some time together, don't you?"

His voice was dark, velvety. Pepper struggled against her long-ago promise to herself not to get involved. "Yes..."

Jim smiled a little. "We've had a lot of hurdles to overcome to get this far, sweetheart."

She sat very still. His hands felt almost hot against her own. She saw the commitment in his eyes, heard it in his voice. "How much time do we have?"

"I'm due back in seven days, shortly after Christmas. If Jason isn't in Maui, we'll have to start the search for him all over again. But by that time, this new team, if they get lucky, will probably know one way or another."

"I see...." Pepper knew she'd made a personal commitment to Jim simply by loving him. She'd already broken her promise to herself, she admitted. In fact, her heart had ignored that promise from the beginning when it came to him, she thought wryly. Yet Jim hadn't said he loved her. But in fairness to him, she hadn't said it, either. Did she dare call it love? How could she not? Fear warred with her instinctive inner knowing.

Jim got up and embraced her gently. The teakettle was whistling on the stove. "I know your relationship with John taught you a lot of good things and bad things, sweetheart. In a way, we have all the time in the world—but I know that hasn't been your experience. You have to trust me on this, Pepper—we've got time. Hang on, I'll get you a cup of tea."

Amazed that he seemed able to read her thoughts, Pepper watched him putter around her kitchen. Jim belonged, there was no doubt. He looked totally at home here. And she had to admit that she'd never seen him as relaxed as he was now with her. The tea made, he held out his hand and led her into the living room, where they sat down on the large merino rug in front of the stove.

Jim maneuvered Pepper around so that he could lean against the end of the couch and still have her nestled in his arms. The fire crackled in front of them. "Better?" he whispered near her ear.

"Much." Pepper sipped the tea carefully as they sat in the early afternoon silence, the glow of red-orange flames dancing around the cabin's cozy interior. Outside, it was snowing again, and the windowpanes were frosted with a thick coating of snow. Setting the teacup on her robed thigh, Pepper sighed and leaned back against him.

"So you can stay for a week?"

"Yes."

"I just never dreamed you'd come back into my life, Jim."

"I never stopped dreaming of you coming into mine."

His voice was filled with irony, and she twisted to look up at him. "Nothing has ever felt so right to me as this," she said.

"Me, either." Jim inhaled the fragrance of Pepper's hair and enjoyed the feel of her, supple in his embrace.

Her robe had slipped off her leg, revealing the length of her calf. He frowned and leaned forward, running his hand across its smooth expanse. "Is that an old injury?" he asked, indicating a ten-inch scar that ran nearly the length of her calf.

"Hmm? Oh, that."

"How did it happen?"

"On the Crown King fire in Arizona a couple of years ago." She shrugged. "If you're a smoke jumper you can expect all kinds of injuries, Jim. That's why I'm glad I met Michaela, with her homeopathic practice. Without her, I'd have been laid up a lot more and a lot longer."

"Where did you get this other one?" He pointed to a scar on her other knee.

Pepper heard the concern in his voice. Setting the tea aside, she turned around and crossed her legs, her knees pressing against his. "What is this? Are we going to compare our war wounds?" she teased with a smile, trying to dispel the worry in his eyes.

"That's a big scar, Pepper."

"So?" She made her eyes large. "You should see the one under my left arm. It's a puncture wound I received at the Patterson fire, just outside of Phillipsburg, as a matter of fact. You remember the Storm King Mountain fire in Glenwood, Colorado, which took the lives of fourteen smoke jumpers?"

He scowled. Who could forget that tragic fire, which had taken so many dedicated and courageous lives? "Yes, I remember it."

"We had a similar situation in the Patterson fire," Pepper said. "It was a hot day—a red-flag day, warning us of high winds. My team and I were moving down into a valley similar to the one in the Storm King fire, and we had a blowout. I had run back down to warn another Hotshot team, because not all of them had radios, when the fire exploded all around us. I got to them and helped them because I knew the woods in this area so well. When a tree fell over, one of the branches gored me. If it weren't for Susan, my fire-team partner, I'd have been dead," she said matter-of-factly. "We were running for it when a burning pine fell across our planned escape route." She raised her arm and pointed to her upper rib cage. "The branch punctured my left lung. I had so much blood in my lungs, I nearly suffocated on the helo ride to the hospital."

Jim captured her graceful hands in his. "I never realized how dangerous your job was," he murmured.

"As if being a Recon isn't twenty times more dangerous, Jim Woodward! And don't give me that pained expression, either. I hope we're not going to have our first fight over our respective careers."

He grinned. "Not a chance, sweetheart. I see enough fighting in my line of work at the Pentagon. I don't want home to be a battleground, too."

Pepper caressed his cheek. "Michaela saved my life when I got that lung puncture. Because we were so close to Phillipsburg, the Forest Service called and asked for her assistance as emergency backup. On the way to the hospital, in the ambulance, she gave me a remedy that stopped most of the hemorrhaging. So you see, I have a homeopathic guardian angel. Too bad you don't!"

Laughing, Jim surrendered to her logic. "Remind me to thank Michaela for giving you the remedy that helped my arm."

"Talk about scars," Pepper murmured, sliding her hands up his newly healed arm. "That was a terrible cut, Jim."

"I had a great nurse—a woman who stole my heart, then took care of it for me. How could I not get well under her care?"

Pepper digested the sincerity of his tone. "I still think you're a figment of my lonely, overworked imagination."

"Finish your tea," Jim coaxed. "Dreams can't make love. I'll take you back to bed and we'll see if I'm a dream or not. Deal?"

Her lips curved tenderly. "Deal." There was desire in his eyes—and in his touch as he moved his hand slowly up and down her thigh beneath her robe. A new joy, a thread of real hope moved through her. In three days, she would take him home with her to Anaconda for Christmas. What would her parents think of Jim? Her whole family would be there. Suddenly, Pepper felt a wave of happiness like she'd never experienced—and she knew it was because of the man who held her in his arms.

Chapter Thirteen

Jim sat with a cup of freshly made hot chocolate in his hand.
Pepper was in her mother's very busy kitchen, preparing the
Christmas Eve meal. He looked down and noted the whipped
cream and cinnamon sprinkles on his chocolate—a thoughtful
touch. A strong burst of love washed through him. From where
he sat, he could see Pepper standing at the sink, preparing the
stuffing for the huge, twenty-five-pound turkey. To her right
stood her aristocratic-looking mother, Mary Sinclair. Though
in her fifties, she was almost as tall as Pepper, her short black
hair sprinkled with gray. Their laughter was nearly identical,
and Jim now knew who Pepper took most strongly after. To
Pepper's left stood Molly Sinclair, Cam's wife, who looked tiny
in comparison to the other two. Molly was blond and delicately boned; it was tough to imagine that at one time she'd
been a navy test engineer on the most modern fighter planes.
All three women were laughing and chatting amiably as they
worked. Unfortunately, Pepper's grandfather had the flu, so
they wouldn't be visiting for the holiday.

Jim smiled and took another sip of the rich, warm chocolate. Happiness seemed to ring through the Sinclair household nonstop. At the moment, Warren Sinclair, Pepper's father, was having a serious talk with Cam by the fireplace. Warren was tall and spare, his hands long and artistic—like Pepper's. He was in his mid-fifties and wore a white cotton shirt topped by a brightly striped red-and-white sweater. Cam was a few inches shorter than his father, lean and obviously fit from his military duties. The navy test pilot had his elbow resting on the mantel, his brow furrowed, eyes intense. Jim smiled to himself. Yes, Cam needed someone like Molly, who was like a cheerful patch of sunlight, to counterbalance his intensity and seriousness.

Molly and Cam's two children, three-year-old Jennifer and one-year-old Scott, played happily around Jim's feet. He leaned over and made sure that blond-haired Jennifer, who decidedly took after Molly, had the coloring book and crayons nearby so she could continue her exploration of creativity on paper. Scott, on the other hand, was the spitting image of Cam, his hair thick and black and his eyes clear, pale blue with a startling intensity to them—just like his father's.

Jim glanced at his watch. It was 1100, and two more families, friends of Molly and Cam, were still due to arrive to spend Christmas with them. Dana and Griff Turcotte were flying in from Pensacola, Florida, where they both worked as instructor pilots. From Miramar Naval Air Station near San Diego, Lieutenant Commander Maggie Donovan-Bishop and her civilian pilot husband, Wes Bishop, were flying in, too.

The Sinclair house was large, a turn-of-the-century three-story Victorian home that had originally been built by Sinclair ancestors when silver mining was at its peak in Montana. Jim had been immersed in the family's stories of the mining era, when the Sinclairs had been among the local elite. But as silver production died off in the 1930s, the family had become destitute like much of the rest of the country. This generation of Sinclairs—Warren and Mary—had turned economic disaster into success. Warren ran a fishing-expedition service with clients from around the world who wanted to fish the state's famous trout streams.

Jim allowed Scott Sinclair to climb into his lap. The boy was tired—he'd been up since six this morning, wanting to touch every bulb and light on the ten-foot-high blue spruce that stood, brightly decorated, in the corner of the expansive living room.

Last night they had all worked together to decorate the tree, and Jim couldn't remember ever having so much fun or laughing so hard. Now Scott snuggled against him, resting his head tiredly on Jim's shoulder and closing his eyes. Jim wrapped his left arm around the boy and watched him drop quickly off to sleep. His gaze returned to Pepper. Again his heart expanded with such joy that it continued to catch him off guard, made him inhale a deep ragged breath as he tried to believe his good luck.

Pepper wore an ankle-length, red corduroy skirt, a dark green angora sweater and comfortable shoes with bright red socks that matched her skirt. Earlier, Molly had placed a sprig of holly and berries in Pepper's hair, and now her cheeks were flushed as she talked animatedly with her mother and Molly in the kitchen. She had pushed the sleeves of the sweater up to her elbows in order to make the dressing. Jim sighed, glanced down at the sleeping tiger he held in his arms and continued to sip the delicious hot chocolate. Life didn't get much better than this and he knew it.

The past three days had been bliss for him and Pepper. Yesterday a brief storm had passed through, dropping another foot of snow, and they'd gone alpine skiing for part of the day. He was sore today from the unaccustomed form of exercise, but it had been a great day. Pepper had packed two thermoses of hot chocolate and a lunch, and they'd shared another snow picnic in the middle of the forest, the towering Douglas firs stately and awe-inspiring around them.

Jim finished the cup of chocolate and saw Cam looking his way. The navy pilot wore Levi's, loafers and a dark green flannel shirt and Jim smiled to himself. He, too, had opted for comfortable civilian clothes: tan chinos, an off-white fisherman's sweater and hiking boots.

"Looks like Scott finally crashed and burned," Cam said as he came over and gently eased his son into his arms. He turned Scott around and allowed him to sink across his shoulder.

"I'd say he's about used up his energy for this mission," Jim agreed as he watched the pilot gently hold his son. It was good to see men who enjoyed being fathers, who weren't afraid to show their full range of emotions with their children—unlike many of the stoic father figures of the past, who'd remained apart from their families in many ways.

"Thanks for baby-sitting," Cam said with a chuckle. He turned, carrying his son down the hall toward one of the many bedrooms to continue his nap. Jennifer quickly got up, leaving crayons and paper behind and followed her dad.

"Playing baby-sitter?" Pepper asked as she wandered in, wiping her hands on a dish towel. How wonderfully handsome Jim looked, she thought. The cream color of his sweater emphasized his dark good looks, and when he lifted his chin, his green eyes narrowing on her, she felt giddy with joy.

"I think the little rug rat just found any old soft spot to call a pillow," he teased, taking the hand she had extended to him. Pepper came to the side of his chair and knelt down, her hand resting in his lap.

"Rug rats—what an awful term!"

He gave her a nonplussed look. "It's an affectionate Marine Corps term for kids."

"Leave it to the Marine Corps to think that that term shows affection." Pepper sniffed, leaning over to gather up the crayons and coloring book.

"Marines aren't usually in the line of being baby-sitters," Jim drawled, teasing her.

She set the items on the lamp stand next to Jim's chair. As she straightened, she muttered, "Listen, I've been around enough military brats, kids who had to grow up in that sterile, rigid place called the Fortress, and I've seen firsthand how little the military cares about the wives and children. Don't get me started, okay?"

Jim grinned and leaned over, placing a swift kiss on her mouth. "Okay," he murmured.

Pepper sighed and leaned against the arm of the chair, content. "This is so much fun. I just love Christmas."

"It's one of my favorite holidays, too." He placed his hand on her shoulder. "And you've got a great family." He raised his eyebrows slightly. "You really take after your mother."

"Yes. She's something else, isn't she?"

"I was surprised to hear she hikes back into those interior places where the trout are. That's rugged country."

Snorting, Pepper gave him a cool look. "Come on! Women can't be good guides?"

He held up his hands. "Remember? I'm still adjusting to the fact that women can do anything a man can. But I have to admit, I can't see any reason why a woman couldn't know good fishing spots, too."

Pepper shook her head. "You're one of those guys who grudgingly gives up ground to a woman, you know that?"

"Maybe so, but I am trying to adjust," he protested lightly.

"Stick around me and you'll change a lot quicker," she muttered, smiling. Jim's eyes were warm with tenderness, and Pepper felt wrapped in a euphoria she still had trouble trusting. The last time she'd uttered those heartfelt words *I love you* John had died. In the past few days, she had realized she was genuinely ready to let go of the past and embrace the present. What she felt for Jim more than rivaled what she'd felt for John. But how should she tell Jim? She wasn't sure if he was ready to commit at such a serious level. Did she dare believe that what she experienced in his touch and his kisses and saw in his eyes was love? After all, he'd never said the words to her. Would he ever?

Sighing, Pepper said, "Molly's beside herself. Her friends from Annapolis and Pensacola flight school will be here in a few minutes. I guess this is the first time they've all been able to get leave, meet somewhere and have a great time together."

"Sort of like a college reunion," Jim said.

"Yes. Molly's told me all about Dana and Maggie—how they shared an apartment in Pensacola when they were there to get their navy aviator wings. I'm excited to meet them myself. Molly has told me so much about them, I feel like I already know them. And it will be interesting to see the men they've chosen as husbands. How they compare."

"Oh?" Jim took her hand and laced his fingers with hers.

"Well, you know." Pepper laughed.

"Is this womanspeak? Some kind of mysterious verbal shorthand we poor males try to decipher, but can't?"

Pepper had the good grace to blush. "Sorry. Yes, it is. I guess I'm curious about the men from the standpoint that all three of these women are very strong, confident people. It's been my experience that most men get defensive or project like crazy around woman like that. It takes a man who is really comfortable with his masculinity, as a total person, to appreciate women like us, that's all."

"So you're going to compare Griff Turcotte and Wes Bishop with me?" He saw Pepper's cheeks grow even brighter red and grinned.

"Not exactly. . . ." she hedged, obviously uncomfortable.

Laughing huskily, Jim whispered, "I know I'm not the perfect twenty-first-century male, but I'm trying. And I think that's what counts, don't you?"

Leaning over, Pepper kissed him quickly on his smiling mouth. The heat in his eyes touched her deeply. "It does count," she murmured. "Besides, you might pick up some good pointers from these guys, especially Wes Bishop. I understand Maggie is a real go-getter. She's one of the first women in the navy to fly the fighters up against the boys—and she beats them on a regular basis."

"Hmm, maybe I will," Jim drawled, holding her laughter-filled gaze, which sparkled with an emotion he wanted to call love. Was Pepper ready to commit to him? To release the past with John once and for all? Jim had seen her seesaw back and forth in the days he'd spent with her at the cabin. Their conversations had tiptoed around the issue. But he'd also seen the deepening of their own relationship. He loved her. Could she put herself out on a limb and love for a second time in her life? Could she do it for him? He still wasn't sure.

The doorbell rang, and they watched Molly fly from the kitchen to the foyer, her long blond hair streaming behind her. Pepper laughed and shook her head. Molly was such a sprite, completely uninhibited, and it reminded her to stay in touch with her own childlike emotions. The woman opened the door, shrieked and flung her arms wide.

Pepper was content to stand at Jim's side and wait until the group shed their coats and gear and came into the living room. Molly's cheeks were pink with excitement, her eyes sparkling with tears as she held the hands of her two dearest friends. She brought them around the room, introducing them to everyone. Pepper and Jim were the last to be introduced.

"Dana and Maggie, meet one of us, Pepper Sinclair. Can you believe it? She made it through Army Ranger school, beat the guys at their own game, was the highest scoring of all of them, and they wouldn't let her graduate? Pepper's a smoke jumper now, for the Forest Service. Pepper, meet my friends."

Laughing, Pepper held out her hand to red-haired Maggie Donovan-Bishop, whose eaglelike eyes seemed to miss nothing. Maggie's handshake was firm, her smile genuine. Dana Turcotte, who possessed an intensity and introspectiveness that reminded Pepper of Cam, shook her hand next.

Pepper was delighted by this unusual chance to meet her "own kind." Though few women had joined the smoke jumpers so far, those who had possessed similar hallmark traits. It was obvious Maggie and Dana had them, too. As Molly introduced Jim, giving a quick sketch of his background, Pepper was able to stand back and observe their reaction to him. Maggie grinned, thrust her hand forward and shook Jim's hand vigorously. Dana was more circumspect, more official, eyeing him with a bit of wariness, or watchfulness, perhaps. Pepper wondered if Dana had had a bad time in general with men, to make her so guarded.

Cam brought the two husbands around next. Pepper liked outgoing and warm Wes Bishop, who was a pilot with United Parcel Service and flew the "heavies," as they called the jumbo jets, all over the world, hauling cargo. Griff Turcotte had a rugged face, a tough exterior, and was more reserved, like Dana. Shaking his hand, Pepper felt Griff was exactly what Dana needed. It was obvious they were happy—she had seen them trade an affectionate glance shortly after the introductions and before Molly had dragged the two women off to the kitchen to give them her late grandmother's recipe for the hot chocolate she'd made for everyone.

Jim went into the kitchen and brought out cups of the famous chocolate for the two pilots. It struck him that the men had formed a loose circle near the roaring fireplace, while the women were in the kitchen, chatting away, laughing and working together on the meal to come. There were differences between men and women, and Jim honored them. He turned his attention to Wes, who pinned him with an interested look.

"Molly said you're a Recon Marine?"

"Yes, a ground pounder compared to you air guys," Jim said, grinning. Everyone laughed. Jim was familiar with the ongoing rivalry between ground troops and the pilots who owned the air above them.

"I won't hold it against you," Wes murmured, his grin stretching wide across his face.

"I'll forgive you, too."

Chuckling, Griff said, "Looks like you have your own tiger by her tail."

Jim stared at him blankly.

Griff motioned lazily toward the kitchen. "Pepper is like Dana and Maggie—ahead of her time, a trailblazer."

"I see . . . yes, she is."

"How are you rolling with it all?" Griff asked curiously as he sized Jim up.

"It's new to me," Jim admitted. "Sometimes I fall into some pretty pedestrian traps regarding stereotypes."

Wes chuckled indulgently. "Tell me about it. Maggie has changed my language from 'man' or 'woman' to 'person,' and I had to learn very quickly that being a man doesn't give you special privileges."

"At all," Turcotte agreed, chuckling.

"I don't think we deserve special privileges," Jim said. "Pepper has taught me a lot lately about the way women have been held down or kept in what's considered their 'place.' "

Wes Bishop sighed and raised his cup of chocolate. "To our ladies, who have and continue to make us better human beings, gentlemen."

Jim had no problem with that toast and clinked the side of his cup against the others'. As he sipped the chocolate, he enjoyed watching the women in the kitchen. They had such a camaraderie—a closeness men simply didn't seem to foster. He liked the way the women reached out, touching one another on the shoulder or arm, or came over and slipped an arm around each other's waist in a hug before continuing on with their kitchen duties. He was struck by how thoroughly the women worked as a team. They didn't fit into the boss-and-underlings structure that men seemed to insist on.

What was most striking to Jim was the way that, although Pepper had just met Maggie and Dana, she was immediately absorbed into their group. He decided there was a lot to be learned from women. Their ability to become warmly personal and freely show feelings left him wanting to be more open with his own gender.

As he stood chatting amiably with the other men, Jim realized that Maggie, Dana and Molly had already rubbed off on their husbands. These three pilots seemed noticeably more open and personable than the men Jim knew. Even more surprising was the way that Wes or Griff would every once in a while reach out and touch each other's shoulder or arm to emphasize something they were saying.

Jim smiled to himself, liking the discovery and seeing how these self-assured women had influenced the men they loved. Most of all, he was struck by the fact that all three men possessed the ability to be flexible and to compromise—certainly the main component to the longevity of any marriage today. These men weren't lapdogs, nor were they battered males with no egos. Just the opposite. These were highly competent men with a confidence and assurance that came from within. It wasn't a show, Jim sensed, but a depth of strength they had about their own masculinity that enabled them not only to support the strengths of their wives, but to push them to become all that they could be.

Finishing his cup of hot chocolate, Jim wandered into the kitchen. Pepper was in the middle of the women, her mother at her side, as she finished stuffing the huge turkey. Luckily, the kitchen was large, in keeping with the old-time kitchens of bygone era. Jim moved to the end of the counter that wasn't being used.

Maggie Donovan-Bishop had spare, lean hands like Pepper's. She worked alongside Molly who was telling her how to make her grandmother's special recipe for Jell-O salad. Dana Turcotte stood a little to the side peeling the potatoes that would soon be mashed into a frothy white mound. Pepper and her mother exchanged warm looks, smiles hovering around their mouths. Yes, this was a happy group, indeed.

Pouring himself a third cup of hot chocolate, Jim left the kitchen and headed back to where the men were standing. His heart was with Pepper. What would she do when she opened his gift after dinner? The Sinclairs opened their gifts on Christmas Eve instead of Christmas morning, Pepper had explained, because she and Cam, when they were very young, had been unable to sleep Christmas Eve out of excitement. So Mary Sinclair had decided they could open presents Christmas Eve, instead, to keep the holiday peaceful.

Jim tried to hone in on the men's conversation, but his mind and heart were elsewhere. What if Pepper took his gift the wrong way? He knew she wanted to tell him she loved him. Hell, he could see it in her eyes, feel it in her touch and hear it in the tone of her wonderfully husky voice. But what if his gift backfired? It could create a destructive split in their new relationship. Should he take the gift back? Hold it until later? His mind and heart seesawed over the possibilities. Finally, exhausted emotionally from the indecision, Jim decided to fly with his original plan. His spontaneity thus far had gotten him Pepper. He had to trust his own sense of creativity and honor his intuition to get him and Pepper to where he so much wanted them to end up—together. Soon enough, he would know—one way or another. The thought scared the living hell out of him.

Jim sat in an overstuffed velour chair opposite the Christmas tree. Everyone was opening gifts, and the room rang with the sounds of paper being ripped off, children squealing with delight and adults making more-subtle sounds of pleasure as they viewed their gifts for the first time. Pepper sat at Jim's feet, her long legs tucked demurely beneath her skirt, a number of already opened boxes beside her. But Jim was having trouble enjoying the happy scene. His heart was pounding in his chest and his mouth felt dry. What would she think of *his* gift?

Pepper had opened gifts from her family—common-sense items such as a new pair of Levi's to replace her well-worn ones, sweaters to keep her warm during the harsh Montana winter, and photos of her niece and nephew to put in her cabin. Jim saw her look back through the packages she'd opened, a puzzlement on her face. Cam and Warren had distributed all the gifts beneath the tree earlier, and everyone had piles of colorfully decorated boxes heaped nearby.

Pepper picked through the surrounding wrapping and ribbons, wondering if she'd overlooked a gift from Jim. She had bought him a Shetland wool sweater in bright red and yellow to remind him of his Marine Corps heritage, as well as a watch to replace the one that had been damaged during the mission. Now, moving the paper aside, the sounds of laughter and surprise still carrying through the large living room, Pepper felt a stab of panic as she riffled through everything once more just to make sure. Jim had gone somewhere two days ago—to Anaconda, he'd told her. He'd been gone all afternoon and hadn't arrived back at the cabin until late that night. Pepper hadn't asked why, figuring that if he wanted her to know, he would have told her. Plus there'd been a look in his eyes that had silently asked her not to question him.

She felt the touch of Jim's hand on her shoulder. Looking up, she met his grave green gaze.

"I think you were looking for this?" he said, his voice low and slightly strained.

Pepper's eyes widened as he placed a small box wrapped in gold foil and a silver bow in her hand. "Oh..."

Jim smiled unevenly, aware that some of the background noise had abated. He looked up to realize everyone was watching them expectantly. How could they know? he wondered, his mouth suddenly dry with nervousness. He squeezed Pepper's shoulder. "Go ahead, open it, sweetheart."

Pepper looked up to see everyone intently watching her. Silence abruptly reigned in the room, except for the soft crackle and snap of flames in the fireplace. She laughed a little nervously and set the small box in her lap. Molly, Maggie and

Dana edged closer, grinning and elbowing each other, as if they knew a secret she did not. What had Jim bought for her? Stymied, Pepper grew impatient with the bow, finally pulling it off with strength rather than finesse.

Laughing nervously, she looked up at Jim. "I'm not very good at opening things."

He smiled back. "I know."

His words fell softly, warmly, across her. Pepper took a deep breath and ripped off the gold-foil wrapping. Inside a white satin box was another, smaller box of red velvet. Her heart plummeted as she hesitantly touched it. No, it couldn't be. Could it? She gave Jim a look of inquiry, and saw tenderness burning in his eyes.

Touched beyond words, Pepper lifted the box in her left hand and sprung the small, gold latch that raised the lid. A gasp escaped her. The other women quickly crowded around.

"Ohh," Maggie whispered, a wicked glint in her eyes as she looked first at Pepper, then at Jim. "He's serious...."

Dana touched Pepper's shoulder. "It's beautiful," she said in a choked voice.

Molly whispered, "Gosh, what a lovely Christmas gift for you, Pepper. How romantic...."

Pepper felt Jim's hand tighten on her shoulder, as if silently asking her what she thought of his gift. Tears blurred her vision momentarily, and she self-consciously wiped them from her eyes. In the box was an obviously antique wedding-ring set. She lightly touched them with her trembling fingers, not daring to believe they were really for her.

Jim leaned down, his voice a broken whisper. "Those were my grandmother's rings. She was very special to me, to our family. Before she died ten years ago, she asked me to take them, to give them to a woman I would love as much as she had loved my grandfather." As Pepper lifted her chin and looked at him, he felt a powerful wave of joy sweep through him. Her eyes sparkled with tears. Reaching out, he caressed her flaming cheek. The silence was complete around them. Everyone's gaze was pinned on them, on the emotional moment.

"I—they are beautiful, Jim. Beautiful..." Pepper whispered.

"There's no hurry," he rasped, sliding his hand along her cheek, smiling gently down at her. "It's not meant to rush you, or what we have. I just wanted something special for you, for Christmas. I love you, Mary Susan Sinclair." He leaned down, caressing her parted lips, which tasted of salt from her happy tears. Her lower lip trembled, and he kissed her deeply, wanting to impart to her just how fiercely he loved her.

The world swam out of view as Pepper surrendered to Jim's long, tender kiss. She clutched the ring box in her hands, stretching upward to meet his questing mouth, to touch him, his heart, his wonderful, thoughtful soul. As awareness that everyone was watching filtered in, embarrassment flooded her. Knowing how private a person Jim was, she realized how difficult it must have been for him to give her these rings in front of everyone, not knowing what her reaction might be. Easing her lips from his mouth, she smiled up into his anxious gaze, touched with his own tears.

"I love you, Jim Woodward," she quavered, sliding her hand upward to touch his clean-shaven cheek. "With my life...."

Much later Pepper sat staring down at the ring box, its lid open. Everyone had gone to bed, and it was past midnight. Jim sat with her on the couch closest to the fireplace, his arm around her shoulders. The house was filled now with a wonderful, peaceful silence. The satisfaction and contentment she felt in Jim's arms had no comparison, Pepper decided. She was dressed in her pink velour robe, her feet bare, though Jim still wore his clothes from the day. She lay back, resting her head on his broad shoulder, and closed her eyes.

"I never thought I could be so happy," she murmured.

"I didn't, either," Jim admitted quietly, looking down at her firelit profile. The house was dark, just the fire offering subtle warmth and light. The shadows dancing across Pepper's face underscored her strength and shouted of her vulnerability. His mouth pulled into a slight, tender smile as he saw her continue to caress the rings in the box. "So you like them?"

"Like them?" She roused herself and faced him, her knees drawn up against his thigh. "I love them." Reaching out, she touched his strong jaw. "And I love you, too."

He met and held her somber gaze. "I didn't expect that from you, you know."

"What?"

"You didn't have to say you loved me earlier this evening. I didn't really expect it, Pepper. I know how you felt about the past. About John and never falling in love again. I gave you the rings because I wanted to let you know the depth of my love for you—the commitment I wanted to work toward, hoping you would want the same thing someday."

With a sigh, Pepper rested her brow against his temple. "I saw how scared you were when you handed me the gift. I couldn't figure out why." Kissing his cheek, she murmured, 'Now I know. That was a hell of a risk you took with me. When I saw the rings, I understood."

"You had every right to say no. To give them back to me," Jim agreed, tunneling his fingers through her loose, dark hair.

Pepper eased from him to meet his serious eyes. "With that group hanging around me oohing and ahhing? I thought Maggie, Dana and Molly were going to grab them right out of my hand. Did you see the wistful looks on their faces?"

"Yes," Jim said, "I did. They were happy for you. For us. I saw it in their eyes and the way they looked at us after seeing my grandmother's rings."

"I know," Pepper said with a sigh, sliding her arm around his neck and placing her hand in his lap. In the light from the flames, the rings sparkled like their own barely contained blaze. 'They are gorgeous. Prettier than any I've ever seen."

"I had a hell of a time getting them out here," Jim groused good-naturedly. "You remember I left the cabin that one morning and didn't get back until late that evening?"

"Yes."

"I made a call the day before, after you'd gone to the grocery store, to a friend of mine who's keeping an eye on my condo. I told him what was going on, told him where to find the rings and asked him to send them by overnight courier. Well, I got to Anaconda, and the place that was supposed to have them hadn't received them yet."

"Oh, no . . ."

"Yeah, well, I was more than a little upset," he assured her. "That snowstorm that hit us a day earlier had grounded all planes coming out of Chicago, and that's where the package was stuck. So I had to wait another eight hours for the plane to finally make it into Anaconda. Luckily, the rings were on it." He shook his head. "I was really sweating."

"No wonder you looked so tired and harried when you got back that night," Pepper soothed. "I almost asked you what was wrong, but that look you gave me told me not to."

"I was a little out of sorts by that point," Jim admitted apologetically, sliding his hand up her arm, feeling the soft firm warmth of her skin. "On top of that, I wondered if I was doing the right thing. I knew how you felt about admitting your love for me after what had happened to John. I knew it was rushing things in one way—but in another, I felt it was the right time."

"Betwixt and between."

Grimly, he chuckled. "More like 'caught between a rock and hard place,' if you ask me." He picked up the ring box and stared at it. "Today I felt tortured. I was seesawing between giving them to you and waiting. I was afraid you'd say no. That you'd turn them down."

"What made you do it?" Pepper asked softly, kissing his cheek, loving him with a fierceness that continued to amaze her.

Laughing wryly, Jim handed the box back to her. "The fact that I didn't have another present for you. I mean, I couldn't sit here with everyone trading gifts and not have something for you. I saw how Molly, Dana and Maggie were covertly watching us."

"Hey, they're old married ladies," Pepper teased, "and we're the new couple on the block. Of course they'd be watching to see what gifts we gave each other."

Jim chuckled. "I figured as much. Still, I felt more on a hot seat this evening when you started to open that gift than when my chutes didn't open on that first HAHO."

"Mmm, that's pretty serious," Pepper agreed. She took out the engagement ring. The gold band held five small diamonds. It might not be an expensive ring set from the size of the stones, but they were precious beyond belief to her because she believed family meant everything. How could she help but cherish these special items, handed down from one generation to the next?

She placed the engagement ring in Jim's hand. "Will you slip it on my finger?"

He sat up straighter and turned. "You have the most beautiful hands I've ever seen," he told her conspiratorially. "They're so long, capable and slender." And wonderful at touching him, making him feel hot with longing, when she caressed his body, he added silently. Taking the lovely fingers of her left hand in his, Jim gently eased the ring forward. "My grandmother was tall and spare, like you. She had work-worn hands with large knuckles, so I figured this ring just might fit you." And it did, perfectly. Satisfaction soared through him as Pepper eased her hand from his and held it out for them to admire. The firelight danced off the small diamonds like rainbows—just as she was his personal rainbow, he thought.

"It's so beautiful," Pepper said with a sigh. She turned, sliding her arms around his shoulders.

"Like you," Jim murmured, meeting and matching the warmth of her lips. She tasted of the wine they'd shared earlier, a toast before everyone, except them, went to bed for the night. Her breath was like the breath of life itself to him. As Jim eased back and met her lustrous gaze, he whispered, "Let's go to bed."

Pepper walked with him, arm in arm, toward the staircase. The house was warm and quiet. Outside, snow fell gently in large, soft flakes, twirling through the darkness of the Montana night. Sliding her hand along the oak banister as they moved up the creaky, carpeted stairs, she smiled gently. The ghosts from the past had finally been laid to rest. All of them. Life wouldn't be easy for them in one way. They still had serious questions to answer about their careers. Jim had twenty years in the corps. Would he want to continue being an officer? Being in the military? And she had to look hard at her career. What did she want? Pepper knew that in another five years she would probably be relegated to a desk job instead of jumping out of planes. The physical demands were just too

extreme, and by thirty-five, most smoke jumpers were tamin͏͏
desks instead of forest fires.

She leaned languidly against Jim as they topped the stairs an͏͏
turned down the carpeted expanse to her room at the end of th͏͏
hall. Their room. The ring felt natural and right on her han͏͏
Never could she have dreamed that she would meet a man li͏͏
Jim on an unexpected mission that came out of the blue. Whe͏͏
she'd lost John, she'd barricaded herself against loving. It ha͏͏
been the wrong decision, Pepper now admitted, but she unde͏͏
stood why she'd done it. Still not believing her own fortune, sh͏͏
knew that no matter what, she and Jim had their love to he͏͏
them compromise and work out their life together. Forever.

*   *   *   *   *   *

Tall, dark and...dangerous...

Strangers in the Night

Just in time for the exciting Halloween season,
Silhouette brings you three spooky love stories in this
fabulous collection. You will love these original stories
that combine sensual romance with just a taste of
danger. Brought to you by these fabulous authors:

Anne Stuart

Chelsea Quinn Yarbro

Maggie Shayne

Available in October at a store near you.

Only from

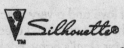 *Silhouette*®

—where passion lives.

Silhouette
SPECIAL EDITION™

That SPECIAL Woman!

D IS FOR DANI'S BABY
Lisa Jackson
(SE #985, October)

Young and naive, Dani fell for the rebellious Brandon
then became pregnant. She'd been forced to give
them up—baby and father. Now she was determined
to find her child and resolve the passion she felt for
her one true love. But could Brandon forgive her for
keeping their baby from him?

All it takes is a letter of love and a very special woman
to mend mistakes of the past and build dreams of the
future. Don't miss *D Is for Dani's Baby*, Book 4 of Lisa
Jackson's LOVE LETTERS series, available in October
only from Silhouette Special Edition!

Five unforgettable couples said "I Do"...with a little help from their friends—especially me, Katie, always a bridesmaid. But now, I'm...

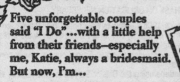

FINALLY A BRIDE
by Sherryl Woods

the fifth and final book of the Always a Bridesmaid! series—only from Silhouette Special Edition.

Katie's finally trading all those taffeta bridesmaid dresses for a wedding gown of her own. Gorgeous single dad Luke Cassidy proposed marriage—a marriage of *convenience*....

Don't miss the big wedding!

OFFICIAL RULES

PRIZE SURPRISE SWEEPSTAKES 3448

NO PURCHASE OR OBLIGATION NECESSARY

Three Harlequin Reader Service 1995 shipments will contain respectively, coupons for entry into three different prize drawings, one for a Panasonic 31" wide-screen TV, another for a 5-piece Wedgwood china service for eight and the third for a Sharp ViewCam camcorder. To enter any drawing using an Entry Coupon, simply complete and mail according to directions.

There is no obligation to continue using the Reader Service to enter and be eligible for any prize drawing. You may also enter any drawing by hand printing the words "Prize Surprise," your name and address on a 3"x5" card and the name of the prize you wish that entry to be considered for (i.e., Panasonic wide-screen TV, Wedgwood china or Sharp ViewCam). Send your 3"x5" entries via first-class mail (limit: one per envelope) to: Prize Surprise Sweepstakes 3448, c/o the prize you wish that entry to be considered for, P.O. Box 1315, Buffalo, NY 14269-1315, USA or P.O. Box 610, Fort Erie, Ontario L2A 5X3, Canada.

To be eligible for the Panasonic wide-screen TV, entries must be received by 6/30/95; for the Wedgwood china, 8/30/95; and for the Sharp ViewCam, 10/30/95.

Winners will be determined in random drawings conducted under the supervision of D.L. Blair, Inc., an independent judging organization whose decisions are final, from among all eligible entries received for that drawing. Approximate prize values are as follows: Panasonic wide-screen TV ($1,800); Wedgwood china ($840) and Sharp ViewCam ($2,000). Sweepstakes open to residents of the U.S. (except Puerto Rico) and Canada, 18 years of age or older. Employees and immediate family members of Harlequin Enterprises, Ltd., D.L. Blair, Inc., their affiliates, subsidiaries and all other agencies, entities and persons connected with the use, marketing or conduct of this sweepstakes are not eligible. Odds of winning a prize are dependent upon the number of eligible entries received for that drawing. Prize drawing and winner notification for each drawing will occur no later than 15 days after deadline for entry eligibility for that drawing. Limit: one prize to an individual, family or organization. All applicable laws and regulations apply. Sweepstakes offer void wherever prohibited by law. Any litigation within the province of Quebec respecting the conduct and awarding of the prizes in this sweepstakes must be submitted to the Regies des loteries et Courses du Quebec. In order to win a prize, residents of Canada will be required to correctly answer a time-limited arithmetical skill-testing question. Value of prizes are in U.S. currency.

Winners will be obligated to sign and return an Affidavit of Eligibility within 30 days of notification. In the event of noncompliance within this time period, prize may not be awarded. If any prize or prize notification is returned as undeliverable, that prize will not be awarded. By acceptance of a prize, winner consents to use of his/her name, photograph or other likeness for purposes of advertising, trade and promotion on behalf of Harlequin Enterprises, Ltd., without further compensation, unless prohibited by law.

For the names of prizewinners (available after 12/31/95), send a self-addressed, stamped envelope to: Prize Surprise Sweepstakes 3448 Winners, P.O. Box 4200, Blair, NE 68009.

RPZ KAL